SACRIFICING ALL PAIN

Book 4 of The Triumvirs

Daniel Dydek

BEORN PUBLISHING, LLC

ISBN-13: 979-8-9874621-4-0

DEDICATION

For those whom no one believes

CONTENTS

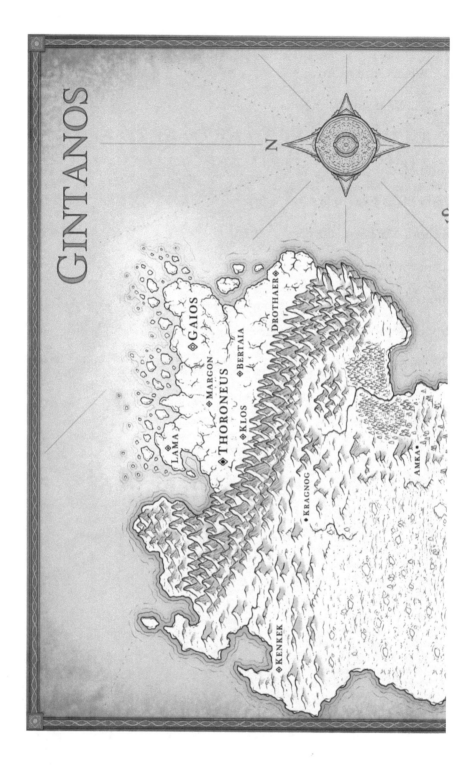

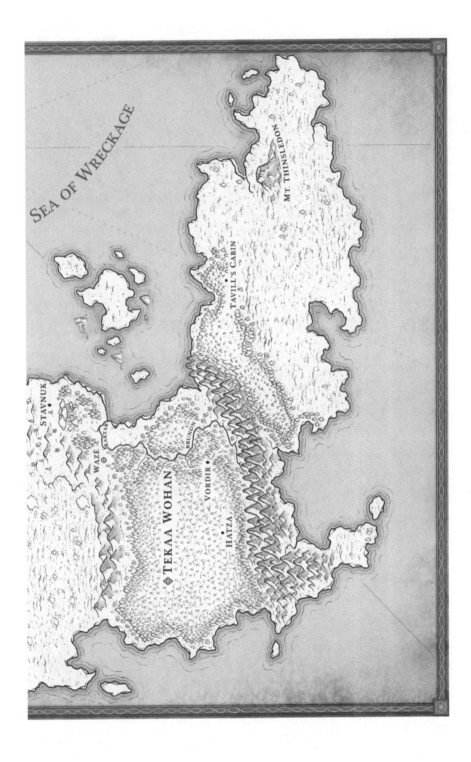

I

THE LEAVES ON BRANCHES

"Should I go?"
"Send Kanala; you stay in Andelen."
"I could handle Gintanos as well."
"But Kanala used to live there."

22 Halmfurtung 1320 — Autumn

Averlynn clung tight as they crashed through yet another seam of undergrowth. Daylight was fading and the low sun barely dappled through the thick foliage overhead. She could hear nothing over the pounding of Tarafel's hooves. But she could see, faintly ahead, the white tail of the deer herking and jerking as it bounded through small patches of sunlight. She needed this deer—desperately, her stomach told her. Before winter, her mind told her.

With a cry, she brought Tarafel skidding to a halt: the white tail had disappeared ahead of her in a large and bright patch of sun. Her eyes flickered, peering around to try to see it maybe off in the woods to either side. Tarafel huffed—winded, but the stallion would not be so easily finished from a chase. She eased him forward, head still swiveling.

Where the tail had disappeared, she stopped. The deer run entered a small glade of breaching rock, and three trails went back into the forest beyond. Two went flat along the ridge, continuing north. The third appeared to turn down the valley toward water. After the chase they had, the animal had to be thirsty.

"And I'll bet you could use a sip?" she said to Tarafel. The gray stallion was quiet, waiting for her command. The sky overhead was still bright, she saw now, though deeper blue as evening approached. High, wispy clouds shone bright, weaving in the sky like threads of silver. She had a little more time, yet—at least today.

This time of year, though, she should be heading south. Tadan È was nearing, and she had almost missed the last one. Her people stood proudly by their ceremonies, or perhaps fearfully. If the gods granted a plentiful harvest it was folly not to thank them. Just as foolish to neglect asking them for it in the beginning of the year, or seeking their guidance when they were at their nearest, or pleading for their return at their farthest, or... She cut off the thought before it ran too far away. She appreciated the ceremonies, but the demands of ranging the far wilds of Wohan often asked for some leniency in how those festivals were celebrated. The elders never gave it. Their life was one spent ensuring the festivals and traditions of their people were upheld, the law followed meticulously, the safety of their people secured in iron bands. Such focus and dedication blinded them to the idea that the Wohan Rangers and Scouts were trying to accomplish the same security, only differently. The elders worried they had failed their religious duties, seven hundred years ago; they didn't understand that Averlynn and the other Rangers felt the same of themselves.

But she did appreciate the festivals, despite what her parents thought whenever she missed them, or nearly. Erion had given her a good, weary-mother's look last time, when she rode into the village only moments before the Harvest music began. Avako had given her far more than that. Her parents always felt like they had failed too, somehow. Except with Aver: he was their pride and joy. And where was he as the Harvest festival fast approached? Running off to see about some sword he had found—as though any of her people would ever actually use a sword.

Tarafel stamped a hoof. Averlynn dismissed the sudden spike of envy for the moment, glancing again across the trails. She had time, though not for that. If worse came to worst, she could make for Amka—it was near enough at hand, and a pigeon from there could let her parents know she had properly celebrated the harvest, even if not with them. They might suffer for a day or two, waiting for curses to come down. As if they didn't worry about those anyway. She nudged her gray to the right, following the run quietly downslope.

Of all the regions she had to visit, the northern wards were always her favorite. The other realms carried their own particular challenges, but nothing in her mind compared to finding her way through the Water Plains, or capturing glimpses of rugged, towering peaks far to the north through the clearings of the Waken Forest. More than once she had thought to truly test her mettle by trying to make it through those rocky warrens—almost everyone said it couldn't be done. But then, those who said it had usually never left their villages.

Her glance flicked through the darkening trunks of maple, cherry, and oak. A stand of spruce to her left blotted the westering sun, casting the splashing brook in a deep gloom. Tarafel paused as Averlynn sat back. The winds eddied; a shot down here would be difficult. But if she could catch sight of her quarry, begin to track it again, she would not have to be as hungry. She breathed deep, but slow, watching.

There: a flicker of movement, thin white against the brown gloaming. Now she saw the outline. The deer had paused from its drink to peer intently into the trees. Averlynn's own browns and pale greens would hide her too, here at the top of the hill. Even Tarafel often only appeared as a slip of fog, though deer would not likely fear him.

It bent to drink again, but still she only watched. She would have to follow it out of the valley first. She might be able to make her shot just before full dark as the doe made its way to bed for the night. Maybe if she could track it to a clearing—especially that one she knew of, to the north and east—the full moon would aid the shot as well.

Her brows knit. Except the full moon had come and gone, over a week ago. She had spent a turn in prayers, as she always did. Shrug as she might about some of her people's ways, she refused to cast aside the gods—especially not when pale Hakana glimmered on the mists the way she had that night. She felt secure in Hakana's pleasure. Most of her people, especially her parents, preferred the nourishment of harsh Praka, making their prayers at his zenith. But Averlynn always found more than enough work that needed to be done at such a turn. Only after her people had gone to their beds, and the land itself seemed to wake gently into soothing song, did she find enough peace to truly hear. Out in the farthest wards, south only of Amka, she found as much peace as she could in this wide land. And yet, it was still not home.

She took another deep breath, stilling that memory for now. That would take her mind too far away from the darkening valley, and away from this much-needed prey. Maybe that was how she had forgotten what day it was. Something still nagged, though; not once in two thousand years had she forgotten something so basic. There was something else wrong here, but her mind was too divided to recognize it yet.

Food first, she told herself.

The doe flicked her tail once more, then moved downstream. Averlynn noted her progress, then nudged Tarafel downslope. She ran a hand down his crest. *Just a quick drink, let her get a little way ahead. Then we circle around to the clearing where her trail comes out.*

She dismounted, taking a few drinks herself as Tarafel slurped quietly, their noises lost below the burbling stream. She gave half a mind to pulling out her second cloak, but knew the land would be warmer out of the valley. She glanced up, seeing a few blots of sky through the canopy westward. They appeared even deeper blue, now, but were still not shot with red or orange despite the high clouds she had seen in the small clearing. And she had even camped without a fire this past week. The warm nights had been pleasant, if a little unusual.

Tarafel raised his muzzle, and looked at her briefly. "Done?" she asked lightly. He whuffled. With a smile she mounted, turning him at an angle back up the slope. She would pass behind the stand of spruce—even Tarafel would contrast too starkly against their dark green—then around the crest. The run below followed the stream for a spell, then leaped up around a knob, over the crown, and finally let out into a long pasture. The doe would probably bed there, so Averlynn would need to set up nearer the entrance. There were often briars on this side, in years past, with numerous breaks near honey locusts between which she might slip an arrow. This late in the year, perhaps the briars would already be falling, with gaps wide enough to shoot through.

Nearing the end of the hunt, it was difficult not to hurry. Pressing the stallion on, though, would not make the doe arrive any sooner, and would more easily scare her away if he quickened his pace.

He almost seemed to know the way, though Averlynn hadn't had him long enough. They had been on one trip northward together since she saddled him, and had not managed to press this far east. The geese and ducks in the Water Plains had been migrating oddly, that year, so she had spent most of her time there. She found nothing she could put a finger on; and when she reported to Harwynn, he had only thanked her, noted it in his book, and she left. Too many of her forays seemed to end that way: wherever she went, things seemed odd—different, certainly, than at any time before. Never anything stark or drastic, no clear sign. Not as clear as a deer run, compressed through overuse. More like an oddly-bent stick, or a tree growing where it did not usually grow.

Her companions said she noticed too much. The Rangers' forays were too short a time and too long an absence to draw conclusions from the things she believed she saw. Oh, they never outright denied she saw any-thing. The day they did was the day she would no longer be welcome as a Ranger—not as bad as being declared *tienko*, outcast, though the shame might hurt her just as much. But a Ranger's usefulness was entirely dependent on being alert, observant, and honest. So perhaps what she saw had been that way before and she just hadn't noticed it last time. Or, if it was new, it meant little. She herself wouldn't necessarily deny that the individual occurrences did not portend catastrophe; but accumulated over the past fifteen years, the pattern was distressing.

At least, it distressed her. So she watched, took note, and reported dili-gently. But Harwynn would only ever thank her, shrug, and write a note. The Rangers she replaced at every cardinal point had made few such notes, avowing when asked that nothing had changed during their foray.

And none of them, she was sure, had ever forgotten what day it was.

She held back a sigh. Food first; failing memory second. Tonight, she could make her prayers again to Hakana. Maybe tomorrow she could pray to Praka too, just in case. For now, she needed this doe.

She followed the ridge-line, keeping well back from the edge. The leaf-mold here was thinner, wetter, quieter. She let Tarafel pick up his pace, to give herself time to find a good gap and get settled. Ahead of her, the forest brightened. The clearing was near. She guided Tarafel left, checking the wind: slight, and always to her right. The doe would come in confidently, as the wind blew along the clearing toward where the trail let out, but it was just enough off-center to carry Averlynn's scent away. She smiled.

She edged Tarafel a little further left, to a small patch of undergrowth. It was not much forage, mostly ferns—he would have better once the hunt was done and they could camp in the clearing—but it should keep him occupied for the moment. She dismounted, loosening the girth a little as she relaxed herself. She gathered bow and quiver, whispered a few polite words to Tarafel, and made quietly for the edge of the clearing.

Almost there, she paused. The briars were towering, and dense enough to completely block her view of the open space. Her breath caught as she looked at the bank of writhing thorns. They had never been like this, especially so near Tadan È! The days were too short, nights too cold—though they had been warm lately. Things were changing, again, just as when she was a child of barely a hundred. Change seemed to chase her people, even if it took centuries to catch up again. She hoped Harwynn would pay attention this time, that the other Rangers were as attentive in their wards.

A twig snapped quietly somewhere, and she froze. It was not Tarafel, it was from the edge of the clearing. She needed to find a gap.

She stole along the wall of briars, glancing furtively. She was already getting too far away from the doe. Where were the honey locusts? Their trunks, though thin, always held off the undergrowth, at least for a space. She shook her head, and ducked down nearly to the ground.

There: back to her right, there seemed to be a breach. She went to it, peered through again. She recognized the trunk, the knot of thorns like clustered spears. It appeared almost dead. Why were they dying? How were the briars overtaking them?

How was she supposed to get this doe?

She froze again, catching movement. Her eyes slid sideways; the doe stood a hundred paces away, staring. Had its own trail been blocked, too?

It bent its head low, seeming to inspect the ground. Averlynn turned slowly, so slowly, knowing the shot was already lost but unable to keep herself from clinging to hope. Usually that was a fault of hers, at least among her people.

The doe looked up again, and Averlynn's eyes pleaded for it to stay. The doe turned, looked away for a moment, then back. A leg raised; the tail flickered.

Just as it was about to run, Tarafel let out a terrific whinny that echoed through the trees. Fear seized Averlynn a moment, until her frantic mind realized there was no alarm in his cry. As her mind cleared, she realized the doe was not so lucid: it stared toward where Averlynn had left the stallion, ears hard forward and legs stiff.

She could waste no more time moving slowly. She quickly drew an arrow, sighted, and loosed. The doe remained motionless, locked in fear, until the arrow sunk deep in her heart and she dropped, already dead.

Averlynn breathed a nearly gasping sigh. She turned toward Hakana's horizon, closed her eyes, and whispered a small thanks. She would do more in the wee turns, before dawn when her pale spirit-bond finally rose above the horizon. For now she would dress the deer quickly, begin to smoke the meat for the remainder of her journey.

She fetched Tarafel, thanking him too for his timely intervention. He merely nodded, then followed quietly as she returned to the doe's carcass. A few quick loops with her rope around its hind legs, securing it to Tarafel's saddle, and she turned for the deer run. Time, too, to find out why the doe had abandoned the clearing.

The bank of briars seemed to remain robust as she worked her way around. At the head, she saw indeed the run end abruptly at its thick tangle. Tarafel stepped obediently behind her as she continued the circuit, the carcass he dragged jolting through the carpet of leaves. The air was still, pungent with the scent of green weeds.

Finally, at the farthest end, the tangle thinned enough for Averlynn to force her way through. It would be good shelter, provided no night prowlers found their way into the dead-end clearing. But the briars would hide her fire, and the natural windbreak would let her smoke rise above the canopy before dispersing.

As dusk fell, she made her camp. Three trips with Tarafel and the rope as darkness fell, to drag in enough wood to smoke the meat, before she finally unsaddled him and rubbed him down with handfuls of grass. She skinned and dressed the doe just outside the clearing, depositing the offal far downwind. Another quick trip outside, this time with a large waterskin to fill at the stream. She paused while cleaning the blood from her hands, listening. Here and there a faint rustle might sound, or the quiet call of some nocturnal creature, but nothing that alarmed her and nothing of animal alarm either. As she made her way back upslope, she saw only the darkness of the hedge, and no light from her low fire.

She returned, swiftly building a spit for the meat. She would cook a small portion and eat, and hang the rest to dry once the fire died down to coals. Tarafel she allowed to roam through the clearing. He would never go too far. While her dinner portion cooked, she trimmed the last bits of fat from what meat she would preserve, and cut it into thin slices to dry more quickly in the smoke. As it was, she would be staying here until midday tomorrow—a further delay, making Amka the more likely place to celebrate the harvest.

She drank, then poured some water into a small bowl and washed the last bits of blood from her knife, arrow, and hands. She skewered the first portions of meat for drying, added some green cherry branches to the fire for smoke, and rested the spit on the higher notches of the uprights so it would not cook too quickly. Tarafel returned and stood behind her as she rested back against the saddle. She pulled a whetstone from the saddlebag, and fell to sharpening her knife.

In the canopy, the breeze picked up, washing through the leaves in a soothing rush. The air in the clearing was still and mild. And now, finally, with her belly full and warm, she began to worry about her lost memory.

Rangering was a complicated life, and only those whose minds were sharpest even had a chance of succeeding in training. It took more work than she had imagined just to find a mentor. A ranger needed to be independent, highly capable, able to recognize a thousand details for what they were individually, but also able to piece them together into a complete picture. One missing piece, or wrong assumption, and the story a ranger told would fall to pieces. And she needed to be able to do that daily for months at a time, and report accurately at the end of it. Then a month back home before making the next foray. Each year, a ranger would patrol through one of the cardinal points—north, east, south, and west—completing a circuit of all the lands they controlled every four years. Her mentor had settled on that plan, when they had arrived in their new home to join those who came before, to help keep fresh eyes on the lands. It was too easy, he knew, for a ranger to miss important clues because they had grown too accustomed to what had been there before.

It was a lonely, tedious, exciting, demanding life, and one which Averlynn thoroughly loved. She had set out on every foray with a heart as light as Tarafel's steps, and eyes as keen as the short Malgus blade she had received from Chief Witko when she'd entered the ranks. And for a century she had been grateful for every single day, even the ones when Harwynn seemed less than impressed with what she reported. Certainly, for those hundred years she had never wanted to be anything else than what she was.

But then they came to this new land, met a new enemy, and she happened onto a patrol with Amrith, a Scout, and things changed—at least, a little bit.

She still would not lie or embellish a story. Others might, but not her. And yet, when Amrith rode up on his stallion—Erglade, he had been at the time—and slipped his way into the enemy camp, observed and memorized three maps and ten pages of battle plans, opened and altered troop rosters and supply lists and flawlessly resealed them, and come back out as the camp was waking up, without slightest indication then or ever of detection, Averlynn suddenly felt the keen lance of desperation for that level of skill.

But if finding a mentor for the Rangers had been hard, finding one for the Scouts was impossible. So far it had been, certainly. If ever she managed to broach the subject (a feat in itself) it was the same story: the Scout ranks were full, and they had no desire to add another. The war was over, the danger passed.

She had been content with that, at first, until one day Chief Witko let slip that Amrith himself opposed her candidacy. Well, Chief Witko claimed it had slipped; Averlynn was not the only one of her family who believed he told her intentionally. Perhaps it was not the honorable thing, but it served Amrith right: his disdain for Chief Witko was an ill-kept secret, at least around Wazè.

Her only hope had been to continue to work hard, bring back good reports, and maybe one day prevent disaster from visiting her people. Certainly if she could single-handedly avert a decimation of her people, Amrith's opinion would matter a little less, and she might be allowed to try to prove herself in training.

So it was not simply *that* she had thought the full moon was tonight, when it had already come and gone a week past: it was *why* she had forgotten. Had she forgotten all of the intervening days? What other signs of the land and sky had she missed, or forgotten? Had she been captured and made to forget, and even now some foreign army was descending on her people while she sat and smoked meat before a fire? Until she could say what had happened, she could not honestly report what had *not* happened.

First, she needed to establish for herself that she had not lost the last days—that some strange enemy had not captured her. She closed her eyes, remembering her prayers to Hakana that night—beginning early, while Praka was still in the western sky, and pausing only while making camp and dinner. Then picking up again when she was at her height and moon-shadows lay like cold lace on the grass. Averlynn had even spotted a wyrgum, a rare and solitary tree that would produce one new pale white bloom every full moon from spring to winter. She had praised Hakana for the sighting, had taken it as bountiful omen. In her mind she saw the tree vividly, could even count the blossoms: seven, perfect and beautiful, and marking the countdown until Tadan È. A week before the next full moon, harvest would be complete and the bonfires would be set, lit from the eternal ember, and she would need to be in Amka.

Had she lost her way, somehow? She thought she had known this clearing, but the briars had never been so thick. And the land was riddled with deer runs that went to water, then to a nearby pasture. Perhaps she had not gone as far north as she thought? She opened her eyes and glanced above the tree-line. She found Wedanka, the Plow; and tall Heradon the reaper with his hand outstretched. His feet were lost below the canopy. If she had lost days of travel, and was further south than she thought, he would be up to his waist.

Best to be sure. Instead she ran through each day of the past week, recalling every rise, movement, and sleep. But it was all still there. So what sign had she missed, to think full moon was ahead of her? She sighed, and again closed her eyes, listening to the wind in the trees.

After a moment, her eyes snapped open: the wind through the leaves. She sat up, looking again at the horizon. In the faint glow of her fire she could see the thick, life-full canopy of the maples and oaks around the clearing. Tadan È was swiftly approaching. Wheat should be turning golden, corn shocks drying at the edges of the largest leaves. A time of feasting and dancing, of standing in the deepest forest and looking up through nearly-naked branches to cold stars tossed overhead.

But with as green as the leaves around her were, they would not turn color and fall by Tadan È. That was the sign: autumn seemed not to be here. The forest still felt like summer.

Averlynn drew up her knees and hugged them. Why would the land be like this? Would the gods be holding back their plenitude this year? She wondered frantically what the fields looked like back home. Had she cursed her people by taking last Tadan È so lightly? For disdaining Praka who helped the corn grow, in favor of Hakana whose only priest was the stingy wyrgum?

Such questions were too far above her. Maybe in Amka she could ask the Isun—a small outpost such as that did not rate a full Sage—and she could cast the bones for her. She would do whatever it took. She hoped Harwynn would grant her a Minor Hangh when she returned to Wazè. It was not common, but she had done so before, back in...

That had been so long ago. Her eyes closed tight, but in vain: a rebellious tear slipped out. She wiped a sleeve across her cheek as she remembered her home—her true home. The rest of the Wohan might have accepted their fate here, but she had too many precious memories of their former land. Or, maybe she clung to hope too tightly. She shook her head, breathing deep to try to calm herself, but melancholy descended anyway.

She lay back again, feeling the earth through her back, letting it cradle her. She had tried to tie herself to this land, but the soil always seemed foreign. It had not raised her, had not taught her the ways of rangering, had not nourished her in the cold and sleet when she thought she might truly die, that she did not possess the skills necessary for the life she desired.

She put her hands down by her side, tangling her fingers in the grass, letting the grit of soil get under her fingernails. This was her home. It had to be her home. She must...

Quite unbidden, verses began to float through her mind:

Undying leaves on branches hang as though possessed by summer's grin,
but glowing fades and decays in days while barring ways to those within.
Full-moon hangs low in following spring below the rolling tempest's roar,
while earthen guardians give out their soul and slide into oblivion's door.

Averlynn blinked as the old song seemed to sing in her ears. How long ago had she heard it? Before they came to this land, she was sure. What could it mean? Why would she recall it now: just because of the first line? It certainly rang true. And spring would be following, so long as autumn and winter both did eventually arrive and pass on.

She sang the verses again, trying to remember what came next. But nothing came. Perhaps it meant little, like all the other signs she thought she saw. Maybe she only yearned for home, wished she could go back and do it right this time. They had been cursed, the Chiefs all said. And how could you avoid a curse?

But it did not sit well with her. Summer remained unusually late this year: she couldn't only imagine that. The first verse was true. What could the second line mean? What glowing would fade? Daylight's glow? Would it get darker? Would the sun decay, casting them in perpetual gloom?

She shivered. *Why did I not pray to Praka? I'll never take you for granted again, I swear it. I'll do anything I must, only don't kill my people.* But Praka was gone until morning, and couldn't hear her.

Unless she read the line wrong. Hakana would still be around—would hang below the tempest's roar in the following spring, according to the third verse. Maybe Praka was not what would fade. *And decay—what might decay? In days? In days when the leaves did not decay as they should? Some other part of the forest?*

The Glowwood. Surely it was not that simple—not in a song from a far distant land. How would they even know about the Glowwood? And yet it fit: the Glowwood was a sacred land, a pocket within the Waken Forest, where between the trunks of bald cypress grew towering, glowing mushrooms—five to ten paces high, at maturity. They were unremarkably white or pale brown during the day, but at night they gave off a floating haze of blue, green, and purple light. The Glowwood thrived most during summer, but persisted late into the cold. Only with the first snow would they fade, the great caps and gills would shrivel, and finally the stems would topple and rot into the ground. In spring, after last frost, they would return, leaping into the sky, some at full height within a hand of days.

If the lines ran true, the Glowwood was rotting already, the great stems collapsed and barring the way through the trees. And Averlynn was near to it—perhaps a day or two east, at most. She knew she needed to go, but she dreaded discovering she was right. She loved the Glowwood perhaps even more than the mountains far to the north.

But she did not love it more than her people. If the song was indeed some sort of prophecy, then events were already tumbling into place. If the Glowwood was fading, they needed to know. If it was hale, she could continue quickly to Amka, make her prayers to Hakana and Praka both, and return with little else to report than a late autumn.

But she did not believe she would find the Glowwood in good health. In her mind's eye, she already saw the colors gone, the caps rotting and stinking, and the stems tottering. Cursed, her people had been. They thought it was in the name, and so they changed it when they had fled.

But curses do not recognize names, it seemed. She only needed to prove it by two days' journey east, and remembering the rest of the song. Then return home and tell her people they could not hide behind the name Wohan. The curse remained, just as it had when they had called themselves Kalen.

2

SIGN OF THE GOAT

"Where is Melnor?"
"Kanala, finally; he is busy in Burieng. Do you have someone?"
"A young ranger, for now."
"Will that be enough, though?"

23 Halmfurtung 1320 — Autumn

Where the forest thinned, Averlynn kept Tarafel to a light canter as they went east. To her right she could hear mighty Raktar pounding down the tumbled stones on his way to the sea. At Gawad she would turn north, though she would miss visiting the high falls. At morning, the early sun could reach through the gap in the forest and dazzle against the mists and foam, and often great herons would leave their high nests to glide over the valley and down into the stiller pools below. Not a bad place to eat breakfast.

But time pressed her on. She had abandoned most of the venison for the wolves, had neglected even to scrape clean the hide, to turn into a new winter cloak when she paused at Amka for Tadan È. As soon as her prayers at Hakana's height were done she had dismantled her camp, packing what precious little meat had smoked, wetting and scattering the coals and replacing the turf. Praka had not risen, though the great trunks began to appear from the darkness in a spectral dawn, when she had Tarafel saddled and they made their way through the valley to a long ridge on the other side.

She hoped to reach Gawad by noon; though she could not turn south to the actual top of the falls, she knew its sound. There the oaks and maples turned to young beeches and black cherry in forest young enough to catch easy glimpses of Praka: she would pause, before turning, to offer her confessions and prayers to him as well.

Though the four verses from last night continued to run through her head, the rest of the song continued to elude her memory. Perhaps the Isun in Amka would remember. Or she could ask the Sage, once she was able to return to her village of Wazè.

She vowed never to take the religious leaders lightly again. She had respected them as her parents had dictated, but were they not beholden still to the Chiefs? She would much rather listen to Chief Witko than Sage Herrada, for certain. Chief Witko might be mad, but at least he was not a lech.

Perhaps that was too harsh. Sage Herrada had never quite done anything to her, not outright. He only seemed too eager for her visits. Now she wondered if perhaps he had only worried about the curses she might bring with her seemingly lapse religion, had been merely hopeful and encouraging. As she slowed Tarafel through a thicket, she closed her eyes; there seemed too much to answer for.

On the other side, she nudged the stallion to a gallop where she could. Penance might come from a timely report. Perhaps if she could discover what threat was nearing, what doom the song pronounced and warn her people before it was too late, the gods might forgive her errancy.

The following afternoon, Tarafel slowed as he seemed to sense Averlynn's hesitation. They rode down a gentle slope, now. Below, the forest opened and turned to black oak, the occasional sycamore, and bald cypress. Here and there the canopy opened wide, and bright sunbeams danced across beds of ferns. More rarely a small pool was edged by pickerelweed, cattail, and sedge.

Averlynn hesitated, knowing the Glowwood was near.

Her prayers at noon yesterday, directly under a bright shaft of Praka where the beeches had bent eastward and opened a hole in the canopy, did not feel as if they had reached his grand halls in the heavens. When she prayed to Hakana, she could feel the vastness overhead, felt as though her voice lifted higher and higher, ascending clear to the pale bosom of the moon mother. But when she had prayed to Praka, yesterday, it felt as though she made her prayers in a closet, her voice going no further than she could reach with her hand and echoing back down to her.

She had pressed on, hoping that with continued speech the sound might pile up and some important word might reach his ear. So she had apologized most, promised renewed discipleship and gratitude. After the first several calls, she had not even bothered making a request, except for forgiveness. She did not want the first word to reach him to be a request for her people. She would not dare to presume so much.

She had left that sunbeam dissatisfied and with more fear and worry than she had entered it. Was that how prayer to Praka was supposed to go? Did his harsh glare beat back the words—did his devotees need more strength of voice and faith in order to reach him? She did not know, could not remember anyone teaching so, specifically. But then, she had attended the temples of Hakana from a very young age, disdaining Praka even in childhood. Perhaps he had actually heard all of it. And so she had continued.

Now, nearing her goal, she faltered once more. She turned Tarafel toward one of the ponds, into the sun. Perhaps if she practiced her renewed devotion, he would pause and hear her.

But as Tarafel drank and Averlynn prayed, she felt no different. She lifted her face, tried to feel the warmth and presence of the sun, but could not. Tarafel's head came up as she raised her voice, and around as she began to weep. Why would he not listen? Was he so demanding? Or was he simply too far away? Despite the warmth of the close air, almost like summer, the presence of Praka on her skin still felt like autumn.

She bowed her head, her prayers ending with a sniffle. She wiped her eyes and sighed, giving Tarafel a despairing gaze. Maybe it was too late, the doom already decided. Even the prayers of the Sages might go unheard, now.

With a final, decisive sigh, Averlynn bent her lips into a smile. "No more waiting," she said to Tarafel. "The truth is out there whether we ignore it or not, and cares not for our feelings. So, let's discover it if we can."

She turned him northward again, weaving among the ponds and bogs on firmer ground. As she went she caught herself now and again straining her eyes forward, hoping to catch a glimpse of the pale mushroom caps in the sunbeams ahead.

As it turned out, she needn't have looked: the smell reached her long before the sight. The rot and decay hid for a time below the brackish malodor of the vernal pools around her, until finally a powerful strain came along an eddy of wind. Her eyes widened as she smelled, and her heart fell—though not far, for her hopes had not been that high to begin with. It felt more like a settling, despair sealing off her mind much like the night sky settled over the land when Praka slid off the edge. On that scent she knew the prophetic song was true, that the curse of Kalen still lived and had come across the sea to visit them again.

By the time she saw the first toppled stem, the great white column collapsed on its side and bruised in black, a grim determination had settled on her despair. In her spirit, the slim figure of young Hakana rested—not bright enough yet to show the way, but still there with the promise of growth. As the song foretold, her path deeper into the Glowwood was blocked by the great fallen trunks, and by the stench. Peering over the top with her mouth and nose tucked into her elbow, she could see the ruin of it. The vast caps were tumbled and broken, deflating in the shade and blackening in the sun. She did not want to wait until nightfall, to make real to her the absence of the wonderful light so reminiscent of the holy cove back home where frogs sung and herons danced, and the spirits of the dead went to rest. She had believed the spirits now came here—the pulsating glow drawing their souls from this land as Iridescent Bay in Kalen had drawn them from that land. Many times, toward the end, she had participated in the great sending rituals, for the souls of the Kalen could not move on their own. They had first to be drawn out of the body in burial, then urged on their way.

Now, depending on the doom that she was sure was approaching, any Wohan who died now would either wander homeless or be forced to try to make their way across the empty waves to that faraway land. She trusted they could, guided by the trails her people had left across the seas when they came here. But it would surely be an arduous journey, and she feared the weak ones who might get lost or slip wearily beneath the cold ocean to some unknown end. Too many even in Old Kalen had not made the journey, their bodies burned or desecrated before the rituals could be performed. She feared the last feast, to look around that eternal table and see chairs empty, old and fast friends forever gone as they were never supposed to be.

It was this thought, perhaps more than any others, that drove her determination on as she turned Tarafel north and west toward Amka. Her prayers alone would not be enough, she knew: she was only one of her people, and one who had either abandoned or driven away Praka. More than that, she needed the wisdom of the clergy, even if it were only an Isun—she, at least, would know more than her of the ways and desires of the gods. Perhaps, she hoped, she could even give her direction in the song, might even remember it herself. If not, then they could seek the spirits together. Whatever it took, she would find the answer to why these portents had come to her, and submit herself to whatever will the gods had.

For three days, Averlynn circled west of the Glowwood, keeping far enough away that Tarafel could not smell it—the first turn of sneezing and grumbling from her stallion helped find that particular boundary. The Waken Forest became all oak and maple again, with some locust, and in the depths retained a deep gloom even at midday. Openings in the canopy were rare, but still she made her prayers as best she could, morning, noon, evening, and night. They went from forage to forage, stream to stream, for Tarafel's sake more than hers. She did not desire to eat often, and her meat lasted.

On the morning of the fourth day the canopy finally began to break apart. Mature black cherry and black oak intruded, and broad beds of ferns carpeted their way. Amka was near.

By late afternoon, the forest edge arrived. Following a stream she knew well, she turned left at a fork, climbed the hill, and at the top broke out into pure, evening sunlight. Southerly, the land sank and glistened in the Water Plains, full of ponds, lakes, braided streams, waterlilies, cattails, sedges and rushes, the occasional hazy magnolia and swamp oak, frogs, dragonflies, and herons. Northerly the lands rose and humped in the Hataki Hills, brown and rocky, tangled, heather, scrubby grass and broomsedge, rushing cascades, roe deer, ravens and crows and killdeer. Faintly on a white horizon rose the vast mountains, their peaks visible mostly only because she knew they were there. There she would sometimes see the white dragon floating almost listlessly on the winds. Aryndurlan, her name was. But she had met her only twice, and she rarely went that far north.

Hard on her right, in the tree-line, was the gateway to Amka. She might have ridden into the east side of it, but she enjoyed this view of the three lands meeting. It was the reason Amka was placed here. From its tallest tower—a massive cypress hundreds of years old—lookouts could see into the first valleys of the mountains far to the north, nearly to the Fleeing Sea to the west, and the green smudge of the Waken Forest where it curved finally west to the cliffs.

She gazed now at Praka, low and red, at his long arm as it rested mottled through the standing waters of the Plains. She knew it was probably her selfish and sinful predisposition that saw it as a virulent arm, reaching out to blight the Waken with eternal summer, to poison the Glowwood. She tried to push these thoughts away, to open her mind in prayer. She turned away unsuccessful.

As she passed back into the forest, into Amka, she raised a hand in greeting, knowing the lookouts had likely seen her when she followed the stream northward a turn ago. It was all silence. It was the custom: new arrivals presented themselves to be seen to the attendant Chief and Isun, were announced to the outpost, and then only if the land was clear could conversation commence.

She weaved her way between the trunks, following roads that appeared only as deer runs. Houses, such as they were, hid behind trees and thickets. Averlynn could only see them because she was Wohan; no other could pierce the minor glamours of her people unless permitted by the Chief. To unwanted visitors and the animals of the forest, they were oak, ash, maple, locust, sycamore, briar, ivy, spotted laurel. To her, they were armory, stable, kitchens, meeting-house, lodges, temple.

She dismounted, turning through the briars to stable Tarafel. She took off his saddle and tack, filled a box with hay, and rubbed him down quickly. After a quick scratch behind his ears she left him, heading east down the street to the meeting-house—a massive sycamore nearly her height in diameter. Brushing aside some ivy she entered.

"I am Averlynn of Wazè, daughter to Avako and Erion also of Wazè, Ranger of Wohan. I have traveled seventy-two days through the Waken Forest and Glowwood, and come here to the northern outpost of Amka of our people to meet with Chief Hathar and Isun Vera, under the watchful eye of Hakana...and Praka," she added belatedly, cursing herself.

Chief Hathar emerged from behind a cherry tree, smiling. As he stepped, the floor beneath his feet appeared, clean-hewn and polished oak. Behind him came Isun Vera as the forest disappeared, replaced by walls and a ceiling. When they stopped before her, table, chairs, and candles appeared, and plates of soup and bread were already laid out. Only now could she smell the roasted onion and warm yeast, and she remembered how little she had eaten of late.

"Welcome, Ranger Averlynn," Chief Hathar replied. "It is good to see you so well."

She smiled thinly; her people were adept at hiding their fears behind a mask of wellness, a talent she had not been able to avoid.

"Hakana's Daughter Averlynn," Isun Vera said, entwining her fingers before her chest; "I had thought it might be you in the north this year, when I did not see you for so long." Though she smiled broadly, Averlynn could not help a brief spasm from squinting her eyes. Chief Hathar politely glanced aside as though to check the preparations of the table.

"I mean to visit more often, Isun Vera," she said. "I have been too lapse in my prayers, of late. Praka has seen fit to chide me and I turn again to him now."

Isun Vera cleared her throat, but Chief Hathar motioned to the table before she could speak. They sat, Isun prayed, and they ate in silence for a time. The soup was hot and flavorful, and Averlynn could not but help dwelling over each spoonful. Amidst the roasted onion flavors were layers of pepper, garlic, butter, potato, perhaps some mild cheese? She believed so. The bread steamed when she broke it, and she let a soft prayer go up with the mist. Sharp cheddar, more garlic, and chives met her tongue in those bites.

Finally, when she believed the silence had gone on long enough, she glanced at Chief Hathar. "Any news from Tekaa Wohan?" she asked. She had met Chief Hathar before, knew he was fifth in line at their capitol city. The chiefs took turns, much as the Rangers and Isuns did, of visiting the outposts to serve as civil leader for the year. Each Ranger was informed of who would be in the ruling council of their outposts before setting out, so they might properly introduce themselves.

"Very little has changed, when I was there," he replied. "Harvest should be plentiful again, or so Sage Jorno suggested. Lota came by—do you remember him? He said he knew you."

Averlynn nodded. Lota had been a childhood friend, and had even spent some time in Wazè when they had come to this new land—had helped build her parents' home. Someone had once mentioned his certain feelings for her. But then he decided to become a trader, and moved to Tekaa Wohan. She had not seen him in fifteen years.

"Typical things: wool is low in the south, meat is low in the west and they grow tired of fish and the eels are sour this year. Of course our vegetables grow fat but do not ripen..." He trailed off, taking a spoonful of soup as though he hadn't meant to mention the last part. Averlynn latched on to it.

"Summer seems to hesitate leaving," she said mildly.

Isun Vera wiped her mouth with a napkin. "The forest feels greener than ever, but I've not been to the north often. It felt warmer than...well, I suppose it felt more like Kal—"

She cut off as Chief Hathar cleared his throat. "This land has long grown warmer in the north than in the south. That is not unusual."

"Have either of you been to the Glowwood?" she asked. "Or have any of the Trackers on mission here?"

"You will have to ask Ka Karaa," Chief Hathar replied evenly. "Unless you mean to make a report to myself or Isun Vera?" he asked with an arched brow.

Averlynn ducked her head. "Of course not, Chief Hathar. Forgive me my impatience."

Chief Hathar rose, then. "Let us announce you to the outpost," he said. "I assume you will stay with us through Tadan È?"

"I will, Chief Hathar, if it is acceptable to you and Isun Vera."

"We should be glad of your company," Isun Vera replied smoothly as she stood. Averlynn refrained from a furtive glance at her unfinished meal, resolving to be thankful for what she'd had. Instead she quietly followed her leaders out into the forest once more. The rest of the outpost had already gathered outside, though they did not cluster. Chief Hathar and Isun Vera stood apart, and she came to stand between them.

"This is Ranger Averlynn, daughter to Avako and Erion, from Wazè," Chief Hathar intoned. "She will remain here for a span, partaking in our fires and dances, and through the Telling, before continuing on her foray to keep us safe from unknown threats."

"She is once-sworn daughter to Hakana, pledged during her Way Tè," Isun Vera said next. Averlynn could not refrain from blinking; she didn't know Isun Vera would know that. That she acknowledged it in front of the outpost was...comforting. "Her spirit will help guide ours who favor Praka, when we make our songs at nightfall."

Averlynn barely noticed as the Trackers began approaching to look at her closer, memorize her features so they would not sound an alarm if they saw her where they thought no one should be. She nearly forgot to hold up her left hand, to display the ring on her forefinger, as the blood thundered in her ears. *My spirit will help guide? Even though I've brought curses down on... Or have I not?* It was not proper to give a military report to civil or religious leaders, but she could certainly discuss religious matters with Isun Vera.

"A goat?" the Tracker in front of her questioned in surprise. She could only guess her shock matched his. They both glanced aside to Chief Hathar, who frowned slightly. Given the decorum expected, that small frown was tantamount to a diatribe. The Tracker looked properly chaste and quickly departed. She would see him later, she knew, deep in the business of some task that should have been below one of his station.

And yet, she had to admit to herself, the sign of the goat on her ring was not much better than, say, mucking out the stalls of ten horses with bowel sickness—not that her indiscretion had ever earned her that task. But the goat was what the gods had given her, and so she wore it. Few knew why their glamour ring was given the sign it was given—or really why any sign at all was necessary. And those who did had never told Averlynn. The most they were supposed to be was functional, helping hide the raven hair, high cheekbones, and sorrel skin of their elven heritage from prying eyes and granting them some small magics, if they had need of either. Isolated in this land, she did not understand why they needed to hide their features, yet most of them did in public. To let down the glamour outside Tekaa Wohan, or one's own home, was often viewed as at least scandalous, if not downright indecent.

Along with the glamour and magics, and more importantly to those passing before her, the rings gave out a mild sense of the person. In the dark, they would know if she was near because of the unique sense her ring would transmit to them. By showing it now, and letting them feel her presence at close range, they would later be able to point to her through a thicket under a new moon. And not shoot her.

The review ended quickly, and the Trackers melted back into the forest and to their posts. Averlynn cocked her head. "When will Ka Karaa return?" she asked, having not seen the military leader with his troops.

"Perhaps a day," Chief Hathar replied. "He took some of the Trackers northward some days ago, following a herd. He did not say why," he interjected as Averlynn opened her mouth to ask. "But come, I will show you your quarters."

Averlynn bowed her head in thanks, falling in behind the leaders. Now that she was introduced, the glamours had been taken away from the interior structures. Those nearer the forest edge would remain hidden, but the risk of being seen to those deeper in was deemed less. They moved silently with sure footing. Deep inside, where a shaft of sunlight struck, they stopped at a small outbuilding. She could tell she would have it to herself. It was not unusual for a Ranger to have such, though she had never stayed in this particular building before. When Isun Vera turned to glance at her, in the Isun's smile she felt the sense that it was precisely because of the sunlight glowing against the pale wood. This room would be best for making prayers.

"Might I speak to you of some important religious matters, Isun?" Averlynn asked, still standing apart. "It will have...little to do with my military purpose in the north," she added carefully to Chief Hathar's compressed smile.

"Of course, Daughter," Isun Vera replied happily. "I have no pressing matters until this evening. Should we join in your room?"

"Thank you," Averlynn replied.

With bows and smiles, Chief Hathar departed, and Averlynn and Isun Vera entered the building. Inside was sparsely but comfortably appointed: one bed with pillows and extra blankets, if the nights ever decided to grow cold; a small dresser for extra clothes, of which she had almost none; a rack for her gear, of which she took immediate advantage while Isun Vera patiently waited. Averlynn briefly observed the small sculpture atop the dresser. Her people never built or made anything without a bit of art. This—a mix, it seemed, of bear, elf, and hawk in lines that joined but also separated each element to the point it was difficult to tell if it were supposed to be one or three—was part of the top, carved out of a thicker plank that had been pared down until the sculpture seemed to rise from it as a fish might rise from the river, jumping after some small insect.

She turned back to Isun Vera. "I thank you, again, for agreeing—"

Isun Vera held up a hand. "Averlynn, we can speak familiarly now. Chief Hathar is gone, and doesn't pry."

Averlynn smiled and sighed. "Thank the gods," she said, sitting in one of the two chairs near the window. Isun Vera took the other, a rocking chair, the sun streaming through the window behind her turning her hair into a silver halo. Averlynn's gaze concentrated, and Vera paused.

"What is it?" she asked hesitantly, patting her hair.

"Nothing, just...your hair isn't yellow."

Vera chuckled. "No, it wouldn't be. I'm glad that's a good thing?"

"Sitting there, even under the light of Praka, it still glows like Hakana instead."

"You're unsure of your allegiance." Vera stated it as fact.

"I wasn't. I love Hakana, find peace in her gentle beams, delight in her soft lay across a landscape. But my parents worship Praka—most of our people do. And things are changing—" She was cut off again as Vera raised a hand.

"I would still not hear your report," she said. "Not until the Ka hears it."

Averlynn sighed shortly, her gaze drifting away. "I'm afraid our people are still cursed—afraid it's because I reject Praka. Summer lingers too long—isn't that his doing? And when I tried to pray, these last days coming to Amka, I fear he doesn't hear me, and what that might mean for the coming times. I thought perhaps I could take a Minor Hangh, if my superior approved it. If he received a recommendation from you...at least it would help me refocus my prayers and thoughts, maybe I could hear again from the spirits. Someone besides Hakana. But then you acknowledged me in front of the outpost as once-pledged—"

A raised hand cut her off again. Vera inhaled slowly. "Why do you believe our people are still cursed? Just a suspicion because the season changes?"

"There are other things that will be in my report—have been in my reports, but didn't seem to mean anything until now. But now there's more—more than what I've seen, but something I recalled...a prophecy, I believe."

"A prophecy from Hakana?"

Averlynn blinked, her eyes widening as she considered. "I...I guess I don't know. It might be. At least, she might have brought to mind...I remembered an old refrain, from back—" she waved her hand vaguely westward. Even she did not like to say the name Kalen out loud. "But I can't remember any of the rest of it, or what it might mean. Actually I hoped you might remember it." At Vera's gesture, Averlynn recited the song. At the first line, Vera's easy smile had gone; by the end she was positively frowning.

"I may have to think on it. It sounds dire indeed, and familiar—though, yes, it has been...centuries, I think. Hmm." Vera looked toward the ceiling with closed eyes for several long moments. Averlynn's gaze drew to the window as leaves began to dapple the sill with shadows. Finally Vera looked at her again, and with a strange reservation as though something occurred to her she was not yet ready to speak aloud. "I had first thought that you might not consider yourself so important, that your disobedience would bring all the wrath of Praka on our people, such that an entire season would delay. And yet, if Hakana brought this to you—did it come under her light, or Praka's?"

"Her's," Averlynn responded promptly. "I was resting before I slept, and...I was trying to convince myself that this was my home." She bit her lip in shame.

Vera's eyebrows climbed. "It is not?"

Averlynn shrugged again, miserably. "I want it to be. I give my life in service that our people might be safe here, as at a home. But I cannot..." She trailed off, palms raised in supplication. "I can't make it feel right."

Vera grunted. "Strange. Odd, too, that a prophecy centuries old, given in a far-distant land, might be seen to fulfill itself here. You are certain it is coming to pass? You've seen evidence?"

Averlynn nodded. "It will be in my report to the Ka."

Vera grunted again, almost a snort. "And I must quiet my curiosity, then. Well—"

"But if it might have spiritual implications as well?"

Vera shook her head firmly. "The spirits will not change in a day. And, according to the verses, we are only at the incipient stages; more must come next spring. We'll wait until you've given your report, and obtained permission to share more with me. For now," she said, rising, "you may stay here and enjoy the sunshine. Praka still warms and lights the way for those who love his wife, as a husband would look favorably on anyone who does not hate his family. Perhaps he does not answer you because he would not impose on the rights of his spouse with their children. So be at peace, Averlynn, Hakana's daughter: this prophecy was not uttered by you, and you have nothing to do with whether it comes to pass or not."

Averlynn bowed her head, clasping her hands in front of her nose; she could do no more to thank Isun Vera than that simple gesture.

Alone again, she sat in front of the window and felt the sun and breeze on her face, smelled the warm green smells of the forest, and rested. She did not try to force her prayers, this time, merely let her mind wander as light and shadows danced and evening fell.

Tomorrow or the next, she would make her report to Ka Karaa. She would speak again with Isun Vera after that. And she would, above all, search out the completion and meaning of this strange prophecy and do whatever part the gods had in store for her as—it seemed—first messenger.

And she would send word to her parents that she was in Amka and celebrating the festival there. Night fell as she hoped that would satisfy them.

3

A Thread of Blood

"You would choose so boldly?"
"As Illmali would wish, I believe."
"You think too highly of yourself, Lasserain."
"You think of yourself too lowly, Hashar."

23 Halmfurtung 1320 — Autumn

K etzler Duamos knelt before the altar, hands held stiff and properly against his thighs, back straight, utterly silent. To the Bader behind him, he knew he seemed astutely in prayer—they thought much of him in the cathedral, had said his name even went up to the Orox in Thoroneus. Each Bader thought they curried his favor by whispering this to him aside, showing no indication that this had become common knowledge.

It was something he had worked hard for, ever since his parents sacrificed him to the God by sending him here. They were ever so pious, offering their youngest to the church when the elder sons had found more profitable trade and did not want the risk of Ketzler inheriting anything. And for the first five years, he had applied himself well and learned everything he could. He devoted himself to quiet times, prayers, and festivals. He believed what he was doing could still change the world.

Then was the day at market, his first time ever in his life. There was no market in his remote hometown of Plomnos, and Pips were not allowed outside the cathedral until deemed appropriate by their Bader. It was some testament to his self-discipline that Ketzler had hardly felt pride when he was the youngest Pip going to market.

He wished he had not been permitted. The people there took one look at his cassock, and turned away at best. Some sneered; others laughed at him outright. At first he thought maybe they believed he was putting on airs: he should have been too young to wear the cassock and be outside. But soon he caught the whispered remarks, truly learned of the Cariste attitudes toward religion, toward what he had bought into heart and soul for most of his young life.

He had cried, he was ashamed to admit; his morning of joy had been dashed asunder by one afternoon in the real world. The Bader tried to understand, to offer consolation. But he soon became annoyed, then angry. By Evening, Ketzler was locked in the crypts with one crust of bread, and told to consider the lives of the saints until starvation and humility reminded him why he was here.

Starvation did its work long before humility, or the lives of the saints. At first, he had applied himself to this punishment with the same fervor he had applied to every task for five years. At the opening of each sepulcher, a plaque had been carved with the story of the saint interred, and Ketzler studied each one. The bread he tucked away in a place of offering, determining to find his humility, to wring it from these stones if it were possible.

By the fourth saint, he began to read more slowly. Tenth, he leaned on his hands against the plaque—a thing he would not have imagined a day before. Fifteenth, he knew the pattern and dreaded finding it in each successive memorial. And by the twentieth, he retrieved his piece of bread and ate in silence. This is what life in the cathedral had become: great deeds locked up, dusty, and forgotten except as punishment—ridiculed by any and all who remained in the light of day, free.

But he knew the words. He had done his reading, as he was told. When the Bader returned to hear Ketzler's submission, the man was impressed and even apologetic, believing he had left Ketzler too long in punishment. As a reward, he offered another trip outside, this time to a tree-filled green-space—one of the few left in any of Gintanos' cities.

Ketzler declined, citing his need to continue in prayers. He believed it was not long after that his name may have reached the Orox's ears.

For five more years he played the role. He hoped, faintly, that perhaps he might find the joy of his religion again. Now, as he knelt perfectly before the God's altar in this little cathedral in Klos, he imagined he never would. Instead of praying for humility and joy, his mind wandered to the pale paneling where the lights glowed. The westering sun shone brilliantly through the cathedral's stained-glass windows, colored the white pine so gloriously when everything else seemed so dank and wan. In those effervescent colors he could almost imagine how beauty might change the world; it certainly stirred something in him. His mind drifted as the lights slid slowly up the wall, and he lost himself in his breathing and in the quiet of the church. For a moment, he could understand the draw of religion, the peace that dwelled here in these silent evenings. He could almost feel as if his soul were opening to the God of All, that revelation might come at any moment, that all the days and years of devotion and worship might actually have some meaning.

A wooden clatter echoed and boomed through the empty sanctuary, and the lights disappeared as they always did when the sun sank suddenly behind The Brynth—towering mountains only a few miles south, and a jutting peak just far enough west to shorten their evening. As bells rang through the city, Bader Losnoss padded up behind him and laid a hand on his shoulder.

"The God bless you and keep you, Pip Duamos. You are his pride and joy, and your worship of him worth a hundred lives."

"Would that I might live them all in His service, Bader," Ketzler whispered back. They always loved that response, and the Bader squeezed his shoulder warmly.

"Would we all, Pip; would we all. He is generous, and you'll find His providence this evening still warm in the dinner hall. You may be dismissed to attend it."

Ketzler rose slowly, his gaze lingering on the God's symbol affixed above the altar: the eternal circle of gold, the interwoven cords of flame red, earth green, white sky, and dark blue water, affixed in the center by a bronze seal etched with the four elements and an androgynous figure of mankind. It was a symbol he loved. Despite everything else he thought of his people's religion, the symbol itself remained untainted and true: he knew his life was caught up in the tangled threads of the elements, and with other people. It was his role, he was told, to travel up the thread of white, linking mankind to the eternal circle and the God of All who lived above to oversee Oren. To come back, bringing down that blessed word and sharing it with mankind.

But then there were the saints interred below. Buried with their deeds and enclosed with stone, they no longer conferred with the God and man. They had long ago left the troubles they were meant to relieve, and Ketzler could detect no improvement in the lives they left behind.

Ketzler made his way down the stone halls lined with rushlights. Another Pip, probably already done with his evening meal, made his way toward Ketzler, trimming the oil-soaked rushes to brighten a hall now devoid of sunlight. They passed with murmured blessings. He was new, and Ketzler didn't recognize him.

A generous God, Ketzler thought as he looked at the plate left alone on the table. Long benches and tables filled the hall. There were not so many Baders or Pips here, but Klos lay between Thoroneus where the Orox lived and the capitol of Gaios, and they often entertained his Holy Excellence and his entourage. Even more rushlights were plastered on the walls, and tall candelabras lined the tables. Here was the second-largest window in the cathedral—the largest and most exquisitely-cut was, of course, reserved for the sanctuary—and bright evening skies helped keep the dimness away from the room.

A pale wooden plate with one crust of bread, a thumb's-length of cheese, and a chicken's wings did little to keep the dimness away from Ketzler's mind. Providence. As he sat and put a finger on the wing—it was warm, but the interior would be cold—he realized too that it was far more than most people outside the cathedral would be eating this evening.

He could not refrain from sending up a small prayer—adequate, he believed, for the portion in front of him—before picking at the small fibers of meat. They were two habits he couldn't break—the prayer, and delaying the end of his meal for as long as he could. It seemed a feast if it could last a quarter-shift, even if it meant things growing cold. It was a habit he began to develop several years ago, when the ever-shrinking portions continued year after year despite promises and prayers of greater harvests.

There were some things Pips weren't meant to hear, which meant they tried ever harder to hear them. Ketzler had heard more than enough. The harvests were not the problem: those increased each year. The problem was the Brynth, and the cursed rugged shorelines and treacherous waters all around Gintanos. That history was well-known: for centuries, Cariste had tried various times to expand southward. Overland, the Brynth was too treacherous and confusing, and too few expeditions sent into it ever returned. By sea, the ships sent either saw nothing but unscalable cliffs, or were caught in storms and dashed against the unseen rocks that littered the coastlines. Eventually the waters to Gintanos' east was named the Sea of Wreckage by those terrified to enter it.

The route overland was abandoned long ago. And when Prince Jorress led a fateful expedition by the western sea and never returned, the King forbade any future expeditions forever, vowing his people could live well enough on this broad, fertile strip between the Brynth and the ocean. That had been during the Age of War. In over a thousand years since, the land indeed proved fertile, but so had Cariste women, and now there were simply too many villages, towns, and cities, and too many mouths to feed from what little farmland remained.

Ketzler finished the chicken, and turned to the bread. Even today he could not eat a crust without remembering the time in the crypts. He still recalled what he read there: Saint Bonetiene fed himself on sunlight and birdsong. *And yet the people do not pray, and turn away from the God; it changed nothing.* Saint Gurvatus led one expedition, and through his prayers reached deeper into the mountains than any other, and returned—one of the few who did. *He returned because at a fateful peak he saw only more mountains, and despaired. It changed nothing.* Saint Karstur received a revelation from the God and harvests under his new farming method nearly doubled, and brought bounty to the land. *That was 500 years ago, and the people again starve. It changed nothing.*

Then what does change things, if not prayer?

Courage; and fighting.

Ketzler gazed at the bread, ate it slowly. Courage, he understood; but why fighting? Fighting for what? The land and food were simply not there. And the king's edict from so long ago still stood, still seemed reasonable—at least, as far as anything Ketzler heard. Despite the value of reason among his people, he judged it no small coincidence that this cathedral in the shadow of the Brynth was so ill-attended. The Baders were devout, but not dynamic. Their sermons droned, uninspired words repeated from almost exactly a year ago each Fastday. Not like when the Orox visited. It was always those Fastdays when Ketzler prayed in earnest, meditated truly, and felt peace all day equal to those few spare moments at any other

Evening. Even the Baders glowed, gossiped in hushed tones of some of their equals in towns near the sea who taught with the same vigor and authority, who were stacked in line to be the next Orox, while they could only hope to tend their small duties without complaint.

No, despite the echoing voices of reason outside the cathedral, the Brynth still cursed, the sea thought little of their courage, and the Cariste still went about in fear of trying to move southward. They fought in pulpits and lecterns, and in the Senate, wrestling the people from one idea to the next. They fought for erudition far more than provision. Thank the God, in the cathedral provision was so plentiful.

Ketzler savored the last of the cheese. Yes, he heard many things he was not supposed to. In his pride, he had judged that the Baders were confined to this tiny cathedral only because they complained so much. Now, in front of his empty plate that mocked his empty stomach, he thought perhaps the people did not complain enough. By accepting their fates they were unable to move on, to enact change. And his name was already before the Orox of Thoroneus, and he would become Bader in a year if he kept to his devotions.

He stood, picked up his plate and returned it to the kitchens. He smiled at the scullion; there was not much to clean from his dish, but she would do it anyway. Cook rested in a chair, cocking an eyebrow at him. He bowed his head demurely and exited.

He was to have one more shift of prayers, just before Moonrise. He had meant to go to his room, perhaps rest and take a drink until the time came. Instead his feet carried him directly back into the sanctuary and he stood gazing at the Eternal Circle. The rushlights were lit, the clear windows black, the stained glass faded as though obscured by smoke.

Eventually, his feet tender through the thin leather soles on hard stone, Ketzler sat. A door opened woodenly behind him, and the heavy footfalls of a Bader approached. Ketzler never took his eyes off the thin tangle of white in the symbol.

"Pip," Bader Losnoss murmured, sitting behind him. "As always, your devotion to the God is unmatched. I have been impressed with you for a very long time, you know." He paused as though waiting for Ketzler's acknowledgement. Ketzler was too distracted to give it. "The Orox is also impressed with you, and we spoke of you at length last time he visited." This time, Ketzler's heart sank too far to do anything but turn his head slightly. "He wants to see you and speak with you directly, on Harvestday feast—in Thoroneus."

Finally, Ketzler responded, turning fully to face the Bader in alarm. "Sir..." he stuttered.

Bader Losnoss smiled warmly. "I have been your Flame far too long for that, young Ketzler," he chided gently.

Ketzler finally regained control. "You have indeed. I am simply caught off guard—I only wished to devote myself to the God of All. I am pleased the Orox has deemed me worthy."

"You are most worthy, Ketzler," Losnoss replied, standing. "But perhaps not yet entirely ready. I have discussed it with the other Baders, and in two Fastdays you will deliver your first sermon. I will work with you until then on what you will teach, and we will practice your speaking," he added quickly as Ketzler's mouth dropped open again. "But by the time you see the Orox you will already be practicing as a Bader."

Ketzler was at a complete loss for words, and the Bader seemed unsurprised. After a few more encouragements, smiles, and a proud hug, Bader Losnoss departed. Ketzler remained standing, now turned away from the Eternal Circle as he gazed at the dark windows glimmering only faintly with rushlight. His first sermon—the first of thousands in a life devoted to teaching about peace and light, wrestling the people's thoughts away from their hurt and hunger and toward the God of All. He would travel the white line interminably, back and forth, fighting dizziness as he turned and turned about between Heaven and Oren, bound to his course.

He was still standing, trapped by those obsidian panes, as the Baders filed in for the final prayers. Behind him he heard the other Pips entering, could almost feel their eyes on his back. He turned mutely, dragging his gaze away; it landed on the Circle, stuck fast on the white line, his life now, as his feet moved him mechanically to the altar. Once there he knelt, in perfect pose. The other Pips knelt alongside him, and they began to chant.

Ketzler's eyes remained on the interwoven threads. There, near the center of mankind and the earth, his Air twined with the thread of Fire before casting off and making its lonely way up to the Eternal Circle.

That's not fire, it's blood—blood is life for all Oren. For the Cariste. For you. Blood must be on the ground.

Whose blood?

Not yours.

Ketzler's perfect chant faltered a moment before he recovered. Why would these thoughts come now? And where did they come from? Now that he looked again, the Fire thread appeared more like blood, dripping away from mankind. He followed it, his mind reciting the chant by rote now as his thoughts wandered: the blood entwined with all other lives—earth, water, and air. Those of the air went to the God, or to the colleges; those of the earth went to farmers, clothiers, carpenters—any and all types of provision; those of the water were sailors or bargemen. All good and peaceful folk, so long as they kept the God above them and mankind beside them.

But those of fire—*those become soldiers.* They would give their blood in the taking of others' blood, keeping Gintanos safe and the Cariste struggling to find a living. There were untouched lands on the other side of the Brynth—the sailors knew it for how long the coastline was. There the Cariste could spread out once more—thousands and thousands of lives spared from torment by men willing to walk the thread of fire, of blood—men willing to spill blood and risk their own.

But how? The ways south were barred.

It didn't matter. Men of the blood thread would fight, would find a way—a far surer and longer-lasting way than the saints buried in forgotten stone. As he considered it, Ketzler found his own blood rising; he fought to keep his chant from rising as well. It would not do to outstrip the murmurs of the other Pips beside him, those ragged few who would continue to chant and preach in this forgotten cathedral. They could not all walk such a bold thread as Ketzler determined to.

But it had to be soon. The threads entwined for only a short time, perhaps for a few days or weeks would the blood thread be near enough to make the jump. Harvestday feast: it had to be before then. If he went to the Orox now he would be caught, imprisoned on his current thread until he died, alone. But at some point, he knew, the opportunity would come, his new thread would wind particularly close, and he would change his life forever.

The chant ended. The other Pips rose and filed out. Bader Losnoss approached again. "Ketzler?" he asked. Ketzler knew why: the faltering chant.

"I beg pardon, Bader," he said. "Your news of the Orox' request was not easy to press down. I feared it was pride. But I think, instead, I am still too surprised to comprehend it."

Bader Losnoss smiled. "Forgiveness is surely granted," he said. "You will be well by morning, and after Dawn Prayers we will begin your preparations. Try to rest for now. A night of sleep will do you much good."

"My gratitude, good Bader and the God's Flame. I take advantage of your dismissal." Ketzler bowed, refrained from looking at the blood thread, and left the sanctuary.

Concentration the next several days eluded him. Each morning between prayers and lunch he met with Bader Losnoss to study the Histories as he never had before. It was not enough to glean wisdom for himself, which could come to him in bits and pieces. Now to prepare a sermon he had to find all sorts of connected writings. Bader Losnoss told him ten separate quotations were an adequate start, and to develop his lesson from there.

For the sake of the charade Ketzler tried to press in—he had to. For a time he could excuse the novelty of it, perhaps some fear of his first public sermon. He knew, as the days wore on, these excuses would grow thinner and thinner, and gradually become a doubt over his readiness for this next step. For a few hours, one day, he contemplated allowing this doubt to seed and grow. Worry of the consequences—perhaps even strict sequestering—soon overcame. And for the rest of the week, that thought cleared his mind enough to focus on the task at hand and he began excelling again in the eyes of his Flame.

As the week turned, he finished writing the sermon and found approval in it. Then began the arduous work of practicing the delivery. For two whole shifts a day—once in the morning, once again in the afternoon—he spoke from in front of the altar while Bader Losnoss sat in judgement from the last row of seats. The Bader would allow Ketzler to deliver the entire lesson, then instruct him to alter his volume or resonance at the start of this such-and-such line, and do the whole thing again. Next, do not be so forceful here, or it will assume too much importance—and start over again.

On top of this, Ketzler found a new worry: that his opportunity had already passed, and he had missed it. The days went by in prayer and preaching, and no chance given to even visit the cathedral gardens. Thoughts of how he was to find any moment to slip away consumed him when he was not practicing, and nibbled at the edges of his mind while he was. He shoved it hard aside when he could, knowing if he did not deliver the message as Bader Losnoss instructed him last time, there would most definitely not be a future opportunity.

And so that week was spent. It was good the food was so sparse, for his appetite abandoned him. The other Pips, if they envied him, did not say so. The day of his first public sermon swiftly approached, and so too the day of his visit to the Orox.

Fastday dawned warm and bright, for autumn. Ketzler blinked a few times in the early light, then closed his eyes. *Please grant me this moment; I find no peace in this thread, in this life. I do not feel that this is my future.*

It is not, came the swift reply, and Ketzler's heart surged. *Be patient. Opportunity comes to those who wait, and seize what is rightfully theirs—to those who deserve it through hard work.*

Ketzler's only remorse, as he leapt from the bed and all but ran to the washroom, was that he had not received that answer two weeks ago. But it was enough to have it now. Perhaps the God granted him that time of testing to strengthen him, to assure him of his ability to persevere. That felt right, as he quickly scrubbed his close-shorn hair in a bucket of freezing water.

He thought, in the preceding weeks, that he would be reciting his lesson over and over, full of fear and worry. To his surprise, he did not. He knew it, front and back. He did not have to consciously recall the Bader's instruction, and the words flowed from him precisely as it had the night before, when Bader Losnoss declared him ready. And as his voice carried through the sanctuary, he sensed the rightness of both the content of his words, and the quality of his delivery. The people listened properly, silently, and seemed to approve of his words. In one corner of his mind he knew they were words only rigorously studied and approved by the Bader, and he wondered what it might be like to speak his own words. As he finished, and Bader Williem stepped forward to deliver the *hestus,* he wondered though if they would ever truly be his words. Under such strict training, it was more likely, he deemed, that all that would ever come out of him would be words approved by Bader, Orox, Madus, and ultimately Grand Tull.

When *hestus* had concluded, Ketzler and Baders proceeded in a file to the entrance, to encourage their followers as they departed. Many of those exiting were recognized by Ketzler as regular attendees. He excused them from recognizing him, as all Pips learned early to fade into the background even when conducting their duties. And yet one man caught his attention: his hair was cropped close like a Pip, and yet he bore a strange scar over his left eye. His grip was firm, and he did not smile.

"Are you new to Klos?" Ketzler asked as amiably as he could, trying not to notice Bader Losnoss' glance. Somehow, he did not know how, Ketzler felt this might be his opportunity—or, at least, its harbinger.

"Depends how you see it," the man said. His voice nearly growled though he did not appear angry. "On my way through. I'm with the unit recruiting here."

"Oh, you are a soldier?" Ketzler said. It took every bit of training over the past week to keep his voice pitched in harmless deduction, instead of the fiery curiosity he felt.

"Yes, Bader..." The soldier trailed off, as if sensing that Ketzler was different from the other four around him.

"I am only a Pip," he confirmed. "But in preparation, if the God provides, to come into that position. Well, at least it is a fine day to make your way back to—I'm sorry, you are outside the town?"

The soldier shook his head. "No, we've been put in the Brynth's Rest, on Haurus Street."

"Oh, close by," Ketlzer replied with a smile. "Well it is a pleasant Fastday regardless. The God sees your attendance and devotion, and grants peace to you who seek it."

The soldier departed with a nod. Ketzler saw from the corner of his eye no suspicion in the smiles of the Baders, and kept triumph from his own as he turned to the next in line.

Though he chatted with each—attendance in so small a sanctuary was not large—he could not, a shift later, remember any of it. He sat on the edge of his small cot, gazing sightlessly at the trunk at the foot of his bed. All his worldly possessions were in that wooden cubit, and he would likely have to leave it all behind. He would also need to find some way of getting rid of his Pip's robe; he doubted he could go unnoticed if he had it on. There was also the matter of how to get to the inn, and to the soldiers, and enlist. Despite all the warm feelings by all the Baders, he would not likely be permitted to leave without escort.

He had gone through several scenarios in his mind of how to convince

Bader Losnoss—even so far as asking outright, of laying his soul bare on his feelings toward the church and this new desire to become a soldier. Each time, he saw the Bader's face growing darker and darker, until he was thrown in isolation until he returned to his humility. He knew they would see his desires as pride, an opportunity to make himself grander than others, to win awards for himself—as if a personal audience with the Orox wasn't grand, or an award for his devotion.

Another imagined criticism came to mind, one that bit deep and was likely true: he was not built physically for soldiering. His gaze now sharpened as he looked at his arms and legs. He had rarely walked further than the halls between his room and the sanctuary, and had never lifted anything more than a holy candle. Even if he had, a Pip's rations would not have helped his build. He had no idea what training would be like, but he could not imagine it was easy even without natural enemies.

His brows knitted as he considered this thought: why was the army recruiting? He had his own suspicions, of course, but no rumors from the congregants or the Baders of any sort of invasion or other threat. Rumors abounded, though, of the increasingly poor farmers and townsfolk joining in order to have food.

Perhaps something was changing. Was this why the thoughts came now, that had never come before? He glanced to the windows, orange with evening light. It made sense—it was his true destiny and life-work to be a soldier, and the God of All prompted him now. Yet must he subvert the Baders, if it was truly the will of the God?

But hadn't he faked his devotion? He considered as he returned to the altar for evening prayers. Perhaps the Baders here too had put on false piety, pretending at religion for some gain, and that too was why they remained stuck at such a bleak and abandoned station. They would not hear from the God of All because they did not ask. Ketzler, though, sought—not by their drummed-up methods, but earnestly in his heart. And so the God honored that. Did not the Histories say he would?

But he must not let them suspect, and so he kept up his posture and chants for the half-shift required. He bowed humbly at their continued praises, and returned to his room with their blessings. He lay awake until the moon rose and lit the small garden outside his window with pale light. He left his robe hanging on the bedpost, instead pulling on a brown winter cloak that did not fit him well but was non-descript. With one final prayer and quick sigh, he eased the window open, crawled out, and dropped lightly to the ground. He squatted there for several moments until an owl hooted somewhere far off, before he stole across the grounds under moonlight.

The inn was only a few streets away, and he would reach it swiftly enough.

4

Captain Arthnoth Blanos Liptieri

"Illmali would see you."
"To congratulate me, to be sure."
"I think he wonders why you waste your time with someone so small."
"It is because I have seen his kind before."

38 Halmfurtung 1320 — Autumn

Ketzler woke stiffly, lifting his head from the crumpled rags in the gutter as something thin but hard prodded his ribs. He swatted a hand; when it met wood it stung, and he squinted up into a helmeted face devoid of a pity he felt he deserved.

"You'd better find somewhere else," the guard growled. "The streets outside our inns are better kept than that."

Ketzler slowly stood, backing away a few steps as the halberd came down, the guard wary of sudden movement. "Better kept indeed," Ketzler whined. He cleared his throat and tried again. "Better kept. Perhaps if they kept their patrons better, they wouldn't end up in the street."

Halberd still ready, the guard leaned forward and sniffed. "You don't smell of alcohol," he muttered. Then, louder: "Why are you out here?"

"I had been trying to find a room. I know the recruiting officers are here, but I came too late to sign up. They were in bed. I asked for a room but was denied, and I felt it too late to find another. And I was tired." He rolled a sore shoulder, trying to work out a kink.

The halberd lowered. "You speak well for someone waking up in a gutter and trying to enlist. Where are you from?"

Ketzler blinked. Claiming his hometown wouldn't alleviate any suspicions, and if he lived here he wouldn't need lodgings. "I just missed them in Thoroneus," he said instead. "My father was against my going and I had to escape—walked from there to here." A little sort-of truth should help.

It did. The halberd came back up, and to the guard's shoulder. "The officers should be awake by now. If I find you in another gutter tonight, it'll be worse for you." He gave Ketzler a glance up and down, a smirk, and turned and went back to the street where his partner waited with a smile. They both glanced at Ketzler again before disappearing around the corner.

Ketzler sighed, looking down at himself. He did look the spoiled city lordling, lost and on his own, and certainly not soldier material. As his stomach shrank, he thought of the breakfast waiting for him at the cathedral. The Baders would soon miss him, and he was not far away.

He turned quickly and went back into the inn, smoothing his rumpled cloak as best he could. The innkeeper cocked an eyebrow as Ketzler crossed the room to where three men sat eating, obviously soldiers. One had a small leather-bound book at his elbow. Their conversation ceased abruptly as he presented himself at their table.

"I, uh..." He faltered, looking into their piercing gazes. These were no men like he had ever known before. He could not say their eyes were lifeless—there were sparks there of a passion he never saw in a Bader. And yet, the life hinted at by those passions was so foreign to Ketzler as to seem not-life. Even as he stood he struggled to comprehend what he looked at.

When the gazes turned to impatience, he returned to himself. "I want to enlist."

He counted two cautious blinks before the smiles crept onto their faces, and his heart began to sink. One of the men—he guessed now to be the highest-ranking—glanced at the others and wiped his mouth.

"Where are you from?" he asked.

"Thoroneus."

"What did you do there? Why do you want to be a soldier?"

"I was...my father was a textiler, and wanted me to be one too. I wanted to do more."

Eyebrows lifted. "I'd have thought life as a textiler would be pretty good."

Ketzler shrugged. "There are worse, for food, shelter, or clothing—"

"You don't care about those?"

"I care more about Gintanos, helping our people."

Squints. "Why do you think being a soldier will help Gintanos more than making clothing?"

"Because..." Why did he think that? The army right now did very little; most comments he overheard—few enough on this subject—said the military was a waste of resources with no persistent enemy to fight. Something that existed only to raise taxes, make the feeblest-minded citizens feel safer against the just-in-cases.

But still, they were trained to fight. "I don't like just sitting around, waiting, being told everything is fine when it's not."

This brought outright laughter from the men. When the leader's chuckles finally subsided, he pointed to a large leather bag sitting just under the table. "Pull that out, please, and pick it up."

Ketzler's brow furrowed a moment, then he reached forward and pulled. With a grunt, he took a tottering step toward the table, barely catching himself from falling over. The leader waved off a few fresh gales of laughter from the other soldiers at the table. Gritting his teeth, Ketzler grasped the bag with two hands, braced, and managed to succeed in dragging it out onto the floor. He gazed at it, knowing he would be incapable of lifting. He knew his soft lifestyle might be a problem. He didn't think it would be proven so quickly.

"Sir..." he said hesitantly, knuckles still white as he gripped the bag.

"What did you say your name was?"

"Ketzler, sir," he said. He tested the weight, shook his head minutely.

"Try, Ketz."

Ketzler took a breath, and strained. He felt the edges lift, and dared hope. But the center seemed attached to the floor by a bolt; if he had not just dragged it from under the table he might have suspected a trick. He relaxed with a frustrated sigh, head bowed.

A chair scraped back. Knowing the leader approached, he took a step back and lifted his eyes. The leader bent a little sideways, grasping the bag with one hand and straightening effortlessly. "We expect a little more from our soldiers," he said, his voice utterly calm. "Even new recruits. I hope you'll make a better weaver."

"Sir, if I could just—"

"We can't waste our time," the man replied. "If you 'could just' lift this bag, then we might talk. Go back to Thoroneus." He turned and sat back down, his posture forgetting Ketzler completely.

Ketzler turned and made for the door. What was he to do now? He had felt so sure...

The door opened, and the patron from his sermon entered. The man glanced him up and down with mild surprise. "Bader," he said. "Were you looking for me?"

"Um..."

"Bader?" the leader repeated behind him. Ketzler turned back, but it was the other soldier who answered.

"I went to the cathedral yesterday," he said. "The Bader—sorry, you said you were actually a Pip—was giving the sermon."

"You said you were from Thoroneus."

"I—I didn't think you would enlist a Pip," Ketzler replied. The glare the leader gave him was murder, and Ketzler cast his eyes down.

After several interminable moments, the chair scraped back again, and heavy boots thudded toward him. He looked up just in time to see the blur of the man's hand, and then exploding lights in his vision.

Then he was on the floor, blinking.

"If you ever lie to me again, you will have a spear driven through you. It is never for you to decide what I need to know, or how I might react to the truth you tell me—do you understand?"

Ketzler blinked through his shifting thoughts, focusing suddenly on that key word. "Again?" he asked.

The man grunted. "So you are smart. And you'll be able to lead the unit in prayers. That will keep you until we've worked the soft years out of you. And, Ketz?" He waited until Ketzler was able to look up at him. "We will work them out of you, but it might kill you. Will you sign?"

Ketzler blinked slow and hard to clear his head, and stood shakily. "Yes, sir," he said firmly.

By the end of the first morning, he thought he might truly die. As soon as he had signed he was given one roll of hard bread and dismissed to join the rest of the unit being formed. Though the recruiters were able to stay at the Rest, junior soldiers—Foot, he quickly learned they were called—and new recruits stayed in a broad field just north of Klos. By the time he was issued clothing and boots, he had to run to the formation, falling in at the tail end as they marched down the road. The man who had signed him—Captain Arthnoth Blanos Liptieri—rode at the head on a bay gelding, with two sergeants mounted alongside. Corporals marched with the snaking column, shouting at those who couldn't keep the line. Before the first shift was over, everyone knew Ketzler's name by rote.

By mid-morning, the column moved off and marched alongside the road, now clogged with merchants and farmers hauling their harvests. Ketzler stumbled and tripped on the lumpy shocks of grass, falling back more than a pace sometimes and scrambling to catch back up. If there was any fortune, it was that he was at the very rear and was not tripping anyone behind him. By noon, the corporal had stopped bellowing and only shook his head and growled.

Unnamed villages came and went, marked in Ketzler's mind only by the sizes of the inns where they did not pause to rest. Most were distinguished by some sort of sign, usually swinging from a wrought-iron arm, but occasionally only nailed to the wall and nearly blending in with the sun-bleached timbers behind it. One larger village had a two-story inn, and a sign whose colors had not yet faded—though he could not remember the name of it through the haze of his mind.

Suddenly they were stopping. Ketzler ran his forehead into the man in front of him before he realized it, but his tongue was too thick and his mouth too dry to even apologize. When he looked up, Captain Liptieri was riding ahead toward the walls of an actual city. Ketzler blinked, trying to think of a map he had seen, try to estimate how far they had come. It felt like leagues.

"Rest, you men," the corporals barked. "Ketzler, since you want to sit, you help take the carts into town for provisions."

Ketzler blinked from where he found himself on his backside. He truly could not remember folding his legs. Everyone else was standing but relaxed. Those nearest glowered down at him, or laughed. Surprising even himself, he stood. "Yes, sir," he managed.

"'Sir?' I work for a living, recruit; Corporal Ardurin to you."

"Yes, Corporal Ardurin." He remained standing, looking around blankly until the Corporal pointed ahead to where several handcarts were being wheeled forward. He stumbled up onto the road, managing a trot to catch up. There, he was guided alongside another recruit, and together they grasped the T-shaped handle and set off.

"What city is this?" Ketzler muttered.

The other recruit laughed. "No city; Bertaia," he said, and Ketzler envied the strength of the man's voice. "It wants to be a city, which is why they built a wall. But the Palos doesn't have enough pull in the Senate." He shook his head mockingly.

Ketzler eyed the walls and the great gate, where the Captain was now a smudge in its opening, then glanced sideways at the recruit. "You know a lot about it," he said.

He shrugged. "Palos's my uncle," he replied, flashing a grin. "I'm Migua Glassos, but most call me Miggey."

Now he said it, Ketzler faintly remembered a Palos Guyron Glassos mentioned, and he colored. The few rumors made him out to be nine parts pride and one part idealism—as a whole, ineffectual in the Senate and laughingstock among the lower classes in Bertaia. If Gintanos had still been a monarchy, perhaps Glassos would have had some power as a minor lordling, but... "Ketzler," he replied. "I guess...I guess some call me Ketz."

"Oh, I heard," Miggey replied, but his merry eyes took out the sting. "You'll get used to the marching in a few days."

Ketzler felt the heat of his soles, knew some blisters were already forming. "You aren't from here? Where did you join?"

"No, the rest of my family moved northward, to Lama, before I was born. I've been with the unit about a week now."

"Where are we going? Do you know why they're recruiting so many?"

Miggey shook his head. "They haven't told us yet, just to keep marching. But we've been constantly moving eastward, whatever that might mean."

"Toward Gaios?" Ketzler offered.

Miggey pressed his lips together and shrugged. "Maybe, though I would have thought we'd take a more northern route if we were."

Ketzler hummed noncommittally. True, the more direct route would have been further north, perhaps through Margon. This road would keep them nearer the mountains and proceed south past the capitol. But perhaps this route took them through more cities where they might recruit more soldiers. He was distracted from these thoughts, though, as they passed through the gate into Bertaia under the watchful eye of one of the sergeants.

The walls were perhaps two paces thick at the base, and another seven or eight paces tall. He could not tell what they were made of, only they were not stone—it almost appeared daub, smooth and tan, and maybe an occasional chip here or there, and spiderweb cracks in corners. If the city thought this would be a defense, he hoped there was at least stone underneath. Considering the Palos who ruled here, though, Ketzler amended his assumptions. Towers were on the corners, and one or two of the other parts of the walls, but erratically placed, and watchmen in glittering armor stood looking anywhere but out.

Ketzler managed to shake his head only once, looking instead toward the cart in front of him as they moved down the streets. It was a clamor he had only become familiar with in the past few months, where hawkers and vendors cried their wares, here a pig squealed as it was slaughtered in the street, there bleating sheep were being herded to another pen for market. Down some distant alley a dog barked, and a cat yowled in response. Someone somewhere beat on a cymbal or bell to attract attention. And over all was the general din of human voices, each trying to rise above the rest.

The Corporal in the lead seemed to know the town well, and led them unerringly down one road and onto another. His turns felt random to Ketzler, until at last the small column stopped. The broader market was several blocks away, now, but ahead the Corporal conversed in lower tones with a large man draped in striped robes, who seemed to know they had been coming. Finally they were all waved forward, and the carts clustered near the house.

"Stay with the cart," Miggey said. "I'll go in and help."

Ketzler nodded, keeping his hold on the handle as one recruit from each team left their cart and went inside. Soon a procession of food began—mostly in sacks, though there were occasional poles of cured sausages or bundles of large, serrated leaves nearly as broad as Ketzler's chest. Miggey pointed to one such pole of leaves significantly, but Ketzler only shrugged. Miggey mouthed something. Ketzler didn't recognize the word, but he nodded anyway.

In short order every cart was loaded, and the Corporal and merchant returned to the street. They shook hands, the Corporal moved out, and the now fully-stocked detachment followed.

"I don't know what those leaves are," Ketzler said quietly, before they reached the market and his voice would be drowned out.

"Oh, sorry. They're for dimbro, it's...you don't know what that is? Well, we'll dry them out first, and then crush it and mix it in hot water. You'll probably be allowed a cup in the morning. Make your legs and feet feel like new. They always restock when we get a bunch of newbies. And with that many leaves...well, we're definitely not done recruiting yet."

Sore as his feet were, Ketzler wondered how a tea could make them feel better. He definitely had a blister now, rubbed raw, and the boot was pinching sharply near his right little toe as he struggled to keep stride. Miggey seemed to be doing his part, hopefully in sympathy. The smile never left his face, never seemed false when Ketzler glanced sideways at him to mumble apologies for stumbling.

They passed back through the gate. The guards there and the sergeant still seemed the only ones alert. West, their column had dispersed and tents were being erected in a broad field. The largest—presumably the Captain's—was half-done near a small copse of young alder: one pole was up, the canvas pulled tight, while the rest of the tent billowed in the mild breezes. All the tents were dun, though a thin pennant of green fluttered from the erect tentpole of the Captain's. Some sort of figure in yellow was emblazoned on it, but the size and distance made it impossible for Ketzler to tell what it was.

"It'll look like a dragon, up close," Miggey told him as they trundled down the dusty road. "But Captain maintains it's a stylized ibex." He shrugged. "I've never seen an ibex with wings, and dragons are more awesome, but he's the Captain."

The second half of the Captain's tent went up when the small convoy finally turned off the road and across the field. The Corporal guided them to what Ketzler assumed were kitchens. "Will we have to unload all this, too?" he asked quietly aside to Miggey.

"No, they've got a detail for that—unless you're assigned—"

He cut off as the Corporal barked: "Fetch your tents and get set up. Ketzler! You'll be with Migua. Ardurin will be around shortly to make sure you did it right."

Taking a deep but quiet breath, Ketzler followed Miggey toward the southern side of the camp. "Sergeant Blass's platoon—sorry, Sergeant Blassner Blassnos to you, probably—is always on the south side. Saves confusion, since no matter where we stop or where we are you can always find us. Sometimes he lays the squads out differently depending on terrain, but usually we're third—so, pretty much in the middle."

"Saved you a spot, Miggey!" someone shouted as they approached. In a grassy gap between tents lay a rolled bundle, poles protruding from both ends and wrapped in white cord a finger thick.

Miggey waved, and knelt beside the bundle. "Set 'em up facing away from the camp, so we wake up looking out," he said. "You'll probably draw a practice weapon after dinner—just a long pole at first. Corporal says we'll get iron heads next, eventually sharpened. We'll get swords too eventually, but we sleep with spears ready. Here," he said, handing Ketzler a tent pole. "Lay it down pointing out. I'll line up mine too."

Ketzler watched, listened, and obeyed. When the poles were up, Miggey stood back and looked along the peak. He shook his head, adjusted the second pole by half a step west, then looked again. "Okay, hold that." He stretched out one side, pegged it, then shuffled Ketzler toward the front as he pegged the second side. "See? Easy. One person can do it alone," he said as one experienced, "but it sure is easier to get it pointing straight with two."

"So's your mom," another solider remarked in passing.

"At least she's not a Captain's tent like your mom," Miggey replied. The other recruit spat, but grinned.

Ketzler caught a faint smell of yeast, just then, and looked up to see cook fires going near the middle of the camp. "So we're here for the day?" he asked, glancing up at the noonday sun. "Is this how it goes—march for the morning then camp?"

"Around here, yes," Miggey said. "Once we're past Gaios though, I think we'll push further—there aren't as many large towns and cities to recruit from, plus we're almost at full strength. Rest your feet while you can—and take care of that blister."

"And my boots," Ketzler muttered.

"Those too; here..." Miggey ducked into the tent, and as Ketzler sat and wrenched the stiff leathers off his feet Miggey reappeared with a small can of paste. "Softens the leather a bit," he said. "Work it into the crease first, get a lot there. You'll want the uppers stiff for support though."

For the next quarter-shift, while his stomach grumbled, Ketzler worked the boots and his feet. Miggey also had lambskin for blisters, and another thin paste for raw skin. "This is mine," he said. "They don't issue this stuff. Hope your feet get tough soon."

A slight commotion to the west brought both their attentions, and they looked up in time to see a tent collapse, stakes and poles flying to the winds. Ketzler frowned, but Miggey started laughing. "They set it up facing inward," he chuckled. "All right, get your boots on. Looks like it's actually the Sergeant coming to inspect our set-up."

Gingerly but hastily, Ketzler pulled on his boots and stood. Down the line, a broad, dark-skinned man was stalking around another tent. He smacked one of the two occupants on the shoulder, and moved on. To Ketzler's relief, he appeared satisfied with most of the pitches. He grew nervous again as the Sergeant quickly drew closer to theirs.

Sergeant Blassnos made a minor correction to the one nearest them—the side should be pulled tighter, and the pegs driven deeper; you want idiots to trip on their way to the pits in the night?—but nothing went flying. He barely glanced at Miggey and Ketzler as he went right past them to the next one. Ketzler looked alarmed, but Miggey only shrugged. After the Sergeant moved out of earshot, he whispered: "He'll probably be back. Maybe he wants to take you to get your practice arms right away. Just stay put."

So they stood, and waited. A convoy of wagons crept down the road in front of them, pausing amid swirling dust as they were inspected, then creaked and clattered through the gates. Another commotion, and two more poles flew out into the field.

"Bunch of idiots," a deep voice growled, right behind Ketzler. He jumped, but did not turn. "Ketzler, your feet okay?"

Ketzler glanced wildly, then caught Miggey mouthing something. "Yes, sergeant," he said, hesitantly.

"Better than your ears apparently. Good set-up, Miggey."

"Thank you, sergeant."

"Thank your recruiter, not me."

"Yes, sergeant."

Ketzler could feel the smile in Miggey's voice, but fear kept his own grin at bay.

"All right Ketz, come with me. Captain wants to see you." This spoken loudly enough that the soldiers closest stared sideways at him.

He turned, tripping over one of the lines and nearly stumbling into Blassnos' arms. He saved himself only by twisting sideways as he fell heavily to the ground. Blooming red, Ketzler leapt to his feet and brushed himself off.

Blassnos only stared at him. "You want a comforting hug, you'll have to go back to your mother," he growled.

"Y-yes, sergeant," Ketzler muttered, keeping his eyes down.

Blassnos stepped closer. Ketzler's eyes came up, locking onto the Sergeant's wide, stern gaze. "When you talk to me you speak clearly, do you understand? And you better keep your eyes up or someone will kill you." With a swift movement, the sergeant's thumb dug into Ketzler's ribs, and he gasped as the air whooshed out. "Stand up straight! You're supposed to be a soldier. You ain't no Pip or Bader anymore, you're supposed to have some gristle in those guts. You keep on like this, we'll find out if you do when a sword empties your innards into some field somewhere. Now move!"

Ketzler all but ran forward, toward the Captain's tent. But after five steps something struck him in the back of the knee and he pitched forward again. Sergeant Blassnos stalked up behind him again, and knelt down. "You're going to make it exactly one day, going on like this," he growled, this time low enough that only Ketzler would hear. "If you ever go ahead of me without me telling you, that rock will split your skull and you'll die a worthless Pip. Get up. And if you hobble in front of the Captain, you'll *wish* for this rock to split your skull."

Ketzler rose. Now his right foot and right knee pained him, and hobbling felt like quite a reasonable gait. But the Sergeant seemed quite unreasonable, and was definitely skilled with throwing a rock, so Ketzler tried to push the pain aside and stride normally. He was thankful at least for the lambskin Miggey had given him before this waking nightmare began.

Sergeant Blassnos did not stop before entering the tent, surprising Ketzler a little until he too was inside. It somehow seemed larger than the outside indicated, though the floorspace was dominated by a long table and chairs. Three maps were spread, and various bowls and cups scattered across them. The rest of the sergeants were there, and someone presumably from the town in flowing silks, though a bit of wool cuff peeked out from the sleeves. On the right end of the long tent was another flap and door, which Ketzler presumed led to a private chamber, and why sergeants could walk in without announcement. A few lanterns dangled from the roof, and shadows swung as the broad canvas caught even small breezes and sent the lights swaying. A low murmur cut off when they entered, and all eyes swung to them; hard glances from hard men who quickly assessed new information and discarded forever what was unimportant. A few nodded at Blassnos, and turned back to the table, and Ketzler knew he was one of the pieces that had been dismissed.

As the chatter recommenced, his gaze wandered, noticing only then a tall, thin woman in pale green and tan that stood at the far end of the table. Her long dark hair lay unbound, though braided cord around her forehead seemed ready to tie it up if necessary. Even in the dim light of the tent Ketzler could tell she was deeply tanned, her face rugged and lined from long days in the wilds. This woman did not seem to dismiss Ketzler, her glittering blue eyes studying him intently. Ketzler tried to match the gaze, but knew his un-hardened features would never convey the same intensity. And yet the woman gave him a respectful nod, her gaze lingering a moment longer before returning to the maps spread on the table.

As Ketzler glanced back, he found everyone staring at him again and his heart squeezed shut in his chest.

The Captain allowed a small grin to creep onto his face, then picked up a nearby goblet and returned to studying the maps. "What did you see today, Ketzler?" he asked.

Ketzler stared speechless for a time, until the Captain glanced up with a raised eyebrow. "Uh, when?"

"Sir," Sergeant Blassnos growled.

The Captain seemed not to pay attention. "When you went into town. What did you see?"

Ketzler's mind still ran through empty fields. "I guess...I saw a lot of things, sir...um, the market, we went and got food..." He cut off as the rest of the men in the tent chuckled. Ketzler glanced aside: the tall woman was still studying him intently. "I'm not sure what you're asking me. Sir," he finished, at a complete loss.

"I know what you *did*, Ketzler," the Captain said gently. "I'm asking what you saw? What you observed?"

"Well..." He paused a moment, trying to think, while everyone looked at him. *What do they want from me? Unless...* "The sergeants—our sergeants needed to be present as we entered, sir, but the gate guards were the only ones watching. The soldiers on the walls didn't seem very alert, sir." He paused again, retracing their steps in his mind. "The market was busy, but there wasn't a lot of goods actually exchanging hands." He couldn't recall seeing one completed transaction, now he thought about it. "And we were supplied by someone outside the market, which seemed strange to me. Sir."

"But you didn't say anything about it being strange?"

Ketzler shrugged, then stiffened when Blassnos growled again. "Sir, none of the rest of the men seemed put off by it; I assumed it was normal. Miggey—I mean, Recruit Glassos didn't say anything, sir."

"What do you make of it? The guards not being very alert, the market being busy but not actually busy..."

Ketzler's mouth gaped again. "I—I would almost think...I don't know, sir. I'm not sure what threat the soldiers *could* be looking for, or why they're there at all. The market...maybe people here are not well-off, there's very little money to buy things with—"

"Would they not just stay home, then?"

Ketzler shrugged again, wide-eyed until Blassnos cuffed him on the back of the head.

The Captain waved him off. "Do you think the Palos might have staged the whole thing, trying to make things appear normal when in fact they are not? Are we in danger of sudden ambush in the night?"

Ketzler did not think his eyes could get wider, but they did. "How should I know?" he blurted. A moment later stars exploded in his vision and he felt grass pressing into his cheek. Amid a general roar from his sergeant, he heard the Captain say wearily: "Just get him out of here." He was yanked to his feet and shoved back into bright sunlight. He moved mechanically, not truly coming to his senses until he saw his tent bobbing into view. Miggey stared at him, concerned.

"Walk the edge, Ketzler!" Blassnos shouted. "You walk that edge—run it! Run that thing and if you're not back to this spot when I reach a hundred you're running it again! Go! Go!"

Ketzler found himself running, not knowing how, barely knowing where except he assumed the edge meant the edge of the camp. His feet screamed at him, the tall grass clung to his boots, and his thighs burned. *What by Illmali just happened back there? Why was he asking* me *if we were safe or not?* But he ran, through pinched ribs and a ragged throat. Blassnos was shouting two hundred when he passed, so he kept running, trying for more speed. By Mid-Afternoon, hungry and parched, he managed somehow to collapse in front of Blassnos as he shouted ninety-nine. But then he had him carry two great buckets of dirt, stumbling around the perimeter again, trying to get back by the count of two hundred.

He never did quite make it. As darkness fell, Blassnos apparently got bored and walked away. Ketzler collapsed to the ground in front of the tent, and just as he drifted off to sleep he wondered if he could slip away and make it back to Klos in time for his visit to the Orox of Thoroneus.

5

LAST OF HIS KIND

"This is a mistake."
"He has survived this long for a reason, Teresh."
"But what if he—?"
"I'll let you know when I return.

38 Halmfurtung 1320 — Autumn

An icy wind blew west across the Great Southern Snowplain and up into the foothills, sending swirls of frost against the thick, smooth trees of the Graytrunk Forest. To any other, such a wind would gnaw skin and bite nostrils. They would find no scent borne on that wind, no warning of what might be hiding beneath the false perfection of the snowscape. But foxes and snowcats still hunted the voles and ermine that found strange sustenance beneath the layers of powder. Cloaked in winter white, the hunters blended perfectly against the dazzling sun-glistened backdrop. He could not see them, but Tavill could smell them.

His interest was not in the foxes or snowcats, or even the voles and ermine, nor yet even in the wind or snow. His back was to the Snowplain, ignoring for now the view of the broad landscape spread out below the tall hills. On clear days like today he might have even been able to make out the steep cone of Mount Thinsledon near the sea. That, though, would have been a long time ago. An eternity, almost.

Instead of that long gaze, his shoulders bent as he split wood in the small cleared space in front of his cabin. Nestled deep enough in the Graytrunk, and made of its wood, it was nearly invisible. He rarely needed a fire: thick fur kept him warm, and the roots, berries, and plants he kept preserved did not require cooking. Besides, the smoke would too easily give him away. He had not noted any other creature except the wild ones of the Plain, animals who were no threat to him, but he had not survived these recent years—and the countless before them—by taking unnecessary risks.

He split the wood, then, because it needed to be split. It was good, warming work. The stone axe was sharp, because he had sharpened it yesterday. And one day he would need the split wood. He always did. When the time came, he would have it, and he would burn it that day because it needed to be burned. Always, eventually, it did.

He settled the last log on his splitting stump and breathed through his nose. A snowcat leapt somewhere; buried beneath the snow, Tavill did not smell the kill. But after a few moments the snowcat trotted off, and he knew it carried a prize in its mouth. He swung, another strike in a countless, endless string of them. The wood split cleanly, his stroke precise. The pieces thudded into frozen ground swept clean of muting snow. Bits of earth were scattered about, speckling the space like a sparrow's breast. He missed the sparrows. They never came this far south. When he had lived nearer the Snowash Mountains, he'd had a couple visit every summer, nesting and growing their family in the trees just outside his home. They had a kind, feathery, stone-and-bark smell that he enjoyed.

But the large, low pass that brought the sparrows south through the mountains every spring also brought the Others, and so he had moved. The Others did not have a kind smell; theirs was iron, sweat, and blood. As they came through the gap he kept far off, observing their numbers and the way they moved—alert, wary, ready to fight. He knew women and young children armed with iron. He smelled, in a long, gusting breeze, their hard minds and knotted sinews. They did not hunt him—no one anymore did—but they would kill him if they knew he was there. Everyone had tried, so long ago.

But even those hardened people feared the Snowplain, and so he had moved further south. Throughout summer the snow clung to hollows, and the heights thawed only enough for the hardiest of mosses, bearberry, diamond leaf, or tufted saxifrage. Caribou came only in the warmest month, returning north through the Graytrunk and Snowash bare weeks after the solstice.

Of all the celestial events, Tavill hated the summer solstice. Days were too long, the sun too warm, and too many prey drifted through the plain below his home. The snowcats and foxes went nearly berserk after new calves and litters, and the plains were dotted with splashes of red where kills were made. After the first year he had nearly abandoned his cabin; he stayed only because the prevailing winds shifted and blew west, carrying the scents toward the sea. More often than not his first alert to fresh kills were the carrion birds that followed the herds, circling high overhead. The brown and gray summer coats of the predators hid them against rock and heath every bit as well as their winters hid them in snow.

But that was a fear far off, now. The summer solstice was come and gone some moons back. The Others, fearing winter, moved north again. He retrieved the split wood and carried it to the western side of his cabin, opposite the prevailing winds. There he placed the quarters individually in a rack he had made years ago of twisted and dried branches. There was no iron around his home—no metal at all. He was not a blacksmith, and never wanted to be one. The smoke alone might betray him, and the ringing of a hammer could roll endlessly across the landscape. Besides, there was the smell. Instead he used clay, wood, and stone. He enjoyed it anyway—made it earthier, and he liked the earth. He hummed as he placed a gnarled hand on the split wood, thankful for it and for the simple work of splitting it.

He knew many others—ancient races, like himself—who bored too easily. Their lives became about finding the novel, the unique, of trying to increase the experience, broaden the range of them, see and do more and more in an unending cycle of falser and falser excitement. Not Tavill. He recognized the futility of that life eons ago, never once set his foot down that dark and finite path. Too many had been swept away. Now he alone remained.

He even shrugged off that thought as frivolous, and too-dark. He could change neither past nor future, alter nothing except the immediate choice. Now he paused to enjoy the view, such as it was. He stood a little straighter, looked out a little further. Mount Thinsledon was visible, he knew: the smear of color was clear and blue, the brown of trees dark and a little more precise. And yet there was something: a thin plume of smoke rose from the mount—probably just from the cold. Still, maybe not. It might be worth investigating, someday, when nothing else needed done. A choice for later.

He turned instead and went inside. The leather hinges still held well, and the stout oaken door opened smoothly. On each side of the door, inside, were poles to prop open the thatch roof and allow daylight in. He set these, flooding the wood and stone interior with clear light. The hearth was clean and bare, swept and wiped several days go and unused since. Beside it was his freshly-ticked mattress.

Across from the hearth was a simple table, and one chair. It did not do to dwell on that. The lone chair had been a reality far too long to feel uncomfortable now. This too was clean, and he had even managed to smooth it recently with pumice he had gathered long ago from the lower slopes of Thinsledon. Against the wall behind it was a small chest, wood and leather only, in which were several pairs of pants—the only part of him that ever grew cold, in the deepest of winters. Sitting on top was a thick, leather-bound tome—a journal, of sorts, though he wrote in it only infrequently these days. It was rare for anything of note to happen, or that he might learn and deem worthy to pen. Besides, since moving this far south, ink was hard to keep from freezing. And, truth be told, as much as he avoided hating anything so trivial, he did not enjoy the close-up work of writing. Aside from the physical strain on his eyes and shoulders, it reminded him too much of what he had lost. Too much.

Today was still not a day to write anyway. Instead, he went to the trapdoor against the wall opposite the main door, and opened it. Made of thicker oak than even the entrance, it made him grunt to lift its bulk. Rather than steps leading down, though, there was simply rock. It alone made this siting of his home ideal: a cave, large enough to admit his broad shoulders and shaggy head, kept a constant temperature above freezing and allowed him to store as much food as he ever desired.

He needed no light as he descended, going more by smell and familiarity than sight. Despite the darkness, his hands fell with certainty on some potatoes, two onions, two sun peppers, a handful of otterscomb—roughage he'd been delighted to find in the clefts of a mountain stream further in the Snowashes—and a bit of seasoning: salt, pepper, dried and ground garlic, and coriander for a bit of lemony flavoring.

He paused, considering. A bit of apple wouldn't hurt his meal either. He vaguely considered the bundle of stuffs in his hands, whether he could carry all of it and an apple or two as well. He juggled a little, tucking a few bits in the crook of his arm, and moved to the appropriate shelf. He reached out—and felt bare wood.

"Hmm," he rumbled. He drew a long, slow breath. There swirled the scents of what was in his arms, earth and sweet and spices. But as he turned his head there was something else, something of warmth, dander, and secrecy. He smiled, and turned back to the center of the room.

Tavill slowly lowered himself to the floor, setting aside his gatherings. He sat crosslegged and silent, drawing the silence and darkness around him until it became part of him, and he of it. He brought it into his mind, banishing thought, until a line could have been drawn across the room, through him, and carried along no change in the silence and darkness. His breathing slowed, needing no more air than the room itself needed to exist. His stomach, no more an empty space than the cellar, did not feel lack in hunger, but simply was.

In this way he sat, no sun or stars to tell the time, no thought or desire to indicate life. He was, as the room was. Slowly, so slowly, a scent began to grow. He did not grasp it, it flowed through him uninterrupted. He continued in silence.

Scritch, scritch.

Slowly, carefully, he returned. The smell now was strongest, and to his left where the potatoes sat. He felt his smile, a warmth of comradeship. Still he kept thought as far at bay as he could, still waiting.

Scritch scritch scritch. Meep!

Quick as though his hand were already there, Tavill picked up the mouse, which struggled for only a moment. "Hmmmm," he rumbled a little longer, thrumming a deep resonance to match the rock around him. The mouse went still, except for its whiskers. "It will be a long winter for us both, tiny brother, if you take all my food," Tavill said. He rose smoothly, drawing his hand closer to his face though he would not see the little creature. His voice lowered, became gentler. "I am glad you enjoyed my apples. Let us see if we can find a solution best for both of us, though."

He returned to his cabin, slowly letting his and the mouse's eyes adjust to the sun. "Hmmm," he rumbled again, quieting its sudden quiver. "It is cold. Let us find you someplace warm." He drew it close, cupping it to his chest as he went outside. He circled the cabin, letting all the smells of the forest flow through him. He went northward, climbing the slopes toward the Snowashes. He knew a place, full of heather and moss and deep turf, where autumn's leaves were piled thick, and huckleberries and powderberries and acorns lay thick through the summer. There were, of course, hawks and owls, skunks and foxes, and even snakes further up in the clefts of breaching rock. But that was the way of nature. Tiny brother could do very well up there, and when his time had come he could nourish others as he had been nourished.

Tavill continued across a broad valley, over the ridge, and down again. The wind eddied, swirling around his legs before rising. His steps crunched through a thick, almost spongy carpet but for the cold. "Here will be your home," he said. He knelt, feeling with his free hand. Even in the cold, the soil felt welcoming. "If you truly need though," he whispered, bringing the mouse close again, "come to my cabin. But ask first, if you will. It's only polite." He lowered his hands into the humus, and felt the tiny feet scamper off, heard the rattle of leaves.

Tavill rose, and glanced up. The day drew late, and he still wished for a meal. He turned and retraced his steps, pausing at the top of the ridge a moment as a strong gust swirled from the east. The weather would be changing soon. He turned his nose into it, letting the wind eddy through, out of his mouth, for a moment going back the way it came before snatching back, running for the west. He thought, briefly, that he could taste the ocean. Bitter and dark, that one was, full of wet rock and krill. Shoals and glimmering spikes kept the whales far out to sea, and only the hardiest of crabs made any sort of home on the surf-blasted shores. Terns sometimes made their nests where there were cliffs; pipers stayed among the thin, hard grasses on the bluffs.

Tavill did not like the oceans here.

He allowed himself a short sigh, then headed down the slope into the valley. He should have known better than to let himself get distracted by that errant thought—as though his opinion of something like birds, cliffs, water, or whales made a difference to them. Painfully he remembered what did matter to him; he missed the changing scent, stepped into a deep bog that the sun had thawed just enough for him to sink near to his waist. Panic hit him before he could stop it. He gasped, floundering, his great arms splashing thick water and mud. Some struck his nose, clung to his nostrils, and the black peat raced through nostril, mind, and squeezed his heart. He lost his breath, sputtered, finally managed to lay still, though suddenly the world around him ceased to exist—there was only the peat, the bog, death. He sneezed, and it echoed down the valley, unearthly. An unharmonized mess of deer-snort and elk-bugle. He quivered in the cold and in the mud.

Slowly, finally, he caught his breath. He listened; all was quiet. But he still couldn't smell, couldn't find a direction. A thick finger trying to clear the mud from his nose only added more. He swiped an arm across, found out it was covered in mud too. The stink of peat grew thicker. He snorted, cringed at the echo again.

He stilled, trying to find the calm he found in his cellars. Very nearly, the panic rose again as he wished he was home already. Wishing didn't help. He reached out his arms, setting his hands down gently. When he pressed, they sank, but the right arm sank a little lower than the left.

Carefully, ears pricked, he moved left. The firm ground below him rose. He continued to sidle, cringing at each splash and ripple. The wet cold moved down his legs, replaced with dry cold. Mocking his lack of smell, the wind blew strong. Was it still from the west, or had it eddied back to the east? Storms south of the Snowashes were finicky things.

He found himself on firm, dry land. He shivered for a moment, then carefully stepped forward, hoping it was southward. Three steps later, he sank ankle-deep again into bog. He stepped back quickly. Dread rising, he turned precisely and carefully walked. Splash. Backward ten steps: splash.

He closed his eyes, wrestling his rising fear. He knew this place. A small island in a marsh, he used to come to the outer edges during the summer to visit the frogs and dragonflies and painted turtles. He had always stayed outside of it; now he was smack in it, and he couldn't smell.

He opened his eyes and looked up. The vague brightness of the sky stretched a mirror image at the top of the valley. One way was east, the other was west, and the air moved along it, but he couldn't tell which way. All he smelled was peat. He sat down. Perhaps if the mud dried enough he could carefully flake it off. Until then, he was as good as blind.

He sat down, heavily this time. Twelve hundred years of carefully-built wisdom began to crumble down, and twelve hundred years of carefully-avoided emotions replaced it. It was not that his people should still be alive—they could, that would certainly be...nice. No, he should be dead. If anyone were to survive, it should not have been him. Pluvik, who had taught him everything—he should have been a viable candidate. His brother Vraden—or, if it could have been anyone, why not Arvalad? By

Harnost, it should have been Arvalad.

A low moan escaped Tavill's throat quite unbidden. His head went skyward again. It was now nearly indiscernible against the darkness of the trees. Arvalad, who it was said had raced across the Plains of Getharmen. Arvalad, who had been the first to summit Tuulos' Crown, who had guided the advance party to the Fields of Annans in that brutal winter, saving the Taur from freezing and starvation. Arvalad, who had married beautiful Kessaria...

Kessaria. With the wreath of hemlock and ivy. No Taur ever had matched her, that day. It was not just that she was Tavill's youngest sister, as the Taur measured age. Everyone sang of her beauty, even the one Tavill had once thought... Well. But for Kessaria a song had been written about her, and often sung in spite of—and sometimes because of—her soft-fur quivering in embarrassment. It had been a wonderful song.

Tavill took several long breaths. A wonderful song, that he had not sung since... Perhaps—perhaps it was time. He considered it a long moment, on his island, in the dark and cold, in more torment than he had been for hundreds of years. To sing it might bring a desire for her to be back—a silly impossibility. He had mourned, as had they all, as they always did after every new battle that saw more of their people slain. Her bones rest now in that far-away. They had fled three more times since then, never finding a home like what they had. She would stay there until time ended, and then would be not even bones, not even memory. Just gone. There was a time when Tavill felt he would be lucky to live until Massar, to be one of the Taur who had lived out every day of time, to be part of the seam that connected Beginning and End.

As more of his people were found and slaughtered, as the remnants of the Taur fled country to country, land to land, mountain to mountain, water to water, he began to wonder. Time would end. Memory would end. The Taur would end—for what purpose? They never knew. Tavill had never been told. Was not time enough of a witness? The Harral? They saw everything, too, and could bear better witness than he could.

He did not know the purpose. And if he did not know the purpose, he could not decide how best to act, to live. It was useless. He was useless. He should be bones along with Kessaria, with Arvalad, with Vraden, and Pluvik.

The world was dark; night had fallen. Tears flowed, and his nose ran.

Vaguely he recognized the peat was washing away. It was too late to care.

But then something stirred in him. He did not recognize it. In a thousand years he had never felt it, yet as it stirred he felt some sort of knowledge, some familiarity. He pressed his hands against the frozen earth.

It was time, indeed. He took a few breaths as his tears shut off. Could he remember how to do it? It had been...

The thing that stirred prompted him on. The rumble began deep, deep within; he had to bring it up higher. It lodged in his throat, where it stayed. He was afraid to go on, so he rested there a while. He let it seep through his body, that rumble, into every muscle and hair, until he felt it begin to leach into the ground itself. He paused, then began again. This time it shot straight into the ground, found some resonance there, echoed back into him until it almost felt as though the source was—always had been—the earth itself.

He hesitated again, but only a moment. As the rumble in his throat filled the night, he bent his tongue. A low, echoing whistle came tentatively forth and drifted down the valley. He held the note, let it grow and fill the space. The night around grew silent, but for this whistle. It spread like water, out and up. It reached the tops of the trees, the top of the ridgelines, and continued until it seemed to find a home in the stars themselves. Tavill, in the center, felt the song pull together earth and stars, joining them into one.

Abruptly he stopped, but the vibrations continued in the earth, the echo continued through the air. He let it fade from his body, and from his ear, and sat in the silence again. Not an empty silence, but one filled with anticipation. Now it had experienced the Tauren song again, it waited. Calm but impatient, eager to be filled again but not greedy enough to fill itself.

Tavill sat in that anticipative silence for several long moments, feeling the presence and the weight of it. Hundreds of years of waiting, that he hadn't realized until now it waited on him. He did not relish the realization, did not feel pride in the necessity of his being. No, there was a certain amount of shame there that—had there not been the anticipation and hope in that silence—would have crushed him under infinite weight. But the silence did not condemn him. It had not the room to do so, for being so full of hope. It simply welcomed him back, as though he had been gone only a moment, and for no fault of his own.

Tavill began again, now with confidence and intent. He leapt into the silence with his song, with Kessaria's song, and this time the silence was instantly full, as though his first tentative notes had saturated it. The rumble went quickly to the depths, the whistle reached the stars the moment that both came from his throat.

He had feared what might come of his singing her song: gloom, for feeling the lack of her presence; guilt, for having gone so long forgotten; elation, at recalling her to mind again. He felt none of these, at least not sharply or individually. All at once, experiencing them merely felt like acknowledging a reality, like recognizing a tree grew where it did. That was reality; but so, too, were his emotions. As he sang the song, it worked on him the way it had the first time he heard it. He joyed when the song was joyful, he wept when the song was sorrowful, he anticipated when the song was hopeful.

He closed his eyes, letting the music recall to his mind what it willed. He saw the sunny days, the days of storms, the days of wind and ice, of planting and harvest. It returned to him a sense of seasons, and returned him to his place in it. He still did not know why the Taur were made the witnesses they were to be. Perhaps he never would. But he could continue until the end...

The song faltered, then died. It fell from earth and sky as quickly as a cut string. Until what end? All the old songs said the Taur would last until time itself ended—yet here he was, alone, the last of his people. The songs had not said anything about the rest of the Taur dying before the end. Was his life guaranteed? What role did he play in his survival? Up to now he had taken it somewhat for granted.

The silence was replaced by the chill of night. He was still in the center of a bog, in the darkness, with no direction home. Surely this was not the night that time ended, but was it the night that he ended? The Taur ended, their witness failed? He was alone—not just the last of his kind, but with no one around to whom he could give his witness. He had spent centuries ensuring it. Was that why? Had he already failed? Had his people already failed, and now the judgement?

His sorrow had cleansed the peat from his nostrils, and he smelled now the stand of firs that he knew lay eastward up the valley. Was that enough? Was this his chance to come back to the road he had left so long ago?

He rose tentatively. But he could not go back among the people—certainly not those Others living nearest him. Could he? Knowing what he was, what the scent would do to him, what he would end up doing to them because of it...

What they would do to him if they could...

He went slowly in the dark, picking his way by scent and touch. Too little moon tonight to help. A full moon would have been better. Little as it would help him personally, it would be something. Instead, he soon became accustomed to the branches slapping his face, the roots and fallen limbs tangling his feet. A dreadful racket he made that night in the woods—certainly not as loud as his song, but far less cleansing to his mind. He paused more than once, resting against a tree he could not see, catching his breath and calming himself. What had been a few degrees of sun-journey yesterday became a night-long slog. A good thing, he realized as the forest began brightening in the east, that he had not started a fire. The smoke surely would have risen above the Snowashes in the clear air, drawing anyone's attention. They may have arrived in the valley, and heard his silly racket. But if they were here, they would not be looking for him.

Partway down the ridge, he stopped again as a thought struck him. Smoke, from fire. He recalled the smoke rising from Thinsledon. If it had been. Could it have been? Or was it merely snow flying off some cornice or other? Could it be waking? And what might that portend?

Perhaps, only that the molten rock beneath was restless. It lay with mortal beings to see sign and omen in basic natural events. How else to guide their short lives through the eons? Still, it might be worth the journey. It had been years since last he visited that tall mount. A walk like that might do him good.

He smelled cut wood, and found his way to the firewood beside his cabin. He entered the dark interior, moved the props so the roof could close, and set them aside. He returned to his cellar. On a crook of branch he had hung a bag; he retrieved it, putting inside bits of dried roots, berries, and cakes of grains he had made some days ago. It would be a long journey to Thinsledon, and with winter so near he would find little forage. There was always some, but he also hesitated to rob the voles and ermine. He hefted the bag; it should do.

He left the cave and laid the sack by the door. He found his mattress, laid down, and quickly fell asleep.

He did not wait for next day's dawn. As soon as he awoke he drank some water, slung the sack over his shoulder, and set out. He wanted to be well on his way before daylight made him second-guess his destination.

There were several valleys still to cross before the broad Snowplain. Heading away from his cabin, he cared less for the noise he made as he moved through the compartments. The birds woke first—less, he believed, from the sound of his passing than from the faint glimmer that began to arise. As he entered the final, deep valley, he knew dawn had come: though it was still dark among the trunks, the forest was echoing with the trill of cardinals and cries of jays.

He mounted the final hill with a degree of trepidation, knowing the sun would be out and his view across the long plain open. The forest ended abruptly at the top of the slope, and nothing but low scrub would stand between him and Thinsledon. Determination was needed.

And yet, he found himself stopping after two strides onto the plain. He gazed across snow that glinted in the sun of a cloudless sky. He had meant to continue. Perhaps the song, and all the memories of last night, affected him more than he thought it would. He stood, still, squinting. Something still smudged across the vision of white and blue—what he hoped was smoke rising from the mount.

He should have died, long ago. All the rest of his kind did, and they were able to see clearly—as Tavill once had. Some thousand years ago, he would have seen perfectly the mountain framed against the sky, and what type of cloud might be rising from it, whether vapor or just windblown snow.

But his vision had faded. Not gone dark, as though he were completely blind; just sort of smeared and smudged, enough that he could see his hand, if he held it up, but not the individual stone of his hearth from across the room.

He should have died, long ago.

6

THE LONG, SHARP BONE

"Will you have time?"
"Travel is far swifter, here."
"But you know the Oldest Race is harder to turn."
"I have the advantage; I have met him before."

1 Fimman 1320 — Autumn

By late afternoon, the Snowplain was covered in a low overcast. Tavill could feel the subtle change in temperature, and appreciated that. The reduced visibility, especially for him, was less welcome. At least the wind remained calm, and did not bite. If he made it to Thinsledon by week's end with no severe weather, he would be elated.

The Plain was clear, and the ground firm beneath the snow, allowing him to eat up the miles with long, sure strides. As darkness came early, he decided to press on as long as he could. He ate snow for drink, and dipped only once into his sack for food.

Today, he liked the darkness. His thoughts had occupied him far too much lately, and he didn't like it. In the dark, he could only ever follow the scents. There were not many out here, and most of the creatures were burrowed deep. But he could still follow the tracks of the wind, and in that there was some relief. The lack of scent was much like the lack of sight: it allowed him, at least, to keep his mind clear.

Sometime, late, the overcast began to break up. Moonlight and starlight bent, however faint, upon the snow. His legs were weary enough, and he decided to rest.

The sun and darkness followed him for the next several days, and he nightly spent time clearing his mind. He was not afraid of the past, and knew still that part of his role was to testify. But with so many centuries pressing in on him, it did not do to dwell too much on a particular moment. He found himself, one night, turning strangely to a time—what could it have been? Over four thousand seasons? How the people had struggled back then. Some sought the help of the Taur, he remembered. Not their wisdom, which would have been a better request, but their strength and size. As if the physical strength of a witness made any difference in the story. He knew what they meant, what they thought they saw: if pressed, Tavill or any of his people could lift one of their warhorses and carry it as they might carry a large wolf—but so could a tree, if the horse stood still long enough. But no tree went looking for things to grow around.

Perhaps that was why so many trees were cut down, though. At the base of Thinsledon, finally, Tavill sighed with that thought. He had found a cleft of rock, and squeezed himself into it as the weather finally turned, and a harsh wind roared across the Plain. Here it swirled, pelting him with frozen snow more ice than fluff, but still not with the violence of the exposed tundra. He would wait out this storm before beginning the climb. He sang, tonight, for the first time since the bog. The whistle did not go nearly so high, torn away as it was by the wind, but the rumble went just as deep, and seemed to bring back with it the warmth of the molten rock. It would likely be active, then. The question would be whether it portended anything more than a new eruption.

The Taur had suffered much in their efforts not to impact the events of the world. Witnesses, Pluvik had reminded him countless times, did not consciously change the outcome of the events. Even now, after running and hiding so long—and, if he admitted it, usually enjoying the solitude—the idea did not sit well with Tavill. It was not just that the annihilation of his people could only be a result of their refusal to fight back, but it seemed strange to him that the Taur would be what they were—endowed with what they were—if their purpose was observation alone. He had to admit they would be unstoppable fighters, if they allowed themselves.

He closed his eyes, breathing in the sulfurous scents around him. Perhaps that was what woke in him such evil thoughts. Even at the height of his anger, watching the people taunt and torment the last Taur before killing him, he had not thought to use his fury on them. Such an act would change nothing, not then. It would not even instill fear, for there would be no witnesses to spread the tale.

He shivered, and quickly changed the direction of his thoughts. Sulfur was too close to metal. A corner of his mind knew he would be safe. He had visited Thinsledon before when the mount was active, and had smelled nothing then. He was here to observe, to see why it smoked now. He would find out in the morning.

As he climbed, the air grew warmer, heated by the rock, and the snow thinned until he could see the crumbled stone of Thinsledon's upper slopes. Near afternoon, he began to feel a mild vibration—nothing yet to fear, but movement nonetheless. Access, he knew, was through a small cave on the far east side. He began to circle around, cutting slant-wise as he continued.

The scent, too, began to change. Most, he recognized: amidst the sulfur, a plain, searing heat; occasionally ash and smoke of burning shrubs; once, even, a bit of burning sage. And yet, every so often when the wind eddied and thinned out the other smells, he could pick up on another. He could almost vow he had smelled it before, yet it was so thin and so long ago he could not place it. It reminded him of deep forest—not the Graytrunk, those were too cold. More temperate—like the leaf-mold and black oaks of, what did the locals call it? Pal Isan?

As he neared the cave, that strange scent thickened. Instead of silk thread it became like a wool yarn, bringing with it a few other tints: apple, yew, and...rosemary? He snorted; he had never really liked that scent. Almost with the thought, the rosemary disappeared, replaced by pine. Why would the scent of the Forests of the Kalen be at this height?

No, not the Kalen. His steps faltered as he thought of it. The memory was not as old as that. He had smelled it recently, when he lived north of the Snowashes, and it had been Pluvik who likened it to Kalen. He stopped, considering. He should have remembered it sooner; but then, the memories after it were far stronger. Perhaps it had hidden behind those. But why was the scent here? Surely the man had not lived that long...

He resumed walking, but slowly. He was not sure he wanted to meet this man again, and not just for the memories that attended their first meeting so closely. There was something...off, about him. Even then, Tavill could not place the discomfort on one thing. But the unease was as complex as the scent.

Tavill paused at the mouth of the cave. What should have been a dark mouth was intermittently lit by what could only be a fire deeper within. His fists clenched and unclenched a moment; last time they had met, Tavill could see much more clearly. Though, if the man's powers had grown since then—and why wouldn't they—no clarity of vision would protect him. Could it be the man summoned him? If he had, could it be for the purpose of killing him?

"Don't stand outside forever," the voice echoed from within the cave.

Tavill started, and glanced behind him. Too late...

"If I had brought you here to kill you..." the voice continued.

Tavill could not restrain a growl, and entered the cave. Past one twist, the brightness of a large fire met him. He could not say he didn't welcome the warmth, despite the shadow that stood beside it, near a table covered with instruments—the shape and colors of the glints, however fuzzy, told him of vials and alembics and funnels and braziers and sundry alchemical tools. He had expected to find as much. "Lasserain," he rumbled.

"Welcome, indeed," the mage said. "I hope you understand, this was far easier than trying to hunt you—" He cut off abruptly. "I'm sorry, wrong phrase. Than trying to come to you. Besides, if I had suddenly appeared at your home..."

Tavill grunted. "Then I suppose I am thankful," he said. "That would have been far more alarming. And who knows what I might have done to you."

When Lasserain laughed, Tavill felt that same unease from so long ago: the laugh seemed easy, and yet there was an edge of contempt that prickled at Tavill. This time, there was another facet, something missing from a genuine laugh, that he also couldn't place. "And why would you want to find me?"

Lasserain's laugh subsided, and he turned to the table. Picking up a glass rod he stirred a powder, allowing it to sift down into a vial of clear bubbling liquid. He watched it turn to blue, then violet. "Various reasons," he said finally, turning to glance at Tavill. "You may choose which one you find most attractive." He checked another vial, made a small grunt—it seemed to Tavill of dissatisfaction, but not surprise—and turned back. "Much has changed since we last met, and you are in greater danger than ever before."

"I was not particularly safe before."

"Ha. True enough. But I have come to you now because I have some options for you. Would you like to hear them?"

Tavill paused, considering. "Tell me the dangers, first."

Lasserain grunted. "Wise of you. First, the Prosan are moving again, and in force." He held up a hand as Tavill opened his mouth. "The Prosan are those you call 'Others' who had killed the rest of your people, who came from across the sea. They will be most alarmed to find you here. You could run away again, perhaps stay here in this mount. But I don't believe one of your...size...will find enough forage."

"What can I do, then?"

"You do not care to hear the rest of the dangers?"

Tavill's shoulders drooped. "I supposed that was enough."

Lasserain barked another laugh. "It might be, but there are complications. Autumn is late in coming to the north." He paused as if it were significant, and sighed when Tavill didn't respond. "It's an old prophecy, from my home but given to the Kalen—you remember them?" He waited for Tavill to nod, then continued. "Doom arrives when a late autumn is followed by a tempestuous spring. There's more," he said with a dismissive wave, "but it seems to be fulfilling here. And the Cariste north of the—how did your people call it? The Labyrinth?" Tavill shrugged; the name was unfamiliar. "Perhaps that was what they call it. Either way, they have grown beyond what their small land can support. They will need to go somewhere, and they know there are untouched lands to their south."

"I thought they weren't able to come south."

"My dear Tavill, when the Cariste need to go somewhere, they do. They are not coming yet, but do you truly think they won't? Superstitious lot, the Cariste—much like the Prosan, actually." Lasserain chuckled as at a private joke, then sobered. "They would not be happy to find you here either."

Tavill scratched his jowl. No one was happy to find him. For supposedly having some divine directive, life for the Taur was rarely guaranteed—at least, not for the past several thousand years. They had been revered, once, before the Wars—so Pluvik always said. The world seemed to have outgrown them.

"You mentioned options," Tavill said finally.

"You can stay where you are, armed at least with my knowledge, and hope to survive. Or you can travel: a moving target is harder to hit, but you might accidentally stumble into someone you don't intend."

"I can avoid people."

"If you are downwind, or when the wind is calm and their scent can spread, yes. How safe will you be in a tempestuous spring? The prophecy sounds quite literal."

Tavill closed his eyes and cursed his vision. There was a time he had sight and smell... That time was past.

"It does not have to be," Lasserain said.

Tavill's eyes snapped open. "What do you mean? And how did you...?"

"I am observant, Tavill," he replied. "I can tell your eyes do not focus. Why do you think I have all this?" He gestured to the array on the table. As Tavill looked, they seemed to come into focus—but only a narrow circle in the middle of the blear.

"How...what is happening?"

"What do you smell?"

Tavill sniffed, harshly at first, then more gently as the scents overwhelmed him. It was something far below the scent of the mount. He tried to separate them—but it was difficult when he couldn't identify what it was. There was a bit of a woodsy scent, still different from the scent that had reminded him of the forests; sharper, a little bit, but with a faint sweetness—like a lily but not as cloying—that rolled through his nostrils right behind the sharp scent.

"I'm not sure," he said. "I have never smelled the like, before. But it—" He cut off abruptly as everything suddenly came into focus. His eyes widened to take in the cave, the roughness of the stone walls, individual dancing tongues of flame in the fire, the grain of the wooden table, the tiny mirrored flames in the host of glassware, Lasserain in his dark cloak...and his face, scarred, like it had not been the last time.

"Did that...did that happen while you were researching this?" Tavill asked.

An expression flickered across the mage's face, a little bit of contempt before a smile. "No," he said. "But my powder is working, isn't it."

"I can see everything," Tavill said, his voice on the verge of breaking. "It's been... But what happens when I leave? Is it fixed forever?"

"Unfortunately, no," Lasserain said, turning back to the table. "You'll need to carry something with you, something I've been crafting more recently. But I need you to test it, and see if it works."

"See if what works?"

"This," Lasserain replied, turning back suddenly. His hand stretched out, and on it lay a large pin: sharp points widened toward the middle until a short narrowing in the center. It was dark with amber flakes that shimmered in the firelight.

"What is that? It looks like..."

"A piercing," Lasserain replied. "Bone, though of course treated with my alchemy. We put it through your nose, and the scent stays close."

Tavill reared back slightly. "Won't it block other scents, or overwhelm them?"

Lasserain shrugged. "We won't know unless we try. I believe once you have accustomed to it, its particular scent will fade away, but the magic behind it will continue to work. As I said, I need you to test it."

"Why?"

"Because I can't know until—"

"No, I mean, why are you doing this? Why help me?"

Lasserain's hand lowered. "Yours is—was—and ancient race, Tavill. You are the only one left. Your vision was already beginning to fail the last time I was visiting Gintanos, and I could not let such a deficit threaten your survival."

"You want nothing in return?"

Lasserain turned away and put the piercing back on the table. "I see," he said, glancing over the alchemical array before him. "This is a lot of work for no apparent return—no benefit to me. What could I ask of you, that would not be worth your survival?" He glanced at Tavill, a strange light behind his eyes—accusation, and pain. "If I asked for your wisdom, would you rather die? Or if I asked you to go north, avoiding the Prosan, and meeting with the Kalen, to help turn away the Cariste?" His head tilted a notch as Tavill considered this. "Do you think the Cariste will treat the Kalen well?" he pressed. "They are not as ancient as you, but the Kalen hold great wisdom that the Cariste will surely hope to extract from them. If I ask you to help protect them, is that too much?"

"I do not want to become a weapon, to you or for you, or against anyone," Tavill said.

Lasserain's jaw set, and he turned back to the table, slapping the piercing angrily away. "Very well," he said. He drew a deep breath, glancing over his shoulder. "I suppose it was a risk I took knowingly. Sorry to have brought you all this way for nothing."

He turned his back with a finality that hit Tavill nearly like a strong wind, and he found himself walking to the cave opening before he realized it. He shook his head. Lasserain could not have dismissed him more firmly short of taking his arm and leading him away. Yet, even as this thought occurred to him, he could not resist continuing resolutely out. Well, he would not be a weapon. Ever. He knew what he was capable of, knew there was no force on Oren—no doom worthy of turning into that.

He stepped out into daylight, gazing out across the broad Snowplain. The effects of Lasserain's magic had not yet faded. He could see, clearly for the first time in centuries, the riffling of wind-blown snow stretching for miles below him, and on the far horizon the faint gray of the forest and the pale blue of the Snowashes behind it. Somewhere over there was his home. Surely, by the time he reached it, his vision would have failed again. It might have been nice to actually see his cabin set in the forest—at least determine if it might truly hide him away from any Prosan—he wondered briefly what the name meant, where they had come from—as they moved.

Why would they be moving, suddenly? Was something drawing them, or pushing them? He might be able to take action, if he knew what it was. Lasserain probably knew. Tavill's steps were already carrying him down the mountain. He wanted to be home quickly. He could think and plan on the way, and decide what else to do. Maybe he could cross the sea, somewhere. Surely there would be minor islands where he could live, where no one else would be interested.

As much as he tried not to, though, he did love this wide, empty land. Since the beginning, the Taur had lived in every country in Oren—but nothing he remembered compared to here. He felt that way even before his people were slaughtered by the Prosan. He could recall no home until he came here. Suddenly, everywhere else the Taur had lived seemed a brief stopover on a long journey back to where he had never been, but always should have. There was just something right about the jagged shoreline, the broad plains, the forests of the mountain slopes, and the mountains themselves. Even though he had been forced south, his cabin in the Snowashes felt like just another room in the same house.

As the sun lowered to the west, his vision began to blur. He wished it would set sooner, that he might see just one sunset. It seemed it wouldn't happen, yet he stopped and faced the west. Just one glimpse...

The wind eddied. A snow fox was nearby, hunting for evening prey.

Clouds were thickening to the west, and the sun would fade, then blaze out. The edges of the clouds were ragged, the holes mere bright spots to his rapidly-deteriorating eyes. He thought he could sense the rays as they stretched their arms toward the snow.

Another eddy. He smelled a hare. It probably snuffled through the snow looking for some heather beneath the snowpack—

Tavill turned suddenly, his eyes casting wildly about. But his vision was too-far gone, and he could not see a white hare against a white snowbank, or the fox that surely prowled closer. He backed up, toward Thinseldon, away from the eddying wind. He prayed it would stop, would blow strongly away from him.

As if in spite, it streamed more strongly toward him. Like thick ropes, the scents of fox and hare filled his nostrils, swirled in his mind. They were close. The fox tensed, while the hare seemed unaware of anything except the trove it had found beneath the snow.

Tavill whined, then turned and ran. The riffled snow, so beautiful in the afternoon, was now treacherous as it threatened to trip him and send him headlong. He dodged sideways. Mocking him, the scent seemed to follow.

He heard the crunch of snow, and the snapping of bone. The snow betrayed him worst, and he fell. Before he could even push himself back up, he smelled the blood. Hopefully—probably—he would be too far away from the cave and Lasserain.

The scent of the blood blossomed in his head, released from the constriction of his nose. It spread rapidly to every corner, and all other thought was shut out. He was filled to roaring as the familiar cloud descended, and he slipped away from his body. He would wander, now, through the vacuum, until his body called him back again.

When he returned, the scent of blood was gone. Much of the snow was gone, too—he could smell bared, frozen flora all around him. He was still panting, feeling as though he had run the length of the plain. He looked around. It was almost completely dark, but behind him Thinsledon still blotted out the slightly-lighter sky. He had run toward it, apparently. It was far closer now than when the bloodlust overtook him.

As his breathing steadied, he couldn't help but weep a little. He had been so careful for so long, had wished and worked to make it never happen again. He had hoped to make it to the end of days without experiencing it ever again.

It had been far worse, the last time. That had been north of the Snowashes, deep in a forest. That time, he had torn down limbs, uprooted trees, and killed hundreds of creatures. Red was everywhere, in the grass, on the trees, in long gouges torn by his fingers. Remnants dangled from what few branches remained. The horror of it painted his dreams for months. And, worst of all, the shattered body of one of the Kalen who had happened upon him in the middle of it. Tavill didn't remember the Kalen arriving, but knew he had not been there when the bloodlust hit. He was probably drawn to the noise.

So, at least, this time there seemed little death but a few small creatures—more than he wanted, but less than possible. And he had not made it to the mountain to kill Lasserain. Odd as the mage seemed to be, surely he didn't deserve that.

And Lasserain had offered him the possibility of escaping this. If Tavill had been able to see clearly, he might have spotted the fox and hare and run more directly away—or at least, out of the windstream that brought him the scent of the kill. And the Prosan were coming, he had said—those who killed, and brought iron, plenty to make the bloodlust return. Perhaps, if he could see more clearly *and* scent them, he might evade their migration and find safety...somewhere.

He turned his gaze back to the mountain. Would Lasserain still be there? Would the offer still stand?

As his feet began to move, there was a more important question, in his mind: would he make it, and be able to find the cave, before darkness fell?

Whether because of his lost time, or some trick of the weather, his pathway back up the mountain remained well-lit enough for him to find his way to the cave. Just as the last bit of darkness fell, he could still see the glow of fire coming from the mouth. He smelled the same scents, heard much the same sounds, as his first time up.

"Why have you come back?" Lasserain asked mildly, when he entered.

Tavill sensed, more than saw, the mage turn to look at him.

"Aha," the mage replied, setting something down on the table with a clank. "If you don't mind my saying, you look terrible. Come in and warm yourself a moment."

The mage seemed to dismiss him, so Tavill sat beside the fire. It had been—too long since he had been so warmed. He lost himself for a few moments in the flickering, blurry light. His fingertips, he realized, were still sore from tearing at frozen earth. As the fire warmed them, they began to throb. He pulled at them absently, then licked them where he felt cracking and dried blood.

"Don't do that," Lasserain said suddenly, pulling him from his reverie. "Here, use this."

Tavill looked over as Lasserain held some small pot toward him. He took it, and sniffed it: ointment, of some kind. Sharp scents of pine and myrtle pricked his nose. He dabbed a finger in it and rubbed them together. They burned, then cooled.

"Keep it," Lasserain said when Tavill held it out. "You'll want it for this next part, too."

"What do I do?"

"Take this." Tavill felt the long, sharp bone in his open hand. "You will need to do it," Lasserain continued. "There will be a soft spot, just behind the ridge, where it will pierce through easiest. You can find it more readily than I. Push it through until the center rests in the hollow I've carved. The skin will close partially around it, and help keep it in place. Then rub that balm on either side."

Tavill held the bone for some moments, considering. The scent rose again to his nostrils, and as he sat in thought the fire came back into clarity. He looked up and saw the glistening walls of the cave, shards of quartz and hematite glittering in the rock.

He pinched the center of his nostrils, feeling. What the mage said was true; he raised the bone and placed the point in the spot he had found. After a deep, steadying breath, he pushed.

For a moment, he thought it had stopped working: his vision blurred far worse than it had ever been, and panic gripped him. Then he felt the pain, radiating back from his nose to echo in his skull.

"No! Keep pushing!" Lasserain shouted, his voice dim in the throbbing of Tavill's head.

He realized that he had begun to draw the bone back out. He stopped, then pushed again. It seemed to resist. As hard as he tried, the hole in his nose would not seem to grow larger, to fit around the last bulge in the bone. Tavill grunted. "You've made it too big!"

"You must do it," Lasserain said. "Hurry! Or you'll never be done with it."

Tavill gritted his teeth, roaring through the pain. The echo became a constant noise, a trumpet blasting pure in his head. Surely Lasserain could hear it! It seemed to echo outside of him, crash against the walls of the cave. He could almost swear he saw dust falling—it was! His own roar threatened to destroy the cave, to bring the rock down on top of him.

He tried to clamp his mouth shut, but it wouldn't budge. When he thought for certain he was about to be buried alive, there was a terrific ripping as the bone slipped into place. To his amazement, he could feel his skin close around the bone. He feared it would be a gaping wound forever.

He gasped, his breath gone again, as he huddled over himself. The echo of his roar, and the pounding in his head, slowly subsided, and his surroundings came slowly back into existence.

"Don't forget the balm," Lasserain said in the quiet.

Tavill wiped his nose on the back of his arm. The bone nearly pricked his skin, obstructing him from clearing the discharge. He sniffed loudly. He dipped a finger in the pot, rubbing the balm around the piercing. Those scents cleared him, and as they slowly faded he could scent the bone, and whatever Lasserain had infused it with.

The walls of the cave were clear, again, the tongues of fire precise and individual. He could see the heat sweeping across the coals of what had already burned. And then, as he continued to breathe, the strange lily scent of the piercing did indeed fade away, but so did everything else: no cold rock, woodsmoke, or any of the elements on Lasserain's table.

Tavill rose, gazing at a wordless Lasserain. He turned and went to the mouth of the cave, and looked up. He swiped at tears again as he beheld the countless stars, could see their faint blues and whites and oranges and pinks, saw some twinkle and some hold forth as adamant beacons. Surely, with normal vision, his need to scent everything else was less important.

He turned back. "Thank you," he called. Lasserain did not respond, and Tavill turned again to the broad snow plain, now faintly white in the starlight. He felt his gaze pulled toward the pass through the Snowashes, so far away and yet seemingly so near, through which he would travel as he went north. Through which, he hoped, the Prosan were not yet moving.

He would find his way through. He would find the Kalen once again. And he would try to help turn away this threat from the north.

He, Tavill, last of the ancient minotaurs, would survive to the end of time, and give his witness.

7

THE NATURAL AND
UNNATURAL

"Why are you moving him north?"
"I fear I am not."
"Then who is?"
"That is precisely what I fear."

7 Fimman 1320 — Autumn

Tavill made his way back across the broad Snowplain. Every day was a new adventure in his returned sight. He spent an hour, one day, in awe of the rusty orange tailfeathers of a slowly-circling hawk. He had not realized how much he had forgotten what things looked like, how beautiful the world was even in something so apparently featureless as the plain, and how much he had missed his sight. He drank in this reborn world.

By the third day, he was hurrying again, eager to see his cabin, the Graytrunk Forest, the Snowashes close up. He had not once seen them clearly, his vision long gone by the time he had moved that far south.

He set out that morning long before dawn, his steps slowing again as the pearl and pink sky brightened. Before the sun emerged from the far eastern horizon it was already casting beams against the mountains. They appeared to breathe, some wind stirring the snow on their peaks. The Graytrunk, below, lived up to its name in the early gloom. The leaves were a deep green, almost gray. They would soon drop, leaving the trunks like unpolished steel stark against the pale gray mountains beyond.

The sun finally rose behind him, a large orange ball that glittered across the snow. He reached the foothills, his eyes searching almost frantically among the trees for his home. But he was still too far away, the trunks too close together and lit by the sun to see between them.

A final hill, and the forest was across the way. Finding his way by sight for the first time went slightly askew, and a little further north-east of his route he finally saw the timbers. He paused, then, and shook his head. He had been lucky—or blessed: the horizontal timbers stood out starkly among the vertical trunks. Only someone as blind as he would not see it immediately, if they came through the woods. Lasserain had come to him just in time.

The thought sobered him. There was still much to do, and he had no idea what kind of time he would have to do it. It might already be too late, so he would have to act as if it were. And yet, he could not skip important steps.

He decided, as he approached his door, that he would do what he could to erase his presence here. If he was able to avoid the Prosan, he would not want evidence left behind. He took a deep breath. All the wood he had split, had been so happy and contented to have against the time he would need it, now would have to be hidden. Split logs did not occur naturally, he thought with disgust, so even scattering them would not hide them.

The rest of the day was spent in hard labor. He unticked his mattress, scattering the straw to the wind. He bundled most of the fabric, but used a few patches to sew in extra pockets on his pack, now that his home would be carried with him. Much of his furniture he was able to simply untwist and disassemble—he had kept iron from his home because it smelled like blood, but now it meant that nothing he owned bespoke of forging.

He unraveled his roof, threw the poles to prop up the thatch deep into the woods, began taking his home down log by log. These took a bit more time. Some of them he was able to bury in the earth, to hide their axe-wrought ends. Others only needed one end buried as he had worked part of the timber and left the rest alone. The stone of the hearth was easier: he had shaped it but little, and those few cut edges buried nicely.

He kept two final logs, appropriately sized for a pair of trails. Some of the limber vines from his thatching created a web between the poles. He emptied his cellar—that took far less than he feared, and he wondered briefly if he actually would have made it through the winter on just those stores—and chucked as much of the split wood into the natural cave as he could. He transplanted a few saplings over its mouth, strewing branches and leaves over the rest.

The remaining split wood and the planks for the doors he loaded onto the webbing, determining to carry it with him until he could deposit it into the bog just north of his home. As evening fell, he glanced over the pad of earth that had been his home for so long. Aside from much trampling that he worked now to obscure, he could not even tell he had once been there. Just like that, from one rising to setting, his presence on the land was gone. Part of him was proud of the fact: outside of their four cities, his people had always lived light on the land. Knowing that, if he died, the evidence of his life would quickly be gone pleased him. But another, darker part of him was saddened by that same fact: that his existence, and the existence of the Taur, could be so easily wiped out.

Darkness descended fully upon the wood as Tavill finished. He stood a moment in the gloom. His pack lay on the ground not far away, ready to be picked up, and the wood sat stacked on the trails he had fashioned. He could leave tonight. For all he knew of the approach of the Prosan, he should. And yet, he hesitated. He could also just as easily leave in the morning, in daylight, when he could see where he was going.

He picked up his pack and slung it. He grasped the trails, settled them on his shoulders, and began dragging them north. The full moon, only a day old, shone brightly down through the foliage and gleamed off smooth-barked trees. He turned a little to his right, climbing over the hilltop. Partway down the next slope was a small clearing. He dropped the trails at the edge, in the woods, and stepped out into the ferns. He pulled the blanket from his pack and lay down, gazing up at the stars. It had been less than a week since Thinsledon, and the sight of the stars had not yet grown old.

The sky was clear, though the bright moon still washed out many of the fainter stars. A cold breeze stirred the branches with a soft rush made more brittle by the dying leaves. The far-off hoot of an owl rose and fell.

Tavill nestled deeper into the ferns, feeling the cold soil beneath him. Of everywhere he had lived since the dawn of time, this had been his favorite for blissfully peaceful moments just like this. He hoped forever to stay in this land, still raw and rugged as it was. As pleasant as the ancient Taur cities were, it was not until after he had mourned their passing and made the wilds his home that he truly felt tied to this land.

A root—like the Prosan—intruded into his peace. He shifted to his left as it dug into his back. The root was part of the land, and he knew where it came from—one of the many trees surrounding him. But so far he had no idea where the Prosan had come from. They had simply appeared in an otherwise barren land, speaking a language he had never heard. Much of its cadence and vowel use had reminded him of people from the east—but those now lived far to the north against the sea, and spoke the language he knew. These were somehow very different.

How long, he wondered, did it take for a people to become part of the land? He had seen for himself the slow migration of plants and other animals to lands they had not inhabited previously. He accepted the root that had been in his back a moment before, though two thousand years ago these hills had likely been as barren as the Snowplain. For that matter, he had not been part of the land two thousand years ago either, and yet it now felt more like home than anywhere he had ever been.

He took a deep breath. He almost wished he could meet with the Prosan, talk to them about the land and how much he had seen it changed, and how well it had provided for him through the centuries. He wished, too, for the opportunity to understand them, understand their place in the land.

And yet, if Lasserain was right, they acted still more as an invader than an inhabitant. He had seen that, too, in the plant and animal world—and perhaps, if he admitted it, in the world of the Taur. The land had not yet reclaimed all of their old cities, and what right had they had to build them? His cabin was gone except for some trampled ground, and the split wood he would soon seek to hide. Within a few years, that too would be rotten and gone, like a flower of the field that died and its place was not remembered. But in places out there, further north, stone columns and lichen-covered walls still gave evidence of the lives of his people, so many centuries after they had gone.

But here sat the forest, older by far than even the Taur cities, though not as old as the land itself. He sighed again; he would think himself in circles trying to discern between the natural and unnatural. It did not ultimately matter if he was more or better an inhabitant than the Prosan: they were here, they were coming, and they would be unhappy to find him here. He could not justify cutting them out, and so like the root that had been in his back he would be the one to move. As it had been for so long.

He awoke suddenly, the stars above him already fading westward. It was a clear day, the branches above bent strongly to the north. It would be a cold day. A good day to travel hard and fast.

He rose, folded his blanket, and stuffed it into his pack. The straps settled against his shoulders, and he anticipated the pumping ache over the next few days as he grew accustomed to that, again. He dragged the trails downslope, across the next compartment. At the next ridge he turned a little right, and down again to the swamp. In went the split wood, his work of many days long ago disappearing with a splash and bubble. He scattered the trails and coiled the lashings, then turned his face fully northward. The easiest way around the Snowashes was along the coast, and he could hide easily in the folds of the foothills and the trees all the way to it. He hoped the Prosan would take the far more visible pass that broke through just to the north—maybe a day's march for him—rather than the goat path by the sea to which he headed.

He followed the stream up the valley as the wind gusted. His hooves crunched through frosted yellow and orange leaves of scattered ash, always the first to drop in autumn. Lasserain had mentioned the season coming late, to the north. Though the air was bitter today, here too it seemed delayed. Tavill stooped to pick up a few of the leaves and twirled them in his fingers, then rubbed a thick thumb across one. It was still hearty and moist, a more recent fall. The next leaf crumbled, desiccated.

An odd time. He thought of his journal, so long neglected. He would need to make himself write in it tonight. The duty of witness pressed against him suddenly. So much was changing, and so quickly. Or had he been distracted by contentment?

He wanted to laugh, except for how strange it was: he had been a blind witness for so long. How could he report on what he could not see? A cruel jest by Elonai to give him a task for which he was so ill-suited.

But now perhaps he could do a better job. His gaze swept through the forest with purpose, rather than for his own enjoyment, cataloging what evidence nature provided. His memory was a little dusty from disuse, long un-oiled, and creaked and groaned as he spun it back to life again. Various bits had to be shaken loose from ancient corners. But by midday, he felt it again running smoothly, information sliding freely in and out of their cubbies and nooks. He would have much to write about, and he smiled.

Stabbing pain shot through his left arm and spun him around. His eyes cast wildly, then lighted on a lone figure a hundred paces back who was quickly nocking an arrow to his bow. Tavill noted buckskin and a furry hood, cast back now; dark, long hair; a black bow.

"No!" he bellowed.

He turned and ran, his legs tingled with fear of another bolt, and he had to force himself not to high-step but simply run, hoping the next arrow would not strike the largest part of him exposed behind his pack. He ducked and dodged behind trees. A dark shaft sped past to his right and caromed off a branch to thud into the ground. He turned left, leapt across the stream, and angled up the opposite slope.

His mind sped faster than his feet. How had he missed it? Because he was too accustomed to scenting, had thought the empty wind meant there was nothing there. Tavill was below the ridge, but continued to turn and jump. He could hear faint cries behind him. By now, though, his long legs would eat up the ground far faster than a human.

He glanced quickly behind him, and saw no one. He slowed his sprint to a long lope, pacing now for distance. He knew these foothills better than the Prosan, knew places to hide overnight and places where thick undergrowth would slow them and make him difficult to track.

His shoulder bounced off a thick maple, and he thought of the arrow. He tested the shaft: the point did not seem to have barbs, and it slid out of his flesh easily. A great blessing, to be sure. But why would it be so? It was not a hunting arrow, at least not for anything of any size. Had he been found and shot by a rabbit hunter? It made no sense.

At least he could not smell his blood, either—an even greater blessing. Lasserain's bone was working.

A hawk cried out. A bird hunter would have a round head on the shaft, to stun more than kill. A migrating people might have outriders, scouts to see a strange land. He wondered that they were so cautious.

The leaves here did not crunch, like the ones in the previous valley. He would be silent, too, then. Except maybe the thudding of his hooves.

The wind had died. His gaze swung upward. Was there movement up there? A squirrel jumped across, then sped to the opposite side of the tree, out of sight. They were cautious too.

Tavill's gaze swept back down. Why would their scouts have arrows without barbs? A great blessing, to be sure.

Hadn't he thought that already?

He turned and looked behind him. The black-haired man in buckskin was there, approaching slowly, another arrow nocked. That shaft had an evil-looking head, two long points trailing behind it, with another two points perpendicular. That would not slide out of his flesh so easily.

How had the man caught up? His legs were so short.

Tavill blinked. Maybe not so short. The man came nearly to Tavill's own height. They stared at each other, eye-to-eye. Tavill had not looked at anyone eye-to-eye since the Taur had gone. No one else had been tall enough.

Tavill looked down at his legs, stretched out in front of him. Ah. The man was not tall, Tavill had sat down. That made sense, then.

Lashings bit into his wrists. Without thinking, he tested them; they had gauged his strength well. There was also a bandage around his arm, so they weren't ready to kill him. Still, he kept his eyes shut, hoping they wouldn't notice he had awoken.

He let his ears and nose wander. There were faint sounds of a camp—cookware clattering, murmuring voices, the occasional soft stacca-to of hammers on wood. Here and there a louder voice as one called across to another. But, overall, quiet and small. Surely this was not the entirety of the Prosan. When he had last seen them, there had been upward of two hundred. This sounded less than dozens.

They had fires going, the smell of smoke far thicker than their own odor. Whatever they prepared, it was simple and not intricately scented—flours and grains, most likely. Someone had a rind of cheese, but even that was not sharp.

A strange voice spoke, suddenly near him. Again, the cadence reminded him of Cariste, but the words were wholly unfamiliar. He was aware, suddenly, of someone else standing near him—his guard, no doubt. That man answered briefly.

Blunted pain shot through his side, and he flinched. He looked up. This man, too, had dark hair, but was not the man who had shot him. Blue eyes studied him below furrowed brows. The man's face was wrinkled and scarred. From Tavill's recollection of the lifespan of humans, he gauged him to be past middle age, closer now to death. But there was also clearly some vitality there.

The man said something sharply. Tavill only blinked. The humans exchanged glances, then the old man squatted down. He said something else, in a different tongue but one still unfamiliar to Tavill. This time, he shook his head. He hoped to convey that he didn't understand, that he was not just being belligerent.

"Are you alone?" the man asked, this time in Kalen.

Tavill glanced at him sharply. He did not resemble that ancient race, not even a little bit. And yet he spoke the language fluently. Only after that realization did the absurdity of the man's question hit him, and he couldn't help but snort. "More than you know," he replied slowly. He had not spoken Kalen to anyone in a very long time.

"Where did you come from?"

Tavill regarded him a few moments. "Do you know what I am?" he asked.

"A myth," the man replied frankly.

"Then I can't answer your question."

The man laughed, an honest laugh that Tavill had caught him in his own words. "Until today, you had been a myth—of sorts. It was hard to believe the stories, old as they were." His face hardened. "Where did you come from, and where were you heading before we found you?"

"I come from here. I was going north."

"Why?"

"To avoid you. Your people."

At this, the man seemed genuinely taken aback—but only for a moment. "How did you know we were coming?"

Tavill considered a moment. There seemed no harm. "A friend of mine, a mage, knew about it and told me."

The man's face hardened more, and he stood and spat. He barked a few words in his original tongue. Tavill's guard responded. It sounded defensive to his ear. Another exchange. The old man was staring hard at him again. Tavill tried to look benign, assuming it was failing.

"Where is this...mage?" he asked, biting off the words.

Tavill hesitated. Where did this man and his people come from? He sounded almost afraid of the idea of a magic-user, but that sounded more like a Rinc Nain superstition.

"Where!"

"The mountain," he said quickly. If Lasserain couldn't take care of himself, he was no longer the mage Tavill had known him to be. "But that was many days ago."

"Did he give you this?" The man held something out, and Tavill's stomach plummeted.

The man held the bone in his hand. How had they gotten it out? *Why* had they gotten it out? "You need to put that back in, right now," he said. His eyes darted around the camp. There were no obvious signs of bloody flesh, but their weapons alone might do it. They once had. He flexed again, testing the lashings, praying they would hold if something went wrong.

The man smirked. "As I thought," he said. "I suppose it gives you some strength, doesn't it. That's how you resisted the poison so long."

"What?" Had he? It had seemed to set upon him quickly enough. "No, you don't understand. That bone is all that stands between—"

"I'm sure it is," the man snorted.

"You have to put it back!" Tavill roared. Less than dozens was still too many. "You risk your life and the lives of your party if you don't. What did your myths say about ones like me? About how we fight?"

The man seemed to hesitate, but only a moment. "No," he said, shaking his head with a glance at the guard. Tavill could almost sense the guard's tension. "No, I think this bone is exactly what causes you to fight the way you do. We have seen your strength with it in place. Now that it is removed, you cannot break free."

"And how many of my kind have you shot with your poison, to know how long it should last?"

"Stop!" the man thundered. He drew a sword and pointed it at Tavill.

"Please, Elonai..." Tavill moaned. He tried to breathe through his mouth as the man glared at him in consternation.

It didn't help. The scent of the iron crept into his nostrils anyway, the tendrils almost crawling, clinging to the skin as they struggled closer to his mind. "Put. It. Away!" Tavill said through gritted teeth.

The man turned his head slightly and barked an order. Red hedged Tavill's vision as another handful of men approached, weapons lowered. He squeezed his eyes shut, waiting to be taken away. He had tried, hadn't he? He had tried to warn them.

But something was wrong. He stayed present, this time. The red grew, pressed in around him, swirled like smoke and stung his nose. His chest buzzed, his ears rang. He opened his eyes, and it seemed he was in a field of red woodsmoke. The man's eyes had widened, but were not yet entirely filled with fear.

Tavill could change that. He had fear aplenty, fear enough to share with this lot. His hands were free, loops of hide trailing long stringers as though he'd walked through a thick spiderweb. Incoherent shouting hit his ears as though dulled by water.

A sword was moving through the air. Aimed for him? That was silly. Tavill brought up a knuckle and tapped the blade aside. How to get fear into the man's eyes? He reached out a hand, engulfed the man's face, and squeezed.

Skulls like berries. That did it. That kind of fear a man never forgot, not for as long as he was dead. But there were more, many more, plenty more. Bones to break, swords to shatter, bows—he laughed. An arrow even now came toward him, lobbed gently from the string. He plucked it from the air, turned it in his hand, and slammed his fist down on top of the man's head. Didn't even have a helmet. The arrow went clean through; that look of surprise would be pinned there, now.

Ribs were like straw. Legs and arms, young twigs. Folded and twisted, like the furniture he used to weave before they wanted him dead. Last of his kind. That wasn't enough for them, though. Kill him? Millennia couldn't kill a Taur.

They came through the red smoke, cries and screams dulled in his ears, lost below the buzz and the ring, their movements slowed by his rage. Clumsy. He turned it all to fear and surprise. He grabbed a kettle and swung it. That was less satisfying, too efficient.

Here came one. A great helm with twisting horns atop it. Tavill supposed the face was supposed to be fearsome, but it looked more like a defective sheep to him. This man carried a massive sword in both hands. Someone of renown, perhaps. A hero of the little people.

Tavill stooped and picked up two swords from the fallen. He swung the first. It shattered against the opposing blade. He swung the second—it too shattered on impact. He was just too strong to keep the blades whole.

But the shock still had its effect. The man's arms went limp, the bones of his forearms shivered. Tavill sighed at how easy it was. This one he kicked; his back broke on a branch twenty paces up, and he fell back to the ground in a very dead clatter.

Tavill's chest heaved and he looked around. There was too much fear and pain left in him, he needed to let out more. But there seemed nothing else left alive. He ran back through the dead, hoping. But they, too, were all very dead. He shouldn't have swung that kettle. Three at once? Too greedy.

He continued to pant. Something glittered among the leaves—not blood. This sparkled yellow like the sun through thick foliage. He stooped and picked it up. Some other clumsy weapon of theirs? It almost looked like a...dagger? No handle. But it was sharp.

Put it in your nose!

Tavill snorted at the thought, and yet it didn't go away. Before he realized it, his hand was bringing it closer. Before he could even blink, he shoved it through. The mist disappeared.

Tavill looked at his hands. They had been bound. He was standing now. But wasn't he—?

His eyes came up and surveyed the camp, and his breath caught in his throat.

He ran, vaguely northeast, his thoughts scattering like the leaves under his feet. They had taken out the bone; he had stayed present during the bloodlust—that had never happened before. But if it hadn't, he surely would not have thought to put the piercing back in. Why had he done that? It seemed a voice had spoken to him, into his mind, telling him what to do.

This had to end. If he was to be a witness at the end of time, he could not continue to endanger anyone and everyone. How to do that? He distrusted this bone, too many strange things attended it. He needed some other solution. From where? Kragnog? Stavnuk?

There might be nothing left but crumbled stone. But there was nowhere else he could think of. Maybe, if the Foldings were still intact...

It seemed impossible. But, so did everything else. The Prosan were coming; the Kalen; the Cariste—everyone was coming, and without a way free from this bloodlust he would kill them all.

He ran on, unseeing through a blur of tears, unhearing through his own wails echoing through the woods.

8

THROUGH PASSES AND CANYONS

"Melnor worries—"
"I don't doubt it."
"What should I tell him?"
"That it is easier to guide an object in motion."

7 Fimman 1320 — Autumn

Averlynn wound her way between the fires, feet stamping with the others as drums beat their rhythm. At the edges of the clearing, the musicians played, so that as the dancers moved the melody morphed. To one side, the harps dominated, their sometimes-frenetic plucking and blending shaped the dance into flowing arms and bending torsos. In the tune lay the memory of dancing sunlight between summer leaves, the falling of refreshing rains, of life and growth. Near the turning fire, the players wore rough gloves and slid their fingers along the strings rather than plucking, turning the dancers' thoughts to aeolian strains as autumn winds rose across the land.

On, and soon the flutes came to the fore; arms and eyes raised skyward as the long cries of hawks and eagles were imitated. As the days shortened, many birds flew north to follow the retreating sun, crossing the distant Wall. Here Averlynn nearly faltered as her heart soared particularly strong with them, though she did not know why. But just as quickly the dancers behind and in front of her pulled her along.

In the darkness, the Kalen were cast in strong light and shadow as fires lit first one side, then the next. Dawn and dusk were represented in compressed time. They approached the drums, and it was all footwork and clapping, their hearts beating in time between the music and the effort. She felt her blood begin to surge as she and the others worked harder and harder. Sweat glistened in firelight—the harvest, working in every moment of daylight available to bring in their abundance. But always moving forward, toward conclusion.

Still on, curving and wending, and they came to the Nunkan, the two-stringed violin, whose haunting sympathies slowed the dance, almost to weeping. The winter stores were gathered and settled in place. The land, once so full of life, was dying. Leaves once vibrant green gave one last gasp of color, then turned brown. Grass withered and wilted, retreating into the earth. The fawn and cub were near-grown, and spent more time in beds and dens. Their time of frolicking long gone, they were wiser and wary, and little seen.

The Nunkan slowed even further, and the dancers came almost to a halt, their movements the speed of freezing streams. As those behind Averlynn caught up, they gathered, sharing in each other's warmth and companionship, bracing for the long winter. A hum rose in their throats, just loud enough to be heard, but not drowning out the harps, flutes, or drums. There at the last fire of the dance it culminated and held as the full moon shone brightly overhead.

Averlynn tilted her head back, gazing at her patron with awe and thankfulness. She had not realized how desperately she had needed the Isun Vera's words until now, when she was free to celebrate the last day of Tadan È without guilt. Her sorrow, with the Nunkan, grew as she knew she was only free to celebrate openly because her parents were not here to keep an eye on her.

As though cut with a blade, the music and drums and humming ceased. Averlynn swallowed, and lowered her face. With her people she knelt on the ground as Isun Vera stood before them.

Now at the heights of her office, the Isun was changed. She wore long deer-hide robes. Her face was painted mostly white, with dark around her lips and eyes, and the hollows of her cheeks. Her hair was loose, and billowing. The male Isuns would wear a headdress of some sort, but Vera needed none. As she raised her arms, the sleeves fell away so that her pale limbs almost glowed in the moonlight.

As she began to chant, Averlynn and the rest pressed their foreheads to the ground. Averlynn felt as keenly as she could each blade of grass against her forehead, felt the solidity of the earth beneath her. If she could, she sent her consciousness even deeper, feeling the rocks far below.

She felt a strange tightening in her throat, and pressed her lips against an involuntary cry. The dancers were to remain utterly silent. And yet...but no! She mustn't.

As soon as she pushed fully away that urge, she felt her mind pulled skyward as though some celestial eagle desired her for its eyrie. Her fingers splayed and gripped the earth. Now her teeth clamped against the whistle that already pursed her lips. She trembled in the tumult as earth and heaven felt prepared to tear her in two.

Slowly, agonizingly, the tearing stopped, and Isun Vera's chant took over her mind once more. Averlynn found herself gasping, and felt more than one elbow in her ribs, prodding her to cease her sacrilege. She took hold of herself, and the elbows retreated. She prayed the Isun herself had not noticed. She would have no idea how to explain herself.

The chant ended in a long ululation, and all the dancers reared back to sit on their heels. Averlynn swallowed again: did the Isun glance at her longer as she reached into her belt to withdraw the bones? Averlynn cast her eyes down in repentance, just in case.

Isun Vera prayed, quietly at first, thanking Praka for their harvest, for the life he had brought to their land yet another year. Her voice rose as she spoke of the following year, begging him to be with them, to remember his loyalty and care and to see them through. Winter, she sang, always threatened to keep Praka away forever. But his power could not be denied, except he chose it.

She ceased suddenly, and her voice dropped to a near-whisper. "See us," she prayed, "though Hakana watches us now. May she be a reflection of your will, of your power, and may you speak to your children through her."

Isun Vera's upraised hand came down suddenly, and Averlynn flinched at the clatter as the bones struck the earth. Dread stole over her, though she could not understand why. The night seemed colder than it had a moment ago. Averlynn tried to look around without drawing attention to herself; something was happening. When she glanced forward again, she saw struck across Isun Vera's face the horror she felt on her own.

Without understanding why, and knowing she should not—it was improper—she looked skyward.

If she could have collapsed, she would have: Hakana was disappearing! Her pale, hard disc had an edge missing, rimmed in red. Averlynn tore her gaze away and fastened it on the Isun, but Vera's gaze still held fast to the bones in front of her.

Averlynn didn't know if she should get her attention—if she even could. She settled for staring hard at her, hoping her gaze would somehow be felt.

As the silence stretched, Averlynn could feel the others beginning to shift around her. They awaited the telling of next year's blessing, and knew it should not be delayed this long. Her hand trembling, Isun Vera pointed at the bones on the ground.

"There is death," she proclaimed. "And...not just one. There is death on the land, death in the air, death in all cardinals, horizon to horizon." She swallowed. "Death in the heavens—" She broke off with a strangled cry as she finally looked heavenward and Averlynn could tell she looked to the moon. Her hand went to her throat. Slowly, her goggling eyes slid down to look dead at Averlynn. "What have you done?" she whispered.

Averlynn's mouth worked, but no sound came out. She could feel the eyes of everyone on her. Finally, Isun Vera's eyes returned to the bones. They focused, and her brow furrowed. "There is hope," she said quietly. She fell ungracefully to her knees, pawing at the bones. "Buried deep, deep below the death. Far beyond the wailing of despair." She thrust the bone aloft, holding it reverently. "Hope!" she cried. "A desperate hope, and it lives in the most ancient times. Something we have not seen, but something that sees all—that has seen all. Has seen time, beginning to end. In its wisdom is our hope!"

"What is it?" Chief Hathar demanded. It was not his time to speak either, but this ceremony had long since lost its sense of tradition.

Isun Vera shook her head. "It will be known when it is seen," she replied. "And yet, it will hide for a time."

"Should we go look for it? Should we send Scouts?"

"I do not know. That will be for the Ka to decide. But it may arrive without our effort." She nodded firmly. Falsely. "I believe it will."

Averlynn knew the disturbance she felt inside would be inside all the Kalen around her. The Isun was rarely so uncertain, especially when the bones spoke otherwise so clearly. She couldn't help but glance up again. Hakana was gone from the sky. Even the fires seemed dimmed, though the flames still danced high. *But glowing fades and decays...*

But if that prophecy was as true as the bones, time was not run out. Winter had not yet come, and their doom fell in spring. If only she could remember more! She knew it was there. But where to find it?

North!

Her head turned. Those behind her still glared, but she was looking over their heads. The Wall was lost in the darkness of the night, and yet she could see it in her mind as clearly as if it were day. As she stared, she could almost see a path through it. There was a pass! She knew there was.

But if there was a pass northward, there was one southward. If she made it through, she might be caught, or followed. But by what? None had gone north of the Wall, it had been forbidden. Their land was plentiful enough, and empty of foes. Why go looking?

And yet the doom she felt indicated a foe of some sort, and from that direction. What if she brought their doom by going to look for it? And yet she could not shake a restless feeling that nearly had her on her feet and mounting Tarafel for the journey tonight.

With an effort, she turned back to the Isun. Vera stared at her, and the hate, anger, and fear that had been there a moment ago was gone. She looked...sorry. And encouraging. Somehow, she knew, and—somehow—approved.

Chief Hathar stepped forward, raising his hands over the assembly. "Praka has indeed blessed us, tonight, by showing us there is a fate to be avoided. Whether we avert it or no, it is now known and we know there is hope. We are not the Wohan if we do not survive again, as we have so many times before." He halted, realizing the paradox of his words: the last time they survived was as the Kalen, and had rejected the name in attempt to reject the curse and put away their history. Now, he tied them tightly back together. He stumbled on, anyway. "Let us rest tonight, and build the strength of our minds and hearts for this coming trouble. The Chiefs and elders will consult with the Ka and the Isun to plan our next steps."

Isun Vera then stood, and finished the ceremony according to tradition. Averlynn barely noticed, her mind filled with thoughts of the Wall, and how she might make her way through it. The land had always yielded many clues to her, and guided her even through terrain she had never visited. But the Wall was more treacherous by far, and in them she had not practiced in decades.

As the Isun finished her last prayers, she glanced up: this time her cry was one of joy. Averlynn was not alone in craning her neck. Hakana was being reborn! The darkness had moved on, and silver light bent down upon the clearing once again. Averlynn felt herself weeping, and she was joined in her praise.

With observably lighter hearts the Wohan returned to their rooms, though it was still not the joy they had during the dance. Their minds would still be heavy, Averlynn knew. Her own was still weighted down by the path before her.

Isun Vera met her at the door to her cabin. "Daughter Averlynn," she said. "Please forgive me. I'm sure you understand the horror..." She trailed off with a tight smile.

Averlynn hesitated, folding her arms. "Isun, I want to. And of course I understand, but...in moments of fear and uncertainty, our true thoughts might show themselves."

Isun Vera laid a hand on her arm. "No, Daughter, our darkest thoughts reveal themselves, and the lies we have tried to silence for so long can come on strong." She let her hand drop. "Of course, I fear that we do better to worship Praka, the source of life. But..." She compressed her lips and shook her head. "Hakana would not be in the heavens if she were not important. Perhaps you, like her, will guide us through this darkness. I faltered, when it seemed she was dying. But now that she is reborn..." She trailed off again, pausing to glance at the moon, full and radiant again. "It is not strictly my place, but I will convince the Ka to let you continue your foray. And I, too, think you must go north. We have hidden too long behind the mountains."

"How did you know that was my plan?"

Isun Vera laughed. "You are not so subtle, Daughter," she said. "And I am not so blind to your spirit. No one looks that intently in one direction without planning to go."

"I'm not sure even you can convince the Ka to let me go there, not as a Ranger."

"*Where* you go is no business of mine to tell the Ka," Isun Vera replied with a wink. "But may Hakana and Praka both go with you, along with the good will of the Wohan."

Isun Vera returned to the darkness, and Averlynn went inside, her heart even lighter still.

However the Isun managed it, Averlynn never learned. But she was given her orders as she always had been, with no mention of what the rest of the Wohan might be doing to address the doom they awaited. She was assured, instead, that her role was most valuable, to keep her eyes on the land and report any more of its secrets. She didn't know if it was her own preconception, or if the Ka's tone actually was just a little patronizing. Regardless, it held no promise they would investigate the Glowwood or her prophecy.

But as she rode Tarafel out of Amka, she didn't care. She was rested, well-fed, and confident that she had celebrated Tadan È well and properly, and that Hakana loved her and cared for her. She let the stallion find his own way north and west. She would wait a day to ride directly for the Wall, lest Isun Vera be not the only one to try to discern her spirit.

For most of the day she tracked along the border between the Water Plains and Hataki Hills. The hills were large and rolling here, and mostly hid the Wall from sight. As the sun lowered, the tallest hill fell abruptly away, and she realized the blessing they had provided. The line of impossible peaks shone at her now, covered in snow and seeming impenetrable on the northern horizon. Part of her knew it was distance playing tricks, that there would be many valleys and clefts. Most of her feared, though. The moon disappearing for a time was not unprecedented, but it had been rare. That Hakana had chosen this time to hide, at the height of their celebration, and that it should accompany her decision to attempt the Wall, was more than unsettling.

And yet her mind was still firm. She turned north the next morning, and even Tarafel seemed to sense it as they rode adamantly forward. At the tops of rises, she found herself glancing back for the familiar green of the Waken as it slowly receded. By the third day, a long arm of the Wall hedged her in from the west, and she topped one final climb. Below her was a wide but shallow plain, littered by rocks and glittering pools. Across the way—she would be there before the sun climbed much higher—the first peak leapt skyward. A small river ran out between it and the next peak that folded against it, filling a long lake that ran eastward. Somewhere among the crags an eagle cried as it hunted along the river.

Far behind her, the Waken Forest was a bare smudge between the brown hills and the blue sky. She expected to feel some sort of pull, a tug to go back where she belonged, where she knew. And yet, she did not; a longing in her head almost like a voice called her into that fold across the way, drawing her through endless passes and canyons until she would see what lay beyond.

She ran a hand down Tarafel's neck. "That river has to start somewhere," she said. "And rainclouds must make it into the mountains deep enough to feed it. Let's go exploring," she finished, almost giddily. That was how to approach such a venture: she was here to explore, to go where her people said no one could.

She entered the valley, and the peaks multiplied and grew on her horizon. Tarafel picked his way well across some rocks beside the tumbling river, while Averlynn only had eyes for the landscape. Cordgrass near the river's edge gave way to bromegrass. Here and there stands of fir and pine struggled in small, sunny patches. Upward, even these soon fell away, leaving largely scree slopes with occasional whitebark pine and gambel oak before balding entirely to rock.

Despite her earlier self-encouragement, her eyes scanned nervously, afraid to miss any clue even though she could turn her head and see familiar lands still behind her. She took a deep breath. She would never make it through with such an attitude. She continued to scan, but repeated to herself it was just observation. Just taking in the new landscape. Weren't the Endolin Mountains back home much the same?

Her eyes roved upward...and upward. *No*, she couldn't help but correct herself. The Endolins were not nearly so steep, and high.

Ahead, the valley was split by a peak. The river was joined from the west by a smaller creek. In the fork, a white and brown hawk perched on an angular stone, a fresh kill in its talons. It stared at her, clearly uneasy. With a shriek it took off, clutching the small trout, and winged eastward.

Averlynn paused. That hawk would prefer lower elevations—she had seen them even among the Hataki Hills—and it followed the larger watercourse. It would not make its home somewhere she could not go. Shifting her knee she nudged Tarafel east, following the path of her avian guide. *If I could fly like him, this would be so much easier.* She thought, too, of the landscape she could see on the wing, the freedom that would provide.

Tarafel flicked an ear, as though irritated by her thoughts. "I know, friend," she said, smiling and patting his neck. "I appreciate how swiftly you can go, too."

She glanced quickly to her right as the shallow plain outside the Wall slid out of view. She was surrounded, now, by towering rock. Somehow, surprising her, she felt more at peace now. She had used the land to guide her, and ahead she could already see the valley winding generally north and east. The sun was still low on the slopes. Though the day would end early, she had plenty left. Before it darkened entirely, she determined to find some high pass she could ascend and try to gain as much of a view of the mountains' layout as she could.

She continued to follow the river. There seemed fish aplenty in the waters, and more than one hyrax bounded away through the underbrush as she passed. As the shadows of the valley finally topped the lowest peaks, she saw her pass: the slope here was gentle, and she could see a stairway like small cirques high up where it steepened to a saddle between two summits still glistening in the sun.

She turned Tarafel, crossing at a shallow, rocky ford, and clambered the slope. His powerful muscles made easy work of the climb, and even where it appeared steepest was not as bad as it had looked from far below. She guided him around a few sparse pines, scattering a family of squirrels and a screeching jay.

She let Tarafel catch his wind at the first cirque, and let him drink a little from the pool that had formed there while she munched a bit of trailbread. When they had finished she pressed them on. She would not want to spend the night high up.

With a series of bounds, the crested the pass, and the rest of the Wall lay out before them—or, at least, much of it did. As terrifying as the peaks around her were, they were small children compared to the center. A long line ran east to west, that even atop this high pass she was nearly craning her neck upward to view. Directly north, the tops were wreathed in thin clouds—higher than any eagle she had ever seen would be able to reach. And, worst of all, her view beyond was completely obscured by rock. She had no indication of how deep the mountains were.

She drew a deep breath. She had expected as much. Even in the Endolins, the edges of the range were the lowest. So if what she saw was the center of the range, she could assume they extended equally further north as they did south.

She glanced behind her, realizing how far she had already come. The valley had run far more north than it had east. She followed it with her eyes; it zigged a bit further on—she might reach the end by next afternoon—and seemed to dead-end in a box canyon. She squinted. There might still be a way out of it. And between the peaks just north of it another valley ran westward, at least for a time. After that, the rocks were too jumbled to discern much direction. She would have to do the best she could. For now, she had a route for the next day or two, and plenty of food below to sustain her.

Tarafel took one step forward, but she stopped him. "Too eager," she said. She gazed down the steep pitch with a critical eye. "How exactly did you expect to make it down that? Without throwing me over your neck?" Besides, it ended in a deep lake surrounded by cliffs, with no way further into the mountains.

By the time she returned to the river the stars were out overhead, a thin spangled patch between black walls. She built a small fire among the rocks, congratulated herself on a successful first day, and fell asleep.

Four days later, she was lost.

After climbing the pass, her journey had gone well, she thought. She had been able to find a way northward out of the canyon, and followed the next valley north and west. That had led her to another valley where she refilled her waterskins and had spent an evening smoking some hare meat for later.

After that, her progress had steadily worsened. The valleys all ran either directly east or west, and more often south than north, and every pass she climbed showed those high peaks in the center shifting but little.

This morning, she climbed another pass and looked down into a valley filled with spruce where she had camped the night before. She swiveled her head, gauging the distance to those highest peaks. They appeared no closer.

The valleys that had seemed jumbled before were indistinguishable now, so cluttered with peaks and passes and canyons it resembled lace more than loose string. Strings she could follow; lace led nowhere.

"I need to get higher," she muttered. Tarafel turned his head. "I know, I know; not on you. I'll have to leave you here for a bit—or, wherever." She continued to glance around, until she spotted—there: a high but attainable peak, and only a few passes northeastward. She thought there might even be a direct line to it, though climbing down and up the compartments might take them another...two days, she estimated.

Or, three.

Maybe four.

She camped early below the peak. Sometime in the night, a fresh layer of snow appeared on the heights, and so she gave herself time to prepare. Under the bright sun, she knew that thin layer of new snow would turn to hard ice, and snowshoes would serve her no purpose. So, while Tarafel ranged to find forage, she unbraided some rope and fashioned spikes for her boots by rebraiding it around small but sharp rocks she had gathered from a scree slope. When she was done she wrapped her boots in it and tested the strength on a boulder. The shards held firmly, scratching lines in the stone without popping free.

The next morning she rode Tarafel as far upward as he could take her, leaving him finally beside a small snowmelt-fed tarn where some short muhly grass managed to grow between the rocks. She looked up and took a deep breath. She took a small belt bag with bread and meat, and looped the thongs of two waterskins through her belt. She coiled the spiked rope for now, waiting to put it on until she had reached the snow.

By the time she had stopped for some food, she was discouraged by her progress. The snowline still seemed far overhead, though Tarafel was a bare dot below her. And the spoiled stallion seemed to be lying down to sleep. Averlynn's breath was labored, and she felt the edges of a headache. She wrapped her cloak tighter around her, took a few sips of water, and lay back against the slope to rest.

When she opened her eyes again, she heard Tarafel's whinny echoing through the valleys. She bolted upright, her eyes searching. He was below, and appeared in no danger, but the sun was far lower than she intended it to be. She must have slept long, and wonderful Tarafel knew she should be moving.

The pressure in her head had lessened, so she turned upslope and climbed with renewed vigor, racing the shadow that spread from the valley below as the sun continued to sink. She reached the snowline, ignoring small hunger pangs as she wrapped the spiked ropes around her boots. Up again, and clawing her way higher. She paused only once to catch her breath and look northward, but shook her head and turned her eyes away; the view she hoped for was coming, but not yet complete. Knowing, at least, she had chosen the correct peak gave her enough of a final burst to finally reach the top. It would be a scramble to get back down; the sun lit now only the snow-cap where she stood, and the rest of the valley lay in darkness.

That low sun had a profound effect on the maze of valleys and peaks now stretching below her. That impossibly high ridge seemed even further away, now, but it also allowed her to see to the other side. Far, so incredibly far away she thought she discerned among a haze and shadow a long, thin, bright, brown line, and on top of that line a razor-thin blue. She blinked, straining her eyes; if she interpreted that right, it was a plain bordered by sea.

As significant a hope as that presented, it paled in comparison to the crosshatch of valleys that spread between her and that far brown. So high, and cast in the contrast of that low sun, it looked to her nearly like a road—a crazy, jagged, sometimes doubling-back road, but a road.

She sat as long as she dared, memorizing the line before her. She saw no peak in the distance that matched this one's height, so she would need to remember her route for the way back as well. Slowly as the sun sank, bits and pieces of the route disappeared completely into shadow. Finally she turned away, hurrying now back down the slope to Tarafel, and to the fire she would build against the chill that had sunk into her while she sat.

She did not attempt the descent into the valley but stayed mid-way, at the tarn. As she warmed herself with the fire and Tarafel's body, she closed her eyes and recalled the image from the peak.

It became a nightly practice, as they continued the circuitous route through the Wall, and she couldn't help but think if she hadn't gotten lost that once, she might never have captured that view. She also realized, as days turned to a week, that without that view, passage would have been impossible. She stopped herself uncountable times from taking a valley or pass that seemed to take her where she wanted to go, remembering that only the one route seemed actually favorable. And, more than once, she found herself on the other side of a pass she had ignored to see that it ended in a cliff beside her, and she might have spent entire days climbing only to be turned back.

Her fortune and guidance kept her for two weeks, before finally failing her. She was in a valley that seemed it had to be near that far brown line, and it ended in a wide box canyon with sheer walls a thousand feet high. There had been no pass out of the valley for three days.

It was otherwise a fertile valley, filled with pine, juniper, tall grasses that did not exist in the south but that Tarafel ate without complaint. Dragonflies skimmed the weeds, and bees wandered among the late-blooming flowers. Jays, warblers, and thrushes flitted among the bushes and hawks and buzzards circled overhead. Marmots, hyraxes, hares, chipmunks, and squirrels scampered among rocks and trees. And late the last evening she saw a bobcat slinking along a stream that emptied from a small pond at the head of the canyon.

But none of that helped her know what to do. By its beauty, she was nearly tempted to stay for a few days just to enjoy it. She knew too firmly, though, that some great threat loomed somewhere over this last—she hoped it was last—ridge.

As afternoon waned once more, and Tarafel foraged through the meadow, Averlynn stood at the head gazing upward at the cliffs around her. Even now, she wasn't sure why she looked. It appeared the same as it had the previous evening, and as it had from further down the valley a day ago.

She shook her head and turned away, when her sliding eyes caught movement. She turned back quickly, eyes scanning. There! It was...

Impossible. Just below the rim of the canyon, and descending, was a goat. Unconsciously she touched her ring as it continued to pick its way down the cliff front. If it somehow made it all the way down into the valley, then she would be able to make it up and out. Not with Tarafel, but on foot. If it was the last ridge, she might see what she needed to see without needing her stallion to carry her. If it wasn't, she could return and figure out what to do then.

The goat continued toward her, and she started noticing the little steps and rocks it used to descend. As her eyes scanned downward, she saw those little foot- and hand-holds continued all the way down.

Tarafel came up behind her, then, as if sensing her thoughts. "I'm going alone," she said. It did seem, often, as though he understood her. And it helped her to talk. "I'll try to come back by tomorrow night, and if not, the night after. But I need to see what's over there."

Tarafel murmured and nudged her, then turned back to the meadow. There was ample forage, and nothing she had seen yet would pose a threat to the war-trained horse.

She walked to the cliff and placed a hand on her first step. She glanced up again, knowing this was a commitment. She would either reach the top before darkness, or she would possibly fall to her death. There was nowhere to rest until the top. She touched her ring again. Guided by a goat.

The next several hours were spent in unwavering resolve. She only ever looked up, finding and reaching for the next hold. A little more than halfway up she met the goat, and got her final assurance: there was a little bit of rope around its neck, dyed blue, and it was not afraid of her. Someone owned this goat—or they had, if this was its escape. She smiled briefly as it bleated at her, and they continued on their opposite ways.

As the sun lowered to the horizon, she pulled herself out of the canyon. It was a broad, flat shelf, and in the distance over the edge she could see the ocean. She was still high up. To left and right were more jagged peaks like broad and craggy knives.

She approached the edge cautiously. The far, far shore slid into view. Her guts clenched, and she dropped to her belly. If this was a sharp cliff, she could be outlined clearly to anyone below. Something lay across the land that began sliding into view, but she couldn't tell what. It almost appeared to be another broad network of peaks and valleys. Was the Wall, then, endless? Had she come all this way for nothing?

She slid forward, then finally reached the edge and looked down. Centuries in the world did not prepare her for what she saw some thousands of feet below.

Cities. And towns. And villages. Countless of them. They were not peaks and valleys but buildings and roads. Here and there were tiny spaces of green, occasionally a broader one in neat rows of farmland—but, surely not enough to support so many people.

She was panting, and wiped her arm across her nose. From the bottom of the cliff to the far sea was a dense mass of civilization. To her forage-trained eye, there was no way the land could support them.

They would be coming south. They would have to. That was the doom hanging over her people.

As she slowly caught her breath, she noticed something else—structures far less permanent, perhaps a mile from her perch and hard by a large city.

Tents. Thousands of them. Tens of thousands. And spangled by glittering steel. She had been there when the Endol massed against the...what had they called themselves? Cariste. Their gathering looked much the same. An army, tens of thousands strong. And more coming from the west, she saw.

She continued to watch as darkness spread across the land below her.

9

NOT EXACTLY A SCOUT

"You should not be helping him succeed!"
"What could you possibly mean?"
"Our job is to destroy them, not build them up."
"And that is why you have failed until I came."

35 Fimmon 1320 — Autumn

In the third row, right, of the long column, Ketz managed to keep his eyes on the road and the men in front of him, even as the camp loomed large before them, and the mountains even larger on his right side.

In the past month, he had run more evenings than he had not. He was assigned camp chores, carried water, pulled carts, rubbed down horses, set up the large tents, dug trenches, trampled thick vegetation down to create pads. Afternoons he drilled with short swords, halberds, bows, wrestled. Always marching, of course. And evenings he cleaned boots, clothes, tack, tarps, cookware, cleaned and sharpened weapons, built, lit, and extinguished fires, loaded and unloaded carts and mules, learned column movements and provisions, and, more recently, led some of his unit in prayers.

When the column halted, he looked down at his boots quickly. Another round of cleaning and polishing would be in order tonight, on top of—whatever else. His eyes came quickly forward again as the Captain rode by, then slid right to glance at the mountains. The peaks across the way were sharp, except for one broad, flat top. The edge of that cliff was remarkably smooth—maybe a tiny hump near the middle, probably just a boulder. At that distance, the cliff must have been some thousands of feet high. It was little wonder no Cariste had been south of the Brynth. In their long march across Gintanos, Ketz had not seen one route through the peaks and cliffs.

And they had not yet been told why they gathered. As they marched, they occasionally met up with another unit, and marched together along the road. But it was nothing compared to the camp that stretched across the plains around them.

It had to be the only bare stretch of land in the region. Villages, towns, and cities compressed here, so near the eastern edge of the country. It was the oldest region, as the Cariste explorers some thousands of years ago landed here from South Pal Isan. By the sign of this camp, Ketz could only assume all of Carist's armies gathered on the eastern shores of the land. As yet, he could not fathom why. Rumors had run wild, especially as the units began to mix: it was simply some massive exercise, preparing for possible invasion; the eastern towns had begun fragmenting, and only a terrific show of force would keep the land together; the Capitol was being moved, and no one liked it; an emissary from Carist had supposedly come, and trouble in Carist itself required all loyal forces to deploy there at once.

Curious by far, though, were the prayers Ketz had been commanded to lead, prayers he recalled from ancient texts preserved from the Age of Discovery. Protections from the God for sailing, from the dangers of the sea. Strength of arm for the foot and horse, and strength of mind for the leaders. Faith that they would be led well.

But only he knew how old the prayers were—maybe also the Sergeants who ordered them prayed, though he often wondered. More often it sounded as if they passed orders they themselves didn't understand, and didn't need to. There were certainly other prayers that could have encouraged the troops just as effectively.

Those prayers, to him, gave greater weight to a final rumor he had heard just the other day: that they were being sent east across the sea to try to find the Abandoned Isles and retake them. Those had been one of Carist's first discoveries, during that age, and their first failure. The Histories said the God of All had struck them with a plague for their arrogance and pride, and hid from them the knowledge of the cure. Everyone on the Isle had died, it was believed. Certainly, when another ship was sent to look, they found countless dead and rotted. In several homes they found written accounts of the sickness—fever, vomiting, gasping for breath, and finally death. When it entered a home, everyone inside was presumed on a course for death, and the bodies did not contradict it. The search party quickly fled the island back for their ships; they seemed to carry no disease with them, as not a sailor fell ill, and they landed back at Carist with wild tales. It was determined that no settlement would be re-established on the islands.

Perhaps something had changed. He was not given more time to think, though, as he was ordered to attend his usual list of chores.

Yet, while he worked, he could not keep his glance from returning to the mountains. They seemed changed, somehow. It was fully dark before he realized the long flat cliff was now utterly flat, the edge against the sky crisp. The boulder he thought he had seen when they marched up was gone—at least, he was fairly certain. It was too dark now to check again.

He had first shift on guard. Far sooner than he anticipated, his relief came. When he returned to his tent, he sat just outside, intending to clean up his boots for the morning. Just as he settled in, though, a shape loomed out of the darkness. He leapt to his feet, one boot off.

"Sergeant Blassnoss," he said quickly.

"Get that back on, and follow me," he said.

Ketzler gripped the sides and slammed his foot into it. "Yes, Sergeant," he said, coming back upright. The Sergeant's eyes glittered a moment, then he turned and walked off. Ketzler fell in behind him, tired but curious.

As they neared the Captain's tent, his heart sank. Why was he being brought here again? He assumed he would not be welcome after his last bungling. He had seen the Captain some since then—the man had even stooped to showing him how to tighten the guy-lines the first time Ketz was ordered to help set up the largest tent. He couldn't help but respect a man of such rank who would do that. But he had never spoken to him.

Unlike before, the guard ducked inside quickly when Ketzler and Blassnoss arrived, and they waited until he came back out and ushered them in. This time, it was only the Captain and the thin woman in green and tan, and both of them quickly fastened their eyes on him when he ducked in behind his Sergeant.

"Ketzler," the captain said. Ketzler gave a short bow, then stood stiffly.

"You have been leading our men in their prayers?"

"Yes, sir."

"What do you know about them?"

"That they are old, from the Age of Discovery, and they were prayed to give the Cariste strength and courage. For sailing," he added, barely keeping he question from his voice.

It seemed simple to him, yet the Captain and the woman looked at each other with significance. "What stands out about this area we are in?" the captain asked abruptly.

Ketzler was careful not to react the way he had the last time, instead allowing himself to think a moment. "We are nearing Drothaer," he said. "Which means we are nearing the sea. There is some land here for farming—not much, yet the cities are adequately supplied. Still, this many soldiers would put pressure on even those stores—" He cut off abruptly, coloring. The Captain had not really asked for assumptions.

And yet he gave an encouraging nod. "Continue," he said. "How many troops are here?"

Ketzler took a deep breath, recalling the sea of tents to his mind. It seemed impossible to count. "Sir," he began hesitantly, then stopped. There were fewer flags on high poles, though, and those he thought he could recall. "It seems to me there were perhaps a hundred Captains' flags that I could see. That would mean...20,000?"

In the heavy silence, he sensed his Sergeant taking a step away. The Captain's and woman's gazes were intense, now. "That is remarkable, Ketzler," the Captain said quietly. "I would have thought you would be too busy with your chores to make such an observation."

"Sir, I believe I have done them all well..."

"You have, your sergeant swore to it."

"And he was setting to polish his boots after his guard shift, Sir," Blassnoss said roughly.

Ketzler barely kept his glance from Blassnoss, and gave the barest shrug. "There felt like ample opportunities to look around while doing work that didn't require my direct gaze, sir."

The Captain grunted. "What is your impression of the mountains?"

"They live up to their name, sir, especially here. I see no way south."

"Should we go south?"

Ketzler opened his mouth, then closed it. "I guess...no, sir, not necessarily. It's just, supposedly we can't, and yet the land—there's too many of us Cariste for the land to support..." He trailed off. That was one rumor he had not heard, and yet it made sense. They needed more land, but they would not try to retake the Abandoned Isles when they were already on a continent that had untaken lands.

"I see what you mean," the woman said quietly.

Ketzler realized his face bore some expression of dawning comprehension, and he worked quickly to hide it. By both of their looks, and her comment, it was too late.

"I trust you to keep this to yourself," the Captain said.

"Sir, I...of course, sir, but—" He clamped his mouth shut and stood still again.

"But what? You may speak freely."

"Sir, I didn't think a route south through the mountains was possible—especially with so many troops as are here."

"As far as we know, it doesn't. Pikaranon agrees."

"By boat, then." Ketzler gave an involuntary shudder. How many ships had Cariste lost in the attempt to sail south and find a shore? "Why now?"

"As you observed, the land cannot support us. We have to try something. Our ships and navigation have come a long way in the past few hundred years," the Captain said drily. "Even if—" He cut himself off, but Ketzler had heard enough as a Pip to finish the thought: *even if our traditions have not...*

"Sir," he said instead, then paused. "If I'm still allowed to speak freely..." He waited for the Captain's nod, and continued. "Why am I here, sir? You know how many troops are gathered here."

"It's a simple test I give to every new recruit," the Captain replied. "Most don't make it past the first meeting."

"Sir, I was..." He colored again.

The Captain and Pikaranon both chuckled. "Yes, you were," he said. "But, you were very new. And you still observed more during an overwhelming time than many others. And you have done so again, and made conclusions from assumptions that almost no one has."

"What does that mean, sir?"

"It means you are most certainly going with us on our first voyage," he replied. He glanced down at the map. "Come over here," he said with a gesture.

Ketzler paused a little longer than he knew he should have, but finally came over and looked where the Captain was. He saw the outline of the coast, much as he had seen from other maps. And yet, those all faded out south of an area called Dead Man's Cliffs. The Captain's continued all the way to a southern point, with a mountain marked on it. And some notation, like a star, on the coast near it.

"The winds and currents to the west are impossible," the Captain said, gesturing to the opposite side of the continent. "And the shoals and shores to the east are impassable—at least, they have been as far as we know. So much wind and water has surely changed the land in the intervening years. You will be taking three boats—about 500 troops—to scout down the coast. If you find anything, one ship will return with a skeleton crew while the rest of you establish a beachhead, and settle in for reinforcements. There will also be spearheads into the interior, to see what the land is like. Most of those missions will be led by Pikaranon, here; she's one of our army's best scouts, and leads by far the sharpest team we can field." His brushed his fingertips across the blank spaces between the shorelines south of the Brynth. "And there will be plenty of land to scout."

"I'm going to be a scout, sir?"

Captain Liptieri compressed his lips and shook his head. "Not exactly. You, and many others who have shown aptitude, will spend a shift or two each day training under her—but just basics. We don't have the time to train you to be both a soldier and a scout. But it is a wide and probably dangerous land, down there. If more of our foot know what to look for, what to call attention to, it cannot help but serve to keep us safer."

"Yes sir."

Liptieri straightened, and looked hard at Ketzler. "I cannot emphasize this enough, which is why I also say it in front of your sergeant: you are still footmen—not necessarily better or worse than your peers for spending time in separate training. You answer to your corporal, and your sergeant. You do not come directly to Captain Pikaranon, unless she happens to be standing by when you spot something. Do you understand?"

"Yes, sir," Ketzler replied, a little surprised to hear Sergeant Blassnoss echo him, though it made sense. "You're not going to be there, sir?"

Captain Liptieri's eyes narrowed. "I am to come with the rest of the main body," he said. "So until I get there, Pike is your Captain once you're on board. I'll be making an announcement to the units in the morning, and you'll start training tomorrow afternoon."

"Sir. Are we landing at that star-mark...?" To his credit, Ketzler observed the darkening of the Captain's features, and shut his mouth. "Yes sir."

Liptieri looked at him a moment longer. "Your comrades are only going to be told of the formation of special units, but not about the plans to sail south. It is too likely they are not ready to hear that yet." He stared hard another moment, and Ketzler gave a short nod of understanding. "Dismissed."

As he exited, holding the flap open for Sergeant Blassnoss, he quickly observed Litpieri giving Pikaranon another look. Just as the Captain made to speak Ketzler let the flap fall.

He expected to run again for his slip-up, but Blassnoss dismissed him as soon as they were away from the tent, and himself made for the guard lines. When Ketz got back to his tent, he found Miggey awake.

"Where have you been?" Miggey asked lightly.

"Sergeant took me to see the Captain again."

"What for?"

"More prayers, and stuff," Ketz said, rolling himself in his blanket. "You'll see in the morning."

He could feel Miggey's eyes, but said nothing more.

"First, let's stop that 'Captain Pikaranon' nonsense. I fall asleep just waiting for you to finish, and we've only got a shift or two a day. I'm Captain Pike—or ma'am, if you must, but I'd rather you didn't. Let's get you into a little bit smaller teams for today. When I call your name, go to your scout."

She began reading, and Ketzler waited for his name to be called.

Captain Liptieri's announcement was met with the expected silence, and yet Ketzler felt a shift in the mood. Liptieri had read the list of names, too, and Miggey almost physically took a step sideways when Ketz's was called.

But then they were off on separate assignments the rest of the day, and Ketzler never had a chance to talk to him. The sun was about halfway down, now, but Ketz hoped to smooth things over once they were in their tents for the night.

Up front, Pike finally read Ketz's name. He would be with Curani Cressador, the male half of a brother/sister duo. The scouts, he was surprised to see, were evenly split between men and women: Alblox and Curani, and Drunae and Sadroe. While they appeared to have no other distinguishing rank, there was clear deference by all to Drunae. Ketzler wondered if she was oldest in the team, or just recognized as best.

But as soon as they were assigned, they split up and began training, and he wasn't able to ask. It probably wasn't important, he decided. Instead, he listened as Curani began teaching on landforms—gateways and edges, and basics on plant growth and terrain. He spoke slowly and clearly. Ketzler got the impression he had taught before.

"A lot of this won't make sense yet," Curani said. "But learn it anyway. Once we get deeper into the field and start talking about specifics, this will give you somewhere to hang your hat. If you don't know what's natural, you won't know what's unnatural. And 'unnatural' is what we'll most often be looking for."

By the end of the training session, though, it still felt like trying to eat soup with a fork: he knew the information was there, but nothing he picked up seemed to fit with anything else, and most of it splashed back into the bowl of his mind.

He crawled into his tent at the end of the night, somehow more weary than he had ever been, even after that one evening he'd had to circle the camp fifteen times. A curious thought, that: later he'd had to circle it 'only' ten times, and it had seemed so easy.

Miggey was there, and awake. "How'd it go?" he asked. His voice, to Ketzler, sounded a little flat.

"It's hard," Ketzler said, and told him the troubles.

"Well, I'm sure you'll get it." He rolled over as if to go to sleep.

"Do you understand any of it?"

Miggey's head turned. "I'm not sure it matters, does it?"

Ketzler shook his head. "It does to me. I know what the Captain said, and his reasoning, but it still seems like we should all be doing this training—at least, everyone going...with the special unit."

Miggey rolled the rest of the way over, and faced Ketzler. "You really think that," he said.

"Of course," Ketzler replied, honestly surprised. "If a handful of us better trained is good, why wouldn't all of us trained be better?"

"What did the Captain tell you? Why were you picked and not me—or the others," he added quickly.

Ketzler gazed at his friend. "Miggey, it's not like that. Well, it might be for the Captain, but you have to know it's not like that with me."

Miggey sighed. "You wouldn't be the first—and so far, you're one of the only. Most of your other scout friends have made comments, or just have that look about them. You all will be elite, better trained than the rest of us, even if not as fully trained as scouts. You were specially chosen, and so you're special. We're not."

"I really find it hard to believe..."

"What did the Captain say? Why did he pick you?"

"Well, he said it was because I observed things that others didn't—"

"More special."

"Miggey—"

"Ketzler, part of what I like about you sometimes is that things like this totally escape you. But so far you're the only one of your friends that don't realize what's obvious to me. You see more than the rest of us, or figure it out better. Why do you think you're not more special than me?"

Ketzler took a deep breath. "It's...think of it this way: you can read, right?" Miggey nodded. "So you could read the Histories, just like I can. But you probably could not teach on what they say, could you?"

"Well, no, but that's because you're..."

"Because I've been trained what to look for," Ketzler finished for him. "Maybe you didn't observe things up to now because you had no reason to. And since my mind has been trained to look for things in the Histories, to make connections between facts that you might see no relation between, I naturally do it with the rest of the world, too. It doesn't mean you can't; just that you don't, because you haven't."

Miggey looked away for a moment. "Well, I like the sound of it," he replied. "But I'm not convinced you're right."

"What if I try to teach you?"

"What, the Histories?"

Ketzler paused, then shrugged. "I mean, if you want me to. I meant about scouting."

A sly grin came to Miggey's face. "Teach me about scouting? From the one who doesn't understand why plants that thrive in wet regions won't be found in dry regions?"

Ketzler gave him a withering look. "I understand the basic principle," he retorted. "I just don't know how it will help."

"How effectively have we moved along muddy roads after it rains?" Miggey asked. "And those are areas that are normally bone dry and hard-packed when it doesn't rain. As an advance unit, you'll be places where there aren't roads. So how easy would it be to move through an area that's normally wet enough to support plants that need lots of water, after it rains?"

"Huh. See, that makes a lot more sense, now that you put it that way. Why wouldn't they just say that?"

"Because you all are so smart, you probably should have made the connection yourself," Miggey teased. Ketzler laughed, and Miggey shrugged. "Besides, there's a lot of the same concern when planting fields. Wheat and corn and the like need some water, but they'll drown if there's too much. So you have to know what you're looking for."

"Thanks, Miggey. That'll help."

They rolled into their respective blankets, and went to sleep.

In the middle of scrubbing out the lunch pots the next day, Ketzler looked up to see Sergeant Blassnos approaching, Recruit Cabalas close behind him. The recruit did not look happy.

"Up, and out," Blassnos said, jerking a thumb into the air.

"Sergeant?"

"Report to Captain Pike. She's got a special mission for your team today."

Ketzler stood and handed the sponge to Cabalas, who took it with a brief snarl, keeping his face turned well away from Blassnos. Ketzler looked where the sergeant pointed, and made his way across the camp.

"We're still waiting for—here she comes," Captain Pike said as Ketzler approached. He turned and saw Karbae Gattaro arrive, her brown braid swinging as she trotted. He gave her a small wave. She smiled in return, then turned her attention to Pike.

"Just a brief excursion," the captain said. "Off into the mountains across the way. Sadroe found us a little route, at least to the top of that plateau.

I wanted you all to see first-hand why we're taking the sea route instead of the land route."

Pike already had small day-packs for each of them, and a few bottles of water. They struck off, threading their way through the rows of tents before entering the small plain to the foot of the cliff. Ketzler glanced upward, at that hard edge that captured his attention the evening they arrived. He looked for the small boulder, frowning when he couldn't see it. Perhaps it was actually set back from the edge.

"Don't worry, there's a way up," Pike said beside him. "Sadroe saw a goat descending yesterday evening. It belonged to a farmer closer to town. Apparently," she continued with a grin, "it makes a habit of wandering off. He didn't find out until now where it went off to."

"Did Scout Sadroe climb up to the top? Does she know what's up there?"

Pike shook her head. "No, it was too close to dark. We'll all get to see it for the first time."

When they reached the base of the cliff, Ketzler still wasn't sure he could see a route. Sadroe went ahead, and began climbing. Ketzler swallowed, his gaze tracing up the thousands of feet to the top.

"Don't worry, we'll be fine," Karbae said quietly, placing a hand on his shoulder.

"I don't know," Ketzler said, his gaze still on the cliff. "It's a long way up. I don't know if my arms and legs will last that long."

"You speak more like the one I saw running our first night," she said with a wink. "You should trust yourself more. You've come a long way."

Ketzler's eyes went suddenly to hers, and he felt his face redden. "I didn't know you were watching."

"I thought for sure you were going to die," she replied, though her eyes twinkled brown. "But I'm glad you didn't."

As Ketzler's mouth hung open, she went forward and took her spot in line, and begin climbing. Her long arms and legs made it seem effortless. The shoulders he once thought were maybe a little too broad for a girl actually fit the woman well in this work. Ketzler glanced over and saw Captain Pike looking at him closely, yet without judgement. Still, he snapped his mouth shut, and let a few others get in line behind Karbae before moving ahead to join them.

If Karbae thought he might die the first day, he knew he would by the time they were halfway up, now. His arms and legs burned, though the hand and footholds were large, flat, and numerous. He had long since stopped looking down, and glanced no further up than the next hold. His breath came in gasps, and he paused often to wipe his hands on his pants.

Further and further up. Soon, the wall became even more sheer, and the team needed to grip tight with their hands to keep from falling backward as their packs pulled them down. Wiping his hands now became a constant battle between keeping a slippery hold on the rock, or letting go entirely to try to dry them. More than once he nearly slipped, slamming one hand back to its hold just as the other let loose.

Now he did look up, desperately hoping they were near the top. To his relief, he saw Karbae's feet just disappearing over the top, and he drew a ragged breath. Five more holds. Four. Two; hands reached over and grasped his pack straps, hauling him finally and quickly over the rim. He moved quickly away from the edge, catching his breath as he looked around.

The rest of the troop had spread out across the large plateau. Some were looking toward the Captain, waiting her commands. Most, like Ketzler, gaped at the rest of the Brynth as it spread jaggedly to the south. Far in the distance a great line spread, impossibly high. He saw, indeed, why they would try to sail south instead of finding a way through these mountains.

"All right, everyone, any questions?"

His breathing almost back to normal, Ketzler managed to pull his eyes from the distant peaks and glanced around the plateau. It was bare rock, with only a few bits of clinging moss in crevices. It was flat, and pitched back a little, but there were still hollows here and there where he imagined water might collect—but today they were dry.

"Why did the goat come up here?" he wondered aloud.

Captain Pike gave him a significant look. "That is a perfect question. Goats like to climb, I'll give you. But a climb like that, just to reach a barren plateau? What does anyone think?"

They looked around a few more moments, then with glances at each other, and as if the idea came to them all at once, they moved as one to the opposite side of the plateau. Captain Pike and the other scouts trailed behind.

They reached the edge, also hard and bare, and looked down another thousand-foot cliff into the wildest and most fertile valley Ketzler had ever seen. There was a pool, and trees, and grass, and here and there he saw the movement of small animals. The valley continued south for miles before butting into another towering peak.

"Could it get down there?" he asked.

Captain Pike nodded. "It would seem so. You can see similar footholds near the top, here, to what we just climbed on the other side."

"So a goat is as smart as we are?" Karbae asked with a grin. "Heading south to find better forage?"

They all chuckled. Ketzler let his eyes wander, and suddenly the sharpness of the edge caught his attention. He glanced behind to the side they crested, looking for the boulder he had seen their first evening—but the edge there was just as crisp as this one. He frowned.

"What is it?" Captain Pike asked.

"Nothing..." Ketzler took a few steps closer. Had he imagined it? "Well, not nothing; I noticed this cliff when we marched in, but I could swear I saw a boulder on the edge. Now it's a hard line."

Pike looked at him closely. "How strongly could you swear?"

Ketzler walked over, while the rest of the team watched him. He felt a strange pressure on his shoulders, the weight of their eyes and expectations. Had he seen it?

"Maybe it was the goat?" Curani offered.

Ketzler considered a moment. "Was it a billy-goat?" He looked at Sadroe, who nodded. "I didn't see horns," he said. As he gazed hard at the edge, he could almost see, superimposed on the cliff, his vision he had seen before. He walked to the point where he knew the boulder had been, then bent suddenly.

"Here," he said. "This crevice; there's moss that's been scraped away, see?"

Pike hurried over and examined it. "So, what do we think this means?" she asked quietly.

"Do the farmers know about this cliff?" Ketzler asked.

Pike shook her head, then paused. "There's always a chance someone knows, but we asked many and no one said anything about it."

"What's the alternative?" Ketzler asked.

"Sadroe," Pike called back. "Would you mind finding your way down into that valley and seeing what you find? Ketzler, do you feel up to going with her?"

Ketzler shook his head frankly. "I'm sure I can get down; I don't think I would make it back up, ma'am."

Pike looked overhead, chewing her lip. "It's getting late anyway. Go with Sadroe; you two scout it thoroughly, but stay the night down there if you think it's safe. Curani, you head back to camp and let Liptieri know what's going on."

"What *is* going on?"

"Hmm. For now, we've found some strange evidence, and we need to look into it further. We'll be back by lunch tomorrow with a full report."

What followed was a flurry of rearranging supplies, to give Sadroe and Ketzler a little more to sustain them for the climb, and setting up an impromptu camp on the plateau.

As they prepared to go over the edge, Karbae approached. "You're even better than I thought," she said quietly, for Ketzler alone. Her smile seemed meant of him alone, as well. "Good luck down there."

"Thanks," he said hesitantly.

She winked and turned away. Sadroe was waiting patiently when Ketlzer finally made it to the edge. "Let's get down there and back first, shall we?" she asked with a knowing smile.

Ketzler flushed, and moved quickly to the edge.

The evening was cool, which helped him not to sweat. The descent was nearly as arduous as the ascent, which helped keep his mind off of Karbae, at least a little bit. He had been a Pip so long, he had learned to ignore women. It was an effort to remember that, as a soldier, he needn't ignore them any longer.

"Can you watch your feet?" Sadroe blurted as Ketzler's foot came down on something less hard then rock. He lifted it quickly from the back of the scout's head.

"I-I'm so sorry," he stammered.

Sadroe shook her head, and they continued.

By the time they reached the bottom, the valley was in deep shadow. And it was so quiet! There was not even a wind, and the forest animals seemed to be heading to sleep. Faintly he heard a short trill, but then nothing.

"Well, this is nice," Sadroe said as they let their gazes wander around the valley. "Where do we look?"

Ketzler let his gaze wander a bit more, then met Sadroe's eyes. "Beside the lake. It's soft ground, and living things need water."

Sadroe nodded, and gestured Ketzler to lead the way. They made their way over together, and began their search.

They found it within a few paces. Ketzler pulled up short, and suddenly couldn't find his breath. Nothing but humans and goats could have found their way south over the plateau and into this valley, and yet... "Is that a hoof print? From a shod horse?"

Sadroe, too, seemed knocked on her heels. "By the God," she breathed. "There's other people in this country."

10

HER TONGUE MIGHT BLEED

"Will you make sure she gets it?"
"I think she must."
"A strange journey."
"Not for one of them."

18 Monzak 1320 — Autumn

Averlynn had never been more grateful for Tarafel's speed and endurance than the past nineteen days' hard riding south from the plateau above the foreign troops. She had thanked Praka and Hakana both, and profusely, as well as her training as she made her way quickly back through the mountains, recalling the turns, valleys, and passes almost by reflex. She paused only briefly in Amka to tell Ka Karaa what she had seen, and he had duly dispatched her back to Tekaa Wohan to report directly to the Chiefs and the Intag Ka.

She could find her way, now, without thinking. The woods deep in the heart of the Waken were as familiar to her as her home. She'd had to bypass Wazè in her haste, sending up a short prayer that her mother and father had gotten both messages, now, and were satisfied. Another festival would be missed with her parents: Wengaka was tomorrow, the winter solstice. Fast as Tarafel was, she would need to rest him after their long flight.

There was no glamour on Tekaa as there was on their outposts—no glamour was strong enough to cover such a city. Since it could not hide, her people made it contrary. Too, she thought, they wanted some reflection of Kalen in Burieng, their first home and capitol.

So, here too, there was no wall. Paths began as compacted earth, then widened into halls of maple, oak, and elm. Stones rose from the ground and became streets. Two slender watchtowers rose like pines, limbless until at great height were set shelters from wind and rain. Lattices had been carved to cover the windows, full of loops and whorls. She had stood behind one, once, marveling at how clearly she could see out. It was nearly impossible to see in, especially so far below.

A long, low horn sounded, followed by the tinkling of of chimes, announcing her approach as a Ranger. A Tracker exited from the bottom of the tower and waited for her, smiling.

"Bekowa," Averlynn said with a slight bow. "It is good to see you."

"And you, Averlynn," she replied. "You're here early?"

"I am. I must see the Chiefs. Is the Intag Ka in the city?"

Bekowa's smile fell. "He is," she replied. "What has happened?"

Averlynn's face clouded, but she shook her head. "Much," she said. "But it is not for idle telling. I'm sure you will hear about it soon. For now, let's gather who we need."

Bekowa mounted her pale horse. She turned and frowned at Averlynn, glancing at her hands. Averlynn removed her glamour ring and tucked it into a pouch. "It has been some time," she said quietly. Bekowa inclined her head and led the way.

Averlynn knew where to go, but it was ceremonial for returning Rangers and Scouts to be led through the city. Something about them finding their own way long enough, that to be led by a white horse would be a blessing and honor. The hurry Averlynn had felt atop the plateau had faded with time, and so she did not mind.

The homes and shops of Tekaa were of primarily white or black stone—never mixed—though some of the newer ones had begun using wrought timbers. Carpenters had begun shaping the trees as they grew, needing only then to make a few cuts to fit the pieces together into the structure of the home. The gaps they filled with carefully-selected branches, and then lighter and smaller stone of myriad colors. Most favored the pale oranges and reds from the far cliffs near the Snowashes to the south, though some audacious families even used blues and bright greens. Many buildings in those styles had been so carefully crafted as to appear just like a cliff's edge where trees sent roots like tentacles deep along and into the cracks. They were a stark contrast to the bluff and fortress-like buildings of pure stone around them, but after a century the style had become accepted and even sought-after.

Anywhere a great tree grew they had turned into a square and a small park. Here the people of Tekaa often gathered for news, music, or teachings. Around the edges of the squares, the walls of the buildings were often bowed to create little amphitheaters, to better accommodate small audiences. Sometimes the events were planned, but more often they let coincidence rule, and many days you could hear a speech in one corner perfectly accompanied by some new or favorite song from another corner. Averlynn remembered most fondly a memorial of one of the Wohan's greatest battles (those were rare, and not often spoken-of), while great drums and low horns played behind her. Somehow, the music managed to swell at just the right times, as the pitch of battle rose to its heights. She had inquired after, and no, the two had not been planned together. The teacher himself could not have been more pleased.

But now, as they rode through, the squares were nearly empty. "Where is everyone?" Averlynn asked. It was noontime, when the squares should have been at their fullest before evening.

Bekowa hesitated, and sighed. "There is a lot of work that needs to be done," she said. "Our harvests, this year..."

"I thought they had been bountiful? I met Chief Hathar in Amka, and he'd said things grew, though ripening was coming late."

"We thought they would ripen in time. But despite the mild weather—or else because of it—blight attacked." She shook her head. "I don't hear as much as some, but I don't see how we'll make it through the winter. Maybe the Chiefs can tell you more, depending on what news you bring them."

Averlynn gave a short sigh. "We're friends, Bekowa, but don't fish. We both know Chata would not approve."

"I'm sorry, Averlynn. I had not meant it. There's just so much fear, these days. You've been gone—"

"We'll make it through," Averlynn replied. "We always do."

Bekowa made a non-committal sound. They continued in silence for a few moments longer before she turned her head slightly. "I don't know if you knew, since you haven't asked, but...Aver is back."

Tarafel stopped suddenly at Averlynn's movement. She leaned forward again, and caught them back up quickly. "I did not know," she said. "I suppose I expected him back...maybe I didn't." Actually, she had all but forgotten. "We didn't know what he would do when he found out about..." She stopped and took a breath. She was babbling, and they both knew it. They also both knew how little love was lost between her and her brother.

As she remembered, she felt a strange urge to see the sword again. Her brother had not let her see it much, but the pale red edges and jagged seam of sardonyx like fractured earth stuck in her mind as surely as if she had looked at it for years. She hoped he had learned something in Burieng, more than what state the land was in.

"Do you know why he is here, and not in Wazè?"

"He just arrived. I did not guide him, but he who did said Aver still had the sword, and needed also to speak to the Chiefs. He will probably be there now."

"Hmm." She wondered how she should respond when seeing him. He might suspect she would be told, but that did not mean he would not want the customary courtesies. He was the elder by an impressive total of fifty years.

She caught Bekowa's concerned glance, and smoothed her face. Her family troubles were not the concern of Bekowa, certainly. They continued in a silence broken only by the clopping of their horses' hooves, the city itself eerily silent.

They reached the Hall and stopped at the massive paneled doors. While Bekowa discharged her duty to the guards there, Averlynn flicked a glance over the ancient marble. This was the first permanent structure they had built, when the remainder of the Kalen left in Burieng finally made the trek across the sea. The earlier settlers had erected solitary cabins, here and there, exploring the land—the Rangers still sometimes used them on their forays. But when she had come across the sea with the remainder of her people, they had stayed in the tents they had brought with them while this building was constructed as their new capitol. Though the Scouts and Rangers had ridden far and wide to gather those preceding, and found no threats, they built the Hall still as a fortress. Their greatest stone-smiths spent years designing it to withstand several times over any known weapons, and barrages from those weapons lasting days. Angles were built in to deflect most shots: it would be a rare missile that spent all its energy on a direct impact. During construction, each stone was thoroughly inspected and tested for durability, and each course measured and remeasured against the plans before the next course could be laid. And once it was done, the city was designed around it to allow maximum visibility by the guards and ballistae at the top of the towers, while minimizing the visibility and approachability of it by any invaders.

Bekowa bid her brief, professional farewell to Averlynn, giving only a slight wink as she turned away from the Hall. Averlynn kept her face still, waiting as she heard the massive bolts being drawn back in preparation for opening.

Directly inside was a small forecourt where Averlynn dismounted and let the groom take Tarafel off to the small stables reserved for the military. Anyone else was expected to stable their own horses before approaching the Hall. She was taken then to a small washroom where she refreshed herself, wiping away the dust of the trail. She found, too, a small tumbler of a light, dry wine. She considered it a moment, shrugged, and drank. As long as they were offering.

From a hook near the door she took a gray, linen, sleeveless sur-plice—anyone approaching the Chiefs would wear it, especially those who had been long on the road. A stiff brush scuffed the dirt from her boots, and she felt as ready as she could be. The Chiefs were easily impressed. It was Aver's opinion that concerned her.

She frowned at that thought, regarded herself one more time in the mirror. She squared her shoulders and exited to a waiting servant, who gave her barely a glance before leading her deeper into the Hall.

Inside, the Hall felt much smaller than it appeared on the outside—due in part to the thickness of stone, but also the narrowness of the corridors and the number of rooms they had carved inside. Most of them, she knew, were empty—distractions and kill zones, with walls filled with arrow slits and portcullises operated from within the walls. She shook off the over-whelming sense of fear that sometimes oozed from the walls of this place. She had been here only a few times before, and hated it far more than the most remote bog in all Wohan.

Up one flight of stairs, and the servant left her at the double doors of the Council. The guard there regarded her barely a moment, then ducked inside to announce her. When she was bid, she entered the room.

Her brother was already inside, and was still turned in surprise where he sat at one of the Petitioner's Seats. She felt a small pang; she had warning, while he clearly had not. So she let a smile come to her, and took an unceremonious step toward him as though excited to see him. His gaze quickly darkened, his face solemn and arrogant again. He would not permit such emotions, even in front of so small a gallery as was gathered at midday in the council chambers.

"It is well to see you," Aver said. She had forgotten, in the intervening months, how grating his voice was, high and nasally, as though he had always just been dealt the most grievous insult. "Keeping us safe?"

"As safe as I am able, with the gods' blessing," she replied, straining to divorce his tone from his words. It would only make her angrier. "I am glad to see you back from the far lands."

He inclined his head only slightly, and turned back to the Chiefs who sat at the head of the chambers. Gone nearly a year, and all he could manage was one exchange. Averlynn took a slow breath, and moved to another Petitioner's Seat, away from Aver.

"Welcome to the Hall, Averlynn of Wazè," Chief Wevrun said. He was fourth in line, and had the duty of Commenter as Hathar was still in Amka. He kept his dark gloss hair in two tails, and thin strands of white now framed his narrow face. A childhood disease had left his skin pocked, and he did not smile much these days. "We will hear first from Aver, as we deem his story the more important."

Averlynn inclined her head. "I thank the Chiefs for their wisdom, and do not know what story my brother brings, but I submit my news may be more pressing."

Chief Jale held up a bony hand. He wore a ceremonial cap to hide his baldness. His eyes flashed as his thin voice strained across the floor. "We have heard some news of you, which will be dealt with in turn," he said with a slight sneer. "It is the wish of this council to honor *obedience*"—the sneer thickened to scorn—"and hear from Aver first."

Averlynn set her jaw, and kept it shut. She should have known. She glanced a little sideways, saw Aver's demeaning gaze, and bowed her head once more.

"No action would be taken today, anyway, so we have time to hear both,"

Chief Witko said. He was, to everyone's consternation, second in line. His broad face smiled easily and often, and he dismissed ceremony as quickly as Jale had dismissed Averlynn. And, she knew, he favored her far above her family. Unfortunately, he was considered quite insane. Still, according to tradition, he could not be deposed without gross misconduct.

Averlynn held back a smile as the rest of the Chiefs exchanged long-suffering glances. Aver, too, looked deflated. She folded her hands, and waited.

"Aver, please begin your tale," Chief Wevrun said quietly.

"Wait!" Witko shouted, and everybody jumped. He glared around the gallery in consternation, as if searching for someone among those gathered. His face suddenly brightened. "The Intag Ka is not present—at least, I don't see him. Shouldn't he be here? I think he should be here."

As if on cue, the doors creaked open again. "The Intag Ka, Onjee," the guard intoned.

The Intag Ka strode in, tall, severe, and wordless. He made his way to the front and took a seat with the council, only slightly apart. He gazed at Aver without expression, and at Averlynn with a brief, slight hardening of features. Apparently he had heard the same news of her as the Chiefs.

Witko looked around pleasantly. "Okay. Go ahead, Aver."

"Thank you. As you all know, I departed Wohan last summer with the blessings of the Chiefs to pursue an inquiry into the strange sword I had found, quite by accident, deep in the forests around Wazè."

"Thank you for reminding us," Witko said. Jale shushed him, but he ignored it and gave a warm smile to Averlynn before returning his gaze to Aver in mock honesty. "We always appreciate your complete and utter deference to those wiser than you."

Someone in the gallery sneezed, and Aver continued. "We took the boat out and made good headway for the first several days before encountering a storm most severe."

How he had managed to get the Chiefs approval for his journey was still a mystery to Averlynn, though she suspected her parents. Avako and Erion were not without influence, when they wished to exert it.

"We were driven back, and northward, for some several more days—the sun and moon were gone, so we were not sure how long we were at sea. When the storm broke, we saw to the east a sight...most disturbing." He paused to let the anticipation grow, even glancing at Averlynn. She didn't give him the satisfaction. "We saw there, a port."

Gasps from the Chiefs, and the gallery. Even Witko seemed appropriately taken aback. "Built by whom?" Chief Hakawo thundered. He was first in line, and well respected. If any forgot, the scar that blued one eye reminded them how he had faced the Cerberus and tamed it, wresting from it the eternal vow of protection. Much good that had done. Averlynn returned her attention to her brother.

"We were, obviously, very cautious, and spent all our glamour to blend in. We pretended to be traders, seeking passage westward. In time, we discovered they were Cariste."

Another wave of whispers and glances as they processed this. Averlynn's mouth twisted sideways as she, too, considered. They'd had some dealings with those peoples, long ago. They had been primitive, at least those that made it to Kalen. Advanced enough for long voyages, but limited in their ability to survive in strange lands. At least, at first.

"In short order, we were able to secure passage on one of their boats. They knew the sea better than we did, and make frequent journeys north to some islands, and west to the far lands. It has changed much..." He trailed off, uncharacteristically contemplative. He cleared his throat quietly. "The entire country, almost, is at the mercy of a mage, Lasserain. He had destroyed their large city of Quaran utterly—only the wall and a few stone buildings remained. He seemed also in power over all but the westernmost lands—certainly over the Cariste people in the east, whose leader had seemed to capitulate to the mage in hopes of appeasing him. They are a most weak people."

"Their king?" Jale asked.

Aver shook his head. "He was the first to fall. The rest of the country fell back into their old distrusts, and either resisted him, or not, separately. It is a most unfavorable land."

The Chiefs, except Witko, nodded as though he confirmed something. Was that part of it, then? Had they sent Aver in hopes of finding Burieng ready for them to return? If so, they had kept it very quiet. As much as she missed Kalen, the idea of return was disconcerting. It still would never be what it was, before those calling themselves the Cariste and Rinc Nain had come.

"There is more," Aver continued, glowing in their attention. "This sword is as unique as we suspected. Only three others were made, and each carries great, though specific, magic. It is called Skyalfamold, and possesses magic of earth."

"The others?"

"They did not say, those of the ancient Kesten who made the sword." A few more gasps, from the elders in the room who remembered the mountain people. Averlynn had never met them, but had heard some stories of their legendary craft. No wonder the sword stuck so fast in her memory. "There was one other, Aerithion, who appeared in the village the same time as I did, carried by a young Rinc Nain named Haydren. That one held the magic of fire. He..." Aver trailed off, and chuckled. "He sought, on his own, to defeat this most powerful mage that had overtaken most of his country."

Averlynn's eyes widened. "And you didn't help him, with your sword?" she asked. The look he gave her silenced her. Of course he hadn't, and she was silly to think he would have. She found herself looking to Chief Witko, who gave her the most sane, sober glance she had ever seen him possess.

"My purpose in that land was not to die," Aver replied for everyone else's benefit. "I had learned what I sought about the sword, and made to return."

"You do not know if this...Haydren...was successful?" Chief Jale asked. Aver quailed a little under the consternation. "That might change the nature of the country, which was your purpose in that land."

"I believe it would not," Aver replied quickly. "The Rinc Nain and Cariste are firmly entrenched, and they have many cities. This Haydren also claimed to have destroyed the Woods."

A heavy silence descended, even over Averlynn. Destroyed? Images of the forest flashed through her mind, the glades, spreading trees, beds of ferns lit by sunlight or wreathed in morning mists. So much beauty...

"Well, then," Hakawo breathed. "Perhaps it is for the best. I declare justice over this Rinc Nain, should he been seen by any Wohan. No ill deed should go unpunished, though by his claim it makes clearer our path forward. Of greater concern now, though, is this port city north of our lands. What do you think of it?"

Aver shrugged. "There may be much to make of it, or very little. It was large, larger than any of our cities. And yet, we have seen none of them come south. It was quite old. I deem they would have come into our lands if they could have. But the cliffs and seas around our coasts seem still to protect us. They treated us fairly enough, under glamour."

"How wide is the land? How many are there?"

"From the Wall to the Fleeing Sea is many miles. But we had no opportunity to see true maps, to see if this was one of a few or one of many."

"It is many," Averlynn said quietly.

Chief Jale glared at her. "Your turn—"

"She seems to speak from knowledge," Witko interrupted. "Certainly more than you have. Maybe we should listen to her report, now."

"First, I would like to hear how she came by this knowledge," the Intag Ka said ominously. "I have heard a disturbing report, concerning one of my Rangers."

Witko rolled his eyes. "Oh, *that's* important. Well, as I said, no decisions will be made today anyway..." He trailed off and gestured to Averlynn.

The Intag Ka spoke instead, bristling. "It may be, enlightened Chief, that she will..." He set his jaw, and his eyes flashed. "She may lie, in order to justify her foolishness."

Averlynn sat back, stunned. He had all but ejected her from the Rangers with those words. "Intag Ka," she gasped, seeking somehow to prostrate herself, though she could not leave her seat until actually bidden. "I have only ever sought to serve my people."

"And has never, ever lied," Witko rumbled. "Or sought her own glory, or done anything to endanger her people."

"Let us hear her report, first," the Intag Ka said. She could tell by his tone, though her eyes were still on the floor, that he was not swayed, and might never be. Unless her words convinced him, this would be her last report.

She gave it, haltingly at first then gaining confidence in the retelling. She told of the prophecy, the Glowwood, the Isun's words—all of them, though some hurt her cause.

"You knew the Isun presented an incomplete petition to the Ka?" Onjee growled when she came to that part.

"You do not command any Isun," Witko cut in. "How she acts—"

"Is of no concern, or import," the Intag Ka retorted. "But the integrity of my Rangers is. She hid her intent from the Ka, with purpose."

"The Ka Karaa gave me no citation when I returned, though," she said. "Surely if he found fault with my actions—"

"I will deal with him in his turn," Onjee said.

"Watch out, Chiefs, the Intag Ka is shaking up our military. All sorts of loyal, proven soldiers getting censured and kicked out," Witko said.

Averlynn did not respond. She feared, instead, that Witko might be worsening the Intag Ka's mood. She hurried on, only briefly explaining how she had made it through to the other side of the Wall.

She paused before continuing. "I was not able to ascertain how their units are ordered," she said, "and so I had to estimate the entire number rather than groups. But there must have been some tens of thousands below me—perhaps twenty thousand, and more coming. They seemed to be moving eastward. And there were so many cities between my vantage point and the sea..." She trailed off for a moment, then continued though the end of the report. When she finished, there was utter silence. She kept her eyes down, feeling keenly the weight of their two reports together.

Witko took a deep breath, which seemed to unfreeze the rest of the Chiefs. "Well, then," he said, as they shifted and looked at one another. "Lunch?"

Averlynn grinned briefly; she was hungry as well. But the rest of the Chiefs seemed disgruntled. Jale fairly growled. "I think we have much to discuss," he said.

"I didn't say we didn't," Witko replied. "But I think we can dismiss those with nothing more to say."

Averlynn glanced between them as they begrudged agreement. Chief Wevrun sat forward. "Aver and Averlynn, you are excused for the moment. Refresh yourselves if you may, but be prepared to return for any further questions. The gallery, too, is dismissed as they wish."

Averlynn took a deep breath amidst the flurry of creaking chairs and footsteps as the Chambers slowly emptied. She didn't look at the Intag Ka—didn't want to see either doom or blessing in his countenance just yet. She followed Aver through the doors, left through another door, and into a smaller chamber where food and drink already sat waiting.

She watched as Aver loaded a plate with grapes and berries, bread with drizzled honey, cheeses, and an assortment of meats. He took a proffered goblet and drank deeply.

He was awkward with the sword as he sat, and fussed with it ostentatiously, she felt. She sat across from him, her plate nearly empty. He said nothing for a time, working his way through his lunch in silence.

"You should eat," he said finally, between bites.

She stared at him a moment. "My appetite is not what it could be," she said carefully. He glanced at her and shrugged. "I fear for our people," she continued, touching a grape with her forefinger, but leaving it where it was.

He shrugged again. "The Chiefs will decide what to do. I am not so worried."

"But if they come south—"

"Exactly," he said abruptly, pointing at her with a crust. "*If.* Nothing either of us saw portends that exact future, does it?"

"They cannot stay where they are," she said. "They are moving somewhere, and they are coming with force. Our military cannot muster even a third of their numbers—"

Aver cut her off again with a raised hand. "You said as much in the Chambers, or we know as much. Do you hope to decide for the Chiefs what we should do?" His smile was derisive. "Perhaps we should let you and this Isun, with all your combined experience and wisdom, decide the actions of our entire people?"

Averlynn bit back several retorts. In all likelihood, Aver would be returning to Wazè after this, and she hoped he would give their parents a decent report of her. "I understand," she managed instead. She smiled. "I spend so much time making decisions for myself, in the wilds, that waiting for someone else to make one for me is...I am less accustomed to it."

Aver did not smile. "I told father and mother that permitting you to become a Ranger was foolish," he said. "Perhaps you have some of the skills for it, but the mentality that is needed...well, you just admitted, you don't have it."

The grape between her fingers popped, and she quickly wiped her hand on her napkin. "I suppose I see your point," she said.

Aver chuckled. "It is no folly to admit shortcomings," he said. "Just to persist in them once they are discovered."

"I suppose we'll let the Intag Ka decide my fate," she said—which didn't make her feel any better, but it did end the conversation.

They finished their meals and returned to the antechamber, waiting for the Chiefs to end their deliberation. As dinnertime neared, the doors finally opened and the Intag Ka exited. Averlynn stood quickly, offering her salute. He returned it briskly.

"You will continue on your southern foray," he said. "Despite my better judgment, the Chiefs prevailed against me dismissing you entirely. But they cannot prevail against the conditions under which you stay. It just so happens Scout Amrith is in the city. You will be attending him, and he will make sure your reports are accurate." He folded his arms tightly. "This is ridiculous, and unprecedented, and an utter waste of precious resources. You could save the Rangers, our people, and probably your parents some amount of shame if you voluntarily leave our ranks."

Again, Averlynn bit back retorts—far more than she'd had for Aver. She thought of invoking Isun Vera again—hadn't her bones also predicted a doom? But then Vera had committed truths on Averlynn's behalf, tainting even that bit of proof. Averlynn put on her humblest expression. "Intag, I am deeply honored by the trust of the Chiefs, and welcome eagerly the opportunity to prove to you that it is not held in vain."

The Intag Ka growled, and turned away.

Averlynn shook her head minutely. She should have expected it; and, in truth, she was grateful that she had not been summarily dismissed. She assumed it was Witko again. She would need to repay him somehow, but without anyone else finding out. She *would* be dismissed if it was known.

Aver stood before her, then, and she looked up. After several silent moments, he held out the sword. She cocked her head, studying his gaze.

"Take it," he said. "You will probably need it before I do."

"I...what..."

"I know your heart, sister," he said. "You won't let this go, and you won't care for the shame or pride of our family in your pursuit."

Her tongue would be bleeding before she made it out of Tekaa Wohan, for all she had bitten it around her brother. But she still managed to say nothing as she took the sword.

"And this, too," he said, holding out a small scroll. "The words to release the magics, and some other instructions they felt important. I didn't bother to memorize it. And I do believe Scout Amrith knows the sword, so you might get him to teach you how to keep from cutting off your own limbs."

"Thank you," she said carefully. It seemed so far outside his character, she wondered...

"And maybe you can talk to him about his brother, too."

And then he turned away, and laughed loudly, and she knew. He dismissed her, as had the Chiefs, the Intag Ka, probably even the Ka Karaa, and likely the rest of the Wohan would as well. Just as they had Amrith's brother.

She wondered how Corith fared, still back in Burieng. He had let them depart, swore he would find a way to rebuild Kalen, convince the people to accept elves. And been outcast in the process. She admired his bravery back then, even if not his full intentions. Part of her had wanted to stay with him. Of course she was too young. And as the years wasted longer and longer with no word, she gave up that particular hope of returning home. Presumably Aver had not encountered him either, or just refused to spread the news.

As always, they simply hid from uncomfortable truths. As they would hide this away, if they could. She hoped she could gather more information before it was too late. For that matter, she hoped she was wrong, that the Cariste would stay in the north.

But her spirit, and the prophecy, told her she was not. And it was now up to her to prove it.

II

SCATTERED PIECES OF KNOWLEDGE

"He is resisting you?"
"The Elders are harder."
"So he is resisting you."
"I don't like your wording. It blames him."

18 Monzak 1320 — Autumn

Tavill sat behind the rocks, looking out over the gray skies and seas. Surf rumbled and hissed far below, and further north on a thin sliver of beach sea gulls cried. The wind, for now, was calm; it had not been so for most of his treacherous walk past the Snowashes.

He had forgotten how narrow that path became, at times—or, perhaps more of it had crumbled away in the intervening years. When the mountains finally disappeared into forested foothills, he had continued along the cliffs for a time. They were easiest to follow, far easier than the broken halls of the forest he had not visited since he first went south to the Snowplain.

And yet, as he traveled, many memories came back strong. Farther out to sea, faintly on the horizon, were broken bits of island and—he thought—perhaps one or two skeletal ships wrecked upon the shores.

He paused now in a small cove of rocks that jutted above the cliffs, and removed the bone to let his nose wander. Though it took time for his vision to fade, the scent always came back instantly. He had taken to wearing the piercing for stretches at a time, then pulling it out. It was far too dangerous to be able to see, but not smell, and it became easier and less painful to insert it and withdraw it each time.

He had forgotten how much more life there was north of the Snowashes. There was not just the rich humus and leafmold, but the warmer air brought him ten kinds of trees, thirty scurrying things, fifteen different nests, ten hoofed and wary animals, seven predators, and hundreds of flowers, shrubs, grasses, herbs...and mushrooms.

After so long in the frozen southern regions, he had forgotten what those smelled like. It was not until he followed the scent and found the colony that it came to him, and suddenly he smelled them every-where—white buttons and brown, sheepshead, beech, black trumpets, pfifferlings like apricot, wood hedgehogs; deathcaps, parasols, and dapper-lings. He sought out each, seeing them again as old friends long forgotten. It was a sensory delight for both nose and eyes.

But as the sun sank on the last day of autumn—the moon and stars had warned him the night before—he knew he was also wasting time deliberately. His journey so far had been treacherous, but not dangerous. He worried, if he turned west toward his people's southernmost city, it would quickly become so. After so many years, surely either the Prosan or Kalen had found it, perhaps even revived it.

He looked out over waters once more as stars began to sprinkle the east. The Kalen, he knew, would likely leave the ruins alone. They were often as light on the land as the Taur had been, and as an Elder race respected history—theirs, and others'. What he had seen of the Prosan were a people bent to use whatever was at hand for their benefit.

There was one small blessing in his being captured, he thought as he finally turned away and sought to make camp westward: he knew their scent clearly, and their sight. And they were not a rustic people. The fact his questioner knew so many languages proved that. Unless he was the only one who could do that, but surely they wouldn't risk such a singular member of their society in such a way.

He walked slowly through he darkening wood. He hoped he had not killed the only one of the Prosan who was capable of such things. For the ninety-fourth time in forty-seven days he wondered again what had happened. It had to be the piercing, he knew that—had concluded that on the seventeenth time pondering it in nine days, as the sun rose above the seas. It was the only thing to change. He knew, that day, that he should have asked more questions of Lasserain on the nature of the alchemy he had used in creating it, how it worked, why it worked, was there anything else it might do...

And for the one hundred forty-first time he saw again the red mists, the blood, the men running at him and dying—being killed by his rage. He saw the trees and rocks painted with blood. The image of his hand wrapped around that man's face, squeezing, flashed again and again and again and again...

He stopped and lowered his head as he caught his breath. He could not change it, he knew. But he also knew that those images had been played out so many times before, his consciousness had just not been there to see it. Always before he drifted away. But not this time. Not the time after he'd had a bone that was supposed to keep him from the bloodlust, and was removed.

Had Lasserain known that would happen? Surely he didn't—couldn't. With no one to test it on...but how did he know what it would do to begin with? It bespoke a knowledge of the Taur that even Tavill couldn't access just now. His memory, he'd found, was overgrown with disuse. While the recent things he had witnessed catalogued just fine and stayed, he struggled often to call up deeper memories. It had been too long since he needed to.

Yet Lasserain had shown him some particular knowledge must exist in the recesses of time. That thought gave him more concern—and more hope—than any other. Concern, even though mages were always inscrutable folk, that they somehow knew more of a subject than the subject itself. Hope, because there might be something Tavill could learn about himself and his people that might ensure he never witnessed the scenes of his destruction again.

Fear and hope were too-constant companions of late, tossing in his mind and frankly making him nauseous. He feared the Prosan would have invaded Vordir, would be waiting for him; he hoped they would not. He hoped the Foldings, at least some of them, would be there; he feared they would not. He feared he would have to journey all the way to Stavnuk; he hoped to see those grand ruins once again anyway, and the grand glowing mushrooms, though they would not be glowing in winter. He hoped he might encounter the Kalen, but according to his terms and the ideal in his mind; he feared they would want to destroy him, or the bone might somehow fail him again and he would destroy them.

He feared the Prosan were tracking him; hoped and feared both that someone had survived.

He found a small bed of ferns on a knoll and wrapped himself in his blanket. The first day of winter was tomorrow, and leaves still blocked his view of the night sky. Lasserain had certainly been right about that—the seasons were drastically off. Tavill wondered briefly what the prophecy was he had mentioned. But prophecies were not generally given to the Taur, to taint their witness. Even warning him of the approaching Prosan and Cariste was strictly against the Taur code, but he understood why Lasserain had done it. He prayed Elonai would, too, when the time came.

Hope, and fear, were finally damped by exhaustion, and he fell asleep.

He awoke early and wet as rain dripped off the leaves above him. It had been a light rainfall, and his blanket was merely damp, but it had been a long time since he had awoken that way. He snatched the blanket off, and shook it vigorously, grumbling. It was not until he was stuffing it angrily into his pack, and heard something deep within snap, that he paused. He was not cold, his thick fur prevented that, and it had been light enough that he hadn't awoken with the rainfall itself. Why was he angry?

He chided himself, tied his pack shut, and set off westward without breakfast. Birds were awaking slowly, their cheeps and chirrups echoing singly through the misty woods. A squirrel perched, legs splayed, watching him pass by from its high oak. He breathed deeply of the wet smells, a few older memories trickling back. He had spent years, decades, in these woods so long ago. And yet he recognized little of what he saw. Saplings when he had been there would be wizened or perhaps dead and fallen by now. He might perhaps remember the terrain, but minor humps and hollows looked much the same all across these woods. And what might have been a stub of stone before might be a spine today.

So too, the smells had changed, but far subtler. The forest itself was not so old as to have undergone complete communal change—or, perhaps more accurately, had not been so young before. And so the scents, to him, were far better reminders of his life so long ago.

It remained so for the next several days as he made his way cautiously west. He progressed slowly, knowing the Prosan and perhaps the Kalen both inhabited these woods to a degree—though, if time proved less-changing, the Kalen would be itinerant, their individuals or small groups only roving. But they could also hide far better, at least they had back then. And they did not change quickly.

By the time the moon had disappeared and reappeared in the night sky, he had begun recognizing the terrain under daylight. It began quietly enough: he thought, perhaps, those branching valleys seemed familiar. But, again, many valleys branched. Then later that day he stopped in the middle of fording a small river, glancing up and downstream. It had widened, and deepened, and the curve just downstream had eaten away a bit of its bank. But most of the channel was in rock, and he knew it. They had named it Kitsturn, barely more than a creek except it flowed for miles. It had grown since then. In a pool, a fish sent out ripples. He trailed some fingers in the water as his eyes welled. It was like seeing a loved child become mature, and wholesome, and vibrant.

"You've done well," he whispered. Kitsturn did not suit it, now. "If I have kept any power of naming," he said, his voice a little stronger, "you are Brunon."

He felt a settling, as if the land agreed with him, and he smiled. Vordir was near.

The next day he entered land as fully familiar to him as his cabin in the Snowashes had been. Each fold and rise appeared to him just as he remembered, could recall in his mind what was over the next hill. Even a few of the groves had retained much of their former composition, if not their exact structure. When he reached a meadow circled by black cherry he paused again, just at the edge, and breathed deeply.

Nearby, to his left, came the faint whispers of ancient stone. This had been their dancing hall, and it called to him now. He longed for summer, to see the rings of black-eyed daisies where the singers might sit crosslegged as they thrummed, to dance where circles of stone had been laid, now obscured by the autumnal skeletons of brambleberries.

But he could not. The land was not safe for him just yet—at least, he had not proved it so. He stepped back into the shadows of the forest, and glanced warily about as he removed the bone. He smelled nothing amiss, and the forest noises had not changed. But after missing their scent south of the Snowashes, he wanted no chances.

He circled slowly, pausing often, cautiously drawing closer and closer to the ruins. It was a battle in his mind; occasionally he glimpsed some stone sitting in the sun, or bramble rose or a bank of whitening ivy that clung to cracks and crevices in the walls they obscured.

As the sun lowered, he was satisfied. He had been everywhere but in the ruins themselves, and scented no sign or mark out of place. Finally he turned and faced the vacant arch, never gated for it was only ever a symbol of passage into the Taur realm. Those who entered had only ever come in peace; by the time war reached them, it was too late.

He walked through slowly, felt the presence change. Some would call it magical, he supposed, though it was far different from the glamours of the Kalen. And it seemed to have little effect on the humans, when they had come, for their senses seemed not to have the time to develop before they died. For Tavill, it was as clear as passing from water into air. A pressure he had forgotten about lifted. His breathing came easier, and the scents of the ruins sorted themselves so he did not have to work to filter through them. The sun itself seemed brighter, without glaring—more as though the shadows were less deep, but crisper so that each line and curve stood in starker relief, and stood out better even to his degenerated vision. The chaos of his mind eased, at least a little—there could still be danger here now, and he knew not to ignore that.

He had thought perhaps visions and memories would come flooding back, that he would replay in his mind scenes of life as it once was. They did not. Though the memories were there if he looked for them, the nostalgia was not. The present state of the ruins was reality, and it impressed on him as though he had never been there before. And yet, when he desired, he could fill in the gaps he needed: where a newcomer might wonder why such was built so, or what that or the other ruin used to be, Tavill knew, but matter-of-factly.

Which meant he also knew where to go, and went directly. Any desire to wander, to relive in his mind, was absent. Though the Taur called it a city, he knew many would not—the buildings were widely gapped, and there was little in the way of roads. Such harsh stone underfoot often hurt after a day of walking or standing. They needed no signs to denote shops, instead shaping the buildings themselves. He passed curving homes with barely a glance—none of his closest friends or relatives had lived here, and the former occupants could only be recalled with effort. He turned right, passing through a veil of autumnvine. The wickermaker's and weaver's now looked eerily similar. In life, they would have been decorated with examples of the work, especially curtains. The former's windows were blockier, he remembered; the latter usually went into an onion-shaped peak.

Potter, with daub walls instead of stone; dyer, with patterned blocks of multi-colored stone; carver, with scrollwork etched all over flat walls by the stonesmith—there, twisting columns around the entrance and at the corners; baker, low and long with a quiver of chimneys at the far end. Herbalist, with dozens of windows, each with a small box for growing their various products.

These all came and went through his mind without lingering, mere waypoints deeper into the city. Finally he reached the Taur Hall; tall central structure with two wings spreading wide, with gardens in front and—he knew, but did not yet see—groves in the back. As a frontispiece, they had fashioned a large slab ten paces wide and tapering to a rounded point ten paces up. The edge was all curves and whirls, and it was carved across the face almost like shingles but less utilitarian—no roofer would spend the time making so many sizes and styles for the mere purpose of shedding rain.

For those who could read it, it was both musical and lyrical notation in the ancient style. The Taur had borrowed it from before the world was destroyed in fire, a people who had called themselves...what had it been? Chunto, or something. Tavill did pause, now, putting the bone in so he could scan the stone. *The Song of Vordir* it was appropriately called, and told the story of its siting and building. He was not as proficient as he had been, and many of the words and notes were lost on him. What a strange, beautiful music it had been—tremendously difficult to compose, as both word and note had to align. He personally only knew of ten songs written that actually followed the true rules. Most bent, or broke them outright, for the sake of having something to play.

He drew a sigh. And no wonder: the climax and conclusion of the song written right before his eyes escaped him now. Usually they were bittersweet, those songs. Ah, Churto had been the name of the style. So what were the people called?

He shook his head. That mattered less now than the Foldings. Enough delay.

It did not surprise him when the doors would not open, at first. Even with the skill of the Taur, their cities were not immune to decay. His hoof slipped only once, and with a grunt of effort he finally managed to swing a door open enough to enter. Daylight pierced through in a stark shaft, the great lump of his shadow moving through motes and across harsh stone edges made soft by dust. A great, horned skull lay on a large ribcage crushed by death and ages—the Halls were always the last defended, with none left behind to clean up. It seemed strange to him that their attackers simply left the villages to ruin, instead of taking up habitation.

But then he saw one of their skeletons, a great gaping hole in a skull crushed by Taur might alone, and he was struck by how small it was. Perhaps it was simple: the buildings were sized for Taur, not humans. They had attacked simply to destroy the Taur, not to claim their homes. It seemed such waste, and yet he knew that's what they so often did.

He glanced around the shadows. It was only the antechamber, a small space to welcome guests and those of the Hall, and not meant to linger. A small hearth, just large enough to chase away the deepest chill without necessarily warming the Taur who would have little need of it, on the east wall. Another set of double doors across, with snatches of the larger song in paints of many hues.

These doors opened a little easier, and inside the darkness was deep—too deep, even for Tavill's eyes. While scent could have guided him through the halls, the Foldings themselves would require light to read. A quick glance back into the antechamber showed nothing worthy of burning. Perhaps he would just find them, for now, and bring them back into sunlight. He removed the bone again.

The ordering of the scents outside did not continue into the interior, and so he set his mind to work. Dust and decay filled his nose at first, and he sneezed. It echoed loudly, and the dust swirled up. He stuck fingers in his nose to hold back another blast until the dust settled again. He wiped it against the thick fur on his arm and sniffed tentatively.

Now the underlying—and more informative—scents came gently. Rotting oak and leather led him through doors; memory led him toward the archives. He entered a broad space—the court where the Hall would meet proper, and often publicly. Wooden chairs were in disarray, leather backs scored, torn, or collapsed at his touch. He saw in memory the dais, the bannister, the runes upon the stones, the great reference books filled with stories and laws both, a factual and memorial history of the Taur.

Behind the dais was set a smaller door, leading deeper into the Hall. Only some select would have been allowed back here. It struck Tavill that he had never been one of those. He paused at the door more out of habit, a strange compulsion years past due that told him he should not do this. He shook his head and opened the door.

He knew the Foldings existed, and what their purpose was. Every Taur did. But it was up to those select few to keep up with them. He wouldn't know where they were, or even precisely what they would smell like. He had seen one only once, late in the war, when it had been brought out in desperation as another raiding party closed in. And he wouldn't be able to recall from memory what the room would look like where they were kept.

It was a desperate task, and this too kept him on the outside of the door, even after the initial hesitation faded away. He breathed deep, but slow, letting the scents of the court fill his lungs. He tried to fix in his mind how it would have looked, as something firm to hold onto, to give him courage in pressing forward.

He was the last. Never again would this court sit in session, no matter what his success or failure was. The mission of the Taur had always been desperate, even if made more so lately. It had been believed they could not 'fail' in their primary mission except they abandoned it by choice. The slow and complete destruction of their race seemed in defiance of that belief.

But then Tavill had survived. It had not occurred to him until now the import of that seemingly innocuous fact. The mission was not failed, the unspoken promise was not broken.

By sheer survival, he was the only one now to decide who should see the Foldings or not. A force far greater than the Taur selected him: history itself, and the one who wrote it before it came to be, had ordered in no uncertain terms his appointment.

The door, to his surprise, opened easily. Even more shocking, the interior was lit. As he squinted in the sudden brightness, he automatically took in the surroundings—close enough he could still make out what was there. Shelves and alcoves lined the walls, filled with books and scrolls with summaries on tags dangling from thread. Three large tables were cluttered over with parchments, bowls and utensils, ink pots and quills, and one skeleton still in a chair but lying across the table as though struck down while scribing. Perhaps he had been recording the attack even as it happened.

The light, he saw finally, came through a long tunnel bored through the walls to the outside. There were six in total, so daylight could enter from any angle. Opposite the door he just entered stood another, smaller door of heavy oak timbers with three thick bands of ashwood. So the scribe had an exit, and chose not to take it.

Tavill went to the table and glanced across it. There was little indication of what the scribe might have been working on before he died—it looked at first as though there were numerous unfinished parchments. As he fixed on and read the texts, his suspicion was confirmed. There were no less than six parchments with uncompleted sentences at the end. Surely he was not trying to write six things at once? Gently Tavill lifted the parchments and set them in a row, and began to read the first:

and so it was Kitrun fell, surrounded by those who hated him. But he spoke nothing except a desire for peace, the words coming slower as the rocks rained down. At last he was rendered unconscious, and the Chief approached and raised his warclub high

Tavill remembered the story, an old one still surviving from the land now called Andelen. Though the sentence broke off, there was not much left to tell. He began to read the second. The parchment, he noted, seemed strangely newer—still old, but somehow a little clearer of text, as though age had not worked as thoroughly on it as it had the others:

Stone is most preferred, but clay properly fired will suffice for those without adequate supply. It is understood that, though periscous rock may be present, rock suitable for the heat required may still not, though this should be rare. The smith is cautioned against lethargy: clay should not be used as an expedient. If rock is available

Again, the rest could perhaps be assumed: *use it, no matter how much more labor is required.* Tavill gazed unseeing at one of the light tunnels, trying to remember what periscous rock was. He could not recall ever having heard the term—but then, his specialty had never been smithing. Clearly something that could be melted, and then fashioned by a smith.

He looked closely again at the page, and then some of the others. He could not discern the quality that kept it looking neater than the rest. The weave seemed perhaps a little tighter, and there was a slight gloss. Perhaps the scribe had somehow preserved it, whether purposefully or on accident.

Tavill vaguely remembered a liquid the scribes had developed, that could be brushed on the page after it was complete, that kept it supple and vibrant. His brows furrowed. The scribe had time to apply such a thing, but not finish his sentences? And why was this one so important, and not the rest?

The next page concluded a recipe for a way-bread that Tavill was familiar with. The fourth contained some notes of geography. And on, and on. All six were truncated pieces of Taur knowledge.

The somber realization hit him: they knew they were being wiped out, and were trying to preserve as much knowledge as they could. They thought, most likely, that this was their witness to the world—or would be. Vordir was neither the first nor the last to be raided, but it had been a time of great uncertainty. The raids did not seem as though they would stop suddenly, or that the Taur would be able to outlast them. So as the enemy approached, they began to commit to parchments what they could, probably hoping those who remained would continue the work.

Tavill settled back and sighed mournfully. He wondered how far they had gotten—if the others had even known what was here. Surely someone had—he had not known only because his was a small band hoping to survive by being nomads. Few thought it would actually work; now he wondered if the others resisted the idea only because it meant fewer Taur to to help in this undertaking. Perhaps, by their separation, they were seen as failing the mission. No one had said anything to him about it.

His gaze swept around the room again. For now, he was still alive to be a witness. Until this, the assumption had been a live witness, not just records. This room certainly held an abundance of written record. He went to the alcoves, began reading the tags. They seemed much the same of what was one the tables: dozens and perhaps hundreds of minutiae, recounting every detail, momentous and mundane, of existence on Oren. Tavill shook his head. It had never been clear what kind of witness the Taur were to provide, but he struggled to imagine it being so...trivial. What would the end of the world care about a hundred different kinds of bread? Or whether there had been fifty in a village, or fifty-one? Yes, that fifty-first mattered to some—perhaps to all the other fifty. And one *could* impact history—but did it? The record didn't say, bore no indication whatever.

He glanced around yet again. The Foldings were—as the name indicated—flat tomes, not scrolls. There was only one set of shelves in the room, their books stacked vertically, and all too thin. Unless the scribe had divided them, to hide them?

But as he searched, he found only ledgers, only more unimportant details that, in the intervening centuries, had come to nothing. If they had not altered the course of the last several hundred years in any discernible way, what use could they be during the Witness?

So much space for knowledge in this room, and as near as he could tell not one piece of it had changed or would change the existence of beings. Perhaps he shouldn't assume that. Perhaps he was only bitter because nothing there could help him right now—or, if it could, it was so deeply buried beneath useless facts that he would never uncover it.

Faintly, he heard a sound like a twig snapping, and he looked at one of the light tunnels. With swift but ginger steps he moved to it, bent his ear and nose to the opening.

A voice. The scent of iron, linen, and sweat. The Prosan were here.

He glanced wildly about, not sure what he was looking for: a weapon? A means of escape? An answer to a thousand questions?

His eyes kept coming back to the skeleton. The third time, he glanced down and spotted a bit of rotted leather on the floor under the chair. Lying against that bit of leather were three bits of sticks unusually twisted: Taur keys. Moving as quietly as he could he fished them out, and glanced at the heavy door at the back of the room. If he was discovered exiting, they would have direct access to a room that had been meant to be hidden—or, at least, not accessed by anyone but those deemed worthy.

But when he glanced toward the front door, he saw the whitened skeleton again. That secrecy had been violently sundered half a millennium ago. What was important now was escape, and the Prosan movements, by their sound, seemed to be toward the front of the Hall.

He put the key into the lock and gently turned. If it stuck, he did not want to break they fragile keys inside. It resisted at first, but as he jiggled he could feel it working free.

He thought he heard a footstep across the threshold, at the main entrance. He twisted suddenly, felt the lock click open. The door swung easily on wooden hinges, opening to a long dark tunnel. He closed the door behind him, letting his nose adjust a moment as he locked the door behind him.

The hall went straight, and shortly he arrived at the door at the other end, this one even thicker and with five bands of ashwood. This lock took longer finessing as he hoped there would be no one outside guarding it. He managed to ease it open, finally, without a sound. He took a deep breath, listened for some moments, then cracked open the door.

Beyond he smelled only forest. No Prosan, but also no wildlife. So the new raiders had probably approached from that direction and scattered the local fauna. Why would they have not left anyone at the exit?

Perhaps they did not seek him specifically. But how would they have showed up here so quickly after him?

He opened the door further and looked out. Dappled sunlight met him, dancing in the wind. He sniffed; faintly he scented iron, and he slammed the bone home.

He exited, closing the door behind him and locking it. He withdrew the keys and squeezed, feeling the wood pop in his fist. No one would enter or exit that way, not without hours of work with an axe.

He needed to go north. Far to the north, to their capital of Stavnuk. Surely the Foldings would be there. They had to be; if the Prosan were hounding him, he might not live to make it to Kragnog.

He moved slowly at first, quietly. As Vordir disappeared behind him, he began to run.

Strange shouts told him his escape was known. He could outrun them, but they could probably track him. He growled an ancient curse. His journey had just become infinitely more difficult.

12

THEIR HEARTS OF BRONZE

"She should know, you know."
"Where is Melnor?"
"Rinc Na. He said he needs to begin there."
"Then I will begin here, too."

19 Savimon 1320 — Winter

Averlynn sat Tarafel quietly, her eyes scanning the forests as they rode. Amrith rode ahead just as quiet, though she sensed a brooding set to his shoulders. He certainly brooded whenever they were stopped, and anytime she spoke. It had occurred to her on the fifth day of their journey south, that Scouts often rode in pairs as well. By her presence here, it was as though they were a team, though she was a nearly-dishonored Ranger. Of course it would rankle a Scout of such prestige as Amrith. And so she endeavored to be as meek as would befit their cavernous gap in honor.

Unconsciously she shifted the sword at her hip. In the intervening weeks, she had still not gotten accustomed to the weight of it being there. A bow and knife had done well enough for her till now. *Till now,* she thought with a rueful shake of her head: nothing at present even indicated she would need a sword. Nothing except a strange pressure in her spirit, and a bizarre, half-formed and half-remembered prophecy.

Amrith stopped, and so did she. He did not stare, but his roving gaze returned often to one particular spot. Averlynn glanced too, and thought she saw it: several broken twigs, though the shards had turned brown with age. Mimicking Amrith, she did not stare either, but gazed around and picked up what clues the forest gave her. A trampled fern. Fallen leaves pale as though pressed into the ground, each instance about the size of two men and spaced at intervals. A camp had been here, some time ago—and not one of the Wohan.

Amrith moved on, and she followed, questions filling her mouth without exiting. She wondered at first that they did not go closer. But as they rode, Amrith began nudging his black in a circle. Finally they stopped again, and he dismounted. He gave her a subtle look of expectancy, the slight hesitation in his movements the only waiting she knew he would do for her. She dismounted quickly and soundlessly. Dropping the reins to the ground, she knew Tarafel and Amrith's black—he never told her the name, and she never asked—would wait immobile until they returned or the horses themselves sensed danger.

She took two steps, then undid the buckles keeping the sword on her hip. It would only clatter and tangle until she knew how to handle it, and would constantly distract her as they searched. She returned swiftly to Tarafel and nestled it among the saddlebags, then turned back to catch Amrith's uplifted eyebrow. She only held his eye a moment before scanning the woods again. They pressed on together.

Jays warbled. A squirrel high in an oak flicked its tail a few times, then disappeared behind the trunk. Two others further away chased each other, the smaller finally escaping across the branches of a nearby maple. Normal sounds and activities of a forest. It would be unlikely an enemy lay in wait.

Averlynn began to distance herself from Amrith, to approach the old camp from a different angle. Low in some brambles she spied a loop of thin vine: a rabbit snare un-sprung and left behind. She paused, peering around. There was no corresponding rabbit trail, and the bush was a berry-less harshleaf—nothing a rabbit would go near. Strange. Surely those able to make such a camp, so far in the deep wood, would know where and how to set a snare.

Perhaps a trail had been there formerly. But her gaze still sharpened. As she continued circling east, closer to where they had first spied the clues, she saw a little lump of leaves poorly covering a pile of excrement, then another. But no more. Here and there a broken twig, but any footprints had faded away. The ground was firm; they had, at least, chosen a dry place to camp. But it left Averlynn no hope of finding a deeper print. She continued on, looking, and listening.

Finally she returned to their first sighting. Amrith had not yet arrived, so she walked among the impressions. She counted ten in a rough oval. There was no fire pit, no strong markers of trails between sleeping pads. They appeared to have camped overnight, moved little, and continued on their way. Which would be, where? She saw no obvious exit, not even a bare trail where they might have marched out together. She circled back, looking closer. On the south-east side she suddenly spotted what seemed to be a cluster of broken twigs, at least compared to the signs elsewhere. As she peered closer, she found luck: one almost perfectly broken in three, its center nudged just further southeast than the two ends. She glanced between the trunks, noting several larger oaks she marked on her way into the camp. The print, such as it was, did not point toward their toilet, so it was not caused by such a call of nature.

A faint noise and motion caught her attention, and she ducked as an arrow zipped overhead and thunked into the tree next to her. She whirled, hands going to her bow, when she spotted Amrith. She knelt, hesitating but not relaxing. Had this been the Intag Ka's plan?

But Amrith stood still, a grim smile just beginning to touch his eyes. He lowered the bow. "At least you're still paying some attention," he said.

"What are you doing?" Averlynn asked, still crouched.

"Testing you. You may stand up, now," he said, slinging his bow again. "What did you find?"

She rose slowly, then came toward him. "Southwest, among some beeches, were only two piles of refuse, poorly hidden and deteriorated—not buried except under some leaves. An abandoned snare, though poorly located. Ten sleeping areas roughly two-man sized, no fire pit, no trails between. It appears they broke camp and headed southeast, but not toward their toilet."

She hoped he would be impressed, but if he was he hid it well behind a mask of disdain. "So you literally found..." He trailed off, and shook his head. "And what are your amazing deductions, based on those findings?"

"On those alone I say they move fast and light, have some woodscraft but not as much as our people. Perhaps accustomed to staying in larger groups but were forced into a smaller unit, on whatever objective they have. But what have you found?"

He glared at her, then his lips twitched in amusement. "Some woodscraft?"

She cocked her head. "They left surprising little sign, to be completely unfamiliar with travel."

"But a snare where there are no rabbit trails?"

"It is strange, indeed," she admitted. "It appears well-formed, but as you said..." She trailed off, then glanced sharply at him. "I didn't say that."

His amusement snapped off, and he stalked toward their horses.

"You made this camp. Why did you do that?" she asked as they reached their mounts.

"As I said, to test you," Amrith replied. "Though, in a way, you have still failed, despite your final conclusion."

"I don't understand," she said. They mounted, and continued on their original course.

"Of course not, because you've blinded yourself. Who would have made the camp, except one of us? Those bumblers north of the Wall? They haven't been able to come to our lands for centuries—not once. The old nomads? We destroyed them utterly. There is no one else here but us. Except you seem convinced there's danger round every bole, some great doom waiting to crash down around us. None of your other Rangers have sensed it or seen a whit of evidence; none of the Scouts have seen anything. But I suppose we aren't as observant or insightful as you."

"I don't say I've seen evidence—not as clear as broken twigs or spoor. Do you deny the land has changed?"

"Lands change, Averlynn! Seasons change, weather changes. Even your beloved 'home' that we abandoned so long ago was different when we left than when we arrived. And I can only imagine how it has changed until today."

"Then why do we do what we do?" Averlynn asked bitterly.

Amrith reined in so hard his black almost sat down. He glared at her for several long moments, his jaw trembling. Suddenly he relaxed and she could see his disdain beginning to return. "Why do you have that sword? You might have left it in Wohan."

"Aver suggested...well, he said you knew the sword, and might be able to teach me."

Amrith's laugh almost perfectly matched Aver's, certainly in style. "And I ask again: why? Why would you learn this?"

"You know why."

"Are you so hopeful?" he asked, sobering a little. She said nothing. Amrith clicked to his black, and they continued through the woods. "So you carry a sword in the utterly unlikely event I would be willing to train you—even though you are not a Scout, will never be a Scout, may cease being a Ranger if you continue with your madness."

"Whether you teach me or not, the sword came to me, and I believe it is for a purpose."

"So you say. And at least you are consistent, if deluded. We have Rangers and Scouts to make our people happy—to feel better about living in a new and strange land. We are not here to serve any function but an emotional one. We do our work because we did it in the old country, and it feels strange to stop doing what one has done for hundreds of years. Should I take up the plow? A smith's hammer? Would you? You want so desperately to be a Ranger—why? To protect our people? From what, a late autumn?" His laugh was light and musical. "Once again, we have seen no evidence of any actual threat to our land or our people, yet you cling to your job because you enjoy the motions. Is that not right?"

She sat back, contemplating. There was truth in his words. She desired no other life, though there had been little evidence of its need until recently. She considered herself working some other job. But, like Amrith, could not. She would miss the forests and plains and mountains, little rivers. Of finding her way across trackless expanses. Of searching grass and twig for spoor or sign. With no clear danger, she could leave it—for what? The council? If they would even have her. To weave and dye fabrics and thread? Learn a trade, and stay in the village with her mother and father? Attend the festivals on time, and properly? She imagined it, picturing in her mind the seasons and times passing in peace and pleasantries, spring plantings and autumn harvests, of worshiping Praka with her people. Safe and secure in the knowledge that Rangers and Scouts roamed the land to assure them that no danger existed anywhere.

But across that vision of bright lands and gentle breezes a cloud began to loom. In her mind's eye the winds picked up; bits of broken grain and leaves scurried on the breezes and trees began to sway. Lightning cracked and thunder rumbled, and far off was the sound of a waterfall drawing closer.

In a blink she was back beside Amrith, considering his smug grin, the lazy way he sat his saddle. It did not seem possible he was the same Scout she had met outside the nomad camp so long ago. He did not seem so sharp, now. Or perhaps she was only seeing him in a new light.

"Perhaps you're right," she said, looking away as his smile grew. "In which case," she continued quickly, "I would still like to learn the sword." She glanced at him as his smile disappeared. "For my emotional function."

He threw back his head and laughed, genuinely this time. "Well spoken," he replied. "In that case, I will teach you."

Amrith proved to be a far more difficult teacher than she could have imagined. For the first two weeks he gave her no actual instruction. He would square up after lunches and suppers and begin attacking her, and she would do her best to defend. While she learned, it was clumsy and slow, and and the sword felt too large. As she fought both Amrith and the sword, she could feel her temper rising. She kept it in check as best she could, afraid if she lashed out he would take it as an excuse to abandon the practice. By the end of the first week, she had wondered if he hoped to discourage her from trying. This strengthened her resolve for a few days, and she focused with renewed effort. Finally she began to pick up common strikes, how he moved as he executed them, and effective ways to deflect them. And, as soon as she did, he would abandon it entirely and began all-new attacks.

At the end of the two weeks, he remained seated after lunch. "You are tenacious," he admitted gruffly. "And clever, to learn what I taught without plain telling. I hoped you would give up by now." She remained silent, seething inside but also triumphant. She tried to let neither show. "So, beginning tomorrow, I will teach you more properly. We'll be in Hatza then, with real training grounds."

As they rode the next morning, it struck her how much she had depended on the changing seasons to ground her where she was. She had never approached Hatza when the leaves were still on the trees—at least, not this many, and few green. It almost seemed a far different place—darker, and more brooding, though that might have been her own thoughts, her own mood. Despite the hope of finally getting formal training from Amrith today, the desire for it nagged. Maybe it was because Amrith had made a jest of her fears those weeks ago. That he disdained her enough to make the effort of constructing a false camp. In the middle of the night, while she slept and he was supposed to keep watch. It had crushed her more than she realized, as she now approached their southernmost outpost, how flagrantly he ignored her warnings, and the warnings of the land. There had been a time when her people heeded the land above almost all else—except, of course, Praka and Hakana. Had coveted its signs and omens for guidance.

But could she blame them? Even she found it difficult to think of this place as home. It had been the woods they had valued, and their home across the sea—not this strange land of unnavigable northern mountains and perpetual southern winters. They had spent so many early years as adrift on the land as they had been on the sea to get here. They could glean no guidance from it, and so had leaned entirely upon sun and moon. It became easier, then, especially for those who neither ranged nor scouted. Her parents, their friends and family, stuck in strange cities and villages, had no other handhold except for Praka and Hakana. And Hakana was absent some nights. And the nights even when Hakana shined were filled with strange sounds none of their people had known for centuries.

They had found peace in their new focus of worship. Praka guided them daily. They supported the Rangers and Scouts because—as she admitted—there was no other work that they knew or desired. But they no longer needed, and now no longer wanted, the guidance of the land. It was a foreign power, a law made for the native-born, and they were not subject. And she came to them claiming this foreign law suddenly required their obedience, but still only obliquely and incoherently. She could not, in truth, actually tell them what was required of them. Just that something was wrong.

She almost chuckled but for the bitterness of it. Because despite all these revelations, she still knew she was right. She only now added the knowledge that she would be able to convince no one, and should not expect to. The most futile of missions was on her shoulders, and she didn't know why.

They were in the outpost, reporting themselves to the Chief and Isun. Averlynn held out her ring mechanically, her mind entirely elsewhere, though nowhere particular. Mostly in a dark depth, moisture suggesting water but no living water, no sound, no smell. Vaguely she was aware that Amrith seemed happy, that he engaged the villagers and other Rangers with a lightness she would envy if she could climb far enough out of her caverns to truly register it. But his was a faint wisp of a cloud, unreachable anyway and therefore of little import. It would hold no rain, shade no sun, impact her in no appreciable way. He simply existed.

The face in front of her didn't move on, the smile on it did not fade but widened. Averlynn blinked, the solitude of her cave erupting suddenly in noise and presence. Her own smile found its way to her face as she took in the chestnut waves framing a diamond face set with emerald eyes.

"Ranger Hamada," she said, now feeling a little ashamed. "I'm sorry, I was..." There was no excuse Hamada would understand, not in this brief time. "We must break bread together later."

Hamada's eyes twinkled. "I suppose you did hear me, then. Worry not, sister-friend. We will rekindle faded bonds this evening."

Of all her people, Averlynn wished she could spend most of her time with Hamada. She most of all understood her moods and mind, even if she did not believe the same or draw the same conclusions. Hamada, even more than Isun Vera, could help her sort through strange emotions and warring desires, intellectually if not spiritually.

The parade passed, each member returning to their duty stations. The rest of the morning was spent reporting to the Chief their movements since leaving Tekaa Wohan, and some of the political and social goings-on that even Averlynn was hearing for the first time. Amrith only quickly glossed over her desire to learn the sword, and only by way of excusing them to the training grounds. A few of the other Rangers were there when they arrived, stealing furtive glances at Amrith. He ignored it all. He was probably accustomed to it. This time, he began not by drawing his sword but explaining to her some foundations of the uses, limitations, and traditions of the blade. Only as noon meal approached did they spar, and limitedly. And yet her movements now, slight as they were, she felt were far better grounded and intentional than the most extravagant counterattack she had ever made on the route there. Whatever else, it seemed Amrith was honest in his bid to train her, and train her well.

A lunch of dark bread and vegetable soup waited for them when they were done. Partway through, a server approached with a small platter of shredded and seasoned chicken. Averlynn was surprised, and assumed it was for Amrith alone until she observed similar platters brought to the others who had been training as well.

Sensing her confusion, the server smiled. "Meat is good to restore fatigued muscles," he said. "As are the penther beans in your soup."

Averlynn bowed her head in thanks. Only after the server departed did she begin to wonder. Looking to Amrith, who dug heartily into the chicken, she decided to voice her wonder.

"Strange, isn't it?" she began. "I have seen more preparation for war in one morning here than...anywhere else."

Amrith rolled his eyes. "Again with this. Habit, Averlynn. Yes, there was conflict here—years ago. And victory, years ago. You were part of it. But by then the habits were built. They train because they did; they learned much during that time, not just training with arms but training the body. So, if you will, be thankful that you came here in a time when you suddenly wanted training. And stop poking and prodding a carcass."

Thankful, indeed. Such coincidence. She chewed silently, though, at the unspoken threat: keep poking, and our agreement ends. "They certainly learned how to make a delicious soup, and to season meat well." She forced a grin. Amrith regarded her a moment before returning the smile. She knew he didn't believe her.

The rest of the day went by in a blur: more swordplay, half lecture and half practice, in between sporadic reports and questions to Amrith from passers-by. Averlynn was grateful for the interruptions. Hardened as she thought she had become by Rangering, sword fighting taxed entirely different sets of muscles. And the sword still felt clumsy in her hand.

Amrith released her just before evening meal to clean up and change. She briefly checked on Tarafel. The groom would have taken good care of her mount, but she also missed him after weeks of constant companionship. She soon found the spring-fed washhouse, her mind exhausted from the lectures. She knew she needed to talk to Hamada, knew she needed to ask specific questions—she just couldn't think of them right then. The cold water helped, but she made her way back to the hall still dazed.

Hamada's mind and body, apparently, was very alert. Her steps were light and her eyes still sparkled as she approached. "You look terrible," she said, but so joyfully that Averlynn instantly smiled.

"I feel it," she replied. "When I wanted to learn the sword, I only saw the goal—not the journey to get there."

Hamada nodded sagely. "Keep your eyes there, on the goal. You cannot make the journey otherwise."

They loaded plates with still-steaming brown bread, a medley of vegetables and mushrooms dripping in a dark savory sauce, and two slabs of pork. "Have you made the journey?" Averlynn asked. "You speak as one who knows."

Hamada laughed musically. "Almost. Almost started, that is. But I saw others going through the journey and couldn't keep my eyes on the goal."

"Why do they commit to such a journey?" Averlynn wondered aloud.

Hamada shrugged as they sat across from each other. "I suppose it's the spirit of this place. It just seems like what one should do, this close to the mountains."

"Is there still a threat here?"

For the first time since she arrived in Hatza, Averlynn saw discomfort on her friend's face. "Of course not," she said, though she sounded uncertain.

Averlynn glanced quickly around, and lowered her voice. "Hamada, if there is something happening, I would want to know about it. I don't like the changes I'm seeing."

Hamada's smile seemed forced. "I know. They told us as much."

Averlynn sat back, stunned. "They told you—warned you against me?"

Now her smile was pained. "Averlynn, you've always been so...focused. Astute. We admired it for the longest time—I did, at least. It's what draws me to you. I can't be half the Ranger you are. But..." She trailed off as her lip quivered, and she sighed. "We also don't need to be half the Rangers we once were. I'm afraid for you, Averlynn. Many of us are."

"Afraid of what?"

"That you've been too focused for too long? That your focus makes you see things that aren't there, or—sorry, not that you're seeing unreality, but that your focus enlarges that which should be small. That you see mountains where the rest of us would see weevil-hills."

Averlynn's stomach grew suddenly hollow. The scented steam from the sauce mocked her. Her determination, once a mountain in her mind, was now truly a weevil-hill. She set herself to die on that weevil-hill. "And the late autumn?" she asked.

Hamada regarded her pitiably. "So it's late," she said. "We've had early winters, and it never aroused your suspicion."

"And the Glowwood? Did they tell you about that too?"

"Probably a direct result of a late autumn—we've never observed it when warm weather lingers, perhaps the gigantic mushrooms cannot support themselves longer. They did tell us," Hamada said quietly. "They told us all your reasons—even the prophecy."

There were no more weevil-hills to die on, if that too was known. "And I make more of that than is warranted, I suppose."

"That prophecy was already fulfilled, Averlynn; it can't be fulfilled again."

That was news. "It was? When?"

"Before either of us were born, back in—the other land. That's what the Ka said."

"No one told me. Why wouldn't Amrith have said something, if it was so well known?"

"Who knows a Scout's reasons," Hamada muttered. She smiled at the shared joke. They had often said so to each other. "Maybe he didn't think you would believe him."

She wouldn't have, she hated to admit. Perhaps his disdain had been well earned: she disdained him first, in many ways. Disdained all of her people, as she had realized earlier. Perhaps she was seeing mountains where there were only weevil-hills. Even Hamada, closer to her than any other Ranger, was seeing it.

"This won't make the journey any easier," Averlynn said, in bitter attempt at levity. She sobered. "What am I supposed to do here, then? What purpose do I serve?"

"Well, you can continue to learn swordplay, for that is a truly impressive sword you carry and you should have skills worthy of it. You can continue to dine with me, and we can discuss far more invigorating topics. And maybe you can build some other relationships within the Rangers, or with Amrith. When is the last time you've visited the Gates?"

Averlynn smiled wistfully. "The Gates" were what they called an ancient ruin—there was more than just gates there, a whole stone city once stood here, deep in the southern realms. But most impressive were the strange gates marked with odd and asymmetrical flat planes across their face. And she had not visited them in some years.

Settling down a little, enjoying her forays again, wasn't an unattractive idea. Strange, and too new to accept without question. But interesting. "When do you go on patrol?" she asked. "I would be honored to accompany you."

Hamada's discomfort returned. "We...don't, really. Sometimes, usually more for forage than true Rangering. But I don't think anyone had planned to do so for some days yet."

Averlynn's fork clattered loudly. "You don't even patrol anymore?" The dining hall went utterly silent, and Hamada glanced around as Averlynn took several deep breaths. She lowered her voice but still seethed. "How can you say I see nothing, when you aren't even looking! How long have the eyes of the south been blind? How can you say nothing stirs against us?"

Hamada glared grumpily. "Where would it come from?" she asked. "Our enemies were defeated years and years ago. We saw no sign of them. Ever again. Beyond the mountains is an endless and inhospitable waste of foreversnow. Or do you think the hills simply sprout an entire people?"

Averlynn calmed, a little. She had a point. The south, at least was likely secure. But had the others stopped patrolling as well? She recalled faintly the words of Isun Vera: *"I had thought it might be you in the north this year, when I did not see you for so long."* It had not been because Averlynn delayed, but because she didn't stay in the village the way the other Rangers did. Vera meant it as a jest. They all jested, while the seasons themselves were in upheaval. Whatever doom was coming, she had to face it and her entire people and their complacency as well. It was too much.

"I'm very tired," she said. "If you will excuse me." She stood up before Hamada could protest and walked out. It hurt to leave her friend like that, but it had been a day full of hurts. And any she thought were friends had abandoned her long ago. They simply didn't have the decency to be clear about it.

She went to her quarters and laid down. She was, in truth, very tired. Tired of the jests and the opposition and the betrayals and the complacency, and of trying to dislodge or call into question any of it. The doubt began to gnaw, too. What if she was wrong? What if these were entirely natural occurrences in a land still strange and new in the nearly-ageless lives of her people. And what if the prophecy had been fulfilled? She wanted to ask Amrith about it, but not tonight. Not when he might affirm it. She would not be able to handle that tonight.

The following days went much the same: lecture and training, hearty meals, and only meaningless conversations with Hamada. It was two days before they even ate together again, and three days more before their conversation became relaxed. Their relationship was still nothing like what it had been, and it pained Averlynn.

After two weeks, Averlynn and Hamada rode out together to forage. The air was pleasant, the breezes slight. She tried hard to enjoy it. If it had been summer, she would have, and so she tried to convince herself it was summer.

But she couldn't keep her eyes from wandering, of picking up every sign and spoor. The land truly lay undisturbed, gave no overt sign of distress or doom. Harts crept through their thickets, heads bobbing as she and Hamada rode through. Hares trembled beneath brambleberry bushes and bolted. A fox paused mid-stalk; when they passed, it pounced victoriously upon some vole and trotted off. Jays screeched at imagined enemies, and warblers sang before launching themselves away from roughhousing squirrels.

"Idyllic, isn't it?" Hamada said. She had been watching Averlynn, who smiled sheepishly.

"It's what I would hope to see," she admitted.

Hamada sobered. "But not in autumn." She sighed when Averlynn was silent. "It's difficult for me to fault you," Hamada went on. "There are times it feels so natural it's unnatural. As if a glamour showed us our highest hope, though completely false."

"But surely no glamour could be cast on an entire land."

Hamada shook her head. "Not only how, but who? There is no one here but us."

"But how much do we know about this land?" Averlynn wondered suddenly. "Remember the magic of Singer's Bay where the lights and land itself play song? Or the Blackmere, portending some cosmic shift? How do we know the land itself does not lie to us, but that in the north that lie begins to crumble? The prophecy speaks as it the land were alive..."

"But the prophecy is fulfilled!" Hamada interjected loudly. She squeezed her eyes shut and shook her head. "Averlynn, we must not conjure such terrible enemies or cataclysmic dooms. By Praka, you'll bring it down on us when it doesn't exist."

Averlynn looked aside. The forest itself had gone silent, the animals seemingly retreating from her reckless talk. "I thought I was only responding to what I see," she said quietly. "I did not invent...this..." She trailed off, only gesturing around at the summer day.

"Perhaps not," Hamada said. She turned her mount back toward Hatza. "But one can still by encouragement bring to harvest that which should have died."

Averlynn watched her go. She should return too: Amrith probably had more training for her. But it would make their silent ride the more awkward if she trailed behind the entire time, and she would not show displeasure by passing her friend at a gallop.

That night, though her mind wanted to race she forced it to calm. She dreamed of darkness, heavy and palpable. Not like nighttime, but like a heavy cloth that would block out even the fiercest of Praka's rays. There was silence at first, yet underlaid by a deepening thrum that suggested a presence, and a portent. Slowly, faintly, she became aware of a glimmer in the corner of her eye. She tried to turn to look, but could not. As she strained it would disappear into the darkness; if she rested, it returned, floating, ephemeral. Gradually it drew closer, and she could make out some sort of lettering. She renewed her focus, trying to trace the spectral lines of the strange script, but they curved and looped so intricately that her mind was lost upon it. She stopped struggling, and the words edged into view:

From the south there grows again a spear to wend and part the bones
There under dying glow becomes a falcon's blood to break the stones.
Across the sea the banners hang while drummers bang the parting knell
And striking deep in hearts of bronze a terrible repealing bell.

She woke quickly, panting. It was the next verse of the prophecy. But why would it come to her, if had been fulfilled? *And* in a dream? A prophecy dreamed carried twice the weight of any other.

And what did it mean? She worried suddenly that this southern outpost was in the most imminent danger—perhaps the idyllic summer day was a glamour. But the verse followed immediately on the heels of the previous, that had referred to the Glowwood. And there was the second line: *There under the dying glow.* Surely a reference to the same. The Glowwood was important. Something grew to the south of it. But would be joined from something across the sea?

The northerners. They could not cross the Brynth. They would be sailing south, striking at their land from a way previously unopened to them. Their ships would have banners. And it would happen just south of the Glowwood. *Hearts of bronze.* Not the strongest of metals. She was not certain it would refer to her people, but it made sense. A terrible repealing bell. Sounding a warning.

She needed to go north, back to the Glowwood, to see what this was about. To warn her people before it was entirely too late. As she rose and dressed quickly, she knew that moment may already have passed.

13

THE COST OF WAKING

"That's not what it says."
"I know."
"You should tell her."
"I will not. Not yet."

18 Fulmatung 1320 — Winter

She hesitated only a moment at Amrith's door before knocking. She knew what his response would be, but knew he would be dead if she didn't try. They probably all would be dead, and her dying thought would be *if only I had knocked...* A stupid regret.

He came to the door swifter than she thought he would, and asked no questions. Had he somehow had the dream too? Did he know she was coming?

"What," he said, once the door was closed.

Perhaps not. "I had a dream," she said.

"What, in your sleep?" he asked with mock seriousness.

She didn't take the bait. "I dreamed the next verses of the prophecy." She would not even ask if it had been fulfilled already; it could not have been.

Amrith considered her for a long moment, and when he spoke again his voice held a measure of respect she had never heard from him before. "Do you know what the verse means?"

She shook her head. "Not entirely. It's still not the end of the prophecy. But what it says tells me to go back to the Glowwood. The doom strikes there." She did not say *our doom*. She would not risk that, not yet.

Amrith drew a deep breath. "This...changes things," he said heavily. "You should go."

Averlynn blinked. "I should?"

Amrith gestured graciously. "I know, it seems I'm turning on a pin. But a dream, Averlynn, is far different from a vision or still-green leaves. Perhaps you are right. At least, I think you had better find out. I still believe it will be nothing. But..." He pursed his lips and nodded. "It should take you and Tarafel...?"

She considered the distance, the landscape. *Too long,* she thought. "Until..." *Until the time of the prophecy.*

He must have made the same connection. "Until the following spring. Well I suppose it must be; if you could arrive there sooner it wouldn't fulfill the prophecy."

"What about my duty to the southern outpost?" she asked.

"I think this takes precedence, don't you?"

"Someone will need to tell the Intag."

He cast her a withering glance, a bit of the Amrith she knew returning. "Well unless I lose my voice and my hands, and soon, I imagine I can handle that."

"My parents," she began, then shook her head. "You would not make the visit all the way to them."

"Do I need to?"

"I would like them to know. Will you see a message delivered?"

"You could send one in the morning."

Averlynn shifted. "I could..." She wavered.

Amrith's head bobbed once. "Sooner off, sooner arrived. You're right. Quickly, write a message and I will give it to a herald in the morning. You will leave immediately?" he asked. She nodded firmly. "Very well. Sit here at my desk and write quickly."

"Thank you, Amrith," she said honestly.

He smiled briefly and turned away, leaving her to it. She wrote a few sentences explaining what she was doing, with Amrith's consent and advice, and when she might arrive back. She calculated quickly: more full moon festivals missed, and Aman È. She closed her eyes briefly; she could not miss that one. No one did, for any reason. She scratched out the last line. *I will be back for Aman È,* she promised instead. She had to find a way to do that. To miss it would mean exile. *But to miss the prophecy might mean death...* She looked back to her message to write one last sentence. *If I do not return, I have died, and so shortly will we all.* Too much? She felt it was not.

She drew her name quickly and sighed. It would be as it would be. Too late now to change it.

Amrith accompanied her to the stables, helped her saddle Tarafel and leave the outpost. He faded quickly from view in the darkness, but she thought she saw him flash one final smile, encouraging her on her way.

She thought at first to ride as straight a line as the Waken would allow, avoiding the villages and cities in the way for explanations would be difficult without some letter from Amrith. *I should have gotten that. Too late.* But the second morning woke her with a shock as a hard frost clung to the ground. Autumn had finally come, and swiftly. Her breath left her in clouds, and a distant Praka hovered in crisp skies.

"The seasons are all awry," she muttered to Tarafel. "For all we know Spring will be here next week." She should perhaps hurry faster. But the way was long regardless of how fast or straight she rode. By afternoon she struck upon a different plan, and edged Tarafel easterly.

"If the threat comes from the ocean, to the ocean we go," she said. Dead Man's Cliffs gave a commanding view of the sea, north as well as east, and perhaps she could spy their doom even far south of the Glowwood.

By the end of the week, the trees of the Waken were nearly bare, and she could see the line of mountains to the south through naked branches. She kept to the line for many days, refreshing her supplies from the many mountain freshets that in the lower foothills had turned to streams. The roe deer were in sudden rut, and many a buck nearly crashed into her so she only needed to hurriedly shoot one in ten to provide herself with meat as well. Her greater concern was Tarafel: glades were sparse enough, and now the winter-blasted grasses offered even less forage.

She rode him carefully, then, keeping their pace light and following around the hills instead of riding over them. It delayed them, but not as much as a famished mount would. She only needed to reach the Cliffs where the forest thinned enough to provide a rich understory.

The winds rose stiff and steady, and thick clouds obscured the skies for days. So it was the crashing of waves that first alerted her to their approach to the cliffs, before the forest began to thin. It disoriented her, nearly to nausea; the land and weather had always been her guide, giving her more information than any other sense, grounding her in her reality. There had been days gone by where she could almost find her way blindfolded, traveling by sense alone, as one would in a home they had grown up and spent their entire lives in. Though inanimate, walls could provide a feeling of presence to one attuned. The trees and forest floor and sun and moon and seasons and hot and cold and wind all did the same for her. But now it was all in disarray, and she went as one who tripped over new furniture and stumbled into empty spaces where familiar walls had been removed. Dead Man's Cliffs arrived for her as one who encountered a balcony where once had been a wall, and it unnerved her. Her survival for centuries depended on knowing there was a wall there, that she could sense it before she even arrived—could turn along it precisely, without even touching it.

She mistrusted the edge. Before, she would ride right to the verge and gaze out over the rolling expanse. Now she reined Tarafel in hard, lengths from the edge.

"Let's wait here a bit," she said. There was grass here. She would give him the rest of the day to fill out ribs nearly gaunt from their ride here. She needed to deal with this discomfort if she was going to be any use.

She took a step closer, forcing herself. To the south she could just make out the narrow ledge that led through the mountains to the forest and plains to the south. She had only been there once, but she'd enjoyed it for how new it was.

But then they'd encountered the strange nomadic people, had fought in fear of what they might be. She met one prisoner, once, and thought she understood the Wohan's fear. Not only were these nomads a warlike people, but something in them rung out like the peoples they had known across the sea. They looked dissimilar, and their language was far removed. And yet, the encounter made her think of some of the flowers they had brought with them, now grown in strange soil and pollinated by strange bees alongside strange neighbors. When compared to their sketches from Kalen, the flowers now looked entirely different, would not be connected in the mind except the florists knew them to be from that original stock. Such were the people who named themselves Prosan.

And so the Kalen fought once for their new land. And had won, completely. The Prosan could not be trusted, could not be guarded against, and so they were exterminated. As Hamada and Amrith reminded her: years ago. Never again to be a threat. Now her people regarded the mountains as a convenient border against the genocide they had committed. Another thing no one talked about if they could help it.

She shivered, and took one more step toward the cliffs. The wind blew stiffer, then fell away suddenly. She blinked, nearly taking a lurching step forward. The waves stood frozen in place. She looked back: Tarafel stood motionless in mid-bite. There was a moaning—high-pitched—that melded into a clarion call, a singer opening a song, to invite instruments not yet playing.

Averlynn looked, bewildered, toward the southern ledge. It was filled, now, with a people—not marching, but fleeing as refugees. Wind stirred their cloaks as they walked with heads bowed. Great bundles hunched their shoulders. There were no beasts of burden that Averlynn could discern. Men and women, young, old, with babies carried, entered the northern land. They turned inland as more came along the ledge.

The singer's voice rose and fell and rose again, and now a drum thumped a slow rhythm. One of the men suddenly looked toward Averlynn and stopped as his people continued to move slowly by. He was so far distant she could not see his eyes and yet she felt his gaze so sharply it almost seemed as if a pale-blue, almost silver stare pierced her.

The note turned mournful as she felt his gaze harden. At his side, a fist clenched hard on the hilt of a sword. The fury of his resolve struck her as now a long horn-blast echoed from the mountains behind the convoy—not as a call to arms but a desperate question.

Those at the head of the column continued as though into a mist, slowly fading into transparency. The man continued to stare, a vibrating thrum rising. The end of the column disappeared, and he turned as if to a dust and was carried away on the wind.

The singer, her voice now alone, trailed away, and as she did the winds rose again, waves crashed against the shore below, and Tarafel's munching resumed. Averlynn's breath slammed into her lungs, held unnoticed as the vision played itself out.

It had been the Prosan. It had to have been. No one else came from there, or looked like that. But why now? Was the vision from past or present?

Was there still a threat from the south? Was she running away from the portents by going northward?

She turned and looked that way. A curtain of sleeting rain met her glance as the thick clouds above finally burst. But the storm remained northerly, and where she stood was dry. Still it obscured her vision. A barrier? Was the land telling her to remain in the south?

Or was it a glamour, as she had wondered during her forage with Hamada? Or, if not a glamour, still the land working against her to deceive her and destroy her people. They had been refugees, hadn't they? Why would the land hold malice? She looked south again. The Prosan came northward as refugees, but were intercepted as invaders and destroyed. Was their doom, then, a punishment—and well-deserved? What if she fought the fates themselves, fought against the justice of Praka and Hakana meted out against the apostates?

If it were, she could do nothing to avert it. Surely she was not so skilled and equipped as to stand against two gods, when the land itself turned against her and her people. Even if she tried. And she would try, just in case they were innocent—well, not innocent, but inculpable.

She stepped back from the edge. There was nothing to prove, not this way. She moved to the leeward side of a large oak. Even in the eddies a fire would prove difficult, and so she would settle for her blanket. She ate cold jerky and hard bread, only enough to strengthen her for the day—a day of rest. Tomorrow if the sleet had abated she would go north. The Glowwood was not so far away now, and the days were growing colder, not warmer. Spring would be some time off, she deemed.

The next morning dawned cold and foggy, but not stormy, and so they began their journey northward. Praka was a dim white disk across a sea less turbulent but grayer than yesterday. Leaves were turning immediately to brown, and the forest seemed nearly dead, but a decaying death not a hibernating one. Though the winds still stirred, all was silent except Tarafel's *clumpfing* hoof falls and sometimes-snorting breaths. If he struck a rock, it seemed to echo sharply through the wood.

Perhaps it was only the fog. That would suppress sounds. And the fog-late and chilly morning would keep animals in their nests and dens longer. Perhaps she was making mountains of weevil-hills. Perhaps her constant vigilance brought visions through exhaustion, not prophecy.

Prophecy. That had been all too clear—at least, the memory of it. There were too many ways to interpret it, though. She had to wonder—and too often did—if she conjured the memory or if it had truly come to her.

Were there perfectly innocent interpretations of the prophecy? She mused; they had many days still before reaching the Glowwood. It could be an interesting exercise.

From the south there grows again a spear to wend and part the bones

Her people used bones at many high festivals to interpret the times, and to bless or curse. And 'south' was often a euphemism for the unexpected. So an unexpected sharpness came again to make their scrying more plain—'parting' the bones could make the message distinct. That would be good.

There under dying glow becomes a falcon's blood to break the stones.

Lots of things glowed. Embers. Stars. Sunsets. A red sunset would occur on a solstice, when the sun would go down between their Season Stones. Not strange.

Across the sea the banners hang while drummers bang the parting knell

Clouds could look like banners, or distant sheeting rain could look that way. And drums would be played during the solstice as well, a type of 'parting knell.' Entirely normal.

And striking deep into the hearts of bronze a terrible repealing bell.

The terrible bell was worrisome. But one constantly gonging also became annoying. 'Terrible,' one might say. Perhaps they would ring some massive, new bronze bell so long and so energetically it would become terrible. At a solstice where a red sun set and there was rain across the sea, and something unexpected would make their bones easier to read.

She sat back. Utter nonsense. Yes, if she tried very hard, she could make the words portend something entirely innocent. But it ignored every sense of the words themselves, and the fact the prophecy was given in the first place, and so outlandishly. The gods did not speak idly, or tell their people of mundane events. Signs on earth and sky were not given to remind the people that daily life happened. Many times the omens of the bones were first clear, then obscure, with no special attention called to when it would be.

No. Far more worrisome was the notion that the doom that approached came from an unexpected quarter. *That* part of the prophecy could ring true—that 'south' simply meant 'unexpected' and by definition she would not be able to predict where to observe its approach. More worrisome by far was that she now effectively abandoned her people on a fruitless quest—she, who seemed the only one to believe something was happening.

But that wasn't entirely true either. Hamada suspected, but shut her eyes to it. Amrith, too, probably suspected, but felt too securely ensconced in his position as a Scout, and her a mere Ranger. If danger truly came, how could *he* not see it, and she did? Very possibly the Intag, and the Chiefs, felt the same. Who was she, and who were they, to have conflicting views?

She shook her head, ducking under a low branch. Who *did* she think she was, to consider herself and her people in such a way? And yet it seemed so clear. Perhaps it began with Hakana; she was automatically put into a position of antithesis because she felt more attracted to moon than sun—already at odds with most of her people, and her parents. Aver wasn't like that...

Aver. So well respected by everyone. Perhaps, she thought miserably, this was all a petulant reaction to her parents' favoritism of a brother who never got along with her. How much of what she was and how she felt was a reaction to him? Aver dutifully worshipped Praka, so she would adore Hakana; Aver was present for each festival, so she would constantly make excuse; her parents wished she was more like him, so she would be nothing like him. And he was the ideal Wohan, the purest example—well, nearly—of what it meant to be one of her people. And so she must be the worst example.

She thought of their last meeting, how he laughed at her when he gave her the sword. He knew the effect he had on her, and exacerbated it. To set himself higher and higher in the eyes of their village and people, he would prod her on to lower and lower depths. While she sought to distance herself from him, from his timidity and adherence to routine, he flourished in it.

Did she truly wish she was wrong, that doom was not coming? Or would she look on the rest with pride and contempt to be proven right? There would be a glimmer, at least, she knew that. There had to be. True, she wanted to be wrong, for life to go on for her people much as it had. Well, somewhat like it had. Except she wanted to return home—their true home. She didn't want them to be destroyed, just...awoken.

But the cost of that waking... She wished, prayed, *wept* for that cost to go unpaid, but knew it would not. She had far overslept, once, and her back felt in knots from inactivity. Her people overslept, and the prophecy told her their backs would be broken when they finally opened their eyes.

Broken, again. It had been broken before, and she felt they had been hobbled ever since, able only to shuffle painfully through history. What would a second breaking do? And why didn't they fear it the way she did? Weakened as they had become, this time could only kill them.

Unless, of course, they were right and she was wrong. *Hakana, prove me wrong.*

The days grew as bleak as her thoughts as they made their way north, step by step, closer and closer to the Glowwood. Snows began, softly at first and usually melting in between. As mid-month approached they stuck fast, a constant blanket softening the stones and hollows and making Tarafel's steps slick. She practiced with the sword to keep warm—though without a true opponent the heavy sword often felt awkward. But it kept her limber, allowed her to clear her thoughts. And, in truth, passed the time. Now she drew near, she hesitated to see the Glowwood again, feared it would be even worse than before.

Then, a week before spring solstice, she awoke to bare ground and a hovering mist—the snows had gone completely in the night. She and Tarafel both stared about in wonder. They seemed to have gone to bed mid-winter and slept near a month until spring.

"I suppose we should hurry, then," she whispered in awe. "Spring seems to be on time, despite all else."

Tarafel sensed her urgency and galloped without her prodding. As the mist vaguely brightened with the dawn, rains fell in torrents. The only thing guiding them were the waves crashing to their right and far below, a dull throbbing roar reminding them the cliffs were near.

Three days of rain passed, then turned to lightning and thunder. More than once a bolt exploded against a tree near them. Once a great branching crown nearly consumed them, hurled to the ground as they rode underneath, the branches sweeping through the air with a terrible rending sound. Tarafel screamed and bolted, coming only slowly back under her control. She reined him completely to a halt, and it seemed the roar was directly below them. She panted, fearing to see through the rain the great cliffs, and them on a softening edge. She backed him quickly away, and when he refused she turned him forward and northward. Only when they splashed through deepening waters did she understand: Raktar, and the falls of Gawad. They were less than a half-day from the Glowwood.

Would it be here? Could she be standing now on the site of their arriving doom? Prophecy was a terrible thing, she realized: difficult to interpret beforehand, but also hastening a dread not yet arrived. Her last time here, she had wished she could stop and see the falls. Many times before, especially in autumn, it had been a place of limitless beauty. She had found comfort here, joy, inexpressible peace.

But now, because of prophecy, she sat in terror as the sky fell around her. Her mind, instead of being filled with images of light and wonder were filled with thick darkness, of battles not yet joined, of scenes of death. Both had felt as real to her as waking sight, in their time. How could it be?

She turned Tarafel back, found a thick stand of maples, and dismounted. She would not brave mighty Raktar in the dark. Hopefully the storm would break, or at least slack enough during daytime to see the land.

For two more days, it did not, and she and Tarafel remained in the maples and in shadow. Full moon was approaching, the time of the prophecy—she knew the clouds had to break, at least on the horizon, for her to see the full moon hanging low.

While earthen guardians give out their soul and slide into oblivion's door. She had not yet interpreted that line. What were the earthen guardians? Spiritually, the Kalen were—placed by Praka and Hakana to protect the world, at least in part. The soul of the Kalen should have been love of the land. They loved comfort, now. And this doom might slide them into oblivion's door. Except that sounded like the fulfillment of the prophecy, while the line was part of the fulfillment. Not the Kalen.

Mythologically, there was a creature referred to only in ancient texts, no longer present or relevant by Averlynn's time. Her people called them the *Anggika*—the Eternal. A strange race neither human nor animal, long since gone from their land but existing—they had to be, or they were not eternal—in other lands far away. What the texts were less clear about was what their role in the world was—why they were made eternal, or what exactly they were and what they were capable of. And, important to Averlynn, how she could tell if they were giving out their soul.

Environmentally. Many things protected the earth—creatures great and small protected their dens, stone protected earth from being washed away, the trees...

The trees protected the earth from the full force of rain, and their roots kept the earth from sliding away in great chunks when the soil was saturated. If the trees gave out their soul—either died, or somehow abandoned part of their role—they and the land could slide into...whatever "oblivion" was. A landslide. It made the most sense given the weather, and the rapid change from summer through to spring.

And, luckily or unluckily, easy to observe. Also easy to get caught up in, if she stood on the land that was sliding.

But how would that allow the doom to arrive? It seemed to come from the sea—she already thought the northern peoples would be arriving by boat. But boats had come south before, and were either shipwrecked or turned back. The great cliffs...

She sat upright. If the cliffs slid away, into the ocean, there would be a new ravine, a route into the interior where there never had been before.

And north of the Glowwood, the rock cliffs gave way to earthen cliffs for a space, in the corner of a large bay. This was doubly disturbing, for 'south,' if not referring to south of the Glowwood, meant something else unexpected—or south from the former lands of the Prosan.

But she couldn't worry about that now. Full moon was coming, sooner than the journey south would take. And the 'expected' inroad was still northerly, only a day or so away.

As if by her wishes—or her desperate need—the rains slacked enough the next morning to begin riding for the bay. The Raktar was swollen, but near the falls still shallow enough to cross. While the rain did not lift, or the iron clouds stretching to the horizon break, it slowed enough she could bring Tarafel to a gallop where the land firmed. She wondered if her people worried about the only-weeks-long winter already turning to spring after so long a summer. Surely, when she returned especially with the fulfillment of the prophecy, they would accept her word. They could turn the tide of whatever was coming if they fought together. They had to be able to.

She veered a little westward for an afternoon, just to skim beside the Glowwood. She wanted to see, to make sure—oddly, it looked as it should, now. As it ever had when winter gave way to spring. Deep in some hollows there were caps the size of acorns already poking through, flourishing in the cold and wet. She hoped desperately for it to grow back the way it was. If all else fell apart, she hoped at least the follies of her people wouldn't destroy the land as well. It had not chosen this, should not be forced to bear the weight of their missteps.

She arrived the following day, looked out across bleakness—a rolling, dark ocean below heavy gray clouds. The rain had picked up again but was not blinding. She paused where the forest thinned, at the last vestiges of rock. It had to be here. Or, if it wasn't, she might spend days riding along the coast looking, and that only if her interpretation was correct.

A great bolt of lightning speared the sky as the winds rose. The thick clouds rolled closer and darkness fell. The trees bobbed in the winds as limberly as dandelions, their branches crashing and clattering. Tarafel's eyes rolled as he pranced. The wind rose to a howl, roaring along the cliffs.

When it seemed the world itself was set to whirl away, suddenly a pale light broke forth, stretching stippled across the ocean and gleaming in her eye. Her protector, her comfort, now signaling doom: Hakana appeared below the clouds across the sea as she began her circuit of the night.

The wind suddenly stilled as though the land held its breath. Then, with a shriek, it struck harder than ever. Before her was a terrible rending as an unseen blow bent the trees nearly in half. It hit her a moment later, knocking her from her horse and against a tree. For a moment she thought she might die beneath Tarafel's hooves as he bolted.

The roar rose, the crumbling of an entire plain. Trees were sucked into a whirlpool of earth like twigs in the Raktar. A great wave was thrust out to sea as dirt poured out of the face of the cliff and across the rocky shoals. A great plume stretched out, and the land sunk.

Averlynn threw herself into the tree's embrace, huddled against it as her terror came to life. While the oak shuddered it did not move, anchored in the rock as it was. She heard Tarafel only faintly distant. He had found a sense of safety as well and would not leave her further.

Finally the roar subsided. The rain only pattered, the thunder grew distant. She worked her fingers loose, took one deep breath to steady herself, and looked up.

Before her was a broad valley, broken by rock and ragged but not steep, its bottom in the sea. She would not walk it now, would certainly not risk Tarafel on its slopes. But it could be ascended.

A way into her land was open to the sea. And pale Hakana, her protector, gleamed dully off a ghostly banner bobbing on the ocean far to the north.

A ship, sails mostly furled, was drawing closer.

I4

A PATCH OF DARKNESS

"He grows impatient."
"Then tell him the time has come."
"He is yours?"
"He will be. And it will start now."

29 Nuamon 1320 — Spring

Ketzler stood near the bow, wrapped in oiled leathers. He turned as the gunwales brightened, saw a pale full moon against blue skies peering through a break in the clouds to the east. He smiled grimly. It would be nice to be wherever that break was, out of this incessant rain.

But the winds here continued to blow, continued to send their ship bobbing like a penitent man first come back to cathedral after a long absence. He had sighed long, though internally, when the captain ordered sails furled. They'd been on their journey long enough for Ketz to get over his sea-sickness, but it made no sense to drive them fast in the dark through seas that had claimed so many other good Cariste boats.

He glanced back, knew the helmsman saw the same pale light that he did. The captain, in his many-windowed cabin, would probably see it too. Ketz hunched against the possibility of letting out sails again.

But the only sounds continued to be the wind and rain, and the creaking of ropes. Maybe with the great storm still in front of them, they would continue to lay off.

Behind him, a hatch scraped open. He looked back and saw Karbae ascending, hooded in her own leathers. She turned quickly to slide the hatch shut behind her, then came and stood beside him. The ship rolled, and though they had learned by now to brace themselves, she let her hand swing over, her fingers only briefly intwining with his before pulling away as the ship lurched back.

He glanced at her, at the gentle curve of her smile. For all of his formative years, girls had been forbidden—would always be forbidden. In the unit, relationships were forbidden. Outside the unit, relationships were near-impossible with the training loads they were made to carry. He hadn't thought those dictates would be a struggle.

Karbae seemed to ignore them, flagrantly at times, and in the presence even of Captain Pike. She didn't exactly throw herself at him, and certainly didn't throw herself at anyone else. But she never let her presence go unnoticed when he was near, and always managed to be beside him whenever they gathered. And Captain Pike neither encouraged nor discouraged her.

At first, he didn't mind. In fact, he very much enjoyed it. He enjoyed the glances between them, the occasional touches—like the one a moment ago—the sharing of joy and apprehension when the orders were finally given to the entire unit. Then they had stared, but only as fellow-soldiers.

He still wondered about this plan, about what it might mean for the soldiers and civilians. For so long the idea had been entrenched in their culture: no one sailed south. For a time, shipwrights were forbidden from even building boats that *could* go into deep waters. The only trading ships permitted were those originating from overseas. That had proved untenable first—long before Ketzler was born, but he'd read about it—and eventually boats were allowed to be built but could only follow accepted trade-routes.

Everything since then had been formed around the idea that Gintanos-that-was existed only north of the Brynth. There was no more land to the south. There were mountains, and then the southern sea. Their people could not be allowed to think that any solution to their problems lay that way. You found a way to get along with your close neighbor, to cultivate denser crops, to raise cattle on less ground. Or you could go to Burieng, or South Pal Isan, or back to Carist. If you could afford passage, and the means to start a new life.

He wondered, too, who had first brooked the idea that they might go south. It had to have been a religious leader. A merely intellectual leader would have a hard time convincing enough others to make it stick. But a religious leader could claim he heard from the God, or at least felt a pressure. There would be enough adherents in the Senates to then give the idea room to grow.

Maybe that was his bias. Karbae always inclined away from his more devout tendencies. She never refuted him outright, but often the conversation would stop as soon as he brought in a religious element. It shamed him that, sometimes, he would keep it to himself for the sole purpose of continuing to hear her voice.

He tensed as she leaned closer, suddenly. "By the way," she said, "you need to report to Captain Pike."

He stared at her as his heart thumped. "Why did you wait to tell me that?"

But she only smiled at him impishly until he hurried for the hatch, muttering to himself. Maybe Captain Pike never said anything because he was to handle it himself. He glanced at her back as he turned to descend, his heart wrenching just a little. As good a soldier as he wanted to be, he knew already he would do nothing to put distance between them. He only hoped she would respect the unspoken boundary.

He slid the hatch shut. The interior was dim, the small prisms meant to let in daylight from above having no daylight to let in. "Where's Captain Pike?" he asked the first solder he saw. He pointed aft, and Ketz went.

He still remembered their first days aboard, remembered the aching shoulders from how often he swayed into a bulwark as he tried to make his way fore or aft belowdecks. Now he was often able to anticipate the roll, could sense the roughness of the seas or not through his feet. He was able to move quickly, now. Nights like tonight were harder, for certain, as storms swept around and over them. But not impossible. He never would have thought it. Of course, ensconced in his cathedral so many months ago, he never would have thought any of it.

He was surprised to find not only Captain Pike but Ship's Captain Prothiar Kareged as well. They looked up when he entered, but resumed their conversation as though un-interrupted. Ketz stood to the side and waited.

"I said this was a fool's voyage," Kareged said. Under his hands was a map of the coastline. "Cliffs the whole way down, at least as far south as anyone has ever gotten; treacherous, changing seas and moving shoals, rocks—"

"I thought this was taken care of, or at least discussed," Pike returned. She sounded frustrated and irritated—and not necessarily at Captain Kareged alone.

"Huh," he said sharply, and shook his head. "If it was, it was not with me. I heard it as you were boarding. Too late then, wasn't it. We might have brought hooks or ladders or something to help us scale, if such a place could be found."

"And why do you bring this up now?"

"Because it was nigh-impossible before we ran into these storms. Now?" He shook his head and glared at the map. "Hard enough to provender a crew. All your troops as well, and in the face of endless storms? Your superior asked—nay, not asked: assumed and told as if mere statement—the impossible. Sail further south than any of our maps show but his own? If we'd fair weather, maybe. But there was a reason we stopped sailing south, you know."

"If you find it hard to provender our troops and your crew, wait until we try to provender our people with the failing fields of the north," Captain Pike replied evenly.

"That's nae my fault either," Kareged grumbled.

Pike sighed. "What do you think, Ketzler?" she asked. Though she looked at him, Kareged still glared at his maps.

It shocked him less and less when he was addressed like this. As it happened, Captain Pike would suddenly ask whoever was nearby what their thoughts were—no regard for rank or experience. So he applied himself to the problem with less apprehension as he did the first days.

"No storm lasts forever," he said, "no matter what this seems. We set sail in what seemed summer, and fall and winter both passed in the space of weeks? A month or two?"

Both Captains looked as unsettled as he felt. He had never prayed so much, internally and aloud for the crews and troops, as he did since they sailed. Weather and wind turned almost immediately, and snows came after a week upon the sea, icing the deck and the rigging. Captain Kareged had been prepared for the eventuality—not knowing how long they would be upon the water—but not the immediacy. Of course they worried the God suddenly rose against their mission. It took every scrap of the Histories Ketzler knew to persuade them that the God would understand and bless their need.

"Perhaps spring will progress as normal, or perhaps it too will pass in a few weeks." An even more disturbing notion. Would the years suddenly pass in the space of months? Would they all grow old and die after a mere year on the sea? "Regardless, there is much change in the air. Why not much change on the land as well?"

The Captains looked at each other. Captain Kareged looked aside first, directly at Ketzler. He'd lost an eye some years ago, and often left the socket empty and uncovered to kill any sort of question someone of the crew might have. It gaped now, but even in its hollow Ketzler thought he saw a gleam. "And why should the land change in our favor?"

Ketzler shrugged to hide his shiver. "Why shouldn't it, sir? Why assume things will end badly? They may just as easily end well."

"Spoken with the arrogance of youth," he growled. "As you grow older, perhaps you'll find in the long years of study that things just as often go badly—or more often."

"This doesn't serve us," Captain Pike cut in. "If they end badly, they do. We must press on with the assumption it will end well for us. Otherwise we may as well dash ourselves against the nearest rock and be done." How Captain Pike stood up to Kareged's blind eye, Ketzler didn't know, but she did, and he finally looked away. "Now," she continued, voice gentler. "What is our plan?"

"I say we anchor," Kareged replied. "It doesn't serve us to sail on in the dark. If the land has changed, we need to see it. If the storms will pass, we need to wait for it."

"But will the ships hold up to such battering?"

"No. Not forever. But if it's to end well, they'll have to, won't they?"

"Captain Kareged, the seas are impossible enough without your belligerence! We need real plans, not sarcasm and idiocy."

Captain Pike's harangue continued, but slurred and faded in Ketzler's ears. The swaying of the ship seemed to slow. He watched the two captains arguing as though from a distance, while he sank below waves that didn't drown him but somehow enveloped him in a safe but freezing cocoon. He panicked at first, sure the water would suddenly break into his lungs. Then it came to him as a curiosity. Somehow he could still sense his ears being buffeted by their shouting, knew his mind was troubled that their mission was already endangered. He longed to reach out and comfort them, calm their storms as well as the storm outside. He had been trying, desperately, through prayers to and for the crew since they weighed anchor on calm shores.

Words came to him, and instantly he was back above the water. "The way south is open," he said.

The captains broke off immediately and stared at him. By their reaction, he almost wondered if it hadn't been his voice: they startled as if they thought someone else was in the room.

"What did you say?" Captain Pike asked first.

What did *I say?* he wondered.

The way south is open.

A thought, not his own, originating outside himself but as sure as the deck below his feet. He repeated it.

"How do you know that?" Kareged scoffed.

In Ketzler's own confused silence, Captain Pike spoke up. "He is our religious leader," she said. Her certainty seemed to grow as she spoke. "Perhaps the God has given him a word to still our bickering." She glared at Kareged again, and for a wonder he again backed down. She directed her gaze at Ketzler. "Do we anchor, or keep sailing?"

"I have no word on that," Ketzler said. He didn't even know where the first word came from, if it had truly come from the God or not. But he latched onto it, if only to keep them from descending into chaos again. "But if the way south *is* open, and this word comes now to give us peace, then surely we will find that way even if we are driven ahead of a storm in the dark. We will have to, if this is to end well," he added, ignoring Captain Kareged's hollow socket as best he could.

He worried he had gone too far with that last. Captain Pike's sharp glance told him she worried at that too. But Kareged seemed content to ignore the barb.

"So we sail on," he said, and the two Captains nodded to each other.

"Is that all you needed?" Ketzler asked.

"No, actually," Captain Pike replied. "We were considering you for promotion—not to lead scout, obviously, only corporal. But as a full scout. You would work directly with Drunae to expand your abilities that you might be more effective once we arrive on land." Her gaze flickered.

"However, there are some issues that you have not dealt with the way a corporal should."

Ketzler's breath caught. *Karbae.* Did Captain Kareged know? He didn't seem to. His gaze on the maps was not forced. So. That was the way.

"Your progress is in your hands," she continued. "You have the ability, the capacity, if you want to fill it. But I will not force you. You must decide what it is you want. Do I make myself clear?"

"Yes, ma'am," he replied quietly.

"That is all."

Ketzler returned numbly to the deck, banging against every bulkhead this time. The rains had returned even fiercer, the sky was impossibly darker, and thunder rumbled to the south.

A hand was on his shoulder. "What did they want?" Karbae asked, her lips nearly brushing his ear. She did it to be heard, and yet...

He turned and looked at her, her face sheltered under the flapping hood, her eyes considering him, concerned for him—loving him? It didn't seem like she could, not so soon. And yet.

He glanced aside a moment. The helmsman kept an eye on the waves and the wind, and in flashes of lighting on the cliffs far away to their right. Between flashes, Ketzler thought perhaps the man watched them. Captain Pike already knew; Captain Kareged seemed not to. He would know, if the helmsman watched. And yet.

He looked back to Karbae. She seemed to wait, the slightest of impish smiles on her lips as she glanced down at Ketzler's mouth and back up. He could be a corporal, grow even further in his new-found abilities, rise higher through the ranks of the Cariste military—far higher than he thought when he'd run away from the cathedral. All he had to do was tell Karbae to leave him alone for a time. Surely not forever—just a time.

And yet.

She leaned ever-so-slightly forward. He felt himself drawing closer, too.

The wind rose to a howl around them. Far away there was a great crashing. They both pulled away and looked landward at the noise. The seas rose underneath them as the helmsman shouted at them to grab hold of a line, to secure themselves. The ship pitched suddenly heavenward, then lurched toward the depths. Clinging to one another now in fear instead of love, they scrambled toward the mainmast. Ketzler grabbed a rope and wrapped it around them both, tying it swiftly onto the pin.

The ship spun one way, then another as the helmsman wrenched frantically on the wheel, trying to keep it erect and cutting through the waves instead of along them. The water itself struggled to follow a line, pitching and bucking as though it wrestled against some deeper foe.

As Ketzler worried he would be sick again, the wind suddenly calmed, though there was a strange, residual roar. He barely noticed at first. To the east the clouds broke, and the full moon gleamed underneath and sent its glow across waves that barely chopped now.

But the roar grew, almost a whine, pitching up as it grew louder. It seemed also to be drawing away, moving across the sea and over land.

There was a terrific thump, as though some great hammer struck the earth, and it echoed across the water. A moment later, a fog raced toward them at dizzying speed. He clutched Karbae tightly as she screamed. He would have as well, except his throat tightened too far to emit it.

The fog bank slammed into them, rolling the boat nearly on its side. The cross braces dipped into the water. The railing came within a handbreadth of the black ocean. But the rope held tight. Ketzler glanced upward: sickeningly now the full moon lay above the top of the mast, though still on the horizon, as the fog continued to race across the sea.

Shuddering, the ship began to right. He thought for sure the mast should break, the top crashing down upon him and Karbae now trapped helplessly at its base. It swung a great arc through the air with a rush as the ship pitched the other way, then came back.

Beneath them the waters rolled and roared and slapped. Quickly, but feeling an eternity, the ship bobbed only as if upon rough seas. Ketzler's breath found his lungs again and he gasped. Karbae's gaze was upon him again, her chest heaving, the whites of her eyes stark in the night. Their attempted kiss was long forgotten.

He looked landward again. A faint roar still echoed, and he thought maybe he heard a crackling like a hundred branches snapping, and the sound of gravel falling in the water.

There were shouts below, and boots thumped across planking. Captains Pike and Kareged emerged from the hatch. Captain Pike clutched her arm, and Ketzler wondered if it was broken.

"Damages!" Kareged roared.

The helmsman, shaken, answered as he could. Pike's glance finally found the two of them, tied to the mainmast. Ketzler undid the rope calmly, betraying no indication of what preceded them ending up together in such a way. Karbae seemed to do the same.

"What happened?" Pike asked. Ketzler explained as best he could, but no one could really understand. "Does this have to do with your little prophecy?" Pike asked, when he finished.

Ketzler shrugged. "It would seem to fit, but..." He gestured landward: what could be made out in the dark was still stark cliffs of sheer granite.

"The scouts may need tending," Pike said. "Lovely that our physician is on the other ship. You see to it."

"What about you?" he asked.

She grinned wryly. "I'll tend to myself when I can. Tell none of them what you told Captain Kareged or myself—only what you saw, if you absolutely must. We don't know yet what this will mean, and I want no speculation. Now get below. Karbae, you stay on watch for a spell."

The glance Karbae gave Ketzler as he turned to descend told him she remembered, now, what had almost happened. It told him, as well, it would happen again. He returned a brief, mischievous grin.

The troops below were as full of questions as Pike assumed, and Ketzler spoke peace to them as best he could. Fortunately for their mission he found mostly bruises. If they made land in the coming days, they would only have five unable to contribute fully. Some would have reduced capability, but there would be plenty of tasks still to occupy them.

Captain Pike came along presently, and he helped set her arm. It was a minor break to her forearm, and they splinted it quickly. When he finished, and gave his report on the injuries below, she sent him topside again.

"You know better than others what you're looking for," she said. "Look for it. And send Karbae to me, please."

"Yes, ma'am," he said quickly. Perhaps she meant to give her the same choice as she had tried to give him. He wondered if it would work, and how far Captain Pike might go to help them choose as a corporal should.

He went up. The air had calmed, the clouds overhead paler. The full moon still shone bright, reflecting off the waves and the granite cliffs. He sent Karbae below and turned to the railing. Along the shore the moon glimmered even brighter, probably upon surf, underlining brightly the rocky shore.

How could they make it onto land? If Captain Kareged had been correct, that sailing for the far southern tip was foolish, perhaps they could have equipped better. Sent a party up the cliffs, the way they had made it over the Brynth so many months ago—at least, over the first pitch. It was no wonder the Cariste had never moved south overland. He couldn't help but shake his head now at the memory. How had anyone even made it to their edge? And with a shod horse? It meant it was possible, he supposed, but after their report and the incredulity even in Sadroe's voice, Captain Liptieri deemed the sea route still the viable one. It was impossible that those cliffs continued the entire way south, true. But how much easier to simply scale a cliff with enough troops and supplies to explore the land? It's not like they had to worry about getting horses up there: they had brought none of those, either.

It put them at a disadvantage, he knew, when they would come across the people who so clearly lived there. A shod horse meant the visitor was not alone; they would have iron, and be able to mine for it and forge it. That one hoof print bespoke a civilization—an entire civilization just to their south, that they had never encountered since they had landed on the continent...how long ago? It boggled his mind to consider it—and yet it was now reality.

Thumping footsteps caught his attention, and he turned to see Captain Kareged pacing across the deck. He gazed at the moon, the seas, the clouds. As Ketzler watched, momentarily distracted from the shoreline, Kareged turned and seemed to sniff the wind, then look toward the helmsman. Ketzler looked too, and the helmsman looked at them both expectantly.

"On deck!" the captain bellowed suddenly. Instantly there was a rushing of feet below as sailors poured through the hatch. "Lower the mainsail; turn us to the wind. We've got ourselves a calm, enough to make a little way. Half the mizzen! We won't risk ourselves too much yet. Up to the nest with you!"

It took Ketzler a moment to realize the captain was speaking to him. No one had been up to the crow's nest in weeks. The seas had been too rough. Ketzler admitted now they had calmed considerably. He leapt to obey.

As he scrambled up the ropes he passed those letting out the mainsail. While he didn't relish the height, he enjoyed it. Yet he could not imagine himself out on the spar, supported only by a shaking rope and one's own sense of balance.

From the top, he could nearly see over the cliffs to the land beyond—or at least felt like he could. Enough to see there were still no mountains: those had ended after a few days' sailing south. Still an impossible number of miles thick, but not endless.

He could also see the white surf, again, but now a little more of their breadth. Instead of thin white underline, he saw now a broader stroke tinged blue, luminescent, that deepened as the wave rushed ashore to break. He thought he had perhaps seen it on other nights, but never so clearly as this. It fascinated him as it stretched along the entire coast, it seemed, from as far north as he could see, all the way—

Except it broke. Further south there was a patch of darkness that spread out, fan-shaped, from the coast. With the strange blue-lit waves it stood out in stark contrast. He continued to stare as he felt the ship pick up speed beneath him.

The land rocked—of course, it was actually the ship, but it felt that way—his eyes fixing on that spot. It neared, would pass by before long. As it came abeam, this strange dark fan, his gaze lifted from the absence of the blue luminescence, seeing the darkness spread upward. A great, dark triangle marring the cliffs—

"Captain!" he shouted down. He looked up again, unbelieving. He could barely make out, in the moonlight, broken and shattered trees scattered across the dark triangle. And he could see more trees near the top—could see their bases.

"Well, what is it? Shoals?"

"Land!" he shouted, immediately feeling silly. He didn't know what else to say. The words finally came. "There's been a landslide! The cliffs are given out!"

The captain's response was much more decisive. "Reef those sails! Drop anchor! Bring me a glass!"

As the sailors scrambled to undo everything they had just done, Ketzler continued to stare. Where had been blank cliffs he could suddenly see deeper into the interior of a land that had been closed to them, it was assumed forever.

No longer. The way south was open. The Cariste would expand, find new lands to harvest and grow. They would survive.

He sobered. But only if their three ships of troops survived long enough for Captain Kareged to return northward for provisions and more troops. With an unknown civilization on that same land, that possibility was far from guaranteed.

15

THERE AND THEN GONE

"This must stop. Illmali requires your obedience."
"He is a fool, and I will not."
"You outstep your bounds!"
"When I am done, he will thank me."

30 Nuamon 1320 — Spring

The next day actually dawned. A red sun rose above the horizon, glowing orange against the granite cliffs north and south. The triangle of landslide, a mere blackness before, was now a tumbled mass of dark brown flecked with gray, chestnut, and stark white of shattered trees.

The ships sat at anchor, bobbing on seas devoid of their previous bluster. A perfect day to launch the boats to shore and make the Cariste's first ever ingress into the southern lands.

Forests in the north were sparse. Those that remained were harvested carefully for lumber severely rationed. The trees grew in ordered rows, planted for harvesting later. Often they were filled with the sounds of saws, the occasional shout just before the rush and thump of falling timber.

The forest Ketzler could see atop the valley was wild, thick, and silent. He knew it would soon fill with the same sounds of saws. They would need to build fortifications, establish their foothold on the land until the return of the ships. But before then he would hear a natural forest, the sounds of birds and animals that perhaps had long been gone from the north.

And there would be a people intimately familiar with land completely foreign to his people. He needed to be sharp, focused, working tirelessly to gain some level of intimacy as quickly as possible.

But Karbae stood behind him. He could feel her presence even after he looked away, and a constant thought nagged at him. He looked forward to every moment together with her, even if their work kept their focus apart. And, if he dwelled too long, he desired to be sharp, focused, and working tirelessly to gain some level of intimacy with her.

He gritted his teeth. Captain Pike had been right: he could never be a corporal at war with his own desires. He had left the cathedral for this! An entire life before him, cast aside for one purpose. But now he was here, his future as bright as the one he left behind, and he was ready to leave this one behind as well? For her?

Her brown eyes and plaited hair flashed before him, and the sight of her walking away, and he knew he would chase her relentlessly. And she would not fight it, would not make him chase too hard.

Oddly, the thought calmed him. It was no question: he would be with her. And in so thinking, he knew he would not have to chase her immediately. She would be there, even if just out of reach. All he would need to do was reach out, and they would meet.

And so he *could* focus on the task at hand. Maybe he wouldn't be corporal, but he could be an excellent scout. He could protect his fellow-soldiers, and so also protect Karbae. He glanced back at her, at those glittering, intelligent eyes as they scanned the shore ahead. She knew he looked at her, and gave the briefest glance, the briefest smile—and yet it signaled a lifetime. He smiled back, then turned firmly toward shore.

"Board!" Captain Pike shouted. Curani, Ketzler, Karbae, Alblox, Zyphor, Fortu, and Mordel clambered over the side and into the boat. Sailors lowered them with block and tackle until the boat splatted upon the water. Curani grabbed an oar and pushed them away. The other ships similarly lowered a boat each. Oars went out, and they crabbed across the water toward shore.

For now, Ketzler pulled as hard as he could, looking back at the ship. Captain Pike stared at him. She had probably seen as he gazed at Karbae. He didn't care. If it became a true problem, he would deal with it later.

The other boats angled toward them, steered each by their corporal as the scouts pulled the oars. They would land first, scout quickly for an immediate threat. Each corporal had a red flag and white: white signaled all was well, and to send the rest of the soldiers. Red signaled retreat, and their sacrifice of death before an overwhelming force. The trick, Ketzler knew, was what constituted an overwhelming force. With barely three Cariste squads ashore, even ten enemies on horseback with either lances or bows could overwhelm them, and certainly hold out against the nearly 500 troops that would come as swiftly as possible across the waters. They would struggle to climb the broken valley, well within range of the archers. If they had them. If they were even there.

He itched to turn and look at the land, to see if he could spot anyone on it. He looked at Curani. The corporal's eyes studied the terrain, but his face was inscrutable. And so Ketzler pulled.

"Ease up," Curani whispered. Discordantly, they eased on their oars. They had not spent much time practicing this part. An oar on the other side, still pulled too hard, clacked loudly against another. Curani's gaze flickered hard, but then returned. He was looking upward, now.

Ketzler's back itched, waiting for an arrow to hit him between his shoulders. "Easy," Curani said again, and they pulled lighter. "Get ready."

Something scraped the bottom of the boat, and Ketzler jumped, nearly dropping his oar. He grabbed at it, splashing water as he got it back under control.

Another scrape, longer. "We're too far out!" Curani hissed. "Pull hard!"

They yanked, somehow in unison, and the boat shot forward. A scrape to the left, then right, jostling the boat. It stuck suddenly fast and everyone pitched toward the bow, oars clattering.

"Out!" Curani yelled.

Ketzler untangled himself from oars and others' legs and leapt over the side. He sank ankle-deep in muck. The shore was several lengths still ahead, perhaps three hundred paces. He struggled to run. His foot stuck, and he fell with a terrific splash. Around him, the rest of his squad had similar difficulties.

The soil was too fresh, disturbed only last evening. He floundered, splashing, taking great heaving steps. They all made their way forward, in complete disarray. He had imagined an orderly jog, onto shore, up the valley, with keen glances deeper into the interior assessing everything expertly and swiftly. This was not it.

As he feared, the soil onshore was little better than that in the water. Up close, now, he saw rivulets still running where water seeped out of the ground. They should have stayed aboard a few days, let the land dry. They worried, with the rains only recently passed, the clouds might return and make things worse.

Now, he wasn't sure how much worse they could get. His breath came in ragged gasps. The other two squads, he saw, fared a little better, managing to get further ashore before grounding out. The scouts, seeing what had happened to the first boat, proceeded more cautiously and intentionally.

The land seemed impossibly steep. If the enemy had archers, they were doomed. But when he looked up, he saw nothing but land and sky. They seemed to be alone.

His gasps forced him to go slower. As a unit, they seemed spent. Even Curani climbed methodically. Surely if they were to be repulsed, it would have happened by now. Below, the other units had already made the same assessment. They straggled, placing each step.

Ketzler looked at his squad, still bunched in some sort of spear formation. "Should we spread out?" he called softly to Curani.

He looked up and nodded quickly. Ketz angled left toward scattered outcroppings, where perhaps the granite neared the surface. It might offer better purchase, allow him to catch his breath before cresting the top. Great oaks and maples stood that way, too.

He slowed further, nearly creeping. As the thunder of blood in his ears lessened, he began to hear the native sounds. Despite the scar on the land, the birds deeper in carried on as they would any other dawn. He recognized none of the calls.

As his eyes finally crested the top, he stopped, hand on his sword. It felt more comfortable to grip the hilt now than it had when he first began training—but was still not familiar.

The spaces between the trunks held no enemy force with bows bent. Wreathing the trunks were thin tendrils of mist—remnants, he supposed, of the storms that had come through. Though wild and disordered, the trees themselves were similar to those he knew. There was perhaps more undergrowth, more fallen and discarded branches. In the cultivated woods back north those would have been cleared immediately.

A squirrel chittered. Ketzler took a few more steps closer to the top. A bird launched itself skyward, and south. He watched it closely. It seemed like any other bird, a crow—larger, perhaps, but still only a crow.

He glanced across, saw the rest of his squad arrayed along the parapet and the other two squads coming quickly behind to fill the gaps. Curani looked at him, got the attention of the rest of his squad: *up and in,* his gesture commanded.

Ketzler pressed forward, onto firm ground among the trees. He kept his hand on his sword, but didn't pull it free just yet. A distant watcher might see the flash of bare steel before they saw his dun clothing. He took a few steps in, still—he knew—in view of Curani. His eyes searched the interior, saw nothing out of place. He looked at his feet.

There was a gash, a bright scrape of rock under the moss. Several scrapes, long, and spread out. He knelt. The moss that remained was thick, putting forth their spring stalks.

But there, beyond the scrapes... He crouched lower: the stalks were broken in an oblong area. Something had lain there. He took a few hurried steps forward, inspecting. Not the same thing that made the scrapes. Those scrapes—if he had to assess their size and distance from one another—were from a horse. This tamped-down area was human-sized—not a large human. He knelt down in the middle of the space. Someone perhaps his size, maybe slightly larger.

His eyes came up again, darting around the forest. Whoever it had been had likely witnessed the landslide. Surely they saw the boats as well? Surely they watched him now? He felt strange, as though such a person stood very near him—impossibly near.

Invisibly near.

He looked up sharply, searching branches in bud but not yet leaf. Nothing could hide up there, not even behind the great burl of the oak nearest him.

He backed slowly away, then signaled to Curani: *important, but not yet dangerous.* He glanced quickly, saw him grip the red flag as he strode over. Curani tapped Mordel as he passed, who followed. The other squads had arrived now, setting up a defensive perimeter along the parapet.

"What is it?" Curani whispered as they arrived.

Ketzler pointed. "Fresh scrapes. Someone sat or lay here, and recently."

Curani scanned the ground. He could tell the scout found it difficult. "I see what you mean, but Ketzler, the odds..."

"Probably a deer, or some southern animal we don't know," Mordel whispered. His voice was low but Ketzler still heard the derision. It shocked him. During training they had never been at odds. Fine if Mordel didn't want to agree with him, but there seemed something deeper there.

Ketzler shrugged. "It is a strange land. You could be right," he allowed. "I didn't say death was imminent, did I?"

"Enough," Curani said, his voice rising. "You were right to call me over. Perhaps it is just some large, hoofed animal. Let's signal the rest, though. If it is a horseman, it is only one, and I'd rather have all our forces ashore before it brings reinforcements. Collapse on the center. We'll entrench for now."

With a final glance back, Ketzler followed. Curani quickly waved the white flag. As Ketzler looked out to sea, the ships came alive with their troops scrambling into boats and lowering away. They would come in four waves, for there was not enough seats to fit all 479 in one launch.

When they arrived at the center, the corporals quickly discussed: there had been no other signs or causes for worry. The land seemed empty except for wildlife.

"Let's build what fortifications we can," Drunae said when they had finished. "Just until the rest of the soldiers arrive. Curani, keep your squad here and keep watch. The rest of us will start bringing trees up here. Let's go."

While the others began scrambling down the hill to collect the broken timbers, Ketzler turned and looked out across the forest. The strangeness of it struck him anew. All their training had been further north, and he felt they had done a good job. But how was he to tell what looked strange here? And it might all be even stranger still, given the bizarre seasons. What might be normal or strange in another month's time?

Captain Pike had taught them well, and thoroughly; they were facing un unknown enemy, of unknown size and equipment, on completely unknown terrain. They could find themselves trapped against a bog, or pinned against a cliff, or simply in this tangled wood—they had practiced fighting among trees planted in rows and cleared of underbrush.

Their position here was far more precarious than he let himself understand when they were only rowing to shore. It was not only today that they faced annihilation—every day until they met the enemy and learned their tactics could be the day they were destroyed. The soldiers that Captain Kareged returned for would come back and find no one. It suddenly seemed to Ketzler supremely foolish to send almost all of their scouts—and certainly all of their best ones—to possible slaughter. Unless their intent was to prove to some faction within the Senate that the way south was still not an option. But that terrified him, and he wouldn't dwell on it. If annihilation was Captain Liptieri's plan, he would just have to do his best to thwart that plan.

Curani was suddenly beside him. "Everything okay, Ketz?" he asked.

He didn't feel like explaining all his fears. "Mostly," he said instead. "I'm eager to scout the land though. Are we moving on quickly once the soldiers get here?"

Curani shook his head. "No, that would be ill advised. We'll scout, and scout a lot—don't worry about that. But Captain Pike wants the soldiers to stay put until we know at least the fifteen miles around us." He glanced with raised eyebrow. "And I mean, *know*. Every fold and crease, I think are the words she used. If we run into a hostile people, she wants us all to know exactly how to move to the most defensible place—know it better, if we can, than they do. We won't survive otherwise."

Ketzler grinned. That sounded good to him. "When do we start?" he asked.

"I hope you've already started," Curani said with another raised brow. "What do you see from here?"

Ketzler grunted. "We'll have a lot more trouble maneuvering around here," he said.

Curani nodded appreciatively. "For sure. I'd guess a few detachments will spend the early days clearing the space around our fort so if we ever need to retreat toward it, we can move quickly. What else?"

"We can't trust the water sources."

Curani's brow furrowed. "Oh?"

"Well, as wet as it's been, a pool or stream might dry up in the summer, now matter how full or raging it is now."

"Well, yes and no. What might be some signs for us that we could trust it?"

Ketzler grinned, recalling the conversation he'd had with Miggey so long ago. "Swamp trees," he said. "Anything older than a year or two that only grows in wet places."

Curani nodded again. "True. And we'll need to learn if there are any new types of plants here that indicate the same thing."

They both fell silent for a time, and Ketzler returned to scanning the forest, looking for movement, listening for sounds.

"What's going on with you and Karbae?" Curani asked quietly.

Ketzler glanced sharply aside, barely managing to refrain from looking at her, a little further down the line. He frowned, and turned back to the forest. It wasn't Curani's business—it wasn't really anyone's business, was it? Captain Pike had laid out the choices.

"You're sharp, Ketz. You see the connections between things better than almost anyone. But you know you can't move up if you're in a relationship with another squadmember."

"Then move one of us to another squad."

Curani shook his head. "It won't help, not now that we're here. We'll be all moving together too often. Besides..." He trailed off, lips compressed.

"Besides, what?"

"It doesn't matter. You need to make your choice."

"I know that. And maybe I have, you know?"

Curani's gaze inspected him critically. "Care to share?" he asked.

Ketzler sighed. *Not really. At least, not in detail. And it's not your business!* "I think I can put my work first," he said.

"First." Curani sighed shortly. "It has to be only, Ketz. I can tell you, from my position, it's worth it."

Maybe to you. "I know. And I believe it will be worth it to me, too. I'm going to try, at least."

Curani gave a tight-lipped smile. "Guess I'll take it," he said. He clapped Ketz lightly on the shoulder and moved on.

Guess I'll have to deal with him too.

Now where did that thought come from?

Ketzler glanced back, across the sea. The boats were on their way, stuffed to the gunwales with troops. It would take them the better part of the day to get all the troops and supplies onto land and to the top of the valley. Not only the soldiers, they would need their provender, construction equipment—saws, hammers, files, measuring ropes, plumblines, trowels, shovels, and buckets. Forging equipment—he didn't envy those that would have to wrestle the anvil up those wet slopes. Even sized small, it was heavy and cumbersome. They had crates of materials for mending; crates of flax seeds and tools for scutching and hackling the flax once it was grown to make linen; seeds for wheat and corn, tomatoes, cucumbers, and cabbage; and enough jerked meat for a hank a day for two months.

And it all had to come ashore and be lugged up the wet slope. If he escaped even half of the work to be done, it was worth being a scout.

As the troops began their slog up the slopes, the rest of the scouts reconvened, having built a low wall of brush and logs to at least hinder any enemy forces who might arrive. The land remained silent and still. Drunae looked them all over. Faintly Ketzler could hear the soldiers huffing and puffing, still pitying them.

"We're going to range inland," Drunae said. "Sadroe, northwestward; Curani, southwestward. I'm going directly west. Obviously, look for signs of whoever lives here—if they live this far south. Curani, take the most caution in case the sign Ketzler saw was true."

Mordel scoffed, and Ketzler wondered again. Drunae's gaze barely flickered; he probably knew even less. He continued. "We're also looking for a good spot to camp. We don't want to stay too near the edge, here. If an enemy attacks, we don't want our back immediately to the sea—but neither would we wish to be easily flanked, or surrounded."

The other corporals' eyes widened, as did Ketzler's. How was that supposed to be achieved? Drunae nodded and raised a hand, acknowledging their unspoken questions. "We probably won't find it. But even if we can find something with good sight-lines, or perhaps difficult terrain..."

"But if the terrain is difficult to flank, won't it be just as difficult to retreat through?" Sadroe asked.

Drunae took a deep breath. "It's less about whether or not we can retreat. Captain doesn't want this ground to give way even further, and he doesn't want the temptation of an escape route. We're here, and—"

"'He'?" Sadroe and Curani chorused. They only knew of Captain Pike, and the ship's captain. Surely he wasn't staying...

"Um. Yeah. Forgot: and it's actually Commander Liptieri now. I found out this morning when Captain Pike sent me in her place." Drunae glanced out to sea, and everyone's eyes followed. The boats, relived of their cargo, had made far better time back to the ships and were already loading with their second wave. Even at the distance, Ketzler could make out the bright banner with the Ibex of Captain—*Commander* Liptieri, and the gleaming helmets of his personal guard.

"Seems he came along with us, but secretly. Made him leader of all forces here and yet to arrive. Even Pike didn't know, or so she said." Drunae shrugged. "Honestly I feel better, don't you?" He fixed the scouts with his gaze until he saw their acceptance, and agreement. "Alright, provision yourselves quickly, and let's go."

"Whistles," Curani said as he turned to his squad. "We'll need to spread out a little, to see as much as we can in this tangle, but also able to respond quickly if something goes wrong. And take some food; there is much ground to cover, and we may be searching for some time. Go."

The squad moved quickly, and by the time the Commander and his boats were halfway across the sea they were prepared to go. Most of the troops and supplies were now at the top. Ketzler watched as three of them still struggled up the slope with the anvil. He whispered a quick prayer of thanks and turned to the woods.

"Ketzler, up front," Curani said. "Wide spear," he added to the rest of the squad, then pointed a direction. Ketzler turned, noting the wind as he looked for any distant landmark to help him keep to the way. He thought he saw a hump of forest between the trees, and fixed it in his mind.

They moved out, entering deeper into the woods. Ketzler picked his way along, careful though the branches, trying to watch a hundred ways at once while also scanning the ground for further signs of what he had seen nearer the cliff's edge.

The strangeness of the land, the uncertainty of what lay ahead and around them, pressed in on him. He almost wished he hadn't seen the sign, wasn't worried about an immediate foe. Suddenly every burl and crooked branch spooked him, every rustle and crackle sent his nerves tingling. It seemed a great weight pressed on his back.

He paused, praying again. *If this is to end well, it must go well. Stop worrying about a potential foe. They either would have attacked by now, or will never. Not soon. It must be so.*

Their mission now was to find a good location for camp, not incite an attack. They weren't even sure the people here would attack. Plenty of Cariste history included landing on strange shores to a welcoming—if suspicious—people. They weren't the Rinc Nain, forcing themselves on natives and decimating or subjugating the people.

He took a deep breath and scanned again. It was just a forest, wilder perhaps but not sentient or malicious. And it was dry, aside from the previous torrential rains—mostly oaks and maples here, scattered ash.

They were still close to the shore, to the cliffs. Of more importance was what the land did as it went westward. He envied, now, Drunae's squad. He itched to see more of the interior of this wide land. The excitement of discovery touched him now, burrowed into his thoughts. A humble former-Pip, on land never trod by Cariste.

The land began to descend. The hump of forest he kept just a little to the right of their line of march rose higher. Here was scattered white oak—not indicative of wet land on its own, but paired with a buttressed cypress was clue enough. He glanced back and got Curani's attention, then made a broad circling motion with his arm: they would need to go around, rather than through, the bowl. Curani nodded, and Ketzler went.

At the top of the next rise—neither prominent or narrow enough for Ketzler to consider it a ridge—the forest thinned a little. Enough to see a succession of similar rises. He wondered, too, if each valley was as wet as the one behind him. Terrible ground, either way. Too many places to move unseen, too much to slow their own movements in anything larger than a squad.

He waited for Curani to come to him, and expressed his thoughts. Curani looked around a while, then nodded. "I agree. Let's strike a little further westward, see what we see. Perhaps—" He cut off as a great flock of small, dark birds to their east launched into the air with a screech. It reminded Ketzler of grackle, with heads that shimmered as they cleared the trees, but smaller.

They looked at each other, sure they were too far away to excite the birds. With unspoken agreement, Ketzler began moving slowly, methodically, that way. Curani made signals to the rest of the squad and they began to converge near the spot.

Ketzler tried to keep his breathing slowed, to calm a heart pounding blood through his veins. He strained his ears, strained his eyes. He kept a hand tight on his sword, until his aching tendons and need for balance forced him to relax.

There was no motion, no strange color that he could pick out. The mist that he had seen when they first landed was nearly gone, nearly burned off in the daylight, but here and there still clung. He stilled his mind against seeing menace in a gnarled branch, a burl, a leaning snag and stump.

Another signal from Curani, and the scouts fanned out, encircling the general area where the birds had taken flight. As they neared, the forms of boulders and breaching stone resolved themselves among the shadows.

Ketzler glanced down, froze, held a fist in the air. The rest of the scouts stopped in their tracks, trading glances between Ketzler, Curani as he moved up beside Ketzler, and the woods.

Ketzler pointed down. There were more scrapes in the mossy rock, similar—though not as scattered—as what they had seen near the cliff. Just off one of the rocks, fresh in the soil, was a shod hoof print.

Curani sucked in a breath. Ketzler's gaze was drawn to the tumble of rocks ahead, a perfect hiding place for a soldier or scout, if not their horse. And where could a horse have gotten? He scanned quickly, but saw no other sign.

There was a scrape, suddenly; a clatter. His sword came out. Next to him, Curani did the same. The semi-circle of scouts rang with drawn weapons.

Ketzler took another step forward. He startled at sudden movement. A squirrel appeared at the top of a boulder, holding something in its paws. Ketzler sighed. He glanced at Curani, chagrined. Curani rolled his eyes.

"A horse still made this sign, though," Curani said. He sheathed his sword, and the others followed suit. With a chitter, the squirrel leapt away, dropping whatever had been in its grasp. "Be careful, but let's check this rock garden."

The scouts moved, all sheathing swords. Ketzler went first to the rock where the squirrel had been. He glanced around for other sign, either hoof or foot. Something more than a squirrel had sent those birds into the air, and a horse would have been spotted by now. None of the rocks seemed big enough to hide a human, either. All he saw was the sticks and leaf-litter he would expect to see among rocks where wind would sweep little away.

He glanced at the top of the rock again, then froze. It was a bit of acorn or some other nut that the squirrel had left, but something looked odd about it—not what a nut would look like if a squirrel had simply discovered it on the ground. He picked it up, rolling it around in his fingers. He lifted it to his nose and sniffed.

"That better not be squirrel dung," Mordel said.

Ketzler shook his head, then held it out to Curani. "It's been roasted," he said. "Someone was here."

"I don't like this at all," Curani said. "We need to have all the troops here, and fortified, before we keep exploring in small groups. Go back. Take

Mordel. Report to the Commander and see what his orders are."

Ketzler nodded, ignored Mordel, and made his way back toward their beachhead. He picked up a light jog, hearing Mordel close behind. He angled eastward, to find the cliff and follow it back. As he ran, he glanced occasionally into the treetops. He looked for the oak with the burl he had seen near their previous sign. He knew it should be visible from the line he ran.

But suddenly the forest ended, the gaping valley below him. He stopped suddenly, and Mordel nearly ran into him.

"What the—?"

Ketzler paid no mind, glancing quickly around. There was the rock with the scrapes, the tamped-down moss. He looked up. That was the tree, he recognized the spread of the branches. But there was no burl. The trunk was smooth and straight.

The image of the boulder atop the cliff, when they had first arrived at the camp so many months ago when he was first made a scout, flashed to his mind. A strange hump, nearly human-sized, that was there and then gone. A large burl, there and then gone.

And as they approached the rock garden, there had been a burl, human sized, near a snag and leaning stump, horse-sized.

"Oh, God," he whispered. He pelted back the way he had come, ignoring still Mordel's shouts. He whipped out his sword as he saw the rocks come into view, gasping a sigh of relief to see the other scouts still there, Curani looking at him curiously.

The relief turned quickly to dread. The burl was gone, though the snag remained. So, not a horse. But still.

Their enemy was here, and nearly invisible—and could not possibly be human.

16

THE FIRST FAINT CLATTER

"The others are on their way."
"Which others?"
"My others."
"That could be helpful."

30 Nuamon 1320 — Spring

Averlynn crouched, breathless, as the young man—how had he been called? Ketzler?—searched the trees. Tarafel was farther south, his gray coat hiding him in the mists. She knew it had been a danger to move when they were so close, but worried Tarafel would come to her rescue if they came toward her.

It took her some time to remember their language. She had learned it when she was still in Old Kalen, what they called Burieng, before her people had abandoned the woods. The accent had changed since then, and some of the words—or it had developed differently here. But it came back to her as they had talked.

Now, they spoke too quietly for her to hear. Their looks and gestures spoke loudly enough: the young man knew her disguising glamour nearer the shore was the same as she'd had as she watched them approach the tumble of rocks. She knew she was in danger wearing it again now. They would look suspiciously at every bole, now.

But she needed to observe them more, see how many were coming, how they organized themselves, if they were prepared for war or not. This small scouting party moved like one, probing as though expecting an attack. Of course they couldn't know the nearest outpost was leagues away, or that those outposts would not be ready for actual conflict. Unless she told them.

She touched her ring, closing her eyes and visualizing the tree she was in with a large, broken branch. A glamour was always a matter of faith, but one she took easily now. As long as she believed she looked like a branch, she would look like one. There were, of course, limits: the glamour had to be something roughly her size. She could not be a squirrel, as convenient as that might be. And she could not be multiple, separate things, like a family of squirrels all scampering different directions.

Secure in her camouflage she settled in, considering. She yearned to ride immediately for home, especially with the approaching festival. She wanted to tell her people both that she was right, and that they needed to prepare. And that was what arrested her: prepare for what? If she missed the festival because she was finding out that a new people came peacefully to the land, seeking trade and foreign relations, she would be expelled outright. If she missed it because she found out that a war-like people were coming and threatened their existence once again, she would be expelled with the knowledge that perhaps her people would survive. If she attended the festival, then returned to learn more, it might be too late.

The soldiers below took up defensive positions among the rocks as the one called Ketzler and two others made their way back toward the new valley. They most definitely acted as though they expected conflict.

But wasn't she doing the same? The only thing those soldiers knew was that some unseen being existed here, one that could look like a tree—or simply did look like a tree. And rode horses. Completely understandable response. She was being unfair. Perhaps she could just approach, without weapons, and talk to them. At least talk to their leader.

One of the soldiers in the rocks below pointed off into the trees. The others looked, too, craning their necks. One took a bow, drew an arrow, and shot. The arrow thunked, dead-center, into a bole on an oak deeper in the woods. The soldiers stared as if waiting for it to fall off, then returned to their watch when it didn't.

Averlynn pursed her lips. That was going a little too far. Shooting without question? Perhaps her misgivings were correct. She needed to learn more about these people—this army, and how it would march and position itself.

She moved slowly, letting the glamour fall away as she climbed down the backside of the tree and trusting in her browns and greens to keep her hidden. She ran lightly to Tarafel.

"Need to keep you out of the way," she whispered. She mounted, riding him further south. Nearer the Glowwood there were a few glens where Tarafel could pasture, at least until nightfall. She wouldn't stay past then.

"Forgive me for keeping you saddled," she said as she dismounted. "We may need to leave quickly." She did loosen the girth a little; she could retighten it even if she fled hurriedly.

As she made her way quietly back, she put on a glamour of a thin mist with darkness behind it. It would not be enough to hide her if they looked at her full-on, but as long as she hid behind trees or among brambles it should be adequate. Maybe even if she moved a snail's-pace between trees, but she hoped not to test that.

She circled wide of the scouting party, wanting to observe the main army. They would move slower, probably be less-attentive, trusting their scouts to warn them of dangers. Even if they were alerted, it was natural to put responsibility on scouts. Her people certainly did.

Even if she hadn't known the way, she quickly would have been able to follow the sounds of clanking armor and weaponry, leaders shouting at subordinates, earthen thumping of hammers driving tent stakes—the general clamor of a large camp as it was erected.

She paused as she first observed the camp through the trees, ducking behind a tree for the moment. They seemed hurried, nearly frantic. She wondered if the report had come back already. But there were no outliers, no one watching for an approaching force. Even with scouts on patrol, there should have been guard posts at least. Soldiers glancing over their shoulders.

The ground here was a little lower, though, and it was difficult to see beyond the edge of the camp. As a mist, she could not climb a tree. On the other side, though, the ground should be higher. And so far their scouts seemed concentrated to the south—thus, their attention would be as well, once the report was given.

She continued to circle slowly, keeping her eyes frequently on the camp, but also the surrounding woods. The activity continued, then seemed to thicken as though even more soldiers arrived. By the time she made it to the north side, she gauged the activity consistent with several hundred people, though she could not see among the tents now for an actual count. But thousands of soldiers would have taken over more ground, felt more like an anthill just kicked than a small beehive.

She found a rise among the trees with a good view between the trunks. An array of tents had been erected in a ring, with the ground in the center left empty except a clutch of soldiers. Occasionally a soldier would approach that center, linger, then depart.

Their leader, whoever it was. He stood a little taller, seemed arrayed a little finer, and clearly the others deferred to him. Yet he stood in the open, while the rest assembled shelters.

To one side stood one who held himself like Ketzler, and she wondered if it could be him. Perhaps he was someone of higher rank than she gave him credit for. And yet he had reported to someone within the small scouting party, as a common foot soldier would have. Surely their scouts would not be led by someone like her Ka? It seemed excessive.

She looked toward the sea, saw smaller boats draw near their ships and be hauled up. It was difficult to see for certain, but it didn't seem as though they were reloading. And those below her nearest the sea seemed to ignore it, as though they expected nothing more from it. Perhaps this was the extent of the force. It was not as daunting as she had feared—certainly not the extent of the doom she imagined from the prophecy. But then, she was never entirely certain what all the prophecy foretold.

A branch crackled behind her, nearly making her jump. But mists didn't jump—nor did they turn, really. So she bent her neck just slightly, very slowly, moving her eyes as far into the corner as she could.

More scouts, coming from the north. They made no sign that they saw her, perhaps didn't even know something was here—still believed the land to be empty. They moved slowly but with purpose, alert.

Just before exiting the trees the one in the lead shouted something—there were still words she couldn't recognize in their speech—and received a return shout from the camp. The leader turned, his gaze lingering a moment before turning back. She watched the scouts meld into the circle of tents. Only two came out the other side and made their way toward the head.

Averlynn marveled a little. They showed a fair amount of experience, moving as though well-practiced. Not every scout would be needed to report, and the rest did not stand idly by but went immediately to tasks. She wondered—prayed not—that they were as experienced in combat. Even a force of several hundred would be a threat if so.

Their sole advantage right now was knowledge of the land. That advantage was diminished by three things: that the Wohan Rangers and Scouts were woefully spread out; many had apparently given up on their forays, and might have forgotten the land; and these invaders—she wondered if they still called themselves Cariste as they had in Burieng, or if they had taken the name of this land—these invaders seemed well-prepared to scout the land and learn it swiftly. Those three factors, she feared, brought them dangerously close to even terms. Add to it her people's unwillingness to fight...

She couldn't think about that right now. She saw the two scouts approach the leader, wait bare moments before he acknowledged them, and give their report.

Out to sea, the ships were unfurling sails. One had already begun to turn northward. No, she realized, this doom was exactly as bad as she feared. They were poised to return north of the Wall for more troops—possibly more ships to carry them as well. An overwhelming force could be here—by Praka, if they mustered every soldier she had observed from that clifftop so long ago...

A few peeps on a whistle floated out to her from the camp. As she watched, the leader with his entourage and the two scouts quickly approached the northern perimeter. Even as they walked another fifty troops mustered, spreading out in a triangular formation. The tip was pointed directly at her.

She was out of time before she even realized what was happening. No mist would move as quickly as she needed to, and no glamour would last against that many soldiers looking for her. One of the scouts must have seen her, or seen something suspicious enough to report it and they figured out it was her. Or, that it was whatever creature could take on the shape of a bole.

She ducked backwards first, trying to slip between tree trunks. But they moved with a purpose. And a glamour relied on a faith she could not hold.

There was a shout from the soldiers. A sword pointed directly at her, and forty others were drawn. But of far greater concern were the nine bows that had arrows nocked.

"Stop where you are!"

Those words were simple enough to remember from Kalen, and—as then—had the same, opposite effect of their meaning. She turned and ran, long legs eating up terrain. She knew these woods, knew this land. It was *her* land!

She heard a terrific commotion from the clearing as the soldiers chased. An arrow or two flew harmlessly by, or *thocked* into trees she had long passed. Above the shouts of leaders she heard a few more shrilling pipes, maybe calling the rest of the army.

She couldn't take a direct route back to Tarafel. The clearing prohibited it, and good sense did too. They could cut off a straight line; a meandering one had to be followed more precisely. She turned slightly west.

They had difficulty following her in the underbrush, she saw. To her, it was not too badly tangled—some of the cleanest forest floor she knew, and certainly in this area. But for some reason the soldiers struggled, and not just because they wore heavier armor. During one glance, she saw a soldier brush the branch of a pin oak, whose limbs are not supple. He careened, and crashed to the ground.

If she remembered, there was something of a grove of pin oaks not far away. Desperately, she made for it. This turned her back to the pursuers, though, and she felt muscles tighten as they awaited a sudden arrow.

They probably could shoot even less effectively than they could run. Within a few moments there were no arrows at all, though the whistles continued to blow.

She slowed to conserve some energy. By the sound of the whistles they were far behind. Either they didn't want to chase anymore, or were worried about a trap. That would have been nice, but no. But they weren't stupid, or overeager. That, too, would have been nice. She risked a glance backward, and saw only flashes of movement. She began to turn southward for Tarafel.

Men and swords were in front of her, sharp and shining. And that same insipid command, now spoken casually. "Stop there."

Rage like she had never known boiled over, and she ripped her sword free. Their faces blanched as the glimmering blue blade caught dappled sunlight—and probably, too, that she was not the easy prey they hoped for.

She crashed into their blades, quickly remembering Amrith's instructions. She cleared her mind, didn't think of the sword itself only what she needed to do. And the sword like a long sharp hand did as she required.

But it was still too heavy, and the tip dragged further and further behind her movements. She recalled magic in it: Aver had told her there were commands to summon it, but she had been too focused on learning basic swordplay.

Even without the weight of the sword, there were too many Cariste, and she underestimated their coordination. While her blade was distracted by one, another reached out and grabbed her arm with surprising strength. Before she could turn her blade against that one, another hand struck and gripped her sword-wrist. They pulled apart. She struggled a moment, flailing until it seemed her arms might pull from their sockets.

She drew ragged gasps, eyes wild. What would they do to her? Their blades held steady, poised but not yet driving into her flesh. One of those not holding her turned to another.

"What do we do with her?" he asked.

"It would be nice if we could question her," he said. "At least find out how many more there might be."

She considered disabusing him of his ignorance. But it seemed better, perhaps, to try to learn more by pretending she didn't speak their language.

"Well, what do we do since we can't, though? She doesn't seem much use otherwise."

The one who was apparently their leader cocked his head. "Not yet, but maybe later. Tie her up for now, and see if you can get that sword off of her without injuring yourselves."

Their usefulness ended. She didn't care what she could learn, she did not want to give up that sword. If they somehow learned about it—she didn't know how they might, but she'd rather not risk it. But how to escape?

On her right hand, her captor dug a finger painfully into her wrist. She gritted her teeth, trying to hold on. If only a glamour actually changed her shape, let her run away! But she was helpless unless she could get them to let go—

She grinned malevolently as she struck upon an idea. The grin alone caused a gasp, and she saw them shrink back at the same time their swords stiffened. Fear was needed for this to work—she didn't need to *be* multiple, separate things, but she could wear them. In her left fist, she pressed against the ring.

They would see great horned beetles scuttling from her wrists. They couldn't touch them, but they wouldn't need to. With cries, the grips momentarily loosened. She wrenched free, now glamouring great wreaths of fire around her as though straight from the Bowels themselves as she sprinted into the woods, weaving behind every tree she could manage.

She was through the failed ambush unscathed. These were more scouts, and kept up with her far better as she ran. But they could not shoot bows while she vaulted and twisted through dead brush, and their swords were already too short.

She felt like laughing. She had managed to keep herself alive without killing any of the others. Until she knew she could not reason with them, or at least discover for certain what their intentions were, she didn't want to sully diplomacy with corpses. Pity many of them seemed not to share the same discretion, as occasionally still an arrow would stray by. One stroke of luck, and she would be dead...

Eventually the arrows stopped, the shouts falling further and further behind until one final barked command. She went several lengths further on before turning to look. They were arrayed in something of a line, gazing after her, but wary. Perhaps they suspected a trap.

She turned and continued, leaving them far behind before she began to turn again for Tarafel. These strange troops, these Cariste, showed boldness and cunning like their relatives across the sea. Though distant, they would be just as formidable a foe, if not worse. She did not remember those in Burieng being as crafty with scouts. Support these with thousands of soldiers, and the Kalen were doomed once again.

She wondered how many more might be in the woods, how many eyes might be following her. If astride Tarafel, she would need to be cautious. She returned to him, his ears pricked toward her though he also watched the forest around him.

She mounted, but sat still, catching her breath and listening to the woods around her. The wind had picked up, its sigh shrill through the naked branches. Squirrels chittered somewhere south. A bird whistled then took flight.

She needed to get to her village. She still had a chance of arriving before

Aman È, and she would need to report to the Chiefs. But she worried about leading the Cariste to them on accident. The only direction she absolutely could not go would be south. If they even glimpsed her heading that way, they might know. It terrified her that they might be that well-trained, and she had to assume they were.

She rode north-west, keeping a near-constant eye toward the sea. Her thoughts shifted as constantly as her gaze. Should the Kalen strike immediately? Drive the invaders off the cliffs before they could be reinforced? But how to mobilize her people? The outposts and villages were too far distant from one another to mass a large force quickly. And it was truly only the Rangers and Scouts who would be prepared for an immediate strike. Between Amka and Wazè they could muster perhaps one hundred—but only by emptying them completely. Trained and knowledgeable of the landscape, they could win. But then what? Thousands more would be coming soon—now they knew the way, and unless they were hindered by more freakish weather, those thousands would be ashore before the Kalen could arrive even if they mustered immediately. They had spread too wide across the land. And they were too deeply entrenched in denial. She didn't think she could convince them right away. They might seek to run, or hide, to wait out the Cariste.

Or could they live together? There were plenty of resources. The Chiefs may be right to seek to divide the land somehow, enter into a treaty of some sort.

Even as she thought it, it felt hollow. Perhaps such a treaty would work for a time, perhaps even a long time. But eventually, given what she had seen north of the Wall, they would consume the land, force the Kalen again from their homes. It would begin here.

She pounded her thigh in frustration. Attacking seemed pointless, a delay to the inevitable; a treaty seemed senseless, a delay to the inevitable. The doom of the Kalen, begun hundreds of years ago, seemed inevitable. What was the use of fighting it? Why not welcome it and be done?

She had seen it so often in trapped animals. Few simply gave up to die. Even those shot by arrows struggled to the very end. Too stupid to know better, she always thought. If not stupid, ignorant—simply unaware what was happening, what was...inevitable.

Once, a trap had been set with a flaw—feeling rushed, the braid had not been drawn properly tight. They found the frayed end, the animal gone. It had struggled and pulled until the cord finally broke. Once in her lifetime, she had seen it. It was a desperate hope. Could she, by struggling, fray a flawed rope—could she in her lifetime see two failed traps?

She had escaped the ambush, hadn't she? Their traps were far from flawless. Their knowledge was imperfect, tainted by countless generations. The knowledge of her people lived perpetually in nearly continuous generations. Many of those alive today—including her—had struggled against the Cariste before. They had lost, sadly; but those they faced now had never faced anyone before. They must react, but Averlynn and her people could *act*. They only needed to know what the Cariste knew, what they planned. Perhaps, by swift and precise strikes, they could force the Cariste to make their weave too swiftly, to cause a weakness in their braid that the trap might break.

As night fell, she knew she would have to return. To find the scouts again, and the soldiers, and see what they were doing—how and where they were placing themselves in the land. It would mean abandoning Aman È; but it would mean *not* abandoning her people, not abandoning hope. And wasn't that what Aman È was all about?

She slept without a fire, just in case, and awoke before dawn. She shed her blanket, for the day was already growing warm. If she was to approach the Cariste, she would need to leave Tarafel again, but she wanted to keep him a little closer this time. As soon as she found what she wanted—or as soon as she was spotted again—she wanted to be fast on her way south.

As light filtered through the trees, she set out. The birds would be waking and calling, except perhaps where people gathered. A pocket of silence might give her an early warning. She made her way from glade to glade, pausing often, staying long, and listening hard. If they moved most of the army, a camp that size would make noise without trying. But how far out would they have guard posts, now they were alert?

She wore no glamour this time, trusting only in her clothes to blend her in. Well-trained Tarafel stepped lightly, for a horse. He could not be silent, but he could be quieter than expected.

The sun rose, great shafts of orange light piercing through the forest. And suddenly, far ahead, it glittered upon something. Averlynn quickly ducked Tarafel behind a tree and dismounted. She peered around the trunk. She began to remember this part of the land, vaguely, though it had been years since she had come to this particular place. They were perhaps half a day's march north of the landslide. Here the land tumbled a little, revealing clefts and ledges of rock. Some ledges were barely waist high while others rose higher than her head would be when mounted. And it was a veritable warren, a place to force troops into narrow—highly defensible—files.

And atop an outcropping, a scout perched, the sun glinting momentarily off a flask of some sort held to their lips. Averlynn glanced quickly around, then led Tarafel to a stand of brush some paces away. His smoky coat would hide him well enough behind the branches.

She returned to the tree, considering. Such a defensible position would also be difficult to escape. And she did not believe it would harbor much of a camp, certainly not with the tents she had observed the day before. If these people intended to establish an actual foothold, it would not be here—should not be here. So what was the purpose?

She thought of the land around the ledges: broader and flatter, with the occasional glade like there were everywhere else, this far north in the forest. Of course, far enough east was the sea. And wouldn't they need to know when the ships returned with more troops?

It was a good spot. Somewhere that her own people would set up an outpost if they felt actually threatened, and had no access to fortifications. Was it what the Cariste did?

She circled slowly, spending more time behind trees than between them, as the sun continued to rise. She saw occasional glimpses of the scouts in the ledges, enough movement to betray perhaps ten soldiers. It served double, she thought: an outpost warning against incursion from the west, and able to defend the place until an alarm brought the rest of the troops into the position.

By noon she reached the far side of the space, where the land flattened again. Here was one last, long shelf behind which she could hide, she felt. She worried they might be watching it too, but now with the sun overhead the base was in deep shadow. She could move quicker, but still carefully.

On the other side, as she came level again with the land, she heard the first faint clatter of a camp. She crouched, peering between the trunks.

The brown of their tents blended in well, though the outposts here were far more visible. It mattered little, as those outposts were so closely spaced there would be no sneaking between them. She spied a small gap between halls of trunks, where perhaps she might gain some height and view the camp better.

It took her near to evening to reach it, as slow as she moved. The guards rotated well, keeping keen eyes out. Tarafel was far enough away, she knew, that getting to him might be difficult if seen, but it was too late now to go back for him. So she made it to a tall maple and climbed up the back. She settled firmly into the branches, then peeked.

The camp had moved in its entirety, every tent spread out below her plus many more. Now there arose a great tent in the center, the leader's tent, a flag limp off the crest. The rest were set in concentric rings. The outermost, she saw, were where the guards rotated to and from. There seemed to be very little motion inside the camp: perhaps they spent their time planning. Perhaps they were intent to sit tight until the reinforcements arrived. It made sense, she thought.

The wind picked up, then, and the flag waved. She studied it a moment. The Cariste made much of flags when she knew them in Burieng, and it might offer insights. This one was green, with what appeared to be a yellow dragon on it. She squinted. What could they mean by that? The dragons here were confined—or content—south of the Wall. And she didn't think they would have anything to do with an invading force—they certainly had not taken interest in the Kalen arrival, or the battle with the Prosan. Aryndurlan had offered judgement when it was sought, but that was rare. Had something changed? Or were the Cariste simply presumptuous?

Movement from the west caught her eye, and she squished against the trunk a little tighter. Two scouts were nearing the camp. One had brown hair back in a braid, the other moved like the one she knew as Ketzler. She watched intently as they parted ways—did they hesitate a strange fraction?—and Ketzler approached a tent and entered. She marked the tent well, fixing it in her mind.

Their hesitation signified something to her. It was furtive, too long to be a mere farewell but too short to pass any real information. But more importantly, it signified that they knew each other well, perhaps even liked each other.

As darkness began to fall, the noise from the camp heightened. Soldiers streamed to a particular, large tent next to their leader's. The man himself exited his tent and made his way to the large one. Smoke rose from a corner, and on a faint wind she smelled cooking. Dinner time.

Then, faintly, she heard a sharp whinny, and her blood turned to ice.

There was shouting. The leader below stopped just outside the tent and looked westward. Everyone looked, including Averlynn.

To her horror, four scouts strained at four ropes, hauling Tarafel toward the camp. Soldiers moved quickly; reports were given; Tarafel was penned and tied down; Averlynn fought for her breath.

And she plotted how to break into the camp and rescue her horse.

17

THE SONG OF CREATION

"Illmali wants you in Rinc Na."
"For what?"
"Your murderer is getting close."
"I must deal with this Elder first."

31 Nuamon 1320 — Spring

Tavill stood motionless, hands braced on tree trunks, scenting the air. There was something new on the winds, tangled with old scents but newly arrived. The smell of the sea had never come this far inland before, not on the strongest of winds. Yet this time it did so on only a faint breeze.

That worried him, of course. But the other scent, entirely new, reminding him of the Prosan but perhaps more recently bathed, worried him more. It had been many, many long years since he had been this far north, true, but the land had always been empty. Now faint scents betrayed the presence of...some hundreds, he guessed.

Hopefully they had not discovered Stavnuk.

Granted, it was difficult enough for him to find, and he had some recollection of where it was. The greatest of the Taur cities, it had undergone extensive camouflaging when their enemies invaded. They had hoped it would never be found, that it could be a last bastion of their people, of their knowledge. Of their memories.

They had underestimated the skill and tenacity of their foes. Small bands had ranged the forests, silently crisscrossing as they crept north. Their scents filled the understory. The Taur were able to move out of their way, slipping behind and between them in ones and twos in the dark, and then making for the city.

But behind those small bands were individual Prosan, naked with leaf-mold and wolf's hair scrubbed into their skin and scalp. Nearly starving themselves to leave behind no refuse. And they had seen the Taur, moved against the wind, and followed them. Only one was ever detected, and by then it was too late; the others brought the rest of the host to Stavnuk. And they pillaged.

But, as with Vordir, there were secret chambers that remained secret even through the siege. At least, there was one that the Prosan never found. The one Tavill had been hidden in during the attack.

But the scents on the wind were not the Prosan. And they were not so near, yet. He made his way slowly along the ridge top, eyes ceaselessly in motion. Though his vision was dim with the bone removed, another sense grew that he had all but forgotten. In the south the smells were not thick enough to form it, he supposed. Perhaps he had just not tried for so long. It was a scent-vision—an image impressed in his mind and colored in by what he smelled. It was imperfect, the colors myriad and unrelated and only of what scents drifted to him on the wind. But it provided some clarity, especially nearby, without being able to see with normal eyes. Still, an advantage he should be able to get used to. Even in the overcast, the bare forests showed him much, and he could see great distances quickly. Nothing moved but branches.

In a dark hollow there was a remnant of drifted snow, the only hint now of that rapid winter. Never since Creation had he experienced such a thing. In the south, it had not been as pronounced, the delayed autumn. Despite Lasserain's warning, it had come as a tremendous shock. Then days of snow, a deep and hard freeze, then...spring. On the earliest bushes buds were forming already. Only a few days past, with the bone, he had seen a tulip nearly opened on a far hillside, a dab of color like a misplaced brushstroke.

Then the storm. Winds and rains like he had not seen in a century. It felt as though the world would come apart at the seams. He wondered if these were the last days, if he would soon be called to give his account. And he didn't know what he would say.

Below him a cascade opened, fed by a spring. The water tinkled down the rocks. It ran its course with certainty, without concerns of where it was or what was going on around it. *To just exist.* Too many did not understand this simplicity. They had to move it, manipulate it, control it, destroy it, bring it into being. But so many things simply *were.*

It was all he wanted. Everything he hated about himself and his life came down to this: *I am.* Those who threatened him could not accept it; the parts of him that strived against everything else that *was* disrupted his own *I am*—even, or perhaps especially, his bloodlust. There was nowhere he could look where he did not find this schism.

He kept moving. Too easy it would be to find some way to destroy these Prosan. If nothing else, he could run pellmell into their camps, piercing removed, and let the bloodlust take its course. There was possibly wisdom aplenty in Stavnuk to help him find this way. But only small minds sought peace through eradication. Elonai themselves allowed these schisms to occur, to perpetuate, to find peace and reconciliation in the face of conflict. Some evil had to be removed, a blight too far spread to save an individual plant; but one would not cut down an entire field of flowers for the sake of even a thousand rotted plants.

It was this wisdom he sought in Stavnuk. First to try to remove the rot in his own self, to try to rid himself of the bloodlust. There had been attempts in their long history, he had been told; none were successful. But this piercing given by Lasserain inspired new hope—at least, a new avenue to explore. If that wisdom failed him, then perhaps something to help him understand the Prosan—at least discover where they were from, why they were here, maybe some indication of what motivated them. The Taur were supposed to be Creation's observers. Tavill worried they had too long ago begun intervening.

He paused as this thought took hold—excited him, in some way. Was it the bloodlust, trying to rise up? It felt different—not as wanton as the bloodlust. Intervention carefully controlled—pruning, perhaps, was a better analogy. Training a tree or bush to grow to be more fruitful. It stirred in him some ancient—not really a memory, but a call to being. And he had not been alone in it. There had been another, very close to him, who had joined him. Who had it been?

He waited, trembling for a time, as the weeds of his memories failed to part. Finally, when nothing came, he looked up again with a slight shake. Stavnuk and the Foldings first. Maybe something there would help him.

Here and there glades opened under the trees. Undergrowth was beginning to emerge, though much of the floor was still a tangle of shattered limbs from the storms. The sun peered through a break in the clouds, sending a soft glow against the trunks. Then, in a meadow, he scented a patch of curespan—small orange starlets that only grew near civilizations. At least, he had never encountered any in the deep wilds. He replaced the piercing; there would be far more to see than smell, until he found what he was looking for.

He had been to Stavnuk only once before, preferring the western lands even when the Taur flourished. So he was less sure of what to look for. He wondered if the camouflage had deepened in the intervening years, or lessened; if he would find bare rock, or find almost nothing at all.

The second clue was barely a cairn, nearly covered in lichen. The sigils had been worn smooth, but even that had created unnatural planes on the stone. By those he thought he could discern a waypost, marking directions toward other sites. But he could not recall which sites lay in which directions.

A fine witness I've become, he lamented. *So distracted by fears and happenings at the time, I can't even recall the layout of our capitol city.*

But then, he wasn't supposed to be a witness of the Taur, but of the world around the Taur. He could recall the approach of the Prosan. By tens and twenties they came, waiting in a ring around the city. Each hour their numbers grew, each hour hope dwindled further and further until none was left. And still they came.

This place had changed far more than Vordir. He knew there had been great gaps between the trees where they could see the Prosan massing; now there were sycamores and maples and oaks. He spotted a wall, far off, jagged with crumbled stone at the base strewn with ivy. He stumbled on a broken floor, shot through the cracks with sassafras, honeysuckle, and morning glory.

He could not orient himself. Nothing was familiar, no sight or sound provoked a memory. The Prosan had not been content, that time, with destroying the Taur: they had somehow torn down the entire city. Perhaps they knew it was the last remnants, that this signified something to the Taur and had needed to remove it entirely from existence. He worried, now, that no wisdom would be found here, or was buried beneath a century of wasted hate.

He stopped and turned in place. One memory did come back again, keenly: the memory of despair. That still lived—thrived—in this space. He spun in mind and place. Frustration blurred his vision.

He stepped in a random direction—it was all the same. A second step, and with a flurrying crash he fell into darkness.

Leaves, dirt, and broken sticks rained down on him, clattered and echoed as if in a cavern. He blinked away the dust and tears, eyes wide. Light struck stones at his feet, reflected faintly around the room but did not reach the corners.

A basement. They had hurried him down a flight of stairs, without even a torch to light their way. The ones who pulled him knew their way without it. To him it had been a blur of yanking and stumbling and swirling scents—now long gone. Dust and decay; earth; rank water, which he still heard dripping far off.

Ahead of him, the light glimmered sharper than anywhere else, and he moved toward it. Crusted and cobwebbed, it still shined. He scrubbed it with his arm and brought it to the hole he had fallen through. It was a platter, and mirrored the daylight almost perfectly.

He tilted it, aimed it around the room. It shined brighter then a torch, illuminating stone walls, tables covered in dirt and cobwebs. Here and there the walls were rent by roots, and cracks jagged up and down. It was a wonder the whole ceiling had not yet collapsed.

There were passages at either end. He cast back in his memory, recalling the sounds. He remembered now, after the stairs, their footsteps echoed tightly as though in a corridor, expanding when they came into this room. But they passed again into a hallway. Which one had it been? And how would he see down each one?

He found a chair, propped up the platter to keep the light on the other passage. That one seemed to head deeper toward the center of the city, and it would make sense they would have taken him that way. He quickly found another platter, cleaned it off, and propped it facing down the corridor.

It was not long, and at the far end opened into another room made cavernous by the dark. Behind him the platter still gleamed, bluing the stone hall, casting his shadow faintly against the floor. But he had no way to extend the light throughout the room.

The platter behind him fell suddenly, sinking him in darkness as it rang against the stones. He was growing weary of this, pulling and placing that blasted piercing in and out. He gripped it tightly. *Maybe it will break—accidentally—and I'll be forced...*

To kill again?

He held still, using his nose to sort through the scents. Mostly it was mold and decay, a little bit of wet stone, some ancient wood. But then he sniffed a bit of earth, a bit of live wood. He reached up; the ceiling was just above him, low enough to reach with a fist. He traced his fingers across as he made his way slowly around the room. A jagged edge, stones rippling downward. He pried gently.

The stones fell and he leapt backward. As in the other room dirt and leaves and sticks cascaded down, and daylight peered in. The room was as nondescript as the previous, with scattered chairs, a table coated with dust and dirt, a small stand tipped over into the dirt...

He stared, a memory tickling his mind. He had been the one to tip over that stand, when he had exited the bolthole where they had stuffed him. He took a deep, steadying breath.

He could of course picture the alcove. There had been shelves of books, cubby holes with scrolls and vials, a desk with quill and ink and loose papers, crates with sculptures and tools. Then they had doused all lights, closed the stone edifice. He heard the scraping of tables that would block the door, make it look like just another wall. And they were gone.

He didn't know why they chose him. Didn't know if it was better or worse than what happened to the rest of the city. All he heard after that were the muffled sounds of a lost battle. Pounding feet. Screams. Earthly bellows and roars. The sucking sound of steel entering then exiting flesh. Bodies collapsing. Skulls cracking. One fell onto the table just outside his door: he heard the hiss of the blade, the cry cut off, the thump, the wooden scrape. The strange silence of one looking around a room, before footfalls departed. His own muffled tears threatened to betray him the way he felt he had betrayed his people. His family.

He had stayed there in a huddle for a long time. It might have been days. Hunger and thirst didn't sway him. If any of the Prosan had remained behind, to take up residence or ensure they had killed them all, their race was doomed.

Of course, there had been a few remaining—a few who had escaped the slaughter and dispersed. When he finally emerged from the hole, the sound of the table crashing sideways nearly undid him, so long had he been in utter silence. It would be years before he would rediscover a few of his family. A few years more until they were hunted again, falling one by one until he was truly alone.

He went to the wall, searched and snuffed until he found a thin crack in the chinking. Fingernails pried, and it scraped open enough to get thick fingers against the edge and wrench it the rest of the way. A heavy mustiness wafted out, and he sneezed against it.

Inside, glittering faintly here and there, was the room of several nightmares. He wondered at the chances of any of the books or scrolls surviving this long. He went in, hopeful that by remaining sealed it had kept some decay out. Spiders could find their way anywhere, and cobwebs draped the corners and cubbies. Mice, it seemed, remained absent.

He went to the table mostly by feel. Papers crumbled at his touch. He tipped over an inkwell that bounced and rolled into a corner. He found a small tin box and opened it. Inside was flint. He sniffed his way to a wall, found a candle of ancient wax. But he dared not light it in here where so much could burn. He went back out to the main room and struck the flint against some of the paper he'd found that had decayed too far to keep legible ink. The sparks burned through. A thin tongue of flame rose, and he quickly lit the candle with it. The wax sputtered and spat, struggling against the coating of dust. He stamped out the paper, then set the candle close enough to the doorway to light the interior.

He moved through the space, clearing cobwebs. Most were empty and abandoned. One cubby erupted in juvenile spiders that quickly dispersed in the sudden light. Tavill sucked in a breath—disturbed by the sudden motion, he told himself. He began to draw out whatever he found.

Journal after wood-bound journal came out, the records of countless eye-witnessed events. He cracked open a few. In the dim light he could make out strong hands, bold lines of ink. They had survived. Gathered by years and not by location. A scribe would have sorted through each individual and re-penned the events in order. It was the purest form of their calling, one long tale of every corner of the world all at once, from Creation until...

It should have been until the present. But the records would falter centuries ago. As the Taur fled from each country, or were killed, the number of journals thinned, covered less ground, obscured from the records yet another race's accomplishments and failures.

Maybe that's why the Taur were persecuted. They told too honest an account. Their knowledge was too exhaustive, too powerful. Too true. There had been a time when, if a judge or court sought a true record of some event, they would go to the Taur. Their word was law. And too many with too much power had lost too much because they had not been able to twist the record to suit them. Too many had focused on the shame of failure instead of the opportunity to learn, and had sought to silence the indelible record. They installed their own historians, worded events as they wished. And the Taur documented that, as well. Shame piled on shame, ridicule on ridicule. And they were slowly forced out, put away, killed. The Taur gave way, hiding everywhere they could, until they had ended up here in vast, unpopulated forests. The last failure they documented was their own.

And Tavill did the same; he had not written in his journal since the bloodlust. He had only run, seeking his own perseverance. His vow to pick up the journal again had lasted...a week? A few weeks? Bare fractions of seconds in the expanse of time since creation. His people had all become faithless.

But The Foldings were not here. He snuffed a great snort as he glanced around the room. The table now was piled with scrolls and journals and books. But none of them were what he sought.

He glanced down at the last book in his hand. A compendium of strange plants, possible generations preceding them, some cultivars the Taur had taken the time to breed. He was familiar with it: he had written it. It was strange to see his own work nearly nondescript amongst so many other writings—in some ways, seeming the least important. He sighed, cast it aside. It landed with a heavy thud on the table.

With a great crash and splinter, the weight of the literature broke through the aging wood, split it in half. Books bounded across the floor, scrolls unrolled through the dust. He stared at it glumly until the wavering light from the candle glimmered off something in the midst of the rubble.

He waded through the piles, reached down and tore through the splintered wood. There had been a secret drawer in the desk, tucked in the middle. It was broken open now, and three thick leather tomes with gold embossing now lay among the rest.

He straightened, staring at them. The Foldings. The only books—of the hundreds they had penned—that told of the Taur themselves. All others were focused on the world, its people, places, events, lives, and deaths. These three books alone focused on the Taur, attempted to explain their existence, roles, societies...and biology. The Bloodlust, surely. Their immortality.

He picked them up gingerly, reverently. If there were answers to how Lasserain's piercing worked, how he might rid himself of the bloodlust, it would be in these.

He carried them outside, grabbing a chair absent-mindedly and placing it under the overhead light of the room outside. He set the books down on the chair, fearing to take his eyes off them lest they disappear. Quickly he grabbed another table, set it up under the light, and opened the books on them. He sat down and began to read.

It began at the beginning. It read not as an eyewitness, but a story retold. The Harral sat in the presence of Elonai worshipping. Their song filled the void, spreading without echo. It was melody alone—words did not yet belong to them. Layers began. Melody became harmony. And in the harmony, words were formed, spoken by Elonai. Words became a story, and soon an echo arose. But rather than complicating the harmony the echo resonated it, heightened it, complicated it. The words spun tale after tale of space and time. With no blueprint but Himself, Elonai created all; the words gave it shape, the music gave it depth. And at the end, as time began, the Taur were formed.

Night fell as Tavil wept. The candle had whispered out long ago, and it was too dark to read. He covered the books to preserve them against the night and the open hole, and took himself to bed. He found some other tattered remnants of cloth and covered himself. The hard stone did not bother him; it too had been formed by word and song that supported him with more joy and beauty than any splashing mountain brook under sunset.

There was something particular, too, about the song that played in his mind. It was not familiar. And yet some aspect of it had been entrusted to the Taur. Not a memory, but a...responsibility, a trust, a protection. Not over the effects of the song—that was a separate responsibility, to protect creation. To steward and shepherd. That was why he had undertaken to study of the plants they had found in this land. At the time it had felt like a discharge of his duty to steward it. He had loved it, had found great pride and satisfaction in the work. It had seemed...important. Not just for the record, but as an anchor in the storm in which the Taur swirled.

But this was different, this charge over the song. The song itself was not meant to be sung, and yet...He growled in frustration, unable to recall or put into words the sense that washed over him as his eyes finally closed, and sleep found him.

As daylight grew inside the room he awoke again. His dreams had been pleasant. The twitter and song of birds filtered down from above, distant. He picked up his head enough to glimpse the shroud over the books on the table. It glowed in the shaft of light, and he smiled. He had no clarity over the Taur role with that creating song, but what knowledge he needed would be in there, he knew. Waiting, at least long enough for him to eat some food.

The sun was in the sky, shining in the first cloudless day since summer finally ended. Buds decorated many of the trees, adding just a hint of color to what had been drab brown and gray. Tavill, still trusting scent more than sight, breathed deep, then snorted.

The new scent was stronger, now. Whatever it was—whoever it was—had drawn nearer. Not so near as to be an immediate threat, but it worried him. It must be the threat from the north Lasserain had mentioned. Tavill had vowed once to help the Kalen, but he was not ready yet. As long as he had the bloodlust, he could only do harm.

He hurried below again, taking a few mushroom caps with him. He gazed at the Foldings for a time, considering. The knowledge he needed could be anywhere in them. They were not large, but they were dense. A single sentence might be all he would find. It could be near the beginning, in the description of their creation, or it might be near the end after the bloodlust had arisen and been investigated.

He sighed. There was nothing to do but start at the beginning and read through. The pages turned slowly. The circle of sunlight from above slid across the floor, edged the table, made for the opposite wall. He paused once to knuckle his back, to pace the room to limber his muscles. He finished one volume, and paused to eat.

He stood against the wall, eyeing the remaining two tomes as he chewed through some roots. It was difficult to retain a sense of urgency, when rushing meant he might miss something. But it was also difficult to focus with the urgency that pressed on him. The scent would not reach him down here—he had put the bone back in anyway, to preserve his vision for reading—but the memory of it was just as near.

And there was something else that worried him, a faint niggling that only surfaced when he quieted the rest of his mind. He was looking for the wrong thing. The song of creation came back to him, in those quiet moments. It seemed entirely irrelevant in the face of all other pressures, except that it was always there, in the background, waiting for him to ponder.

He returned to the table, re-opened the first Folding, and began to read again. There was something in the third chapter, a phrase he had scanned quickly because it had nothing to do with the bloodlust.

Here. *The sky descends; the earth rises—a star rains down; rock and tree reach up. Solitude decays. Connection brings life. The words describe, but the song fills the space.* Surely that spoke of Creation Song. *Deep within us, we yearn for this connection—as was put in us by Creator. If we forget, all forget, the music will flee, and space collapses.*

When the Taur used *us* in that sense, they meant the Taur alone. It hinted at their duty—at his duty, as the lone surviving Taur. A duty to not just remember, but to remind *all*. That *all* meant not just the Kalen, the Prosan, the invaders from the north: all *Creation*. Remind everything under the sky of connection. Connection to the song? But how?

Tell them.

But how? If I go among them, I might kill them.

Only those who reject the connection.

Tavill blinked. That didn't comfort him. And yet, too, the Foldings did say space would collapse if music fled—would that not be death as well? If death was the eventual end of forgetfulness anyway...

This still didn't answer the question of the bloodlust. He had thought by seeking this answer it would resolve the other. There was something else there. The Foldings were not large, but dense, as much information crammed into as little space as possible. Structure mattered as much—if not more—than words.

Reference to the 'Connection' came before the reference to the Creation Song. He read it again. Sky and earth, seeking each other, but never touching except a star falling from heaven. He had seen that many times, though never where or if the star finally met the earth. Aside from that, the connection never occurred, was only striven after. At least, not physically.

But it would have occurred before, in the midst of the song while everything was forming still. While the words still described and the melody filled, heaven was touching earth through the song. And just before the connection was sundered, the Taur were made. Some primordial instant in their birthing left its mark, for they had sensed the connection, had been part in it and born of it. Thus the Taur never reproduced, for that inception never repeated, was not made to be repeated.

And they were made to live until Creation collapsed once more, when existence roared together. They were the link between the first connection and the last. They were not *the* beginning and end; but they were to be witnesses. And they were made to hold together the ends, the sky and the earth—not physically, but in their memories—to keep them from flying apart forever, until reconciliation at the end of all things.

Perhaps their witness was not even to be given at the end. They were witness *during* as well. A witness to the desire of Creation for connection. Heavens and earth. For the high to descend to the low...

A deep rumble began in Tavill's chest. He stood, looked up toward the hole in the roof as the last orange glow shone against the wall. As the rumble continued he closed his eyes, began the throat-song. He sank within himself, tried to immerse himself in the song of Creation. Its streams and rivers flowed through him, guided him. There was life in the river—not just in its power and energy, but actual life. Like a fish it leapt out. His tongue shaped the whistling overtone, and the fish became a bird that vaulted toward the heavens. The river leapt with it, borne on melodic wings, yet still within its coursing banks, shaping the sounds, guiding his song. The bird hovered in crystal sky, one slow wing-beat away. Tavill held the notes; reflected above the bird was a pool, a fish upside down in it slowly rising to the surface—an image of the fish that the bird had been. The wings unfurled, the beak tipped up, gently rippling the waters above while the river and earth were just below.

The notes in Tavill faded as the image effervesced. He remained standing, head tilted upward. In the stillness his blood thrummed in his veins as it did during a bloodlust, yet it kept within its banks like the river. He let himself be carried along for a time, felt the incredible power that he somehow kept contained. He feared to move, that unbridled strength might be unleashed on the room, that he might lose control forever. And yet it seemed wrong as he thought it—that the control was not his, it had been in the song.

His eyes blinked open. Control was not his, it was the song's. It *was* the answer to the bloodlust. Maybe. Difficult, *dangerous,* to test.

But even if it were not, his purpose for living was still deepened by this. And complicated. He was the last of his kind, the last that could witness at the end of time. If he walked among people, tried to re-awaken their spirits through the throat-song, would they not try to kill him again? And what would be the good in that? He would still have failed his mission, his people, his Creator. He would fail his purpose. A long, bold plan, instantly come to ruin.

He sat. It was not his plan. *Not my plan, not my control.* It didn't make sense, though. Surely if he and his people had simply allowed what happened, they would have been destroyed sooner and utterly. Not even Tavill would have been left alive.

He shuddered. Why had they been hunted so fiercely, for so long? Even with only a few left, surely they were no longer a threat. They would have learned...what lesson? To leave people alone? To finally cure themselves of the bloodlust? But if they were in hiding, not within leagues of anyone they could kill, free to live at peace, the bloodlust would have been no threat to anyone. So...Why had they been hunted to near-extinction?

18

A Hornet's Nest Stirred

"Melnor is still waiting on his wizard."
"I never took you for a gossip, Teresh."
"There's nothing going on."
"There is always something going on."

34 Nuamon 1320 — Spring

It seemed impossible.

She had spent a night and a day observing their camp, trying to figure out a way inside. But their guard was too tight, their watchfires too close together. By day they kept not only a standing guard, two per post, but other pairs roving together at intervals, always within sight of those behind and in front. There would be no space to slip through, no chance of neutralizing one guard and reaching Tarafel before anyone noticed.

Tarafel they kept near the center of camp. For a time they had tried to keep him with the other horses, but he proved too difficult. He stood now aside, tied firmly to a post. They treated him well, if warily, still providing food and water. That was the second obstacle: even if she managed to get inside the camp somehow, she saw no way of getting back out, through the lines, and far away without being shot or captured.

As night descended again, she sighed. Daytime was definitely out. What was made difficult by firelight would be impossible by daylight, and when nearly everyone was awake. If there would be an opening at all, it would be tonight.

The watchfires bloomed around the camp, roared high. From where she hid in her tree, Ketzler and another guard were the closest. He glanced occasionally, she noticed, toward one of the roving guards as she walked by. The glance was returned. About the third or fourth pass, Averlynn recognized the roving guard as the young woman she had seen Ketzler with before. A wild plan began to hatch in Averlynn's mind. She just needed an opening.

As the nighttime deepened, other guards began to filter out from the camp to take their places by the watchfires. They did not all come at once. And increasingly, one of the watchfires was left on their own. The guards there began to glance back occasionally toward the camp.

Now.

Averlynn slid down the tree, making her way as swiftly and silently as she could toward that fire, praying incessantly that this might work. If the replacements came too soon, she would fail. If the guards resumed their watchfulness, she would fail.

As she approached, she fixed the Cariste dress and deportment in her mind. She would need know every inch of it. She crouched just out of firelight and waited.

Distracted by their late comrades, the guards forgot to stoke their fires and the flames settled. Urgent whispers passed between them, and their backward glances became more frequent and prolonged. She waited.

Finally there was a rustling clatter from the camp, and the two tardy soldiers hurried forward, fumbling with sword belts and apologies. Averlynn pressed her ring, believed herself to look like a Cariste, and stole forward.

The four guards bickered long enough that she was through the line before they finally sorted things out. She walked purposefully, as though she were on important assignment. That part was easy.

In the interior, darkness reigned. The light of the fires died between the tents, even the flickering shadows fading in the lack of moonlight—Hakana had not yet risen, the full moon nearly a week old. She made her way to Tarafel first, to check on him and let him know she was safe. But she wanted to talk to Ketzler if she could, to see if she could find out from him what their plans were. She also needed to figure out how to escape when all was said and done.

Tarafel had no guard, and managed to keep his surprise at her presence to a low whicker of joy. She patted him, checked him over quickly; he shivered, ready to run.

"That will come," she whispered. *Somehow.* She untied his rope and led him quietly away. The camp was silent, except for occasional snoring as she passed a tent. She neared Ketzler's, and dropped Tarafel's rope.

She fixed in her mind the appearance of the guard Ketzler admired. She just needed him to wait before killing her, to let her begin to talk. She hoped she would remember enough Cariste to have a good conversation.

"Ketzler?" she called softly, just outside his tent. She heard rustling, then the tent flap opened. His head popped out, but he stopped short upon seeing her.

"Karbae," he said, hesitantly.

That must be her name. "I wanted to talk to you," Averlynn said. "Uh, alone if we could. Could I...come in?"

He looked at her curiously. He had to be able to tell her voice was different, her syntax. He had to know.

He ducked back inside and said something gruffly. Then another emerged, only looking coolly at Averlynn before walking off. Taking a steadying breath, Averlynn went inside.

Ketzler had his sword out, pointed unwaveringly at her. "Karbae never asks," he said, harshly but quietly. "Who are you?"

"A friend, I hope," Averlynn replied. "I mean you no harm, I promise. I am sick thinking you mean us harm."

"Who. Are. You."

With a deep breath, Averlynn let her glamour drop. "My name is Averlynn," she said. She waited as Ketzler's eyes went wide, then narrowed again. "My people live in this land. I am afraid you come to kill us."

Ketzler settled back. "Will you kill us in return?"

"I don't know. I don't want to." She paused. "In times past we have only run away. We might run again."

"Are the rest of your people outside the camp? Are they near?"

Averlynn shifted uncomfortably. She had come in here to try to get information from Ketzler, not give him all her information. "No," she said. "How many more of your people are coming?"

Ketzler smiled. "Good point." He took a deep breath. "What is it you want?"

"I want to be able to talk to you—for our two people to talk, to figure out a way to live together."

Ketzler was silent a long moment. "Why did you come to me? I'm just a scout."

"Scouts among our people are held in high regard," she said. *Just' a scout? Let Amrith say those words...* "And I knew your name. I overheard it once. And I had seen the guard you favor..."

"You've been watching us a long time," Ketzler accused.

Averlynn lowered her eyes. "I'm sorry. But I needed to know what, if any, threat came against our land. We have not been around other nations for...a long time."

"What do you propose, then? How do we get our people to talk?"

Averlynn pursed her lips. Another thing she had not actually puzzled out just yet. "Perhaps it will be enough to let me talk to your leader, to start. But eventually you will have to meet our..." She could not remember the Cariste word for 'chief'. "Our leader. At least, one of them."

"And how do we know this isn't just an attempt to kill our leader? Strike the first blow? Your ability to hide, to change shape, is...well, evil, but also a great concern."

"Evil?" She sat back, then shook her head. "I do not change shape by magic," she said, remembering some of the old laws. "I change...how you see me."

He stared at her flatly. "That sounds like changing shape."

"My body is the same," she said. "If you were to reach out and touch it, the shape is the same. Only your eyes are tricked."

"That doesn't change the concern. I don't even know if this is your true form or not."

She held up her hand. "To change how you see me, I connect through this ring and believe you see me as I want you to. So, if I were to take it off..." She slipped it off, then back on. "You see?"

"I could claim the same about taking my shirt off," Ketzler said drily. "But without proof..."

Averlynn pursed her lips. She imagined a glamour, then repeated the process.

Ketzler shook his head. "Again, I have only your word that it is the ring doing it, which we have not trusted yet."

Averlynn sighed. "Perhaps this was a mistake," she said.

"If you give us all of your weapons, perhaps give us the ring as well..." He paused when she drew back. "So, it's more important to you than your weapons," he mused. *"Indefron.* Perhaps that is the key. If you give me the ring to show to my Commander, I'll make your case for you."

Averlynn quailed. She had revealed too much. He had no idea what he asked: they did not easily give up their ring even to other Kalen. And with no concession on their part! "You cannot ask this without some promise in return. Give up something you value."

Ketzler spread his hands. "Such as?"

Averlynn cast about in her mind. What would they value? Safety, certainly, while waiting for their reinforcements to arrive. Knowledge of the land and its interior. "What if I promised to be a scout for you, instead?" she offered. "Let me keep my ring, and I'll help you with maps for places for shelter, food..."

He shook his head. "And lead us into a trap? I don't think so."

"Do you trust nothing?" she demanded. A spark came to her—the possibility of a mediator. "What about dragons? Your *k'mander* has one on his banner."

Ketzler grinned. "It's not a dragon, supposedly. *Commander,"* he enunciated, "says it's an ibex."

Averlynn froze. A goat. A goat that was on her ring; that led her out of the Wall; that she was bound to. She found her breath coming difficult.

"Why do you ask?" Ketzler asked after a long moment of silence.

She had meant to seek Aryndurlan, to bring their two parties before her to witness. But only if the Cariste trusted the dragons. She wasn't sure they ever had, or if they would now—they would probably not have had contact with one since they had settled here centuries ago. But she had hoped, maybe, with a dragon on their banner some remnants of old loyalties were re-awakening. That was something she could trust. Now she was being asked to trust something far less tangible.

She found herself gazing at the ring, twisting it slowly. It slid up her finger, sticking a moment on a knuckle. One last chance to change her mind. With a shuddering sigh bordering on a sob, she took it off and held it out to Ketzler. Her hand trembled, but she gazed at him hard. "Take this to your...leader, and tell him everything I've said. If he's agreeable, he will send you, alone, to the Glowwood—you'll find it a day's march south-west. It is a forest of mushrooms—it cannot be mistaken," she added as Ketzler frowned. "You will know it when you see it."

"That is a long way to go alone," he said.

"It will be small loss to your army if you don't return," Averlynn said harshly. "Be sure he gives you whatever authority is necessary to deal with us."

"If he doesn't?"

"We will assume you intend us harm, and will strike first."

"And what if he wants to come himself?"

"That is his risk to take."

Ketzler paused a moment, chewing his lip. "When do we meet?"

Averlynn stifled a sigh. There was no way to make it for Aman È by this point anyway. "One week—a Cariste week is eight sunrises, yes?" Ketzler nodded, then cocked his head.

"What are you? Obviously not Cariste, but how do you speak our language and know our calendar?"

She cocked her head. True, her people had maintained their glamour a long time, but for this scout not to recognize an elf when he saw one..."We are of the land you call Burieng, but long ago," she said.

"Oh. What are you called? So I can tell the Commander."

"Call us the Wohan; calling us by our name from Burieng will not bring peace."

Ketzler's eyes glittered. "I cannot promise that. But I know he will want to know what your people were called in Burieng. To know of the history of our interactions."

Averlynn bit her lip. No telling how that would be received, who would be blamed or feared. But Ketzler's demand made sense, and would most certainly hinder negotiations if she denied it now. Admitting it would only possibly hinder them. "We were called the Kalen," she said.

She saw a flicker of emotion, but too swift to read. She cursed this man's ability as a soldier to keep his reactions damped. Solid rock gave more sign than he. But it was too late; he nodded solemnly and took the ring from her hand. She felt simultaneously as though a great weight had been lifted from her shoulders, but had been set down tenfold on her spirit. She feared how that ring might be used against her, or her people. But the sign of the goat helped her to only nod and rise to her feet.

"You have one week," she said. "After that, the full fury of my people will descend upon you." It hollowed her inside to know how empty that threat was. Before her face could betray her she exited the tent.

Tarafel waited patiently outside. There was no sign of Ketzler's tent-mate, no sign of any stirring in the camp whatsoever. And she still had to figure out how to get out of the camp.

Nearby she spotted a bundle of torches, with jugs next to them. She quickly tore some of the rags from the torches and wrapped three of her arrowheads with the rags and soaked them in what she assumed was oil. She sniffed them as they dripped: definitely oil.

She mounted Tarafel, clutching two of the arrows and nocking the third. She kneed him to a walk, approaching the ring of fires slowly and quietly. In just the right position, she waited, loosing an arrow.

It *thunked* into the logs, the oil-soaked rag bursting into raging fire. The guards glanced quickly at it, drawing swords. Averlynn turned and loosed the second arrow into another fire. It too flared up, drawing attention but not yet alarm as the arrow shafts went unnoticed. Those guards too were distracted, and—she knew—would be sight-blinded by the intense flame.

Just as the roving guard left the third fire she loosed her final arrow; they heard the arrow hit, turning in time to see it burst aflame. They glanced into the camp, from where the arrow had come.

Averlynn dug in her heels, and Tarafel shot forward—her fourth arrow. They were through the lines before the call could be raised, a streak of gray only momentarily lit by fires. They were in the darkness of the woods before the first answering arrows sank harmlessly into the trees behind them.

Averlynn ducked low, trusting Tarafel to keep his head from knocking any of the branches. He knew this land as well, if not better, than she. But, when she glanced behind and saw no pursuers, she eased him off. No sense risking a broken leg, or being thrown from him.

She guided him through the woods for a time as the camp grew silent behind them. She hoped Ketzler was quickly reporting to his Captain, or at least the Scout leader, that the hornets' nest she had stirred would quiet down and she could make her comfortable way south to the Glowwood.

It was not until the fires and the guards and the clamor and the lights had fallen far behind that the enormity of what she had done truly hit her. To her knowledge, no Kalen had ever given up their ring. It was not just her source of glamour, but how her own people would sense her. They would know as soon as she arrived what she had done—because they would see her, but not feel her. It would feel so wrong to them that they would likely kill her without asking, assuming somehow someone or some thing had taken over her body, or had made itself look like her, in attempt to sneak its way into their village. She had essentially cast herself out of her people—self-*tienkan*. Dead even though alive. Her only way back in was if Ketzler returned the ring when he came to meet her—and she had not even demanded he do so. Regardless of how the meeting went—*if* it went—she would have to have that ring back. If he did not show up, she would have to find a way back into the camp again, and try to find the ring. All because of an ibex.

She shivered, then, and looked up. She missed Hakana. Tarafel stopped underneath her as she prayed to the blank sky *save me from my own stupidity*. She should never have gone into that tent. She should have saved Tarafel and simply bolted.

She sniffled. Everything she prayed her people would not do to her, she had essentially done to herself. And everything she wished not to do to her people—to consign them to death, perhaps, from lack of knowledge—she had perhaps just done. Averlynn drew a deep breath. All hope was not yet entirely gone: Hakana would rise soon. Curiosity alone might drive the Cariste to meet with her, to at least hear what she would have to say, see what relationship might be forged between their peoples. Or they might come in hopes of capturing her. Either way.

She guided Tarafel forward, began a long loop to the south to come to the Glowwood. She would not rest this night, putting as much distance between herself and the camp as possible.

It was a long and dark night, to her eyes and to her mind. She knew they had not traveled fast, had made perhaps less headway than if she had simply waited until dawn and rode Tarafel hard. But she would not have been able to stand it if they had not made even what little progress they did.

Finally the sky began to gray. Trees loomed dimly around her, almost more a physical sense than a sight at first. They grew more solid in the glowing. To the east the sky pinked; birds began to awaken and the forest echoed occasionally with their trilling.

Tarafel stopped, swiveling his ears. Averlynn sat erect, hearing it too. From somewhere came a deep rumble, as though another landslide shook the ground far away. But the sound did not come from the east. She and Tarafel looked south, and suddenly a faint and echoing whistle joined the rumble, seemed intertwined with it. They both sat staring as the sound rose and fell like a song. Almost as one, Tarafel moved forward cautiously just as Averlynn wished to draw closer to the sound.

They wove between the trees, Tarafel stepping carefully and quietly as the sound grew louder. Averlynn's gaze swept the forest, still uncertain of where exactly the sound came from. As she looked west, she suddenly stopped Tarafel and stared.

There was a cairn, of sorts, deep in the woods. It would not have belonged to her people. She had never seen it before, and yet it looked ancient. Somehow, in all her Forays, she had never been to this spot.

She guided Tarafel to it, the song present but momentarily forgotten. She studied the cairn, noticed the yellow map lichen spreading across it. She gauged the growth of the lichen: by its size, the cairn had been abandoned before her people had arrived in the land. *What people had lived here?* She could recall no evidence of a ruin such as this before—neither here nor in Kalen. There appeared to be patterns—glyphs of some sort, long since faded but too regular to be natural erosion.

She looked around the forest for other ruins—was this simply a way-point along some ancient highway? Or was there a city nearby? As she neared the cairn, she saw remnants of some stone floor now overgrown. And then, amid the stones, a gaping hole.

The song, seeming to emanate from that hole, ceased suddenly mid-note. She sat breathless, waiting for it to resume. But the trees were only filled with the occasional trill of birds still waking.

She gasped. In the depths of the hole a pair of great eyes blinked glossily at her. Her hand strayed to her sword momentarily, but she sensed no threat or evil just yet, and she placed her hand back on the reins with an exaggerated movement.

Slowly the being bobbed into view, and she stifled another gasp: a massive bull's head poked through the hole. Great sinewy and muscled arms, hirsute, pressed against the ground as the creature climbed out. Equally muscled legs bulged in linen trousers, and as it stepped up onto the broken floor she saw the legs ending in hooves instead of feet. The creature stood before her, eyes level with hers though she sat atop tall Tarafel. It bore no weapons.

"*Bur tō asvad?*" he rumbled.

Tarafel pranced back a step as Averlynn gaped. She knew what he was, though she had never seen one. They were people of legend to her people, nearly myth, not worshiped but deeply honored. She couldn't help but bow her head. "*Anggika,*" she said breathlessly.

When she glanced up she could tell he was taken aback. "You know of me?" he asked in perfect Kalen.

"Of course," she said. "Our people still sometimes sing of you, though only in our oldest songs. We didn't think you still existed..."

She saw bitterness and sadness in his eyes. "We nearly do not," he said. "I am the last."

Her mouth worked silently for a time, shocked that so magnificent a race of beings should end so. "How?" she managed finally. "Why?"

He was silent for a long time as she saw myriad emotions pass through his weary eyes. "We were feared," he said finally. "Dangerous as dragons, but more easily defeated."

"Feared by who? And dangerous how?" She felt no fear of him, only reverence, and he stood demurely enough despite how massive he was. And his song had been so beautiful...

He spread his hands. "By many. We were chased from every country where men lived until we found this land. Dangerous because..." His gaze went distant and he absently rubbed his nose where a great bone pierced it. "Our minds can be taken over, and we kill..." his voice dropped to a whisper: "everything."

That had not been in the songs—only great wisdom, and some heavy burden. Or was that the burden? A type of curse? She tried to recall the verses. It struck her suddenly, though any time the song had been sung it was of a thing to be pitied, not feared.

"The bloodlust," she said.

He glanced at her sharply. "You know of it?"

"Only vaguely. In our final songs of you, it was a hindrance to your duty, an accident—like, sneezing when you're trying to hide, or breaking a branch when you need to be stealthy."

He snorted disbelief and irony. "The reality is far more brutal."

"It usually is," Averlynn said quietly. "Though, if that sneeze or broken branch alerts an inferior force, incites a slaughter..." She trailed off, and they shared an understanding glance. "Did you come to this land alone?

The ruins here indicate not."

He shook his head. "No, there were still hundreds of us—perhaps a thousand. We had thriving communities. This was our capitol." He spread his hands as he glanced around. "It was the Prosan who ensured our demise here."

"You fought the Prosan?" she asked sharply.

He shrugged. "Not really. We tried to avoid them. We just wanted peace, to be left alone. Though I suppose that was a rejection of our duty anyway."

"Do you know where they came from?" Part of the legend of the Everlasting was their vast knowledge. But he shook his head.

"They had rarely spoken to us. They knew this land well, though; perhaps they are simply from here."

"You sound uncertain."

He shrugged again. "There is something about them that they seem descended—far descended—from an existing people."

Averlynn nodded; it had seemed so to her as well. "They should not bother you so much anymore," she said. "I'm afraid my people did fight them long ago—one of the few times we ever fought anyone—and they are destroyed."

The Everlasting eyed her for several long moments. "They survived," he rumbled. "They still hunt me now."

Averlynn stared as Tarafel danced under her, feeling her terror. "Where?"

"I encountered...slaughtered a small raiding party south of the Snowashes, but they followed me north. They found me again, though I escaped. But they are determined. I assume they are able to track me still, somehow."

From the south. Averlynn trembled at the thought of their ancient enemy, likely still infuriated and now coming north in some numbers. She remembered her vision near the cliffs, wondered if it had been a vision of the past, present, or future. Had they already found one of the outposts or villages? *The Prosan from the south; the Cariste from north and east.* It was Burieng all over again, her people caught in a tightening vise of war. Why was it their doom?

"You must come back with me, to my people," she said. "You must tell them what you've told me."

He was shaking his head, stepping sideways away from her. "I cannot," he said. "I cannot until I know if the throat-song..." He shook his head again, his eyes squeezed shut. "I don't know how," he lamented, more to himself, she felt, than to her.

"Is that the song I heard?" she asked. "It was beautiful. It felt so..." She struggled to think. "It felt...natural. Born of earth and sky..."

He was gazing at her again, seemed to have calmed. "It is that, and much more, I think. But I cannot be sure. I cannot think how to be sure, without risking everything and everyone around me. But the duty..."

"What duty?"

"To be witness. I am supposed to be a witness to events, and yet I threaten every event, threaten to turn it into slaughter. With the bloodlust..."

"What if I could help you cure it?"

His eyes snapped to her. "Is there one?"

"I—I think so. Doesn't there have to be? How else could you be witness, if that's your duty?"

"I have wondered the same. How could you help me find a cure, then, if you don't know one exists?"

"There is a woman, nearly a legend among our people—Old Raina. She is old even by our standards, and her mind is still sharp. I could take you to her, see what she knows..." She trailed off as he shook his head emphatically.

"For now, this piercing does as much," he said. "I will risk no one until I know how to test the throat-song."

Averlynn sighed desperately. "My people need to know about this," she said. "I don't know if they'll believe me anymore—especially about the Prosan. Can I tell them I met you, that you are the one who told me?"

He was silent for a time. "What proof would you offer? You cannot bring them to me."

"What is your name? And what do you call your people?"

"I am Tavill, of the Taur. I will be moving on, so if you must you can bring them to these ruins. I have the important things." He turned slightly, and she saw the pack on his back. "But below you will find even more. Please do not try to find me. I fear, more for your people than for me."

"I am Averlynn," she replied. "And I promise. Beware of the Cariste as well. They have landed on our shores, and are barely a day to the north-east. More will be coming. I've invited them to the Glowwood, and I fear they will come in force. I'm trying to find a peaceful way to coexist, but they know nothing of you or your kind, I'm sure."

Tavill glanced that way, then back. "Thank you," he said. "I'm sorry I cannot help you."

"And I'm sorry I can't help you," she said. "Or spend more time with you to hear some of your witness. Of all things..." She shook her head in wonder. "It has been a very strange several months."

Tavill rumbled. "Indeed. It seems everything is happening at once. Perhaps, one day, we may meet again and you may tell me of the Kalen."

Averlynn gaped. To do so would make her part of history she had never imagined, never considered or really even wanted. And yet... "I would be most honored, *Anggika*."

Tavill smiled grimly. "Call me only Tavill," he said. "I am far from everlasting just yet."

"Be careful," she said. She was loathe to turn Tarafel away, but wondered if Tavill would feel safer if she departed first. He might not want her to see which direction he headed. So after another bow of her head she guided Tarafel around and rode resolutely south, never once looking back. Though she kept her back straight, a tear slipped from her eye.

19

A Chance for Ketzler

"Here is a good opportunity."
"At least you recognize it now."
"How will you do it?"
"I will twist his faith."

35 Nuamon 1320 — Spring

Ketzler sat outside the Commander's tent, fingering the ring the strange woman had given him. He knew without doubt it did what she said—she could not have feigned her reaction. He just had to convince the corporal, and in turn the Commander of it.

First, he had to convince himself of whether or not he trusted her. It might not matter—the Commander would make up his own mind as well—but how he presented their conversation would influence it. She had seemed earnest. And he knew a little of the Kalen from Burieng—mostly myths and tales of elves—that they had not been a warlike people there. But if they found themselves cornered again, would they simply turn and run again? Eventually those who were bullied would have enough of it.

Assume they would fight: what kind of threat would they be? She had managed to sneak through their lines—a thing Ketz had thought impossible last night. And she had escaped again. He watched her do it, marveling at her inventiveness and the speed her horse made through the darkness. If the Kalen had an equal number of troops as his people, and all as skilled or nearly, they would be destroyed. If they had half the number, they were in danger. They had the advantage of knowing the land. He wondered about this forest of mushrooms. It was not far away, and yet she gave him a week to get there. Would she take a week to get there? Or would she be waiting? He wished it could have been ground of his choosing—not that he would necessarily know what ground to choose. And without this ring, if it did what she said, she was already at a disadvantage.

He blew out a short sigh. He was desperately curious, but he had to think of the safety of his people, too. He would be a poor scout to endanger them for his own curiosity.

The blood thread calls a sacrifice.

He had left the white thread long ago—though not entirely. The Commander had made him cling to it, still interwoven. But if he would ever make his own life, walk his own thread, he had to abandon it. Not abandon the God of All—never that, surely—but abandon his walk as intermediary. He must become a soldier. A soldier owed his allegiance to the army, to his people—not to some strange people he didn't know and who might threaten his army, his people.

He gripped the ring tight. He put Averlynn as a being out of his mind: she was a threat, a danger, an enemy. If not now, then eventually. Resources *would* be limited again, eventually.

The flap before him opened, and Curani beckoned him inside. He stood, and entered.

Commander Liptieri stood before a map, some of the ink still wet as a cartographer filled in what they knew. All the corporals stood to one side—and Captain Pike also, though nearer the map. They all looked at him when he entered.

"Ketzler," Liptieri said, straightening from the table. "You have something to report?"

"Yes sir," he said. "The intruder came to my tent, and we talked."

Even the cartographer looked up in silent shock, and the room went utterly still.

"You were unable to capture her?" Liptieri asked, his voice a threatening calm.

"Sir, I thought I should learn from her what I could. And she made a proposal that required her to leave in order to fulfill."

Liptieri leaned forward again, his gaze boring menacingly. "You've done very well as a scout, so far," he said. "But this may grossly overstep your bounds. Speak quickly for yourself."

Ketzler took a deep breath. He knew he had made the right decision. He relayed their conversation, placing the ring on the table as he spoke of it and her attitude toward it. They looked at it skeptically. Liptieri picked it up and examined it.

Ketzler paused his retelling as they focused on the ring. "A mage might be able to tell us if it's magical—"

Liptieri cut him off. "We brought none."

"Sir?" With this Averlynn using what appeared to be magic, this seemed a supremely large oversight.

"Why is this significant?" Liptieri asked instead, waving the ring.

Ketzler mentioned her genuine reaction, the effort it took her to hand it over.

"For a ring?"

Ketzler paused a moment. Why were they hung up on the ring? The only use Ketzler could see was its importance to the Kalen. The Commander was losing the thread, and he needed to bring him back to it. "She said, sir, she was Kalen."

Only a few of those gathered reacted visibly, and the rest then seemed to wonder why it was important. Liptieri's own gaze pierced Ketzler again, all humor gone from his eyes. "Was she?"

Ketzler took a breath while he considered. "I've not heard many stories," he allowed. "And fewer still bother to describe them. And most are from long ago and prone, probably, to exaggeration. But this glamour ring would seem the least of their powers even if half the stories are half true. If she is—and it seems possible to me—they could be a powerful enemy, sir."

"And, again, you let her escape."

"She acted in desperation, sir," Ketzler said, summoning all his confidence. "And earnest. With her presence here alone, and risking so much to sue for peace—sir, if she wanted them to attack us she would have never let her presence be known, if she could help it."

"So you think they do want peace?"

Ketzler was shaking his head before Liptieri had even finished. "I think *she* wants peace, sir. I don't think she has the support of her people."

Eyebrows were raised all around the tent and murmurs rumbled. "Explain," Liptieri said over the hum.

"As I said, she was desperate. She said we would 'eventually' have to meet her leaders—why not right away? They fought our people long ago in Burieng, before being chased from their homeland, and they have near-eternal life—likely she herself was there. How much bitterness do they hold now that we come again into their lands? And where, now, would they go? There are no more uncharted countries for them to flee to."

Around the tent he saw looks exchanged that showed agreement with his opinion. He had, after all, been their mediator with the God of All for months. Such a position always came with some power and authority, explicit or not.

Liptieri studied the map, gauged the distance between their camp and their landing spot. He tapped a blank space. "She said this Glowwood is a day southwest? And she would be there in a week? Why the delay?"

"Perhaps to give us time to consider," Ketzler said. He flattened his voice. "Or perhaps time for her to prepare an ambush—at least to be there first and see if I come alone."

Liptieri glanced at Pike and received a barely-perceptible nod in return. "Then you had better hurry," he said. "Corporal Curani, take your squad and go with him, but stay back. Your job will be either to rescue him, or report on his capture. Or death."

Ketzler's stomach slammed down like a stone. "S-sir?" he said weakly.

"To be a leader, you must often make life or death decisions," he said, gazing at Ketzler steadily. "Decisions like whether to capture a prisoner or not. Since you have made that decision, you will see it through to its end."

Ketzler's back stiffened. "Then, sir, if you are not coming, I will need the authority to treat with her—as she said."

However he did it, Ketzler managed to meet the Commander's gaze eye-to-eye. Finally a measure of respect appeared in Liptieri's eyes. "We will not come to them—we do not know the land and will not be put at disadvantage. Outside of that, let us test your judgement."

"Sir, do you think that's wise?" Pike asked, casting a troubled glance at Ketzler. "Perhaps I could go with him as well."

Liptieri shook his head. "I'll risk none of my leadership. We knew there were people here before we sailed—knew we would somehow or another come to meet them, and test our fate." He shrugged. "Perhaps it is the providence of the God that it has happened so soon. Ketzler, as soon as it is daylight, head out."

"Yes sir," Ketzler said, sparing a quick glance for Pike before turning and exiting through the flap. He paused just outside and heaved a steadying sigh. He had all but ensured war between them; it would only take tactful bargaining in the Glowwood to ensure it.

The flap rustled again and he turned to see Captain Pike straighten from it. "Are you sure you know what you're doing?" she asked without preamble.

Dawn was near, and her face against the pearling sky showed genuine concern. Ketzler felt a flicker of anger: he knew far more than she gave him credit for. "With the help of the God of All," he said demurely instead. "He can give us words to speak in a moment that may not even make sense at the time, because He sees their effect in the future."

She gazed at him a long moment, and he worried she saw through his words. Curani exited the tent, and Pike glanced at him. "I'd rather not send the entire squad," she said. "Perhaps leave...Karbae here; she has the least fighting experience, and we don't want to throw her immediately into harm's way. Do you agree, Ketzler?"

Ketzler hesitated, nearly agreed, then caught Pike's hardening gaze. "I think she is quite capable," he said, "and will be in no danger. This Kalen, this...Averlynn...wants peace and will try to talk me into it. She won't strike the first blow just yet. But it isn't my squad."

"Very well," Pike said. "You seem confident of the safety of the squad; they will all go." She turned immediately and went back into the tent. Curani cocked an eyebrow.

"Something going on between you two?" he asked.

She is becoming more difficult—and suspicious. If anyone is in a position to hinder my growth as a soldier, to stand between me and my heart's desire, it will be her. Ketzler shrugged. "Not for my part," he said. "What do you think?"

Curani's mouth twisted. "Ketzler, you've been strange since you arrived here," he said. "I try not to mean that in a bad way. But you were a Pip, soon to be Bader. And suddenly you're a soldier?" He shook his head. "I prayed you wouldn't be in my squad when I first saw you. You've done well, I admit now. But the Commander's deference to you, that you still lead us in prayers... Now you're our ambassador? Sometimes I don't blame Captain Pike. I'm not sure I would know what to do with you either." Curani shrugged, and walked off before Ketzler could think of a response.

It wasn't his fault what he had become within the unit. He only tried to excel. Was he to blame that excellence came—not easy, he had worked hard for every step—but without delay? He couldn't explain Liptieri's deference either, and wondered if perhaps the Commander was more devout than he let on. It was Liptieri's choice to promote religious pursuits in the unit, not Ketzler's. It was odd, for Cariste in Gintanos. Oh they valued religion in its place, but only as one of many voices offering wisdom and ideas. Even those who would never miss a Fastday sermon were just as likely to never miss a session of the Senate.

And yet Liptieri now sided with Ketzler over another of his captains. It could have been anger and punishment, as he expressed, but it seemed an odd and long leap—potentially risking the entire expedition, while giving Ketzler an opportunity to prove himself even worthier.

And he would prove himself even worthier. It settled firmly in his mind. Averlynn may seek to surprise him, but he would surprise her instead, and quickly turn the ground of her choosing to ground of his advantage. While she was off balance, their army could strike mightily, put the Kalen so far on their heels they could not recover before the ships returned with even more soldiers. And then would come even greater opportunities to prove himself, to rise so swiftly through the ranks he would be an example through the history books. Examples of action, of change—not merely curiosities in a catacomb.

He smiled and went to outfit himself with supplies. He found Curani already with the quartermaster, and after he'd been given a pack and began filling it out the others of the squad trickled over. As the sun cleared the trees they were ready.

"We're going to look for a forest of mushrooms," Curani said, turning toward the squad. "Supposedly, we'll know it when we see it. The rest of us will wait north and east of the mushrooms while Ketzler advances to meet with this strange person. Ketzler, you will either shout 'away' or 'come' depending on any ambush, and we will respond accordingly. If you can shout any other information, before we charge in to our deaths, I would appreciate it." He paused only a moment to glare. "Let's go."

They stepped out. Ketzler let most of the squad pass him by before falling in line. Karbae waited too, falling in just behind him. He tried to ignore the prickling between his shoulders, the constant desire to turn and look at her. After a time he spared her one glance, one smile, to tell her he was not angry or distant, just focused. She wrinkled her nose impishly at him, and only by sheer force of will did he turn back around. The prickling increased.

The forest was quiet, the birds, it seemed, still disturbed by the sudden presence of a large camp. He saw no boles, then remembered Liptieri still had the ring. He considered that a moment, and regretted it. It would be a powerful sign of trust to return it, an ironclad shield of his true intentions. Too late now.

Once they passed the rock labyrinth they moved out of column and into wedge formation, spreading wide to see as much terrain as possible without losing sight of each other. It was a dynamic formation: as they passed over or around ridges and valleys they closed or opened ranks. Here and there the forest thickened or thinned, and they were forced to respond in kind. And between all that, to keep eyes on every rock, tree, fold, or rise. It allowed little time to think.

Around noon they stopped to eat. Ketzler spared Karbae only quick glances between bites of way-bread and smoked pork. Some days she controlled herself. Others it seemed she taunted him publicly on purpose, almost to try to get them in trouble. He didn't understand it. This day, at least, was one she controlled herself.

The squad spoke little, facing out more than in to keep eyes on the forest. They all knew ambush was possible, even if Ketzler felt it unlikely. The reduction of their forces by only a squad was hardly a tactical advantage—would only stir the hornets' nest.

Ketzler found himself wondering endlessly how the Kalen might be positioned—how many were in the country? Were they in pockets or one encampment? *Would* they be more willing to fight than they did in Burieng? He considered what he might say to Averlynn when they met, how he might pry this information from her without her knowing.

There are many ways to get information. It takes one committed to finding the truth by whatever means.

Capture her. Interrogate her. A different set of 'tactics'—perhaps blunter than he hoped for, but could achieve the same results. Before he could think too long on it Curani was motioning them to their feet.

Despite her display of control this time, Ketzler still moved to the opposite side of the formation. Maybe this time, he didn't trust himself.

The forest eventually began to darken, and they had seen nothing of any mushrooms—certainly not what could be called a 'forest' of them. Typical white caps under fallen and decayed trees; an odd shelf or two; chicken of the woods, which they gathered swiftly. Furthest out on the western wing of the wedge, Ketzler first noticed it on an eddy of wind, almost as if he held a mushroom just under his nose and sniffed. A deep, rich, earthy smell, though the leaf mold here was no thicker or wetter than what they had seen the rest of the day. He hesitated, sniffed again, but it was gone.

He glanced at the others. They moved without hesitation, still observant but with nothing to attract their interest. Curani, in the lead, glanced at him, checking. He continued forward until another eddy, stronger and more durable, and the earthiness nearly overwhelmed him. He stopped, made a low bird-call. Curani glanced back sharply, and Ketzler angled a flat palm toward the west.

Curani made swift gestures, and the squad halted and sank to their knees. He made his way toward Ketzler, eyes still roving. Some paces away the wind stirred again and he halted; he smelled it too. He glanced at Ketzler and approached.

"That smells like a lot of mushrooms," he whispered.

"I thought the same—perhaps even a forest of them. But it's perhaps too dark to investigate right now?"

Curani scanned the forest, then nodded. "Let's move to a little bit better of a hiding place. We can find it in the morning."

The squad huddled, and Curani gave his orders. They found, a little further east, a small glade on higher ground screened by thick trees and undergrowth. Curani set the watch, and after a quick meal they bedded down.

Ketzler lay awake, peering through the canopy opening at the spray of stars overhead. There was no moon yet, but the starlight lent a faint glow to the trees. For most of Ketzler's life, he had slept indoors or in a tent, or lately they'd had watchfires burning. It had been rare for him to see the stars so plainly, and so many. Some nights, late on the decks of the ship; or winter evenings back in Klos when he'd been permitted outside. But then he thought of Averlynn, who had clearly been watching them for some time—roamed, it seemed, most of her life. There had been no tent in her horse's saddlebags. She would sleep under such a brilliant canopy almost constantly. Her knowledge and intimacy with the land would always outstrip his. He found he envied her, in a way. Part of him still envied those back in camp, around warm fires or out of the wind, certainly. But there was something to be said for the beauty of remote lands, of the competency to live in it without dozens or hundreds to support you.

He closed his eyes, nearly drifting off when he heard motion nearby. His eyes snapped open, worried somehow Averlynn had slipped through the lines and came to kill him.

The stars were blotted out in the shape of a person. As his head came up, the figure knelt down. He recognized Karbae's smell. "My watch already?" he whispered.

She shook her head. "I couldn't sleep," she said. "You're going to negotiate with this person tomorrow, or someday soon, and we don't know what she intends—if it'll be ambush, or..."

He grinned. "I'll be okay, I promise. She had her chance to kill me already."

But Karbae shook her head. "You can't guarantee that. And I can't...I mean, if you..." She gave a short burst of air, then lurched forward and kissed him. It was not quick, but it was not long either before she leaned back and gazed at him.

Blood thundered through his ears as his heart raced. He sat up, trembling a little, then grasped her firmly and pulled her back to him, leaning into the kiss. It was awkward at first—he didn't exactly know what he was doing, and their movements never quite seemed in unison. But it was thrilling, all the more so as the squad slept around them.

Finally they parted again, nearly panting. His hands traced her face, her neck, swept back strands of her hair. He tried to stare into her eyes in the gloom, saw faint blue reflected in her brown eyes. He frowned, suddenly: blue? He glanced around, spotting as he twisted toward the west a faint glow through the trees.

"What is it? Did I do it wrong?"

He turned swiftly back as she withdrew a little. "No! Of course not, that was..." He let out a trembling breath. "I definitely can't die now," he said with a smile. She giggled, but he sobered. "Sorry, but is there a faint blue light coming from over there that wasn't there before?"

She looked with him. "I guess there is, but...Is that more important to you?"

His eyes darted to hers. "I mean, not necessarily more important, but...It is still important, isn't it? And strange?"

He could not read her expression in the darkness, and he was confused. Of course that had been thrilling and incredible and everything he'd wanted for a long time, but did she truly expect him to just ignore everything else?

He stared as her lips compressed, and she stood suddenly and crept slowly away. Part of him wanted to chase after her, show her how important she was to him, how eager he would be if they could find time and space alone.

But the strange glow dragged his attention away. There would be time for that later. He would ensure it, somehow. He moved the blankets aside and stood, buckling on his sword. He moved to the watchpost, found Mordel there.

"Can you tell what that is?" he asked, nodding his head toward the faint glow against the trees.

Mordel shrugged. "Just moonlight, isn't it?"

Ketzler stared across, taking a patient breath. "The moon does not rise for some hours, yet," he said. "When did that glow appear?"

"Distracted by something else?" Mordel sneered.

Ketzler swallowed, then frowned. "Yes, sleep," he retorted. "You're on the watch, not me, remember?"

"Oh, did the glow wake you?"

He held back a sigh. "I'm going to go check into it. Don't shoot me when I come back, please?"

Before Mordel could reply he strode forward, quickly but still careful not to make too much noise. He descended the rise, trying to fix in his mind the trees that would guide him back.

He made his way across flat ground, the glow before him steady but taking on a greenish hue—not sickly, and still primarily blue, it reminded him some of the glowing surf. But he could not tell where it came from.

The forest was silent, not even a breeze stirring the branches. He could see little, but felt no danger. Then, faintly ahead of him, he saw strange humps, and the glow seemed purer as though they emanated from those humps.

Suddenly, the ground below him fell away into a broad valley, and he could see the stalks below the humps, and he gasped. A forest of mushrooms, indeed: man-height or a little better, with caps the size of shields, the mushrooms below glowed in blue and green, and something like glow-worms drifted in the air around them.

He forgot the land around him, forgot that he was alone, forgot there might be a strange people waiting to ambush him. He descended the slope, eager to be among the mushrooms, among the lights that hung almost magically. He reached the bottom and the soil felt springy beneath him but not muddy. He wandered slowly, gaping around. The scent was only a little stronger, and he quickly grew accustomed to it. He felt something near a presence—or at least, not as strong as a sentience but a knowing. The concept skittered around his mind without being caught. He lacked the focus to even try.

Finally a fear occurred to him, and stuck: was this why she chose this spot? He shook his head, tried to shake the enchantment that clotted his thoughts. But the wonder of it pressed in, and with little effort his focus wandered again.

He made his way through the halls, bouncing slightly on the springy turf, saw a figure off to the side—the glowworms seemed bigger than they should, almost like large butterflies. Not butterflies, but dragonflies that did not zip and dart but floated along. He stared at one as it drifted. Was that a small human-shaped body suspended between the wings?

The figure drew closer, hand on the hilt of a sword.

What were these, then—sprites, from the fairytales? Their wings shimmered the colors of the rainbow, reflecting in infinitesimal shards the glow from the mushrooms. But he thought sprites would scatter, would hide long before he blundered along.

"They are the spores of the mushrooms," the figure said.

"Oh," Ketzler replied distractedly. They looked like they flew... His eyes finally snapped over. Fear and surprise overwhelmed the wonder and he scrabbled for his sword.

Averlynn's eyes darkened, but her hands were steady. "You're early," she accused.

Ketzler finally swept his sword out, but it wavered in his hand. Staring at her, the enchantment of the Glowwood finally seemed to dissipate. "So are you," he retorted. "A week, I thought you said?"

"I was being generous."

"Or you needed time to prepare an ambush."

She lifted an eyebrow. "Do you think that would have been necessary, now?"

His sword dropped further. "I suppose not."

The stood in silence for a few moments. Ketzler finally sighed and sheathed his sword. "How do we proceed?" he asked.

"You are ready to pursue a peaceful meeting?" she asked. Ketzler nodded. "I will return to my village. It's nearest. If I can, I'll convince our leader to come out and meet with your leader. I'll come again to your camp to settle on a location, and bring you and your Kammander to the meeting." She paused. "I will need a symbol of your trust."

"What would that be?"

"I need my ring back."

Ketzler's heart thudded. "I—the Commander still has it, at our camp. It would be another two days to get it to you, unless you come back with us."

Averlynn's lips twisted. "That is not ideal," she said.

"It is what it is, though," he replied. "I can't change..." He trailed off as her gaze sharpened, and she glanced quickly aside. "What is it?"

She frowned. "Setting up your own ambush?" she asked, backing quickly between two trunks.

"I don't..." He trailed off again as he saw Curani wandering toward them, the same gaping wonder on his face that had presumably been on his. Now he saw it in someone else, Ketzler was disgusted: he came like an imbecile, and surely Ketzler had looked the same. She had made a fool of him—what would stop her from doing so again? This time perhaps in front of the Commander?

"Curani!" he snapped.

His corporal's gaze fell on him, barely registering. "What is this place?" he breathed.

Ketzler rolled his eyes as Averlynn stepped out once more. "This is the Glowwood, sacred to our people," she said.

Ketzler watched as the enchantment fell from Curani's eyes, saw only a slight hardening. He waited patiently for his corporal to say or do something that wasn't idiotic.

"Averlynn?" he said.

She nodded once. "And you are?"

"Curani," he said. "I lead the squad..." He cut off, too late. Averlynn's eyes flashed to Ketzler.

"You were to come alone."

"I was alone," he said angrily. "You surely didn't expect me to walk a day's journey into this forest by myself, did you? I still came into the Glowwood alone."

"And unbidden," Curani said. "Once again you overstep your bounds. You should have told me you were going."

"What difference would it—"

"Much difference!" Curani nearly shouted. He took a slow breath. "I was to give you a bargaining item," he continued in normal tones. He reached into a pocket, and when he withdrew it and held it out Ketzler saw a ring in his palm.

Averlynn stared at it, then into Curani's eyes as she slowly reached out and retrieved it. She held it up with a slight bow as if in thanks, then turned to Ketzler. "Our bargain is struck. I will return as soon as I can with one of our leaders, and we will talk. Look for me in a week's time—a true week, this time," she added with an apologetic smile.

She backed a few steps away, then turned and departed. Ketzler watched her, then turned to see a triumphant look on Curani's face. "So," Curani said. "Perhaps we will have peace."

His blood must be on the ground. The blood thread demands a sacrifice.

Ketzler gritted his teeth. His blade flashed, swept across Curani's throat. He delighted to see that insipid, triumphant grin turn to shock as blood bubbled from the death rattle.

"Come! Come!" Ketzler shouted desperately. He took out Curani's sword and clashed them together a few times, shouting over and over. He placed Curani's sword near where he'd fallen, then drew his own sword across his forearm. He sat, scrubbed the blood from his sword, then waited.

A few short breaths later, he heard splattering footsteps as the rest of the squad charged through the mushrooms. Whether the enchantment had been Averlynn's doing alone, or his shouts of danger warded it, they showed no signs of befuddlement as they approached.

"She demanded the ring," Ketzler gasped, clutching the cut on his arm. "When we tried to negotiate, she attacked." They glared in horror and sadness at their fallen comrade. Karbae's gaze went to Ketzler's wound. "When I started shouting she ran. She had managed to take the ring from Curani." He heaved a sigh, forced a few tears. "I don't think they plan on having peace between us."

20

ANSWERS TOO LONG DELAYED

"What will you do now?"
"...I don't know."
"There's nothing else?"
"Perhaps. But it is not easy to do."

10 Tetsamon 1320 — Spring

Tavill lifted his head, sniffing the air. The currents swirled and danced through his nose: a doe moved across a ridge; chickadees darted after one another; crabapples were deep in bloom; his own footsteps released humus-scent. The stream he walked beside carried a mineral tang, its headwaters springing from limestone, wherever it began.

The stream for now angled north and west, and so he followed it. He recalled it little, though he vaguely thought it would eventually bend eastward. Before then he would cross it, striking almost directly west as he made for the ruins of Kragnog.

As he thought back, he could not recall specifically visiting the place when it was alive. It was sometimes with difficulty that Tavill could distinguish between what he had read and what he experienced. The more recent the memory, there more would be specific emotions or thoughts attached to memories that separated knowledge from experience. But too far back—perhaps a few hundred years—those would fade, leaving him the knowledge only.

So he recalled Kragnog, in a way, but more so because he had read about it in Stavnuk. Or perhaps Pluvik had told him, long ago. That happened sometimes, too. But isn't that why the Taur wrote everything down? Isn't that what Pluvik had...?

Tavill had meant to leave, to steal away quickly after Averlynn had gone. But her trust and respect in not looking back eased him, and he had stayed a little longer. She had reminded him again of duty—or, reaffirmed it for him. He had not been called 'Everlasting One' since he had fled across the sea with his people. It stirred in him some of those ancient memories. He was surprised to remember a time when the Taur were known, their habitations in groves and fields marked by the nearest human settlements. Often people would come to find wisdom. The Taur had not hid, but neither did they insert themselves into people's lives unbidden.

And so he had gone back underground in Stavnuk, to read through not just the Foldings—which he took with him now—but every scrap of written work he could find. It came back to him though he remembered it. Knowledge is a thing hard to drag up by itself—it must be attended by some problem or question. Or so he found. Though it seemed sometimes his memories were gone, he had only to face a particular point and everything he had stored away came flooding back. So it was as he read what the Taur had committed to writing. Even as he read, other bits came back. Slowly, at first, to be sure; but in increasing amounts until he had to put down the writing for a time to sort through all that washed over him.

It was after some time that he came across references to Kragnog. It was a third affirmation for him, after his own and Averlynn's. For those who settled in Kragnog had been those who lived in the plains of their former countries. Many Taur preferred mountains; others the forests; still fewer enjoyed the deserts. The last had found no similar place in this country to build and live, and had dispersed as they could. But many had found the plains and marshes to the north and west and re-created their old homes as best they could. It would be not of stone, but of earth. He worried that it would have been erased entirely, eroded away by wind and water. But he needed to see for himself. For the Taur had tucked away in each place memories and knowledge specific to those places, and specific to those histories. The Foldings had told him much; but much was still missing, and those memories were still buried and would not be called up.

Despite blurred vision, he saw the valley begin to bend eastward. He followed it for a time. The breeze shifted, floating down into the valley from above, and on it he still scented a limestone tang. It was not yet the hard eastward bend he sought. And so he stayed beside the stream.

The second night after meeting the elven maiden, he had gone through most of the writings that he could find, that did not crumble to dust when he touched them. And, his eyes felt strained. That night, he went up to the surface to gaze at the stars sprinkled across the sky, let memories drift through him as they would. And then, when even those faint lights pained him, he took out the bone and let his nose wander.

He didn't even wait to see his vision fade; he closed his eyes completely, letting the smells around him paint the landscape for him in his scent-vision. It still surprised him—and frightened him, a little—to find the vision jumbled and disarrayed at first. Now he had used it several times, he remembered it used to paint vivid and clear pictures. Now the scents invaded him, presenting themselves at random and according to strength rather than location. It unsettled him that he struggled so much after such a short time, and worried again that there was more magic in that bone than Lasserain had told him. But the mage had never before given him reason to distrust, and so he attributed it as a lack of practice. His other skills had atrophied with disuse, why not this one? And so he calmed, let the scents sort themselves out, did not try to force the image. And slowly it came to him, stronger than ever before. Of course the moon and stars would still be gone, for they had no scent, and he missed that. Much of what was downwind was a blurry space, and he feared that, feared an arrow suddenly coming from that darkness—shot accurately, this time. He twisted the bone in his hand, fidgeted to put it back. But it came to him again that his duty had not been taken on, but assigned. His poor vision had not been taken on either—he had not blinded himself. And so these things must somehow work themselves out to keep him alive. He hoped.

Once the scent-image firmed in his mind, clearer then even before, and when he felt he could navigate it confidently, he was loathe to let it go. And so he had traveled these past days by scent alone. The bone lay secure in a pouch, within easy grasp and never far from his mind, but left alone.

By late afternoon, the valley and the scent both bent eastward. He forded the stream easily, pausing once in the current to bid farewell to the still-icy waters before mounting the ridge on the other side. Great cherries, oaks, and ashes surrounded him, their leaf-litter thick—and slippery, he discovered. He finally made the top, panting and with leaves still stuck to his fur from when he'd fallen, but invigorated.

To his dim sight, the pale brightness of the day turned slightly yellower and he thought the sun must be westering. The breeze was dying off. He faced the light as directly as he could and wove between the trees. The ridge was broad and he walked easily for a time, but a heaviness began to settle on his mind. He was in un-remembered lands, now—more than before. He thought of his cabin below the Snowashes, how safe and hidden he had thought it was until he saw it. He could not risk camping for the night without seeing his surroundings. He wished now he had not delayed in Stavnuk. Well, he could not quite say that. But he worried that the Cariste might move quickly, sending out scouting parties wide across the land. The Taur had done so, when they'd gotten here, tried to learn as much of the land as possible. With two extra days to gather themselves, they might already be close on his heels—not intentionally, but accidental or not could still kill him.

He shook his head—it had been a thought too-often present to simply reject now, even if he began to think it false. He reached into his pouch, felt the hard smoothness, the sharp points at the ends. Not only to see his campsite, but he would like to get some height, see the lay of the land. Perhaps not yet. It was some time until evening.

A bird squawked; he faltered, sniffing. Ah: pungent fox. It squawked again, a short call, and he listened intently. Grosbeak. He sighed, and removed the bone from his pouch. Grosbeak meant the forest edge was near.

The bone slid in easily, once again. It seemed impossible it had hurt so much the first times, but those memories still brimmed with experiential tones. The scent of it swirled, built, inflated, then faded. He blinked in the light, each branch and twig coming into focus. The sight of everything tore at him as the fox scent faded away. His scent-vision tattered away on emotional winds, replaced by cold but precise true-vision.

The sun was lower than he thought, and he could see now—faintly through the trunks—a broad, brown land of undulating hills. There would be little cover for him out there, except in the folds and hollows. The terrain would be too jumbled to follow those, and he would be forced up and over the crests in full view of anyone. He shrank back, glancing at the safety of the forest.

The fox departed. The grosbeak, after a time, began its melodious chirping. It had worried for its survival, too, and the survival of its friends around it as it called the alarm. Tavill had no friends—no like species to warn. And of course, no more Taur could be made. If two Taur bonded it was because of a shared purpose given them—no off-spring could come. For Kessaria and Arvalad, it had been a bonding of help-meets, to share with each other the task of...something. For Tavill, he recalled no bonding, except—was there a desire? He thought so.

It rose again, the pull toward intervention—toward pruning. To aid the flourishing by cutting away that which damaged the health. Had he been a gardener? It didn't seem right. And the name of the other...Zus—something? He pawed through his mind, forced a few extra letters...

And yet, did it matter? Every individual worried about its survival, didn't it? The grosbeak had no great desire to be eaten by a fox, or any other creature, whether it be one of thousands or the only one. The loss of the last might impact the world, but only if that one in turn had impacted the world first. What loss would there be, truly, if Tavill were no longer there? For the better part of a millennia, no one knew he existed. Averlynn had said it: the Kalen thought they were a myth. Already departed from the world. No longer relevant except in ancient songs—they did not even bother to make any new songs.

His head came up and he stared hard across the open ground ahead. To be missed, he first had to be known. To be known, he had to figure out how his people had dwelt among other civilizations. He didn't know how he had forgotten it, why those memories were gone so deep he couldn't recall them. But he needed to find out. He strode forward.

Evening waned, and the first stars glittered in the east. He made his way into a deep fold of ground. Pursuers would have to come up that exact ridge to see him, and he deemed the plains a little too wide for that chance. He could risk no fire, though, and so he simply laid out his roll and sat.

He removed the bone again, tucked it away. For too brief a time he enjoyed clear sight and unmuffled scents. There was a sharp evergreen scent here. He thought perhaps he had seen some small shrubs clinging to the crowns here and there, tiny splashes of green sometimes like necklaces on the far hills. The crispness of the evergreen, though, was wrapped in blankets of the scents of grass and moss. Far below that, hidden except to those who sought the hardest, was rain-wet stone and the pale dustiness of lichen. It was a hard land of small creatures and soaring hawks.

He drew another breath. Darkness descended as his sight blurred. He placed his palms on the ground, feeling first the press of grass, then the drought-packed earth that soaked in the rain and sponged it quickly away from the surface to bedrock below. When his senses reached that plane, not so far below the surface here as it often was in the forest, he began his throat-song.

He had taken to singing it more often—not always nightly, but nearly. Stanzas he had long forgotten came back, now and again. If they didn't, he simply hummed. Mostly he sang songs of calm, or connection with the land. Throat-songs served different purposes, performed some different functions—could, in some cases, interact with and change physical things. Those he stayed away from, especially now. In the past days he had learned that the bone inhibited the song, as though he felt the trunk of a tree through a woolen blanket. To make changes he would want a fine and gentle touch. And there were few changes he would dare risk, just yet.

The thrum massaged across the bedrock below, spreading like ripples in a pond. Tavill reached down with his senses, felt as though his fingers themselves brushed across the rock. It was not as solid as he thought it at first. The plates, though smooth, were thin. If he tried to dig it up it would shatter, and small roots and shells were trapped between the layers.

His tongue curled, sending the whistling overtone skyward. It leapt higher and higher, faster than ever now that there were no trees to recognize and sense. He felt the vastness of the vault overhead, felt as though time slowed—or, if not slowing, mattered less. Deep in that void the tiny bits of time constructed here were pointless—there was very little that happened up there that did not take a long time. Here a leaf might fall in a moment, or a bird might light or alight in an instant. But there, far removed from the concerns of the world, far removed from dawn and dusk, one could float for eons and see no change.

Tavill felt himself in both of those spaces, caught between the two like the mollusks in the shale below him, a sign of temporal life in between hard plates unbound by time. And yet his existence, alive in a time of fleeting moments, was as equally unbound by time as it was in fact bound. His was a life made up entirely of overtones, of a deep rumble interwoven with an echoing whistle.

The throat-song faded as his eyes dragged open. It was a difficult harmony, unduplicated to his knowledge except by a chorus. That was the way of humans: through almost limitless numbers, their song could be as complex as a forest of birds, each singing their part and—with guidance—blending to a harmony unmatched by any other species. But short. So short, and though so often complex and unique it too often changed between and sometimes within a generation. Younger generations rejected the harmonies of the elder, seeking their own song—sometimes selfishly, discordantly—until a new harmony never before heard might finally come forth. But there was too often almost no continuity, nothing to tie the race together, to see where they had come from as they plotted their way forward. So enraptured by their own fleeting existence they could not see to draw meaning from the time and people which surrounded them.

Unbidden, the thrum began again in his throat. This time, though, he kept his tongue still. He reached down, and then out, spreading his sense as far as he could. He felt it grow thin, stretch, not to a breaking point but dulling the sense until it brought him almost no information. He deepened the thrum, put into it whatever power he could manage, and felt the sense thicken. It had spread, he discovered, over the hills and spilled down into the hollows around him. He found a thread of water, a small burrow of hares; he felt little wriggling things with soft bodies and things with hard bodies scurrying through their little tunnels.

He felt, suddenly, the soft press of feet. His eyes snapped open as the thrum instantly ceased. He bundled his blanket in his arm and stuffed it in his pack, fearing the soft rustling noises it made. He sniffed; the wind was from the wrong direction. He put the bone back in as he lay flat, shivering until his vision cleared.

They had been in the hollow to the east. If they had heard his throat-song, it may have folded around the hills oddly, not giving them a clear sense of where he was. He considered the valley, that it opened to the south. He glanced around the rim above him, saw a small saddle to the north. He crawled as silently as he could, casting surreptitious glances to the crest to the east, fearing to see a head peering over. He had no idea whether they would have paused when the song ceased; he thought perhaps they would have. He could almost see them looking at each other, waiting for the noise to begin again. Surely they could not imagine he stopped because he had sensed them.

He made the saddle and scuttled through it. He paused quickly on the other side, looking below. As he caught his breath, he saw a flicker of movement south; a single scout came around the bottom of the valley, crouched low with an arrow nocked. It was difficult in the moonless dark to see what kind of clothing the scout wore, but it seemed to him the movements were like the Prosan. They had managed to follow him. He nearly whimpered, but kept it in his throat: why were they so tenacious? Why could they not simply chase him away and be done?

He crept away down the other side, then circled around and struck westward again. He wondered, briefly, if he should even continue his quest. He was certain to lead them to those ruins as well. But whether they found it or not mattered little. What history he might find there, what help it might give him, mattered much more.

He drew a breath as he descended the next compartment. He had gone nights without sleep before. He could be tenacious too, tenacious in pressing ahead through exhaustion. He would want at least a day between himself and the Prosan when he reached Kragnog. One day to read as much history as he could.

In the dark, he could move freely. As the eastern sky began to pink, though, he knew he would begin to stand out on the tops of the hills, and he faltered. All they would need to do is look over the top of whatever hill they were on, and they would see him—however much of a speck, a speck still that moved—and their pursuit was nearly guaranteed.

He knew, from the writings in Stavnuk, the ruins were still some days ahead. And he had learned through the past night of running something of the lay of the land. Invariably, the valleys and hollows ran northwest to southeast; always open on one end or the other. And the hills were all of a similar height—so the Prosan would not suddenly be able to climb to an observation point. He would not need to stay in the deepest part of the valley, just far enough down not to be seen. If he kept perhaps twenty paces below the crest, he felt he could move without detection. He would still meander while they could draw a straight line, but he would not need to zig zag. There were, he thought as he turned to follow the contour, no other real options.

He continued that day at a light jog, pausing only barely to retrieve food from his pack before continuing to run as he ate. Occasionally, still, he would need to descend a valley to cross and make a saddle between hills to keep to his westerly course. As the golden hour approached he passed through another saddle and stopped: below him the land flattened and glittered. He glanced wildly for a moment. He could see the brown lands and hummocked hills stretching away north and curving east. But the writings made no mention of this lowland. Perhaps it didn't matter. It wasn't where he was trying to go. But it did mean he'd lost something of his bearings. What if he had already passed the ruins?

With something of a despondent whuffle he turned north and ran, angling downhill until he felt the ground begin to soften. He jogged again up to firm ground and continued. But his legs were beginning to ache. Desperation drove him to run through the night, but his body protested. Surely he had gained some time on his pursuers. But a nagging thought reminded him of their tenacity and hardiness. For all he knew they had run through the night as well.

Ahead of him, one of the valleys emptied into the lowlands, and water trickled down stair-stepped stones. He paused, scanning the hilltops and up the valley, then bent to drink.

"Kenis!"

His head came up, eyes wide. Stepping around a rock up the valley was a Prosan, bow raised and arrow to his cheek. Tavill's eyes flickered. More figures rose atop the hills. Some descended to circle him. All had their bows raised, some with arrows only nocked, others already bent. He marveled for a moment how well their dun clothes blended into the hillsides. Perhaps they had been almost on top of him all night and day, watching him in amusement as he fled.

They did not seem amused now. Nor did they seem tired. Indeed a hardy folk. It was a shame he couldn't get to know them, to learn about their history and people. Surely theirs was a story worth the telling—worth remembering at the end of time. Not that he would be there to see it.

He straightened slowly, keeping his hands calmly at his side as they completed their half-circle. He wondered, briefly, that they didn't enter the lowlands, seeming content to surround him only on the hillside. Not that it was an opportunity to run away. Maybe they knew that, and didn't bother to get their feet wet. A practical people as well.

"*Efitlos,*" the first man said. He lowered his bow and straightened. That left only...five arrows pointed at him. Tavill fixed him with his gaze.

"Why do you hunt me?" he asked.

The man blinked, glanced around the circle. Tavill followed his gaze, fixing on another Prosan as he—she?—lowered her unbent bow. Five still remained bent. He hadn't expected to see a female among his pursuers, but he supposed it wouldn't matter. She had clearly been able to keep up.

"We must," she said. Her Kalen was awful, but he could understand it. It surprised him again that they spoke it.

"Who are you? Where do you come—" He cut off as she hissed. Her knuckles were white on her bow, and her other hand tightened on a dagger at her hip. Surely she didn't think one would be more effective than another.

There was a burst of their language from the first man, and she backed away a step. She took a steadying breath. "Are more there of you?" she asked. When Tavill's head drooped a fraction, a light came to her eyes, and there was another scattering of their words among them.

He blinked away tears. Unbidden, the thrum came to his throat, a dirge he had sung over Kessaria. It was slow and gentle, but woolen now. He tried to add the overtone but it was as though his mouth were stuffed with that same wool. He paused, noticing that the Prosan held still as though enraptured. If there were ever a time to test the throat-song, it might as well be before he died.

He took the bone from his nose, began the thrum again. Now it rang in him and through him pure as silver bells. The overtone came with hardly an effort. Earth met sky as the sun sent its final burst over the far western horizon.

The tableau held: Tavill at the center singing, beginning to sway faintly; the Prosan in a half-circle, listening as though disciples being taught by their master. Bowstrings creaked as arrows were lowered. The world seemed to go silent before the song, and time ceased.

His vision faded as the smells began to fill in. The Prosan around him were prickly points of musk, sweaty from their long chase. The water trickling over the rocks became a thread of minerals—not limestone this time, but something of sand and clay.

The wind eddied, and he caught a whiff of the lowlands. He blinked.

There was death in that water. Not immediately, but if it would be drunk or seep into a wound it would fester quickly. Had they known that? And if they had, how?

There was a sharp twang, and searing pain lanced through his arm. The dirge ended in a bellow. His fingers, numb, dropped the bone. As his cry echoed away, it ended in a sob. The blood dripping down his arm swirled into his nose. Gone was the musk, the thread of sand and clay; only the death remained.

This time, blessedly for him, he did not remain aware. He awoke on his back. The sky overhead was foam on coal, the stars blurred to him. The breeze was steady, now, and from the north. He lay for a time, not seeking the scent-vision, but it intruded regardless. Musk and copper both were scattered around him. His arm throbbed where he had been shot, and he grasped it. The bleeding had stopped, and the arrow was gone—probably he had used it to...

He wiped his eyes. Could he not have stayed in his cabin? Would it have been worse than this? He had never incurred a bloodlust while he had lived there. Now, in just five moonturns he had slaughtered two bands of men—and women. He wondered how many were left, how many might still be pursuing him. And why not come after him all at once? And why come after him at all?

He sat up slowly. His legs trembled, still weary from the past day of running, and probably from the killing as well. She had said "we must." Was it some sort of duty, then? Who had laid it upon them?

He didn't know if Kragnog would hold any answers. He didn't know if any answers were even to be had—much of life didn't, he had found. Answers were invented, where necessary, the strain of continuing on without them too much for most to bear. And if answers themselves weren't invented, the hope of finding them was.

He heaved a sigh. Weariness was making him cynical. Answers too-long delayed were making him bitter. And yet, too much more of this and he wasn't sure he would want to keep fighting it.

He reached into his pouch. Just for a time he wanted to feel safe from the bloodlust, though there was likely no further threat. His fingers shuffled through empty space. He thrust in his entire fist. Nothing.

He had dropped it. Horror invaded his mind as keenly as the arrow, blossoming like the bloodlust. He scented; he had ended up north of the stream, for he could no longer smell it. Groping and shuffling he worked his way south, recoiling when his hand fluttered against one of the dead. He splashed through the stream, barking his knees against the stone. Where had he been? He felt through the grass, bent low hoping to smell it. He found a loose arrow: had he pulled it out immediately? Or was it another that had shot wild? That wouldn't make sense.

He whimpered, fingers scrubbing through the blades of grass. He found only dirt. He gripped the grass, yanking it up as he whined. Where could it have gone? Had it rolled, somehow? His head came up as he looked downslope. If it had—it was not a small piercing—it might have ended up in the poison waters below. He made his way down, hands weaving desperately, finding nothing. The smell came to him, the deathly water. His hand splashed and he leapt back, hoping the water didn't land on his arrow-wound. Panting, near tears again, he crept forward again. The stream cascaded directly beside him. If it had rolled, it should be some-where here. But he was loathe to search the lowland, and he had found nothing.

He rested on all fours, still panting, his head drooped. It was gone. His sight was gone. Only the threat of the bloodlust remained. And a faint and wavering hope that there might be some solution to it.

If there was, the throat-song was not it. The strewn bodies above him proved that.

21

SPIT IN HIS EYE

"How many of these do you have?"
"A few more."
"Why not just end him?"
"In death, he is useless to us."

12 Tetsamon 1320 — Spring

When Tavill finally stood, the rim of the hill above him was faintly white with sunlight. He breathed deep. The wind had died in the morning calm, and the scents now floated to him of their own will. It often allowed him a clearer picture, rather than when they were rushed along and jumbled by some breeze. The picture this morning was a blanket of death.

He stood over one of the Prosan, staring down at the inert form. It was not as—splattered—as some of those he had killed in the southern woods. He knelt. His nose could distinguish the scent of hair from the scent of boots, and he touched the head. A small hole was in the temple. She had probably been the first, killed by the arrow. He wondered if it had been hers. Idly he counted the arrows in her quiver. Her sheath, he found, was empty. If not the arrow, maybe he had killed her with her own dagger. It wouldn't have mattered to her.

Her body was arched as she lay overtop her small pack. He rolled her over, working the pack off her arms. He felt through it. Some small amount of food—incredible if they traveled on so little. He wondered if they took a vow of near-starvation. "We must" she had said—must, before they died? He felt deeper. A thin blanket, a few coiled leather bands, a whetstone, a...necklace? He pulled it out, held it close. A token of some kind, a flat ring with grooves across it. He held it closer so he could see. There were threads etched on it, but not in any recognizable pattern. He put it back. There was nothing else inside. He sniffed the food, detected no poison or strong scents, and put it into his own pack. He stood up and moved to the next blur.

That one, too, carried little. The same number of arrows. The same assortment, plus a quarter loaf of bread. Perhaps he ranked higher. On he went to the third body, the fourth, the fifth.

It was the sixth body that struck him, because it carried something none of the others had: a water skin, and it was nearly empty. He considered it for a time, sloshing it back and forth. There was traveling light, and there was traveling feral. This seemed the latter, now. Aside from the trickle now emptying into the lowlands, he had seen few streams on his way across. Plenty in the forest. Perhaps they were as surprised as he to leave those environs for a waterless waste.

Or perhaps they had a camp closer than he realized. He picked up the sixth's foot, inspected the boot: well-worn. No holes, but when he rubbed the sole it felt thin, almost brittle. They had to be far from home.

He dropped the foot and it thudded to the ground. He sloshed the skin again, and uncapped it. He sniffed, then recoiled and blinked. Not rancid, and not poisoned—at least, no poison he knew. But nearly pungent. He dribbled some on a finger and touched it to his tongue. Even that drop sparkled across his tongue, awakened his nose, peeked through a curtain of weariness he didn't know was there.

So. No ordinary water, but something that would drive them on and on relentlessly. He sighed, and checked the rest of them listlessly. All the same. The tenth was missing an arrow. Not that it mattered.

All twelve had the same token. Something bound them all, but without further context it could have been anything: clan, purpose, unit, religion... He peered close again. Threads. If threads had been bound around the flat circle, they could have been made to join in the center. The grooves might have held them in place.

And yet, he couldn't place why that was significant. It was a religion, but which one? Where had he seen it? He gripped his head and shook it. Was he simply tired? He had thought that memories always needed a trigger, or some sort of focal point, to be brought up—there were too many to simply call up whenever he wished. But now. Now it seemed like it was simply gone but for the vestiges. He knew he knew—or that he had known at one time.

As he strained to think, a darkness seemed to roll into his mind, a pain long forgotten. A throbbing ache, nearly like loss. He staggered away, still clutching the token. He had to make it to Kragnog. He didn't know why.

He drove himself on most of that day, collapsing finally as the sun lowered again. His chest heaved as he lay curled on his side in a hollow. "I am Taur," he croaked. "I am witness to the end of time."

Failed.

Failed witness. What was he witnessing but his own despair? The slow destruction of a race of people, twelve at a time, as they hurled themselves against him? Perhaps the destruction of another race of people, the Kalen? Averlynn had seemed to think it impending. But he could not help—the Taur were never supposed to help, only witness. The throbbing ache, a permanent companion since this morning, intensified a moment. *We cannot help. We cannot interfere.*

We must let evil happen.

There was a different timbre to that last thought. Perhaps it was a logical conclusion, made on his own. But the first two thoughts felt musty, decayed, a long-buried command. The ache sharpened almost to a point. He had argued, but weakly. And for some reason he could not possibly recall he felt as though he'd argued on his side, just as he now was.

As though his body moved on its own, he managed to wrestle his pack off and pull out some food. He ate, the bread thickening in his mouth as he tried to chew it. Too dry. He sipped some water while his mind still wandered almost feverishly, his thoughts seemingly not his own. He shivered as the land darkened. Again without thought or conscious volition he pulled out a blanket and covered himself.

Slowly warmth seeped back in, first the blanket and then back into his skin. He swallowed the last bit of bread, and slept.

The next few days were marked by drifting thoughts and consciousness. He barely knew when he ate or drank, and struggled to remember how many sunrises dragged him barely to the surface before he sank again. One afternoon he blinked awake, instantly and fully alert. But then he lay there, his mind blank. He scented few animals, though a lean deer grazed most of the afternoon across the north. He felt as though he could scent individual blades of grass in front of him, as though each possessed its own particular amount of grass-ness. And then, as quickly as it had come, consciousness departed. His next thought was a fuzzy evening as the sun flashed underneath a cloud bank before it set, and he ate a few more bites before sleeping through the night.

As far as he could recall, could trust he had come to consciousness at least once a day, he awoke the fifth morning since the bloodlust. Whatever had plagued him seemed to have gone. The ache was gone. The sun just peeped over the land, a warm yellow glow in his eyes. He felt hungry, and ate—there was little left. He would need to find some forage, somehow.

He sat up, wiped his mouth with the back of his arm, and tried to remember the past few days. Whatever had come upon him had never happened before—not in response to a bloodlust, or from eating something spoiled. He wondered about the drink in the waterskin. But that had been barely a drop. It seemed to him like the malaise had come from trying to force his way into his memories. Had he dug too deep, touching things not meant to be recalled until he officially bore witness? Was it some sort of barrier installed by Elonai to prevent too early a recollection?

But that too felt wrong. Whatever it was, it was past, and he had a destination. He rose, shouldered his pack, and set off.

But now he was not entirely sure to where he set off. He had lost most of his bearings, lost any of the landmarks the writing had mentioned. Far to the north he spied white peaks. He remembered there was some mention of mountains north of Kragnog, but not real distances. It spoke of folding, wrinkled lands; he was most assuredly in those. Vague mention of the lowlands and marshes, far to the south. And several day's journey from the forest. But if the forest had grown since then...

He finished the last of the food in his pack at midday. Though he trusted the strange drink, he still hesitated to use it. He hoped, instead, for forage of some kind. The grass, he found, held little nutrition, and sat on his stomach as though it took more energy than it gave.

The land changed more than it seemed from afar. The valleys first grew deeper, then longer. By evening he found one that dove all the way down to water, and he paused to drink. When he settled back, licking the drops from his chin, he scented a berry bush. It was too early in spring for berries, but the sprigs and shoots held the promise of them, and filled his stomach far better than the grass.

The days were warming, and he sat without fire or blanket as darkness fell. He took a breath to clear his head. He looked up at the fuzzy sky and missed the stars, and reached into his pouch before he remembered the piercing was gone. He rubbed his nose with a thick finger.

He felt his vulnerability keenly. He was entirely at the mercy of the bloodlust again—even a rabbit killed by a fox or wolf could bring it on. It seemed these hills were empty of such large prey, but he did not intend to stay here either. He had wanted to return to his duty—his entire purpose for going to Kragnog was that pursuit. But what would it matter if he would kill everyone he met? He couldn't expect humans to stop eating meat, or using metal, as he'd had to.

And the throat-song, he realized, hadn't worked. It had held them off momentarily because they didn't know what it was—had seemed even to spell them for a time. Which could have been fine, if his only purpose was to escape a chance encounter. But he longed to dwell among them again. And, ultimately, the spell had broken.

He could perhaps find Lasserain again, except he had not even intended to find him the first time. And could he ask for another piercing after losing the first? Could Lasserain even make another one? And then what if he lost that one? Eventually Lasserain would die, and mages such as those rarely passed their secrets on to another—certainly not only for Tavill's sake.

That left Averlynn, and her Old Raina. He nearly scoffed; what could she know that he wouldn't? True, some of his memories were strangely buried, but he thought he remembered the past millennium at least. How old could she be?

But, as he thought about it, he remembered too the Kalen were an ancient race. Not immortal, but perhaps a millennium as well. And if she was considered old even for her people...

He considered which would be harder to find: Averlynn, or Kragnog. Kragnog, at least, was static—it wouldn't move to somewhere he had already searched, and elude him either purposefully or accidentally. And, if he was honest, he had more hope of answers from there than from a people he could barely recall.

The next day just before noon, a strange smell came to him—not quite a carcass, and not quite reptilian, but reminded him of both. It passed quickly, and though he searched he could not find it again. He found another small stream, another smattering of bushes and even a few wild leeks. It felt like a feast.

When he ascended the valley again, striking vaguely north, the carcass smell struck him again—not blood, thankfully, only rot. This time he looked around in time to see a faint pearlescent glimmer streaking across the sky. He stared as it slowly wheeled, the shape twisting as though it wormed its way through the sky. It drew nearer. The scent struck him as it twisted again, nearly overhead, and he realized great wings flapped.

Once again, a vast emptiness in his mind suddenly flooded with memories—memories of dragons. One still lived in the south, and he had been amazed it lived in such cold reaches. He had never met it, or spoken to it, but he had scented the same long before, vaguely attended that scent to a memory even further back, before his vision had gone. The two races often intertwined, back when both had been revered by humans.

This one wheeled again, closer. Tavill sat down, let his pack slip to the ground, and waited, watching.

With a great blast of wind, the scent nearly suffocating, the dragon landed heavily in front of him, and the head lowered quickly toward him. He couldn't help but flinch, though he felt no danger from it.

"Excuse me, master Taur," the dragon said as her neck arched, her voice a high almost breathy timbre, but—it seemed—carrying a sliver of a deeper boom as well. A complex voice. "I don't land as lightly as I once did. How are you?"

Tavill sat in shock a moment. He had not been prepared to answer any question, and certainly not that one. How was he? "Alive," he responded.

The ground trembled as the dragon settled on her haunches. "That I can see. Is that all?"

"That is all I can say for certain, master dragon."

She shook her head as though ridding herself of a fly in her ear. "Oh, forgive me. I am named Aryndurlan." The dragon seemed to wait expectantly.

"Tavill."

"Well met, Tavill." She paused. "Is something wrong?"

Tavill realized he had been torn between holding his breath and taking only shallow ones: the carcass smell far overpowered the reptile one, and his scent-vision seemed overcome by the idea of dead animal. "Forgive me, Aryndurlan," he said. "My nose is very sensitive."

The dragon's head reared back further, and the cloying faded some. "Of course it is! Forgive me please—consequence of my diet. The deer out here are rangy and sometimes stick awfully in my teeth."

"What are you doing out here?"

"Why, I live here. Don't you?"

Tavill shook his head. "My home was far to the south—"

"Oh, have you met Wynthuel then?"

Tavill glanced up. "I have noticed—him? From afar."

"Ah yes, it is difficult isn't it. I suppose I sound like a female dragon. And in many important ways I am. And in many important ways Wynthuel is a male dragon." Aryndurlan nodded sagely. "Yes, it is often difficult." Her neck curled as she gazed south.

The silence stretched, both lost in their own thoughts for a time. Suddenly Aryndurlan glanced sharply at Tavill. "You said your home *was* there. Where do you live now?"

"Never in one place for long." He glanced over the highlands. "Have you perhaps seen some ruins out there?" he asked hopefully.

"Do you mean Kragnog?"

Tavill looked up excitedly. "Yes! You have, then?"

The dragon shook her head. "Not for a long time."

Tavill frowned. "But you know where it is—or was?"

"Oh...dear. Let me think..." Aryndurlan laid down, stretching her neck out and resting her head on the lower slope. As Tavill stared, the dragon closed her eyes. Soon she began to snore.

Tavill closed his mouth, settling in to wait. There was no rushing a dragon, nor waking one up. That was a good way to have your head bitten off—accidentally, of course.

The afternoon wore on, pleasantly warm and sunny. He found himself repeatedly glancing toward the mountains. Even blurry, they were definitely vaster and taller than the Snowashes. He wondered if he could lose himself in them, at least for a time. He missed the opportunities to explore. Though the Taur retreat to these lands was marred by fear and failure, a part of him had quickened to the idea of wandering.

But more often he returned to the idea of finding Old Raina. He shook his head. It was an odd pressure—not quite a thought, certainly not one he could pull out and examine. Not like some others that also came unbidden. But there was something there, something he worried was worth considering. Perhaps it was his own fears, or desperation of seeking every possible avenue.

He stood and walked to the edge of the ridge, carefully side-stepping Aryndurlan's tail. The breeze had swung somewhat westward. Without sight, finding the ruins seemed impossible. The landmarks in the writings mentioned no scent, and what landmarks it had given would not have a particular smell. If the dragon could not remember—could not guide him to it—what hope did he have? But if he returned to Stavnuk, waiting in hope the Kalen would come to him for proof, he could be led to Old Raina.

He drew a wavering breath. To have come so far, just to slaughter another band of Prosan... But they had likely followed him to Stavnuk first, so if he had stayed there he would have killed them there. Probably. But then he might also not have lost the piercing.

"You know, I think I have," Aryndurlan said suddenly. Her head came up. "Where are you? Did you leave? I say, someone asks a question of an old dragon who needs a moment to think—"

"I'm here! I'm here," Tavill said, hurrying around to where the dragon could see him.

"Ah, there you are. I have seen Kragnog."

Tavill's shoulders sagged. "You told me that already," he said. "But do you remember where?"

"Oh, yes." Aryndurlan nodded, drooped her head back to the earth and closed her eyes. Tavill sighed, waiting to hear the snores again and nearly decided to walk off. "It's north."

"Aryndurlan," Tavill said. He clamped his mouth shut and turned away for a moment.

The dragon's head came back up. Her voice suddenly lost all bass—she sounded entirely feminine. "What is it?"

Tavill closed his eyes. "I cannot see," he said. "At least, not far past my nose. I cannot find it on my own."

Aryndurlan was silent, her head curling a little closer to Tavill. "When did that happen?"

"Long ago. It began, I think, before we came here."

"Your people are not known for this," she said carefully. Tavill shook his head bitterly. "Do you know how it happened?" the dragon asked. Again he shook his head. Aryndurlan stooped even closer, her breath washing over Tavill. He let the carrion scent swirl through him until he no longer recoiled, but simply allowed it to be what it was.

Aryndurlan sat back. "It has been long since I've known your people," she said, his voice complex once more, but only slightly less compassionate. "But it seems something deep and dire has happened to you—for you to be both blind and forgetful is a dreadful twisting of your purpose."

"I know," Tavill croaked. "It has not mattered for some time, though..."

"Tavill, it always matters." The voice now was deeper than ever, and boomed across the highlands. "It always matters when what has been created is bent away from its purpose."

Tavill gave a bitter snort. "My people bent away from their purpose long ago, I fear, and through our own choice. Although..." He trailed off, letting that bitterness blossom a little more. "Although to choose otherwise seemed impossible at the time—seems impossible even now..."

"Why?"

"We were supposed to witness," Tavill said, the bitterness continuing to grow as he spoke. "But those we were supposed to witness wanted us dead."

"My kind have often been hunted, too," Aryndurlan said, nodding wearily. "It is often a struggle to keep up our numbers."

"But you can do so!" Tavill nearly shouted in anger. His bitterness was quickly becoming rage. "There are none of us left, and the Prosan are hunting me now relentlessly—"

"None of you?" Aryndurlan asked suddenly. "You have been all over the world, every inch, and know this for certain? You've been far to the east?"

A sudden hope pierced his rage, deflated it in an instant. "You know of others? A remnant besides me?"

Aryndurlan tossed her head. "Of course not, I live here and do not travel much. I merely present the question." She leaned a little closer. "And by your response I can tell that *you* do not know for certain either—you believe so, only."

Tavill opened his mouth, then closed it. He had been told that those who came here were the last—he could remember...but could he? Or had that been lost with time, too? And all that remained was what he believed, what he had been told—reminded of—by others. Had theirs been belief only? Or had he forgotten an important nuance? How could he know?

He glanced away, frustration again watering the root of bitterness. For so many years, south of the Snowashes, tucked safely away in his cabin, he had thought his memories were always there, always present and clear, he just never bothered to stir them up. There were no hooks with which to dredge them up, he told himself. But surely, at the end of time, he would be able to. At least, as far as whatever memories he had.

His bitterness, for a moment, turned on Lasserain. If the mage had never told him of the approaching Prosan, he would be safe in his cabin still. But he knew that was hollow; either they would have come and killed him, or their presence would still have brought him down this long road. He would have realized eventually that something had changed.

"What's happened to me?"

Aryndurlan rumbled. "That is a good question," she said. In the silence, the wind picked up again. A storm threatened. "Do you know," the dragon continued, her voice nearly soft. "That dragons are granted a measure of healing?"

It took a moment, and Tavill swung his head around slowly. Hope, long forgotten, pulsed. "Will it? Is it...possible?"

"Many things are possible. But—" Her head tilted in warning. "This is a strange thing—it is not a simple physical ailment. I do not know exactly what will happen. But if you wish, I will try."

"If it doesn't work, will it...is there a chance of making things worse?"

Aryndurlan shifted. "Do you know," she mused, "I'm not sure." She stamped her feet and hummed. "I can't see why it would, or how it would..."

"Just—" Tavill held up his hands. "Let's just try."

Aryndurlan cleared her throat, a great barking noise. "Now, this might be uncomfortable, but..." Tavill saw the head draw near, the great tongue snake out. The carrion scent threatened to overwhelm him again, and he closed his eyes.

Suddenly a thick wetness splatted on his head, and he tried desperately not to cringe. It slithered across, then down each side, and finally swiped across his nose. To his shame he gagged, but quickly fought it off.

There was silence again, broken by a low rumble of thunder in the distance. Finally, and almost comically tentative, Aryndurlan asked: "Well...what happened? How do you feel?"

Slimy.

Tavill mentally shushed himself. He had felt nothing, felt now no different. His memories, memories of where he had been or what happened to him, were still hidden. That left...

He scrubbed his nose with his arm and sniffed. The scents were still there—dry grass just turning to spring green; the snake-like filminess of Aryndurlan before him; petrichor. He was not worse.

He cracked open an eye. The day was darkening, probably below the storm clouds. The breeze was stiff and steady. The dragon stood uncertainly, her head cocked, her eyes concerned. Tavill opened his other eye, and blinked.

Something was different. He took a shaky breath, trying to sort it out. He could see, after a manner, but it was unlike having the bone in his nose. The colors were all wrong—almost black and white, except his mind could shade in what he knew. But it slipped sideways, sometimes—the brown grass leached into Aryndurlan, or the pearl-and-yellow topaz of her scales would blend into the sky.

He blinked a few more times, seeing if it would clear. It made it worse, his eyelids smearing the colors further. If he held his eyes open, they steadied for a time, then slowly dripped down like paint on a wall.

"I hope it doesn't stay like this," he said. He looked at the dragon, and gave a faint smile. "It is no longer blurry like it was, but the colors..." He trailed off, then tried to explain.

Aryndurlan came close, peering hard at him. "Oh," she said suddenly. "Well that's...strange." She cleared his throat again. "So, Kragnog you're looking for? Hmm. I may be able to guide you there. I won't walk, though," she said with as much consternation as Tavill had ever heard. "But I can fly ahead and see if I can find it—"

"Master dragon," Tavill cut in. He blinked again to right the colors, and saw Aryndurlan's apologetic gaze trying to hide behind bluster. "What is strange?"

"Yes. Well, it seems there's some saliva still in your eyes," she said, trying to sound normal. "I think it's holding your vision steady—I mean, as much as it can. But it's...I mean, it moves around, you know. And so..."

Tavill looked away, couldn't help but snort a chuckle. Then he sighed. "So it won't last."

"I'm afraid not. Perhaps while you sleep, or..." She broke off at a sudden crash of thunder nearby, the bolt of lightning casting the broken landscape in stark relief. "Or when it rains. Let us find what shelter we can for now from his storm. And I will stay with you until we find what you're looking for."

They retreated to a hollow, sharp and deep. Aryndurlan curled in the bottom, extending a wing and resting it on the hillside. Tavill crawled underneath. Nearer the dragon's body he was able to sit upright, and watched as the rain swept across the land. It ripped through the hollow in an instant, nearly like a waterfall. Rivulets ran down the hillside, puddled here and there, then ran off further down the hollow.

Aryndurlan's head poked in suddenly, nearly missing Tavill. "Oh, forgive me," the dragon said. Her eyes were already closed, her breathing deep. "I didn't realize it would be raining this hard..." She trailed off, muttered a bit more, then seemed to sleep.

As the dragon relaxed he folded a little tighter, and Tavill's small window to the outside world shut. He sat in a shimmering amber gloom, the dragon's wing translucent enough to let in some light. After a time, the glimmer brightened and the hammering of the rain on the wing lessened.

Tavill settled back. He didn't want to sleep. He didn't want to let the dragon's saliva be squeezed out and to lose even this strange type of vision. He went through his pack, taking quick inventory. He wouldn't need his blanket. The heat next to the dragon was already almost unbearable. He went through his pouch, his fingers feeling the flat ring the Prosan had carried.

He pulled it out by the string, holding it dangling. It was harder to see now, in the failing light. But he stared, seeing if some hook might drag up a memory, however distant or dry.

"Is that the eternal circle?" Aryndurlan muttered.

Tavill looked sharply at her. The dragon's eyes were still closed. "How did you know?"

"Hmmm, I can feel it, I guess. Never thought you would have one, who knows Elonai personally. Hm, well...*knew*, I guess..."

Tavill sat back. The eternal circle. Emblem of the Cariste—so, it had been threads. Were those, then, Cariste, not Prosan? He shook his head. He had gone through their things, had seen them face to face—and nearer the Snowashes, long before the Cariste came near Stavnuk. But then why did they have them? Where had they gotten them?

And how did he remember that's what it meant? He could dredge up no specific memory. Except he knew distantly he had seen it before, knew that's what it was. Aryndurlan said she felt it...did it communicate with her somehow? Tavill felt nothing specifically from it.

His hand dropped, and he sighed. Kragnog. There, hopefully, was knowledge. This constant running of questions wearied him, and his eyes sagged shut. As the rain drummed on, he slept.

22

NINE MORE THAN BEFORE

"You know what is waiting for her."
"I do."
"Will she survive?"
"This long, Teresh, and you still ask? I cannot know."

15 Tetsamon 1320 — Spring

Averlynn let Tarafel walk a slow pace. She was weary, and knew he was too. Odd, it seemed to her: she should have felt some sense of urgency. She should be tearing through the woods, desperate to get to the village and raise the alarm.

She had heard the outcry, the clash of weapons, and had snuck back and overheard Ketzler's words to his companions. She was amazed, didn't want to think that he had killed his own comrade—couldn't imagine he harbored that much hate against her people to incite war. Was it hate? Or just fear?

Did it matter? He had done it, and nothing she could say or do would change it—change their minds. So war would come. She didn't know when. They would still have to find their villages, find their Rangers. Her people would not be powerless, if it came to it—not unless they chose to be.

And, as she changed direction again to confuse pursuit, she was nearly certain they would choose to. It fit them too well, a life of running and cowering. Right now she wouldn't mind that life either. She had little strength left to fight.

Tarafel walked despondently, as though sensing it. It didn't matter that spring was upon them, that the trees budded and the black trunks of the forest were speckled in green, that brooks babbled and chuckled in their rocky beds, and rivers roared with rain and snowmelt. She had seen just yesterday the first fawns, still awkward and brightly spotted. And in her mind she saw it slain by an invading army.

And yet she had to try. She knew, if she projected defeat, her people would latch onto it. Somehow, some way, she had to find an ebullience that seemed impossibly distant right now. She would have to find something within herself, some spark, to light the flame of the courage of her people. She knew they had it—before the war turned badly in Burieng they were a fierce people, proud of their heritage and abilities, willing to sacrifice whatever it took to preserve it.

But then the war exposed the truth: they were not willing to sacrifice everything. Much, perhaps. But soon the toll rose higher than they could have believed. Village after village was swallowed up, their people harried and killed and lost. Too many. They had been misled by their pride. They should never have resisted. If they had only run from the start, they would not have lost so much.

Why was it different now? Why should they risk, again, everything they had, everything they were? It was this question that she had to answer before she returned home, a question that had worried her from the first day she left the Glowwood, the question she was no nearer answering now.

But there was another question, one which cropped up only now and again, one for which—for her parents—there would be no answer: why were you not here for Aman È? She doubted they would even ask. It was the worst of fortunes that her home was the nearest village. If only she were nearer Amka—or Tekaa Wohan, if she were truly wishing. Instead she would have to face her parents, face those she had grown up with, and worry she was already banished and forgotten. *Tienko.* Never to be sended to their eternal home upon her death. Eternally isolated.

Hopefully her letter through Amrith had reached them in time, that between the letter and the news she brought she might be forgiven. Or, if not forgiven, at least somewhat excused.

She turned again after crossing a stream. She needed more time. She doubted the Cariste were pursuing her already. The turns now were to delay the inevitable, to make Wazè that much further away. To give her time to think, to dredge up some form of courage she could share with the others.

If only it was as simple as needing swiftness. If they could strike first, they could destroy the landing party now. Leave some evidence of their destruction for the next wave, as warning. Or leave the land completely empty, make them wonder and worry what had happened to the first force. That might deter them. Or set a defense on those shores and actually repel the next wave.

But it would not be swift. Word would have to be sent to Tekaa Wohan. The council would have to sit and discuss. Maybe, finally, the order would go out and the armies would *begin* preparing. But plans for the defense of each village and outpost would have to be formulated—should they even defend the outposts? Or collapse on Tekaa Wohan and defend it alone? But what of the homes of those from the villages? What of the lands they had grown attached to?

Had they attached to the lands? Or should they abandon all and flee again? More orders would be sent out rescinding the first. The outposts and Scouts and Rangers would be in disarray—some of them may act on their own, various Kas taking matters into their own hands. And she would not be there to lend her voice. She didn't hold that sort of power anyway. She would make her report, and whatever unfolded, unfolded. And she would be awash in the tide of orders along with the rest.

She considered the various Kas, which of them might be most likely to support her. Perhaps if she approached one of them, she could sway him, at least have some splinter of their forces acting in a way that made sense. She had nearly run the list in her mind when one stuck out: Ka Ouwa. So revered he was sent to the port where Aver had departed—probably the only Kalen to have used the port since they landed. His troops would support her out of sheer boredom. Was she that confident that her opinions made the most sense? To risk the lives of Kalen who might join her only for something to do, not because they believed she was right?

Tarafel stopped, and they both bowed their heads. He, to drink; her, to look inside herself. Why did she think she knew best? Just because she had kept herself most open to the land? And why did she wish to stay? She didn't even like it here that much.

Her head came up as she took in the forest around her, so different from the woods of Burieng. Wilder, in many ways. But also younger. The forests of home held so much more reverence, such a weight of age that worship came easy. That forest predated her, gave her a sense of place by existing before her, of holding such wisdom that she wished to sit at its feet all her life.

Not here. There were ancient enough trees here and there, but most would have sprouted during her lifetime, had come from parents that sprouted during her lifetime. She knew by tree and soil that this forest had once been open plain, indistinguishable from Hataki Hills below the Wall. As such it felt more like a younger sister, something for which she was responsible. It sat at *her* feet, bright-eyed perhaps and eager to learn her wisdom, but too close in age to be worshipful. Not that she desired to be worshiped anyway, but...

Perhaps that was why she stayed. She loved old Kalen, but she was responsible for new Kalen. She knew these lands in part, and loved in part, and that knowledge and love would increase. But only if she stayed. Return to old Kalen was impossible—Aver's story told her that much. She did not want to start over. Perhaps that would be enough to convince her people.

She galloped on, now, until dark. She set her camp with no fire—the nights were beginning to warm anyway. As she lay awake, her mind and body tossing and turning, in the times between she fiddled with her ring. Finally exhaustion overtook her and she slept.

For two more days and nights she traveled deeper into the heart of Waken Forest. By morning she arrived where the smooth-trunked sychar trees filtered in among ash and cherry, and slowed. Wazè was near, and Rangers and Scouts could be anywhere, coming or going. But also she still worried.

The long cliff near Wazè rose on her right. She felt again the soft change that came when she entered the borders of the village, layered below her churning stomach. They would know, as well, that she had entered, feeling the ripples of the magic in her ring. Much preferred, she supposed, than entering unannounced, and yet...

Her mother and father strode toward her, and she felt the whiplash shock of their rebuffs. Tarafel whinnied, sensing some of it, nearly sinking back on his hocks.

"How dare you!" they shouted, their voices full of power. United in spirit—apparently—and in wrath, even the branches near Averlynn shook as though in a violent wind.

She felt herself pale: this was far beyond what she even feared worst. "Please, let me—"

"Begone! You are no longer Wohan; you are no longer our daughter. You have abandoned your people, murdering them in the sight of your existence. What made you even countenance returning now?"

"I thought...my letter..." she said weakly. "And I've seen it, seen the doom—"

But they did not hear her. "Your letter?" her mother, Erion, seethed, nearly apoplectic. "Your letter explained much indeed! How do you think we knew you had rejected your birth? Rejected everything you swore oaths to?"

Averlynn felt a little color returning. Erion's words made no sense. "Rejected my oaths?" she repeated. "I said I would hold to my oaths as tightly as I could—including the one to protect our people!"

"And now you lie, as you try to skulk back. We have your letter!" Avakó said, now waving it in the air. Of course he would have it: evidence for banishment would be carried by the instigators for a period of years, until all record of the banished was otherwise erased.

But as he read the words, they were not hers. They spoke of regret at following the Chiefs from Kalen. She dismissed their rule as just—dismissed, therefore, the authority of the Intag Ka. That any oaths made to these were non-binding. And, finally, that she considered herself free from her people to act as she chose.

Beneath the weight of her confusion she felt a tiny prick of anger; did they know her so poorly, to think she would abandon them that way? Did they think she spent the time away from friends and family, patrolling the wildernesses of Wohan, for anyone's sake but theirs? True, she enjoyed it, but it was never purely for that. And the torment of the prophecies, the fear of what would happen to her and her people...

"I am permitted to see the evidence for my banishment," she found herself saying, far more firmly than she felt. It was a dangerous gambit, because it acknowledged the banishment.

Her father stalked toward her and held it out. She took it and scanned it quickly. It felt like the parchment she had used. She could not deny her handwriting, her signature, her seal. How, then...?

She closed her eyes. Amrith. The Scout who had gone into the enemy camp and changed their reports, their tallies—had done so in a way that they couldn't detect. Amrith, the legendary—almost mythic—Scout.

Her hands trembled as she opened her eyes. "Listen," she began, before her mind convinced her of the futility. "Amrith, he—"

"Oh yes, he told us how you snuck out in the middle of the night," Avakó said, dangerously quiet. "Taking your sword and fleeing, nearly taking off his arm as you fought him. And when they searched the possessions you left behind, found this letter." He snatched it back and tucked it in his pouch. He held out his hand, palm flat, and waited expectantly.

It took her a moment to register. He waited for her ring. Banishment meant being stripped of all privileges granted the Kalen. She looked to her mother, but Erion had turned away—as though Averlynn were already gone from the village, and from her memory.

But they had to know—she had to show them the enemies near their havens. Tarafel shifted, as though already sensing what Averlynn only now began to consider. "Our shores are breached," she said quietly, looking again at her father. "Forces have come. The Prosan—"

"Hssst!" No more words were permitted to be spoken to her. She was not supposed to speak any.

She tightened her lips, and looked hard into her father's eyes, trying to convey by sheer will what she could not say. But she saw no softening, no shifting, no understanding—or capacity to understand.

Almost without command, Tarafel whirled and charged from the village. She didn't think they would let her go; one such as they perceived her was dangerous, still in possession of a ring. Perhaps they had been unprepared, expecting her to give it up willingly as the letter indicated she should. Perhaps the gods protected her.

As she galloped she shouted. "The Cariste are coming! The eastern shore near the Glowwood has fallen into the sea. I have heard from their own lips they intend war." Far outside bowshot now, she turned and looked back on an empty forest—but she knew they were there, knew some would be listening. "And I have met one of the *Anggika*—he names himself Tavill of the Taur. I have proofs of him. He told me the Prosan are marching, and already there are raiding parties north of the mountains. If any would preserve our homes, if any would take up the responsibility we owe these young forests, come with me."

She turned Tarafel and dashed away. She knew her words had reached some ears, but could not know if they had any effect.

As the sun sank, she wondered what she truly thought would happen—if any would follow her without question. As she waited in a small glen she wondered why she thought any would show up. She thought how silly that they might magically know where she went. If she were lucky, an armed party would arrive soon to take her ring by force. They were not prone to executions, but in her case exceptions might be made.

Tarafel grazed, unconcerned. She paced; he laid down and rolled in the grass. She folded her arms tightly and glared. "I'm glad of your sympathy." He tossed his head with a light whinny.

She felt a tickle, and whirled, her hand going to the hilt of her sword. She sensed another's ring, but unfamiliarity kept her from identifying the owner just yet. She searched the trees, but in the failing light saw no movement.

Faintly, like a tendril of fog, the ring's presence grew. When she knew who it was she blinked, almost in disbelief. Of anyone to support her, though... But is that what his coming meant?

Finally she saw him, riding sloppily—he had never been a good horseman, and in his old age cared even less for form. Chief Witko, perpetually second in line, rode into full view. His glance held concern, with the hint of wildness he always carried. Some of the younger Kalen called him withered, and not only in body.

He reined his horse to a stop—she couldn't remember a name, and wasn't sure it had one—and looked at her for some time, hands folded on the saddle horn. As the silence drew on, Tarafel came to stand beside her.

Finally, Witko drew a short breath. "Well," was all he said. The wildness flickered a moment, almost playful, and he dismounted. Without another word he set about gathering firewood.

Averlynn joined him silently, and they made camp. Witko had brought two small shelters and an array of food. As darkness fell their fire crackled merrily and the glen faded away behind the globe of light.

When they had eaten, Witko reached again into his saddlebags and brought out a small bottle and two simple wooden cups. He poured into each and handed one to Averlynn. She raised it to her nose a moment and sniffed; a light summer wine, and she wondered how he had it. She sipped as they watched the flames.

"I told them I would bring back your ring," he said.

She had wondered, but made no comment. It didn't even really surprise her. "The Kalen are going to run away again."

"It keeps us young," he replied.

She snorted. She was one of the few who still found wisdom in Witko, despite some of his shenanigans, and so she reacted less strongly than others to some of his comments. "Is that why we live so long?"

They were both silent again for a time, and finished the cups. Witko poured a little more. "I didn't know you were in Wazè," Averlynn said.

"Hmm. Tell me about the letter," he said.

"Is that why you were there?" Witko didn't answer but she felt a settling. She shrugged. "I wrote a letter, with Amrith's urging to come to the north and see if the prophecy was true, explaining what I was doing and why. I hoped to return for Aman É, but I was held up."

"He's never really liked you. A lot of them don't, but he was special."

She suspected as much, but it still hurt to hear it out loud. "Well, it seemed he had begun to change." She clipped off the end of the word, felt how silly it sounded as it came out of her mouth, and took another sip. "I want peace, too. But we aren't going to have it." She glanced at him sharply. "Do you believe me about the letter, then?"

"That boy is a *kissik*," Witko said. Averlynn spluttered; even she wouldn't have thought Witko would use such a word. Or would call Amrith a boy. "Well he is. Hero, ha! He rowed his boat up a small stream and told tales of mighty rapids, is his kind of hero."

Averlynn chuckled a moment, then sobered. "He'll be the hero of the Cariste and the Prosan, soon."

Witko flashed her a quick glance. "Plenty of those," he muttered. Averlynn looked the question at him, but he seemed lost in thought. His head drooped a moment. "They'll be worried about me."

"You're not riding back tonight?" she asked. It was full dark, and his horse didn't seem the type to travel well at night through the forest.

His head snapped up, though he did not look at her but across the glen.

"Of course not. They don't worry about me that much. Might do them a convenience, actually." His lips curved into a smile at the thought, and Averlynn saw all the wildness in his eyes she was accustomed to. For a brief moment, she wondered if his friendship had hurt her more than it helped. But she dismissed it. She would rather his alone than a hundred of the others. Except she needed an army.

"Do you think any others will help me?" she wondered aloud.

"Not from Wazè," he said frankly. But then his glance gleamed again. "But they're the only ones who know of your exile."

She frowned. "How did that happen? Shouldn't word have been sent out already?"

"Oops."

She turned to him in amazement. "Witko, what did you do?"

He feigned innocence. "Why would I interfere with the supremely wise decision to wait until we had your ring back? I'm just a crazy old man anyway, Chief only because my age demands it." He shook his head. "No, better for me to remain silent. At least, once the idea had been put in the right ear."

She shook her head in wonder. But a problem still persisted. "I don't know how much that will help me," she said. "I don't know if anyone from Amka will believe me either."

He groaned as he sat up and stretched a hand to his saddlebags again. "Here. Umph. Take this to them." He withdrew and handed her a letter. She opened it and read, then read again.

"Witko," she said, then dropped her hands to her lap. "The council cannot actually support me in this."

He cocked an eyebrow. "Of course they don't!"

"But their signatures!" She waved the letter. Witko's eyes never left hers.

"Well who do you think taught Amrith how to forge a letter?"

She gaped. She wanted to throw her arms around him, knew he probably wouldn't mind, but worried she would knock him over. His grin returned a moment, then he sobered.

"You should probably leave tonight," he said. "I can delay perhaps one more day, but word *will* go out if I don't return soon."

"What will happen to you, though? Won't they be upset with you that you didn't return with the ring?"

Witko drew a deep and dramatic sigh. "I don't know what happened, I guess you didn't trust me as much as I thought. I couldn't well overpower you. If they truly want it back, they may need to send some Rangers in force to—where was that Taur village?"

Averlynn shook her head. She always knew Witko hid something behind his crazy demeanor, but had never realized how much. She gave him directions. "The Cariste are not far from there, either, or they weren't when I left."

"That's a lot to remember. I hope I can recall everything you've said, but you know how my old mind is." He shrugged. "Here, take this." He handed her the bottle. "I can get more, and I doubt you will for a long time yet. Get on your way."

She stood, then paused to watch him at his ease beside the fire. "What of the Prosan?" she asked. "Tavill said they are coming."

Witko shrugged, seemed uncomfortable. "Well, I don't know if...I mean, they're all gone though..." He stopped, twiddled something with his thumb. "Averlynn..." He paused, tried to smile and failed. "They won't be after us," he said heavily.

She gazed at him. "They aren't supposed to exist anymore."

"Well...right."

"You're not surprised they still do."

His glance flickered. "We have been keeping something of an eye on them—special task force. We didn't want anyone alarmed."

Averlynn closed her eyes and sighed. She felt a little betrayed, true; but part of her was relieved her people had not completely annihilated them. "And I wasn't on it?" she asked playfully.

Witko's grin was weak. "No," he said, his voice low. He cleared his throat. "But you need to go. Your journey is not a short one."

She had Tarafel quickly saddled, and with little else to say rode off with a brief goodbye. She hoped she would see him again, would be welcome in her village again, would maybe even rouse her village to fight.

But that was perhaps far off, and little in her control. Maybe Witko could contrive something; she would have to trust him with that. Her task still lay in Amka, and gaining what Rangers she could. Which presented her with her next problem: how many would she get? That depended on how many were there, and how many the Ka would want to keep up the outpost. And how many did she need? That depended on what her plan was—did she want to track the Cariste only? By subterfuge lead them in circles? Destroy them?

The letter gave her command of a "small war band." It would be up to the Ka to decide what "small" meant, at least in part. She tried to remember which Ka would be in Amka, but her mind was muddled with her travels. She had not been on the normal rotation schedule for a time, now, and wasn't even sure if they would have changed it when they decided suddenly to send her south. That would have to wait until she reached Amka.

She pushed Tarafel nearly to his limits over the next few days. Forage increased as spring settled on the land. The buds grew and some trees came to early leaf. She worried what was happening where she could not see. She didn't realize until now what small amount of comfort came from keeping eyes on the Cariste, in the midst of the horror of it happening. She didn't know how fast they could sail, when the reinforcements would arrive, how soon they would move, where they would move to...

All she could do was press on toward Amka as swiftly as possible, gather what forces she was granted, and pick up the trail once again. If others saw, if they engaged the Cariste in some way, the intent of the enemy would be known and her people would have to react.

She did not pause to see the Hataki this time, but went directly to the outpost. For a time, everything felt normal: they did not seem to know about her banishment as Chief Hathar greeted her. His surprise was only at her unscheduled presence. They neglected the review of the guards this time as she relayed the urgency of her mission. He agreed cautiously, but escorted her into the main hall.

She froze upon entering. Scout Amrith sat at his leisure, a cluster of grapes in his hand. His eyes hardened and he leapt to his feet.

"You were banished!" he shouted.

Hathar turned, eyes goggling at first, then turning quickly back to Amrith in scorn. "She still has her ring," he said.

"She must not have been back to Wazè to return it," he said. "But I have come from there. I delivered her letter rejecting our people, and heard the pronouncement of our council on her banishment." He glared at her, and she thought she saw spark of defiance—and confidence.

Hathar turned back. "Is this true?"

Averlynn desperately smothered her fears. "I cannot speak to the letter's origin that Scout Amrith claims to have delivered," she said, only thinly hiding her own sarcasm. "But I have no banishment over me."

"I tell you, I was there!"

"I do not deny it," she said as smoothly as she could. "But I convinced the council that I wrote no such letter, and that there is now a threat from the east as well as the south." Witko was on the council, after all, so she was not entirely lying.

Something flickered in Amrith's gaze—was it surprise? But it seemed more like surprise that she knew it, not that threat was there.

"Our council is not so easily swayed," he spat. "And not when it is your word against mine."

She raised an eyebrow. He rowed his boat far indeed. "Well, I have also just come from Wazè and I bear a letter from the council there." She pulled it out and handed it to Hathar. He unfolded it and read it.

"It bears their signatures," he said. "And supports her claims."

"Letters can be forged," Amrith scoffed, lowering his eyes briefly as he realized what he had said.

"Indeed, they can," Averlynn said coolly.

Hathar glanced between them. "Perhaps we will need to decide this for ourselves, with what evidence we have before us." As Amrith's fists tightened on the table, Hathar turned to Averlynn. "Refresh yourself for now. We will convene the council this evening."

"We should delay as little as possible, Chief," she said, bowing her head. "Our enemies have had some weeks already to reinforce their positions." *And a message may too soon arrive proclaiming my banishment.*

Trust in Chief Witko.

When she returned as daylight faded, she found Hathar, Amrith, Ka Urlan—she thought he was at least neutral to her—and Isun Vera all in attendance. A fifth—for a council could not be less than five—she struggled to recognize. She thought perhaps he was a Tracker, which Hathar quickly confirmed.

"Edda," he said, nodding to the man. "If you go, you will take a contingent of Trackers as well, and he is familiar with those regions. Now, let the council be aware first of my discomfort in making this decision so near the end of my term." He glanced sternly around, sternest at Averlynn. "I do not wish to leave him short of bodies without his knowledge. However, the letter brought by Averlynn—"

"Shouldn't we determine if the letter is real, first?" Amrith broke in.

"Did the Chiefs of Wazè do so?" Averlynn asked.

Hathar pounded the table, his face now completely dark. Averlynn lowered her eyes in apology, but when she looked up Amrith sat as proud as ever.

"It occurs to me," Ka Urlan said in the silence, "that if the news Averlynn brings is as dire as it sounds..." It was his turn to glare as Amrith scoffed. He continued: "It would be best to send our detachment while we also investigate the truth of the letter, rather than waiting."

"Agreed," Hathar said firmly. To Averlynn's surprise, Amrith shut his mouth. "For one, I have seen these signatures enough times and they appear authentic. While Scout Amrith's word is not questioned, events as Averlynn described them seem plausible—"

"She claims I lied!" Amrith shouted this time.

"And her claim will be investigated—if you so graciously permit us the chance?" Hathar's voice was thick with scorn. Amrith was overextending himself, and only he seemed not to realize it. The entire council shifted uneasy glances toward him now as his jaw worked soundlessly. Finally he let some tension out of his shoulders. But not much.

"Of course," he said.

Hathar shifted. "Ka, what would you have the nature of this detachment be?"

Ka Urlan chewed a lip as he glanced at Averlynn. "With the wisdom of this council," he said finally. "I would still verify Averlynn's claims first before committing to engaging these forces. Perhaps ten, including her."

Ten. Nine more than she had before. It was a pitiful start. Ridiculous, even. She tried to think of the distance by sea, and how soon fresh forces might arrive.

"I want to be on this detachment," Amrith said suddenly.

Averlynn cast as imploring a gaze as she could, but Hathar was too busy suppressing a sigh. He glanced at Ka Urlan, who nodded.

"Of course," the Ka said. "But per the letter from the council, Averlynn is still commanding it." He held up a hand as Amrith puffed up. "There is wisdom in it. She has seen the enemy, knows their locations and some movements. Unless we prove her banishment, I see no reason to disregard that wisdom."

Amrith ground his teeth, but remained silent for the rest of the deliberations. He found her afterward as they prepared for an early morning departure. "I know you forged that letter—or if not you, someone else.

You are banished, and I will laugh to see you put out."

"And I know you forged my letter—you yourself," she shot back. She paused. "And you will not laugh when you see the forces arrayed against our people."

23

A TRACK LEADING NORTH

"Illmali approves of your haste?"
"It is not haste, only the culmination of long-laid plans."
"How soon until they are destroyed?"
"When the time is right."

1 Elfumon 1320 — Spring

For his heroic actions defending Curani and determining the intents of the Kalen, Ketzler was promoted to Corporal and given his squad. Of course they regretted the loss of the ring back to its owner, especially under the circumstances, but it was hardly Ketzler's fault. And, they determined, it got the unit's blood up, which would serve them well in the coming patrols. For the Cariste were now at war with an unknown enemy of unknown size and location, and they would need to be cautious but determined in their intelligence-gathering until their reinforcements arrived.

Ketzler emerged from the tent, his emotions roiling below the mask he had managed to maintain during the Commander's judgements. The thoughts and actions had come so quickly at the time, he had not been able to truly process them until it was too late.

He had killed one who trained him, who selflessly and devotedly taught him everything he knew about scouting. Had kept him safe numerous times, shared joys and triumphs, but had not withheld discipline when it was necessary. Curani had managed to keep an air of superior in rank while also being a friend—something Ketzler was not sure he could duplicate. Through Curani's guidance he had achieved everything so far that he had wanted when he left Klos to become a soldier. And, he was sure, he would have attained Corporal eventually, and probably more.

Ketzler paused, flailing at a guy wire to keep himself from falling as the import of what he had done washed over him. He drew ragged breaths, fought to keep tears out of his eyes. But when he closed them, he saw again Curani's surprise as the sword went through his neck. Over and over it played, from the moment Ketzler drew his sword till it cut—Curani's eyes widening—his hands coming up to his throat as his mouth opened—

Ketzler went to a knee and forced his eyes open. He drew a deep breath, then another. Curani had begun to change. He too disapproved of Ketzler's and Karbae's relationship. He would have sought peace with the Kalen. He would have died eventually, along with the rest of the Cariste. *The blood thread requires a sacrifice,* the thought had come—and it was true. It had to be. Better one of them, and early, than all of them and late. The Commanders' determinations were true: it was better now for their blood to be up.

Ketzler swallowed and stood. Some of his soldiers were nearby, had seen his actions. He knew by their glances they thought he mourned the loss of their former Corporal. As his gaze hardened, he knew it was not right to mourn. Curani's death was not unnecessary—it was entirely necessary.

"Gather our squad," he said to the nearest one. "I'll need to brief them."

They arrayed in front of him, not quite in formation but attentive enough. Most had not heard yet, and looked at him quizzically. "It's not official yet," he began, though he kept his voice firm, confident. "But I'm going to be your new Corporal." A few glances were exchanged. He watched them closely for disapproval, but saw none. Karbae looked almost mirthful, though he thought perhaps there was some true happiness for him. Not ridicule. Surely.

He continued. "We are going to have a hard road ahead of us," he said. "The Kalen intend war. We're going to give it to them."

"Hayep!" the squad shouted.

Ketzler grinned. Necessary. "We need to figure out where they are, first.

We know they can hide themselves when they wish, and they know the land better than we—so far."

"How do we find someone who's invisible?"

"How do we *fight* someone who's invisible?"

Ketzler held up a hand. "They are not invisible. They can make us think we see something. If they move, we can spot them. If they try to look like us—well, we'll have a few clues built into our dress and speech so we know quickly if it's one of us or not. I don't worry about fighting them." He let the silence drag a moment. "The true difficulty," he continued finally, "is finding where they live. It is there we will strike them."

"So how do we do that?"

"We track them," Ketzler said simply. "The one who killed Curani rode a horse; horses leave hoof prints. It will be our job to track them to their homes, observe what we can, and report back to the Commander."

"We don't attack them?" Karbae asked.

He smiled, appreciating her enthusiasm. "Not by ourselves. But our reinforcements should be arriving soon—our weather comes from north and west, and has been fair. Captain Pike believes the ships have had fair weather as well."

"How many are coming?"

"We are not to be told. We cannot give anything away that we don't know. But Pike says that it will be enough." Ketzler grinned, and the squad mirrored him. Pike had a knack for understatement.

"When do we start?" This from Karbae again, and Ketzler nearly glowed.

"Tomorrow morning."

There had been some small ceremony the evening before they left, attaching the rank of Corporal and giving him the squad. He worked out with the Captains a small colored badge that they would change at intervals, and key words attached to each that could be worked into a sentence—so, the badge and the key word had to match, and be given by anyone out of sight for even a moment. To an observer, they thought, the badge would be meaningless and only casually duplicated if it was at all.

Ketzler, though, wondered. Averlynn had watched closely enough to hide behind the visage of one he knew well, would trust almost without question. But he agreed with the thought that not all of her people would be so observant. First, he only needed to find Averlynn's prints near the Glowwood.

But it was not, to his chagrin, as easy as he made it out to the squad. Perhaps he had not truly thought it. The squad had needed to hear it, and he began to believe it himself. But much was obscured by forest quickly coming to leaf. All they knew was that the Kalen would not live to the east, he chuckled to himself.

At the Glowwood, they were able to track Averlynn's prints for a time, but those quickly disappeared among fallen trees and rock. She knew her craft well—Ketzler never doubted it, only hoped.

Something nagged at him, a thought he couldn't shake. Averlynn had always come from the north, and fled that way. Even when she came to him in the Glowwood. His first thought was that she must live with her people in that direction. But the nagging told him the opposite—that she would always loop around to head the opposite way. So when her prints disappeared and never resurfaced, he took his squad south and west at angles.

They carried everything they needed on their backs. Spring wore on and forage appeared, and there were several accomplished hunters with them. A newer member, a last-moment addition to Ketzler, was one of the cartographers. It made sense, but he was also only barely versed in warfare, and not at all in moving quietly through a wood. He was observant enough, a far as geography was concerned. But more than once he nearly walked into a tree for how distracted he was by some prominence or other.

On the fourth day, just as Ketzler's confidence struggled a moment, they found a hoof print beside a stream where they stopped for water. He inspected it closely. There was no distinguishing mark on it—if it was Averlynn's she kept him well—and yet it recalled to him the print he had first seen inside the Brynth.

They followed the water for a time, but saw no other print either beside it or departing from it. By evening, as they set up camp, he decided to continue his south-west movements.

He lay awake in his tent that night, listening to the sounds of the woods and the wind gently stirring through the leaves. It had seemed so long since he'd heard such a noise. The nights were still chilly, but they risked no fire.

When the wind stirred just right he could see the waxing gibbous moon, its pale light chilling him more than the wind. There was something menacing about it, silent as it was. The shadows it cast were furtive, sneaky almost.

A dark figure approached his tent. It moved like Karbae. She was on first watch with Juris and Mordel. "Why aren't you at your post?" he asked gently when she was near.

He could sense her hesitation. "The night is, um...*an throt* Ketzler, purple grapefruit," she finished with a frustrated sigh.

He stifled a laugh, knowing the sound would carry. "The sentence doesn't have to make sense," he whispered.

She came close and squatted down. After another moment she sat and laced her hands around her knees. "Ketz..." She trailed off, and gazed into the night.

"I'm sorry, about the last time," Ketzler said. He reached out and stroked her thigh. "I guess sometimes I can't help it. It has nothing to do with how important you are or aren't."

"I know. And it's not exactly your fault I'd been planning that all day." She picked at one of her fingers, then looked at him and smiled. "At least the first part was how I imagined, even if you completely shattered what the second half was supposed to be."

His hand stopped and he swallowed. His mind went wild with what the second part might have been. She laughed at him. "Your fault," she chided.

He forced himself to chuckle. "Now I'll never know."

She leaned over and her hair fell around his face. She gazed into his eyes, the playful spark making him nervous. "At least not yet," she whispered. Before he could reply she kissed him and left.

He stared unseeing at the leaves and moon, sleep escaping him utterly.

He walked the next morning in an exhausted daze, letting others take the lead. He felt he had done his part so far, finding the hoof print and setting their strategy. Still, he understood some of the glances, much as he also hated them. Of course Karbae didn't judge him, and seemed to enjoy his discomfort. She did that a lot.

They came across another stream, its waters clear, cold, and deep. Without ceremony Ketzler plunged his head into it, holding it there until his lungs burned. When he finally sat back, he felt better—more awake at least, as the freezing water dripped down his chest and back. He scrubbed his scalp quickly to shake free as much water as he could, then stood up.

"Okay," he said, his voice clearer now than when he'd given the orders this morning. He looked around the woods afresh, noting the trees, the terrain. It was changing again—the terrain, that was. The valleys were broader, the ridges lower and fatter. This stream, though deep, meandered across the broad floor. And it was brighter under the canopy.

He scanned the trees again. Ash and cherry made up most of the woods here, with occasional maple. And something new—a smooth-trunked and fat tree with wide glossy leaves.

"Does anyone know what these are?" he asked, placing a hand on one of them. None of the squad made a comment. It had been in none of their trainings—though, they anticipated encountering new species when they went south. But that they appeared now, sporadically, indicated some kind of change. He wondered what kind.

The end of light is in the west.

Ketzler splashed across the stream, twisting the sheath at his waist to keep the sword out of the water. The water came about thigh-high in the center, the current strong and threatening to topple him.

"Is this really the best leader we can have?" Mordel called loudly. On the opposite bank already, Ketzler looked back to see the squad staring after him. More than a few looked like they agreed with Mordel.

Ketzler looked at them all patiently. "What has our route been so far?"

Many shifted. "South and west," Karbae replied suddenly. She, at least, seemed still to trust him.

"And which direction have we been heading the past day or two?"

"West."

"And only now are we seeing these trees." He glanced up into the canopy. "Which means the land is changing to the west."

"So what?" Mordel spat.

"So, civilizations often arise at the junctures of changing land," Ketzler explained slowly. "To offer the city, town, or village or whatever, access to multiple resources. Could you plant wheat in the forest?"

Understanding began to dawn on the rest. Mordel, he felt, clung to ignorance out of spite. "No," he muttered.

"Then those we seek might likely live near open land. Perhaps these trees indicate we're nearing such a place."

Most of the squad began to cross, leaving Mordel there. Karbae cast him a triumphant glance, but he sneered. "You're only guessing. We don't even know what these trees are."

Ketzler shrugged amiably. "Nope, but it's the best guess we have for now." He set off again without looking back, and chuckled to himself when he heard Mordel's tardy splashing across the stream. Ketz took the lead again this time, his eyes roving.

The next two valleys were dry, but the third held another, smaller stream. As they descended the gentle slope they came to a small flat space. Karbae, a few paces to Ketzler's left, called a halt.

"What is it?" he asked.

She shook her head as she knelt. Carefully she picked at a few leaves, uncovering the earth beneath. Finally, with broad strokes, she brushed aside a large area and looked at Ketzler.

The ground beneath was compressed in two places, roughly the size of seated individuals. Ketzler knelt where he was and searched through the mold. Under it was blackened earth, and a few charred stones. "A fire," he said.

The squad fanned out, searching through the area. Mordel found a hoof print to the south, and Oridin found another set, larger than the others, next to Mordel's. Juris and Fortu found a single set northward.

"But only two sat at the fire," Ketzler mused. "A small meeting, and they departed separate ways?"

"It would seem," Mordel said. Now they had further proof, he seemed in a more agreeable mood—as agreeable as stone could be. "Which way do we go?"

Ketzler drew a deep breath. The signs clearly pointed north and south. The thought earlier had been west, and nagged even now. But how would he justify it to the squad? Why did he feel he needed to?

"We'll remember this place," he said slowly. "But I don't relish the idea of fighting in the forest with a people who can make themselves look like tree-boles. If this does open into a plain of some kind, I want to find it." He nodded firmly as he said it; it was not an excuse. He glanced at the cartographer. "I imagine you would like to fill in more of that map?" he asked.

"We have the sign now," Mordel cut in. "And it's aging fast. We should follow it."

"I didn't realize it was up for a vote, Senator," Ketzler said, stepping closer.

"I didn't realize you knew anything about war, Pip," he shot back, stepping up as well.

"*Corporal,* footman," Ketzler replied.

"Mordel..." Karbae said in warning.

"You get away," Mordel said, glaring. "You can have your say when you two are in bed tonight."

Ketzler's fist lashed out as Mordel began to turn back. Fist and nose met in the middle, and blood sprayed as Mordel fell to the ground. His eyes flashed as he wiped the blood on his sleeve. He leapt up, his hand going to his sword—but Ketzler's was already out and pointed unwaveringly.

"I will report this to the Captain when we return," Ketzler said. "Maybe she'll find you a place among the mule train. But for now we go west to find good ground to fight from, if we can. Then we can draw the enemy out if we want—not before. That's what a good commander would do."

Mordel growled, wiped his nose again. But the fire seemed to be gone from his eyes as he moved toward the back of the squad. Ketzler sheathed his sword and turned to the rest of the troops. "Let's go," he said.

They moved out, silently returning to their positions in formation. Karbae flashed him a reassuring smile, with just a hint of the playfulness she'd showed him the previous night. He returned a faint wink, spoiled as his jaw cracked into a yawn, and Karbae laughed. At him, this time; definitely at him.

By the end of the day, his faith in himself and in the thought began to wane again. He sat alone at the western edge of their camp, staring off into the trees. Karbae was asleep. Mordel nursed his grudge, Ketz assumed, at the far eastern edge. That problem would rear its head again, as soon as Mordel realized he could report Ketzler for improper conduct. If he hadn't thought of it already. But that problem would require a little more tact than Curani. It would look suspicious if another of Ketzler's squad were suddenly killed.

But Mordel could tell no one while they were still on patrol. He did not have an indefinite time—the Commander wanted him back before the month was out, whatever he found. Which meant they needed to find something worth reporting in the next several days.

Thus his waning faith: south would have otherwise been the logical choice. In all probability there was some sort of village or outpost that way. He needed more than a thought, nagging though it was, to report to his squad and to report back to the Commander.

At a faint rustling, he turned, praying it was not Karbae coming to distract him again. Then he realized if it were her, he would not have heard her coming from so far away. That left one, and he rolled his eyes.

"Sir," the cartographer said when he was near.

"Elirose, I told you, I'm not a 'Sir' I'm a corporal. And you're supposed to give the password."

There was a sniff. "But you already know who I am."

Ketzler held back a sigh, too tired to explain—again—why that didn't matter. "What do you want?"

"I've been going over my map so far." *Shocking.* "I don't know if you've noticed what's been happening?"

Ketzler turned to look at him. "Why don't you tell me, in case I haven't noticed the same thing you did?"

"Very good, sir." Elirose sat beside him and pulled out the map, and a single sheet with notations scribbled across it. "I've done some calculations—rough, of course, without a second person. There should be two of us, really, with our guide pole and sextant. I tried to explain to the Commander the necessity of not just marking the terrain but being able to measure its altitude as well as length. I fear this map I'm botching will be no help, no help at all, or if so only barely able to—"

"Please come to—!" Ketzler cut himself off. He forced a smile and lowered his voice. "What is it you've noticed?" he asked.

"I'm sorry sir. But the land is gradually rising. Over time. Each ridge is a little higher, each valley a little less low."

Ketzler only stared at him. Of all his problems, this was not one—or a solution to one. Was it? "What does that signal to you?" he asked.

Elirose blinked owlishly. "Nothing to me, I suppose. I just mark it down. But it's something hard to notice without figures. I thought you should know."

"Thank you, Elirose; you're dismissed." He didn't even bother to watch the man go. The land was rising. Good. They weren't descending into a bottomless pit. Or perhaps the forest would end in a mountain range—perhaps the Brynth extended all the way down here, and all hope was lost.

This patrol was not going as he hoped. Karbae was back on good terms, but that signaled probably greater trouble not less. Mordel launched a full-scale if not mass mutiny. They had spare sign of their quarry. And he had a nagging thought defying logic. And they had not found any other indication of where these people lived. With how things had gone so far, they would be nomads and whatever camp he found would be gone long before he could return in force. Or they kept their cities so well hidden by glamours his squad would walk right through it without noticing.

There's a thought...

Perhaps they had passed it already. How could he know? They could be living in these strange trees, for all he knew. He glanced up, with just enough moonlight shining through the gaps to see the canopy. If they built their homes there, would he see them? If they made them invisible...

But that wasn't how Averlynn said their glamours worked. She could not change her size, or not by much—she could not be a willow branch or a mole. She was a little taller than Karbae when un-glamoured, but not much, and all the boles she hid as were human-sized. Surely if they glamoured their buildings, it worked the same.

And if they lived in caves? He wrinkled his nose at the thought. Something would have shown. Things that lived in caves were sickly, pale, didn't do well on the surface—probably smelled of nasty underground smells. Averlynn conducted herself supremely well on the surface. And, if he was somehow wrong, then they would find an abundance of sign where a cave-mouth would be. He didn't think they lived in caves.

Unless they came to a mountain range like the Brynth in the next few days. Then he might think differently.

They did not encounter a mountain range the next day. The forest, Ketzler thought, grew brighter hour by hour. The strange trees thinned, though, until they no longer saw any, and again his decision not to go south worried at him.

Then, as evening approached, he could see the sun peering straight at them between the trees. It took him a few moments to realize it had always shone through canopy—that the vague haze between the trunks ahead of them was undergrowth, and beyond that was a shimmering brightness that was not sky. And as the songbirds began their dusk-time calls there seemed to be hundreds.

He fairly sprinted forward, no warning of caution coming to his mind. His sword banged against his leg and he gripped it. He heard the others of the squad matching his pace.

He pulled the sword free to cut through the undergrowth trying to tangle his legs, then thought better of using it for such. He slowed instead, picking his way carefully through.

And with that, he stood on the edge of the forest. Ahead and slightly below him was a broad marshland. Broad did not even adequately describe it: it was massive, stretching nearly to the horizon as far as he could see. Faintly—so faintly, to the south he could see the green of the trees as the forest curved westward. To the north those trees continued in a hard line, the sudden drop into the marshes preventing outriders that normally would expand the reach of the trees. His squad was just exiting behind him, forming their own hard line as they blinked in the sudden sunlight.

Ketz's gaze swept the land again. This would be a terrible place to fight—aside from being able to see their enemy. No glamour would hide them there, but such treacherous footing would make assault impossible. And if the Kalen had no special defense against arrows, neither did the Cariste. The only comfort from seeing this came from the knowledge the Kalen village would not be out there. If they needed somehow to screen their buildings, they would need either trees or rocky ground.

Or undergrowth. He glanced back worriedly. Surely it would still need to be tall—he reminded himself that they could not make things invisible, only hide it somehow.

"Well," Mordel said lightly. His gaze, though, was hard. "Good thing we came all this way to see an *adderos* marsh."

Ketzler tried to make his own gaze hard, but he lacked the confidence. "We know for certain they're not out there," he said.

"They've not been anywhere we've been!" Mordel said, his mask falling away. "We weren't sent out here to find out where they're *not*, but where they *are!*"

Ketzler took a few steps forward, his confidence returning. "We were sent out here, Mordel, to figure out where we can best face them. And in order to figure out where they are, it is very helpful to figure out where they are *not*."

"I'll see you explain that to the Captain when we return," he sneered.

"'Yes, Captain Pike, we spent the month not finding anything. That's what good scouts do.'"

"Mordel," Ketzler said heavily, drawing a hand down his face. "You wouldn't know a good scout if you saw one—because you would never see one. He would come and go while you preened and felt proud of yourself. We need to learn everything we can about our enemy—everything. Including what kind of terrain they favor, how they live in the land."

"And how do we know how they live, since we haven't *seen* any?"

"I foresee two possibilities: they are nomadic, which is bad; or they aren't numerous, which is wonderful. Regardless, they are likely light on the land—they do not alter their surroundings very much."

"And how do you know that?"

"First of all, the camp; at first glance, it was just a flat space on the side of a hill. Karbae recognized what it was, and we still had to dig to find the rest. Our camps are as hidden, but we've been trained to do that. Second, there have been dozens, hundreds of places where we might have found *Cariste* settlements these past days, if it were us living here and the Kalen invading. Sources of water, areas where trees could be cut down and the land cultivated, easy passage in and out of valleys but with prominences where we could post guards—everything we would look for to live. But there is not a mark. So, either they're nomads and we'll never find a settlement; or they only build where the land needs no alteration, especially for cultivation."

"The confluence of lands," Elirose said, coming up beside Ketzler then.

"Exactly."

Elirose pointed. "That way."

Ketzler gaped at him a moment, then looked north. He squinted, but saw nothing different. "I don't see it," he said. He ignored Mordel's smirk.

"It was easier when we first came out," Elirose said. "But there was the barest line I thought might be mountains. But even if not, look at the marsh there: see it? Right at the edge it doesn't glitter anymore."

Ketzler glanced at him. "I think that's just the distance," he muttered. But Elise's gaze was firm. He was the cartographer, after all, trained to cast one glance at the terrain and draw it. He should recognize things Ketzler did not.

"Are you serious?" Mordel said, probably sensing the shift of Ketzler's shoulders. "The tracks went *south!* As should we!"

Ketzler gazed at him. "Tracks also went north," he said. "And if they went alone, they were likely not going far. Aren't you eager to see our enemy?"

Mordel only glowered, but the glance he cast between Ketzler and Karbae worried him. He would need to do something very impressive to keep his position as Corporal if Mordel reported him. Perhaps bringing back a prisoner—especially Averlynn.

He hadn't said anything, but he had recognized that same hoof print in the tracks going north. There was still no identifying mark, which was why he kept silent about it. But when he saw it he knew—something about the press and the angle of it.

Beyond that, he felt he and Averlynn were drawn together somehow. She had been in the mountains, he had seen her head peeping over the cliff's edge so many months ago. *But I don't know that...* It must have been her, to have conveniently been where they landed, observed them, and had come and spoken to him personally. And now it was her they tracked, though Ketzler was the only one who knew it.

As he led them back inside the forest's edge, inside the undergrowth and onto a northerly track, his confidence had returned fully. They had to come west to see the land, to know that north was indeed the best route. And as far away as the marshes stretched, he felt they should be able to make their edge in time to return to the army before they were overdue.

All he needed to do was figure out how to tell where their settlement was, if they had glamoured it. And what to do about Mordel. And Karbae.

Especially what to do about Karbae.

24

NOT ALL HAD DIED

"I thought we weren't to give them memories."
"I won't."
"But what he scents there..."
"Just because I know it does not mean I cause it."

12 Elfumon 1320 — Spring

Aryndurlan landed with a thump, and Tavill prepared to camp again. The dragon was prone to tiring, and during the subsequent and sudden naps Tavill would sit with his thoughts. Occasionally he would nap too, because the days were warm and Aryndurlan did usually remember to wake him before taking off again. Sometimes she didn't. But she always came back.

They had been days wandering the highlands. Perhaps nearly a moon turn. Tavill had foregone any further 'healing' licks from the dragon, once the first wore off. And, without being able to see the moon phases, he had lost track of the days. Aryndurlan had led him from water to water, and he was able to find increasing forage as spring wore on. It had taken them several days to figure out their process. First the dragon had flown too high. Then, though lower, she would turn erratically and Tavill would lose the scent. They tried letting Aryndurlan fly for half the day searching and come back for Tavill—that worked until Aryndurlan forgot to come back for two days, waiting for Tavill to catch up.

Now Aryndurlan stayed low, would not turn on a new heading without calling down to Tavill, and stayed generally close enough to keep up with. But it tired her wings to fly so slow, and naps were more frequent.

And Aryndurlan could not remember *exactly* where the ruins were—she never paid them much attention once they were abandoned, and they had always blended in well with the landscape anyway. So they wound their way generally north, mistaking natural piles of rock of ruins sometimes, and one time thought a cave was an entrance. Fortunately the bear inside was more afraid of Tavill than he was of it, and he was able to exit the cave and be on his way.

He laid out his blanket and sat down, closing his eyes a moment. A few times he had throat-sung on their journey, and the thrum seemed to have some sort of healing effect on his mind. Or at least it seemed to shuffle his memories together, un-scattering them some. But it never brought back old ones. The oldest were still only facts, and everything before that was behind a gray veil.

Only, last night, he thought the gray might have whitened a shade. Just barely, as though it drew thin, but still implacable. It would have comforted him more if something seemed ready—or trying—to burst through. He could not touch it, and it hung limp. But thinner.

He began the thrum now. Aryndurlan never seemed to mind, or waken, when he did it before. This time, though, the dragon cleared her throat.

Tavill's eyes snapped open as he went silent. "Yes?" he asked, a little testily. He respected the wisdom of dragons, but—

"I thought you would be more eager, is all," Aryndurlan said.

Tavill cocked his head. "Eager?" His eyes widened.

"Oh, I'm so sorry. How do I keep forgetting. We've found the ruins."

Tavill felt like he should leap to his feet, but he didn't. His breath came shorter as doubts assailed him. If he failed here, if there was no special knowledge, if he had wasted the entire journey...

Then he would return to Averlynn. Somehow. As long as he was alive he had to keep trying. His breath steadied and he rose. "Where is it?"

Aryndurlan's face loomed large, and before Tavill could stop her, her tongue stabbed into his eyes. He nearly fell over backward with a cry.

"I didn't think you'd let me do that if I asked," Aryndurlan said as Tavill blinked quickly. "Also I think you should see this."

Once the pain receded and the colors stopped running, Tavill looked where Aryndurlan was gazing. He stepped out from behind the dragon to gain a better view.

She had brought them to the top of a hill, and a broad valley stretched out below them. Near the far end was a lake, and a river glittered on its way south. From here there was no obvious source feeding the lake, other than the high hills around it. Scattered here and there were the remnants of stone buildings—large, uncut boulders that would have blended into rocky terrain but here stood out by mere fact of the otherwise unbroken grassland around it. A few sycamores and willows clustered around the lake, but the rest was the same brown scrubby grass that carpeted the rest of the highlands.

He blinked again as he saw how near they had come to the great wall of mountains to the north. He had always loved the Snowashes, only realizing how accessible they were now that he saw these monoliths. Snow still covered every peak, though a few of the valleys glittered with flowing water.

But his attention quickly came back to Kragnog below him, and he drew a deep breath. That close were either answers or not.

"I'm going to enjoy some of this sunshine," Aryndurlan said quietly. "But I'll stay here until you return."

Tavill looked at her quickly. "Thank you," he replied. With another bracing snort he set off down the slope.

On the first stone, on the leeward side, he found some of the ancient patterns. Wind and weather had washed them nearly away, and too far gone to read, but they were there. He ran his hands over them, the first Taur to do so in ages. There was a familiarity, he thought—still not from him being there but from being somewhere similar. He paused and cast his glance around the terrain, noting the curve of the hilltop as it mounted away, Aryndurlan at its top with wings flared, massive mountains just peeping over the northern rim. There was something so...fitting, about it all, as though the tableau was laid out exactly as it should be. Vaguely in his mind there was a stirring, a sense of accomplishment that had come after weary eons.

He turned to the rest of the ruins, making his way among the scattered stones. Even they were not truly scattered. He knew that particular left turn would come after so many paces, would then turn right—though that stone was tumbled down and partially blocked the path.

He made another turn and froze. Between blinks he saw a fire, saw bodies—not Taur—lying in the spaces. Another blink, and a cobblestone road was there and dark rain clouds thundered overhead. He looked back, saw carts in disarray, household belongings cast in and roped down haphazardly.

He took one step toward a cart he felt was his own, and the sun was shining again and he was surrounded by tumbled down stones. He looked at Aryndurlan. Had her healing somehow brought back memories, as well? But when he tried to think, he could not bring up the images on his own.

He looked down. There had been a cobblestone road in the vision, but here was only grass and dirt. He knelt, and dug down. The turf was hard. He placed a hand flat and began the throat-song. As the rumble went down it soon hit the same plate-like stone as he'd felt further south, though soon beneath that were the roots of the mountains. But certainly no remnants of road. So why was the layout so familiar?

He rose and continued his walk. None of the buildings were intact, no rooms closed off against the elements. If there were writings here, they would be long gone.

He came to the southern end of the village and stopped. The warmth and sunshine contended with the desolation behind him, gone not by violence but the long, quiet wearying of time. There was a deep, unruffled silence about the place, and he felt lost in it.

Down at the lake, the leaves of the sycamores wagged. He walked slowly toward it, letting his nose wander. There was so little life here, beyond the grass itself. A beetle buzzed by, nearly crashing into him. A tiny honeybee floated among a small patch of daisies. As he neared the trees a chipmunk darted away. But very little to scent, no larger animals browsed or preyed.

The lake was still, and a thick scum covered the northern end. Further away where the sun hit eventually there were lily pads, and a faint burgundy where deep Rotelgil grew. A faint wind ruffled the surface.

He found a hummock where the roots of both sycamore and willow tangled, and sat down. Dragonflies skimmed the cattails near the eastern shore, and his thoughts darted with them but gradually lagged further and further behind.

He blinked awake. The sun was far lower, and the lake was in shadow. He shook his head; perhaps he had gotten used to Aryndurlan's naps. The color—and clarity—of his vision was now seeped nearly to the bottom of his eyes. He blinked a few times, rubbed them, managed to spread the saliva back around. He tried not to think too much about that.

Peeping between the cattails was the largest animal he had seen so far, but not by much: a chevrotain leaned out and drank. But it seemed at ease, as though it knew no predators were around.

Tavill rose. He still saw no source for this lake, and it seemed too large by far to be merely rain-fed. The cattails and Rotelgil told him the level of water did not vary by much.

It was only now he noticed a small gap in the scum near the shore, a patch of clearer water that bellied out. He went to it, gazed at it. It rippled here without a breeze, nudging the scum away. It dipped his hand into freezing water, felt a faint pulse to it like a current. He stuck his arm in deeper, ignoring the icy grip. There was a hole, far deeper than he could reach, down into the earth and angling back toward Kragnog.

He stood and shook the water off. An underground spring, and a large one, originating under the city. He made his way slowly back, the air chill now as the sun dipped below the rim and cast the valley in shadow. Aryndurlan was a faint lump on the hilltop, probably fast asleep, the sun still glittering in a halo around her.

Tavill walked unerringly to a spot near the center of the ruins. It was exactly where it should be: a well, covered in a stone. At least he wouldn't fall into these ruins. He feared they were deep indeed.

He wrestled the stone from the opening, felt a swift rush of air as it plummeted into the hole. In the faint light he could see handholds carved into the stone sides of the well. From far below he heard an echoing drip, a plonking of water falling from height into a pool.

He sat on the rim, casting one last glance at the dragon before beginning his descent. He had no light, but suspected he wouldn't need one. He couldn't recall why he thought that, but somehow he knew.

He descended into deepening darkness. The light above him was a crisp circle of darkening blue. Below him was a formless and incalculable darkness. The steps as he went lower were ragged, filled with detritus and things he'd rather not think about. A hoof slipped. He caught himself, but pushed backward until the opposite wall nearly brushed his back before continuing.

He went on for what seemed an hour. The light above him became barely a pinprick. The wall behind him suddenly curved away, and he nearly fell again. Handholds that had felt so sure were crumbling, sloped to shed his grip. As he scrabbled, dust arose and he sneezed once, then again, and he fell.

He had barely the time to gasp before he struck water, deep enough he sunk over his head. When he emerged and sucked in a breath he felt a sense of motion, of bobbing along a powerful current. It was dark as pitch. Occasionally his hoof would brush something hard, but if he reached for it he could feel no bottom.

He managed to turn forward as the current carried him further. Faintly a blue light grew, and with it the sound of rushing water. The bottom rose suddenly and he tripped on it, sliding headlong down some sort of greasy rock, and back underwater. When he came up once more the current was gone and he merely floated in some kind of large pool. Behind him the waterfall still churned, short and quiet.

The light now was bright enough he could see a set of stairs descending to a shelf beside the waterfall along the wall of the cave. There was probably some sort of walk alongside the stream he had missed in the darkness. He swam for the stairs, heaved himself onto the shelf panting and shivering.

As he lay there, it occurred to him that this was entirely unfamiliar—not like the rest of the ruins above. Whatever memories were nudged up there, it did not extend to these caves. At least, not in particular. He still knew the light would be there, somehow.

It glowed around him now, sourceless as near as he could determine. It simply was, and cast very thin shadows. He stood, shook the water from his fur as best he could, and looked around.

The walk continued around the rim of lake, which was smaller than the one above—or was it abreast? Was this the source of the lake in the valley? He felt he had surely fallen too far, and yet the valley above sloped sharply as well. It had to be on a level.

But for the moment, he was not really seeking a way out, but a reason for this walk to exist. He went along it, and as he went he noticed in the strange light certain folds here and there in the rock wall. Coming to one, he saw a cleft on the other side comfortable enough for him to walk into.

He reached toward the inky back of the cleft, but his hands felt only air. Suddenly the blue light winked on in the cleft, showing a large room. He entered, staring around as the space opened before him.

The air in here seemed somehow nearly dry. In the lake room it had not been exactly damp, but certainly more so than in here. The walls were lined with shelves, mostly empty. A few books lay scattered here and there but draped in webs. He touched one, felt it crumble. He tried to read the script on the spines and covers, but the gilt had faded and the leather decayed so far the impressions were obscured.

There was nothing else inside, so he returned to the lake. The sourceless light behind him went out again as he exited. Now when he looked around the lake he recognized dozens of the folds, and across the way could see the clefts themselves, all dark.

In each, the blue light came on when he entered and snuffed out when he left. Each one showed nearly the same decay as the first. Some were libraries, others held tables with strange apparatus in various states of disrepair and disassembly. Some were simple tools for woodworking, cloth making, or farming. One contained instruments of metal, and only the thick dust of decay damped the scent enough he was able to duck back out before his blood raged.

He stood beside the doorway, panting as the light went out. Why would they have such things here? How could any withstand the scent? He had seen them only briefly: a short blade, a pair of tongs, and two pieces like scoops lay on a small table next to a larger table probably long enough to lay on.

He searched beside the lake, found a fist-sized rock. He hefted it once, then tossed it through the door. The light came on again; he could only see the one edge of the table, where widely-spaced holes held remnants of some cloth or leather. The wall held other similar objects as the table, displayed as for use. They glinted in the blue, still retaining some original luster despite the dust.

The light went out, and he continued. The next, almost directly across from the waterfall, had an even stranger air to it, almost warm but not humid. When the light came on, his eyes widened. The largest of all by far, it was lined with shelves and books that were perfectly preserved.

When he stepped fully into the room, he felt as if something closed behind him. He turned quickly, and the lake room appeared to him to shimmer as though he viewed it through a summer haze.

He turned back and began to read. These were organized, allowing him to scan quickly. The first rows held histories grouped by country and time.

The next were myths, legends, and tales—also, it seemed, organized by country and time. He passed a hand over these. He could track, if he wished, how stories changed with the telling and the people.

Behind that were tomes on practices of manufacturing, agriculture, silviculture, and animal husbandry; governments; magics of the world; general flora and fauna; medicine.

Behind even that were three rows of shelves of different wood. The books there were slate black with silver lettering that seemed alive—the light in the lettering was clear and moved within the symbols as though a luminescent ink still flowed. Tavill reached out a finger to withdraw a tome; it struck an invisible barrier and nearly burned. He pulled it back with a yelp, staring as the light in the letters flared. Only then did he read those letters, and gasped anew.

These were from before the Rivening. Human scholars spent lifetimes digging back through centuries of documented histories, and they had barely found anything dating *to* the Rivening. The Taur had some memories—*had* had some; those seemed lost to Tavill now—but they had kept those too from those who asked. It was irrelevant. Five thousand years made sure of that.

His breaths came in great, difficult lungfuls. He would have thought these would be in their Capitol, but perhaps the rest of the Taur thought so as well—knew the tomes would be in danger there. Instead they were here.

And they were guarded. He was permitted in the room, clearly; but he was just as clearly not permitted to touch them. Why did they exist, then? Were they to be unsealed only at the Witnessing?

Another memory lost to the veil. He drew a deep sigh, struggling to drag his eyes away from those beautiful, terrible shelves. In those, too, he might have found the information and memories he sought.

He wandered almost listlessly between the other shelves, now bereft of wonder. He paused at one, plucked a random book from the shelf that drew his eye. A treatise on medicine. He thumbed through it, through the many sketches of medicinal plants, regions where they might be found, some of the tools used by practitioners—

He stopped suddenly and went back a few pages. There, facing the text, was a full-page rendering of the room with the strange instruments. He scanned the words. *It may be necessary to restrain the patient, for the pain*

can be very great—enough that bonebreak is ineffective, and even uncon-
sciousness brought by novistrine broken through. The extraction of the koridin
is imperative; fatality is complete for those from whom it was not withdrawn.

Tavill blinked, and the book fell from his hands. For the second time he
found even the shallowest breath difficult. In his mind, a rip appeared in
the veil, a sliver of clarity. He peeked an eyeball through, watching the scene
play before him filled with every emotion attached to it, as though he were
experiencing it for the first time.

There was thick, oily smoke boiling into the sky, the acrid smell of burning
pitch and flesh making him cough. For a vision of clarity, it struck him that
it began with smoke. It next struck him that he was on his back.

He jostled rhythmically, making the pain in his head worse. At times he
felt his skull would detach and bounce down the street—that if it did it
would be a blessing. His ribs ached from coughing. He gripped the side
of...something. A table? A door, ripped from its hinges?

A blast of heat struck him as another house went up in flames. Through
the pain, the clamor of battle came as through thick water. Screams, battle
roars, the sporadic clatter of arrows and spears, the general din of swords
against shields. Was it a blood-lust? Why was he unaffected?

A *thok* nearby, a grunt, and the boards carrying him dipped suddenly
to one side, and he crashed to the pavement. It was not a blessing: pain
wracked every joint and he nearly lost consciousness. The boards raised
again, unevenly, and he swayed. He managed to pick up his head: two Taur
and two humans were around him, carrying him. The Taur wore no armor,
but one carried a bow and quiver slung on his back. Another carried a
great-axe. The humans were unarmed.

We were never war-like... The thought bounced around a moment before catching up in the smoke and swirling away. He felt, then, the sword
at his own side, still strapped to his waist.

A face appeared above his, one of the human faces, worry lining her eyes
and mouth. "How did they find it?"

Tavill blinked. Was she asking him?

"How did they learn to use it is a more difficult question," the archer
grunted.

Tavill suddenly realized he was no longer swaying. The sounds of the
battle were distant, behind walls. But the sky was still overhead, the roof of
the building gone.

"And how they used it without being infected by it."

"I think they probably are," Tavill heard himself say.

The Taur archer looked at him sharply. "How do you know?"

He couldn't shake his head, but twitched it to one side. "I don't *know* Miktar, but they fight as those dying." He closed his eyes, seeing a vision within the vision of slain Taur, of humans battling among them. "Like those berserk," he whispered.

A silence settled over the room as each considered the implications. He was one of those dying, he knew. How many millennia had he lived, how many great events had he seen, taken for granted? To be reft of seeing any more... Death was considered a failure among the Taur; how would Elonai consider him when he arrived too early?

A hand was laid on his shoulder. "Peace, Tavill," she said. *It was her...the other Taur. Zus...Zusamin?* "We will do everything we can for you."

"It has never been enough for others," he said bitterly. He didn't even think prayer could help him now. The hand departed. Tavill sighed and let unconsciousness come.

He thought the vision would be over, but the darkness passed and he heard voices. He still couldn't remember the human names, though their voices were familiar.

"We have to try."

"Well we cannot do it here."

"Miktar, he will not survive the voyage."

"He has already borne more than most," said a newer voice, one he recognized immediately. *Pluvik!*

Miktar scoffed. "I don't doubt he can handle the pain. But will he bear it enough for us to remove it without killing him?"

"What difference will it make, then?"

"What are you plotting?" Tavill asked, his voice thick. He was surprised at his banter. The pain in his head had lessened. The battle, he realized, had either ended or moved further away. The sky through the broken roof was deep blue, un-smudged by firesmoke. The first Taur—Zusamin—was gone, replaced by Pluvik.

The human face appeared. "Removing the *koridin*," she said bluntly.

He felt a hollowness open inside him as his eyes widened. "Can that...can that be done?"

She shrugged. *Who was she?* "It is not unheard of," she said. She hesitated, and looked away.

"Tell him," Miktar rumbled.

She drew a breath. "There will be consequences from this, ones we don't entirely know. How a Taur reacts to it is...well, we have almost no experience to guide us, and what little is there is contradictory. It signals to me that you will respond differently, and we won't know until the changes come."

She said 'we'—her and the other? They both had an air of familiarity, inside and outside the vision, that he couldn't place.

"Will I stay eternal?"

"As far as we know, yes. But for the other attributes..."

"Do it," Tavill said. "At least try."

She hesitated again. "Tavill, this pain will be unlike anything you've ever experienced—in magnitude or even type."

He frowned. "Type?"

She gave a short sigh of frustration. "I mean...This will not feel like a cut, or a broken bone, or anything like that. It is a pain wholly different, or like every kind of pain all at once. And removing the *koridin* is...difficult. I know you will not be able to hold still, but you're going to have to do your best, to keep us from killing you. And Tavill, you must be sure you are willing to sacrifice anything for this. No matter what you lose or gain, you will be eternal still, and your first duty remains."

He shifted, glancing quickly at Pluvik and Miktar. "She knows of this?"

They nodded somberly. Who was she to be trusted so? *Did* he trust her? What might he lose? He thought of what made the Taur different: their heightened smell, their strength, their memory...

By Elonai, Tavill thought outside the vision; *that's what I lost...*

He found himself considering the Taur around him. Pluvik trusted her and the other, clearly. And he trusted Pluvik above all else. He looked at her a longer moment. He realized, suddenly, her face was not entirely human. Nearly, very nearly; and yet there was something there...was it so long ago? Had humankind changed so much since this memory? He didn't actually know when it was taking place, now he thought about it. The Taur were practically ageless. Or was it something different about her? She spoke Taur flawlessly, and that was difficult for human voices. The other did not speak, but he could tell she understood. As he gazed into their eyes he saw an age there that did not match the face—in neither human.

"Do it," he said. "Whatever comes, I will do my duty."

Whatever comes. None of them predicted what would come after they fled.

She stood away from him, began rolling up her sleeves. "You three will need to hold him down as best you can. Give me that." Now she had his permission, she was swift. The archer handed over a short blade, dripping clear liquid.

He nearly cried out when the others knelt on his limbs. Whatever battering they had taken in the fight had not gone entirely while he was unconscious. And the pain to come was to be worse.

As she hovered over him with the blade, a small whimper left his throat. But her eyes bored into his, radiating determination and confidence—in her competence, but also in his ability to withstand. And, he thought, a note of assurance that all would be well.

Pluvik spoke. "Hurry, Raina..."

Tavill was kneeling on the floor of the cave, gasping and nearly retching with remembered pain. She had not lied; it had been like nothing he had ever experienced. Wave after wave of it. He felt the walls of that little room had to have shaken with his roars.

But somehow she had done it. He knew she did. Whatever infection he had gotten, whatever had to be gotten out of him, was gone. But with it, until now, was memories.

Hurry, Raina. How could it be that Averlynn's Old One was with him in that moment? Had known what to do—had known the Taur and their first duty? He knew for certainty those events had not taken place in Kalen.

He buried his nose in his arm as he wept, trying to keep snot from dripping onto the books as he scrunched into a ball as tight as he could. The weight of that duty, of all the Taur dead since then, of the Prosan dead since that first battle...

He hiccuped. That was it: they had been battling the Prosan. Memories flooded back, too fast to sort. On...what had they named them? They were Islands, between here and Carist. But some plague had swept through it, something native to the land. The Taur had suppressed it somehow...confined it. But the Prosan had weaponized it. Or had the Taur? They weren't warlike, that wasn't their first duty...or was it their second duty?

The *koridin*. It wasn't a physical thing, like a body part. It was the infection. They called it the *koridin*. Raina had called it that. What did it mean? He couldn't remember the word, if it was Kalen.

The Taur had found it, contained it, but somehow it had been discovered and had infected the Prosan. But the Taur didn't help them. They left. Tried to leave. The Prosan had tried to make them stay. The Taur had abandoned the Prosan to the disease. *The Abandoned Isles.* It would kill them all, especially without ships—they couldn't risk ships, couldn't risk taking the *koridin* anywhere else in the world.

The Taur hadn't cared. Or, they knew they were less susceptible to it. They had centuries of collected medical knowledge, knew how to identify its early stages, knew—apparently—how to remove it. But no human could live through that. So the Taur had left them all to die.

But they had not all died. Some had either survived it, adapted to it, or were naturally immune. But they eventually left the Isles, followed the Taur here, but remained hidden until they had grown their numbers again.

Tavill sat back with a heavy sigh, jostling the bookshelf. And once they had an army, they had picked up their battle with the Taur where they had left off.

25

FAR FROM THE LAST

"We are worried you are slipping."
"Remind me what you do?"
"You know we are with the dragon-son."
"And how is that progressing?"

21 Elfumon 1320 — Spring

K etzler stood just inside the wood-line, arms folded, gazing out over
the highlands. He could see the line of the Brynth—the backside of
them, this time. To those who lived here though they would be considered
the frontside. Funny, that.

Despite the great distance, they appeared no less impressive than they
had on the Cariste side, and no less impenetrable. How Averlynn had
found her way through it so long ago—*it had to have been her*—and with
a horse... Not for the first time he wished, in some small corner he still
refused to acknowledge aloud, that he could spend more time with her,
learn of her abilities.

His gaze slid south, across the marshes they had bypassed. It was an
interesting land, here. Much less hospitable than his homeland. But then,
his homeland reflected years and years—generations—of taming. Could it
have been that his ancestors had met just as inhospitable a land so long ago,

when they'd first arrived on Gintanos? It made sense, but was difficult to imagine.

The rest of his squad was hunkered down behind him, hidden in the forest, eating a quick meal. They were near their goal. They had to be. The high trees here offered excellent vantage points to a people clearly alert—at least, Averlynn had been. If one wanted to see far, to apprehend approaching enemies, this would be the place. From height they would even be able to see encroachment from the mountains—just in case the Cariste had finally found a route through the mountains. He almost wished to find it, or have Averlynn show it to him. He smiled grimly; he did not think she would show him that even if he threatened her entire people.

Wouldn't hurt to try...

Karbae might be jealous though. So far she was the only female spending any length of time around Ketzler. It warmed him that she had her pick of men, and chose him. But it complicated things that she took even his mildest distraction as impending unfaithfulness. Not that they had promised any real faithfulness, not out loud.

Something in him growled, as though frustrated with his thoughts. He blinked, uncertain. It seemed to come from the same place as the urge to go westward, a week ago. He heaved a sigh. To be a man was to be torn between everything that desired you—the Baders had said so, though they talked about the soul. It pertained, though. Karbae desired him—he quavered at the thought, and banished it; the army desired his sword-arm; the Cariste desired his tactical mind; the Commander desired his prayers.

He had not prayed in some time, he realized. Maybe once since making Corporal. Perhaps that was why Karbae caused him more mischief now. She was never comfortable with his religion, and delighted in his apostasy.

His gaze had drifted, unseeing. It sharpened suddenly, seeing a dark speck against the sky. He squinted. It appeared very small, but also very far away. And it drifted on the currents of wind like something large. But so far away...it had to have been massive.

He watched it for some time as it circled. The stories of dragons had all but disappeared from Cariste lore, at least here on Gintanos. There had never been a sighting of one, that he remembered reading. His histories were not that of a scholar, but things like that tended to make their way into folklore too, and that concerned the Baders very much. But none had been seen or talked about, and it was thought—a hundred years ago or so—that perhaps none existed on Gintanos. Now they were not even thought about.

Until Averlynn thought the ibex on the Commander's banner had been a dragon. Why else would that matter to her, except such a creature still lived on this side of the mountains? And why would it be significant to her, even then? Was it possible the Kalen had some relationship with one?

He shook his head. If a dragon is even what he saw out there as a mere speck on the horizon. Yet, somehow, it felt right.

He glanced up toward the sun as it peered through the trees, flickering as the leaves rustled in the wind. And, for just an instant, he saw a silhouette of someone else looking toward the speck on the horizon.

He swallowed, his hand flying to his sword. But he did not draw it. He stared only an instant longer, until he was sure it was only a flicker that would likely not return.

He went swiftly but quietly back to his squad. "Up!" he hissed. They looked at him, saw his stance, and were on their feet, eyes darting around the woods.

He scanned the forest as well, still not sure what he was looking for. His heart pounded: they could have arrows pointed at each of them already, and would they know?

Except they would have attacked by now, wouldn't they? Perhaps that lookout had been the extreme southern one. Perhaps they were not so vigilant.

Perhaps they felt too secure in their glamours.

They would need to explore further. But how? What to look for? He knelt, and the squad joined him in a circle.

"I saw a lookout, up in the trees," he whispered. "We don't know exactly what their outposts will look like, but we know they might be glamoured. They can't be invisible, so there will have to be *something* there—Averlynn hid as a bole, but still human-sized. They themselves may appear as tree limbs or trunks, perhaps rocks..." He trailed off and shrugged. "As I said, we don't know *what,* but always human-sized. And if they have buildings, they'll have to be screened by underbrush or trees or something." He paused and glanced around the canopy. "Keep your eyes up as well as around," he said. "If you suspect something, signal me, and stay as hidden as you can. We'll circle east for a time. Elirose." The cartographer scooted closer. "Let's see your map." He spread it out; he already had some of the surrounding terrain sketched in. Ketzler studied it for a time. "With lookouts in the heights, this may not be a full-sized village," Ketzler mused. "That would take a lot of lookouts. So let's circle about his far out"—he gestured on the map—"and consider sweeping north after that, if we haven't seen anything."

"Are we supposed to attack?" Mordel asked. He seemed eager. In truth, Ketzler was as well. It felt strange, to share desires with Mordel.

But he shook his head. "We need to observe, if we can." He paused and looked each of his squad members in the eye—saw there the same glint. Had he fostered it? He certainly hadn't done anything to get rid of it. He had one last flash of Bader Lossnoss, so long his mentor, inspiration, advocate. What would he think of their thirst for blood? Their eagerness to destroy a people they had not known existed a mere few months ago?

But as he looked at those around him, his squad-mates, the family he had chosen even while surrounded by his former family, he put the ideas and preferences of Lossnoss behind him. All of northern Gintanos was behind him. If they were to survive in this new land, under this new threat, he could not long for home. He had to be fully committed. And his troops had to be fully committed as well. He set his jaw.

"Let's see what we're dealing with first," he said. "And if we have an advantage..." He trailed off, but grinned fiercely, and they each knew what he had not said. "Drop your packs here. Let's go."

They moved off with purpose, Karbae lingering the longest. She gave him the most dedicated smile he had ever seen from her, a smile that spoke of so much more than happiness or approval. And there was, just at the end before she turned away, the glint of mischief in her eye. He shook his head and moved out.

If they had hoped to hide here the most effectively, they had chosen poorly. These trees were smooth-trunked and healthy, and should be impossible to hide in. The canopy was thicker now as summer came on, and most of the trees were full-leaved—enough to perhaps screen his movements from their lookouts. His squad spread out in a thin line. Elirose stuck next to him without crowding.

They slowly circled east. Ketzler kept his eyes mostly north, though he occasionally scanned south for an outrider. The forest was silent but for the occasionally washing of wind through the trees. His troops moved efficiently and carefully, and he never heard a twig snap or the crunch of leaves.

He glanced up again, noted a broken limb near the top of a tree. He tapped Elirose and pointed: it was about the girth and height of a human—Kalen—and looked strange on an otherwise hale oak. Elirose nodded, making a mark on his map. Ketzler studied it, gauging distances.

A warbler sang out ahead. Ketzler's head snapped up; Fortu pointed overhead to the north. Ketzler nodded, glancing again at Elise's map. He raised an eyebrow. Elirose pursed his lips as his head wagged a few times. Then he gestured a circle and mouthed "one hundred yards."

"Outpost," Ketzler mouthed back. Elirose considered, then nodded. Ketzler moved up beside Fortu as the rest of the squad waited. He peered between the trees, spotted the same grayish bark against an otherwise normal brown cherry tree. Fortu had good eyes to spot that and Ketzler placed a quick hand on his shoulder.

Three lookouts in a gradually-curving circle. Where was the outpost itself, then? And if the squad had seen them, surely they had seen the squad? Else what good were they as lookouts?

But so far they didn't move. Ketzler didn't know how they would pass messages, but presumably it involved moving or making noise. They were either unseen or unwarned—either way, the outpost didn't know they were there.

"We circle a little bit longer," Ketzler whispered, lisping his "s" sounds to keep them even quieter. "Come at them from the north. I want to see this outpost—or whatever there is of it—before we attack."

They nodded, Mordel reluctantly, and moved on. They counted four more lookouts by the time the sun was moving to their right. Each had hidden differently, but always some human-sized chunk of different. They formed up again.

"Seven," Ketzler said. He shook his head minutely as he gazed toward the center of the circle they had drawn following the lookouts. The outpost had to be in there somewhere. "That's not a lot of lookouts. One of our cities would have dozens just on one side."

"What are you thinking?" Oridin asked.

"That this isn't a large outpost. I would have expected more..." He trailed off and bit his lip. What could it mean?

"Unless they're all hidden inside," Karbae offered.

"Or they don't exist," Mordel sneered. Whatever agreeableness he'd had apparently had worn off. "What have we seen? A bunch of trees and bark, and this one's word that's how they hide." His voice rose with his anger, far past a whisper. Ketzler was not the only one to look at him in alarm. Whether they agreed with Mordel or Ketzler, it was shocking after so much silence.

Mordel glared at all of them. "Have we seen another track?" he demanded. "Any other sign? At all?"

Ketzler tried to shush him, glancing nervously into the forest. Mordel slapped his hand down. "No!" he fairly roared. "And I have *had it* with this idiot, this...*Pip!*" His jaw shook as he spat the word.

Ketzler's eyes widened. Overhead, the tangle of branches shifted though the wind hadn't stirred. "Mordel, shut it!" he hissed.

Mordel stood, fists clenched. Ketzler, a little to the side, saw the arrow appear suddenly in the air in front of the tree. With a wordless cry he launched himself forward, tackling Mordel to the ground. Fire erupted along his back as he hit the ground.

Fortu was swift, loosing his own arrow toward the tangle. Ketzler glanced up, saw the shaft disappear into it. The branches dissolved, became a man who fell from the tree and thumped to the ground below.

Ketzler wrenched Mordel's head around, not caring if he hurt him, forced his eyes to see the dead Kalen up ahead. "Now shut your festering hole, and let's go," he said. He stood and worked his arms. The pain in his back had quickly dulled. "How is it?" he asked Karbae, turning his back toward her.

She picked at his shirt. "Just skipped off. I don't think it was barbed. Most of it is just welts."

"Lucky," he said, his glare meaning both he and Mordel were. "They may know we're here now. Either way, let's move in. Elirose, you stay here. If it goes badly, take the word back to our armies."

This time it was Karbae who looked at him warily. "Are you sure that's a good idea?"

Ketzler sighed. "I'm tired of not knowing, of not seeing our enemy. Maybe if we flush them out..." He shrugged, then freed his sword. "Let's go."

He strode forward before anyone could say otherwise, though he kept his eyes alert for any other differences. As he went forward, the space between the trees seemed flat to him, as though he was not truly looking through the trees, but at a—very realistic—painting. And one that didn't shift the way it should as he moved.

He paused by the dead Kalen, studying him a moment. The eyes gaped up at the canopy. If the stories of the Kalen were true, those eyes had seen more than Ketzler ever could. Not anymore.

He bent down and worked the ring off the man's finger. A bird was imprinted on it, wings spread as though soaring. The rest of the squad had reached him, were keeping eyes around the forest. Out of curiosity, Ketzler put on the ring. He fixed Karbae with his gaze, pressed the ring with his thumb, and convinced himself he looked like a stump.

Her expression never changed. But suddenly, faintly, he felt as though something tapped him once. He studied the ring; it came again, a soft thump, familiar and yet he couldn't place it. *Thump...thump-thump.*

His eyes widened. It felt like a heartbeat, but beating on the outside of him. Was it the dead Kalen's heart, somehow tied to the ring? He made to remove it, but stopped when it was halfway off the knuckle. He panted, forced himself to take a deep breath. There was something else there. A...not a pull, but a sense of direction, as though a string had been tied to him and he could feel the weight of it.

He took another deep breath, slid the ring on, and closed his eyes. He felt the weight, got used to it. It was tied to...a pig? No, wilder. A boar. He wondered what an animal had to do with the Kalen. Were they all the same sense—just a race of boar-people? Or did they differ?

Either way, Boar-Kalen was nearly two hundred yards to the west, and alert. As he grew familiar with the sensation he started to feel it in other places, pulling other directions. Each was a different animal. Strange. What had Averlynn's been? Was she here? A worry for an other time.

"There are not many," he whispered, looking to his squad. "I can feel them through this ring," he explained. "Most are alert, but they don't seem to be moving yet. Perhaps they think they can hide."

Feeling the strings, he began directing the squad. The Kalen would be able to feel him too, but not the rest of his troops. "As we kill them, gather their rings but don't put them on yet," he said. "We can use those in future, perhaps, but for right now we need surprise. Once you take out the guards, converge there." He pointed ahead where most of the strings clustered, deep inside the thickening. "Swords out for that one. If we strike hard we can probably drive them off, those we don't kill. Try to force them west."

Four of the squad moved off as directed, toward the guards. Ketzler waited with the rest, eyes closed and focused on the strings.

Snip.

A string slackened then dissipated like smoke. He waited, not daring to breathe: the Kalen would feel that too, begin to worry. Maybe begin to take the threat seriously and attack. It seemed an eternity.

Snipsnipsnip.

"Now," he said.

They ran forward, swords drawn. A shout threatened from Ketzler's throat but he held it back. The closer they could get before...

Arrows zipped from the brush ahead, but the volley seemed hurried and most went high or wide. One thunked into a tree just as Ketzler wove behind it. The four who had eliminated the guards returned a volley, and almost miraculously another string was cut.

The 'painting' shimmered and faded, and they could see scattered buildings. Ketzler couldn't help but marvel. Their glamours seemed to work far better on structures than people, and the interior of the outpost was nearer than he had thought. The Kalen appeared, too, now mostly in flight though it was a fighting retreat. A few would turn and kneel, loosing arrows while the rest moved back.

But they were too formulaic, too predictable. Ketzler could time it, duck behind a tree while the arrows flew, then return to the chase. But they were not gaining ground.

"Shift left!" he shouted. He threw caution to the wind and charged to the east, trying to maneuver to their flank. He wanted to force them toward the treeless highlands. Surely they would perceive that threat, but...

His squad obeyed, and they worked their way left and forward. Some had kept out their bows—against orders, but it made sense now. He had expected some actual resistance, but the Kalen offered little. His scouts were able to loose a few shafts, and more strings were cut. It was a strange sensation, now, as sometimes the string was cut as the Kalen fell, other times the man would fall first and the string weaken, dissipate, then cut at the last moment.

With a growl he leapt forward, head low. A war would never be won if they only chased and chased. The Kalen before him wavered, loosed a wild shaft, and Ketzler was on him, sword swinging. The fool clutched his bow, swung it like a staff. Ketzler's blade shattered it, the tension in the string snapping the broken ends back around the Kalen holding it. He had barely begun to untangle himself when Ketzler's sword bit deep.

The thrill this time was far higher than Curani. Pure. Righteous. It didn't stink of murder the way the other had. Both had been necessary for the safety of future Cariste, but this would not bother him with complicated justification. The God himself would have done this same to protect his followers.

The sun was ahead of him, not quite in his eyes but lowering. He charged ahead again. His squad was around him, the enemy before him. Everything had fallen into place the way it needed to. They still fought their delaying actions, but they were shaken. He felt it more and more, as though someone tremored the strings. They felt almost brittle now, and one felt like it broke before it was snipped by another Cariste arrow. They hadn't expected the attack. Not just today: they seemed to have never expected it.

Now Ketzler shouted. Roared, really. His squad around him roared too. Weeks of nothing, of boredom, of uncertainty, released. They had found the enemy and utterly routed them.

And they weren't done. They reached the edge of the trees as the Kalen dropped all pretense of defense and simply ran. "Bows!" Ketzler shouted, unlimbering his own. They shot quickly, and five more fell into the grass. Only the Kalen's fear and the uneven terrain saved them now as they ran pell-mell and were too quickly out of bowshot.

Chest heaving, Ketzler stopped and felt for the strings. All of them were before him and fading—spindling away until they were too thin to feel. None were left behind him. The other lookouts must have joined the rest on the ground at some point. He had been too busy harrying them, he thought. The thrill of the attack, of victory, kept him from contemplating that frame of mind.

"Ketz!" Oridin called. He turned swiftly; the tone of voice had said it all. He saw Oridin kneeling, Fortu's head on his leg, Fortu's face sweaty and pale. He rushed over, saw the arrow snapped off near the skin. He must have fallen on it and broken it.

Ketzler knelt, placing his hands gently. Fortu's stomach heaved as he gasped. "Hey, it's okay," he said quietly. Fortu's eyes went to his, locked in. "Listen to me," Ketzler continued, leaning down. "We did it. We found them, and we crushed them. Curani is well-avenged." He knew the two of them had been close, had worked together more than the others. "You did very well, I knew you would. That's why I sent you after the guards, all right? I knew I could trust you. I'll send prayers for you. And I know none of us will forget you."

"Ketz...ler..." Fortu gasped. His face was going slacker.

"Yes?"

"Just...shut up."

Ketzler stared, then saw the faintest beginning of a smile on Fortu's face before it went stiff and his stomach slowly deflated. Ketzler sighed and closed Fortu's eyes, then stood.

"We don't really have a way to bury him," he said. "So, let's see if we can gather some rocks or something."

Oridin nodded, laying Fortu's head gently on the ground and standing up. He headed deeper into the forest without a word. Ketzler glanced around; the rest of the squad had gathered, their gazes in various directions. Mostly not at him, except for Karbae.

"This is going to start happening," Ketzler said, keeping his voice gruff. But they needed to be prepared. "Curani might have been the first. He will be far from the last."

"Does that make it easier, for you?" Mordel asked harshly. Ketzler bit his tongue. He knew this did not come from any care for Fortu. It amazed him, still, that Mordel could use such moment to continue to dig at him.

"Perhaps it does, in its way," Ketzler replied. Now a few glances swung to him. "If we take every death as hard as we can, we will fail. We *have* to find a way to cope. But you can choose your own way—if through bitterness or anger, only be careful where you direct it. Be angry with them," he said, nodding his chin toward the fleeing Kalen, through they were too far away now to see. "But not with each other. Mourn him, but don't let it keep you from what must be done. Rationalize—we took far more of them than they took of us. In our first meeting with the enemy we have come out enormously on top. I find hope in that, and in knowing we will be capable of doing what we must here to ensure the survival of our people."

They were silent, though he thought he noticed a few faces lift a little. They would each need to work it out on their own. For now, he would give them something to look forward to. "Once we tend to Fortu, we'll spend the day here and rest. Tomorrow we return to our camp and report."

They moved, now, to find what they needed. Ketzler made his way back to Elirose. The cartographer had evidently figured the battle went well, and he had returned to sketching the terrain.

"We lost one," Ketzler said. He didn't need to report to the man, and yet it felt right. Elirose looked up.

"That doesn't seem so bad," he said.

Ketzler's brow furrowed. "It isn't," he said hesitantly.

Elirose kept scribbling for a time, then looked up. "I've been with the Commander for a long time," he said, as though explaining something. Ketzler folded his arms as he listened. "My mother had died of disease when I was young—she and I had been very close. Most people are surprised when I tell them how she doted on me. She was not Cariste, in that way." He gave a half-smile that faded fast. "My father fell from a roof a few years later. I was there, held him as his breathing failed him. He wasn't able to say anything to me, though he was trying. He and I almost never spoke to each other, and I could tell he finally wished he had." Elirose shrugged. "I was too young to live on my own, but I had no close family. So I made my way as best I could, sometimes stealing, sometimes not. Oddly enough I found myself on the roofs of Padaer—that's where we lived. Maybe I wished my father had spoken to me more as well, and thought I might find some connection to him by roofing." Another shrug. "Instead I started drawing what I saw from those heights. I carried many of the drawings in a little envelope in my pocket. It was a hard habit to keep, writing implements costing what they did. That was what I began stealing the most. Then, one day, I tried stealing from Commander Liptieri. He wasn't even a Captain then, and he caught me and struck me. When I fell, some of the drawings fell out too. He saw them, appreciated them, realized what else I could do with such an eye."

"When was this?" Ketzler asked, brow furrowed.

"Oh, ten years ago. Maybe more. Fifteen."

Ketzler turned to face him. "I would have thought the land north of the Brynth would be well-drawn by then."

Elirose's eyes flickered. "I have seen many of the maps—practiced with them, even, to hone my craft."

"Elirose, are you telling me Commander Liptieri knew we would be coming down here before he was even a Captain?"

Elirose looked at him patiently. "It takes a long time for things to move through the Senate, you know," he said. "Especially things that need to contradict Kings' edicts."

"I didn't think our resources were stretched that thin, that long ago."

Elirose shrugged, and sketched a few more lines. "Maybe they weren't, but one could probably see where things were heading."

Perhaps. But Ketzler didn't like it. It took piecing through the stories from the vaults below the church of Klos, through the historical prayers, and seeing what was excluded to sense it, but the Baders had made sure he'd spent plenty of time doing just that. Perhaps it was why he was a good scout, now.

What was excluded was any recognition of impending want. If anything, the Cariste were gluttonous. And unlikely to have large families. Elirose had spoken true: parents were rarely affectionate of their children. They were a necessity only to prevent decline. As near as he could tell, the number of Cariste on Gintanos had not increased, causing the shortage: they simply took up more space and more resources with their lifestyles. Poorer families, perhaps, increased more than they should. But they wouldn't contradict a King's edict for the sake of the poor. And they wouldn't have been paying so close attention nearly fifteen years ago. If Liptieri had been looking for a skilled cartographer that long ago, there was some other reason.

A twig snapped behind him and he turned as Karbae approached. He stepped away from Elirose for the moment. "How is it going?" he asked.

"The same," she said quietly. "Mordel thinks you don't join in because you don't care, or because you're above the work, and he points it out to everyone. But we also aren't finding much stone."

"I suspect you won't," Elirose called out. "It isn't quite the right terrain for it."

They both looked at him, but he was engrossed in his sketching again as he wandered toward the forest's edge. "There's another way," she said after he'd gone. Ketzler cocked an eyebrow. "Burn him," she said. "We used to—our people, that is."

"That was a very long time ago," he said. "I don't know if they'll accept that."

"It's better than leaving him lying there, or trying to take him with us." She hesitated as his gaze wavered. "Ketzler, we cannot take him all the way back with us. He'll rot by then. We have even less to embalm him with than we have to bury him with. Fire we can make. And I believe you could make a proper ceremony of it."

"Perhaps," he said with a sigh. "But..." He trailed off, a thought striking him. "Okay, I want you first to gather the rings off the Kalen," he said. He held up his own. "I could sense where the others were through the one I took. It could come in very handy if we could all do that. Then tell Mordel to start piling their dead just away from the edge of the forest. Unceremoniously." Comprehension dawned in her eyes, and she smiled. "And then once he's done with his tirade, quietly tell a few of the others to help him. The rest of us will build a bier for Fortu."

She bowed slightly to him, then stepped forward and kissed him before he could stop her. He shook his head as he watched her go. They would be very dangerous together, if they could ever be together. He was becoming just as devious as her, sometimes.

And, increasingly, he was enjoying it.

26

THE ONE BECOME TWO

"This seems like a mess."
"How so?"
"They're going in different directions!"
"Parallel paths never converge, Teresh."

1 Haschina 1321 — Summer

Amrith had been quiet their entire journey back toward Amka. True to Averlynn's prophecy, he had not laughed when she had brought them to the Cariste camp. Nor had he seemed surprised—or, not as surprised as one should be who had denied the threat for so long. It nettled her for most of their return journey. His surprise seemed more like one who had expected chicken and gotten venison, not like one who had not expected a meal in the first place and was treated to a feast.

And for the war-like, it would have been a feast. The first reinforcements had arrived while they were there. The ocean seemed clogged with boats, large and small, as the Cariste poured ashore like ants coming from a kicked nest. The guard posts had been tripled, and there were more armed soldiers in the forest than there were trees. They had barely been able to get close enough to see the banners of the leaders, and only briefly, before another roving patrol inadvertently chased them off.

It was possible that Ketzler simply hid among the masses. But as they neared Amka it nagged at her that she had not spotted him anywhere. Scout patrols came and went from the camp while they watched, but none of them were his. On the last day they had watched the ships disgorge the last boats, and after reloading turn north again.

"Surely they won't bring more," she muttered, barely aware it was aloud until Amrith answered her.

"It is most likely," he said quietly.

"They won't *fit*," she nearly spat—not frustrated at him, specifically. Generally, yes, but also at her people. There would be no turning those forces around without great and concentrated effort. If more came before they could win the impending war, no amount of concentrated effort would matter. At least, so it seemed to her at that moment. And all because they refused to listen, refused to consider they might need to act. It came to her again the futility of her calling, of devoting herself to Rangering for a people who long ago stopped caring about her reports.

That didn't matter any longer. They were in this time now. Hopefully her vigilance still earned them a chance, now that they knew—now that they finally believed her. Amrith himself had seen it. Certainly it nagged that Amrith had to see it before they would believe her, that they essentially only believed him, not her. But the safety of her people was paramount. Right?

"We'll need to approach this carefully," Amrith mused. They neared Amka, now, would reach it shortly. Apparently close enough he felt he needed to speak, and take control of whatever happened next.

She glanced at him warily. "But decisively?" she asked.

"Well, we still don't know if they intend war," he replied.

"But Ketzler—"

"Oh yes, and this one scout controls that entire army?"

She thumbed the reins. "He doesn't have to control it, so long as his is the prevailing attitude."

"And are we sure it is? If we act to reinforce his attitude, we might make prevailing what was only incidental."

"But they sent him as emissary," she countered. "Intended for him to speak on behalf of the leader—to make a treaty! Whatever he is, he holds some sway there. He only needs to influence their Commander, which he seems already to have done."

"Hmm, because you went to him, perhaps? A fine choice you made."

Of course she had considered that, but having it brought into the open by another jolted her. What had she done by going to him, specifically? She had no way of knowing at the time, of course. One fateful choice might just have set them on this path more surely than anything Ketzler could have done on his own.

But they didn't know. For all her meetings with the enemy—she couldn't help but consider them that after the Glowwood—she knew very little about them. Didn't know why they were here, how many there were, how they were organized—was Ketzler's Captain head over the entire army? Or would someone higher have come with the reinforcements? There had been a host of new banners, but they hadn't been able to get close enough to see who came and went from which ones.

Amrith stopped suddenly. Averlynn, distracted by her thoughts, reined up short and stared at him in confusion. Then she looked beyond him, around them, and saw: Amka was right before them, all the buildings visible, but they felt no one.

Her eyes widened and she spurred Tarafel forward. "Averlynn, hold!" Amrith shouted in vain. She kept her eyes about her, looking for ambush, but the forest was silent. She dismounted before Tarafel fully stopped and charged into the main hall, sword drawn. Empty, though the hall had been ransacked. The tables were missing their legs, and the chairs were gone—why would they take chairs? There was not a parchment or book in the place, which made some sense as long as they had someone who spoke Kalen. She didn't think they did. Perhaps they hoped to learn it.

"Averlynn!" Amrith called again. He seemed less angry this time. She exited, found the rest of her team roving through the outpost. As she watched them she realized there were no bodies lying around. If they had all died, wouldn't there be something?

"Over here," he called again. He had gone toward the Hataki. She went after him. As she neared the edge of the forest she saw some sort of structure, burned but not destroyed—one that had not been there when they left.

But there was far, far more. She stood next to Amrith, staring at the charred structure, and at the pile of blackened bones not far from it. The first was a bier—they had built enough of their own, though not to burn their dead. The second, she could only imagine were the bodies of the slain

Kalen.

She sat down, unaware as the rest of her detachment slowly made their way to the gathering. It didn't seem possible. There would have been no one here that she had not known for hundreds of years, had gone through everything the Kalen had gone through, together. Ties that had the comfort of ages gone and ages yet to come had snapped suddenly. Snapped and desecrated, trampled upon. How had he found the outpost? How many were with him, that he was able to overpower the entire camp? How had they not been spotted long before arriving?

Through the haze of sadness, anger came knocking. They should have been prepared. She recognized some of the laziness in herself, in her surprise that Ketzler had found the outpost. Probably they had thought the same thing—the danger was far away, and even if it were near it would not find them. It was an attitude born and bred over the centuries they had been here. They thought they had found an empty land, that there was no threat between the mountains. They ranged, just to be sure, but it grew unnecessary. Then there was the annihilation of the Prosan, and they were alert for a little bit. But that was long, long ago. And even that race had never really found any of the Kalen villages or cities—had never actually attacked. They just couldn't be allowed to roam free.

So now how many had died, because they thought they were safe? Because they thought life could only get more and more comfortable? That even when someone tried to warn them, when things were beginning to change, rather than face it they would rather silence the alarm.

"Do you still think they don't intend war?" she asked.

"They left many alive," Amrith said.

She glanced sharply at him, then looked over the charred bones. There were not many there, now she looked closer. Certainly not all Amka's worth. "Where are the rest?" she wondered aloud.

"They probably fled."

She snorted. Of course. It's what they did best, perhaps better than ignoring warnings. But it still didn't answer where they had gone, and why they hadn't returned. Would they return? Or would they simply go to Wazè?

But if Ketzler had found one, he could find another. Their cities would be no haven, not anymore. They had to take the fight to the Cariste, the way they had the Prosan. *Which Tavill said had risen again.* She'd almost forgotten them in the whirlwind of the Cariste threat. They would need to scout the Prosan as well—if they had not already struck at the southern outposts.

There was so much she didn't know. It should not have been her duty to know it all, but she seemed the only one curious. "We need to find them, the survivors," she said.

"They will have gone south, to Wazè or Tekaa Wohan," Amrith assured her. She had meant the Prosan, but really both. Tekaa Wohan would have been better, probably; they had fought the Prosan before and might be able to win that war much faster, while she and her detachment learned as much of the Cariste as they could. But that might be for others.

"Did you sense any threat in the south, before you came to Wazè?" she asked.

He glanced at her, puzzled. "Why there?"

"I told you there was a threat to the south," she said. "The Prosan have returned."

"Oh," he said, as though relieved. "No, there is no threat from the Prosan."

Now it was her turn to be puzzled. "You sound certain. Have you seen them?"

He looked away. "I have my methods," he replied. "We should retrieve their rings," he continued, gesturing to the bones.

It seemed worse, to root around through their remains like some feral animal, but Amrith was right. She and several of the others began, but after sifting through much of what was there, Averlynn stood. "They're not here," she said. She glanced at Amrith. "Would he..." She chewed her lip. She had told Ketzler about the ring, and a little about what they could do. "Can others besides Kalen use our rings?" she asked.

Amrith shook his head, but he didn't seem certain. "They are only a focal point for our magic," he said. Despite his uncertainty she felt some scorn in his voice. "Why don't you know that?"

"It was never my forte," she said absently. Why would he take them, then? "Could they have melted in the fire?" He glared at her now. That was a no. "Why would they have taken them, then?"

"Because they're shiny little baubles? Because they think maybe they could use them somehow, if they study them long enough? Because they take trophies?" His shrug was exaggerated. But he had a point. There could be any number of reasons why an enemy force would take something off those they killed, especially when they held the battlefield.

But it made her uncomfortable, him having those rings after what she had told him. They searched a little longer just to be sure, but there was nothing there. She stood.

"What now?" Amrith asked. She glanced in surprise, but she was technically still in charge. She took a breath, more to think than anything, as she gazed around the Hataki. She paused as she saw a small, flying speck. *Aryndurlan,* she realized. She wondered what she was doing out there. Normally she kept to the mountains, more. She watched her for a time. Was she growing larger? It certainly seemed like she hovered without flapping, as though she were heading either directly away from them, or directly toward.

"I wonder if she brings some news," Amrith muttered, just as she decided for herself that she was indeed flying toward them.

But then she flared her wings and sank to the ground and disappeared behind one of the hills. They watched a little longer, but she did not reappear.

"We should bury them," she said, looking again over the scattered bones.

Edda, leader of the Trackers, looked up and studied her. "What good will that do? Without their rings, we cannot know who they were. We cannot send them even if we did. And when did you start caring, anyway?"

She stared at him. "I have always cared," she said.

"Oh, is that why you were around so much? Why you took time to talk with us, share even common daily times with us? Why you attended nearly every festival?"

He couldn't know how much his sarcasm hurt her—but probably she could not know how much it hurt them either. "That wasn't my intention," she said. "I was trying to keep us safe..."

"We are all trying to do that," Amrith said. "Some of us take the time to still be part of the community."

"Well they won't be part of the community anymore, because I had to prove I was right. What part of the community was I allowed to be?"

"Maybe we would have trusted you faster if you had been around more often," Edda replied. His voice was soft, though. He was not angry with her. "It was difficult to ignore the idea you no longer wanted to be part of us. Of course I see the error now, but don't lord it over us that you maybe perceived it first."

From Amrith, maybe she would have denied it, or at least fought harder against the condemnation. But from Edda... She had barely recognized him when she saw him. When she thought of those assigned to Amka, she knew few of them, and none of them well. In Kalen, she had. She grew up with them there, played for endless hours with them, refused to leave the celebrations even when they were ended, always felt the sharing bond of the reverences to Praka and Hakana. She had even caused a certain amount of mischief together with Akanowa, Ofron, and Chata. What had changed?

She had, she knew. She disagreed with the decision to flee their home. Hated them, for a time—certainly for the entire journey across the ocean. She had pouted in her cramped seat on the boat—they hadn't been able to build anything luxurious, and the quarters had been small and shared. And it was on that ship that she had begun pushing them away. First the Chiefs, then anyone who agreed with them. Those she considered friends here had either agreed with her, or had not vocally agreed with the Chiefs. She leapt at the chance to conduct Forays here, she thought for the opportunity to learn this new land—maybe come to love it. And she had come to love it. But the Forays had also conveniently given her excuse to be alone most of the time.

She wondered if it was too late, now. Would she fail to raise the army because she had been selfish? Was it selfishness now that drove her to raise the army? She gazed at Edda, knowing the past moments of emotions all flooded through them. He seemed to recognize it, perhaps begin to accept it. But he said nothing.

"Well," Amrith said, folding his arms. "We're still waiting for your commands."

Averlynn closed her eyes briefly. "I still don't want to leave their bones like this," she said. "The Cariste wouldn't have treated their bodies kindly. It won't matter to them, or anyone else who comes by I suppose. But it matters to me."

"Fine." Amrith stalked away, perhaps to get shovels from the village but perhaps to avoid the work. Edda's gaze was softer, perhaps even held a note of respect. It was a start.

By the time they were done, the sun was nearly set. She let Amrith lead the prayers to Praka. When he finished she offered a few more to Hakana.

They set a small watch—the Hataki and Waken both seemed silent, their enemies long on their way back to the coast to report on their victory.

The next morning, Amrith came to her again. She had thought maybe he was finally listening, maybe trusting her a little. Now he nagged her again. Maybe it was just because of what had gone before, and she was misreading him. And yet he seemed intent to remind her at every occasion that they were waiting for her, that every moment she didn't make a decision or give them a command was a small failure.

"Wazè," she said as soon as he neared, before the question could leave his lips. "We regroup there, hopefully the survivors have gone there too. And we let the Council decide how to handle this war."

A small gleam came to his eye, she thought of triumph. Was she simply too hurt by him? Or did he have some other plan that he was working on? She wouldn't have suspected that, except he seemed so earnest that she investigate the prophecy only to accuse her of abandoning her duties. Maybe he hoped that, in front of the Council, her banishment would be upheld. He may have been right.

A small, flying shape caught her eye again, and she stared. It was Aryndurlan, still flying toward them, though it seemed she started her flight closer than where she had ended it yesterday. In fact, she gauged the dragon would arrive before the sun was above the treetops. If she didn't suddenly stop for half a day again.

She cocked her chin toward him. "Actually, we might wait to see what she wants," she said.

She was flying even faster than Averlynn thought. Shortly after breakfast she landed, though heavily. She bowed her head quickly, then seemed to be catching her breath. Averlynn stepped forward and bowed deeply, then waited.

"It will be soon," she said.

Averlynn's eyes went wide. "What will be?"

Her eyes suddenly focused. "Oh, I do apologize. Talking to myself is an odd habit I picked up, out here on my own mostly. Until recently! Now it seems the entire country is coming to my lands."

"Who? More of the Kalen? You've seen them?"

Aryndurlan settled onto her haunches, then curled her neck and laid her head down. "How I wish I could take a nap," she said. Averlynn could hear the weariness in her voice. It went far deeper than lack of sleep, or hard flying. She went to her, laid a hand on her scaly head. An eye opened and studied her.

"You may, if you wish," Averlynn said quietly. "We can wait for you."

Her head rolled a little. "That is very kind. I fear, though... Well, no matter. I saw some of you out on those hills—are you calling yourselves the Kalen, again? That would be good..." Her sides heaved like bellows.

"I guess I have," she said. "I want to be that again."

"Hmm. Well, whoever you are, there are two dozen or so camped out there. You should go to them."

"How did you know to come here? Did you know we were here?"

"Oh, no. I hoped those creeping attackers would be here, I'd teach them a thing or two. Killing all the elder races like they're trying to do!"

"All of them? Are they after you too?"

"Oh, probably. People have always been trying to kill us. Then you. Then the Taur—"

"You've seen Tavill?" Averlynn asked excitedly.

"Oh, yes. He's such a dear. Troubled—so troubled, within and without. But I think I was able to help him with that, at least a little. It may seem worse for a time, but wounds have to be cleaned before they can heal. Yes, he's out there. But I saw the Kalen fleeing something, knew I had to come help if I could. So many in need of help, these days. If you find Tavill, though, tell him he did well. Tell him it was a true honor escorting him through these hills."

Averlynn trembled. "Aryndurlan, will you come with us?"

Her head rolled a little more. "I would so love a nap," she mumbled. For a moment, Averlynn thought perhaps she did sleep. But after a deep breath, she sighed: "I wonder who will replace me."

Her side deflated slowly to rest. Averlynn backed away a few steps as a faint thrum rose. It reminded her some of Tavill's throat-song, but this filled the air as though the world itself sang it. Aryndurlan's wings shone, turned translucent and shimmered like dragonfly wings. The thrum rose in pitch, grew louder. Aryndurlan's body began to glow, seemed to grow young again, the skin and scales tightening. Averlynn could picture her like a topaz thunderbolt through the sky in her youth, how high and far she used to fly, the might of her. It almost seemed to come back, now, and yet it was temporal.

What happened next she would hardly be able to describe later, though she tried to commit it to the songs of her people. To her knowledge, none had ever seen a dragon die of old age. But as she watched, the keening whistle like Tavill's throat-song rose, seeming to split Aryndurlan, but not in any physical sense as though she were cut in half. Rather it was as though her essence divided, one becoming two. And somehow she knew their names: she was Arykorin, he was Endurlan, and they had known each other before the Kalen came to Gintanos. Averlynn felt a warmth in her spirit, a thankfulness and a knowing from them.

Her body grew brighter, sleeker, younger. Their spirits began to mist, neither rising nor blowing away but simply dissipating. The thrum and the whistle harmonized a complicated but slow tune, and the body took on a quality like stone, hardening to crystal. As the last particle of their spirits faded, she saw in the long crystal two bodies interred, faces heavenward. He with long jet-black hair that flowed around a face of firm angles, a sharp nose and deep-set eyes. Her, near his height, with flaming hair that framed features a little softer but no less noble. He had one wing wrapped around her, the other tucked to his side, and between them their hands clasped together.

All this she saw in a moment before the crystal hazed over, obscuring them and turning the rock to near brown. As Averlynn lifted tear-filled eyes she saw the Hataki littered with so many rocks. Most were too small to be sepulchers, but she wondered at some of those that were of similar size.

She placed a hand on the stone, felt warmth slowly fade as the song died away. On the other side were the small graves they had dug for the fallen Kalen, the fresh-dug earth a warm brown now in sunlight.

She took a deep, calming breath as she wiped her eyes. There could be no better monument—perhaps it was even too-worthy. But she felt a small chuckle in her spirit, as though Arykorin and Endurlan did not think so.

Another breath. There was work to do, others who needed to be able to die of old age. She looked at Amrith, who seemed strangely unmoved by what had just happened. His gleaming eyes, instead, focused on her.

"Well?" he asked.

She said nothing, simply went to Tarafel and mounted. She wouldn't let his little barbs dig in anymore. She couldn't figure him out, and wasn't sure she wanted to. Whatever his motives, she didn't share his actions. She clicked her tongue, and began riding northwest, where Aryndurlan had originated yesterday. The rest of the detachment fell in behind her, Amrith the last.

She would have loved to gallop, to push them to the refugees as swiftly as possible, but the Hataki wouldn't allow it. The Wall loomed to the north, and as she let Tarafel find his own way over the sometimes rocky and always rough terrain, she found herself studying those peaks again. Memories of her journey through them came back again and again. It could be a place of strength, that warren of valleys. But the idea stank to her of cowering, letting the Cariste simply take over the rest of the land that had so long been theirs.

Perhaps that was what the survivors of Amka had thought, and why they hadn't fled south. Perhaps the Water Plains simply worried them, an obstacle too hard to surmount. And, truly, there were no paths through the marshes. Routes changed with the season, and the water was often sick. Trackers wouldn't help.

Her brow furrowed. "Edda," she said, falling back to talk to him. "Where are the Rangers for the north?"

"They should be either behind us or in front of us," he said.

"But I didn't see them when I first came."

He gave a little grin. "For that, Avako's daughter, you are to blame. Isun Vera chastised the Ka for his soldiers being lax in their duties, after you departed last time."

Averlynn stared. "That was not really her place," she said. It wasn't; spiritual leaders *never* directly influenced military leaders.

Edda shifted uncomfortably. "No, it wasn't. Well, there were words before. The Isun..." He glanced at her quickly and sighed. "The Isun defended you after she had overheard some words. In that defense she faulted the Ka for endangering the worship of the gods by endangering the Wohan."

"Because the Rangers rarely left the outposts," Averlynn finished. Edda nodded. So, things were changing. It was a small measure of hope, to which she clung. Still, strange for an Isun so well-versed in their faiths—nearly a Sage—to stand up so.

As evening fell, she felt the first tenuous senses of the survivors. Now she did push Tarafel, wanting to reach them before darkness came. The threads grew stronger, clustered just to the west. As she rode she sang an old Kalen song of triumph and praise. It thrummed along the connecting threads, and she started to take stock of who was left. Vera was there, as were Rangers Lakana and Akanowa. She didn't sense Chief Hathar, then remembered he would have gone at the end of the month she departed with her detachment. She sorted through the ring-signs, but none of them were Chiefs.

Finally she reined in at the top of the hill, her song dying away as she saw the impromptu camp below. All the Wohan were standing looking at her, at her detachment. Isun Vera stepped forward.

"Welcome, Hakana's Daughter Averlynn," she said, her voice husky. So few were there. More than she thought when she had first seen the charred bones. Far less than she thought when Aryndurlan said there was a remnant.

"Thank you, Isun Vera," she called down. She led her troops quietly down the hillside, then dismounted and clasped Vera's hands. She glanced around again, tears welling. Her eyes widened with realization as she turned back to Isun Vera. "The Ka Urlan?" she whispered.

Vera shook her head. "He was one of the last, after ensuring the rest of us had gotten away." She cocked her head. "Did you not find them?"

"The Cariste had...burned them. We could not find the rings to know who was gone."

Isun Vera's hand went to her mouth as she shook her head. "This is a terrible thing!" she said.

"Why?"

Akanowa stepped forward. "They are able to use them to sense us," she said. "Their leader...he took Withlow's ring and put it on. It was...disturbing," she said with a shudder. "We felt the connection snap, knew Withlow had died. But then suddenly it re-wove itself." She shook her head. "It was Withlow, but also not Withlow. As though the ring-sign trembled against the spirit of the wearer."

"Was he able to do anything else with it?" Averlynn asked, trying not to look at Amrith. Had he knowingly lied, or just been confidently mistaken?

Akanowa shook her head. "He did not use it otherwise, but whether or not he can..." She shrugged. "We didn't even know he could re-weave the thread."

"So if they took what they found, then everyone lost is an opportunity for them to feel us at distance."

"But also we can feel them," Amrith cut in. "That would be a benefit."

"It didn't seem to benefit us," Isun Vera said quietly.

Averlynn was glad she said it, instead of herself. It would have been cruel. "Only one of them had it," Averlynn said. "It could give a false sense of confidence, make us think an attack is coming from one direction while he communicates our positions to those we cannot see."

"Do we abandon our rings, then?" Amrith asked scornfully. His eyes raked her up and down with a glint. "Will you abandon yours?"

"Scout Amrith!" Isun Vera thundered. Averlynn only looked away. His barbs would *not* dig in.

"Were you heading to the Wall?" Averlynn asked.

Isun Vera shook her head. "We were only trying to get away—as far as we could. They circled south of us at the outpost, so when we came to the Hataki we only continued running." Her lip trembled, and Averlynn sensed her shame. But if the Cariste had attacked so effectively when they were least vulnerable...

"It was the right thing," Averlynn said. "*Is* the right thing, for the moment. But I think we cannot run forever."

"We'll let the Council decide that, Ranger," Amrith said boldly.

Averlynn and Isun Vera both turned to him. "Was she not given command of the detachment?" Isun Vera asked. It still shocked Averlynn, a little, how easily Vera assumed her role as leader.

"The detachment is no more," he sneered. "We have gone to the Cariste camp, and returned to give our report to the outpost. Command is now mine."

"Is it?" Isun Vera mused. "I recall the council giving her command of the detachment until they proved or disproved her banishment."

Amrith's mouth worked silently a few times. "And have they not?"

Isun Vera's brows arched. "I have heard no word, yet. And as I am what remains of that council—" She broke off tremulously. After a moment she set her jaw. Her voice was husky again as she spoke. "Then until we hear for certain, she remains in command."

Amrith glowered, but had no recourse. He led his mount away in silence.

27

THOSE TORMENTED BY
PROPHECY

"I thought...the call..."
"Yes. It is odd."
"Odd? Catastrophic, I would say."
"We knew things would begin to change."

10 Haschina 1321 — Summer

Averlynn walked beside Tarafel. The rest of her people were un-mounted, and it felt strange to ride when they could not. Isun Vera was beside her as they made their way west.

Amrith had taken the rest of the detachment toward Wazè to report, and start the Council until she could arrive. Averlynn worried about that, worried he might turn them against the idea of war before they got there. Isun Vera was all for it—well, perhaps not eager for the conflict, but understood first-hand the intentions of Ketzler and his people.

That had been another surprise the Isun relayed: that Ketzler led the scouting party that had attacked. He had certainly not led when the Cariste first arrived on shore, so he was rising through their ranks. Was that why she had been drawn to his tent? Had the gods known he was more important than he seemed, able to sway policy?

And yet why had he killed his fellow? If it had been to instigate war, then there had to be more who didn't want it. Surely the leader of one scouting party wasn't the only one.

She sighed. What did it matter? War was coming—she hurried them toward it herself. They made their way now for the hidden port of Kenkek, where Ka Ouwa led, to collect the troops there. They would need every body they had scattered around the lands.

"The winds themselves eddy enough," Isun Vera said with a grin. "Even without your help."

Averlynn glanced at her, biting back another sigh. "I'm sorry," she said.

"These times may call for it," Vera said. "But we must focus on what we can control, and what we can do. For the rest we must pray."

Now Averlynn smiled, ashamed. "I'm afraid I have not been making my prayers lately."

"You do not abandon them?"

Averlynn cringed at the alarm in Vera tone. "No, not at all. And I know it is times like these where I need to press even further in my prayers. I can do nothing without their help..." She sighed again, unable to help it. "Isun, I wish I had been able to undertake my Minor Hangh back when I first wanted to. Every day brings new terrors and changes, and I'm too swept away by it all to even take the breaths I need. If there was only some way to get away for a while."

"Take the time now," Isun Vera suggested.

"I don't know if I can quiet my mind enough. And, besides..."

"'Besides' what?"

Averlynn thumbed the reins she carried loosely. "I've missed Aman È. I've missed most of my prayers. Even before this I felt as though my prayers to Hakana were falling short, as though she wasn't hearing me anymore."

They continued in silence for long moments. Finally the Isun spoke. "I am not yet a Sage," she said carefully. "Though I am perhaps not far from it. But do you think the god's ability to hear is limited by your feeling?"

Averlynn's brow furrowed. "What do you mean?"

"Well, they are gods, aren't they? If you believe they are."

"Of course."

"Praka rises and sets without our will. Hakana waxes and wanes in her time. Clouds or mist may obscure them—but reason tells us they are still there, yes? Still shining even if we cannot see them."

"That makes sense. But then—"

"So if their nature remains true regardless of us, then their abilities remain unhindered by us, aren't they?"

"But as you say, clouds or mist may obscure them."

"And yet the light of Praka still accomplishes its will—we can still determine that it is daytime."

"I'm not sure I see the point, Isun."

"Missing the festivals, or missing your prayers, may have thrown clouds over the light so that *you* cannot feel them, or may not be able to point to them to say 'there they are.' But they are still there, still doing their work—and part of that work is hearing our prayers, I think."

Silence descended again except for the tramp of their feet, the swish of the grass around their ankles. "I've not heard that before," Averlynn said eventually.

Now it was the Isun's turn to sigh. "And that is our fault," she said with a furtive glance. "It is hard to admonish our people to dedication if we start saying dedication may not be necessary."

"Only if you just want the gods to do things for you that you can't," Averlynn replied.

"Explain," Isun Vera said.

"As you said, they are the sun and moon," she replied. "We could maybe live by torchlight and firelight forever. As long as there were other powers to give us everything we need, we could survive without their light. And yet..." She looked around the Hataki, the folds of hills, the brown of the grass hued now with bits of green and scattered with blues and yellows and reds as daisies and paintbrushes and foams and sages were blooming their little, delicate blooms. "As you said, they exist with or without us. We can ignore the tree in the forest if we want, until the point we try to walk where it is. Then we cannot help but crash into it. I don't want to ignore it. I want to fall completely into its embrace, to know it from acorn to trunk to branch to bud to leaf."

Isun Vera smiled. "Are you sure you want to be a Ranger?" she said. "I think you would make a fine acolyte."

Averlynn snorted. "After missing something so basic and important as Aman È?"

"You may have missed a festival," Isun Vera said. "But you have more than understood the intent of it. I did not even give so eloquent a homily at the festival you supposedly missed."

"Then why don't they hear my prayers?"

Vera laughed in exasperation. "What have we been talking about? You've done everything you can to warn us of the danger that has reached our shores, and despite the opposition you've managed somehow to succeed. What were you praying for? That the Cariste simply wouldn't come? Or else what makes you think your prayers aren't heard?"

Averlynn walked in silence for a while after that. Was it simply that she thought she should feel something when she prayed? She had, on numerous occasions, 'felt' like her prayers went somewhere. But had they had any effect—visible effect? What good was feeling like they were effective if they were not actually effective?

And what had she prayed for? Was it the right thing? Was it something possible? *Should* it have been something possible? Or was it better to ask the impossible of a god? Maybe they only responded if she asked the impossible, so she would know it was them. But then if they didn't respond, was it because they couldn't do it? Or they simply didn't want to? What, then, was the point of asking?

No matter what Isun Vera said, she was no acolyte. She didn't understand faith in the least—or, didn't understand what the gods demanded or how they operated. And her desire to know was only a product of her general curiosity. No; far better to let those who would be diligent seek out the truths and tell her. Just as she needed to seek out the truths of their environments and give the answers to those who needed them.

"What happened to you at Tadan È?" Vera asked quietly.

Averlynn blinked. It had been a long time ago now. And had she ever been certain?

"I know we never talked about it," Vera continued. "And that was my failing as your spiritual guide. It was a strange time, I guess. It still is..." She trailed off and set her jaw.

"Something...I don't know," Averlynn said frankly. "I remember feeling pulled into the ground, but also pulled to fly to the highest reaches. Like I was both at once—in both places at once."

"Were you in both places at once? Or part of both?"

She tried to think back. "It was so strange, I'm not sure if I could tell—no, not just in it. At least, not as though I were simultaneously some sort of burrowing animal and also some sort of hawk."

"Don't necessarily think only of how you felt physically," Vera said. "What you experienced was clearly spiritual—your body stayed where it was the whole time, though you were not moving as tradition or ceremony dictated," she added drily. "What about your spirit? *Were* you stone *and* air at the same time?"

She gave an exasperated sigh. "What difference would it make if it was one over the other?"

"It would seem to me that if you were only there, as an observer, then perhaps it was a vision of some kind." She paused a moment. "But if you were the things, at least spiritually, it shows a deeper connection—may show something about your nature that shouldn't be ignored."

"I felt torn in two," Averlynn said finally. "That's as best as I can remember. I sought to feel the earth—I had for a long time. I thought maybe if I could sort of sink down into it, become part of it, it might feel like home. And in that moment it gripped me as if to pull me deep into its environs. But when I recoiled, suddenly I felt torn into the air as though by great eagle claws. But I was never actually in or part of each, just that each desired me for its own."

Isun Vera's eyes were wide. "Oh," she breathed.

"What does that mean?"

"Nothing. Or rather, I'm sure it means something, I just..." She took a breath. "That's not what I was expecting to hear."

"It's not what I was expecting to feel."

Vera chuckled. "I can imagine. And now you explain it like that, I must confess I applaud your restraint. I would have abandoned every vestige of ceremony if I was in the middle of that." Her brow furrowed suddenly. "And yet, it reminds me of something. Who was talking about it? I think even while he spoke it reminded me...Lakana!" she called backward suddenly. Lakana looked forward. He had been talking with Akanowa. He trotted up to walk with them. "What were you reciting to me some days ago?" Vera asked.

He thought a moment. "Oh, that! Just a bit of song I had been working on."

"Sing it, please? The part your sang to me."

His gaze darkened. "I don't know if it's appropriate," he said. "It was meant for a time of joy..."

"Please? I want Averlynn to hear it from you."

He pressed his lips together, and Averlynn thought he might continue to refuse. Finally, with a scratch of his neck, he began:

The dancers dance, they run, they jump, and twist and turn to thumping drums.
The stars above are scattered wide and hide the dark till morning comes.
But one falls swift and streaks the sky—a flying torch from grander height
Than all below; and yet she knows the depths of earth will hold her light.

Averlynn trembled as he finished, and felt Isun Vera's eyes on her. "Are you sure...I'm sorry, but—you wrote that as original?" Averlynn asked.

Lakana nodded. "The rhyme and meter are familiar to me, though I can't think from where. Something from the Old Country. But the words themselves—do you like it?"

"When did you write it?"

He made an off-hand gesture. "I've been working on it for a time. You know how it can be—a word here or there, an idea, some concept of what you want..." He trailed off as he caught both Averlynn's and Vera's expectant gazes. "Right. Probably...Tadan È? I had the idea of a falling star coming to earth before then. Then the first line came to me during the festival. And when Hakana went out!" He shuddered. "Such a strange darkness. I felt like it shook the heavens. Certainly shook them enough to dislodge a star...that's kind of the idea, anyway. I need to keep working on it."

"Thanks," Averlynn said faintly.

Lakana hesitated. "You never said if you liked it."

She blinked at him. "Oh, no it's very...well-written."

Vera only glared at him until he fell back with the rest of the refugees. "So I was right," she said. "I have a few thoughts, but I'd like to hear yours first."

"I fear it feels too proud," Averlynn replied.

"That this latest verse is about you?"

"And is it part of the original prophecy? Did he just forget the words already existed?"

"Hmm. Or is the prophecy being added to?"

Averlynn shook her head, denying the possibility. "I know little about prophecies, but they are never fulfilled so close to their inception, are they?"

"They are not subject to the whims of elves, that is certain—neither the speaking nor the fulfilling."

"Lakana is also not finished with it, he said."

"But he said the idea is there."

They continued in silence as the sun slowly fell before them. "There was another time," Averlynn said finally. "Another thing—a song, I heard, that also seemed to tie heaven and earth. Tavill—the *Anggika?*"

Vera glanced sharply at her. "You truly saw him?"

Averlynn nodded reverently. "I couldn't believe it. Our songs have preserved their appearance quite well—I knew instantly what he was. But he was doing this thing, he called it the throat-song. It was at once like the grinding of great rocks against each other, and an echoing whistle that reminded me of the highest mountain peaks. It was incredible, and beautiful. He thought it might suppress the bloodlust, somehow—" She paused as Vera's brow furrowed. "You remember, from *The Lay of Wathantha*. His quest was nearly ruined by inciting the bloodlust of an *Anggika*."

Vera rolled her eyes. "That's a little oversimplified, isn't it? You speak of the bloodlust as some inherent trait when the Lay speaks of a kind of disease."

It was Averlynn's turn to look confused. "That isn't how Tavill spoke of it. He spoke of a compulsion that would take him and he would kill every living thing around him—and it existed as part of being Taur."

"Interesting," Vera mused. "I should have liked to meet him, then, to learn more about this. Isn't that also what *Ek Ikowa Lers* also talks about? Some hindrance to their duty?"

"I imagine."

Vera shrugged. "I always thought it was something they encountered, not part of them, that hindered their duty. It would be fascinating to learn it was this, instead. Terrifying, of course. But it would change so much."

"I wish I could learn to throat-sing," Averlynn said quietly. "Isun, you should have heard it..."

"Can't you?"

Averlynn paused. "Well, would it be appropriate to? Who am I to try to sing such a thing?"

"Well, if Lakana is to be believed, you're a star falling from the heavens knowing she can light the depths of the earth," Vera replied with a twinkle in her eye. Averlynn chuckled, but then Vera sobered. "But, even with what you said you experienced at Tadan È, you already are somehow tied to earth and sky together. You already are this throat-song."

After making camp that night and sharing a cold meal—they did not want to risk open fires, which could not be glamoured—Averlynn stole away into the hills. When the sense of her people was thinnest, but still present, she stood silently under a canopy of stars. Hakana was gone from the sky for now, farthest from her lover. Despite her lapse in prayers, Averlynn still attuned quickly to the moods of her favored goddess. She felt, too, the bereavement, the fear of darkness, the smaller losses of the stars. Each of them, minuscule ice chips in the void, were also without their swelling mother on these nights.

Her mind drifted to Lakana's poem. Why had he composed it? Surely not for her sake. Just there, though, a star fell. Most didn't reach the ground. They winked into existence, flared, and disappeared. Often it was how the Kalen perceived the lives of humans. She wondered if that was how the Taur perceived the lives of elves.

She closed her eyes, let her senses curl inward and downward. She felt as though a funnel of darkness opened in the front of her mind, drained into it all her thoughts, carried them first into her insides, then flowing out and into the ground. She tried to thrum in her throat the way Tavill had.

A squeak startled her, coming from her throat. The funnel rebounded and she shook her head. Silly. This was foolishness. She grit her teeth, delved her senses deep into the earth again. And squeaked again.

She growled, her eyes flying open in frustration. She hummed as deep as she could. It sounded closer, though still far too high in pitch. Hers sounded like bees, not rocks. She stopped humming and folded her arms.

Useless. She wasn't who Vera thought she was—what the silly song of Lakana's alluded she was. Deluded was a better word. She sighed and closed her eyes. If she was deluded about that, what other high positions had she simply taken for herself? Had assumed that *she* was the one to do it?

She only did what no others wanted to, or seemed to do, she thought bitterly. Was it her fault, truly, that she had pulled away from her people? Should she have valued community over what was right? And yet why was she so certain she was right?

Because the signs said so. Didn't they? Hamada had said the prophecy was already fulfilled. Was that why Lakana added to it? Was the prophecy renewing?

Averlynn turned and went back to the camp, making her way to Isun Vera. The Isun was awake, and sat up as Averlynn approached. "Daughter?" she asked tentatively.

"Was the prophecy fulfilled in Kalen?" she asked.

Vera arranged her blankets. The nights were still cold. "I told you they are not subject to the whims of elves."

"That doesn't entirely answer my question."

"The chiefs thought the prophecy was already fulfilled, yes."

"When."

"When we fled. Do you remember? The Endolin came from the south, the Cariste and Rinc Nain came from across the sea. We, the guardians, gave out and slid into oblivion—here."

Averlynn sat back. "Are prophecies ever fulfilled twice?"

Vera shook her head. "I can't imagine."

"So either it wasn't fulfilled, or this is something else. And the prophecy can't help us."

"Or it's still not being fulfilled. There are a few lines that don't make sense. Even if the return of the Prosan is the spear, what falcon's blood breaks the stones? This is my point, Hakana's Daughter: prophecy cannot guide us anyway—it is not subject to our whims. You must choose what is right, and once it is done the prophecy will either be fulfilled or not."

"Then what's the point of it?"

"To display the power of the source—so we know that whoever gave the prophecy is supreme."

Averlynn took a slow breath. "So who gave the prophecy? Praka or Hakana?"

Isun Vera glanced aside, lowering her voice to a whisper. "And why are you sure it was one of them?" As Averlynn gaped, Vera snorted. "This is why I am not a Sage yet," she said drily.

"But if it's not, if we worship false gods...and you're a spiritual guide...how...?"

Vera held up a hand to still her stream of questions. "I have only come lately to it," she said. "But think of it: what god is so easily comprehended? Subject to mortal whims? Or is it easier for us to relate to a god who is closer to one of us? What might be called a false god might also be called a fraction of a true God—a finite aspect of an infinite being—created by us or others to help us understand the incomprehensible. So some worship a god of war, another worships a god of justice, another a god of creation, another a god of wisdom, because it is difficult to imagine one god being in nature all those things at once."

"A God of All?" Averlynn said.

Vera gave a short sigh. "I don't like to use such a name," she said.

"I can imagine."

Vera looked sharply at her. "And that is exactly why. As soon as you hear it, you close your mind—why?"

"Because those who worship that one are this moment threatening to destroy us—again! All they know is destruction and selfishness. I will worship no god that they do."

"And do you think Amrith is acting in the best interest of our people?"

"What? That's...different..."

Vera smiled grimly. "Of course it is; because you know the teachings of Praka and Hakana, and know that Amrith isn't fully guided by those teachings. All you know about the Cariste god is a name—what difference the name? Call him Elonai if you wish. But because of that name and those people, you reject the mere possibility."

"So we should just convert? Surrender to the Cariste so we can learn about their god and begin to worship it instead?"

Vera looked steadily at her. "Do you think that's what is right?"

"Of course not!"

"Why not?"

Averlynn's mouth worked silently a few times. "Vera!"

"First, I am still your Isun. Second, I'm making a point. Your incredulity at such an idea has nothing to do with their god, and everything to do with them, yes?"

Averlynn calmed herself. "Yes, Isun."

"Thank you. If you earnestly want to learn the truth, don't hide behind ridiculous suppositions. And my proposal that there is one supreme god —above both Hakana and Praka—was not based on the Cariste at all, was it?"

Averlynn sighed. "No, Isun."

"Daughter, please don't sound so defeated. It is not a competition.

What if there is no god at all? Everything just happens? We might need to consider that as well."

"Then there wouldn't be prophecies."

"There wouldn't be *fulfilled* prophecies—nothing more complex than 'the sun will rise tomorrow,' anyway. If prophecies are not real, they seem real only because they are so general that almost any event will fulfill them, or they are so narrow that it is merely a safe assumption—or, they are never fulfilled. But if they are true, they will be fulfilled no matter what you do to oppose it, no matter how complex or specific it is in its details."

"And we cannot be guided by it, to know what to choose."

Vera shook her head. "It is for knowledge only—when we see it fulfilled, we will know that what is, was meant to be."

Averlynn's brow furrowed as she thought through that. "It's not complete, is it," she said finally. "Even with Lakana's addition."

Vera glanced at the stars overhead, then slowly shook her head. "I believe it is not. It paints no clear picture, does it? It doesn't tell us *why* these things are happening, or what the object of the prophecy is. So far it is just a telling of events."

Averlynn folded her arms. "And I haven't ruined everything by thinking I was doing what the prophecy told me."

Vera smiled thinly. "Only if prophecies are given falsely," she said.

"Unless this prophecy doesn't apply to now."

Vera laughed. "What a dreadful circle," she said. "How much better off would we be if we simply didn't have them? Perhaps that's why—" She cut herself off, smiled grimly. "Well, not everyone is given prophecy, to be tormented by it."

Averlynn's lips quirked in a half-smile that slowly faded. "It raises an interesting question: why is it coming to me now?"

Vera pursed her lips. "What is it you hope for?" she asked.

"Peace for our people," she replied quickly.

Vera's eyes glittered as she studied her. She shook her head. "No. Deeper than that."

Averlynn felt a tug in her throat. "I want to go home," she whispered.

Vera smiled grimly. "Do you think that is promised to our people?"

Averlynn shrugged miserably. "It doesn't seem like it."

"Hmm. And yet you do not feel settled here, for all your efforts."

Averlynn shook her head, then cocked it. "I did have a moment, a little while ago, of the need to defend this land. A responsibility, because of love for it, to protect it from those who only look at it for what they can get out of it. As one might defend a home."

"Or anything they have been put in charge of," Vera replied. "I don't discount your feeling—I think that is a right feeling. But prophecy is also something to attach faith to, to await the fulfillment in either dread or excitement."

"Dread?"

"Indeed. A promised punishment if we do not depart errant ways." Vera grimaced. "Did we sin to give up our home so easily? Will we sin again to give it up this time? Or did we sin in defending it?"

"How would it be sin to defend it?"

"Was it ours to possess? Or were we given oversight for a time until someone else came along?"

"According to Aver, it was destroyed by some would-be hero of the land, a Rinc Nain." She shook her head, even nearer now to tears. "There is no home to return to if we could."

Vera reached out and touched her hand. "Daughter, I believe this prophecy comes to you to offer some hope, once we parse out what it is. Do not despair just yet. Great forces are at work in you, and such forces do not work in vain."

"What should I do?"

Vera withdrew her hand in thought. "I think we must seek to understand these forces better, first. Perhaps by re-creating, or re-entering that position you fell into during Tadan È. Maybe learning the throat song..."

Averlynn scoffed and wiped her eyes. "I already tried. It was humiliating even alone."

"Oh, well, as long as you've tried once," Vera replied, though she smiled. "Averlynn, Hakana's daughter, apply yourself to this as you apply yourself to Rangering until something happens with a little more finality. But, maybe after you've taken some rest."

Averlynn forced a smile. "Thank you for that, at least," she said. She returned to her bedroll. Tarafel had finished grazing and was asleep standing up nearby. She smiled, eager to join him. And yet, as she lay down, she continued to watch as occasional stars burned themselves out through the sky.

The next night, she departed the camp again and went just far enough away that the threads were there. She lay facedown as she had been at the festival, splaying her fingers in the earth. But the thrum did not come—or, at least, was no deeper than when she simply hummed deeply. She sat back again. Was it the land itself? Perhaps she needed trees…and yet, the thought struck her as ridiculous as soon as it came.

And why did she think so? It felt almost as if it were not her own thought, but as though whatever 'force' it was Vera spoke of were chiding her. She stilled herself, trying to listen, or at least to feel, opening herself to the night around her.

But the elven threads nagged at her, distracting her. Blinking, she rose and walked deeper into the Hataki until those threads faded to nothing. Hopefully the Kalen on the watch wouldn't worry too much. With a wry grin she realized her difficult relationship with them gave her perfect excuse for any strange behavior.

She knelt again, utterly alone. That pose felt strange, too. She rotated, sitting down with her knees drawn up to her chest. She placed her hands palm-down, wove her fingers into the grasses, felt every blade and grit of dirt.

And yet, as she opened herself again, something was off-balance. The stars and the sky surrounded her, and she felt nearly as if she were on some precarious perch, a thin spike of rock held high above a valley below. Displayed as an offering to the voids above.

And yet she knows the depths of earth will hold her light.

She wrestled her boots off, settling her bare feet into the grass. The earth sucked her down, and she could barely gasp before it closed over her head. It felt still as though she were falling through space while the dirt and rocks pressed around her. She wanted to scream, but dared not let out the air that might become so precious to her.

A flying torch from grander height than all below.

She buoyed for a moment, her descent slowing. Frantically she stilled her mind, eased her chest. She reached out, welcomed the rock, found herself among it. Then she carefully opened her throat and began to hum.

It was only barely higher pitched than the Taur's. His voice was of vast rocks, commensurate with his size and the weight of his years. Hers were only slightly smaller, but felt to her to be manageable. She held it for a time, pitching it up and down only slightly in a tune that came from both inside and outside her.

Then, carefully, afraid to break the spell, she moved her tongue. The thrum warbled and wobbled, then steadied as a whistle buzzed and stopped. She approached it again, working her way toward a slight curl.

Suddenly the whistle came sharp and loud as the sides of her tongue touched her teeth. She held it for a moment as she burst from the earth and into the sky, then bobbed as she changed the notes.

She strained to hold it in balance, to hold the song while paying attention to what it brought her—it was not the violence of Tadan È, but some sort of broad connection with the land around her. It placed her strangely in it, almost as a thing not there.

It wavered as she began to feel a strain. She pitched and rolled, and before she could right herself again she felt a strange pressure from northward. She slipped sideways before it, lurched as from a heavy blow, and sprawled on the ground as the song died within her. She lay gasping for a few moments. As the experience itself faded away, it left behind strange bits of uncorrelated knowledge like driftwood. But she had not the strength or presence of mind just yet to gather it.

28

FACTS, DRY AND DUSTY

"You are losing him."
"It was always possible."
"Are you giving up then?"
"There is one chance remaining."

10 Haschina 1321 — Summer

Tavill sat in the sun, still waiting for Aryndurlan to return.

He knew the dragon needed frequent rests. And if she needed to fulfill some task after investigating the disturbances, it could take her even longer.

But this seemed something else. The days drew on, and Tavill was convinced the dragon would have returned even briefly to tell him what to do. And yet she had not, and Tavill sat with only his scent-vision, and waited.

He might wait one more day. There was comfort in not moving, sometimes. It reminded him a little of his mountain retreat, of enjoying the little things. He had made no friends of mice here, and there were other odd little creatures that he smelled now and again. He had investigated much of the rest of the ruins, though he never went to that deep pool again. Once had been enough. He thought several times that it had been more than enough—but it had been necessary. Like the pruning of grapevines, the cutting away hurt at first, and yet allowed so much more growth.

And fruitfulness. He shifted, letting the sun warm him. A strange fruit, though, unless he only misunderstood it. The duty came back to him, and he wondered why. *Why* was it their duty? What purpose could it serve? The Harral and Elonai both saw everything—had *already* seen it, if some of their most ancient songs were true. He assumed they were true. And yet he had this thing—this blank space, this veil over so many of his memories. So cleanly veiled he only realized it recently.

Or was it only because he'd abandoned that duty? He had not searched his memories for so long, only assumed they were there for unlocking later. Too long had he sat complacent.

And yet here he was, still sitting complacent, letting Aryndurlan take responsibility for whether Tavill sat or moved. He drew a deep breath. But what would happen if the dragon returned and Tavill was gone?

That was not the true hesitation: Aryndurlan, from a height, would see Tavill traveling from far away and would catch up. The problem was that Tavill didn't know where to go.

He could perhaps go east, try to find Aryndurlan or the Kalen that the dragon sought. That might take him back toward the Prosan though, or the Cariste. Without sight, and with a prevailing—he sniffed—west wind, that could be most dangerous.

North? Aryndurlan nested there in those massive mountains that had teased Tavill's view of the horizon when he could still see. It might be interesting to visit those monoliths after he'd grown so accustomed to the Snowashes. And yet, finding the dragon in what had to be warrens of valleys and peaks was daunting. And the way wind might swirl...he did not relish that idea either.

He could go south again. Back home. That smacked of retreating, of abdicating his duty once again. It wouldn't be, necessarily; but the temptation would surely be there. And all that pruning would be for naught.

He rose, rolling his shoulders. West it was, then, for no good reason. At least, for no bad reason. Perhaps he would reach an ocean and simply begin to swim until either he died or found a new land. Why not?

And yet, as he gathered his pack and set off, there seemed something very *right* about going that way. Not as though he gained outside permission or approval, but had somehow internally simply felt an assurance. Perhaps some outside approval had already existed and he aligned with it in this decision. Like a note suddenly coming into harmony with another.

Maybe the Harral watched and silently gave their approval.

He walked directly into the wind, giving himself the clearest picture of what lay ahead. He did not want to stumble, or encounter a surprise—he worried even that would be too insurmountable an obstacle. The slightest hindrance now would bury him in self-doubt, and he would second-guess himself into an entirely new path.

At least no one seemed to pursue him. After so many days spent with Aryndurlan in the ruins, and then alone, another patrol of Prosan would have shown up if they were going to. The more he thought of it, the more it felt right: that last party was near the end of their supplies. They had ranged far from their main force to come after him. It had been a desperate attempt. And until they returned positively in either victory or defeat, the rest of their people would have no idea where to find him. And the Cariste didn't know he existed, yet.

He continued into the night for a time, until only the nocturnal creatures left their scents as he passed. He had begun singing the throat song every night. A new song had come to him along with that terrible memory, and he allowed it for himself only occasionally. He began to notice, too, different reactions to different songs. Some brought him lower, some took him higher. But far more than that, the responses from sky or land differed. After one song, he had returned to himself and scented a dozen animals around—a few deer, a hare, several voles, and a rangy fox who seemed strangely un-interested in the prey all around him. As the song died away, they simply got up and left.

He sang something safer, this time, just wanting the practice. But it raised interesting questions: was there a better song to quell the bloodlust? Or to mesmerize the Prosan? Was there perhaps even a song that, when it was done, they would simply walk away as though only briefly interrupted from their daily life?

It seemed improbable. But, it was a pleasant dream. He needed more of those.

The winds had shifted a little southward during the night, and he decided to follow it. Without a guide, without sight, without knowing where the Kalen were, there were certain things he simply needed to trust to the wind.

He did worry about the dragon. Aryndurlan's naps had become longer and more frequent. A small seed had begun to germinate in Tavill's mind by now, a reason why the dragon was delayed—might be delayed forever. But he knew the fruit of that seed would be grief and so he watered it as little as possible.

There were plants, in the desert places of the world, that managed still to flourish in parched lands. That seed must have come from such stock. By nightfall, he was all but certain of what had happened to his newest-found friend—whether through violence of some kind or the forces of nature. And so, as he settled in under a black sky, he decided tonight's song would be a dirge. And he thought he might try composing his own.

As he thrummed he thought of Aryndurlan lying curled in the sun, or of walking with her ponderous bulk—she had done that at times, either to move short distances or to give Tavill some company as they journeyed. But as he whistled, he wanted to imagine Aryndurlan as a young dragon, her wings fresh and new, her muscles well-corded and powerful as she sped through the sky. On the wings of the song, he soared to incredible heights, spied curiosities with keen eyes, then plummeted faster than a falcon to pull up at the last possible moment and skim the earth. He and his shadow were one in those moments, earth and sky met.

Suddenly a fierce wind met him, slowed him almost to a stop. His wings bucked once, twice, before the slipstream slid him sideways along its front and he tumbled to the earth.

Tavill's eyes snapped open. He turned to the south and west and scented the wind. There was the barest salt tang to it. The sea was near. But there was something else, something small but pointed, a wandering tendril.

He rose and moved silently toward it, following the thread as it danced back and forth. After he climbed the next rise, it hit him coarsely.

Trust not the wind, but the one who sends it.

Averlynn. He moved carefully, still not sure why she was all the way out here, and what she had done to his song. Through the next valley and up the following hill, until at the top he paused again. Her tendril, a thread of winter's wool now, was joined by a host of thinner scent-threads from further off. She had come here with her people, perhaps the survivors from the fires Aryndurlan had observed so long ago. At the thought, his nose sought frantically—but there was no scent of carcass and reptile.

Perhaps Averlynn would know. Maybe the dragon had simply gone off in another direction for some other reason. He continued through that valley as well, and at the top of the ridge he paused. Averlynn was below, by her scent, and she was struggling with her breath.

"Averlynn?" he called softly. He did not want to surprise her in the dark. Was it as dark for her as it was him?

Her breath slowed, he thought. Alert. "It is Tavill," he said. He took a few steps forward and waited.

"I wasn't expecting you," she said.

Her voice was weak. Something was wrong. He came forward in urgency, though he tried not to rush. He still wasn't sure how she would take that. "What happened?" he asked. He reached her side and knelt down. She was sprawled sideways, and with his help sat up.

"I'm not sure," she said. She trembled in his arms.

"Please don't think of me more highly than you ought," he said. "I am just a creature."

She shifted. He could barely make out her face turned toward his. "Oh, it's not that. I mean, it is a little bit of that. It's not every day, even for an elf, to be comforted by...I'm sorry, you wished not to be called that. It is difficult not to think of you that way." She paused and took a few gasping breaths. "But no, it is not entirely that. I—I was able to sing your throat-song," she said.

With that she leaned into him—not quite fainted, but her consciousness rested on a precipice. He continued to hold her gently while the blood thundered in his ears. How had she done it? To his knowledge, no others but Taur could sing that song. And yet it made sense that his own had butted against hers. When Taur sang together it was a dance, their voices always sliding between and among the others.

It made sense, too, that such a collision would impact her so much more profoundly. Neither had expected it, but he was the master singer and her not even an apprentice. If she had learned it—and he did not doubt she had—she would need instruction and practice.

He picked her up as he stood, then turned toward the scents coming from her camp. She mumbled a word he didn't recognize, but as he stepped forward he kicked something. Feeling with his hoof he realized they were her boots. He knelt, grasped them clumsily as he tried not to drop her, then continued toward the camp.

His heart thudded as he neared. She had accepted him well enough, but now he needed to announce himself to another group, with her nearly unconscious in his arms. He hesitated as he scented the nearest of them. There were no lights ahead—they would have no fires. And the night was dark.

"Honored Kalen," he called out. The night erupted with scattering sounds of the camp awaking, hoarse whispers, a bow creaking? "I am Tavill of the Taur," he pressed on quickly. "I bring back to you Averlynn of your people, who is known to me."

"What happened?" asked a strong, feminine voice.

He turned toward the sound. "I do not know your learning, honored one," he said carefully. "But her throat-song collided with mine."

"Oh. So she learned it, then?"

His ears pricked forward at the tinge of eagerness in her voice. "I would say she stumbled upon it," he said, keeping the growl from his voice. She meddled in things she did not understand and nearly killed herself, he thought. Perhaps that was too harsh.

The female elf stepped closer, and he scented her better—had something of an idea of her. "Is she alive?"

"Yes, but she will need rest."

"Very well, set her down there."

Tavill hesitated. "I am afraid I am nearly blind," he said hoarsely.

"Oh," she said, gently—pityingly? As much as he hated it, he also appreciated it. Suddenly she was nearer, and lifting Averlynn from his arms. He stooped quickly, catching vaguely the sight of her even in the darkness. She was clearly concerned for Averlynn, but also seemed respectfully curious of him.

He stood aside as they arranged the young elf on her bedding. Then the first female approached again. "Are you sure she will be okay?" she asked.

"I do not fully know the way of elves," he said. "But I have never heard of one dying from the throat-song."

She drew a breath. "I am sorry, Everlasting One, I have not told you who I am. My name is Vera. I am a spiritual guide of my people. And I confess a curiosity: Averlynn and I have spoken of you, and of the Taur."

"Did you encourage her to the throat-song?" he asked.

Her hesitation said enough.

"You should not have done this thing," he said—growling, this time.

She bowed to him. "May we speak apart, please? Over here." She touched his elbow, guiding him gently away. "Akanowa, please watch over Averlynn and fetch me as soon as she awakens," she called behind her as they walked.

Some space away she stopped, and sat down. He lowered himself as well, folding his legs under him. She began. "Tavill—I can call you that? I confess our ignorance, and apologize. But also understand there is something at work in Averlynn that is—I would say uncommon, except I have never heard it happening in any of that Kalen. But I wondered, before we might discuss her, if you would tell me of this bloodlust."

He sniffed sharply. "Why?"

"Perhaps call it personal curiosity," she said. When he didn't reply, she continued. "Averlynn told me she offered to help you find a cure. I wasn't under the impression that there was one—that it was a disease. And one that often killed."

He followed her until the last part, then looked at her sharply—at least, in her general direction. "Why did you think that?"

"Some of the old songs I think have preserved some of your lore that we still had, and it doesn't mention a Taur living with this thing."

Tavill sat back, considering. It was strange, so suddenly, to be around others—to perhaps confide in them. And yet, if he intended to do what it was he came here to do, they would need to know. "I...am no longer certain," he said.

"But...you are...I thought that the Taur preserved memories..." She trailed off as he waved his hand.

"Averlynn mentioned someone: Old Raina, she called her."

"Yes, she still lives."

"Averlynn mentioned perhaps, if there was a way to suppress it, Old Raina would know it."

Vera shifted. "She may have spoken in haste," she said carefully. "Old Raina is just that—old. Chief Witko is sometimes thought to have lost his mind, and Raina was old when Witko was born. I do not know what faculties she might still possess—"

"I knew her, at one time," Tavill said quietly.

"But the Taur have not been in Burieng since—oh. Oh!" He heard Vera shifting again, excitedly this time. "You were one of those! Oh Tavill, I have heard—I am so sorry." Her hand was on his arm suddenly. He might have pulled away but for shock.

"One of which?" he pleaded.

"You truly don't remember?" Vera's voice was soft. Near tears, if he had to guess. "I heard her stories from so long ago. I was a mere child too, then, so she left out the worst bits, I can only imagine. It was a terrible thing even so, the plagues, the panic, the war...the Taur, she said, had chosen to do the unspeakable—to create weapons. Some of them. It caused a terrible division. I am so sorry, Tavill."

He was silent a long time, disturbed. Recoiled, a little: felt a thread of anger as though she interrogated him rather than comforting him, or reminding him. She couldn't know that most of the memories—those that had faded to mere facts—colored in with his own emotions, his own experience of them at the time. The guilt and shame when they had reached this land. The fervor with which they returned to their duty—but still an empty fervor, for there were none here to observe, no history to chronicle except their own. They had sought the throat-song, had sought to write down every scrap of every thing they could remember or imagine from every epoch.

Except for some of them. Except for him, who could no longer remember. He was one taught, as though his mind had addled. Reminded of every piece of history. But only told it; he could not live it himself, ever again. Facts, dry and dusty, like oatmeal set out too long in the sun.

Then his sight began to fade and he was drawn even closer, protected even more, sheltered and coddled like a gigantic infant. And bit by bit, day by day, battle by battle the glory of the Taur dimmed until it shattered and he alone was left.

"What happened to the others?" he asked hollowly. "Those who still refused to fight?"

"I—don't know," she said. "Not for certain. But Tavill... Raina never mentioned them. And our songs of you turned to legend and myth for all but Raina."

"I must see her," he said. "Maybe she will know. Maybe she can help me..." He broke off and bowed his head. For all his uncertainty of his sudden place within this community of elves, he wept aloud.

Vera held him as best she could, and rocked with him gently. For a time he allowed himself once more to be an infant, gigantic though he was.

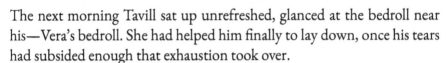

The next morning Tavill sat up unrefreshed, glanced at the bedroll near his—Vera's bedroll. She had helped him finally to lay down, once his tears had subsided enough that exhaustion took over.

Another elf was before him, squatting. "Master Tavill?" he asked.

Tavill blinked blearily and grunted. "Yes, Master...?"

The elf laughed. "I am no master," he said. "Only Edda. Averlynn is asking for you. The Isun Vera has told us some about you, so I came to lead you to her."

Tavill grinned, and sniffed the air. "She is over there," he said, pointing unwaveringly.

"Perhaps the Isun was mistaken," Edda said slowly.

Tavill shook his head. "I am unkind, sometimes. I never told her how much my scent makes up for my eyes. It still might be helpful for you to lead me so I don't trip over anyone."

"Very good."

They rose together and Edda led him. When he arrived Averlynn was sitting up and eating something with a hint of wild onion in it, and perhaps some type of fowl. Whatever it was, he had not smelled it cooked before.

"How are you feeling?" he asked.

"Mostly grateful," she said. "I was told you brought me back here."

He knelt, trying to look very serious into her eyes. "Averlynn, how are you feeling?"

She hesitated. "Tired, I guess. Almost as if I hadn't slept last night."

He couldn't help but grin. "I know that feeling," he said. "But your body: you can feel everything? Move everything?"

"I—yes, I haven't noticed anything."

"What about your mind? Is anything missing—blank, maybe?"

"Tavill, you're worrying me. What happened last night? I mean, I remember singing the throat-song, and then...I don't know, hitting something. And there was..." She trailed off.

"There was what?"

"I don't know. Knowledge. But scattered. Unconnected parts. I haven't been able to recall it."

Tavill nodded. "What about emotions? Any gaps or new lack of control?"

"'New'?" she echoed.

Tavill smiled disarmingly—or tried to. He wasn't sure how it came across to an elf. "Well no one perfectly controls their emotions, and many struggle to have particular emotions. I am making sure you feel completely yourself except for being tired."

"Is it something that might show up later?"

"Not in the sense that it will develop later. Perhaps you might not realize a change until something which should occur naturally does not."

"Then as far as I can tell now, I only feel tired. Can you tell me what happened?"

"Our songs collided."

He could sense she was staring at him, waiting for a better explanation. But he hesitated. This song was not supposed to be for others. She may never be able to handle it, and explaining things to her, perhaps encouraging her? It may not end well. It may end very badly.

Yet Vera, who would know her better than he, said she was special somehow. And if he left her with no response, she might continue to badger him. Might continue trying to do it on her own.

"Why did you try this thing?" he asked.

"There was something beautiful about it, when I heard you doing it," she said. Her voice was low, but passionate. "And...I don't know if soothing is the right word. But as though it offered some kind of comfort to me particularly."

"It probably entranced you," Tavill said. He didn't want to be harsh, but his voice lent itself well to it. "I think that is part of what it's supposed to do. It did it to the Prosan, too, when they attacked me some time ago."

He could see her well enough in the brightening dawn to see her shake her head. "It felt deeper than that," she said. "I know that might sound silly, and I know you know better than me, and yet..." She trailed off, but he heard determination in her voice.

"Will you try this again even if I discourage you?" he asked.

She drew a sigh. "I don't want to. I want to respect your wisdom, of course—"

"Why 'of course'?"

She set down her bowl. "The wisdom of the Taur is well-known, at least to me. I mean, it may have been nearly legend, but now you're here. You're not…I mean, you're real. The things we've sung about you—"

Finally his shaking head interrupted her. "I am not what you have heard. I may have been, at one time, but no longer."

"Because of the bloodlust?" she asked quietly.

"There's more than that. Something that I'm hoping your Old Raina will know."

"So you'll come with us, then?"

"Yes."

"But you won't teach me about the throat-song."

He couldn't hold back a low, rumbling growl. And yet she waited. "I will tell you as much as I know, but only on the condition you will not try it again unless I think you are able. It taps you into forces you may not be able to imagine."

She smirked. "I guess I learned that last night," she said.

"That force was me," he replied. "And I did not expect you there—I did not expect anyone there. But the song itself contends with both the mountains and the stars, and either one—if given too much—can swallow you forever."

"Isun Vera said you have never heard of the throat-song killing anyone," she said.

"I have never heard of an elf singing it," he replied. "And that is not what I mean. I have touched the stars once, when I was new to it. Through the craft of my people I was able to return from that void. But for us it is a void not wholly unknown, and so I was less overwhelmed by it. If one such as yourself fell into that nothingness…"

"Oh," she said—appropriately breathless, he thought. "I think I know a little of what you mean." She described to him the event at Tadan È. When she finished, he grunted.

"Your Isun Vera said something strange attended you," he said. "She spoke the truth. I will teach you what I can as we go." He paused a moment. "Where are you going?"

"Kenkek," she said. "It was our port to set out to sea if we needed. It's where we first landed when we came here."

"Why there? Are you fleeing?"

She snorted. "No. Not if I can help it. But we need troops—everyone we can. The Cariste have been reinforced since you and I met. I intend to bring them back to Wazè."

"And is that where Raina lives?"

"No. She did, for some time. But...it was difficult, they said, as she grew older and older. Eventually she went to live on her own."

Tavill frowned. "How was it difficult if she is able to live on her own."

"Well, our Chiefs are supposed to be the oldest of our people—the wisest and most knowledgeable. It is uncommon for that to be a woman. And, to be fair, there are other duties of the Chiefs—visiting the outposts and things like that—that she was unable to fulfill. And..." She hesitated again. "She sometimes seemed like her mind might not be what it was—or should be."

"Vera mentioned something similar," Tavill said. "And you still believe she might know a cure?"

"Vera mentioned you two knew each other, at one time."

"That doesn't mean she knows a cure." And he had never been specific about her role last time he remembered her. So Averlynn shouldn't know that.

"No, but if she knows what happened..."

"Would she not have fixed it already?"

"I've not heard a better idea from you," she said testily.

He glanced away. "I'm sorry. Perhaps I don't want too much hope for myself. So we go to Kenkek and gather forces, then return to Wazè, and then find Raina and see what happens. And I teach you about throat-singing along the way."

"Sounds like a plan to me," she said. He couldn't see, but he felt the smile in her voice.

29

FOUR THINGS ARE NEEDED

"What is this meeting?"
"A portent."
"Of what?"
"Oneness."

20 Haschina 1321 — Summer

She did not mind riding Tarafel the rest of the way to Kenkek. Her strength was slow to return, and she once—to her great shame—fell asleep while Tavill spoke of the throat-song. He told her not to worry, reminded her she was perhaps lucky to be as alive as she was, and halted her instruction until they were on their way back toward Wazè.

She was pleased with the success at Kenkek. There were no chiefs, and Ka Ouwa felt useless—Aver had been the last to use the port. He quickly accepted Averlynn's report of what was happening. As she remembered, he was sympathetic to her, trusting her perhaps the most of anyone in their military. And, he said, he had begun noticing a strange and rapid spread—he called them blooms—of algae that killed the fish.

By the time the Waken Forest edged the horizon again she was able to walk most of the day. They kept hard beside the Water Plains, following it south to enter the forest nearer to Wazè. They had no idea where the

Cariste were, what maneuvers they were making. Their entire force could be on the Hataki by now, or just inside the trees. Ka Ouwa wanted space to maneuver first, and then as short a run as possible to the village. And he did intend to run.

That night, still in the Hataki, Averlynn led a small team of Trackers ahead of their line of march. Hakana was nearing full and the sky was clear, and she could see all across the Hataki and Water Plains. The Waken, though, was a dark smudge ahead of them.

She hoped, as they moved forward, that Ketzler would still only possess a rudimentary knowledge of the rings—that perhaps she could sense the thread fainter than he could, have some early warning of his presence.

But the night was quiet and still. They paused just inside the tree line, and Edda came up next to her.

"Seems quiet enough," he said. "But they might come at any time."

She nodded grimly. Might come, and might not wear the rings until they had a target. She couldn't let herself rely on that sense.

"Should we stay out and keep watch?" Edda asked.

"That wasn't what the Ka wanted."

He tilted his head. "But the Ka also has only been in charge of an unused port for the past several years."

"Edda," she said, her tone a warning.

"I'm only saying, you were supposed to be in charge until we got back."

She frowned. "What did you have in mind?"

"We set up on a line to the north, kind of a corridor. As the main unit passes, we fall back into it."

She hesitated. "I'd rather the Ka knew about it," she said. Edda only looked at her. She glanced around the forest, the dark trunks and hidden hollows. If they refrained from wearing their rings, they could be hidden in any one of them—or in each of them. "Okay, do it. Just far enough north so you can still feel as we go past. I'll let him know."

Edda grinned and relayed the orders to the rest of the Trackers. They took it well enough in stride, and only a few seemed concerned that Averlynn gave the order. In the end, she told herself, she was a Ranger and still ranked higher than they.

When she returned, the Ka only glowered. Isun Vera was nearby to help make her defense, which seemed only to make it worse. In the end practicality prevailed. "Perhaps I am only angry I didn't think of it myself," he grumbled. But he said it only loud enough for her to hear, and stomped off.

As the sky began to brighten the next morning they were off. She rode Tarafel at the front, keeping a loping pace. As she went she felt each thread of the Trackers, mentally plucking each one to make sure they were alert.

Tavill was beside her, running easily. She was amazed he didn't hit any trees, for supposedly being nearly blind. Occasionally she thought she heard a thrum from him, like the beginning of a throat-song. But none of his teaching suggested he could use it that way. None so far.

She longed to be able to enter the song again. Despite the near-disaster at the end, the rest of the experience had been exhilarating—and fulfilling, somehow. As though she were indeed meant to sing it.

The first of the Trackers had pulled back to the rear of the column. He sprinted up to her and caught his breath.

"The night animals all seemed content," he said. "No disturbances."

She glanced at him. "Tell the Ka Ouwa," she said. He bowed his head and fell back.

"They see you as a leader," Tavill observed.

"They shouldn't," she said. Did he smirk? It was difficult to tell on that Taur face. She sometimes had trouble figuring out what expression he was giving. Usually she could resort to his eyes, but that was harder at a canter.

They passed through the forest, and none of the Trackers reported any disturbances as they each fell back. Finally they reached the sychar trees scattered near Wazè. She turned them slightly south, then hard along the cliff. She slowed, letting Tarafel pick his way down a natural chute to the valley floor below. Tavill fell in behind her, and the line strung out as they navigated the narrow walk.

The threads of her people began to pick up in front of her. Isun Vera hurried forward, as did the Ka Ouwa. Her own heart began to race, then. They all recognized the uncertainty of this meeting.

Flashes of recognition came along the threads, and several of them thickened quickly. At the towering oaks the Chiefs appeared—all except Witko—belligerent glares all on her. Behind them, still hidden, she sensed Amrith.

"You are—" The words died in their throats as they beheld Tavill. The great Taur stood silently, a living relic, only a little bemused. As Averlynn glanced at him, she thought she saw growing consternation in his eyes and wondered why.

The Chiefs shuffled, suddenly, eyes looking everywhere but at her or Tavill. Ka Ouwa stepped forward. "Chiefs of Wazè," he said formally. "We, the remnants of Amka and the wasted talents of Kenkek seek entrance to Wazè." Averlynn startled at the bitter tone in his voice. He was more frustrated over his command at the port than she realized.

And, it seemed, perhaps not the ally she hoped for. With a new fixture for their ire, their eyes all went to him. "Wasted?" Hakawo asked. "Wasted because if we need to depart these shores, and do it safely away from the Cariste invasion, we hoped to have a place of security? Can you vouch now, wisest Ka, that if we retreat to that port, we will not be met with disaster?"

Ka Ouwa eyed them critically in return. He seemed unperturbed. "Retreat?" he asked. "To where? Back to Kalen? Or do you intend to sail on non-existent boats the entire southern route around this country and head further west?"

Two of the Chiefs hissed; the other two folded their arms. "That is not the point," Hakawo replied. He did seem perturbed. "You have abandoned your post without consent of any Chiefs or the Intag Ka. And not just you but all our forces."

"Is it the Chiefs' intent to run, then?" Averlynn asked. "To take all our people once again—"

"We know your thoughts on the matter!" Jale sputtered. "You have made us sick with it since we left Burieng!"

Averlynn clamped her jaw shut. Hakawo raised a hand to silence Jale as he kept his eyes on Averlynn. "Scout Amrith has told us everything," he said.

Averlynn's eyes blazed. "Has he indeed?"

"Yes, *tienko*," he seethed.

Averlynn gripped her reins as Vera gasped. They confirmed it again, and again lay on her the burden not to speak.

But she had plenty to say. "Scout Amrith has lied and deceived many. He forged that letter, after encouraging me to go north to investigate the prophecy. He has at every moment tried to make me doubt that prophecy, and doubt that danger was at hand. Tavill can confirm my worries about the Prosan. Isun Vera can confirm the attack on Amka, as can the absence of the Chiefs from there, and many of our people. Our glamour cannot hide us: the enemy has some of our rings, taken from those they killed, and they can sense us as we can sense one another. They will find this place, will find all our villages and our city, and destroy us all. We have no where to run to—what country is left to us to hide in? The world has grown up while we buried ourselves in obscurity. The only way to retain our elvenness is to take our place in time and keep it."

Hakawo continued to glare at her. Jale still scoffed. Horuk suddenly seemed undecided, and Bakara looked sick. If Witko had been present, she would have pushed for a vote, and perhaps won. She assumed that's why he was not there, and wondered how they had gotten rid of him.

"I was told the wisdom of the Taur was once valued," Tavill said in the silence.

Hakawo's eyes flickered. "It was, once," he said. He folded his arms tighter. "But you have been gone a long time. I doubt not your wisdom was deepest, but I wager no longer relevant."

The growl caught even Averlynn off-guard, and Hakawo goggled. Bakara shut his eyes. "No longer relevant?" Tavill repeated. His snort echoed through his massive nostrils. "Perhaps, though not because of time, but because of idiocy. I have heard enough today to tell me the wisdom I could give would be applied about as judiciously as a boar might apply twigs to a sparrow's nest!"

It seemed Hakawo would not be bullied. He unfolded his arms only to clench fists at his side. "Permission to enter Wazè is not granted!" he fairly screamed. "You, all of you, are hereby *tienko*." He grabbed the shoulder of the nearest Chief, who happened to be the unfortunate Bakara, and shoved him back in between the oaks. The others hurried after him, leaving Hakawo alone and puffing. "Stay out here longer than moments, and arrows will fly. You are considered an invading force!"

"Does that mean you will run from us?" Tavill asked.

Hakawo's face went red, then purple as he held in whatever retort he might have thought appropriate, and simply backed between the trees and disappeared from view.

"I think he might have been serious," Ka Ouwa said. He looked at Averlynn. "Though they forgot to take our rings."

"They cannot trust them anyway, if our enemy has them."

A light of respect came to Ouwa's eyes. "Well, if we are all *tienko*, then I am no longer Ka. As one of the eldest, I recommend you lead."

"I second," Vera said immediately. Tavill only looked at Averlynn with the same smirk he had before.

"I'll argue with you later," she said, still a little numb from the turn of events. "For now, we go east and south. Go."

She led the column quickly east, a direct line away from the village. She did not doubt Hakawo's sincerity in the least—for him to stand up to them all like that would not be a bluff. And she knew the finality with which her people could turn against one they considered outcast. It was utter: there would not even be the thought that they killed 'one of their own.' They were no longer their own. Even the threat of it would have an effect—who now even remembered Corith's name? Few enough. The rest had left it behind, like the name 'Kalen' itself—left him behind, because he wanted to try to work with the Cariste and Rinc Nain and Endolin, to keep as much of Old Kalen intact as they could. At the time, she had disagreed with him, in part—keep Old Kalen, yes, but fight for their exclusivity. And so she had not thought much of the threat of *tienkan* at the time. Now that it became personal, that she felt for herself that barrier—an antagonistic and complete separation—she worried she had not taken the time to understand him that she should have.

That she was not alone did not comfort her.

Finally the senses of Wazè fell far enough behind to disappear, and she turned south. Old Raina was perhaps a day's ride away. They would regroup there, seek her wisdom and the wisdom for Tavill. News of their *tienkan* would spread quickly, faster than they could go to another village or outpost, or Tekaa Wohan itself. Her only hope was that, as the Cariste attacked, her people might change their minds.

She glanced back over the column. It was pitifully small, compared to the forces she knew had landed on their shores. What did she expect to accomplish? They were a briar thorn attempting to bring—well, to bring down a Taur. Her eyes flicked to Tavill. She wished he could be an ally. But he had told her enough by now that she could not countenance turning him loose on the Cariste. For one thing, he was not some mere tool to be turned loose. But for another, he would not necessarily stop with just the Cariste. From his intimations, he generally did not stop until all life with blood in it around him was destroyed.

But what if Raina had a cure? What if he could be restrained just enough? Would it be enough to save her people?

She turned forward again. The questions bothered her, but not as much as her fear. They would all need to turn into ultimate weapons to turn the tide that was coming at them. Not just him. Not just her. Thankfully Amrith had taught her enough of combat in arms to be useful. The Trackers and troops from Kenkek should do well enough, and they would learn quickly.

Either that or they would be utterly destroyed in their first engagement. A briar thorn.

"What's your weakness?" she muttered.

"Otterscomb," he said.

She stared at him. "Otterscomb?"

He continued in silence for so long she thought she had misheard. But then he turned his gaze just a little left of their route of march. "Yes," he said. "It is hard to find, but you can put it in almost anything. I'd forgotten it for a long time. Do you know if it grows here?"

"I'm not sure. I've never heard of it. What does it look like?"

"The leaves are like large dandelion leaves. When it blooms, it grows a long stalk with a spiked flower that looks like a sea urchin."

"We call that kagersthorn," she said. "And I'm afraid it's further south, in low-lying areas."

He shrugged. "I thought I would ask. Why did you want to know my weakness?"

She pursed her lips but decided against explaining the metaphor. "Not yours necessarily; the Cariste."

He gave a slow nod. "You cannot win this war," he said quietly, with just a hint of question.

Averlynn dared not look back again. And looking didn't change their numbers anyway. "Not like this," she admitted. "Our one advantage might have been knowledge of the terrain. But now they can sense our presence with our own rings…"

"Most armies don't have that ability, you know," Tavill said. "Perhaps you will need to learn that as well."

She shifted uncomfortably. "But we've been used to it for so long."

"You've been used to peace for so long."

She snorted. She knew that was right.

The first sign something was wrong was when she smelled woodsmoke. As evening came on, she soon saw the smoke lying in drifts below the canopy. The winds were calm and so it only blossomed from its source, pushed out further under its own pressure. She walked faster.

Finally she saw the cluster of cottonwoods where she knew Raina had stayed. Witko sat beside the fire, fast asleep it seemed, while his cookfire ran rampant. Averlynn shouted, running ahead and beginning to beat the flames as they licked against some saplings. The rest of the troops joined her as Witko came out of his slumber with a shout.

He glared at all of them. "What are you doing here?"

"We could ask you the same thing," Averlynn said, nearly gasping. The flames were out, but many of the trees were charred. And Old Raina's hut had lost its glamour.

Witko's gaze finally came to rest on Tavill, and his brows climbed. "I didn't expect to see you," he breathed. Tavill only watched him. "If only Old Raina could see you too." Witko shook his head sadly.

"What happened to her?" Averlynn asked. "Is she...dead?"

"Oh, no," Witko replied. "But she went south. Couldn't take the warmer temperatures, she said. Winter was far too short, in her estimation, and she needed more snow. Why?"

"Tavill needs to see her," Averlynn said. She wiped a hand down her face and sat. She looked blearily at Ouwa for a moment. "Ka, set up a perimeter. We'll still stay here for the night. Perhaps you and I and Tavill—and Witko—can take counsel later. Get some food first."

As Ouwa bowed and left, Witko glanced at her with a gleaming eye. She tried to wave him off. "We'll talk about that later. Did she say exactly where she's going? Or how she'll avoid the Prosan?"

Witko shook his head. "South. I think she intended to go beyond the mountains though. And old as she may be I think she can avoid a few stragglers." As he said it though, he seemed to avoid her gaze.

"Besides, there's a special task force watching them, right?" she said.

Witko grinned. "Right. She'll sense them first, if she even crosses paths with them."

"I do not think your force tracks all of the Prosan," Tavill said.

Witko's grin tightened as he glanced at the Taur. "Oh. No?"

Tavill shook his head. "Two detachments came after me. Yet Averlynn told me I was a myth to your people. Would not such a task force have seen me, too, and reported it?"

Averlynn watched Witko, the force of his presence like a rabbit pinned under an eagle's gaze. "Well, perhaps they missed a few here or there," he said.

"Witko," Averlynn said. "I have long considered you a friend. And I cannot deny you've supported me far longer than anyone else, and that has meant to the world to me. But Wazè has closed its gates to us—all of Wohan has closed itself to us. And yet we few are all that stand between the Cariste, the Prosan, and the certain destruction of our people. We cannot plan if we don't know what we're planning for. Do you know how many Prosan still live, or not?"

Witko looked at her miserably. "You had to go and say such nice words, didn't you," he said. "Last we knew, there were some thousands—perhaps five."

Averlynn's mouth gaped. "Five... And how long ago was 'the last we knew'? Don't we still know? Isn't there someone watching them?"

Witko shriveled even further in his seat. "Averlynn, you have to understand what pressures the Chiefs were under—are under. I was young enough that I still aspired to Head Chief, back then..." He broke off and cowered as Averlynn's eyes widened even further.

"Witko, that was fifty years ago!" she blurted. "They may have thousands more since then!"

"They won't attack us," he said weakly.

"How can you know that?"

"They won't! Just...your plans don't need to include them."

"Witko," she seethed. "Stop coddling me—"

"We paid them," Ouwa said, suddenly beside them. Averlynn's horrified glance took in him, and then Witko again.

"We did, what?" she said weakly. "Why?"

"We needed to be safe from them," Witko said. He glared at Ouwa, who only shrugged as he sat down. Witko shook himself, and continued. "When the war was almost over, we sent a delegation. We had been utterly destroying them, so we figured they would be...pliable. We offered to stop slaughtering them in exchange for a yearly tribute."

"Why, if we were beating them?" She hated to ask it—she didn't want them annihilated, but it just didn't make sense.

"Hakawo's son had been killed," Witko said simply. "We didn't want any other Wohan dead, if we could help it. So we offered peace, in exchange for dictating which lands they could use to live in."

"And what were those lands?" Tavill asked.

"Oh, a long stretch along the mountains."

"North of them?" Averlynn asked, surprised. She had forayed often in those reaches.

But Witko shook his head. "South. Not stuck in the snow, necessarily. Not all year. Those ranges still see spring and summer."

"Not much of either," Tavill rumbled.

Witko swallowed his smile. "Yes. Well. More than they would see in the grave."

"And what was the tribute? Food, I imagine?"

"Of course. Since the land was not ideal, we supplemented them with grains and such."

"And in fifty years, did the tribute ever increase?"

"Of course not! We couldn't let them eat us out of hearth and home."

Averlynn sighed.

"If they choose to have more babies than they can feed, that's not our fault. We agreed to the conditions. They did too."

"I'll be sure to remind them that as they're killing us."

"Listen here, young lady, don't get all high and mighty because you're scrapping for a fight and think you could lead this people better. I've been doing it a long time, you know—all the Chiefs have."

"Too long, perhaps," Ouwa said.

Averlynn laid a hand on his knee. "I'm sorry, Witko. You're right, I was not there. And it doesn't help us now anyway. You still haven't said why you're out here."

Witko's lip trembled. "I am *tienko*," he said.

She barely blinked. It shook her, but too much had shaken her already. "Why?" she asked, already suspecting the answer.

"Hakawo sensed instability in the Chiefs," he confirmed. "Knew if I was there, and too much was said, he might lose control."

"But he couldn't simply banish you," Ouwa said.

"Amrith was very persuasive," Witko said bitterly. "I think we both underestimated him. He said he had observed me helping you, and would support you to the detriment of our people." He shook his head. "He really doesn't like you!"

"So I'm realizing," Averlynn said tiredly. "What do we do now?"

Witko shrugged. Ouwa was pointedly silent. As Averlynn glanced around she saw every eye on her. And yet, there was no overwhelm, no consternation, no fear. As if she had asked a thought out loud, knowing she was the one to answer it. She glanced at Tavill who merely observed. Of course he did—that's what he had been made for. His duty had been established along with the sun and stars and moon. Perhaps hers had too.

"This isn't much of an army," she said quietly, intending it primarily for Witko. "At least, in numbers alone."

In those quiet words she knew she was setting their course. And she saw as Witko's eyes lit with faint mischief, knew that in setting that course she gave him hope. "Perhaps," he said, "when the enemy sees the Kalen actually defending themselves they'll simply faint with surprise."

She couldn't help but grin. Perhaps they could do this. Painfully optimistic, since the war had not even truly begun. At least, they had not contested much yet. She straightened, easing stiff muscles as she glanced around at her—could she call them hers? Should she?—unassuming army. From each of their eyes she saw the same gleam of hope only faintly recollected from before the Endolin attacked so long ago. Perhaps they could.

"We should still take counsel," she said, glancing meaningfully at both Witko and Ouwa. She didn't need to look at Tavill. That left...she looked around, saw Vera attending a few who seemed uncertain. At least, their gestures were less controlled than a Kalen's usually were. She frowned, worried what might be upsetting them. Besides being Marked.

Then she realized: those had family in Wazè—new family. She sighed heavily, rubbed her lip in frustration. Amrith had much to answer for.

"As bad as that?" Witko asked. She knew he did it only to prompt her into speaking, and cast him a wry grin.

"Those," she said, gesturing. "Only recently covenanted under Praka," she continued. "Too recently to add *tienkan* to their life-bond as well, I guess?"

Witko frowned as well. "Yes, they would be." He shook his head and glowered.

"Could we rescue them?"

Witko's grin twisted, then fell. "Rescued from acceptance by our people. But are you sure they want to be rescued?"

She hunched. "Maybe that's what they're asking." She chewed her lip, glancing sideways at Witko until he gave her a cross-eyed look and she chuckled. "Okay, fine. Do we attack the Cariste first or the Prosan? Or let both of them come to us?"

"Ideally we can not be found."

Averlynn shook her head firmly. "They have already found us once. At least, the Cariste have. And the Prosan have found Tavill more than once."

"Perhaps I should leave," Tavill said.

Her reply died in her throat as she caught his eyes. There was genuine fear there—for whom, she couldn't tell. Perhaps everyone. "That time may come," she said gently. "You need to find Old Raina, and we might not be able to send anyone with you. For now, I would like you to stay if you can."

His eyes glittered. "To what end?"

She spared a glance for Vera and the others; they still spoke, though their gestures were more subdued now. "Do you remember any wars?" she asked.

When Tavill remained silent she searched his face. There was something else there, something he wasn't saying. Or didn't know? She thought the Taur's memories were perfect—had to be, even. Yet he was troubled.

"Are you not allowed to interfere?" she asked.

His muzzle wavered, though he remained troubled. "We are, and we aren't," he said. "I can't help but think, though... Perhaps if someone had interfered when my people were being destroyed..."

She held up a hand. "We must all fulfill our duty," she said. "I am sorry others did not fulfill theirs, to bring the Taur to such devastation. But it doesn't mean—"

"Unless they did," he interrupted quietly.

She glanced quizzically at him. What could he mean? The Taur were supposed to be destroyed—or nearly, anyway? Surely...

He drew a sigh. "Forget I said that. You want to know how diminutive forces stood up to larger ones." She gave him a worried grin. It seemed so selfish. But he drew himself upright again, and the trouble seemed to pass. "First, they must have hope," he said. He glanced between Averlynn, Ouwa, Witko, then finally and firmly at Vera and the three Kalen with her. As if on cue, she could tell by the set of their mouths they had finished speaking as Vera glanced over. The Isun took in all four gazes, cocked her head, and approached.

"Did you overhear?" she asked as she neared.

Averlynn shook her head. "We suspected. They want their covenanted out of Wazè?"

"Yes and no," Vera replied. "Oh, they want them here. Who says they'll come, is the problem. And with the Cariste approaching..."

"Do they approach?" Averlynn asked, alarmed.

Vera shrugged. "Oh it's not a foretelling. But that's what they're here for, isn't it? And with our rings to guide them..."

"Tavill seems to have an idea, though," Averlynn said, looking back to the Taur. "An idea about hope?"

"Four things an army needs, if it is small and seeks to destroy a larger force," he continued as though he had not stopped. He ticked off each with a raised finger. "To believe they can do what seems impossible; to learn to fight without rings to connect them to their people; and to accomplish one small, impossible thing—like bringing three of their own from within one of their cities."

Averlynn's mouth gaped. She knew from the silence—and the task he suggested—everyone else's did too. "You cannot be serious," she said. "You want us to sneak into Wazè where discovery means death and try to pull out three people who might not want to come? Who might kill us on sight, too?"

Tavill sighed heavily. "The fourth thing it needs is to be prepared for some to die."

Averlynn blanched. She turned mutely to Witko and Ouwa. And she could tell by the set of their mouths, now, that they agreed. And yet they still looked at her as though she could guide them.

She looked again at Tavill, her eyes pleading. He couldn't ask this of her. But she only saw in his dark eyes one who had already endured it. He did not ask lightly. She closed her eyes a moment, sending a prayer to Hakana. But the prayer seemed only to hit the top of her head.

"Call them over," she said without looking at Vera. "And let's see if we can plan a rescue mission."

30

THEY STARTED THE FIRE

"Do you know why you are failing?"
"Am I?"
"You are too proud to know you have chosen poorly."
"Then why are you failing, too?"

1 Mantaver 1321 — Summer

"C aptain Pike wants you. Now."

That was why Ketzler stood outside the tent, waiting to be admitted. Because it was urgent, supposedly.

It had been a long and complicated report, when they'd returned to the main settlement. There was a lot of news to work through, and he struggled to organize it in a cohesive way. At least, a way that didn't lead them down fifty rabbit trails before one of his answers finally made them realize they hadn't needed all the questions in the first place.

When finally he'd been released he had collapsed into a cot just outside Commander Liptieri's tent. The horizon was the faint gray of a not-too-distant dawn. When he'd been awoken, it was pearl and the sun had still not risen. He hadn't even enough time to dream.

Now he stood in a haze, his focus drifting in and out. It took him a few breaths after the tent flap opened and shut again to force himself upright. And yet he was still not summoned inside.

He blinked slow and sighed. The sun was now up. The camp around him was eating breakfast and looking well-rested. He knew the orders would come soon, and he would be part of the group leading them south again, following the second trail as they sought the next Kalen settlement. One would think he would need to be awake for that.

"Corporal Ketzler, get in here," came Captain Pike's voice finally.

He rubbed his eyes, tried to look awake, then waved away the thought. Let her see what she was doing to one of her best scouts.

He wandered in, stood at her travel desk as she looked over a few parchments. "Reporting, Captain."

She looked up and inspected him. "Not like that, you're not. I think you forget yourself." Her eyes blazed with a fire he didn't know she had. She couldn't have slept much either, could she?

He took a deep breath and forced his back to straighten. "I apologize, Captain," he managed. "I was unaccustomed to such a lengthy...debriefing."

She grunted. "You probably would have been better off not even trying to sleep," she said, a little more kindly. "But, not why I brought you here. I have a few reports here I wanted to discuss before taking them to Commander Liptieri."

"Reports?"

"You may consider them anonymous. You haven't broken your relationship with Karbae. In fact, it seems—in complete defiance of my orders—you've deepened it."

Ketzler's mind buzzed, but like hummingbirds in a fog. "I don't know who told you that," he said.

She barked another laugh. "I just told you as much."

"It's not true. And I don't remember you ordering it—"

"Ketzler, you've been in my unit long enough to know that a suggestion from me is an order. Do you intend to continue this relationship?"

"It's not only up to me, you know," he said, bristling.

"Are you saying this is Karbae's fault?"

Ketzler set his jaw. He could put the blame on her, actually. Very rarely had he initiated anything. It depended on who made the report, and what they had seen. But then, if Karbae found out... "I am only saying it is difficult to—"

"With so many of our scouts leading us south, Commander Liptieri wants two Sergeants to lead them. You are most qualified to fill this spot. Unless it is too difficult for you."

His hands clenched. "I'll talk to her," he muttered.

"Good. How did Curani die?"

Ketzler blinked. They had gone over this a hundred times when it had first happened. He said as much.

"So this suggestion that you killed him to advance yourself is..."

Now he gaped. "I...don't even know how to respond, ma'am," he said. "Curani had taught me more than—I wish he had not been killed either, but to cast such a bizarre accusation with no evidence..."

"Is there none?" Pike asked. Her hand fell to one of the parchments in front of her, adjusting it as she waited for his answer.

He was far too tired for this. He couldn't form an answer, and he hoped that would be answer enough. Pike drew a breath. "Fortunately, most of our forces are mobilizing for this operation, so I will get to keep an eye on you personally. If I see so much as a fond glance between you and any other member of my team, I will see you demoted. And if this evidence should bear itself out—" her gaze flickered to the parchment "—I will see you hanged for mutiny and murder."

So. This is what it is like to gaze upon a dead woman.

Ketzler paused as he studied Pike's face. He could tell she was serious. There was something written on that parchment, something someone had seen or figured out. Well. War was a serious business. "I assure you, it will not, ma'am," he said.

"Then congratulations, Sergeant. You will receive your assigned soldiers later today."

"May I ask who the other Sergeant is?"

"Mordel, of course. You didn't see him leave?"

"Ma'am, I'm not sure if Mordel—"

"Dismissed, Sergeant," Pike said firmly.

Ketzler fairly chewed on his tongue. But he retained the presence of mind to snap a salute. "Thank you, ma'am." He turned and left, thankful there was not a door. He probably would have slammed it.

His first stop was Karbae's tent. "We need to be more careful," he said in hushed tones as she sat in the doorway.

She glanced sideways. "Who?"

Ketzler shrugged. "It doesn't matter. For the next little while though, can you stop—" He clamped his mouth shut just in time. "Sorry," he said with a smile. "We just need to be careful for a while. Unless you don't want a soldier as a partner."

She looked him up and down. "I guess a Corporal will do," she said with a mischievous flash in her eyes.

He held up a finger. "Sergeant, now."

At the look that came to her eyes then he fled, not trusting her to be discreet. He couldn't imagine what she would do if he rose any higher in the ranks. He'd probably have to find a way to marry her.

He made his way to Mordel's tent next. The overbearing soldier stood cocksure outside it, swaggering somehow without moving. And he had his rank already on his chest. He must have known beforehand—or just assumed it and had a uniform ready. Probably the latter.

"Congratulations, Mordel," Ketzler said, as earnestly as he could manage. "You proved yourself well out there."

Mordel's eyelids flickered. "Of course. Why shouldn't I?"

Ketzler held his hands up placatingly. "No, of course. Your prowess as scout, your keen observations and ability to see things where no one else sees them—truly impressive."

"Indeed," Mordel replied, though Ketzler saw the hints of glowering behind the swagger now. He wasn't so stupid as to miss what Ketzler was saying.

"Anyway, I look forward to fighting alongside you. I promise, my squad will always be there to protect your flank."

The glowering turned a little to fear, but Ketzler left before he could respond. Mordel the Moron, making enemies of people who might need to save his life one day.

He returned to his own tent, now, and lay down on top of his bedroll without removing a stitch of his uniform. Just a little more sleep before the work began in earnest.

And in earnest, it began. He had to work out his own uniform, then attend two assemblies before lunch. The first introduced him to his foursquad—Karbae, thankfully, was not in it. That might have made it easier, except she was in Mordel's foursquad instead. He could only hope her wits would save her where Mordel's stupidity might endanger her.

He was given a training schedule, and watched like a hawk as he relayed the information. Then it was into the Commander's tent for a briefing on the plan to assault the Kalen. A bit more information was pried out of him—and in truth he offered a few best-guesses as though they were actual fact, but no one seemed to notice or mind. But the plan Commander Liptieri and Captain Pike came up with made sense, and he had no real arguments. Then it was back to his foursquad to brief them as much as he could, and then see they ate lunch. Then it was setting watch rotations, drawing supplies and rations, and enforcing the watch rotations.

By the time they were set to march south and west, the glamor of being a sergeant was gone. But in its place was still a feeling of contentment and belonging. Hard as it might have been a few times, the men under him did obey. If one or two had a hint of fear in their eyes, did that matter? Better than thinking they could argue against him. But he wondered if Mordel had let his suspicions slip to some of how Curani had actually died.

But then they were marching, the scouts in the lead with the Kalen rings, and there was too much to worry about the strange woods around them and whether the rings would actually work or not, or if the Kalen had some way to counteract or defeat them. With the weight of the army behind them, instead of feeling more secure they worried they might inadvertently lead them into an ambush and wipe out the first Cariste presence in southern Gintanos ever.

By the end of the week, Ketzler was feeling better. They moved into a routine and settled in it. They had good scouts, good soldiers behind them. They made and broke camp efficiently and quietly, set good outposts. It was far slower going than when it was only the scouts, but that was to be expected.

They followed the same route they had before, so it was terrain Ketzler and the scouts were familiar with. Captain Pike made sure almost every night. She seemed far less certain than he, but—he told himself—she had not been there before. Most of it was empty lands. Perhaps the Kalen would be on greater alert now, but more likely they were terrified. Averlynn had seemed like she felt alone. Probably she had been. Alone and desperate for peace. And why peace, except her people were afraid to fight?

They reached the spot where the trail had seemed to split. As Ketzler explained it to Captain Pike, Mordel stood aside with a triumphant look on his face.

"I think Mordel was right," Ketzler said, gesturing. "Probably their scouts came from the south and went north, to the outpost we destroyed. If so, the other end of that trail will be their village. So, it's a good thing we didn't go that way or we might have tangled with a far superior force."

Ketzler kept his face calm as Mordel flustered. "Well, I didn't say we should attack or anything," he said.

Pike nodded. "That's fine. You might not have had a choice, but either way. Disaster was averted." She looked to Ketzler. "Make sure to give plenty of notice if those rings start to tell you anything."

"Of course." He turned immediately and went to his foursquad, fanning them out and moving them generally along the line of the trail. He himself stayed on it, keeping line of sight with at least one of his scouts, to change direction if necessary.

Finally they came again to the valley where the cliff ran along a stream. He called a birdsong to Mordel to get his attention. "We don't want to get pinned against that," he said quietly. "Can some of your foursquad go on top? I'll send a runner back to the main body to alert the Commander."

"I'll send a runner," Mordel said quickly.

That will weaken him. It could threaten the entire flank.

There aren't that many of them, and they aren't willing to fight.

And, my foursquad will still be strong.

Ketzler nodded. "Fair enough. Let's keep pressing forward though; I think they're nearby."

Mordel the Moron nodded and quickly moved to carry out his plan. Ketzler looked to his left, nodded to Oridin and gestured him forward. They crept on. Occasionally Ketzler glimpsed Mordel's foursquad atop the cliff. They were bunching. He wondered what might be up there to make them do that. Just as he was about to whistle another birdsong he felt it: a tiny tug, just a hair's-breadth wide, coming from the south. He thrilled a moment, and as he continued to move he felt the hairs thickening and gathering.

He held up a fist, waited for his scouts to stop. To the right, Mordel's foursquad had almost all clustered together. *Idiots. They can feel us too!*

He made a few quick gestures to his troops to hide themselves well, then motioned pulling his ring off. He would keep his on to sense if the Kalen drew nearer, but keep his foursquad from being sensed in return. Maybe, if they did come out, they would focus on Mordel's.

The sergeant came over to him, eyes alight. "They're there," he said, barely keeping his voice in a whisper.

"Of course they are. Did you want to send another runner? Or wait for yours to come back?"

"I'll send another," he said. "We should attack today. Would you like to be first with me to see if they'll come out?" Mordel fairly hopped from foot to foot in excitement.

"Probably should wait for the army," Ketzler said coolly. "Whether we attack today or not should be Commander Liptieri's call."

Mordel pouted, still grinning. "I guess you're right. I'll settle in my soldiers."

"Good idea," Ketzler replied. As Mordel turned to leave he shook his head, glancing back up to the cliff-top. He caught Karbae's eye, and the brief grin flickering across her lips. He mimicked removing the ring to her, too. With a quick glance around, she showed him her hand: she had already done so.

So smart. He pursed his lips just briefly and she waggled a finger at him before turning back to her squad.

Mordel climbed up a natural chute in the cliff and disappeared over the top. Soon the rest of the foursquad disappeared from sight. Ketzler made his way forward.

"There's a lot," Oridin whispered as he approached. Ketzler nodded, feeling as though a rope were attached to his finger, now. Not dragging at him, but definitely present. None of the threads thickened or thinned. They seemed to be staying in place.

Their glamour will still hide them. The army was going to have a cursed time tying to fight an enemy they possibly couldn't see. He wondered what plan Liptieri had for that—beyond just knowing his scouts could sense them.

They sat in silence, eyes scanning. There was occasional true birdsong, sometimes a harsher cry. Mostly the forest was still. It was growing hotter, but was not yet stifling. At least it was shaded. A breeze would be nice, though. Not strong, but steady.

"Oridin," Ketzler whispered. "What would you think about slipping ahead? Get to a place where they and I feel the same distance apart, but they are directly west of you?"

Oridin's eyes darted, and he grinned. Wordlessly he moved off, slipping on his ring after he had gone several lengths away. His alone felt like a rope now. Ketzler concentrated, measuring Oridin's steps and how the sense thinned as he went. High above the leaves fluttered, then stilled.

Finally the lines felt equal. Ketzler calculated quickly in his head. He would get a better account when Oridin returned but he guessed it was perhaps half a mile. Not far. Oridin's line began to slowly thicken again as he returned.

Mordel crept over from the cliff. "What are you doing?" he demanded.

"Scouting," Ketzler replied without looking at him.

"You're going to give our position away!"

Ketzler glanced at him sideways. "And having all your squad on top of each other, all still wearing their rings, wouldn't have done that already?"

Mordel chewed his lip, let loose a curse. "I don't want to be blind, though..."

Ketzler held up his hand to show the ring. Mordel cursed again and turned away. Ketzler was surprised he didn't start shouting orders to his scouts. He shook his head.

Another flash of movement: one of Mordel's runners had returned. The other should not be far away.

Whether by chance or design, the runner came to him first. "The army is on its way," he said. "Pietros came as I was getting set to leave and gave his report," he explained quickly. "Hold fast until they arrive, and make sure no Kalen approach."

Ketzler only nodded. *A wise man is our commander.* Ketzler brushed off the voice, turned forward just as Oridin's ring winked off. Another few moments and Ketzler saw him slipping between the trees.

"Twelve hundred paces," he said, barely winded. He was a good scout. Ketzler would need to make sure he stayed alive.

"How large did it feel?"

Oridin tilted his hand. "Much larger than the outpost, but not anything to rival one of our cities. Perhaps if they've not spread out, it's a few hundred paces across at most."

Ketzler nodded. Averlynn had said to maintain the glamour they couldn't move. So all he had to do was get them to move, somehow. A lot, and all of them. Maybe Liptieri had a plan.

But the army was taking longer than Ketzler thought. By the time he saw their outriders, he knew it would be nightfall before they could be ready to attack. No, they would camp tonight. Foolish, since the Kalen would know they were there.

Sure enough, as the main body began arriving, they started setting outposts and pitching tents. Ketzler shook his head, rolled his eyes at Oridin. "Let's hope this is all part of the plan," he whispered.

Oridin only sucked in his upper lip.

Captain Pike herself came for him, this time. "Commander Liptieri wants us all. Leave your outposts in place, but come with me."

Ketzler nodded to Oridin and followed. Liptieri was in a smaller tent, this time, only twice the size of the two-man tents the rest of the soldiers had. Just enough room for the small table his aids were constructing beside his bedroll. With Pike, Ketzler, Mordel, and the rest of the sergeants from the army—Ketzler had never bothered to learn or overhear any names—it quickly grew crowded. No one there were the soldiers he had trained with. He wondered briefly where they were.

"Is this the place?" Liptieri asked without preamble.

"Yes sir," Mordel responded quickly, curtly.

"One of them," Ketzler amended gently. "It's large enough to be a proper village, but my scout said too small to be a city."

"You've already scouted it?" Liptieri asked. He seemed surprised. Pike seemed furious.

"Not exactly, sir," Ketzler said, lowering his eyes. "But with the rings we can sense them, how many there are and how they're scattered. I sent Oridin wide until his sense back to me was as thin as his sense to them, then calculated the size of the triangle the three of us created..." He shrugged. "It's twelve-hundred paces from our outpost—so, fifteen hundred to this tent. Sir."

Now both superiors seemed impressed, and Mordel was the one who was furious, though more quietly than Pike had been previously. The rest of the sergeants only looked on: it was scout business anyway.

"Well then. Our attack commences in the morning. Ketzler, those rings work both ways, correct? Good. The scouts, then, will make several maneuvers encircling the village tonight as though surrounding it. Then, at first light, continue their circle—oh, thank you, Solmon." They moved to the table and glanced over the map Elirose had drawn. "Continue south, taking up a position behind it. You'll have less than a shift. As soon as it's bright enough to see, we attack from the north."

That's not an awful plan. "With the Kalen glamour, sir, our men may still not be able to see who they're attacking. Or where. They could pass straight through the village and not know it."

"I'd bet with that many soldiers descending on them, they'll run," Liptieri said with a grin. A few of the sergeants joined him. Pike considered Ketzler for a moment.

"Do you have a suggestion, sergeant?" she asked quietly.

A storm is coming.

"There's a storm on the air," Ketzler said. "We should have some strong winds by morning. We could set a fire in front of it."

"Burn the forest down around us, Ketz?" Mordel said with a condescending grin. "Not sure what that would prove."

A few sergeants chuckled, but Pike and Liptieri glanced at each other. "If it's a storm, the rains would put it out soon enough," Pike suggested.

"That seems like quite a risk," Mordel said. "Just because he said there was a storm."

"We've been risking since we left, Sergeant," Liptieri said. "And...Sergeant Ketzler has been right so far. If we have the wind at first light, we'll try it. If not, we'll follow the original plan."

"Who sets the fire?" Pike asked.

"We will," Liptieri said. "I want to call it off if I need to. If you see smoke, shift the scouts to watch for runners. Otherwise they sit tight in the south until we get to them."

"Yes sir," chorused through the tent.

Ketzler left when dismissed, went to his outpost to brief the rest of his foursquad. "Put your rings back on," he said. "And let's go. Oridin, take point. I'll be in the middle."

They spread out in the gathering gloom, threading south through the woods to circle the village.

They passed the night quietly enough, though Ketzler sometimes worried the Kalen would do the same as his foursquad by taking off some of their rings. But then, he would have sensed it, and likely they wouldn't risk dropping their glamour. Perhaps they even needed it to maintain the camouflage on the village—Averlynn hadn't ever mentioned. He wondered, then, if she was in there as well. As he studied the threads, making sure none of them came or left, he sorted through the subtle differences between each. He wondered again if the difference came from the ring or the wearer. So much he hoped to learn, if they could take a prisoner. Not that they would necessarily tell him. Perhaps he could make them.

If it was part of the ring, would they know the ring he wore was stolen? Presumably their own people wouldn't come to a village, encircle it, and do nothing, but still...What if he wore a ring that was special to a particular person? Might that enrage them? Might it anyway—wearing magical items stolen from those they had killed? Probably.

Blood must be on the ground.

He didn't understand that phrase, or where it came from. But it tugged at him in a strange, enticing way. Blood of a sacrifice, perhaps? He thought that's what Curani had been. But maybe the Kalen had done something to enrage the God of All—

The thought of that name shocked him, repulsed him just a little. He had not used it since...he couldn't remember. Long ago. Strange.

To the east, songbirds awoke. Ketzler picked up his head—had he slept? It didn't seem like he could have. But the forest was gray, now, the trees and boughs colorless in the too-early light. He shook his head. There was no sky visible above the canopy, though the leaves tossed...

There was a breeze. A strong one. He sniffed the air. A faint hint of rain was on it, but not immediate.

He got up and stole quickly from man to man, gathering them up to begin their shift to the south. He wondered what the Kalen would make of it—perhaps that there was a weakness to the south that had suddenly been discovered. More likely that whoever was out there was trying to deceive them.

And yet, there was chaos and confusion among the threads. He didn't know how he knew—maybe because they felt as though they vibrated slightly, wove amongst each other as though the villagers didn't know which was to move, where to prepare. He grinned.

He spread out his squad to the south, attack formation just in case the Kalen would recognize it. But they held, waiting to see the smoke Ketzler knew would come. The weather and the forest were perfect for it. And the Kalen would have to run like rabbits.

"There it is," he said quietly, urgently, pointing at the plumes that quickly lit from underneath in bright orange. He pounded his thigh in excitement. "Keep watch," he said. "Wait to see if they run."

"Shouldn't we shift west?" Oridin asked.

Ketzler glanced that way, hesitated. They had been ordered to do so, and yet something was wrong. *Those rings work both ways, don't they?* The Kalen had not survived thousands of years by being stupid. But he couldn't outright disobey orders. "Yes, a little. Oridin, I want you to stay here though. I'll assign six to you. Keep an eye to our east. Things go too easily in our favor, right now."

"What do you think will come?"

Ketzler shrugged. "Reinforcements," he said.

31

Because It Was Insanity

"Reckless. Both of you."
"One can never be too sure."
"With this other Triumvirate though..."
"If we managed before, we will manage now."

09 Mantaver 1321 — Summer

Averlynn closed her eyes and let out a mixed sigh. Two of her soldiers smiled, spoke closely with their bonded. One stood apart, pitied certainly but with a grim understanding. Witko had said it well: they had hoped to rescue these from acceptance by their people. Newly bonded, it was a miracle the two had even come—were devoted enough to their men that they would give up life within Kalen community to join such a tenuous war.

Perhaps the greater miracle was that the third raised no alarm. Her eyes had grown wide when they entered her home, her back stiffened, but she listened silently as Tuwon made his offer. When he finished she sat no more than a few breaths before shaking her head and turning resolutely away.

Tavill approached, his hooves crunching through the leaves. Averlynn glanced at him and gave a thin smile. "We have three of our four requirements," she said.

He glanced over, took in the Kalen separately. His gaze lingered on the Tuwon. "He feels the fourth," he rumbled.

Averlynn rubbed her jaw. "True enough."

"It is well enough," Tavill continued. "You understand, as you continue down this road, the fourth will come to all."

Averlynn nodded, closed her eyes again. "I don't want to think about it," she said. She looked up. "We've already lost some—more in the last few weeks than in hundreds of years. They accused me of not caring, did you know? And maybe I don't care as much as I should—"

"I think not," Tavill interrupted. "Until the Cariste change their intentions, you must remain determined. Perhaps you, more than those, are prepared to do that."

Averlynn snorted, shook her head. "I don't feel prepared," she said.

A half-grin curled Tavill's mouth. "I did not say you were prepared—just more than they are."

Averlynn shook her head, looked toward Witko and Vera. They had approached the three now, sharing smiles with the two. Vera left and went to Tuwon, grasping him and touching her forehead gently to his as she spoke to him. It hurt a little, as their supposed leader, that she could not do that. It would mean nothing to Tuwon, that close gesture, coming from Averlynn. She watched him weep, comforted by Vera. She wondered again if she was truly the best choice, no matter what Tavill said. Surely there were others better able to lead—even Ka Ouwa at least had experience. Witko, despite his occasional bend into insanity, which Averlynn rarely bought as more than an act, still had more wisdom in one finger than she had. Tavill, for that matter—why could he not lead? At least direct, even if he needed to stay some distance off from battle?

Vera straightened, turned and looked at Averlynn as though hearing her thoughts. Confidence and encouragement radiated from her, and Averlynn set her jaw.

Vera's gaze shifted to Tavill, and she frowned. Averlynn turned to him. Her stomach dropped. "Tavill?" she asked.

He was staring westward, nearly shaking as his nose twitched. He snorted once, twice, and his fists clenched.

"Is someone coming?" Averlynn asked, wheeling Tarafel. She saw no one through the trees, expected an army, or at least Ketzler.

Instead she saw a far-off haze lifting and spreading through the canopy.

As she watched it billowed, spread across a long line. She felt the breeze at her back, then.

"Ka," she called, managing despite the rush in her veins to keep her voice only loud enough for him to hear. He trotted to her side. "Form them up, but quietly. No rings. Hurry."

He ran off, calling in low tones. Averlynn glanced at Tavill. "You stay here," she said firmly. When he looked at her, she shook her head emphatically. "I will not risk you. Stay back, and we'll find you when we're done. If there's any of us left..." She set her jaw again. They both knew, if Wazè was under attack, it would not be a small force.

She glanced sideways, saw her troops arrayed. Wordlessly she led them out back they way they had just come. Skyalfamold stayed in its scabbard—she could barely wield it on foot, she would not risk it on horseback—and readied her bow instead. The rest already had theirs out. Vera, she saw, was with them, staying in the back of the line but near her.

"Don't wait for my command," she ordered. "As soon as you see a Cariste, shoot them. Let them know."

Vera nodded quickly and ran down the line. Averlynn watched her go, marveling a little. For an Isun, she had adapted to their fighting group swifter than any other, and fit herself to Averlynn's command. How many times had she gone to the Isun for guidance, and now Vera acted almost as an aide? Had taken on the role unbidden?

Averlynn could smell the smoke, now. She flexed her fingers on her bow, peering through the undergrowth. Then, to the north, she saw movement.

"*Hitht!*" she cried, pointing with a flat hand. Ka Ouwa looked, nodded quickly. He split some of their troops away. Averlynn shook her head: it looked like ants when their hill was scooped away. It had to be the entire Cariste force.

A horn sounded, and Averlynn's gaze whipped south and west. There was a thin line of Cariste there—an outpost, it looked like, as if waiting for her to arrive. She halted Tarafel, nocked and let fly. One of the outpost staggered and fell. "Now!" she shouted, and those with her surged forward. She held back, knowing she would be too tempting a target on Tarafel. And she wanted to see if Ketzler was there, how the battle unfolded.

"They're pushing them west," Vera said. "Using the fire..."

She didn't need to finish. Averlynn nodded, spurred Tarafel south to gain the other side of Wazè and see what was happening. She signaled a few of her troops to follow her.

Past the fire, she saw her people fleeing, saw the Cariste on the other side like an anvil to the fire's hammer. With no rings she could not quickly tell who ran, who fell. She thought perhaps she saw Aver, but he was half-turned away, and alone. Surely he would have stayed near their parents?

Taking a deep breath to fight away tears, Averlynn began to loose her arrows as she could. It felt pathetic—for every one she or her troops loosed, it seemed a hundred arced from the Cariste. And soon it was only sword-work on the Cariste side.

Suddenly she saw Hakawo, arms spread as he stood before Ketzler. Surrendering, of course. And why wouldn't—?

Suddenly Ketzler ran his sword into Hakawo, turned swiftly away to move against her troops now circling around the northern end of the fire line. Averlynn could only gape as Hakawo bent around his wound, staggered, and fell.

The forest was filled with clashing arms, screams, the rush of the flames. Something broke in her at seeing Hakawo's still form huddled on the ground. She turned her gaze woodenly away, staring at the village. The glamour was gone now, her people still extracting themselves from the wreckage of it. So few had weapons—those fought back as best they could but they were gnats before a hurricane. Those unarmed either ran, cowered, hid among the un-glamoured homes—or were killed outright. The sea of Cariste to the north swept down, blades and armor gleaming among the trunks and ferns, boots trampling plant and dying Kalen alike with equal disdain.

Some of her people, somehow, escaped the net and fled westward. Any Cariste that tried to follow she and her southern detachment managed to shoot down. She knew they would be making for Tekaa Wohan now, knew also that if they were followed their doom was sealed.

Her quiver neared empty. She saw one last Cariste pursuing those fleeing, quickly nocked and loosed, exulting as it sped unerringly into the back of the Cariste. The female Kalen he pursued spun, managed to catch Averlynn's eye for the briefest moment. She could not place who it was, but something felt familiar as the woman nodded her head once and loped away.

Averlynn allowed herself only the briefest moment to draw breath.

There was at least a remnant. She turned back to Wazè, saw the battle was all but over. Her troops were being pushed back, gave way by increments only. She motioned to her detachment: it was time to disengage, save themselves for the rest of this war.

As they circled around the east side of the village again, the fire had nearly burned through its entirety. The smoke had not laid too thick, blessedly, but she fought away a fear of any who had burned alive trying to hide. She paused to scan the forest for her soldiers again.

Just to the north she spied Ketzler, and she grit her teeth. There was no doubt in her mind he had caused this—pushed for the war itself, and had been able to bring his army to her village.

Vera was by her side once again. "Take them north," Averlynn said. "Let's get away from this army."

"What about you?"

"I'm right behind you," she said. "Just get them moving."

Vera nodded quickly and ran off, calling and signaling as she went. Averlynn's eyes locked onto Ketzler, began maneuvering Tarafel toward him. He was the cause. He must be—no matter what standing he supposedly claimed.

He was running, eyes toward one of her archers. She nudged Tarafel to a canter, angling to cut him off. She saw her archer draw back, oblivious to Ketzler's rampage, and loose. The arrow sped toward a knot of soldiers who seemed to be protecting a kneeling Cariste—a female. In that brief glance she could tell it was not the one he called Karbae, but some other—perhaps of important rank?

But then her eyes were on Ketzler as Tarafel pulled up in front of him, rearing. Ketzler skidded to a stop, eyes wide as Averlynn's own arrow pointed unwaveringly at him. In the midst of her fury, seeing him so close, seeing how young he looked—his lifespan surely was short enough for his own people, how short was it compared to hers?

She loosed, and as she felt the string slide on her fingertip he dropped to the ground, somehow ducking her arrow from less than two strides away. *Could he possibly have known?*

Her quiver was empty, and his army pressed their attack. In disbelief she wheeled Tarafel and leapt away into the forest. She spared one glance back, to see Ketzler start to head over to the knot of soldiers, saw the female fallen with an arrow through her throat. Why had he not called a warning? Surely there had been time, and Cariste archers aplenty.

Tavill was ahead, watching her approach. She shook her head, gesturing as she turned Tarafel northward, and together they ran to catch up with her tattered army.

The fires of Wazè crackled, then hissed as rain began to fall.

Averlynn sat chewing her lip as night fell. The 'army,' if it could be called that, camped restlessly around her. Witko, Ouwa, Vera, and Tavill sat pensively around the fire they allowed themselves.

They had done a lot of retreating over the past few days. In true Kalen fashion they had abandoned their home and fled in the face of an enemy. That it was such an overwhelming force mattered little to Averlynn. History was repeating itself, and she was supposed to be in charge.

If she really wanted to be thankful, she admitted pulling the Kalen bonded out of Wazè had some of the benefits Tavill wanted. It had prepared her troops to maneuver without the rings. It put them in position to return and wound Ketzler's forces. And so, without the rings, they had been able to approach the Cariste unnoticed.

It had not, however, prepared them to die. Contact with Ketzler's forces had done that. And when they retreated, they had not been able to retrieve those fallen, which meant even more Cariste would wear rings they were not intended to wear. Now that her soldiers were bloodied, they feared the upcoming war even more. Averlynn had not even had to listen close to hear talks of abandoning the effort, of fleeing deeper into their territory and trying to hide in Tekaa or one of the remote outposts. The only thing that appealed to Averlynn was the possibility of recruiting more soldiers—at least more Rangers, maybe a Scout or two. Scouts would have been highly useful. Even Amrith. She wondered briefly where he had been, if he survived the attack or if he had already departed elsewhere by the time Ketzler had shown up on their doorstep.

That bothered her, too. The rings still had a limited range, and the territory south of the Wall was massive. How that man had managed to find an outpost and a village in so short a time terrified her—terrified her that Amrith was selling them out, or some other Kalen had been captured without them realizing it. Perhaps it wasn't even Ketzler, though he kept popping up where she never expected him.

She worried how he had ducked at just the right moment. Battlefield luck, maybe. And yet, with everything else he seemed to pull off that should have been impossible, this grated perhaps the worst. Not only because she had hesitated—doing that too often would get her and probably others killed—but because he seemed to know she would hesitate, had somehow read her mind as her thoughts whirled in that sudden meeting. And if he had, she worried what he had found there.

And, to top off everything, they still had no idea where the Prosan army was. Presumably that threat still loomed, waiting to fall somewhere.

She closed her eyes and sighed. When she opened them again, Tavill was studying her with his deep, sad eyes. She knew he didn't mean it, that he wasn't sad specifically at or with her. But it was a constant reminder that her problems were not the only ones in the world. Sometimes that knowledge helped, actually—that at least the entire world was not actually riding on her shoulders. Right now, though, it added to her responsibility because he would refuse to leave unless she demanded it. And, truthfully and selfishly, she wanted him around.

"What are we doing?" Vera asked. She looked at no one in particular.

"Waiting for direction from the gods," Averlynn murmured. Vera's gaze snapped to her, and she shrugged tiredly. "It would be helpful, at least."

"Should I perform hunim, then?" Vera asked.

Averlynn cocked an eye at her. Was she testing her? Maybe not intentionally. The end was the same. Did she still believe in the gods? Consulting the bones was an easy and time-honored tradition—one that had become largely ceremonial. She could blame that.

But it wasn't the true reason. Her connection to the gods had been waning, truthfully since before this began. She had made her prayers, but only dutifully. There had been a faint re-ignition once, when she had thought of requesting a Minor Hangh. And a slow but inexorable slide into apostasy after that. She hadn't meant it, had not sought it. And now she was here she didn't even regret it. Almost as though she had known, at some point, she would arrive here.

That left what to do now. She looked at Witko, expecting him to agree to a hunim. But he stared at the flames. Ouwa would only do what she told him. His acceptance of her command...well, he had not let her deny it.

She lowered her eyes, shook her head mutely. "Let them guide us silently, if they must," she said. "Or turn things out as they see fit." She drew another breath. "Tavill, you must go find Old Raina." She fixed him with her gaze. "Our paths are not the same, yet."

Some of the sadness was replaced with puzzlement. "Is that all?"

She paused, then shook her head. "I'm hoping, if you are able after meeting with her, you could scout for the Prosan and report back to me."

"Where will you be?"

All eyes were on her, now, waiting for her orders. "North. We have to make sure no more reinforcements arrive. Although I'm not entirely sure how."

Tavill's gaze flickered. "I think your Chief Witko will have an idea."

Averlynn glanced quickly at him, her eyes widening as he didn't deny it. "What is it?" she asked.

Witko glared at Tavill. "I had hoped never to use that again," he muttered.

"You also hoped never to be threatened with extermination again," Tavill said.

"Huh. True."

"What are you able to do?" Averlynn pressed, nearing exasperation.

He held up his hand and waggled his fingers, making obvious the ring that was missing. Averlynn still hadn't gotten used to not wearing hers all the time. It felt chill, like abandoning a piece of clothing. "These can do a lot more than hide us," he said. "It's difficult to explain. But if you can get us through the Cariste lines, you'll see well enough."

She pulled on a finger. "They don't allow us to hear another's thoughts, do they? Somehow?"

Witko pursed his lips. "Not exactly. It is a magic born in the mind though." Then, as if realizing the implications of her question, he frowned. "What happened?"

Averlynn glanced away. "Nothing important," she said. "Strange luck, I suspect."

Much as the Cariste had, Averlynn sent outriders with rings to begin to feel their way north. It was slow going, and she worried constantly that Ketzler would leap on any sense between them. As far as she knew, he would not know of any other Kalen settlements—and the nearest was Tekaa Wohan deep in the Waken Forest. The problem was that the nearest settlement was *the* Tekaa Wohan, and Ketzler shouldn't have been able to find even one settlement. She hoped, in part, that this movement northward might draw him off. So she wanted to make contact, but also wanted to be well clear of their main forces before she did.

It turned out not to be up to her. The third day the birdsong rang out, warning that rings had been felt from Kalen they knew to be dead. She mounted Tarafel quickly, trusting in her senses and the few of her soldiers with rings rather than wear her own. She had appreciated Ketzler's surprise at seeing her in more than just a practical way.

At an answering song she turned left, searching the forest. Their uniforms blended in well to the landscape, but not perfectly—and to one who had spent almost every day in that land it was just enough. She loosed an arrow, turned grimly away as the flash of too-chestnut brown fell to the earth.

It was a small band that quickly turned and fled into the valley. She counted perhaps ten, wondered if it would be enough to draw their attention. Wondered, too, if they had already planned to strike deeper into the Waken, or if Wazè had been their only objective for this foray. She desperately wished for Scouts.

"Shouldn't we pursue them?" Ouwa asked as she turned away from those retreating.

She shook her head. "Not yet. Let them report a small force moving northward. Hopefully they won't send their entire army."

"I doubt their army is maneuverable enough," Ouwa said.

"We'll find out. Let's keep going."

If their army was not, they had raiding parties that were. Twice more the Kalen were nearly ambushed, but it seemed their familiarity with the terrain worked in their favor more than the Cariste. Each time the Cariste left the field bloodied, and the Kalen were left to continue.

As night fell Averlynn ordered all rings removed, leading them harder eastward to a sharp valley to hide for the night. She set outposts that would be able to spot any Cariste coming over the ridges and let everyone else settle in.

"Do you think they harry us intentionally?" Witko asked. They had decided to hold council nightly—well, Averlynn had suggested it, after Tavill had gone, and enforced it.

"What would be their purpose?" Ouwa asked.

Blank glances were given around the dark circle. Averlynn spoke first. "They could be keeping us from moving quickly while also keeping in contact, as they set a larger ambush ahead of us. Unless you truly believe their army isn't that maneuverable."

Ouwa shifted uncomfortably. "Not the entire thing. But yes, they might have taken a portion—enough to overpower us—and are setting up a barrier northward."

Averlynn nodded. "I don't like that they seem to appear out of nowhere. Like they wait to put the rings on until we're close. They're tracking us some other way, they have to be."

"But how?" Vera asked.

More uncomfortable glances. "I don't want to say we have a traitor..." Averlynn trailed off, waiting to see if the heavens fell at her suggestion. It chilled her more when there seemed to be grim agreement. "Any ideas how to find out?"

"We assume it's no one here," Vera replied.

Averlynn folded her arms and sat back. Finally she shook her head. "We can't function if we do," she said. "So let's figure out how to test everyone else until no one is left."

"We need to send scouts north to see if the Cariste are laying an ambush," Ouwa said. "Who would we suspect the most?"

"Anyone close to Scout Amrith," Averlynn replied quickly.

"Maybe one of those we rescued, or bonded to them," Vera said quietly.

Averlynn looked to Ouwa. "You know your people best."

He picked at his lip, shook his head. "There was one who seemed impressed by Amrith—reverent, almost. The rest I would swear by."

Averlynn shifted uncomfortably. She had been like that. But, without any other indicator... "Okay, so those. What's your plan?"

"We send them along with five others to scout the Cariste position ahead. Tell the ones we distrust that we are taking our forces further east to escape the Cariste patrols."

"But we head west, try to slip through the lines and give us more room. How do we check it?"

"We'll send one of us east, and see if the Cariste show up."

There was silence for several moments. "That one will likely die," Averlynn said quietly. "Or at least get captured. And we won't know the outcome."

"That's why it will be me," Ouwa said. "I might look old, but I have greater faith in my sneaking abilities than you seem to."

Averlynn lowered her eyes. "Of course, Ouwa, I'm sorry. The good thing is, if this works, we'll also clear our road northward."

Ouwa cocked an eyebrow and hummed agreement. "Yes, it is a brilliant plan, isn't it?" He sobered. "Except for one possibility: the traitor is in this circle, or is not part of the group we have chosen."

"And who goes with the other group, then?" Averlynn asked. "We need at least one that we trust."

Glances were exchanged, and Vera drew a breath. "Well, I'm not the consummate warrior, but these past few months have taught me a thing or two. I guess I'm one of those going."

Averlynn wanted to protest, but knew it would do no good. And, truth be told, Vera might have made an excellent Ranger if she had applied herself differently. "And Ouwa? What three of your Trackers do you trust the most?"

"Jara, Hekteth, Arrida."

She nodded. "I believe I remember them, the few times I made it to Kenkek on patrol."

"They think well of you," Ouwa confirmed. "They do not, perhaps, revere you," he added with a grin, "but your warnings had stuck with them more than any others."

Averlynn was a little flattered, and was thankful for the darkness that hid her face. Of course she had wanted her warnings to be heeded—she was nearly useless otherwise. But not to be remembered for them. "I thought it was what we were supposed to do," she muttered. "That is all."

"It was," Witko said. She looked at him, trying to read his expression in the dimness. "I know it probably doesn't mean much, but I am sorry. The Chiefs did wrong by all the Trackers, Rangers, and Scouts. I can't even tell you why, probably. And they never took me seriously anyway. So I hid. That was my fault."

"As you said, it seems they were all part of it. Are still a part of it. For now, let's get what rest we can, and launch our plan in the morning. And hopefully we're wrong."

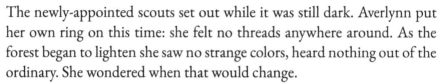

The newly-appointed scouts set out while it was still dark. Averlynn put her own ring on this time: she felt no threads anywhere around. As the forest began to lighten she saw no strange colors, heard nothing out of the ordinary. She wondered when that would change.

"How do we do this next part?" Witko asked as the remaining Kalen gathered in the bottom of the valley.

"We're going to have to rely on our eyes," Averlynn said, her voice low. She pulled her ring off again and tied it securely in a pouch. "We cannot remotely risk the Cariste sensing us through these. We move slowly. If it takes us a full day to move through two valleys, I don't care. I think we have some time, here." She looked at each of them, ensuring they understood her. "Spread out, plains formation." They would each only be able to maintain visual contact with two other Kalen. "It'll be hard in the forest, but that's why I don't care how slow we move. I'll lead. Keep Tarafel in the rear with my sword. It's too heavy for me anyway." She paused, grimaced in frustration. Such a beautiful sword. But impractical. "Let's go."

It was harder than even she imagined, and she waited sometimes what felt hours until a second Kalen appeared in her line of sight behind her. They moved forward like an inchworm, the last of them moving forward first, then once contact was made the next several. Finally Averlynn would move forward through the trees, slowly, looking ahead and behind, until she could see only one other. Then hand signals were passed back and the process began again.

But it forced everyone to pay attention, to become attuned to each foot of forest before they would move. If anything changed while they waited, they would be able to tell. And she did not think the Cariste would be that patient.

As evening approached, they had managed to cross their third valley. As Averlynn knelt behind a thick maple at the top of the next ridge and prepared to give her hand signal, she caught the barest movement ahead of her. She froze, giving a slight gesture of halt. Her eyes scanned while her body remained motionless.

It took everything inside her not to duck even further away when she saw a face appear from behind a tree halfway down the slope. She knew any movement could be caught and so she held utterly still. The face moved slowly, watching the forest. She didn't recognize it specifically, other than it was a light-skinned Cariste. But it wasn't Ketzler.

After agonizing moments, the soldier came further into the open. When his face was averted, Averlynn sidled further behind the tree, but still able to watch. The soldier made his own signal, and she saw troops like ants all detach from their trees and move forward. They were incredibly patient, she realized, as they made their way northward almost as slowly as her soldiers made their way west. She permitted herself a begrudging respect: she had half-expected them to clear roadways through the forest to allow their large army to move swiftly, if not lightly.

Darkness continued to fall, and she worried they would halt and make camp. But something drove them onward, and they continued up the valley. She counted fifty of them, but felt the weight of perhaps hundreds more behind them. It was not the main army, but definitely a movement in force.

At twilight, birds began to sing again, heralding the closing of the day. In the midst of it she heard a warble, a missed note—a warning from one of the Kalen behind her. She turned cautiously and wished she could disappear.

The main force was in the valley behind her. When she had called the halt, the Tracker behind her had the presence of mind to hide well. He was now nearly surrounded by five hundred or better troops. These moved slowly, but less cautiously, presumably relying on their scouts on either side.

If only we could wear our rings, she lamented. They could each glamour themselves to look like saplings or rotting logs. But with that dratted Ketzler stealing the rings and learning how to use them... *I gave him the key, though.* She waited, praying to anyone who would listen to let them keep moving past.

They showed no signs of stopping or setting up camp. When she looked forward again, the scouts on that side were gone from the valley, just disappearing out of sight ahead. The main force still moved behind her—she could hear the occasional snapped twig, a susurrus of leaf litter underfoot. Birds continued to sing even as crickets and the occasional cicada began their nighttime chants.

A breeze stirred, letting a little more skylight filter in through the leaves, just enough to let her see the back of the army continue further north. She watched them carefully, found a thin shaft of sunlight, and flashed a quick hand signal: *come to me.* They would go no further tonight.

They camped spread out, though not as far as when they moved, and made no structures for themselves. After the passing of the Cariste, Averlynn did not even allow leaves to be piled. The nights were not cold, so it was not a difficult command. But even as a Ranger she had regularly allowed herself little comforts like that.

At best she dozed, though every rustling leaf brought her alert again. That army had such a bad habit of being where they shouldn't. She wanted to move a bit further west tomorrow, then north as fast as they possibly dared. She missed the council, but only her and Witko remained anyway. Though it had only been a day, she hoped Tavill was well, and well on his way to Old Raina.

Then, suddenly, gray light filtered into the forest and the songbirds were beginning again. She lay still, listening, letting her eyes adjust as her gaze roved around the valley. She slowly moved into a crouch and made her way to Witko.

"Take them west. I want to linger back a moment and try something stupid."

He inspected her a moment. "You truly cannot read thoughts with them."

She smiled briefly. "I'm okay with that. But I want to see if I can sense any rings anywhere. Just quickly. If I do I might lead them away from you and try to circle back later. If not, we'll move faster and head north soon."

He nodded, turned to a few of the Kalen faces peering quietly from the bedding spots. He made the appropriate hand gestures, and they moved off into the forest.

Averlynn continued to wait as the forest brightened and the birdsong began to fade. Finally, as she thought perhaps the sun might be above the horizon, she slipped on her ring.

Energy shot through her as a faint thread sprang up, then almost immediately broke. As thin as it was, it was probably at the very edge of its range—surely the wearer had not pulled theirs off so quickly. If it was Ketzler, he would know it was her. She trotted forward until the thread sprang up again, thickened as she paused. Then she walked away, south and slightly east, then broke into a run. As soon as the thread became tenuous she pulled off the ring, sprinting west in a long loop to take her back to the main unit.

She caught up to them by catching sight of Tarafel. She whispered to him as she drew near, and when he turned the Tracker with him turned as well.

"That might have accomplished nothing," she whispered quickly. "But it might have done a lot. We need haste now more than stealth, but still we'll be as quiet as possible."

She mounted and let Tarafel gallop a few strides, his thudding hooves capturing the attention of everyone even in plains formation. Then she gave rapid hand signals as she led them at a light trot into the next valley.

At the bottom they turned north, arrow formation, at a brisk walk. She wanted to make as much time as possible while the Cariste hopefully debated what to do about the Kalen ring that had suddenly appeared directly behind them. She hoped that, at least for half a day, they might be able to move freely.

The valley narrowed, and she gestured firmly for them to mount the sides. Even with hope, she wouldn't let them bunch. They slowed a little while they waited for those who needed to ascend the slopes. A Tracker on the east slope lost his footing a moment. Her eyes snapped to him as the leaves rushed as he slid. And if he had not slipped, she would not have seen a Cariste near the top of the slope.

"How?" she cried, mostly to herself. Then: "Ambush!" She nocked an arrow and let it fly, her anger and frustration venting a little as the shaft found its mark. She turned Tarafel and charged, looking for more targets.

They appeared in ones and twos as arrows began to rain into the valley. But her people were archers too, and had not lost the knack for shooting from cover.

"Forward!" she cried again. She wanted to hurt them badly this time. Not just out of frustration, though for now that emotion would serve her well enough. As she topped the ridge she slung the bow and drew the sword.

Now it flashed in the sunlight, the jagged sardonyx rending armor as a quake would rend the earth. It felt solid in her grasp, unshakable, unbreakable. Perhaps her adrenaline gave her the strength to overcome its weight—but for how long? She pushed the worry aside, harried the enemy as the rest of her people kept up their rain of arrows. The Cariste began to flee.

But Averlynn was tired of it—tired of the fear, the worry, their enemy showing up at every turn, of their superiority. She chased them down—none had horses, and as she swooped down on them, blade ringing, she began to see the fear in their eyes. She wanted this detachment annihilated. Let no one return, and see if Ketzler and his superiors thought twice before raiding again.

With iron strokes the last fell bleeding. Tarafel snorted as Averlynn gasped for air. The solidity of the blade was pure weight, now, and threatened to fall from her grasp. She searched the woods closely, but saw nothing out of place. She turned back, saw Witko and several other Trackers watching her closely. "Search them for rings," she said.

"We have," Witko replied. "Many had them."

Averlynn permitted herself a grin. Good. Whoever had sent them probably felt them dying—at least, felt the connections sever. They would suspect there were no survivors. "Give me one," she said.

A Tracker—she believed his name was Athlek—jogged to her and handed her one. She inspected it briefly, not recognizing the bird etched on it, and slipped it on. She felt one presence, middle-strength. They were not too far away. Then she simply removed it and handed it back. "Let Witko carry them," she said. "We can perform the rites tonight." It was perhaps not enough, but they would try. "Let's keep north."

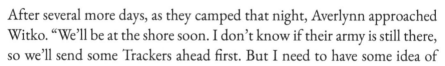

After several more days, as they camped that night, Averlynn approached Witko. "We'll be at the shore soon. I don't know if their army is still there, so we'll send some Trackers ahead first. But I need to have some idea of what we're doing if we get there."

"Of course. Well, we'll be making a circle." He paused, waiting to see if she knew what he meant. She did not. "Do you remember when we left Old Kalen? I thought it might be just a little too long ago. And most of what we did, we did after you had gone. Another reason all our rings bear the marks of animals is that we can draw on their spirits, and on them, to help in great need. To determine if the need is great enough, we need to have a circle of at least twenty."

"Because only if the world is ending would twenty of us agree on something," Averlynn said with a wry and bitter grin.

"Hmm. Yes. Well—as to what we can do with it: if you were to go back to Old Kalen, you would find a city in ruins. Now, at this point, that's natural enough. But what we had done was make a circle and draw the forces and help of the land itself to tear it down as we were leaving—so it was in ruins though we had only just abandoned it."

"So..."

He nodded once. "We should be able to make the shore where they came in look ancient and overgrown. They may miss it entirely, or at least struggle to land."

"How large of an area can we do this?"

"It's limited only by the size of the circle."

Averlynn's eyebrows climbed as she glanced around their encampment. Witko chuckled.

"Oh, yes, we should be able to cause some havoc with all of us."

"How long does it take to do this?"

"That, unfortunately, is the difficult part. We'll need most of a night."

Averlynn stared at him. "A full night, wearing our rings—near their camp!—without being attacked."

"Ah. Yes. I was supposed to give you this when we got to this point." He dipped his hand into his cloak and pulled out a folded parchment.

"Where did this come from?" Averlynn asked, reaching out.

"Tavill," Witko said.

Her hand froze on the letter. Why would he write to her about something, and not just tell her—or tell Witko? After a breath she unfolded it and began to read. As she read, the reason became clearer.

Because it was insanity.

32

NOT EXACTLY A PIP

"This is almost fun to watch."
"Which part?"
"How you dig your grave deeper and deeper."
"I must make it deep enough for all."

30 Mantaver 1321 — Summer

K etzler lay comfortably in the tent. Well, mostly. He had not quite made it his own yet, but at least most of what had been Pike's was gone.

That had been a bit of a whirlwind. All he had seen was the removing of an obstacle that annoyed him. But it seemed Liptieri saw an equal, and only a few short weeks after making Sergeant he was suddenly a Captain. The hardest part of it was how to punish Mordel without making it obvious. A fun challenge.

He had also needed to still go slow with Karbae. He wasn't sure how much Liptieri knew or didn't know. But he had made sure she knew his intentions as soon as he felt safe. And she had shown her deep appreciation—things he had never imagined as a Pip in a monastery.

He rarely thought of those days, now. Of course he had applied himself there, and done reasonably well. Everyone saw that as a sign of one devoted to the God of All. Now that he had joined the Army and done as well, if not better, he began to realize it was just part of who he was—the applying himself and doing well. Now that he was here, in this tent in these woods, with all his successes behind him, he almost laughed at the tiny aspiration he'd had as a Pip. No, here was where he belonged. Not imploring men, but commanding them. Not attempting vainly to inflate the faith of those who would have it anyway, but committed to a cause that would actually help his people in a real way, whether they had faith or not.

He smiled to remember the series of successes harassing the Kalen led by Averlynn. Ketzler still wasn't sure how he'd pulled it off, except he seemed to know from time to time exactly where they would be. A little voice he might once have attributed to the God of All guided him. Now he wondered if it was perhaps just his good instincts. Perhaps that was all anyone ever had, or not.

Creeping right past them, and then a bloody and failed ambush, set him back a little. But, truthfully, he was tired of the games—all the little, almost nit-picking raids. If Liptieri wanted some space before Ketzler could convince him of a grand and decisive plan, Ketzler would see it done. So now they returned to their main camp by direct and bold routes.

He still itched for more. Not a lot, but some. An actual company, not just scouts. He turned over in his bedroll. Did he want Liptieri's position? Perhaps only if Lip wouldn't initiate his plan. He did have one, or at least most of one. It might need the next round of reinforcements—probably, even. It couldn't hurt to have more bodies. But it would see them spread across the land like wildfires—like the fire they had set outside that village, only this one wouldn't be damped by a little rain. In its wake, the Kalen would be all but gone, the land ripe for Cariste settlers. There was so much good land, here. And he would be key in securing that land. It made him giddy.

Sleepless, even. What to do about Mordel? He was a sergeant, so his options were limited—no digging latrines, even though he deserved it. Make him an aide, a runner? He grinned; that would be almost the reverse of what one might expect—nearly a place of honor, except in Mordel's case a constant reminder of how far superior Ketzler was. And he could keep Mordel running with endless and inane messages, which might be enjoyable. But in the reports, they wouldn't know that. And the little tuft would probably do well at it and gain some amount of recognition. All he

DANIEL DYDEK

was actually good at was inane tasks.

Ketzler rolled onto his back and stared at the black roof. Perhaps that was the key. Give him some of the highest-level—and highest-visible—responsibilities and let him torch his own career. Ketzler chuckled at the thought. He couldn't make him more than a sergeant, but he could stack his foursquad with some of the least-competent scouts and give them important missions. Not so important as to cripple the army, of course; Ketzler would do absolutely nothing to endanger them. But just important enough that a good soldier would distinguish himself, while poor one would be reduced back to Foot. That's where Mordel belonged.

Then, when Mordel was a mere Foot, he could begin to risk a relationship with Karbae. Ketzler smiled, remembered her gratitude, and finally fell asleep.

The next day they came to lands he recognized better, knew they would reach their base camp sometime the following morning. He began to build Mordel's roster—didn't want to risk anyone too useful, but also not make it obvious. Karbae he would move to a new, elite squad he wanted to propose to Liptieri. Surely the man would listen! They needed a quick but effective unit to find the settlements, with light, quick forces soon behind them to engage the enemy as soon as they were found. The squad would report almost directly to him. At least, one of them would be his most trusted liaison.

When they camped that night, he prepared his reports and went to see Liptieri. One step at a time, he told himself. You're still new to command, don't overstep your bounds.

Liptieri was expecting him, offered him a light refreshment. Ketzler had only had it once before—another memory from the monastery life he had all but quelled. Not because he didn't enjoy it, and it tasted much now as it had then.

"Thank you, sir," he said, setting it on the little transportable table Liptieri loved so much. Ketzler still hadn't gotten used to seeing that thing, though it made poring over maps slightly more convenient.

There was no map tonight, just the glasses. Ketzler took another sip, waiting for Liptieri to start. His rosters were still rolled in his pocket. The Commander had a faraway look as he scratched a knuckle absently.

"A shame," Liptieri muttered.

"Yes sir."

Liptieri grunted and sat forward. "The next boats should be here in a few weeks. We're going to recover and reorganize a little bit, get ready for the new wave of soldiers. They'll need to integrate into our existing units." He paused to sigh. "As far as I know, they didn't train any new scouts. We'll have to do that once they get here. Only, I don't know who has aptitude—if any of them do. I assume some will, like you did. With these raids..." He set his jaw and shrugged.

"We're strong enough for now, sir," Ketzler said carefully. "If we use them carefully and properly."

"You've had no further contact with the Kalen pursuing us?"

Ketzler bit back his first reply. Liptieri wouldn't be that comfortable with him yet. "Not yet, sir. But I still believe in the barrier we set up."

"You're sure the force that hit your last raid was the largest group?"

"Yes."

Liptieri's stare went flat. "Explain."

"It's been the same group that has been after us since the village," Ketzler said. "If there were more places to get reinforcements between there and here we would have found it. It's still them, and only them."

"And so they split up to seem bigger?"

Ketzler nodded.

"Big risk."

"So is what we did."

"I didn't think the Kalen were risk-takers."

Ketzler snorted. "Averlynn is, sir."

Liptieri nodded once, took a sip. Ketzler drank as well. "What's in your pocket?" Liptieri asked.

"Mmm. I did want to reconfigure the scouts a little, with the changes that have occurred recently. And, as you say, to prepare for reinforcements."

Liptieri was already shaking his head. "Too much change, Ketz. Let them get used to having you in command first. We can discuss changes once the reinforcements arrive. Once we settle on the next phase of this war."

Liptieri's eyes held warning. Ketzler ignored it. "Sir, these changes will prepare us precisely for that next phase. Unless the next phase is to sit and do nothing for a year."

Liptieri cocked an eyebrow. "And if it is?"

"Is it?"

Liptieri watched him, but Ketzler neither moved nor blinked for several breaths. Finally, he said: "Elirose told me an interesting story, sir, that you should be familiar with." Liptieri was silent, but cocked an eyebrow. "He told me, sir, that you recruited him some fifteen years ago, knowing you would need cartographers. Is that true?"

Liptieri drank, and didn't deny it.

"Our resources were not so thin fifteen years ago that we would have needed new lands," Ketzler continued. "Nor were there any new maps to be drawn—in the north, anyway."

Liptieri idly turned his glass on the table, but remained silent.

"Sir, in order to advise you as best I can, and guide my troops as best I can, I need to know why we're actually here, in these lands."

Liptieri drew a long breath as he stared at his glass. "Twenty years ago, I stole a ship," he said. He cocked an eyebrow at Ketzler. "I was younger, bolder perhaps. Bored out of my mind, mostly. So I forged some orders, took over a small but capable boat, and set sail." He took a drink and leaned forward. "See, all our expeditions—back when we could make them—followed the coastline. Treacherous place it is, with all the rocks and currents and storms. This time we sailed further east, out of sight of land, and then south. South until we started to see ice and snow. Then we came west again. You are familiar with the story of the Abandoned Isles?"

Ketzler shrugged. "Some. I know we abandoned them—obviously enough. I wondered for a time if that's where we were going—some of the rumors in the north, anyway, were about that."

"Well. I discovered some old book or other, supposedly fiction, written perhaps a hundred years ago, telling the story of those who were left on those Isles." He waved a hand distractedly. "In some old library in Gaios or somewhere. The problem was," he said, saluting Ketzler with his glass, "that my family had handed down old letters—rewritten when the originals were fading beyond recognition—sent from my forebears who governed one of those settlement. And the plan that those letters told about were shocking close to these 'fictional' accounts in this book I had found."

"Plan, sir?"

"The plague did not wipe them all out," Liptieri said, leaning closer. "Some got off the islands without disease. Obviously they didn't go back to Carist or South Pal Isan, or we would have known. Everyone thought they had been completely wiped out because we never saw any of them again."

Ketzler nodded: it was old history.

"So where did they go?" Liptieri asked, sitting back and taking another drink.

As he pondered, Ketzler's head notched downward. "They're here?" he asked in quiet disbelief.

Liptieri grinned. "Twenty years ago, my little boat and I found land again, far south. Still massive caves and unrelenting seas. Except one small cove, where low tide opened a cave. Inside that cave was a boat—nearly brand new. And yet it perfectly matched the shipwright's abilities from some several thousand years ago."

"And so we came south, to..."

"We are going to meet with these people—there are many left—and with their help take over the rest of the land. We made contact with them, so long ago, and promised to bring our people south." He leaned forward again and pitched his voice conspiratorially low. "Seems they had some trouble with oppression by a race calling themselves the Wohan."

Now it was Ketzler's turn for a flat stare. "You already knew we would meet with resistance when we got here," he said. "You knew there was an enemy here—before we found the hoof print in that lake behind the Brynth."

Liptieri waggled a finger. "I knew they were here; I didn't know their capabilities, how many, their locations—any of that. That's why we needed so many scouts—good scouts. And also why we brought no mages."

Ketzler squinted. "Sir?"

"While my interactions with the Prosan were brief, I learned they had no magic-users—hated them, it seemed. I wanted nothing with us that might provoke them."

Ketzler sat back. "That still seems like a terrible risk, sir."

Liptieri nodded. "It is. Still, there was a little bit more. Nothing I could take to the Senate, but enough to convince me."

"What was that?"

"A prophecy."

Ketzler managed to keep from rolling his eyes. "May I ask what the prophecy was, sir?"

"Of course. You should know, actually, because it concerns you."

Ketzlers eyes widened—in fear, and not just for unreasonable expectations. Was his rise to power some foretold thing? Had the God of All not let him go, yet? "Sir?" he asked, failing to keep the trembling entirely from his voice.

It didn't seem that Liptieri noticed. "Late one night, beset by doubts when all my preparations and haranguing of the Senate had gotten me nowhere, when I was nearly giving up the whole mission, I went to a cathedral. Utterly desperate. But there was a strange woman there—the Bader confirmed later she was a known prophetess. She came to me almost as soon as I walked in the door, as though she had been waiting for me. She told me: by ship's captain I began my journey, but by ship's captain I would see my destiny fulfilled."

Ketzler mulled it over. "'But,' sir?" he echoed. "It doesn't make much sense put that way—"

Liptieri's finger came up as he launched himself forward again. *He's feeling his wine, isn't he...* "Exactly! Exactly. I worried over that for a long time too. Eventually resources grew scarcer. Senators were hearing too much grumbling in their cities, they didn't know what to do. I proposed, once again, an attempt to go south. I told them what I had found. And I received only tentative agreement. Not enough to launch the mission. But I began recruiting. Then, one fateful morning, a strange boy came along looking to enlist."

Ketzler squinted, but waited silently for the continuation. Liptieri smiled. "I remembered the woman's words, and the pattern of speech. She had a slight impediment, I think. What she had actually said to me was: By ship's captain I began my journey, but by Pip Captain I would see my destiny fulfilled." He sat back triumphantly, raised his glass in toast. "You're my Pip Captain now, Ketzler!" he continued. "Obviously, I tested you thoroughly. So even though I knew there were people south, it wasn't until you found the hoof print that the Senators believed it—enough to grant my mission request."

"You're saying all your recruiting, all your posturing of our mission and organization, was completed before you knew we were even going to do this?"

"That's my point! I did know. It did not have an official, external seal yet. But as soon as my soldier said you were a Pip—I knew."

Ketzler sat stunned. Absolute and utter nonsense, as he suspected. Liptieri's faith was built entirely on what he already wanted, already believed would be true. And he was in charge of this expedition!

"That's...incredible, sir," he said. "I fear you think too highly of me." *I was all but a Bader, so not a Pip Captain anyway...* "I thought I was only here for the men, those who might need such things."

"Well, we all need to believe in something."

"I believe in relieving the pressure on our people, of giving them a wide new land to settle in and prosper from. Let the Baders only pray for the oppressed; I will give them bread and meat—from heaven if I must."

It sounded slightly sacrilegious when he said it, and he quickly swallowed another drink. In the silence his head hummed—perhaps he'd had too much too quickly.

But then Liptieri was staring at the door, head cocked as though listening. "What...?" Ketzler began, cutting off as the humming grew to a rumble. They rose and went out into the night.

The rumble continued almost to a roar. Ketzler expected to see a mountain of rocks rolling down on them, except he knew this part of the country didn't have any—or, not enough. Then, beneath the roar, a hum came again almost like a long growl.

More soldiers exited their tents, looking wildly at one another as the night filled with the sound. Then, above it, there came a whistle like eagles high overhead, growing in volume and pitch till Ketzler's head hurt from it. As he fell to his knees, Liptieri was on the ground next to him. He felt the earth would swallow him deep into a cave and seal it shut, or that a great winged beast would pluck him up and carry him to eyries above the clouds. His nose was bleeding, and hurt as though he'd been punched by a golem fist. He was screaming, but couldn't hear it—only that his throat was raw and his lungs near empty.

How long it went on he was never sure, and none of the soldiers around him could recall. He sank into an oblivion of pounding fists and shearing talons and utter darkness until finally, agonizingly, the echoes faded and there was light again. As though waking from sleep, it was dawn and birds were twittering their morning songs and the ground was covered in fog. Ketzler sat up slowly, every joint stiff and fiery.

"Ketzler?" Liptieri called. His voice sounded like Ketzler felt.

"Yes sir."

"What was that?"

A thousand thoughts ran through Ketzler's mind, not one of them a good explanation. The only thing it could be, he wouldn't allow. "I don't know, sir." It would not be the Kalen. They were not that powerful. They could not be.

It seemed Liptieri thought the same thing—wanted to deny it equally. "Check on the camp. Check your scouts. Let's make sure we're fit to move and then get moving."

"I don't know if *I* can move, sir."

But when Liptieri growled, Ketzler struggled to his feet. "Sergeant Mordel!" he bellowed. This wouldn't seem improper. "Mordel!" he shouted again. His calls rattled the still morning air, a pale echo of whatever had happened the night before.

All the tents were still erected. There was not so much as a new fallen leaf—only soldiers, fallen as leaves in autumn, groggily coming to their senses and sitting up painfully.

Finally through the mist Mordel replied. "Ketz?" The sergeant sat up against a tree. He didn't seem hurt, at least not more than the rest.

"Mordel—sergeant, take a detail and inspect the camp and the soldiers. Make sure everything is fit. We need to march on as soon as we can." Ketzler waited for him to respond, but the sergeant only stared sightlessly into the mists. Curious, Ketzler approached. "Sergeant?" he said, quietly this time.

Mordel whimpered as Ketzler knelt beside him. His trousers were soiled, judging by the smell if not the sight. His breaths were still ragged. And his eyes were milky.

Ketzler laid a hand gently on Mordel's shoulder. "Sergeant, what happened to you?"

Mordel's head wagged minutely. "I don't...I heard a noise—"

"We all heard the noise, sergeant, but we are not all blinded."

Mordel shrugged, and Ketzler glanced suddenly as he scrabbled at his finger. He had one of the Kalen rings on.

"Did you have that on last night?" Ketzler demanded.

Mordel whined, still tugging at it. The whine rose to a shriek. "It burns!"

Ketzler reached down and wrenched at the ring, but it seemed fused to Mordel's skin. Ketzler growled, pinned Mordel's hand to the ground, and stabbed the joint with his knife. It separated the finger cleanly, and for a wonder Mordel fell silent as though that hurt less than the burning had.

"What happened?" Ketzler asked.

Mordel drew a few ragged breaths. "When the earthquake started, I thought maybe it was a Kalen attack. They've been quiet for a while, since that last patrol never came back. And I worried for a few days that they would be waiting for us at camp. So when the earthquake started I put the ring on to see if I could sense them." He fell silent, leaned his head back, and closed his eyes.

Ketzler waited for him to continue, but he did not. "And did you sense them?" he prompted finally. Of course Mordel would still be worthless.

A tear leaked out of Mordel's eye, and he shook his head. "Not like we used to," he said, his voice cracking. He swallowed a sob. "I'm going to die here, aren't I?"

"Mordel, this is important. What did you feel?"

Mordel opened his eyes and stared at him. Ketzler recoiled; the whites were blood-red and the milky irises had jagged cracks across them. His voice was strangely deep and resonant. "You've done well for yourself, haven't you little Pip? Look what you've become—from hiding in a catacomb to Captain in the army." Mordel smiled, his teeth dripping red. Blood leaked from his ears. "You've walked the blood thread indeed, now, through Curani and Pike and the bodies of the Kalen. And where will it take you next? Do you even know? Can you grasp it?" He laughed breathily, then coughed on more blood. "Oh, what I felt—I felt you, the most promising murderer. Your slain will number in the thousands, and you will bathe in the blood of hordes. Their viscera will be the laces of your armor."

Rantings. "Did you feel the Kalen?" Ketzler asked ruthlessly.

Mordel's mauled hand came up and grasped tightly to Ketzler's shirt as he pulled him close. "I felt the seraphim," he whispered. "She calls them down to crack our skin with scorching heat. I felt the golems as she called them up to crush our bones and burst our bodies. She will catch you in her cosmic vise and—" he paused to wheeze a few laughs "—pop your skull like a grape." He cackled, choked, and went limp.

Ketzler took a steadying breath, unable to tear his eyes from the crumpled sergeant. Nothing he had planned to punish him could compare to what he had just suffered. Mostly he was horrified, but a tiny part of him marveled at what Averlynn had been able to do. It had to have been her. Somehow.

"What did he mean about Curani and Pike?"

Ketzler whirled. Karbae stood behind him, face pale. He had never seen her so shaken. He rose and took her in his arms, but though she didn't pull away neither did she relax.

"Mostly rantings, I'm sure," Ketzler said soothingly. "But in a ruthless sort of way, it was their deaths that opened the opportunity for me to get where I am."

"Did you kill them?"

Her voice was shaky. She wasn't certain, didn't want to believe it. He pulled back just enough to gaze into her eyes. "Karbae, I loved them both. Curani taught me more than I thought I could know, and Pike molded my character to match the skill Curani gave me. I would give anything to see them alive again."

Karbae blinked, placed her hand on his chest. "Okay," she whispered. Her eyes centered on his until he was all she saw. "What are your orders then, my Captain?" she asked with a tentative smile.

"Can you check on the units, make sure everyone else survived? See how fit we are to march."

She drew a deep breath and stepped back. "Yes, sir," she said, offering a salute with more of her customary impishness.

Ketzler returned the salute with a roll of his eyes. "Get going," he said. "Bring your report to Commander Liptieri's tent."

She turned and left, and he allowed himself one admiring sweep up and down her departing form before turning back for Liptieri. This changed everything.

As he approached the tent the fog was almost supernaturally lifting. A soldier stood nearby, dazed, staring around. Ketzler cocked his head. Something about the man...

The eyes met his, sparked. "Ketz," he said, almost in wonder.

Ketzler's steps faltered. "Miggey..."

A ghost of a smile appeared. "I'd seen you here and there during this attack. I never—well, I guess I did think a little—"

"Where is your squad?" Ketzler asked abruptly.

Miggey swallowed his smile, and he gestured vaguely southwestward.

"Get to it, then. I imagine we'll be marching out soon."

Miggey blinked. "Yes, sir," he said hollowly. But he didn't move.

"What is it? Are you hurt some way?"

"No, I guess not. Just... You've come a long way. I told you, you had something I didn't."

Ketzler snorted. "No, Footman Glassos, we both have it—as I told *you*. Only one of us did something about it though, I see."

Before Miggey could respond Ketzler strode off, back on course to the Commander's tent. As if sensing him Liptieri exited the tent as he neared. "How do we stand?" he asked.

"I sent Karbae to inspect. Sergeant Mordel has died, sir." He relayed some of the details, adding only that he had rambled. "I fear we cannot use the rings anymore," he concluded. "If they somehow open us up to attack..."

"How do we find them, then?"

"I found the first without the rings, sir," Ketzler said. "But it might behoove us to try and capture someone, next time we meet them in battle."

Liptieri looked closely at him. "Is there something else?" he asked.

Ketzler considered a moment. The time did not feel ripe. There was something in the air, some other doom they had not realized yet. "No sir. If we are able, we should return to camp first."

Liptieri nodded. "Are you sure this was the Kalen?"

"Mordel talked as though this was done by Averlynn, sir," he reminded him. "He spoke of a 'she' as though we both knew who he meant. And it was through the Kalen ring he was assaulted."

Liptieri folded his arms. "Let me put this plainly: whatever plan you come to me with later must include that woman—some way, somehow. I am not asking for your opinion. Is that clear?"

Ketzler straightened. "Yes sir." What did Lip think he had been talking about this whole time? Idiot.

Liptieri glanced away and waited. Ketzler turned and saw Karbae approaching. "Gentlemen," she called out. She offered her salute, which they returned. Her eyes remained fixed on Liptieri. Good girl. "Sir, we are in good shape, otherwise. Most report the same event, and suddenly waking in the morning. But aside from some stiff joints there are no injuries. A few sergeants already had their foursquads packing awaiting orders to move."

"Excellent. We'll do just that." Liptieri turned to Ketzler. "As soon as you can, get your scouts out front and get us home."

Ketzler snapped a quick salute. "Yes sir. See you back at camp."

He felt rushed, as though Liptieri had given the most emphatic order. Perhaps it was the event of the night before, perhaps it was his new captaincy. It might have even been a desire to be settled in where he could explore more of his relationship with Karbae. All good reasons. And yet none of them—even combined—equaled the buzzing in the back of his mind as he waited restlessly for the units to form up.

Finally he could wait no longer. "They'll have to catch up," he snapped. Oridin inspected him, but he set his jaw. "Start them out, normal scouting formation. No rings! And you, get as far ahead as you can and report back to me as soon as you get back to camp and see what shape it's in."

He had only enough self-control not to take the lead himself, but positioned himself in the middle of what would be their arrowhead formation. They were too far ahead and to the sides to see, but they were there. And he had no idea what was outside of them. Perhaps the rest of Kalen. Maybe Averlynn had managed somehow to rally them.

Despite his assurances to Liptieri, he wondered at the idea of being able to find the Kalen again. Without being able to risk the rings, they could simply move from one place to the next. He could chase them forever—it was a wide land, with too much forest to manage. Could they simply set up fortifications, let the settlers come and farm and raise livestock, and wait for the Kalen to move?

Perhaps, but it wouldn't replace those slain by them, both before and into the future. He needed to finish what had been started in Burieng. The Endolin had erred to let them survive. Ketzler would correct the error. Somehow.

The forests grew brighter, and warmer. He caught a brief glimpse of one of his scouts, and shifted position. He was letting himself get too distracted, to let that happen. He tried to re-focus, but all he could see was Mordel's bloody grin, and Averlynn's horse rearing as she nearly shot him with an arrow. She was the linchpin. To succeed here in the south, he needed to capture her, make an example. An extreme one. And figure out how to send that message to the Kalen everywhere. Make them think surrender was their only option. And then—how had Mordel said it? It was strangely lyrical, in a gruesome way: pop their heads like grapes.

He saw the back of another scout, startling himself out of his reverie. This one was on the opposite side, and he took half a step to readjust before he stopped, brow furrowed.

"Pawlos!" he called, heedless of how his voice carried. The scout whirled, and Ketzler saw the uncertainty in his eyes. "What are you doing?" he demanded.

Pawlos shrugged. "I don't know, sir, it's..."

Ketzler blinked, looked around. Lands that should have been familiar were strange. He couldn't tell where they were. He strode forward to find Oridin.

The scout was on one knee, leaning forward as he peered through the trees. He turned as he heard Ketzler approach, and rose. "Something's wrong, Ketz," he said quietly. "There's the tree you spotted our first day ashore." He gestured, and Ketzler stared. Except for the bole that had been Averlynn, it was indeed that strange oak. But it should have been near a cliff: now the forest stretched around them.

Ketzler went to it, placed a hand on the trunk. It felt real enough. "They couldn't cast a glamour so large, could they?"

"They cast one on their village," Oridin said.

Ketzler grunted. He could order Oridin to move forward, see if he suddenly fell off a cliff. Or Pawlos. Better if none of them did. "Come with me," he said. "Pawlos! Report to Liptieri and tell him to hold. The land has changed."

While Pawlos scampered off, Ketzler and Oridin went forward slowly. At a low branch, Ketzler wrenched it off the tree, held it backward. "Hold on to this in case I fall," he said. Oridin grasped it solemnly, and they went forward again.

There seemed to be light ahead, an end to the forest, and perhaps the sound of waves crashing. Ketzler paused, listened close. It was still faint and ahead of him. He went toward the light gingerly, feeling each step before setting his foot down. Finally he paused beside the last tree. He could see the ocean ahead and far below. He held onto the trunk and leaned out.

The forest spread across what should have been the bare valley but was now ancient oaks and vines and hanging moss. Massive, sharp rocks littered the water's edge. He looked up and down the coastline, could pick out some of the promontories and distinguishing trees he had observed when they first landed. It had been here. But their ingress was gone. Their camp was gone. It looked now like land untouched for hundreds of years.

"Oridin, would you recognize that land from out at sea?"

Oridin glanced down, and shook his head. "Not with all of that there, and not when the ships left it was bare dirt. And what happened to our camp?"

Ketzler shrugged, looking around the forest as though rows of tents might suddenly step out from behind the trees and laugh at them. "Let's report back to Litpieri for now," he said. "We'll have lots of time to figure out what to do next, I think."

When they returned, the new camp was already being erected in what clearings they could find. Ketzler set his scouts in outpost positions and went to Liptieri's tent.

"Sir, what have you been told so far?"

"Well some of it I was told, the rest I could see for myself," Lipteiri responded. "I had spent some time in the woods around our camp, and I know we should be about in the middle of it. Any sign of any of those we left behind?"

"No sir," Ketzler said. "And the forest and rocky shore has been re-formed. I don't think we can get reinforcements anymore."

Liptieri's lips set in a grim line as he stared at the map. Suddenly he roared and swept the parchment off the table. "We should have tried to make peace until we found our ancient people!" he shouted. "What kind of enemy have you made us tangle with?"

Ketzler felt his own rage erect its battlements. But rather than attack, as he had before, he felt a strange safety and calm as he bunkered behind it. "It was not me who forced this, sir, but Averlynn."

Liptieri's nostrils flared as he bellowed air. "Are you sure you want to stay with that story, Ketzler?" he said quietly.

He doesn't know as much as he pretends. Ketzler maintained his calm. "Our only chance now, Commander, is to strike our enemies faster and harder than they can imagine. We must reorganize to be swift and limber. It's only us, now, and our skill in battle."

"To what end, Captain? It's not like we're securing a new land for our people."

"Not yet, but perhaps another opportunity will come. At the least, we'll secure this land for ourselves. We *are* our people, Commander."

Liptieri ground his teeth a moment, but Ketzler could tell his anger was fading. "And where do we start, then?"

Ketzler took a breath. *One comes.* He blinked and turned toward the tent flap as there was a brief commotion outside. The flap was suddenly thrust aside, and two scouts entered with a woman held firmly between them.

Ketzler's blood thrilled for a moment until he realized it was not Averlynn. And yet, she was definitely Kalen.

"Who are you?" he demanded.

"You may call me Ravun," she said. "And you can let me go. I've come of my own free will, and have no intention of leaving."

Ketzler glanced a question at the two scouts. "She came from our trap to the south," one reported. "They brought her in just now."

"Why?" Ketzler asked.

"To take you to the Wohan—who you call the Kalen," she said calmly. "To end Averlynn's stupid war she's trying to fight."

33

KNOWING THE CORRECT COURSE

"You withdraw now?"
"Something isn't right."
"It is never right."
"We are not alone in his mind."

15 Thriman 1321 — Summer

Tavill rested, his eyes closed against a throbbing headache. It would seem Averlynn had read his letter and followed it. It was also still clear she had no idea how to handle the power.

He could only assume too, then, that the way the Cariste had come ashore was now closed. Part of him hoped she had not killed too many. A selfish part hoped he would never see them again. The more he interacted with the world, the less Taur he was becoming. That had surely not been the intent.

So he nursed his occasional headache—throat-song pains came and went for a few weeks—he hummed sometimes to himself, and smelled as much of the forest around him as he could. He would not be ready to throat-sing for some time, but he could work his fingers into the dirt, feel the roots lacing underneath, make way for the worms and grubs and beetles. He could listen to birdsong, to deer bellowing. He knew he was drawing near the Snowashes because he even heard the faint bugling of an elk. It reminded him of his cabin, when his mind would stay on positive things; it reminded him of the Prosan when his mind would not.

So far there had been no sign of anyone. A small comfort, though it also meant he had not yet found Raina. At night, when he closed his eyes, he would see her again. Never did more of the memory return—and he never remembered the other Kalen who had been there. Something about her seemed very familiar, though her features were foreign. She must have been important to his story in some way, but perhaps before the memories disappeared. All he had left was the notion she was someone he knew, and knew well.

Today's headache began to fade, and he breathed deeply. Time to move on. The air was changing—getting colder, but with autumn on the horizon that was expected. But it was a little cleaner, and little clearer. The land had been rising. Very faintly he smelled a deep cold, and pine. The Snowashes were near.

As the wind eddied, he snorted. There was more than just cold pines. Wool. And that peculiar sweat smell. He hunched, sniffed again. They were east of him. But not too close.

There was a rustling nearby, downwind. He moved himself behind one of the big oaks. Dead leaves had a way of making a chipmunk sound like a moose, but better to be cautious. He peered out, fingers exploring the rough bark while he waited.

A twig squeezed before it snapped, a little closer. So it was something bigger. He sifted through the scents, but there were still large dark areas. And whatever moved out there was in one of them.

He closed his eyes, letting the scent-image grow and become vibrant. He gauged the winds. Then he bolted, tree to tree, the rush of wind and the thudding of his hooves and heart deafening him for a time. He weaved between brilliant chestnut hues of trees, leaped an obsidian fallen log full of decay and beetles. Some of the holes filled in.

It was a person—but not Prosan? He nearly stumbled; the sweat wasn't quite right, the woolens a finer mix. How had a Cariste made it all the way down here? He had left Averlynn as they went north barely two weeks ago. He had traveled a little slower, more carefully, but for them to have turned...

Well, it wasn't a 'them' so far. A scout of some kind. One that didn't pursue him. The scent winked into darkness again as the wind changed, but the whole time he had run the figure had not moved. Surely if they had been creeping up on him, they should not have been surprised by him. Was it possible they were friendly? There was no guarantee they wanted to kill him.

Better safe. He wove between a few more trees, stopped suddenly and crouched. His capacity to run had certainly improved since leaving his cabin so long ago, and his breath came back to him in a few moments. The wind between the trees remained unsteady, and the blind spots winked in and out. But he did not see the figure again.

If the Cariste were down here, was it possible Averlynn had come with them? He wished they had some way to communicate. The throat-song would not do that for her yet. He vented a frustrated sigh, wishing he had stayed longer to teach her. He still marveled sometimes that she could do it.

He scratched his arm. He wondered if he could influence her dreams somehow. The trick with that was knowing whether or not she received it. If she was not nearby, he would be singing to the earth—not the worst thing, but might unnecessarily expose him as she would not be the only one to hear it.

Perhaps he was panicking too soon. For now he needed to find another way south. And try to scout the Prosan positions. It might not matter, if the Cariste were here...so perhaps he needed to scout their possible position as well.

Another whine slipped out: he should have just stayed with Averlynn. But it was useless to think so.

He stayed in place, letting the winds carry to him what they would, as darkness fell. Finally he set out, scenting his way carefully eastward, being especially wary of blindspots that lingered too long. A few night animals scurried here and there, and the crickets were still awake—though, this late in the year there were only the hardiest or most desperate.

Long before he found the Prosan, he found their fires. Cooking was done, but there was still warmth to give. It wasn't until then that he truly felt the chill. Autumn was arriving early even for the foothills of the

Snowashes. And the Prosan would know they wouldn't be bothered, if their bargain with the Kalen held.

He paused a while there, letting the winds eddy and fill in the blank spots. It was a large camp—he thought perhaps two thousand here, though he sensed there were more scattered across the forest. There was a difference, something nearly tangible, between a camp that was alone and one that had brothers and sisters nearby. There were a few outposts, but the Prosan stationed at them seemed equally prepared for friend as foe. The fires, too, were more likely to be banked if the entire camp was bedded down for the night. But too many communal fires still blazed.

He moved east along the perimeter, firming up its size. They were proper nomads, with broad, low tents that looked like hummocks in the woods. Even a Kalen might pass by a hundred paces away and not notice. Well, Averlynn would notice, but she was unique.

He paused behind another tree, wondering what drove her on. How she could maintain such faith when every last one of her people tried to convince her to leave things alone. It spoke on the one hand of a strong-willed tenacity, of seeing things in a true light with no regard for the lies shouted by others. It might also have spoken of an incredible arrogance to believe so firmly that what she thought was true, was. And yet he couldn't see that in her. At least, he didn't while they were together.

An eddy, another strange scent. Different—it was the Cariste again, also scouting the Prosan positions.

Tavill melded almost unconsciously into the shadows of the big fir, watching with seeing eyes and with his scent-vision. The Cariste approached an outpost warily, but intentionally. Just when he was near enough to be spotted, he called out in a low voice.

The two at the outpost stiffened, peering into the gloom cast by the fires far behind them. They responded. The Cariste came slowly forward, arms and empty hands visible. He said a few more words in the Prosan language, though Tavill could tell he had difficulty with it.

They were on full alert, now. They rattled off several lines of speech in hushed alarm, spears at the ready. Tavill inspected those spears: all wood, no iron cap or point. Strange.

The Cariste held his ground, but kept his hands out front as he struggled with a few more words. The outpost approached, spears lowered. Finally, one of the Prosan lifted his spear, searched the Cariste under the suspicious eye of his partner. He grasped at his tunic, squeezing it into bunches. The Cariste said a word; the Prosan barked in response and continued grasping. Finally he froze near the Cariste breast, dipped a hand inside the tunic and pulled out a scroll. He retreated quickly to inspect it. While the Cariste held utterly still, the Prosan opened it and read it.

Even from the distance, Tavill could see the smile quickly spread across the Prosan's face. He stilled it quickly as he continued, then eyed the Cariste. He rolled it up again, said a word casually to his partner.

In one swift thrust the spear went into the Cariste, right where the scroll had been. Tavill stiffened, testing the breeze. As the Cariste groaned and crumpled Tavill turned and ran before the blood-smell reached his hiding place. Heedless of the noise he plunged through the woods, north and east, using his scent-vision as best he could—but in headlong flight it was nearly useless. He cradled his head in he arms as he ran.

Blood pounded through his ears as branches whipped his arms and legs. One—from a pin oak it felt like—snuck through and stabbed him in the snout. Mucus ran, clogging his nostrils as the world went black now. He staggered a few more steps, tumbled, and rolled into what felt like a small hollow. He gasped, trying to fill his lungs again, to slow his breathing so he could hear.

Just as one thumping eased, he heard a new thumping—drums, from the Prosan. A few staccato beats, then a horn sounded a peculiar series of notes. His breathing slowed, and he heard an answering call echoing far on the wind. Then another from a slightly different quarter. And a fourth, further west.

He blinked tears away, rubbed his snout on his arm. He was no good to the Kalen this way. He found where a bit of branch had speared him like an oversized thorn and pulled it free. Gently, quietly, he snorted—trying to sound like a deer, if he could—clearing the snot from his nose. Another good rub, a quick snort, and faintly scent-vision came back. There was not much on it, but he felt safe where he was.

The horns ceased and a low clamor arose. A few shouts. Hissing as fires were quenched. A clatter of pots here and there. He searched deep in what memories he still had to recall the sound of an army striking camp. Four camps, probably all similar in size, packing up in the dead of night after a strange visit from a Cariste, now assassinated, his body not even chilled. Tavill was no Kalen Scout, but he wished he knew what the scroll had said.

As he lay listening and scenting, they began to move. Scouts first. And they were not heading toward him. He yearned to go after them, to learn what he could and report back to Averlynn. But he would continue to be mostly useless, if not a danger, with his bloodlust intact. And his way south was opening up, now.

As dawn began to filter through the trees the Prosan were gone. Swift and silent as a mist, their mark had been erased as though they had never been there. Tavill shivered and continued his journey toward the Snowashes.

In their shadow the next day, he had begun to notice faint sign—a bit of lichen broken off here, stems of some herbs and ramps with cleaner breaks than a foraging animal normally left. Beyond that there was a forest that bespoke an inhabitant unaccustomed to its environs.

Through breaks in the trees he could make out the peaks of the Snowashes shining in yellow sunlight, their highest tops already capped in snow. A cool wind stirred the branches, and leaves newly fallen littered the ground. He breathed the scents in deep, letting the scent-vision enhance what his eyes could faintly make out. Memories of his cabin flooded back, the simplicity, only the most basic of responsibilities. A place to retreat from a world spinning wildly out of control.

He sat, closed his eyes, saw again the Cariste soldier standing firm as he was killed. He began his throat-song. He let himself soar first, flying up to the peaks where he might see over the breadth of the Snowashes, to far Thinsledon across the dazzling snow plains. Higher into the thin blue, to the heavens themselves where he could look down and see hawks as pinpricks against the ground. Impossible heights.

But then he returned to the ground, as he had to. He burrowed deep until he struck water, searched across it as it flowed down from the mountains, down runnels and freshets and springs. He wove around roots in whirling dance, bubbled out of another spring, filtered down through gravel and rocks. He ran along the mountains westward, each new spring bringing its peculiar blend of minerals from the rocks above.

Then it dove again, down deep, and suddenly he was in the bottom of a hole where a bucket dangled. He paused there, unable to fly for he'd been too long underground. He waited until the bucket dunked then lifted, then raced back to himself.

The last rumble faded from his throat, and he looked up. Evening was coming. He *could* wait until tomorrow. No one would blame him. No one would know.

He rose, took steady strides west. Questions had gone too long unanswered. The light held for him as he went, the wind steady in his face and painting lurid pictures of the land around him. Woodsmoke came to him—cherry, he thought. Leeks, potatoes, salt, pepper, and rabbit boiled.

And otterscomb.

He stopped short, his breath caught in his throat. He whined lightly, let himself breathe in the scent of the otterscomb.

And then she was there—bent, nearly hobbling. She sat herself beside the fire and, after a few moments, cocked her head toward him. She straightened slowly as she stared.

"Well," she said. "I never..."

He walked forward slowly. "You remember me?" he rumbled. A silly question, but he couldn't think of any other.

"I have seen your face in a thousand dreams, Tavill," she said. Her voice crooned, full of her years. "I'm sorry for what I had to do to you."

He stopped short again. Her tone carried the weight of mountains, as though the words had been in her mouth for all those centuries, wanting to be said but his ears were not there to hear.

"I have lived much since then," he said.

She eyed him a moment, then turned to the fire as her hunch returned. "No you haven't," she said huskily as she stirred the soup. "No Taur lives without their *koridin*. Not truly."

Now he sat. "Removing it took my memory."

The stirring ceased, and her hand trembled. She withdrew the spoon and hurled it into the forest with a furious cry. Her hands balled into fists as she wept.

Suddenly she was at his feet, grasping at his fur, babbling words that sounded like an apology. He let her vent it all as tears leaked from his own eyes. Somehow he had known it was worse than he thought. He thought he had been the last Taur. Now it seemed they had died out long ago, and he was too stubborn to admit it.

Had this been the plan? A duty unable to be carried out? Proof of some kind that only the Harral could witness all of time? Could offer some kind of wisdom borne of ages? It seemed unfair—cruel, even, to burden an entire race with an impossible task. Condemning them to be a living failure.

Old Raina cried herself to sleep in his arms. He moved her gently onto a bed of moss, went into her hut and found a blanket and wrapped her in it. He would not sleep yet, and he was famished. He hoped she wouldn't mind. She probably would be upset if he didn't, consider herself to have failed him in even the simplest task of feeding him. So he poured a bowl and drank it slowly.

He marveled at how expertly flavored it was, but realized she had nearly as much experience as one could have. The otterscomb interwove with the rest, rising and falling on his palate like a dance. It was so easy to add too much or too little. But not in this. As he ate he felt bolstered a little. Perhaps he had not lived as he might have since that war. But then there were moments like these, small moments of beauty if he paused to enjoy them. But one had to look, had to be aware and watchful. And then not throw them away just because everything surrounding the moment was less beautiful. A flower did not care if it bloomed in a tangled wood, nor did the wood diminish the beauty of the flower. On the contrary, the flower made the wood a bit more beautiful. So could all moments of beauty if they were allowed.

He stoked the fire, kept the soup warm without burning it. He hoped she would wake soon: otterscomb could only take so much before it became too thick with cooking.

A smear of stars appeared overhead, and Raina stirred. He poured her a bowl, helped her sit up and handed it to her. She sighed as she took it, risking only a quick glance at him. He did not smile—not yet—but he tried to convey some warmth with his eyes. She bent to the soup, closed her eyes as it hit her tongue.

"You cook superbly well," he said quietly.

She stared at him as she chewed. "Thank you," she said faintly.

He let her continue eating in silence. But, eventually, the waiting was enough. "Why don't I remember anything? How am I to be a witness if that is gone?"

She stared again, startled this time. "Witness to what?" she asked.

It was his turn to stare. "I thought you knew everything about the Taur," he said.

She ate another quick bite, then set her bowl down. "I'm not sure anyone can know *everything* about the Taur except they themselves. But I pride myself some on knowing the most of anyone else."

"But you don't know about our first duty?"

She shifted. "Before I answer that, Tavill, let me ask you: how do you remember me?"

"Kragnog," he began. "I found...strange things in the ruins. Chronicles. Rooms of..." He trailed off, wrinkling his nose. "Rooms I didn't believe Taur could be in. Full of metal. And I had a memory there, of what happened to me in the Abandoned Isles. You were there. Averlynn told me to come find you to see if you could remove the bloodlust." He paused, recognizing in the fire's glow a look of complete bafflement on Raina's face. "It was you, there? You did apologize..."

"Oh I was there," she said quickly. "As were you. But everything else you're saying... What bloodlust? Why can't you be in a room full of metal?"

"I thought... Didn't all Taur have that weakness? Is that not why we were hunted down?"

Raina sat in stunned silence for long moments before finally shaking herself. "Oh, Tavill, I fear you have done more than lost your memories. Someone else has come in and filled that head with a lot of nonsense. A lot of nonsense! How on earth could you fulfill your first duty—your actual duty, not the one that's been planted in you—if you couldn't be near metal?"

"The Taur were not created to witness to the events of the world?"

"Oh Praka bless us." Raina shook her head, cradled her face in her hands a moment. Finally she looked up. "I suppose you could do that. No, that's not fair. You should do that. But—did you expect you were to sit in some gallery and watch the whole time?"

Tavill nodded dumbly. It had seemed to make perfect sense before, and he still wasn't sure why it should be questioned except that Raina took an alternative for granted.

"The stars do that, Tavill, and the trees and—why, even the Kalen do that, as much as we can. Probably more than we should," she added with a bitter edge. She shook herself again as if to chase off an unpleasant thought. "Tavill, what is wisdom?"

"Knowing the correct course," he replied.

"Isn't that what knowledge is?"

He shook his head. "Knowledge is just knowing things..." He began, he thought, to see where she was going. "Wisdom is being able to apply knowledge appropriately," he said slowly.

Raina placed a finger alongside her nose. "And wisdom always entails action of some kind. For the humans, even the wisdom of the Kalen is worth seeking, if all they want is a peculiar knowledge. Few enough even want that. Taur wisdom is for those desperate enough to seek *help.*"

Tavill sat for some time, staring into the flames rendered a bright pink by his scent-vision. He had gotten one of his answers, and the implications staggered him. He had failed his duty far more than he had realized. And only with Averlynn had he barely begun to fulfill it again. And then, in perhaps her greatest need he'd run off again—prompted by her, to be sure, but how could she know?

And yet, that duty still could not be fulfilled as he was. Back to the task, then. "When I smell blood, or iron, I go into a frenzy and kill—everything. Usually I am not aware of it until after. But one time I was aware of it. I have incredible speed—I plucked an arrow out of the air when it was shot at me. And I can grasp a helmeted head and..." He trailed off and made an emphatic fist. He drew a breath. "That is the bloodlust."

When Raina was silent, he looked over. She had a hand to her mouth as she stared at the fire. She seemed to be thinking, so he let her. Finally she looked up. "What you speak of came of the plague that swept the Isles."

"That took my memories?"

She shook her head. "No, removing the *koridin* did that. We knew it might. I desperately hoped it wouldn't. But I thought, even if it did, you would have what remained of your people to help you..." She trailed off and shook her head. "What happened to them?" she asked quietly.

"The Prosan," Tavill said quietly. "They pursued us relentlessly, here."

"Who?"

"The Prosan. They were not far from you, yesterday. Four camps of them. Though they suddenly moved north and west, I'm not sure why."

Raina shook her head, cursed, and shook it again. Tavill smelled the salt of tears in her eyes. "Where did you hear that name?" she asked, her voice thick.

"A mage who was a friend of mine, on occasion. And Averlynn confirmed it."

"Of course she did," Raina said harshly, then bit her lip. "That was also unfair. Averlynn is...well, she is unlike most of her people. I'm sure she only repeated what she had been taught as well. We do love to change the names of things, thinking that will erase the past."

"Who are they, then?"

"They are Cariste."

Tavill gaped, then shook his head. "Impossible. I saw them assassinate a Cariste who had come to their camps. I have seen them myself! They are..." *Not far different. Not their scent, nor their features.* His whole argument failed as the pieces suddenly fit together. "They *are* far removed, aren't they?"

Raina nodded somberly. "They are Cariste who had discovered the Abandoned Isles in the Third Age. They lived and thrived there until the plague. They built an incredible civilization—some of their technologies may never be recreated, not in the same way. And it was destroyed in a matter of months. They sent to Carist for aid—but when it was told that it was a plague that threatened them, Carist sealed them off. Forbade any ships to or from the Islands. They abandoned them—so their histories say. It usually neglects to mention the people they abandoned there—left to die."

"But they survived?"

"Some seemed immune to the plague. They took the last ships and sailed west. East was closed to them, so they sought a new land."

"And they found this place."

Raina nodded. "Still a miracle, since the Cariste who settled in the north couldn't find any way south."

"Until recently."

Raina shivered. "I'd heard rumblings of that. There are small clefts and coves nearer the Snowplains, but it's a wretched place to try to land a large boat. What few landed here scratched a living. They came close to extinction several times in those early generations. Finally they found their way north of the Snowashes and thrived. Until the rest of my people came here, anyway."

"The Kalen?" Nothing matched what he had been taught, and he was quickly getting used to abandoning what he thought was the truth.

Raina nodded. "We mistreated them. Badly. We had just fled one oppressive regime and didn't want to permit another. We didn't know how bad off they were, just that they were here."

"Why did they attack the Taur, then? Did we do the same to them?"

Raina rubbed her nose and sniffed. "No, Tavill, you did maybe far worse.

You were supposed to help them, in the Isles. That was the Taur duty. But as far as we know, the Taur weaponized the plague. The Cariste created it—or, found a way to distill it from native plants. It was one of the Taur who spread it—we never found out who, or why."

Tavill sat numb for more long moments. "Is there anyone in this land that the Prosan wouldn't want to destroy?"

Raina snorted appreciatively. "No, I don't think so. I'm left wondering how they'll play this war to get what they want out of it."

He was torn, suddenly, knowing all that had happened. The Prosan had a point—several—against both the Taur and the Kalen. Except both had not fully exterminated them. A fuzzy line, but drawn. And a line the Prosan did not seem to share. He had seen one of four camps, had experienced himself their murderous power. He sensed no amount of restraint in their retribution. They would have to be slowed, if not stopped.

"What I am," he began slowly. "What I could do—what I *did*. Why am I like that? Why does the scent of blood put me in a frenzy?"

Raina shook her head. "The plague had that effect, at least on the Taur. That was why we remove the *koridin*—to remove the plague. It was something we could only do to the Taur. There was no cure for the Cariste: they either contracted it and died, or they never contracted it. But Tavill, no Taur lived long after infection. Those whose *koridin* we couldn't remove died. Their bodies could not sustain the energy it took. So if you still have it..." She trailed off and shrugged. "I cannot understand it."

"What is the *koridin*?" Tavill asked. "I thought, at one time, that was the disease. But you talk about them separately."

She heaved a sigh. "I'm not sure where to begin to explain it to you. Biologically, it is a knot of tissue and fibers set roughly between your eyes. We found we could reach it through the nostrils. With the right conditions and tools—which, I believe, is what you saw in Kragnog—it can be removed with some ease. In the middle of a battle, in a hurry, in a crumbled-down building...well, it can be done, obviously." She closed her eyes as if remembering, shook herself violently and reopened her eyes to banish the vision it must have presented. "As far as what it does...it seems to facilitate some sort of extra sight, beyond what your eyes can normally see."

Tavill's ears flicked forward. "Do you mean the scent-vision?"

"I wasn't sure if you would remember it."

Tavill blinked hard. "Raina. I have it."

She stared at him. "You cannot. Surely."

He closed his eyes and breathed deeply. Colors popped into existence, the layout of the entire camp. Raina rising quietly and stealing away. He turned his head to watch her go. But soon she disappeared into a black spot. "Your scent does not reach me," he said, opening his eyes.

She came back to the fire and picked up her bowl again. "Fascinating," she said. "Not perfect, but...fascinating."

"Not perfect?" Tavill echoed.

"No, it was not entirely based on smell—or, at least, there should be no places where you can't still see me. So it was affected—"

"My normal sight was affected too, eventually. That took longer to go away."

"Hmm." She took a few more spoonfuls as she considered. "So either we didn't get the whole thing out—which I really felt we had. And we'd never had one come out piecemeal before, so we never thought it could. Or it re-grew, somehow. Hmm."

"What do we do, then?"

Old Raina blew out a long, weary sigh as she stared at her fire. "We go back to Kragnog," she said. "And study the Taur. But—" she looked up with a thin smile. "I'll need a little more rest, first."

"One more question, at least?" he said. When she nodded, he continued. "What were you doing there, so long ago? I thought your people were in Burieng."

Her eyes went distant again. "We were. Some of us traveled, though rarely. But I was there because you were there—well, not you specifically, but the Taur. I was studying you. Your people had already left Burieng by then. When I heard of a community still living..." She trailed off and shrugged. "We had to look into it."

"'We'?"

"My apprentice and I. Vera." Raina smiled again with a distant smile. "She was so bright, so eager. Clever. She found out more than I just by piecing bits together better than I did. She would have made a fine scholar."

Tavill nodded. "Until she became an Isun, instead?"

Raina gave him a puzzled look. "She didn't...no, she died in the Isles. We thought perhaps we were immune from the plague, after we had been there so long. We were wrong."

"I'm sorry," Tavill said. "I met a different Vera, then."

Raina rubbed her palms on her knees. "Tavill, one thing we Kalen pride ourselves in, as few as we are: we don't share names. There was only one Vera, and only ever will be."

Tavill stared at her. "But I met her—she's with the Kalen army, with Averlynn. She said she was Isun Vera."

"How old was she?"

"She appeared older than Averlynn, I cannot say by how much."

Raina shook her head emphatically. "I know all the Kalen from before Averlynn was born. It's impossible."

Tavill could still only stare. "Then who is with Averlynn?"

34

THE TAUR BATTLE CRY

"I suppose they must meet?"
"It cannot hurt."
"They are still far away."
"They can be brought nearer."

30 Thriman 1321 — Autumn

Averlynn leaned back, closing her eyes. She shifted as the scabbard pressed into her back. She had taken to leaving Skyalfamold on Tarafel's saddle, relying on her troops and her bow when she was dismounted. The sword was simply not sized for her, and she had finally had to accept that. Perhaps she would return it to Aver, if she saw him again. Hopefully he wouldn't laugh.

She no longer cared. Her arms and back ached, her neck was strained, and there was a pressure building behind her eyes. Faintly she could hear around her the same fatigue settling across her army.

If their march north had seemed hard, this was impossible. There was no other way to look at it. Every move they made seemed to be watched, and ambushes set up well in advance. As much as she tried to change tactics, change directions, it was as though Ketzler knew a week ahead of time where she would be and had forces ready. And they were getting boxed tighter and tighter together. She could only imagine how much longer they could hold out—like imaging how long before a stick will break as you apply more and more of your weight to it.

Even Tarafel was worn. He'd been lucky to escape their engagements with minor wounds—a scratch here or there as an arrow came uncomfortably close. This time he'd taken quite a slice from a sword. Weary as she'd been, as soon as she had been able to disengage their forces, she'd tended it. He nuzzled her, seemed equal parts thankful and dismissive of the wound. And as soon as she had finished, he curled himself up and slept.

"Averlynn?" said a quiet voice.

She didn't look up, but made a small acknowledging gesture with her hand. More of a flop, really, but it was all she had.

"It's Witko."

She cracked an eye. She could tell by his voice, of course. But without their rings many in her army had taken to announcing themselves. Awkwardly. They had over several centuries become unaccustomed to not knowing who was nearby.

"I'm worried none of those we sent north, earlier, have come back. They can't all be traitor, can they?"

She closed her eyes again and let out a quiet sigh before she spoke. "We're moving around too much, and they don't know where we are—can't know. They're as good as lost, Witko."

"So." He was quiet again until she finally, with a monumental effort, raised her head. "Well, it just means, we don't know if these ambushes continue because of one of them, or from someone still here."

She studied him, his bent posture, his folded hands wringing. He wanted to say more. Or, wanted her to say more. But what was there? Her leadership was their idea, and she was far more comfortable studying flora and fauna than tactics and commands.

He took a short breath and held it. That sign, she understood. "Speak your mind, Witko."

"We're doing no good here," he said in a rush. "So we've delayed their reinforcements. Maybe. But we're not trampling them under our feet. And...I know I brushed aside the Prosan, but I also know you did not, and yet..."

She clamped her teeth to keep from screaming. As if she didn't know! But without her people behind her, far more of them than were here, what else was there? They couldn't attack, they could barely fend off the ambushes. After several, long moments she managed to press her ire down deep again. Her voice, when she spoke, surprised even her with its calm. "I'm open to your advice, Witko. You're all the council I have left."

His voice lowered. "We are not accustomed to our rings being gone. We need somewhere we can see—far. These woods are no longer to our benefit."

She wiggled herself into a more upright position. Tarafel shifted behind her but she waved him off. Of course Witko was right. She had been so focused on being able to maneuver behind cover, to have somewhere to hide while they fought—not just her personally, but her soldiers too. It was where she felt at home.

Except she hadn't felt at home since leaving Kalen. She had derided her people's attitude of just hiding from their problems or things they feared, and here she was employing the same tactic against actual threats. "The Hataki," she said. "They might be able to see further, but so can we."

"And, once we've gotten used to it, we might be able to maneuver north, start using the Brynth. If we can learn its warrens."

She tilted her head back and forth. "I'm not sure it's as warren-like as would be best, but..." She took a breath to think. "We'll see if we can rest at least a little. If I need it, Witko," she said quickly as he drew a breath, "the rest need it even more—I've been able to ride, at least sometimes. Before dawn we run west for the Hataki. And, Witko—" she paused again, then nodded her head firmly "—take everyone's rings from them for this maneuver. If anyone resists too much, we'll blind them and leave them for whatever finds them first. Make sure they know, from me."

A spark came to his eyes as he nodded. "If nothing else, it will get some people's attention," he said with a grin.

As he moved off Averlynn shook her head and leaned back against Tarafel. What an army they had become. Perhaps if they had not bargained away their security, felt safer trusting in the land or their payments than in Praka or Hakana...

She chewed her lip, remembering her words with Vera what seemed ages ago now. And her more recent reticence to relying on the old gods of the Kalen. Could they be so easily abandoned? Should they? So much of what they did, the celebrations and observances, bound the Kalen together far more than shared blood or experience. And yet factions still moved in.

Kalen like her were ostracized if they could not be brought back under control. There were still dissensions, perhaps under the surface but no less alive—or active. Amrith's face flashed across her mind and she scowled. He was one who decided on action. She wondered if anyone approved of what he did, if he had told anyone. Perhaps he had even been ordered to do what he did by the Intag or the Chiefs.

She closed her eyes again. None of it mattered—not pragmatically. Her faith in the Chiefs had been shaken far before her faith in Hakana. Perhaps one had led to the other, even. But she didn't miss Vera less, or her parents.

A tear escaped her eye as she finally drifted off to sleep.

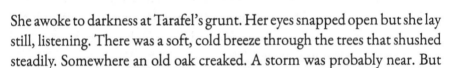

She awoke to darkness at Tarafel's grunt. Her eyes snapped open but she lay still, listening. There was a soft, cold breeze through the trees that shushed steadily. Somewhere an old oak creaked. A storm was probably near. But that's not what woke Tarafel.

She turned her head slowly. His head was up, ears pricked forward. She followed his gaze, but between a waning moon and the foliage the darkness was nearly complete. She realized Witko had set up his bedding near her, but he lay silently.

Tarafel's head ducked as though he had been mistaken, then snapped back up as a thin whicker bubbled in his throat. Averlynn continued to stare: he would not do that if there were danger.

Suddenly she whistled a call, nearly sitting upright but deciding to wait. The response came, and a figure appeared in the darkness. Averlynn was on her feet, running into the embrace.

"Vera!" she whispered. Then she backed quickly away. "Are you okay? Where are the others?"

Vera gave a thin smile. "It is good to be welcomed so. I'm fine, but I'm afraid I'm the only one I know of." She shook her head. "They knew, as they always know. I cannot understand it."

"Ouwa?" Averlynn said faintly.

Vera shook her head. "I cannot know. They appeared out of nowhere, and we scattered. He urged me to come find you, as I was furthest west. But I neither saw him fall nor escape. But if anyone could..." She trailed off, wavering slightly on her feet. "It's been a long journey," she said wearily. She flashed a faint smile. "You hide well."

Averlynn caught her as she fell, lowered her to the ground. She pulled a flask from her saddlebags near Tarafel, wet a cloth, and pressed it to Vera's forehead. Vera stirred faintly but still slept. She would probably need it. Averlynn sat back on her heels, rubbing her jaw. This might hinder their morning escape. If they were unlucky, the Cariste would attack while they camped another day. The needed a respite.

Averlynn moved to Witko, shook him gently awake. "Can you bring me Jutek, Kehwynn, and Antath please," she said. "Vera has returned but she needs rest. As do we all."

"What's the plan?" he asked as he rose.

"I'll explain it to you all when you come back," she said.

After he moved off, she went back to Vera. The Isun was wan, almost frail. Averlynn checked her over just to be sure there were no wounds the Isun neglected to mention. Aside from a bruise on her side she appeared fine. Averlynn continued to check.

She gasped. Vera still had on her ring. Why would she risk that? Or was she the traitor? Had she already led the Cariste here? Averlynn knelt and tugged, wrenching frantically as the ring stuck on a knuckle.

Vera muttered, then woke suddenly, grasping Averlynn's arm with a cry as the ring slipped off. Averlynn fell backward, scrabbling until her back banged into a tree. Tarafel leapt to his feet, snorting.

A glamour had fallen, and in Vera's place sat a Taur. Averlynn barely registered that such a glamour should be impossible. Forefront, instead, was that it was not Tavill.

Her mouth worked, but no question came out. They sat and stared at each other for long moments, until finally Witko returned with the three Trackers Averlynn had requested.

"Ah, Tavill, you're back!" Witko said, approaching from behind. The Taur's chest still heaved as it panted. When Witko came closer, his stride broke. "You're not Tavill." The Trackers tensed, just short of pulling bows and arrows.

"Who are you?" Averlynn said, a little out of breath herself.

The Taur sat a while longer, blinking. "I'm sorry," it said. Though still a rumble, it didn't grind like rocks as Tavill's did. "I've been Isun Vera so long... Zusamin was my name. I like Vera better—"

"How long have you been like this? Where is Vera?" Averlynn demanded.

"Averlynn... I'm so sorry. You never knew Vera. The one you knew as Isun Vera was always me."

Averlynn's eyes went wide, and her breath came short again. "But you've...you mentored me for..."

Zusamin nodded. "I know. I've become quite fond of your people, your culture." She shook her head. "It will be hard to distinguish myself again."

Averlynn looked hard at her. "Tavill thinks he's the only Taur left."

Zusamin's eyes glistened. "And since Stavnuk fell, so did I. I didn't know about Tavill until he showed up."

"And you didn't say anything?"

Zusamin shrugged, palms up. "He had changed so, still seemed sick. And I thought maybe it would be better if still no one knew there was one more. Then there might always be one of us."

"But where did you come from?" Averlynn asked.

Witko answered. "The Abandoned Isles," he said slowly.

Zusamin looked at him and nodded. "I knew your real Vera while she was there. I had become something of her pupil, as much as I was her subject. She studied me and my people, and I studied her and yours. When she died during the plague that broke out, there, I...stole the opportunity to become one of you."

"How did you hide for so long, though?"

"Your Old Raina was the only one who knew Vera had died, and she was a recluse. I stayed out of her way whenever I could, figured as a mere Isun my name wouldn't travel too much. I thought I would have been caught long ago, to be truthful."

"Vera was a good choice," Witko said drily. "Few remembered her before she hared off to the Abandoned Isles with Raina. When you came back, it was easy to assume you'd found religion, especially with the stories coming from the Isles. Now I realize I don't think I remember what Vera looked like, actually."

"But how did you make yourself smaller? Glamours shouldn't do that."

Zusamin shifted uncomfortably. "Oh. Well, they don't. For that, I admit I've been a bit... I came across some spells while we were investigating the blighted cities. I was able to cast one of them first—of Shape—then use the ring for the glamour."

Averlynn regarded her for a moment. "Couldn't we use that—?"

But Zusamin was already shaking her head. "Shape magic is forbidden...I—I was desperate. I shouldn't have, but..." She looked imploringly at Averlynn, as though for forgiveness but it was not Averlynn's to grant.

Averlynn took a breath. "Well, you've probably been alerting the Cariste to our location this whole time, so—"

Zusamin waved a hand. "Not for a while now. Not since you used the throat-song to attack the Cariste."

Something in the way the Taur regarded her caused Averlynn to duck her head. "Was it wrong to do that?"

Zusamin hesitated. "Yes, it was," she said. "But...Tavill instructed you to do it, I suppose."

Averlynn toyed with Vera's ring. "Well, sort of," she said. When Zusamin straightened she continued hurriedly. "He didn't tell me to what extent to use it, just to cause a distraction with it. I was desperate too, you know. They had to be distracted for so long..."

Zusamin relaxed. "Yes, I know. Perhaps we both need to stop using each other's magic to such ends."

Averlynn nodded. "But you say the Cariste aren't wearing the rings?"

"I've sensed none of them since that night. I don't know why."

"That could still be helpful," Averlynn mused. "At the very least, we don't need to fear them anymore. Well, since you are all here, we can at least for now move forward with breaking free of the forest."

"What did you plan?" Witko asked. The Trackers behind him had relaxed, and now paid her all their attention.

"I was going to use the throat-song to feel out where the Cariste are. Is it okay if I do that?"

"As long as you sense only," Zusamin said, but not harshly.

"It can do that?" Witko asked.

"Some, at least for me. Enough if they are in larger groups. Unless Vera...Zusamin can use it better...?"

"I could," Zusamin said carefully. "It's been a long time since I've done it... Perhaps we could both sing, and help each other as we need it."

Averlynn hesitated. "I've never done that before...or, when I did, Tavill and I collided..."

"I was there," Zusamin said with a lopsided grin. "But that was an accident. I should be skilled enough still to avoid crashing into you, and

I deem you are as well."

Witko glanced between them. "So what do we do, then?"

Averlynn glanced around the group. "We'll feel out where they are, and then send three groups as feints to different sections while the main body threads whatever gap we can find. I know this land well enough to draw a map for everyone."

"That, I can help with too," Zusamin said, sitting forward. She brushed aside the leafmold and placed her hands palms-down against the dirt. The Kalen watched curiously.

Zusamin began to hum, and Averlynn immediately felt a charge moving through her. It was as different to Tavill's throat-song as Averlynn's was. Zusamin's buzzed a little higher, with the overtone a little lower, and wove in tighter circles. It thrilled in Averlynn's chest and she was nearly overcome with a desire to join in.

But then she saw the dirt under Zusamin's hands begin to shift and knew her song would destroy what the Taur created. Averlynn bent forward in fascination as she molded the humus into a perfect relief of the surrounding terrain. Averlynn could identify every ridge and valley and knob.

Now the buzzing deepened and Averlynn recognized a searching song. Now she did join in, gingerly. She bumped Zusamin no harder than nudging elbows, then followed her around the landscape. Occasionally she would feel herself dive too deep, and Zusamin would reach down and pull her up. Other times they drifted apart and she could feel Zusamin stop and wait while Averlynn got her song under control.

Then suddenly she felt her physical hand pulled over and down, and placed on a portion of the relief Zusamin had created. She hesitated, her sense spinning in circles for a time. Then she felt Zusamin shaping the song and followed suit.

The Cariste positions began to surface, and in her body she could feel the dirt moving under her hand. She was distracted a moment, felt the sense slipping. Then it was Zusamin gripping her tight so she wouldn't drift. She fought to overcome her awe at this feeling, of being in her body but also far away, of singing this incredible song. When she finally mastered it she zipped around the forest, brushing past Cariste with the touch of butterfly wings. There were many, and they were not as spread out as she hoped. Still she went on until she neared Zusamin's side of the circle. She tapped her elbow, then, and raced back to her body.

Averlynn's song stopped a few moments before Zusamin's did, and she lifted her hand to see the completed work. It was fascinating: every Cariste stood like a tiny banner pole, tipped in yellow clay against the dark humus.

Zusamin took her hand away and they inspected the completed work. "Here," Averlynn said immediately, pointing to where a smaller group had gathered.

"Probably here," Zusamin said, a thick finger pointing to a smaller spot. "They'll expect a knowing enemy to hit where they're weakest. They'll wonder how you knew, and worry."

"And then here," Averlynn said, pointing to the largest grouping. "Maybe they'll think the other attacks are the feints, and that is the main assault."

"And where do we escape?" Witko asked quietly. The ring of soldiers seemed nearly complete.

"Here," Averlynn and Zusamin said in unison, then smiled at each other. "They're tired," Averlynn explained. "They were the ambush we survived yesterday, and they haven't slept well. Attack your positions with swords, too, so we hear the sound of battle. Once we're through, I'll send a small contingent to attack the larger group from the rear. When you hear Tarafel, disengage and make for the hole we'll have created. Oh, and I think we can wear these again." She held out the bag of rings Witko had gathered. Witko received it, quickly withdrawing his own and slipping it on. She watched him carefully, but he soon shook his head.

"I sense no others."

"Good. Begin when you're ready."

Everyone nodded and moved off. Averlynn held Vera's ring toward Zusamin. "Perhaps you should wear this until we get through their lines—I don't want special attention brought to you."

Zusamin looked at it a moment. "This might be strange, but...I promised myself once I took it off I would never put it on again. I suppose I imagined my situation would have changed enough by then that I wouldn't have to. And yet..."

"You're ready to be Zusamin again?"

The Taur's dark eyes snapped to hers and glistened. She nodded mutely. Averlynn smiled and pocketed the ring. "Will Tavill recognize you when he sees you?" she asked suddenly as they gathered their few things.

Zusamin looked troubled. "I don't know what he remembers or doesn't.

Before the plague struck him, we were near bonding..." She faltered, sighed, and looked up. She forced a grin. "I can imagine he'll be overjoyed that another Taur still lives, regardless."

Averlynn nodded. She couldn't imagine. Even on long patrols, on long nights in winter when she had not seen another Kalen for weeks, perhaps over a month, she still knew they were there. Even in societal exile, she had her remnant. And, though they had banished her, she had not banished them—still protected them, whether they knew it or were grateful.

She slipped her ring on, felt the senses of those around her, some growing faint as they moved to follow her orders. She closed her eyes, wanting to whisper a prayer but only allowing herself to think good thoughts, as much of a cry for help as she could muster, regardless of where it went. Maybe it went nowhere. She knew that some of those she sensed now, their threads beginning to break by distance, she would never sense again. Their ring might come back. More than likely Ketzler would take it. Maybe to be used by the Cariste if they ever realized she would not use those threads to kill again. Maybe to be destroyed if they feared them so much. She thought—prayed, if she could—it would not be too many.

She opened her eyes, looked at Zusamin who studied her. Mere hours ago she prayed for Vera to come back. Then it seemed Vera was actually gone—had never been there. And yet it had still been Zusamin, hadn't it? What might she think about all this? Why had she started to change her words, her direction, away from Praka and Hakana toward the God of the Cariste? For a brief, gutting moment Averlynn wondered if she was still the traitor. She had only Zusamin's word, and her faith that the Taur were who the legends said they were. Who Tavill and now Zusamin said they were.

The last of the threads disappeared. Moments later, the sounds of sword on sword drifted under the canopy. Too late now.

She leapt onto Tarafel, spared the barest glance for Zusamin, and broke into a canter. "Follow me!" she shouted—unnecessarily, for the rest of her band had already gathered and followed swift behind her. Zusamin outpaced them all, falling in beside Averlynn's stirrup. Over the thudding of Tarafel's hooves, over the rushing of wind, she heard the beginnings of a Taur song, what could only have been a battle song—the cadence and thrum of it permitted no other possibility. And the hope that soared in Averlynn's chest matched it—hope, and determination. She found herself humming the chant, finding the melody if not the power.

They broke upon the Cariste line as most of their enemy still stumbled blearily with weapons wagging uncertainly. With a shout their pitiful and minuscule tide pierced a breach, beat soldiers back, killed some. But their task was to break through, not destroy, and so they pressed on. One Kalen fell to an arrow in the back; most missiles went high or wide. They were through.

With a command, the Kalen fell silent, ghosting through the woods minus Tarafel's hooves. They knew how to run lightly, and if she closed her eyes Averlynn felt alone with Tarafel. Even Zusamin seemed to know how to move her vast height and solid bulk like a mist.

Down into the valley and over the next ridge they moved, hardly breaking stride. With quick hand signals, she hurried them onward while she circled back to pull their diversions back. As she went, Zusamin went with her. For a moment she thought to urge her on, but knew the Taur did not make the decision lightly. So they rode on, Averlynn intent on her ring for the first glimmer of another Kalen.

As soon as she felt it, she slapped Tarafel's neck. He reared and whinnied mightily, his voice echoing like thunder through the woods. Zusamin made fists and roared. Leaves fluttered around them and branches quivered. Tarafel came back to the ground, hooves slightly splayed. Averlynn, too fell onto his neck and gripped as the Taur battle cry seemed to shake the very rocks.

Averlynn stared in wonder as Zusamin's eyes sparked with life. There was a joy in her countenance unhindered by the fur on her face. How long had she hidden as Vera, now free?

Threads laced to her, line after line of Kalen filling her sense through her ring, growing thick fast. Another roar from Zusamin, not as long but every bit as powerful, and they turned back to meet with the Kalen ahead of them. They still needed to escape to the Hataki.

Satisfied that her people followed, Averlynn galloped ahead. She would be the link between the two parties, drawing them toward each other. Able to use their rings, able to see the Cariste if they followed, and now with Zusamin with them, hope flamed to life again. And if the Cariste did not follow, they would train and try again. They had to. By dint of their combined power they had sealed off the ocean approach the Cariste had used before. If they could hold the Northern Cariste off, maybe the incursion would fail. Maybe Ketzler's band would seek terms of peace rather than destroy themselves.

The rest of the day was spent in flight, and by nightfall they were returning to lands so familiar they continued into the dark and the cold. Averlynn knew the Cariste had not pursued too closely, not after the otherworldly bellow Zusamin had let loose. She considered stopping, of entering the Hataki tomorrow. But even her people pressed on—not that salvation necessarily lay in the bare and brown hills, but more to prove that they were not a beaten people. That they chose to run, and ran with full control and disciplined pace, not pell-mell in fear. And so they loped on under a dim moon, under a failing canopy of leaves, until the trees beside them fell entirely away.

As though on command, though Averlynn gave none, they stopped under the bright stars. No one panted. No one rushed. They stood, faces lifted, basked under the open skies. There was no cloud above, no shadows beneath. A silvery glint lay across the land. Finally, when the silence had been allowed to spread as long as it needed, Averlynn gave the quiet order to make camp. They would wait now to see if the Cariste followed them.

Averlynn awoke to birds chirping, a faint stirring of wind through the grasses, and low murmuring conversation. Zusamin lay outside, across the door to her small tent. No one could disturb her without going through the Taur first—and, as yet, no one would. They held Zusamin in too much awe to try.

The sun was not yet above the forest edge, though the sky was bright. Averlynn knelt, gripped Zusamin's shoulder briefly to wake her. The Taur blinked and rose as though fully awake. Maybe she had been. She looked at Averlynn, brought a thick finger up gently to smooth a part of Averlynn's hair, and smiled.

"You slept well," she said. It shook Averlynn to hear so much of Vera in Zusamin's voice. She wondered if she would ever grow used to it. But then Zusamin's face grew serious. "No, really, you slept well. Go back in and make yourself look like a leader before you come out again."

Averlynn glanced down. If her rumpled coat looked anything like the rest of her—she ducked back inside. She was a leader. Everyone saw her as one. It would not do to be rumpled.

She emerged feeling better, more awake anyway. Zusamin was standing and holding a crust of bread and a bowl. She looked Averlynn appraisingly up and down, and handed over the breakfast—dried grains and fruits in goat's-milk, wherever they had found that.

"Are you my aide, then?" she asked playfully as she took the food.

"Yes," Zusamin said plainly. "As I was before."

Averlynn paused to chew and swallow. She could think of no one better. "Thank you." She looked out over the army—they were barely a unit, at this point, but it was what she had. "Anything need my attention?"

"Eat first," Zusamin replied. "But, yes."

The Taur waited patiently as Averlynn scarfed the food, impervious to Averlynn's demands of what was going on. Finally she fell silent and only ate. She slurped the last of the milk and held the bowl toward Zusamin. "Now: what is it?"

Zusamin turned slightly, gesturing Averlynn to walk ahead. "Our northern outpost seems to have seen something."

"That seems rather important, Ver—Zusamin," Averlynn said in exasperation as she strode along.

The Taur bent to hand the bowl to someone washing up, barely breaking stride to keep up with Averlynn. "It is not so near as that, and they were instructed to report immediately if the issue became pressing."

Averlynn slowed. A little. "Oh."

They reached the outpost and Averlynn gripped the Tracker's shoulder. "What is it?" she asked.

He pointed across the hills. "There," he said. "A strange mound that wasn't there before."

She looked, and grew still. Aryndurlan's mound. She glanced at Zusamin, then at the Tracker. They had picked him up in Kenkek, so he didn't know. "Yes, we know, it's—"

"Look closer," Zusamin rumbled.

Averlynn turned and bent her gaze on it. Suddenly her eyes widened. Someone was there, kneeling by the rock—two people. She blinked. They were utterly still, and yet one hung a little further back as though more a visitor than the other.

"Who do you think it is?" Averlynn asked.

"We could go find out," Zusamin said.

"Right. Sure. Um..." Averlynn turned, spotted two more Trackers who weren't engaged. "You two, bring your weapons and come with us."

They made their way across the field. The two with bows held them low, unthreatening. Something about these two ahead did not speak of the Cariste. Something about the way the nearer one knelt at the rock made Averlynn recognize some familiarity, though she couldn't figure out why.

The one further back spotted them first, rose with some alarm. Her hand went to her side—they were near enough now Averlynn could tell male from female—though she drew no weapon. The one nearer the rock turned his head, rose more uncertainly. Was it a cloak he wore against the cold? It lay funny, Averlynn thought. Definitely not Cariste, though.

They paused, just out of bow range. "Who are you?" Averlynn asked.

The two only looked, though maybe some communication passed between them. The one in the cloak called back—Averlynn barely recognized the Rinc Nain words.

"Did he say his name? Or was that something else?" she whispered to Zusamin.

"He is behamian," Zusamin said, breathless in awe. "His name is Deuel."

35

HE THEIR BADER CAPTAIN

"He becomes hesitant."
"He will find his way."
"With your help, no doubt."
"No. He's been on this path long enough to find his own way, now."

10 Halmfurtung 1321 — Autumn

Ketzler stood just inside the tree-line, gazing across the brown, scrubby hills outside their first victory. Karbae was beside him, a respectful distance—always when they were working—waiting his command. Which she did on and off duty. Unless she was more ornery than usual. Now that he was her captain, she had lost much of that. Just enough that he enjoyed the break, and enjoyed it more when she fell into a mood. At the moment, he appreciated her silence.

Averlynn was out there. And the beast he had seen with her, or so he had been told. He wasn't worried about that, yet. The report was unreliable at best, possibly untrue, most likely exaggerated, and definitely irrelevant. Averlynn, though—that report was far more interesting, and verified. He knew she was the key—not some horned beast of myth. If it were a minotaur, it mattered little whether it was alive or dead. The Kalen would not stand or fold for a minotaur. They would likely fold if Averlynn was taken.

Every Scout knew that was his mission—and, thus, their mission. The only one of importance who didn't know was Liptieri. His command was eroding, though. After the botched attempt at pushing Averlynn into a trap—a full third of the army sitting on its heels while she remade their ingress was the height of embarrassment, and the beginnings of incompetence, in Ketzler's mind—and after haranguing about some mythical creature barely spotted twice, the whispers had begun. Then their envoy to the Prosan grew weeks late, presumed dead, and probably killed after alerting the Prosan to the Cariste presence and location, and a few whispers had grown louder. Now that the army was split as one group went with Ravun to meet with the Kalen chiefs, and Ketzler's went after Averlynn, most of the talk was that their expedition south from their homeland was in shambles. And Ketzler agreed.

But there was yet a chance. Liptieri was gone, and couldn't bungle the job with his interference. Averlynn was out there. He had his best scouts with him. Once Mordel had gone he had his pick of fighters and trackers, and built what was to him the most stunning fighting unit since he had joined. Pike had let too much slide—including, he remembered with an ironic smile, his 'forbidden' relationship with Karbae. If Pike had truly wanted an elite fighting force, she should have stopped that instantly. Ketzler allowed no such laxness in his unit now. Karbae was in her place, and was comfortable. Anything he didn't like in his soldiers, or didn't want, he eradicated without question or protest. And the men and women loved him for it. For how much it might hurt sometimes, they knew they were honed to that much finer an edge.

All he needed to do now was take Averlynn's head to Liptieri's 'negotiations' with the Kalen and throw it on their bargaining table, along with the promise to do so to any others who opposed the Cariste expansion. Their chiefs would do what was necessary, at that point.

But he had to find her. She came here for a reason. Maybe it was more comfortable to her. Or more familiar. There were not many places to hide—maybe some little folds in the ground. Was that the point? Draw them out where they could see them more easily?

A smile curled his lips, bent into a sneer. So pitiful. Well, if she wanted to see them, then see them she would. At least, some of them.

"I wonder how many of us she thinks there are?" he wondered aloud.

"Depends on whether she knows the rest of the army went with Ravun,"

Karbae said. "If she doesn't, no amount of us will make her think she's seeing all of us."

Ketzler raised a brow appreciatively. "Very true. How do we use that?"

"Sometimes using brute honesty is the best tactic," she said.

He eyed her. Did she mean more than she said? But she looked at him squarely, without shifting eyes. Perhaps she didn't have a devious bone in her body.

I think she has many...

"If she thinks we would only show part of us, she'll hold some back, or at least keep a wary eye behind her," Ketzler said.

Karbae nodded. "She'll never be fully committed. And with speed we can overwhelm her before she realizes she's wrong."

"But we need to know where they are."

Karbae swayed her hips a fraction, smiling when his eyes darted. "First things first, my love," she murmured. Then, louder: "Where would you hide?"

Ketzler let his eyes linger an appreciative moment longer before turning back to the brown rugged hills. Where indeed. Flat as it was, there were many places. South, if he recalled, were marshes. She wouldn't want to flounder in there. North were the backs of the Brynth. He paused again as he recalled how long ago he had seen someone poking their head over the top of a cliff. A lifetime ago, it felt sometimes. In the Brynth, if she knew this side well, the Kalen could hide almost interminably. They would want that stronghold where they could get to it. And before that, they would want to see their attackers coming—wasn't that the whole reason for being here?

His eyes scanned and swept back. The rocks could just be rocks, or they could be Kalen wearing their rings again. Or the rocks could be real and could hide them without rings.

He drew a breath. Sometimes strategy could go in circles. Those who would win eventually stopped drawing them and attacked. And there was one easy, if risky, way to know.

"We move north first," he said. "I want to cut them off from the Brynth so they cannot hide there. Then I slip on a ring to see if I can sense where they are and shoot an arrow—no, my love, it must be," he interjected, cutting her off as her mouth opened in protest. "It needs only be a moment, just enough to sense them. She will not be expecting it, or able to kill me so quickly as that. When you see the arrow, everyone press the attack as swift as you can. Do not let up! I'll join you when I can." He turned again with a lascivious half-grin. "And perhaps we can celebrate our victory."

She blushed slightly, only murmuring again, if a little huskier, "first things first, my love." She turned and moved back to their camp with more than a slight sway to her hips this time.

Ketzler turned back. The only way this would fail is if he could not sense them from here. And yet he was sure they were using the rings again. Such coordination to escape their trap could only happen if they knew where their comrades were. Somehow, some way, for some reason, they wore their rings again. Perhaps not after today.

As he waited, he wondered. How had they rebuilt the forest? He had heard of such magic used by many Cariste, but that scale should have been impossible—or so he thought. Why else wouldn't the Cariste have used such magic to make a way into the interior to begin with, after all? Was there some other way of achieving such a thing? He wished Liptieri had brought at least one mage with them, forget the Prosan—especially if they rejected the Cariste envoy anyway! As he thought: a terrible risk. But too far past that anyway.

Perhaps the Kalen could also somehow give something tangible to their glamours? Nothing Averlynn had mentioned before indicated such. And Ravun had few answers. Perhaps it was something new to her, as well.

Ketzler still worried about that one. It seemed terribly convenient, at a terribly inconvenient time, for Ravun to show up supposedly offering the Kalen on a platter. Of course he had raised his concerns—remember the last meeting with the Kalen, sir? And how that turned out, sir?—but Liptieri had dismissed them. He was a coward. He was scared, and didn't have the mind to grasp the type of campaign Ketzler envisioned. So let the fool walk into the trap. If he was killed, so much the better.

That left the remainder of Ketzler's questions, though, and more kept piling in. Every last one a question that he needed a Kalen to answer—ideally more than one, for Ravun couldn't be trusted. Perhaps Averlynn couldn't be trusted either—her capture would be more symbolic, though useful in its own right as well. And the beast that traveled with her. Supposedly. And when he was done with Averlynn, she would be useful again in pieces.

A brief glint caught the corner of his eye: Karbae signaling they were in position. He took a breath, pulled the ring from its pouch, and slipped it on.

Senses flared up, dangerously close. No time to take the ring off, he nocked and arrow and shot into the next fold. To his surprise and delight one of the senses winked off.

Then, to his horror, the beast arose from a fold he had not spotted and roared, almost close enough for him to count the teeth in its mouth. He nocked another arrow and loosed, but it went just wide.

He heard his own army roar, and though they were dozens the sound paled in comparison. He had sent them too far away. He took one steadying breath and nocked again.

This one went wide as well, as a dark shape suddenly shot skyward and he jerked his eyes to follow it. He had never seen such a creature—was it something unique to this land as well?

As he watched it twisted, turned, and hurtled earthward again. Wings opened and it shrieked, banking toward him with the speed of a hawk. A very large hawk.

Ketzler ducked into the trees, trying to keep his eye on this new creature. Fire shot from it and splashed against a nearby trunk, close enough he thought his eyebrows might be singed. A dragon of some kind? If so it was tiny.

He heard the rushing of wind, peered out long enough to see the thing turn along the wood-line. It was human except for the broad wings, and Ketzler caught a quick glimpse of strange weapons in its hands. The tip of one pointed, and suddenly lightning crackled toward him. He did not have time to duck, and the bolt splintered the tree he hid behind. With a shout he fell to the ground, pain searing his left eye.

He heard another shriek—more like a scream this time—thought he recognized Karbae's voice in it. He growled and pushed himself to his feet. He raised a hand tentatively to his eye and wiped away blood. Gritting his teeth he forced himself to probe his eye.

It was mush. He cupped the empty socket with his hand and knelt, trying not to be sick. Perhaps it seemed worse than it was. He would have to wait until his soldiers returned to him.

He raised his good eye, peered out onto the plain. His forces were now completely engaged, most fighting with swords, some hand-to-hand. He clenched his fist and growled, unable to help. Most of the slain he could see were Kalen, but there were enough Cariste to enrage him further. He forced himself to stand, to ignore his ruined eye, pick up his bow again.

Someone else was shouting commands, someone besides Averlynn. He wished anew for his other eye as what he observed appeared to be a Rinc Nain woman, well protected by Kalen, gesturing north-westward as she shouted. The Kalen line shifted just as Cariste topped the rise that direction and ran head-first into the shift.

Ketzler growled again, glancing skyward. The flying man was circling now, observing. Was he somehow able to communicate with the Rinc Nain woman to direct their defense?

Karbae appeared suddenly near him, shouting something. Her eyes were wet! Of all the times! "Kill that Rinc Nain!" he shouted at her, pointing. "Or capture her at the least, but be actually useful!"

Karbae pulled up short, staring at him. He growled, and sighed. "First things first, my love," he said, barely throttling the rage he felt. It was not, after all, directed at her. She stared only a moment longer, then quickly nodded and turned back to the battle.

To his horror and amazement Karbae bolted directly for the Rinc Nain. Apparently the Kalen were amazed as well, and two fell before they realized she was not pretending. But by then she was among them, her swordplay dazzling even Ketzler—and he was not even her target.

The Rinc Nain pulled a small sword out and fought back at first, but Karbae seemed almost superhuman as she fought. Suddenly she backhanded with her sword, knocking the Rinc Nain on her head. She crumpled bonelessly.

The flying man was beside them, swords out and teeth bared. With a bit of his own superhuman effort, Ketzler drew another arrow and loosed. The pain in his eye radiated through his skull as his blood hammered through his veins, but the arrow still struck in the man's leg. Karbae leapt forward as he staggered, striking both blades from the flying man's wrists—they were attached somehow by a cuff—and pressing the point of her blade to his throat.

If his eye did not pain him so greatly, Ketzler might have taken Karbae right then. He had never seen her fight so brilliantly, move so fluidly or strongly. And she had captured two enemies almost single-handedly!

All they needed was Averlynn...but as he surveyed the battlefield he saw there would be no capture. She was with the rest of her troops, and that beast, and retreating southward. His army, he could tell, was wearied.

"Karbae, call them back," he said hoarsely, waving his bow toward their troops.

Without taking the sword from the flying man's neck she bawled the orders. Ketzler sat down and waited for their doctor—gods help them if he had been killed. The darkness in his left eye spread across his right, and he fall backward with a thump.

He awoke slowly, the sounds around him coming as though water and the light through a veil. Some pain still thumped through his skull, but it had dulled. He blinked, raised his hand to his left eye. He probed the stiff cloth there. He felt no wetness of blood.

"Ketzler?"

He looked over, saw the doctor—Movrus—sitting on a stump someone had brought into the tent. "Is it still there?" he asked.

"No. Whatever hit you had taken it before I got there."

Ketzler glanced up at the roof of the tent and sighed. "And the troops?"

Movrus shifted. "Ten killed, half wounded. We may lose one of those."

"Who?"

"Janiver."

Ketzler nodded. He would get the full roster later. Not bad, considering. "And the prisoners?"

"I don't know about those," he said.

Ketzler turned swiftly, closed his eye briefly against the pain. "One of them is wounded, too."

"Your second refused to let me look at him."

Ketzler growled and rotated himself to his feet.

"Sir, I cannot recommend that..."

Movrus trailed off as Ketzler glared with his good eye. He hoped it wasn't twitching as the room spun. He took a breath to steady it, and himself. "I will take most of your advice, doctor," he said. "But I still have an army to command."

"I assumed that's what your lieutenant was for."

"And yet she hasn't performed quite as I hoped, at least in this instance.

Do what you must to attend to the wounded prisoner, please, short of losing your life."

"Then perhaps you should come with me. By the way, there might be more drainage, but don't be alarmed. And don't scratch it if it itches."

Ketzler looked at him steadily and rose to his feet. "Anything else?"

"I'll still be taking care of you for a while. I'll see if infection sets in. Don't let water sit in it. And stay out of the rain."

"Really?"

Movrus nodded as he held open the tent flap. "I've seen it happen before. Healing just fine, thought he needed to ride out in a drizzle. He didn't come back, and when we found him his socket was rotted out." He shrugged. "Maybe it was just his time."

"I don't like the rain that much anyway," Ketzler muttered as he walked outside.

They had set up camp inside the trees again, though the brightness of the plains still shone through the trunks. He could tell the perimeter was set, and there was the sightly-reduced bustle of a camp set up and preparing to stay for a time. He would address that later.

"Come with me," Movrus said, moving northward through the camp. Near the edge they had built two hasty cages of stout branches, and six guards watched—four looking outward and two inward.

Ketzler paused with Movrus outside the circle of guards and observed the prisoners. The dark man with the wings seemed none the worse for wear. He had removed the arrow himself, it seemed, and had a piece of torn cloth wrapped tightly around the wound. He had been stripped to his underclothes, and his wings sat at odd angles off his back. Not broken, it didn't seem, but perhaps he was unused to having them exposed as they were.

Ketzler ignored him for now and turned to the woman. She had been permitted some dignity, at least, though she still wore barely enough against the approaching winter. Her eyes were still bright, and showed no harm except a bruise and lump near her hairline. She wiped gently near the edge of the wound as though cleaning it. There was a restrained wildness to her, he thought. And—not an arrogance, but a confidence that worried him. And because it worried him, he hated her.

"Who are you?" he demanded.

They both stared blankly at him. Well, they tried; but in the man there was a flicker of understanding. And Ketzler's head throbbed.

"Lastar, she's useless to us," he said casually. "Please kill her."

"No!" the man shouted, lunging forward and gripping the bars. "I speak. I can speak to her."

Ketzler waved Lastar off, appreciating the look of worry that clouded the woman's face as he turned to the winged man. "Who are you?"

"I am Deuel; she is Catie. We were seeing my brother."

"How did you get here?"

Deuel ruffled his wings.

"You flew over the mountains? From where?"

"Not all at once. We came from Andelen."

Ketzler raised an eyebrow. "Just to visit your brother?"

"I longed to see him."

"Why are you helping the Kalen?"

Deuel settled back and glowered. "They are an ancient people."

"So are the Cariste."

"But you do not belong here."

Ketzler smirked. "We 'belong' wherever we can find, wherever we can go and make ours."

"They were here first."

"But not originally, yes? They came into this land just as we did. If anything we arrived first, but had been limited to the north. Yes?" Deuel's glowering silence answered him. "Well, we're not limited now. We will not be limited except by force. If this land belongs to them, then they can fight to keep it."

"And I can fight to help them."

Ketzler chuckled. "Well, that was true until this afternoon."

The woman said something in Rinc Nain, and Ketzler glanced at her.

"She wants to know what you will do with us," Deuel said.

"That depends on what use you are to me," Ketzler replied. Deuel didn't respond. "Can you think of any? Because I assume you will want to eat, at the very least. And we must distract some of our army to watch you," he continued, gesturing to the six guards. "So whatever it is, it must be highly valuable and worth the risk, and the expense."

"I think that is your problem. I don't know what you want."

Ketzler sighed. "Yes you do, and my head hurts. So let's do this: I'm going to move your friend here—and whatever else she is to you—to the other side of the camp. Just so you get used to the idea of her not being around. And you have until nightfall before she is executed. If you don't offer me something before then." He gestured to the four guards, who inserted poles into brackets and lifted her cage.

"Deuel," she called as they moved her off. But he only gazed at her. Except Ketzler could swear there was more in that glance—a whole conversation, perhaps—and she seemed to settle into the swaying of the cage.

He turned back. "If you'll permit him, the doctor here will take better care of your wound. If you harm him, your friend dies and you will sit with her rotting body until you die too. If you cannot think of a use for yourself, your friend dies and you will sit with her rotting body until you die too. If I suspect you two are somehow communicating, she dies and...well." He smiled coldly and briefly, appreciating the grimace that flashed across the man's face in confirmation. Ketzler turned. "Doctor?"

He moved off, intending to go back to his tent. Except he had been in the doctor's tent and not his own. One of the guards—Pentus—came up beside him quietly. "We set you up over there," he said, pointing.

"Thank you," Ketzler said. "Get a few more to replace those who are watching the girl—Catie. I want to see his weapons, too."

Pentus shook his head. "He threw them, sir, and the Kalen recovered them before we could get them."

Ketzler managed not to growl. Another missed opportunity. "Send Karbae to me, please."

"Sir, um, I believe she's already in your tent."

Ketzler pressed gingerly on the patch over his eye. The empty socket throbbed. "Thank you," he repeated, moving slowly off.

When he reached his tent, the guard outside was gazing a little too resolutely forward, and Ketzler suppressed another growl. He stopped directly in front of the guard, staring up at him with his one good eye. "How long has she been in there?" he asked.

"Most of the afternoon, sir."

"Did she tell you anything?"

"No sir."

"Well at least that."

Behind his throbbing eye, a thin light went through his mind. Command changed you, he decided. He was prepared for it as much as he could be, but a mere month or two ago he would have hummed with excitement at the prospect of Karbae alone in his tent and no one around to tell him no. Now he warred with the idea that she had abandoned all of her duties for an entire afternoon to await him.

And yet, he had been promising her for the better part of several days. She might not wait much longer. He could restrain his anger, and ignore his socket, for a few moments at least.

He went in carefully, closing the tent flap quickly behind him. She lay on the cot, turned her head to look at him. "Are the first things done?" she asked. By her tone, it seemed she expected him to say no. Perhaps she even expected the anger that he was quelling as best he could. But that could wait.

"The earlier ones, yes," he said gruffly. Her eyes widened momentarily, until he smiled. "Now there is a new one."

She squirmed deeper into the blankets with a giggle and cast him her most mischievous look he had yet seen.

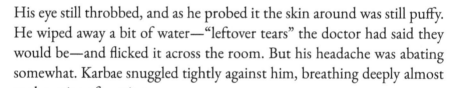

His eye still throbbed, and as he probed it the skin around was still puffy. He wiped away a bit of water—"leftover tears" the doctor had said they would be—and flicked it across the room. But his headache was abating somewhat. Karbae snuggled tightly against him, breathing deeply almost to the point of purring.

"My love?" he whispered.

"Hmm?" That was a purr.

"Am I a good Captain?"

She tilted her head and kissed his neck below his ear. "The best," she murmured.

"Why?"

She paused, shifted, began to twirl his chest hair with her fingers. "You're serious."

He waited.

"Ketzler, the scouts love you. I love you. They would obey you if you told them to cast themselves over a cliff."

"That sounds more like a charlatan," Ketzler said, rubbing his good eye. "So I've fooled them, deluded them."

"No, not like that." She shook her head against his arm, gave his chest a quick kiss. "They would do it because they know that even if you ordered something like that, the God would bless whatever plan you had to make it succeed."

"The God." Ketzler had not even thought much about him in some months. "What has the God to do with this?"

She shrugged her free shoulder. "Doesn't he?" When Ketzler remained silent she continued. "Do you know what the scouts call you? Around their fires at night, and when they see you maybe far off directing an attack, they call you their Bader Captain. They know you stand between the God and them, mediating, guiding their fates—and certainly far better than Liptieri ever did. Or Pike." She said the second name quietly and went still.

Or Pike.

The Cariste could spread out once more—thousands and thousands of lives spared from torment by men willing to walk the thread of fire, of blood—men willing to spill blood and risk their own.

Echoing from what felt his distant past he remembered those early thoughts in that tiny cathedral. Well, he had walked the thread—continued to walk it. Along the way he had found many who walked it for the same reason he did. Many of those now served him. Some—like Pike, like Curani—were simpler-minded, could not grasp what it took to save their own people.

Could Karbae? His headache pulsed again with the memory of what he had done to ensure the war between Cariste and Kalen. He wanted to tell her—tell someone. Would she still love him?

"What about you?" he said.

"What about me?" she asked, tracing a finger along his cheek.

"Do you call me 'Bader Captain'? Would you throw yourself off a cliff if I ordered it?"

"Mmm, yes to the second part," she said, then gave him a playful flick. "And you know what I call you."

He smirked. Of course, there was that. And yet... "What about in front of the scouts?" he said.

Her hand splayed across his chest as she levered herself up to look into his eye. Her hair cascaded down around his face and she quickly swept it to one side. "You are our Captain, Ketzler. The one who will save us and our people."

"And yet this morning you nearly defied me."

She looked away, but he could see the tears brimming in her eyes. He longed to reach out and draw her back, and yet this must be done. For the sake of their people.

"I thought you had died," she said hoarsely.

"I will one day, most likely."

A tear dripped. "It was worse than that. I saw you standing, but thought you might die if I left you. I can't do that, Ketzler. I can't come back from a defeat—or worse, a victory!—and find out you were killed."

"Karbae," he said gently. He cupped her face and turned her back to him. "Our lives are not ours to direct. But for what it's worth, I don't believe this campaign ends in my death."

"Everyone believes that," Karbae retorted.

Ketzler let his hand drop, shaking his head minutely. "No, this is more than that. When I set out on this path, back in the cathedral in Kloss, whatever it was directing me to abandon the white thread and take up the red assured me my blood would not be spilled."

Karbae studied his face a moment, but he could tell she took special note of his eye.

"Technically, I caught that blood in my hand," he said.

She rolled her eyes and flicked him a little harder this time.

"The important thing is that I need to know if you trust me, if you would obey my command even if I order you away while surrounded by our enemies. That no matter what action I take—or have taken—you know it is for the best. No matter how it might affect you. Or how...evil it may seem at the moment." He said the last part quietly, desperately.

She lowered herself against him again, but kept her gaze on his eye. "I do, Ketzler. At first I found you interesting. Something to have fun with. I thought because you had been a Pip...well, I enjoyed watching you get flustered. I guess it made me feel good that... I mean, most men seemed put off that I thought I could be a scout. So any reaction I could get... But it became more than a game. More than just fun. Because eventually I saw that you were not a Pip. You were a captain. And yes, I trust you fully."

He bent his head and kissed her. "Thank you." Then, after a sigh: "A Kalen arrow took Captain Pike, but I allowed it. Or, I took no action to stop it. It might not have helped if I had, but still."

Karbae looked away, then lay her head on his chest. "I understand."

"And I killed Curani. He came while I was at the first meeting with Averlynn. He was not supposed to be there. He might have made peace, if I allowed him, and I know there can be no peace if Cariste and Kalen try to live side-by-side. So when Averlynn left, I killed him."

Her fingers twined his chest hairs again. "I know."

He glanced down. "You do?"

She nodded against his chest. "I told him you had gone off. I knew what he had planned. And I knew you wouldn't agree. I guess I didn't know for certain what you would do, but I thought I saw it in you that you might."

"Then why did you send him?"

"Because by then, you were already my captain."

Ketzler wrapped her in his arms and kissed the top of her head.

36

A Bit of Elderstone

"It is no shame to admit defeat."
"Defeat depends on when you end the story."
"What next, then?"
"Let me write just one last page."

16 Halmfurtung 1321 — Autumn

Tavill sat back with a frustrated sigh, a lamp above him flickering in the breeze. His eyes hurt from so much close reading, and it had gotten them nowhere. Averlynn was still on her own, or near enough, and he had no idea how that war was going.

He'd been able to do some throat-singing in the evenings, which had helped. There was so much more to Kragnog than he'd explored the first time. Some of it, Raina remembered. Other parts he had found during the song. But for now the room with all the books interested them most.

Raina sat in an opposite corner. It had been a long journey from her cabin in the woods to Kragnog, and for the first day they had sat together for long stretches. He was amazed she could do it at all. Averlynn had been right: though Raina could not compare to Tavill's age, by Kalen standards she was ancient. By the second day she had found her strength, it seemed, and their rests became less frequent. Even now she sat with a posture exuding a vitality that amazed him. At least, when he bothered to notice. Too often he only sat with hurting eyes and mounting frustration.

Raina had gotten used to his sighs and stopped looking up when he expelled them. He worried, from time to time, that she was fascinated simply by all the knowledge there to obtain, whether or not it was relevant to his bloodlust.

"Are you sure that what we seek isn't in there?" he asked, not for the first time. By now it had become something of a joke, at least for him. A dark bit of humor. But one he couldn't avoid.

"No, it is perhaps in here," Raina said, looking up from her book—the first time in a long time she had looked at him to respond to his jokes. And for a moment he only stared.

"What do you mean?"

"Here is our problem: we know the plague attacked your *koridin*. We know we removed your *koridin* and it affected your memories. We know, without the *koridin*, you should not still have the scent-vision—and yet you have it. So something of the *koridin* must remain. And, more than likely, the plague is still in it and still causing your bloodlust."

"You said it had never come out piecemeal before."

Raina shrugged. "There is always a first time."

"How do we find out?"

"I will have to look for it."

"Will that hurt?"

"Immensely."

Tavill hunched. "As bad as the first time?"

Raina's eyes glittered as she watched him. "At least."

Tavill scratched his nose. The pain would fade again, at least the memory of it. And if the bloodlust was gone... "What about my memories? Will I lose all of those again?"

"It's very possible."

Tavill growled. "And I thought you said what you did, no Taur truly lives after that is done."

Raina sighed. "Maybe I was being a little dramatic. So much of what makes the Taur the Taur is tied up in it though. But if you're ever to help Averlynn, ever to affect change in the world again, I'm afraid sacrifice must be made. Or at least risked."

"Easy for you to say," Tavill said bitterly. He couldn't imagine losing his memories again—everything he knew now wiped out *again*. Blank slate. Maybe he could sit here in Kragnog for a few decades and read everything. Put it back as dry, historical fact. No emotions or senses attached. He would maybe remember the fact of his cabin in the mountains, but he wouldn't remember the bright cold mornings with fresh snow blanketing the plain, the winds gusting fitfully through the pines, the curl of smoke from the chimney, the little mice that tried to make homes in his storeroom. All the trees and plants and rocks and dirt and lichen from here to his cabin where he had sunk his fingers or sung the throat song. All the tension and strivings of Averlynn and the Kalen, of spending days with her and trying to study her as best he could—not just what she said and did but what drove her and what held her back. It would be like meeting her anew—would he still be a help? Or was he abandoning his duty once again for his own sake?

"Are we sure the throat-song doesn't hinder the bloodlust? Help stamp it down? If I lose everything again, I won't be able to help any more than if the lust is still there."

"Are you sure about that?"

Tavill's shoulders drooped. "Perhaps at least I won't want to."

Raina closed the book. "Thank you for being honest, at least. The choice is, of course, yours. It always will be. Whether you help Averlynn or not, whether you remember or not, whether you are as perfectly Taur as you can be or not—if it means ridding yourself of a plague, of an evil set in you by someone else that turns you into the anathema of what the Taur were meant to be... Tavill, what are you truly sacrificing? What are you giving up compared to what you are gaining?"

"But the throat-song—"

"The throat-song is of the earth, Tavill. It distracts you well enough for a time with its near-supernatural experiences. It gives you control that others do not have, an insight into the world that others do not, perhaps even a...an intimacy that benefits you and molds your character and nature in a way almost no others have access to. But it will not get rid of the plague. It masks it only. By cutting out that part of you—"

"It grew back before, though."

Raina snapped her book shut. "Very well. That is a fair point, actually, and well made. I can investigate that first, if it would make you feel better."

Tavill blinked. "Y-you can?"

"Of course. But it still means going to the room that you now detest."

"How do we do that?"

Raina set her book down and picked up another. She leafed through it, then backtracked. "Here. If you trust me to make a tisane to render you unconscious, I can do some probing to see how much is left and perhaps if it has grown back or was merely missed. Do you?"

"Yes."

She pursed her lips. "You are very certain."

"I trust you to be a Kalen of your word," he said. "Not that your word is always infallible." He grunted. "I trust what you say, but not that you necessarily know what you are saying."

"Well, I'll try to take that as a compliment," she said drily.

"I meant it as the truth, not necessarily as a compliment."

She set the book on the table beside her and stood. "That makes it better, then." She waved a hand. "Meditate if you will, I'll be right back."

He watched her shuffle by, then closed his eyes. He searched his memories while he waited, thrummed a little to himself in case it might help. He went back to the scenes in the Isles, trying to remember everyone there. If the other Kalen had been Vera, then the one he met with Averlynn was far different. The problem was he still could not recall her as being Vera in the Isles. Something else was wrong.

Without realizing it, his thrum deepened to a proper throat-song and he instinctively bent his tongue for the over-tone. As it echoed around the chamber, though, it soared in volume. He cringed, lowering his voice, let it meander through the room like a cloud of mist, taking shape and filling what corners it chose to. When it brushed the wall it paused, almost felt as if it ran hands along the surface. Then, almost playfully, it reached as though through water and splashed.

Tavill's eyes snapped open, seeing the ripples along the field as it settled back into place. He got up and went to it, placed his own hand on it. It was as firm as ever.

"What happened?" Raina asked.

Tavill whirled, startled. "The throat-song. It can reach through the wall, through the barrier."

"Oh," Raina said, glancing down at the tea she had brewed. "I suppose you want to ransack all those tomes before we get down to business? If you can."

"Shouldn't we?"

She set down the cup beside Tavill's chair and re-took residence in her own. "Well, the plague happened *after* the Rivening, and those were all written *before* it. But, by all means, put off the inevitable for as long as you can."

Tavill glanced back at the spines of books, the hordes of knowledge calling to him. And yet, she was right. No matter the outcome of what he had to do next, the tomes would be there. He went back to his seat and lowered himself into it. He clasped his hands a moment as he studied the steaming liquid. When he picked up the cup, he saw Raina watching him patiently. He raised the cup in salute and drained it.

He blinked, and Raina was still in her seat, looking pensively at the floor now. There was a tool in her hand that she drummed absently on her leg.

"What is that?" he asked.

She stopped drumming, studying the instrument a moment before tossing it across the room. "I wonder, Tavill, how you ended up with Elderstone in your blood."

Tavill shook his head. "I don't...what is Elderstone?"

"A regenerative, apparently. I've never come across enough to do so, it is incredibly rare. Though according to this it didn't use to be. Well, it was still rare, but the Taur were rumored to have some quantities."

"Why would they have it? What did they do with it?"

Raina shook her head. "I don't know. Perhaps that will be in those books." She waved toward the barrier. "But there were hints in this one—" she held up another she had been reading perhaps a day or two ago. "It's how I knew what I was looking at. That, and the fact your *koridin* is almost completely regrown. And still infected."

"But, how..."

"That's what I want to know."

"What did Elderstone look like? I've been to every Taur ruin in the past few months, maybe I found some by accident."

"Perhaps like gold, though yellower. Because it was difficult to find, and to mine, it was often in flakes—"

"Amber flakes?"

"Yes, I suppose you could call them that. You did find some? Where?"

Tavill's gaze went distant. Could it have been? But then, why? "You say it was a regenerative. Would it restore my eyesight?"

"I said it apparently was one, because it otherwise shouldn't be in your blood and your *koridin* shouldn't otherwise have regrown. But, given those factors, I would say yes. But I thought you couldn't see."

"Well, my sight would get worse after I took it out."

"Took what out?"

"A piercing, given to me by a...friend." *I think.* "He said it would restore my vision, and it blocked my scent so the smell of iron couldn't affect me."

Raina turned to face him squarely. "Who is 'he'?"

"A mage, Lasserain," Tavill said. When Raina blanched he sank back. "What?"

"This piercing...that's what made the hole in your nose?" she asked hoarsely.

Tavill nodded, dread already creeping up his spine. "He was not a friend, was he."

Raina gazed at him, her eyes glistening. "No."

"The piercing had Elderstone, enough to restore my infected *koridin*, temporarily improve my eyesight, but that was it."

She nodded. "I assume so."

"Why?"

Raina considered a moment. "I have heard only second-hand tales of the devastation the mage Lasserain wreaked on Burieng. He seemed intent on starting wars. Perhaps he wanted to use you to stir up the Prosan again. Which..." she looked grimly at him. "He has done."

"The camps around your cabin."

She nodded. "Yes. Granted, don't take it too personally: they have been chafing under the Kalen yoke for some years now. You were perhaps the trigger. And, set loose and wandering around all of Gintanos..."

"I might instigate wars between the Kalen, the Cariste, and the Prosan." Tavil buried his eyes behind his hands.

"Curious, though. Lasserain was supposed to have died in Burieng almost a year ago. When did he give you the piercing?"

Tavill shook his head and let his hands fall. "I had not kept track of days for some time. When the autumns were running late."

"Might it have been after Halmfurtung? Maybe. Interesting. Strange times." Raina picked at her lip, then finally shrugged. "Well. Would you like to go about removing your *koridin* then?"

Tavill's gaze was on the sealed books. So much knowledge, so much history. So much that even when he was younger, people wanted to know, sought desperately to know. All right there. Mysteries of millennia could be solved. *Strange times* she said. Time again for another Rivening, perhaps. Could the world handle it? Societies, cultures? Could there be another upheaval and reset? He sighed. From deep in this ancient ruin, his vision was far too limited for that. It felt like it, but he truly had no idea how other countries fared. Perhaps Gintanos was the only one. Still. It might be fun to write everything down he could, seal it off with the rest of these, for whatever eventuality arose.

Keep delaying the inevitable for as long as you would like.

"If it goes badly, could you please find Averlynn and tell her how sorry I am?"

Raina's head came up. Her eyes were glistening again.

"Tell her I did truly want to help. I would have offered as much wisdom as I could, taken part as much as I could—provided I was not a danger to her or her...your people. Would you tell her that?"

"Of course," Raina said. "I must do that, if nothing else."

Tavill nodded. "What do you need me to do?"

"Drink that next tisane," Raina said. Tavill looked down, surprised to see another cup on the table beside him, full now but not steaming. "I'm sorry it's cold," she continued. "I didn't know exactly how strong to make the last one..."

"What will this one do?" he asked.

Raina took a steadying breath. "It should relax your muscles enough that you won't kill me when I try to take out your *koridin*."

Tavill's hand went limp as the impact of her words hit him. "Raina, what is the danger to you?"

"Oh, considerable, I guess," she said. "I'm not as young as I once was, and I don't have two other Taur to hold you down like I did. And given the strength and speed you claimed to possess at the scent of metal..."

"But—"

"We must risk it, Tavill," she said, her jaw firm now. "I see no other way."

The sealed books flitted through his mind, but didn't stay. He lifted the cup and drank it down. Or tried to. He coughed once or twice at the taste. Some of it came back up, but he swallowed again quickly. Raina looked at him ruefully.

"Sorry about that. I thought it worse to forewarn you. Come with me, quickly."

They got up and he followed her out of the room and into the cavern. They made their way quickly around the lake. Tavill's steps slowed a moment as he realized what room she was taking him to, but when his knee buckled slightly he hurried on.

"Be good ifthese tis-tisane's weren't so shtrong," he mumbled.

Raina ignored him, bustling him through the door and onto the strange, cold table. Scents wafted over him, maybe a strain or two through him that nagged but nothing stayed. His nose twitched involuntarily, and belatedly he felt a pinch around his wrist. He tried to lift his head but couldn't. There was a tightening around his ankles, then his knees, around his waist, his chest, his forehead. Then he felt something like large blocks slam into the sides of his head.

"Sorry," Raina said. She was above him, then. "I'm afraid I must do this." She reached down and yanked a bit of hair from his snout. Though pain blossomed through him, he couldn't make himself move.

"And for this, I'm even more sorry," she said quickly. Another tool was in her hands resembling long narrow pincers, in the same shiny steel as so much of the rest of the room. He closed his eyes, tried to tell his mind to relax. And, for an instant, he thought it worked.

Suddenly it felt as though a great iron spike was driven through his head, top to bottom; then a rope tied onto its middle and pulled toward the tip of his nose. Waves of pain and nausea radiated through his skull. Surely his brain must be liquifying as the spike pulled through it. Bones separated before it and found their way irregularly back together behind it. The sinews of his shoulders strained and tore; his waist bucked up and down and tendons ripped free of their joints as his muscles leapt suddenly into action.

He screamed and roared, deafening himself. He thought he heard glass shattering and rocks tumbling, his voice bringing the mountain down around their ears. His jaw unhinged and flapped before the depth of his cry.

Great hammers went to work next, rhythmic as they thudded against the inside of his nose and pulverized his cartilage until it was limp as torn flesh. Great pulses of pain like flashing lights throbbed, slower and slower, until finally with one great gasp it was over.

His body went entirely limp against the table. Every joint shrieked with pain remembered, every breath hurt as though his ribs had all fractured, and he sobbed as the sharp ache in his snout slowly, slowly ebbed away.

A hand laid on his arm, cool to the touch. He reached his mind for it, tried to spread that calm to the rest of his body. That coolness rippled languidly like a slow tide, lapping against the fire in his joints. His breathing slowed, deepened, as the pain diffused. He lifted a hand, realized the restraint dangled from his wrist, and wiped his face. "Are you okay?" he croaked.

"Aside from a little deafness," Raina murmured.

He cracked open his eyes, observed her wan face. "I didn't..." His tongue was thick, his throat raw. He lifted his free hand and waggled it.

Raina stared at it as if trying to comprehend it. Her shoulders sagged as she drew a breath and turned away. "No," she said. "We were done." Another breath with a broken sob at the end. "I'm so sorry Tavill."

He lay quietly, listening to her whimpers, listening to his own breath swirl into and out of his lungs. With each draw, the pain lessened and receded deeper into memory. As the stillness grew, he thought he heard the splashing of the underground river. And something smelled wrong, but he couldn't place it. "Is there still some in there?" he asked quietly.

Raina turned back suddenly, eyes red-rimmed. "Oh, no, not that. Just...watching you go through that twice—being the one to do it, even. Oh it's a terrible thing. But it's all gone this time. I was able to check to make sure."

"So, then..."

Her hand was on his arm again. "We'll find out in time. For now, at least, I'm heartened by the fact you're not going berserk surrounded by all this metal."

He glanced wildly around, each gleaming surface and edge nearly blinding him. And yet, they were sights only. It was what smelled wrong—he had not smelled deeply of metal since...

The Isles. Flashes came to him of armed Taur, massive soldiers on the lines, roaring defiance at row upon row of troops across a rolling plain. Behind were more of the same troops—the same peoples. Some Kalen mixed in, but...Cariste. Cariste to the rear, Cariste in front of them. But something else was wrong with the Cariste behind them. They seemed...frenzied, in a way, though more the way a child gains sudden energy as evening falls. It was an energy borne of desperation, of staggering weariness that had to be overcome.

"They were sick," Tavill said. The import staggered him—both of what the rest of the story was, and that he remembered it. Not as dry facts he had read in a book, but the memory was his own. It had been a cold day with a bleak sun overhead. The wind carried scents of juniper. He was afraid, but also enraged. "We hadn't abandoned the sick Cariste, but the healthy ones. The healthy ones who wanted to destroy those with the plague."

Raina was blinking at him. It seemed she did not know this part.

"Weren't you there?" he asked.

"But they weren't...they had no signs of plague, or at least weren't separated by it..."

"They were. It was not a plague that confined you to bed. It did affect both of us the same—the Cariste and the Taur."

"Tavill," Raina said wearily. "I was there. I treated many of them. They had fevers, boils, aches, exhaustion. Thousands of them. Nearly all of them."

"Then who did we fight with?"

Raina looked up and away. "No one, Tavill! The Taur were on their own, I swear to you. Well, with some few of us Kalen, but all the Cariste on the Isles were opposed to you—and you, to them."

Tavill searched her face intently but saw no deceit. He sighed, closed his eyes, went back in his memory. He was there, with a whole troop, swords and axes and massive bows, bronze armor...

Bronze? That would have been... He thought back further on that day. They were in a town, not a large one, intently eating breakfast, fueling for the anticipated battle. They knew thousands awaited them outside, knew their hope of surviving were slim—so slim, after years and years of fighting. He squeezed his eyes tighter. The plague was sudden. This war had run on...

His eyes snapped open. The war in Cariste. He was not remembering the Isles, but even further back—decades further back, when Cariste went to war with each other over the expeditions to Rinc Na.

"They're back," he whispered. Raina cocked her head, but his eyes were shut again. Long before The Abandoned Isles he was somewhere else...

Another set of Islands. Tropical—it was so hot and muggy. The Clana-soes, except the locals called it Okaden...

In Burieng, when there were only Endol and the Kalen were barely a tribe...

Andelen and the Beltraths—well, so they were called now. Before colonization they called themselves Yngit—The Ones. Nomads even back then...

So far back, years and years and countless lives of others. How far back? He had not heard of Burieng, for none lived there: the Endol first called it Turfiril, referring mostly to the mountains where they lived, a name that lived on in Dubril. The Kalen had not yet been made. The Kesten lived in the north. And the Werine had not yet fled from Andelen...

There were so few people in the world, nomads at best except for one ragged group collected in a remote village in Cariste. If there had been maps it might have barely registered as a dot on it. Garmegil. Meaningless, filthy, infested, unimportant—except that from there would come wizards...

Further back he tried to delve...

Except his memories ended in a thin veil like a high waterfall plunging from the depths of time to that point. He could not pass through, or see, or even hear. And yet there was a knowledge there, and his people were still strong. But somber. Such a great sadness weighed on them in those days! Not guilt, it was nothing they caused or could have prevented. And therein lay the remorse—all they could do was watch. Their intervention had ended, or paused at least for a time, as was commanded them.

Tavill's eyes bolted open again and he sat up. His other hand was free, and he undid the rest of the restraints. "Come with me," he said, fairly leaping off the table. Raina, silent but bewildered, followed as he returned with swift strides to the room with the books. He stopped and gazed at the barrier between him and the books, those ancient, impossible tomes, those answers to thousands of years of mystery. He felt himself begin to sweat. Surely not he...surely this was not the time, after so long.

He scratched his jaw with trembling fingers as he took a breath. Absently he gestured Raina to sit as he took his own chair, closed his eyes, and began to thrum.

It came so quickly it nearly startled him out of the song. The thrum and whistle braided and twined and shot through the veil. He reined it back just in time, managed to just brush one of the books. He felt something like power surge from it, a brief shock only before a warm embrace. Through the song he tentatively reached forward, opened a book, and traced the pages.

It had been written in ridged ink, so he could feel the letters as though he traced over them with a finger. And yet he could lay the song across entire pages at once. And the words and the memories flooded off the pages, rending the veil of water in his mind that had separated him from the Taur's life before the Rivening.

After what seemed only a few pages the song died in his throat, the memories and knowledge nearly knocking him unconscious. He reeled in his chair, tipped it over backward as he crashed onto the floor. Breaths came in gasps. He glanced over, saw Raina watching him calmly.

"It's a lot, isn't it," she said.

All he could do was nod, bury his eyes in his elbow as he slowly caught his breath. Suddenly he looked at her again. "You knew about this?"

"Ah, Tavill, for one so old you have so much to learn." She tisked, shaking her head. She held up her ringed finger and touched the band. "Oh, it doesn't matter I guess," she said suddenly, dropping her hands as her form changed into that of Lasserain. "I thought about putting a show on for you," he continued, standing from the chair and walking over to the veil. He shrugged. "But it probably would have only raised too many questions."

Tavill leapt to his feet, glancing around for a weapon or something. But then... "I thought Raina said...I thought..."

"Oh I know, old friend," Lasserain said over his shoulder. "I have been in your thoughts for a long, long time. Such a gold mine! I don't know why I waste my time anywhere else. Well, I suppose duties call. But very, very rewarding, I must say."

"Are you dead?"

Lasserain turned and gave a dramatic bow. "Extremely. At least from this world. What you see is an image only."

"Then...how..." Tavill's hand went to his nose that still ached with re-membered pain.

"Ah. Well. You were becoming quite useless to me, with all your inten-tions of ridding yourself of the bloodlust. But I suppose it had to be done. And no, I cannot do anything physically—just make you think I am. So don't thank me for removing your *koridin*." Lasserain's smile broadened. "That was all you."

Tavill stared, remembered the dangling restraint. "My free hand..."

Lasserain closed his eyes and nodded. "I just had to make you think I tightened a restraint, then a little guidance toward the implement, a little guidance toward your nose..." He stuck his finger in his mouth and then pried it out with a *pop!* "Everything you lost comes back. Well, I hoped so, anyway. And I was right."

"But...why? Why do you use me—"

"Oh don't get the wrong idea, Tavill. I use everybody. Absolutely everybody. Nothing personal for or against you. I used you, I've been using that...what's his name in the Cariste army—well, several of them, actually. Amazing how many will listen to me, I was honestly impressed. For seeming to be so devoted to the God of All, they are a massively corrupt lot. Well, almost everyone is, doesn't matter what beliefs they claim. Then I've got a few very good friends in the Islands, one absolutely delicious slave in the Pal Isans, a batch in Rinc Na..."

"Why? What have you become?"

Lasserain gazed at him silently for long moments. "Not 'have become,' old friend; 'am becoming.' And you will not recognize it when I get there. Much like you didn't even recognize Old Raina to not really be Old Raina."

"When?" But even as he asked it, he knew: her sudden renewed energy on the second day. Lasserain had been with him since then. Raina, then... He gritted his teeth. "What have you done to her?"

Lasserain waved him off. "Oh, very little. She'll realize where she is soon enough. And wonder, of course, why she's there. But she'll be perfectly safe. And you are as well, for now. I got what I needed." He turned as if to leave, then turned back. "Oh, if you could, would you mind stirring up the Kalen a little more? I'm worried they aren't taking the Cariste threat quite seriously enough. We need more..." He made circular motions with his hands. "War. Chaos. Distrust, at the least. Things like that. I would appreciate it."

Tavill growled as he stepped forward, fists clenched, but Lasserain disappeared in a blink. Tavill stared at the books on the other side of the veil, saw the one tipped on its side and opened. The lure to read it was gone—not if Lasserain could be in his mind at any time and steal the information in those books. Powerful a mage as he might have been, and whatever he was now, he did not seem able on his own to crack them and read them. So Tavill would not give him that satisfaction.

What was it Lasserain wanted, then? Why, when he couldn't use Tavill to fan the flames of war, did he seek his knowledge instead—reversing entirely his course of action up to that point?

Tavill sighed. His head still hurt. But the bloodlust was gone. He would rest for now, then try to find Averlynn. She would still need his help, need his wisdom—and perhaps the knowledge that an evil mage desired this war she was fighting.

37

THE GATHERING OF SCOUTS

"Illmali wants you."
"I assumed."
"He seemed displeased."
"He has been displeased since he was cast out."

20 Halmfurtung 1321 — Autumn

H e had her this time.

He had been long laying his plans. Long sending out scouts, using the rings for brief moments to verify. He had arranged his troops just so. Karbae was with him, double-checking his logic from a woman's perspective—it was a failing of Liptieri to view the Kalen too separately from the Cariste, and to distrust women unless he had seen specific evidence to trust them.

Ketzler didn't care who he used, just as long as they were useful. Now, in the morning, Averlynn would be his.

Yet he paced his tent. Karbae had fallen asleep, one bare leg sprawled from beneath the blankets. He only occasionally allowed himself to be distracted by it. Well, mostly he wouldn't be distracted if a herd of elk trampled through his tent. So perhaps he reminded himself to be distracted by it from time to time, to make sure he didn't overlook her beauty for too long. She was one he would not merely use. Could not merely use. He knew her quality, that if he reduced their relationship to utility she would leave, perhaps without slitting his throat. No, he wanted her close and wanted her loved. And he did, as best he could.

But right now the plan took precedence. He went over it again—who would be on the line, and who would be the pushers. He recalled again their frequent, small engagements over the previous week, how the Kalen reacted, where they moved to break off. The beast was indeed with them, and was not to be touched. It towered over his most formidable soldiers—he didn't have many, they were supposed to be fast and light scouts, not berserkers. And it was well acquainted with and...eager, he felt, to use its axe. Ketzler still wasn't sure where it had gotten it from.

No matter. The beast was not entirely his concern. He didn't want to capture that thing. He wanted Averlynn.

And he knew the key. Each time they engaged, there was a battle on the Kalen side to protect Averlynn without entirely protecting her. Even Liptieri, if he had been there, would have realized she was important to them. Well, maybe he would have. With minimal help. Ketzler wondered briefly how the negotiations were going. Well, if his luck was still against him. He refrained from rubbing the temple by his empty socket. Plans.

Early in the attack, she would be near the front, fighting with everyone else. As they disengaged, she would be hustled toward the rear, behind a screen of archers and swordsmen. And that's when he would get her.

Well, not him—he was forced now to watch from afar. Turned out, he was important to his scouts just as Averlynn was important to hers. But now with his eyepatch he was relegated to plans and tactics only. He wasn't entirely upset about that—despite the kills to his name, he had never been very good at front-line battle. Scouting suited him far better, and captaincy even more than that.

But his plan would catch her. They knew where the Kalen had camped, knew the ground, knew how to press them and how hard. Two factors caused him to pace: the beast, and the horse.

The towering beast, if too close to Averlynn, would make capture costly, if not impossible. As desperately as he wanted the female Kalen, he would not risk more than a few of his troops to get her. One key and unpredictable component was the ability to get the beast to move away from Averlynn, even for a moment. They had experimented—carefully and briefly—in the last attack, and Ketzler was confident that an arrow barrage, well-timed and well-placed, could hinder it for just long enough. Karbae was in charge of that—the only one he knew he could trust to balance his desire and the safety of the troops.

As if hearing his thoughts, she shifted in her sleep and her hand reached out to clasp empty blankets. But she soon relaxed, and he wanted to pace a few moments more. *First things first, my love.* He knew it didn't help to pace, at least not directly. But for now it made him feel better.

The second and most difficult factor was the horse. She was astride it as often as not, and he had been unable to predict in ten straight attacks when she would choose to ride or not. If she was astride her horse, she would be gone long before his capturing party could get to her. And if his scouts tipped their hand too soon, she might realize she was a specific target and take measures to prevent capture. And they were drawing too near the Brynth. If the Kalen made it inside that craggy warren, Ketzler would be forced to return south empty-handed.

Well, not entirely. But he still had not found a use for Catie and Deuel.

Deuel had made something of a convincing case—potential to manipulate dragons, he had wondrous knowledge that could be useful, and...something else. Nothing Ketzler had a desire for. And Catie, separately, had all but deconstructed Deuel's arguments. She seemed less interested in saving either of them. Ketzler was almost happy to oblige her, especially after she had made him feel the fool, thinking she didn't speak Cariste—apparently her flying companion had taught her, somehow. But something stayed his vengeful hand. Something in the looks they each gave him told him there was some other, far greater value they simply didn't want to disclose. He would keep them around until he could figure out what it was.

Ketzler turned one last time and sighed, gazing at Karbae's shadowed and blanketed form. He had put it off long enough. Dawn would come, their attack would commence, and what would be, would be. He undid the clasp of his robe and let it fall, only briefly feeling the chill night air through his underclothes before slipping into the blankets Karbae had kept warm and easing himself against her back, pulling her tight against him.

Dawn came with a bite as first frost whitened the grass. Ketzler gazed hard at the paled plain, back toward the far away forest only half-bereft of leaves. Was it a bad sign? Should he hold off?

"She won't be on her horse," Karbae said, her cheer cutting through Ketzler's mood.

He half-turned in anger, then understood the implications. "She won't risk him slipping on the frozen ground, breaking a leg," he said. Karbae nodded triumphantly. Ketzler ran a hand lovingly down her arm. "Go get her," he said with a smile.

Karbae gave a slight and impish bow and turned to leave. Ketzler took his time appreciating her retreating form, as well as the attitude she had displayed just before. Maybe that was why Liptieri failed so utterly: he didn't have a companion to admire, whom he could trust. Had it been Pike? Did Ketzler inadvertently set up more than his promotion to Scout Captain with his opportune silence in battle?

An interesting thought. Maybe when Liptieri returned he could explore it, carefully. The end result was the same, regardless.

Ketzler stayed near the tent at first, watching Karbae and her retinue slip out of camp to take up their positions. Out on the open plain, they were not near enough for Ketzler to watch the whole thing unfold. But if they were successful, a lit arrow would be loosed and the outposts would inform him. He had strengthened that front as well, in case the Kalen counterattacked to try and retrieve Averlynn. Every avenue he could think of had been considered.

Finally they disappeared behind a fold. Ketzler let his gaze wander further away, up to the massive Brynth dominating the horizon. So close. He hoped, this close, the temptation to run and hide inside it would be more powerful than the temptation to rescue Averlynn. That was part of the anvil as well: once that fire arrow launched, everything else Ketzler had would swarm the Kalen, pushing them toward the mountains. He could see it in his mind. If only she wasn't on her horse.

He blew out a gust of air, watched it drift briefly in the cold. He turned back for camp, for Catie's gibbet. Time to see if they survived the sudden cold.

The guards ringed the cage, far better and more warmly dressed than its occupant. She sat, clutching her knees to her chest. But despite the occasional tremor wracking her, she actually looked content. Well, if not content, she at least managed it well.

"She's pretty," Catie commented in a low voice as Ketzler neared. He turned briefly back as if he could catch a glimpse of Karbae somewhere far off. She would not be back so soon, though.

"And fiercely capable," Ketzler replied.

"She would have to be," Catie said with a smile.

Ketzler quirked an eyebrow. "Why do you say that?"

"To capture both Deuel and me. He should have struck from a distance, but I guess he was worried about hitting me..." Catie trailed off, blushing. She cleared her throat and nodded toward the plain. "And now to capture Averlynn too. That's a lot to ask any person. Especially since you didn't fare too well."

Ketzler glowered, and Catie—to his surprise—looked chagrined. "I'm sorry," she said. "It was cold last night and I'm grumpy, I guess. If it helps, I'm sure Deuel would rather he had killed you."

Ketzler snorted, catching a guard suppressing a chuckle out of the corner of his eye. "Would you not have rather that as well?"

Catie shrugged. "It doesn't matter. We'll get back to what we were doing eventually." She leaned back and closed her eyes as though fully convinced of it.

"Having dreams of escaping, are we? I think you'll find that harder than you imagine. My men are—" Ketzler cut off as Catie looked at him suddenly, her gaze piercing with a glint of knowledge that stilled his tongue.

"No, no plans," she said, the glint gone as swiftly as it had come. She sat up a little, peering at him with curiosity. "Do you know who the Ekllar are?"

He blinked rapidly. "I—no, not at all. Should I know them?"

Her shoulders slumped. "It would be nice if you did, that's all."

"Listen, whoever you think these Ekllar are, I think my troops are more than capable of handling... What is it?"

Catie was trembling again, this time with her own suppressed chuckle. "Sorry, I wasn't threatening you. I don't know who they are either, I just...have a sort of memory, that's all. I'm trying to figure it out. If you hear of them, will you tell me? If I'm still here, anyway."

"How are you so certain you'll escape?" He hoped it didn't show, but her confidence was beginning to rattle him. Annoy him, at least.

"That's...hard to explain as well. I guess we'll both find out when Deuel and I are gone."

Ketzler's fist clenched. Annoyance quickly turned to rage at how little she must think of him. "We'll see how easy it is to escape if both of you are dead!" he seethed. He yanked free his sword and stepped closer. Still, somehow, she only looked at him as if she knew the blade would never fall.

"No, you'll need to be alive for this," he muttered. "Make sure she watches!" he called behind him as he turned for Deuel's cage. Much better punishment for her insolence if he killed her friend—or did her blush mean they were lovers? So much better. As he approached, Deuel shifted himself to watch him come. The strange dark man gave one glance toward Catie's cage before watching Ketzler with the same lack of concern she had.

His fist tightening, Ketzler raised the blade, ready to ram it home and tear asunder that smug, insufferable confidence. "He's really very good," Catie called out behind him, almost as if in warning as though preventing some horrible fate from befalling him.

He stared at Deuel wide-eyed. How could they be so confident? What possessed them? *Did* they know something he didn't?

"Captain!" one of the guards shouted.

Ketzler looked wildly away, saw the burning arrow as it arced back toward the ground. And he could already see several forms running across the short ridges toward them, could hear a faint cry behind them. The shaggy beast rose up near enough Karbae to take off her head, and as the axe rose glinting in the early sun a swarm of arrows descended. The axe faltered and dropped, and a moment later a roar of anger and frustration rolled across the plains. The beast itself did not fall, but it turned away. Faintly there came the sounds of battle—clattering swords, the occasional shout. But it drifted away. He thought he caught a glimpse of forms retreating over some far ridge toward the Brynth.

Ketzler turned triumphantly back toward Catie, teeth bared. "She is beautiful and terrible and far beyond your capabilities, is my Karbae. I'll let her decide what to do with the two of you." He rammed the sword home and returned to his tent, waiting outside of it a moment.

"Have her bring the Kalen directly to me," he said. "At least four of you inside guarding against her escape until I've done with her. I have her! She's mine!" He continued exulting as he swept the tent flap aside and entered.

He poured water into a basin that stood near his bed, where he and Karbae together had wrought their perfect plan. Soon enough he heard their triumphal entry, heard the guards outside give instructions to Karbae. And then they entered.

The she-Kalen had the decency, at least, not to appear defiant. Karbae had already knotted cords around Averlynn's wrist. Her belt held no scabbard—he did not see the strange sword anywhere. Blood dripped off Averlynn's hand, and Ketzler realized she did not wear her ring. He resisted every temptation not to go to Karbae and kiss her hard for her brilliance. He had not thought to mention such a precaution, but of course she had.

Other than that, Averlynn seemed intact, at least physically. "So," Ketzler said. Her eyes came up wearily and warily to meet his. "How have you been?"

"Better. And worse," she replied.

Ketzler cocked an eyebrow and laughed. "Haven't we all." He motioned to Karbae, and she came to stand near him. He took a rag and dipped it in the basin, gently cleaning Karbae's face of dust. Her bright eyes were on only him until he finished his ministrations. He gestured for her to sit, and then sat beside her.

"Anything to drink?" he asked, pouring himself and Karbae a light wine. It seemed appropriate for the time, and he had been saving it.

"Water, please," Averlynn said.

Ketzler gestured to one of the guards, who complied with her request. "Who will lead your people, now?" he asked quietly as she sipped.

She paused to look at him, then finished the cup. "Perhaps Zusamin will. Or any of the chiefs, really. I don't think I led them as much as you seem to think."

"Oh, your chiefs," Ketzler said. "I don't see any of them around here. They are, I believe, hosting our Captain Liptieri as we speak, providing terms for your surrender. Liptieri seems to think we can live peaceably together." A spark lit her eyes—of foolish hope, he didn't doubt. "But I think you know me too well for that," he chided.

Averlynn's eyes slid sideways to Karbae, and back. "You have become..."

"Captain," he enunciated. "Of the scouts. For now." None of the guards shifted or even blinked at what he implied with those words. Karbae had been right about that, too.

"Do you know what I am?"

Ketzler paused. She said it quietly, demurely. Brokenly? He assumed she was of little rank, perhaps she amounted to nothing more than a Scout Foot, like he had been. And yet had they not both risen among their ranks? That she led her force was unquestioned. "I find it matters less what you are as much as what people think you are."

She raised her bound hands to point one finger at him. "That is true. But your soldiers all think you are a Captain, and of more than just your scouts. Don't they."

He gave her a small salute with his cup before taking another drink. She nodded confirmation, and her eyes returned to the floor. "Only those left in my band think of me as a leader. To the rest of the Kalen I am outcast—I don't exist, in their eyes. Oh you can kill me, behead me, take it and give it even to my family if you want. They will thank you, for they have already put me to death in their minds."

Ketzler felt Karbae go still beside him, but he smiled and set down his cup. "Ravun indicated much the same, at least the way she seemed to think of you and what you were trying to do."

Averlynn's head came up. "Who?"

"One of your people," Ketzler said with a dismissive wave. "She came not long after you regrew the forest—how did you do that, by the way?"

"I didn't."

"Hmm." Ketzler drained his cup and stood. In one quick stride he was in front of her, the backhand with his cup catching her full on the side of the head. She cried out, managed to keep from falling entirely to the ground only with the help of two of the guards. A trickle of blood leaked down her cheek as she blinked away stinging tears.

"The others did it while I used the Taur song," she said. "Witko didn't explain it to me in detail."

Ketzler stared at her, but couldn't find any deceit in her gaze. Perhaps they had hid it from her. He inspected his goblet, saw the bit of blood on the rim. He lifted it and wiped the blood off on her cheek. She wrenched her head away too late.

Ketzler turned back for the table, casting a quick glance at Karbae. He hadn't meant to lose his temper like that. But she gazed unblinking at Averlynn, and did not seem put off by his outburst. He returned to his seat.

"As I was saying, she came to us to try to avert the war you were starting. Liptieri went with her to broker a deal. So yes, I can imagine you are a rogue among your people. And yet you gathered something of a following in a short time. And should the terms of the deal fall apart, should war become imminent, who else might your people look to except one who has already engaged the enemy? Unless that course is no longer open to them. You see what I'm driving at."

Averlynn lifted her bound hands again to wipe the blood off her cheek. "I see what you think you're driving at. But your goal is misplaced. You'll learn that soon enough, I imagine."

Ketzler only barely kept his teeth from grinding together as he stared at her. He was growing weary of his prisoners and their cocksureness. Perhaps it was time for a true and violent lesson.

"Put her away, please," he said to the guards. "And wait for me to come to you."

They turned her away and exited, leaving the tent empty. Ketzler sighed and turned to Karbae. "I love you," he said.

She smiled, scooted closer to nestle under his arm. "It was close," she said. "Your scouts deserve as much praise as I do—more, even. She was a few steps only from her horse—she had her sword in the saddle, for some reason—and might have been gone. Mandros risked the beast to prevent her."

"I'll commend him to Liptieri along with you."

Karbae went still. "He paid the price for his risk, Ketzler."

Ketzler closed his eyes. Of course. "How many died?" he whispered.

"Five. Four are wounded."

"Just in trying to capture her?" he asked, alarmed.

Karbae shook her head against his chest. "No, only Mandros of the capturing party died. The others died in the feint to draw the rest of her troops away."

Acceptable losses. Unless... "How many of *them* died?"

Karbae shrugged. "I didn't get a firm count, yet. The corporals should be back by now, I can go—"

As she started to move to get up he stopped her, pulled her tight again. "I wanted to do this when I saw you had removed her ring," he said, tilting her chin toward him with his finger and kissing her hard. Her hand went behind his head and tangled in his hair as she returned his passion.

When they parted, she smiled. "That reminds me," she said, putting a hand into her pocket. She pulled out Averlynn's ring and dropped it into Ketzler's palm. "She won't be able to attack anyone with a ring on, now."

Ketzler smiled and held up the ring to inspect it. What was her animal, then? There was an image on it—a goat? His mind cast back to their first meeting, of telling her Liptieri's blazon was an ibex. Was that why she had decided to trust him, because of a goat? He smirked. Foolishness.

"Catie and Deuel seem to think their escape is imminent, though she claims not to be planning anything." He rolled his eyes when Karbae looked puzzled. "I don't know either, but it's annoying. I was set to kill Deuel when the fire arrow flew. I promised them I would let you decide what to do with them."

Karbae's smile was uncertain as her eyes studied his. "Why me?"

"You and I are one. I stand behind your decisions just as surely as I would stand behind my own."

"And what if I told you to release them?"

Ketzler sat back, cocking his head. "Why would you release them?"

"That's not what you just said."

"Karbae, if you're doing this just to test me, I'm not sure—"

"Then perhaps we are not as 'one' as you think."

He paused, rolling the ring around his fingers. If she did want it, she would have her reasons. Surely. Just as he would have his reasons. "They are in your hands," he said. "Though I may not know your heart, I have told you mine. Do with them as you will."

"Give me your sword, and stay here," she said.

As soon as she left he stood, unable to refrain from pacing. She wouldn't set them free with a sword, so he wasn't worried about that. And yet there was the strange way she was looking at Averlynn. Did she have some design for her, instead? Surely not. He was being silly. She knew his heart, knew what he wanted—had known it long ago and had helped feed it to him with Curani. He could trust her. He had, up to this point. Whatever would happen—

There was a shout outside, a flurry of noise. Was that flapping wings? Was Deuel thrashing in death? No, more shouts joined in. Something had gone wrong. Or had she done something else?

He ran out, looking immediately at Deuel's cage. It was empty, the bars cut through. He rounded his tent until he could see around it to Catie's cage. The winged beast was atop it, reaching through a hole to draw her out. Why was no one shooting him? Where was...?

Karbae was huddled on the ground. He ran to her, gripped her shoulder and moved her. She was crying! She clutched her arm, blood dripping through her fingers. It didn't look like too much, though, not enough to hurt her so badly.

"I'm sorry," she whispered. "I'm so sorry."

Ketzler looked up. "Shoot him! Shoot them both!" he shouted.

When his men only stared at him, he looked up. The winged creature and the girl were both far overhead already. Faintly on the breeze he heard the girl shout down "I told you he was very good!" As he watched them angle northward and fly off something sparkled as it left Deuel's grasp then disappeared against the clouds. He searched, but couldn't see what it was.

There was a whirring sound. One of his men shouted, and he looked up again barely in time to dodge as his sword fell from the sky and nearly impaled him, sinking almost half its length into the ground. He gazed at it a moment as it waved back and forth with a faint ringing.

"You shouldn't underestimate things you don't understand," Averlynn said quietly from her cage. Ketlzer double-checked, but she seemed secure, her guards' attention still fully on her despite the disturbance around them. He knew he had chosen well.

"I failed you," Karbae said quietly.

Ketzler knelt back down. "What happened?"

She sniffled, gave him only a quick glance. "I went to run him through, just as I imagined you would do. He moved his wings just in time, was able to grasp it somehow and wrench it off me. Next thing I knew he had cut through the bars with he sword. I think that's when the blade nicked me."

"You're okay, then?"

She peeled her hand away to peek at the wound, then nodded. "He moved so fast, Ketzler. Don't blame your men. In one leap he had cut the top off her cage and took her—well, you were here by then. It's my fault—"

He laid a hand on her arm. "Hush. He would have done the same to me if I had tried it, I don't doubt. And they were merely a bonus. You obtained for me my true prize." He bent and kissed her head. "Go get your arm bandaged. We'll stay here one more day before we see if we can harass the Kalen all the way into the mountains."

She bent her head to touch his shoulder with it then smiled. "Yes, Captain."

He helped her rise and watched her make her way through the camp toward the physician's tent. He went to his sword and pulled it free, thumbing the dirt off the blade before sheathing it. He made his way to Averlynn's cage.

"Perhaps you were right," he said. "I notice Deuel didn't make even the slightest effort to free you. Maybe you mean less to them than I thought." He raised a finger in warning. "But you mean very much to me, and it will be my pleasure to extract from you as much knowledge as I can. For instance, the location of each of your towns and villages." He held up a hand as he saw her back stiffen. "Oh don't worry, I don't expect you to just hand them to me. That would be foolishness. Just know that you will, in the end, hand them to me." He turned to one of the guards. "Get a bucket of water, please, and douse her with it. Thank you."

He returned to his tent, lingering outside only long enough to hear Averlynn gasp and chatter as the freezing water hit her. Winter was almost here, and it was fascinating how the cold could destroy someone's resolve.

As night began to fall, he had them build fires near her cage—just close enough that she wouldn't freeze, but not enough to actually keep her warm. Four guards faced inward, six faced outward. He would not risk escape or recapture. The pickets were over-manned as well.

He sat next to one of the fires, watching Averlynn hug herself in vain. Karbae sat with him, finishing a leg of chicken. He sipped some water, blowing out a misting breath into the night air.

"I told you, you can kill me—"

She cut off as he raised a hand, ducked her head against a slight but chill breeze. "I haven't asked you yet," he said. "There is nothing I want from you but for you to sit there. So just relax."

Her eyes like chips of ice glowed at him, firelight dancing in their depths. Yet she remained silent.

"Someone comes, sir," one of the guards said. "One of the pickets, escorting... It appears to be Ravun, captain."

Ketzler rose, unsure. Karbae tossed the bone aside and stood with him.

"What is it?"

"She says she brings news, sir," the picket said.

"We've been betrayed," Ravun said. She glanced at the cage, seemed to recognize Averlynn. She ground her teeth, then spat. "You! Well, I can't say I'm saddened to see you in there. After all you've begun!" Ravun took a step forward, fist clenched, but the guards stopped her.

"Please," Ketzler said quickly. "We have her. Tell me what happened."

"She's poisoned their minds, that's what happened!" Ravun seethed. "The chiefs seem to think they can actually stand up to your army. They've rejected the terms, nearly destroyed all of your Commander's detachment in an ambush. Only I and a few others escaped to come warn you."

Ketzler's head tingled—Karbae seemed to think the same, for she gazed at him with sparkling eyes. "What happened to the Commander?" he asked Ravun's escorts.

"He's dead—one of the first to fall, sir."

"They thought by striking him down they would bring you to the table on your knees," Ravun seethed.

"You're Commander of the army now," Karbae whispered.

"Why do you not stand with your people?" Ketzler asked.

Ravun scoffed. "It isn't just me. Very few actually oppose you."

"You can show me where the villages and towns are?"

Ravun nodded. "Right now, if you want. You have maps?"

"Of course. Thardus, take her to my tent immediately, please, and see she has everything she needs. Pluvius, you go too. I'll be right there."

They departed, and Ketzler turned back to Averlynn, who still shivered as she stared at Ravun's back. "Do you know her?" he asked quietly.

Averlynn tore her gaze from Ravun and fastened them on Ketzler. "She's a Scout. Scouts are the highest ranked of us, just below what you would call Captain I guess."

Ketzler nodded. "Very good. Don't freeze to death." He turned and went to his tent, Karbae close behind him. Now he could turn the army into what he envisioned—a fast, mobile force that could easily and quickly dispatch the Kalen. This war was all but won.

38

WHEN ONCE AN ACORN

"Is every road...?"
"The God of All still works even while we do."
"Makes you wonder what we're here for."
"To do the work He gives us."

20 Halmfurtung 1321 — Autumn

Averlynn watched the party depart, hiding a shiver not entirely from the cold. She had not lied about Ravun being a Scout. And if she did not tell the truth as to Ravun's real name...Ketzler had not asked, had he?

But that left her wondering alone. If he had shown up as he actually was, that would be one thing. Then she would know he was indeed still working against her, that he intended to try to hand over the Kalen to Ketzler and his army. That her people were still fully opposed to her, saw her as dead.

Instead, Amrith was masquerading as a female Kalen named Ravun. Why?

Had her people turned? Would they make a stand? And would that change her status? It seemed too much to hope, and the cold still bit too deep into her bones. She had to begrudgingly respect Ketzler's method. Pestering her with questions would give her something to harden her resolve against, make her feel like she was winning a war. At least a battle.

But to have him sit there with his woman, quietly observing her suffering, refusing to even let her speak defiance. She knew he did it to wear her down, that eventually he would begin asking questions. That knowledge didn't help when the next bucket of icy water doused her and the breeze picked up again.

She focused on Ketzler's tent, tried to imagine what was going on in there. What 'Ravun' was telling him. If it was all a ploy, there was danger of it being exposed. Surely Ketzler would be wary—why should he trust this Kalen and not the others? What had Amrith told him?

She thought of the look on Ketzler's face when the woman, Karbae, confirmed he was now Captain of their army. Maybe that was what Amrith promised—or, if not that specifically, something else that Ketzler desperately wanted anyway. But not in an obvious way.

Just like Amrith had done for her. Had she not taken the bait, snare and all, when he offered it? Some of her old reverence for the Scout returned. He was exceptional at his craft.

But she couldn't quite forget how he had used that craft against her. As another chill wracked her, she fought again the urge to spit out his name, give the Cariste something to reward her with. If they knew Ravun was false, perhaps she might be permitted some warmth.

She squeezed her eyes shut, thought of Witko and Zusamin and Ouwa and all the rest—and Catie and Deuel, now. Perhaps they would be able to rescue her. She almost wished they wouldn't, or at least wouldn't put themselves in danger over it. She wasn't lying to Ketzler about that: she was truly not that important. And if she gave them Amrith, they would want the next thing, and the next. She would have to replace the promise Amrith represented—a key inside all the Kalen villages, so Ketzler could destroy them.

The tent flap opened and Ravun emerged. Averlynn knew that walk, that posture, even his general mien was not so different—just the hair and cheekbones, and the garments. But only she would know that after the time she had spent with him in the south.

He stormed toward her, flanked by two guards. He pulled short just out of arm's reach of her cage and glared at her. "There you are," he said in Cariste. His mouth twisted. "You...*pay close attention*."

Though he spat those last words in contempt, he spoke in Kalen. Averlynn managed to only shift her eyes in response. What was his plan? Hopefully she could figure it out as he went.

Amrith-as-Ravun continued, still in Kalen and with a scowl on his face as though berating her. "The chiefs send their greeting, and apologies that it took so long to realize the truth of what you were trying to say to us." He switched back to Cariste. "I've given Captain Ketzler everything. I just want you to know so you can give up this ridiculous hope, this...*be strong!*...whatever you think you'll accomplish."

"What are you going to do?" she mumbled—in Cariste—as though broken in spirit. Was this just another one of Amrith's tricks? A way to make her suffer?

He sneered. "I've given him our biggest city. Tomorrow I'm leading him personally to Orthrindel and handing him the keys to the gates."

Orthrindel. Where Burieng made the pact with the Kalen to honor their lands. Now a lost city, a mythical city, a city the Wohan maintained didn't exist. He intended to lead them to the middle of nowhere. And, knowing him, abandon them there.

Or, ambush them?

"You know you'll die there," she said. "When they no longer have a use for you—"

"Ha! Unlike you, I will remain very useful, not only to the Cariste but our people as well. Once we've gathered all our people at Orthrindel we'll bow in obeisance to the Cariste. And your little war will be done, *make me mad.*"

"It is not my war," Averlynn said, trying to make her voice stronger. The chills still in her bones made it difficult but she had to try. "You are a leaf to the Cariste winds—no better than flatulence."

Amrith scratched his jaw as though his patience was wearing thin. He paced one step to the side, his shadow cast across her from the fire behind him. Averlynn pressed on.

"In the annals of our history, Ravun, you will not be. You will die and no one will mourn you. You will float away, a vapor, a cold day in summer quickly forgotten. Traitor to your people, I name you *tienken!*"

"You are already *tienken!*" he shouted. She barely caught a glimmer in his mouth before he spat at her. Something struck her in the stomach, and she managed to let it drop into her hands as she turned away, cowering.

It was a ring.

"Your own curse will be on you," he seethed, taking a step closer to her cage. The guard on his left placed a hand on his arm to hold him back. Amrith shook it free, still glaring. He heaved a dramatic sigh, before switching to Kalen again, this time with deep regret in his tone. "Raina sends her greetings as well. She said you are to go to the Abandoned Isles. The next step on your journey lies there. She said to remember these words:

"The Ancient and the Elder race alive with those who should be dead
Still share a bond in time beyond the silken veil all mortals dread.
The time entwined the elder age to those who come again at last,
And fires roar to mold the door to walk in present future past."

Averlynn stared as though mortified—it was not a difficult act. A fourth verse to the prophecy. How did Raina know it? And how did she know it meant going to the Isles?

Amrith gritted his teeth, his anger returned. "I said 'do you understand?'" he growled in Cariste. Averlynn nodded quickly. Amrith sighed again. "If you were not stuck on this course, Averlynn, you would have made an excellent Scout. Too bad neither of us saw it in time."

As Amrith turned to leave, the tears that she should have shed at his disappointment were easily replaced by the respect he acknowledged he finally had for her.

"Maybe one day," she called out in Kalen.

"If it can, it will be," he called back in Kalen—with a sneer for the benefit of the guards.

At least, she hoped it was for their benefit.

She remained huddled, cautiously fingering the ring still in her palm. She felt the outline etched in it, knew it was hers. *How had he possibly gotten hold of it?* Catie's words as Deuel flew overhead echoed in her mind. Amrith was very good as well. And he said she would be an excellent Scout. Had he only said what she wanted to hear? Did he hope she would try to escape, only to be killed and no longer interfere with his other plots?

She mewled a broken sigh. It seemed like him. And he might have made up the poem, said it was from Raina knowing that would get her attention as well. All of it could have been made up. Even pretending as though it were subterfuge—he had done that before, too.

She glanced up when Ketzler emerged from the tent, watched him approach. Was there anything he might say that would convince her? How could she know whether Amrith was being truthful? He knew how to wrap mystery in deceit inside another deceit.

"My men say Ravun spoke to you," Ketzler said as he neared.

Averlynn looked away. She almost wished 'Ravun' hadn't.

Ketzler chuckled. "She really didn't like you. What did you do?"

"I thought I could be a Scout."

"Hmm. She mentioned your aspirations. It is a difficult life." Ketzler went silent, and his gaze went distant for a time. "Difficult decisions must be made to get there, and stay there." His eyes focused suddenly. "He mentioned taking us to Orthandirl—"

"Orthrindel," she corrected automatically.

"You've been there?" he asked.

"I've been all over our kingdom," she said.

"Can you show me on a map where it is?"

Her eyes flicked to his. "No."

He gave her a withering look. "Ravun has already pointed to it. I just want your confirmation."

Her heart sped up. She would have no idea where he would have pointed. If she pointed to the wrong place, they would be caught. Where would he have said? Somewhere remote if he was planning on abandoning them; somewhere they could easily ambush if that was the plan instead.

"Get her out," Ketzler said wearily.

As the guards moved to unlock the cage she slipped the ring into a pocket. One of them hauled her roughly out. Her legs barely supported her after being bent for so long. But she was nearer one of the fires and the warmth eased her momentarily.

Ketzler's fist seemed to materialize out of nowhere, and she doubled over as the air rushed out of her lungs. More blows rained down—not all of flesh and bone—and soon stars danced before her eyes. She tried to shield her head, but her wrists were grasped tightly and her arms bent behind her. Just as she was sure she would black out, the blows ceased and freezing water doused her.

"Where is it?" Ketzler said, not shouting but loud enough to cut through her mental fog.

She gasped for air, felt the stings of a hundred cuts and bruises, tasted copper in her mouth. Somehow an ancient word flashed through her mind, and the stupidity of saying it aloud escaped her. "Apollyon."

She believed the next few blows came from booted feet, and darkness followed rather than water.

She groaned awake, still feeling the hammering of blows—or thought she did. As she became more aware, she realized she was on her side in the cage, and it was her own rhythmic pumping of blood through bruises.

She took shallow, careful breaths. As though feeling each tender spot she led gentle fingers down her Ranger garb, not pausing as she felt the small circle of the ring still in her pocket. Nothing seemed broken, but she doubted she could run very fast.

"Where is Orthrindel?" Ketzler demanded from behind her.

She startled, and groaned as she pulled weary and sore muscles in the movement. Even her gasp hurt, and she wondered again if she had not at least cracked a rib.

"Get her out," he said.

"Wait," she mumbled. She couldn't live through another session. He didn't truly need her, and her death would never cross his mind again. "I can show you."

"Bring a map," he said quietly.

Her mind reeled. *Where would he say it was? What was his plan? Why hadn't he told her more? Was he tricking just her, or both of them, or just Ketzler?*

She heard rustling, and the map was in front of her face. "Where?" Ketzler demanded.

She peered at it, rubbed her eyes as though still weary and broken. *Where?!* her mind screamed at her.

"I will hand them the keys to the gates."

Kalen cities had no gates. *The Gates.* The ruins—the Taur ruins?—with the strangely-planed gates. Now that she had met Tavill and Zusamin, it made sense. Amrith would lead them past Hatza to those ruins.

Please, she prayed, extending a shaky hand. *Whoever it is above us, help me.* Her finger came to rest in the blank space where The Gates would be.

The silence was deafening. She dropped her hand, waited for death to come. She couldn't even bring herself to look up. *Amrith, what have you—*

"Feed her," Ketzler said quietly. The map was withdrawn and a bowl replaced it. She blinked stupidly, noting the steam rising from the broth within. It was not thick, but it was seasoned. Her hands trembled as she cupped the sides of the bowl and lifted it to drink.

By the time she finished and looked up, only her guards remained. Perhaps the soup had been poisoned. It didn't matter to her now. She had either helped Amrith guide the Cariste into a trap, or she had accidentally sprung it too early. She wasn't sure it would be possible to escape anyway, so if her mission to the Abandoned Isles was truly given, she could not accomplish it.

She gripped the ring through the cloth of her pocket. Her senses slowly returned as the broth worked in her. She feigned lassitude for the sake of the guards. Well. Perhaps Amrith was tricking her again, goading her into attempting escape when he deemed it impossible.

There were many things she had done that he had deemed impossible. Perhaps she could disappoint him again by succeeding. Only, how to do it?

She awoke moments before the freezing water hit her again, though still not enough time to prepare for it. As she sat blinking water from her eyes, her mind was a whirl. Had it been poisoned, or at least tainted? Or had she just been that tired? Was she still imprisoned?

She was. She felt the bars of wood beneath her a moment before she looked through them into a cold dawn air. Fog lay around the small valleys and the sun was a pale white disk on the horizon.

Why was she suddenly being tortured again? Had Amrith been caught? Had she? It took everything not to reach for the ring. Not yet, in case they watched too closely.

"Get her out." It was Ketzler again, and he seemed angry.

Hands grabbed her roughly and hauled her out. Again her legs refused to support her and she collapsed. She rolled a little, using the flurry of motion to surreptitiously check the pocket. It was still in there.

"What's wrong?" she asked, her tongue thick in her mouth. They must have put something in the soup.

"I'm afraid your usefulness is at an end," Ketzler said. "You've confirmed what I needed. And, frankly, I don't want to worry about you escaping or being rescued. It's one shoulder I don't want to constantly look over. And we need to be swift. I won't spare guards to watch you."

She looked up, gaze boring into his. He was being serious. Another man flanked him, one with sword drawn and no spark of conscience in his eye. Karbae, she noticed, was also not around.

"Your...woman...does not approve of this," she commented, rolling to her knees and upright, as though kneeling before him. She didn't like the image she presented, but it worked for now.

"Approving it and wanting to see it carried out are two separate things," Ketzler replied. He glanced at his man, and some of the other guards. "But, as it happens, she has other duties anyway. Oridin, if you would, please."

The man stepped forward, sword coming up. Averlynn held up a hand, knowing it wouldn't stay the blade. But it couldn't end like this.

Ketzler's hand came up, and Oridin paused. "What?"

Averlynn let her eyes wander. "Please," she said. Could she explain it to such a man? "I am a Ranger—"

"So what?" Ketzler demanded. "Oridin..."

"No. Please wait..." She trailed off, taking in as much of the world as she could. Just in case this didn't work. "I've wandered through forest, across plain, through rivers and streams. I've known rocks and trees. Do you know there was once an acorn I saw fall to the ground and take root...I could lead you straight to it." She paused to point unwaveringly to where her little oak grew, though it was a day away at least. "It's...birds nest in it now, you could climb up in its branches if you wished. I've watched it grow each time I patrolled the north."

Ketzler sighed. "So...what?"

Tears came to Averlynn's eyes. "I've been a part of this land for so long, Ketzler. It never felt like home. But now..." Her lip trembled. It had started as an act. Except it was true. "I'm afraid for it, as you would be afraid for a child to grow up without you. I know you have to kill me, but..." She looked him in the eye. "If I could just touch it one more time, to say goodbye before I go."

Ketzler sighed, waved Oridin back. "Whatever barbaric ritual you feel you must..."

She only bowed her head in thanks, shuffling her feet around. She lost her balance, tipped over and squirmed a little to get her legs back underneath her. Finally she made it onto her backside, legs in front of her. She pulled off her boots and socks, let her feet settle onto the cold ground. She closed her eyes and bowed her head again, drawing a long breath.

The God of... She squeezed her eyes shut. She couldn't say the name. *Elonai, if you approve of this, what these people who call themselves by your name, are doing—let them kill me. If not, protect me now. May this song be for you, and let the music come swiftly to me.*

Any other time, she had to work her way into the throat-song. Thrum first, then the overtone. She did not believe she would have time. Oridin was nearly overtop of her. And she knew Ketzler would know what she was doing.

Her hands were clasped in front of her, the ring finger tucked into her fists to hide it. She let out her breath, opened her eyes to look at the muted colors of the world around her, the grass and broomsedge with its veil of frost, the foggy air, the pale sky. Another deep breath in, and in one swift moment unclasped her hands and placed them on the ground as she unleashed the song.

As thrum and whistle rolled out of her, she saw Ketzler's eyes widen, his mouth begin to shout. Oridin's hands tensed, tendons springing in sharp relief against his skin as the sword descended. The other guards around her reaching for arrows or swords.

But the thrum seemed to hold them while the whistle gave her unnatural speed. She rose, ducked out of the way of Oridin's sword. She aimed a careful punch to his hands, knocking him and the blade off course. She leapt forward, striking Ketzler in the chest and knocking him backward. Still he seemed to move like a fly in molasses.

Something told her she didn't have the time to wonder. She spun to her left, ducking as an arrow loosed silently from the bow. She moved under it, the song unwavering as it poured from her, chopping the bow in half with her hand.

She grabbed her boots and socks and ran, dodging around astonished soldiers and tents. One arrow she didn't see coming grazed her arm from behind, but she flinched and it sped the rest of the way harmlessly by.

Still she sang, feeling the very ground pulse to her beat. Above, it seemed as though hawks and eagles attended her, lending her their flight as she left the camp and soon the outposts far behind.

The Wall rose before her in the mists, guiding her way. She thought perhaps of reaching behind her with the song, doing to some of them back there what she had done to the other who wore a Kalen ring. But then she realized she felt no sense of rings, in front or behind.

You promised you wouldn't said a voice in her mind, and she smiled grimly. She had promised. She let herself only run instead, until the Wall loomed nearer than Ketzler could pursue her in a day. She slowed first, came to a stop in the bottom of a valley. She sat, placing her hands on the ground again and bowing her head before she stopped singing.

As soon as the last note echoed away, fatigue washed over her and she fell asleep.

She came awake on her own, lying completely still as she listened to the world around her. Birds twittered faintly somewhere, and she thought maybe she heard a trickling stream. Out of some far away valley an elk bugle echoed, and the scream of an eagle followed.

She opened her eyes. It was not as cold as it had been the past few mornings. There was no fog, no frost, but winter was still on the cusp. The sky above was crystalline, a thin but resilient blue. Peeping over the top of the hollow where she lay were the whitened peaks of the Wall. She breathed deep, then craned her head before sitting up.

She was alone. She worked her legs a few times, less cramped now that she had been able to sleep without being permanently curled. She stretched down, gripping each foot as she worked the kinks out of her back. She sat up again and sighed.

All she needed was Tarafel. She gave a quick prayer of thanks to Elonai that she had left her sword on his saddle. Even if she couldn't use it yet, she would hate to lose it.

Averlynn stood. She doubted she could use the throat song again to speed her way to their rendezvous point. Even if the laws of creation didn't allow it, she would feel more than scandalous at such a use of it. So she set off on her two perfectly-capable feet.

She was nearer the Wall than she realized, and was actually near the river flowing out of them where she had entered so long ago to try to find her way north. When she reached the gravel bank, she saw sign of both

Tarafel and Zusamin. She glanced over her shoulder, but saw nothing on the distant horizon. If Ketzler was to take over the army, surely he wouldn't be pursuing her anyway. She continued north.

At the fork where she had gone east, she turned west, trusting Zusamin and Witko to find adequate places to hide the army until they could recoup. She thumbed her ring as she walked, slowly twisting it on her finger. She came to another fork, and paused.

More water came from the mountains here, but beyond that she had no idea which direction they would have gone. She inspected the ground for sign, but there was a lot of rock and very little vegetation.

She stared at the waters, noticed in a pool some fishes swirling. After a time one departed, swimming further upstream. It turned right at the fork, nosing its way northward. Averlynn shrugged and followed.

When the sense came, it felt strange again. She had spent so long accustomed to it, then afraid of it, she nearly took the ring off. Then she recognized the personality of Witko and smiled. She continued, her legs refreshed.

More senses came, but before she saw any of them there was Zusamin running at her from over a low saddle. Averlynn ran to meet her, bowing in respect and gratitude.

Then the rest of the Kalen appeared and she received hugs, warm handclasps, and hurrahs. It overwhelmed her: no one had been so expressive around her since she had become a Ranger.

"How did you escape?" finally became the question most often repeated. She glanced at Zusamin with twinkling eyes.

"The throat song of the Taur," she said.

Zusamin cocked her head a moment, her lips quirking into a strange half-smile. "It gave you speed?"

"It did. I didn't know it could do that."

"I didn't know it could do that for one who is not a Taur, but I suppose it will do everything for you it does for us."

Averlynn's eyes went wide. "What else can it do?"

Zusamin laughed. "That will take some training. For now, what do we do next? Deuel and Catie departed only moments ago to rescue you. What state did you leave the Cariste in? Is Ketzler still alive?"

"Very much, and in command of their entire army."

"You should have killed him," someone muttered from deeper in the ranks.

Averlynn shook her head. "I promised I wouldn't use the song for that. But there is more. I believe our people have seen the value in fighting the Cariste. It is possible Scout Amrith leads the Cariste now into an ambush."

Witko's eyes glittered as he stared at her. "Surely he does not."

"Why not?"

"After everything else he did?"

Her mouth twisted. "I'm not sure," she admitted. "But some of what he did..." She quickly related to them the manner of Amrith's deception and how he gave her the information.

"As you say," Witko said, "his layers of deception run so deep..."

"We could try to find Raina," Zusamin said. "If she did not give him the prophecy to give to you, he is false."

Averlynn nodded. "I considered the same thing. Finding her might prove very difficult, though."

"If I know Raina," Witko said, "and if Amrith is telling the truth, she'll be near the Gates. Not close enough to get involved, but near enough to receive word. She makes a show of backing away from the Wohan, but she still cares. We should go there. Might be able to help ourselves, if ambush is real. And that will confirm—"

"What is it?" Zusamin cut in. She had been watching Averlynn's face, undoubtedly saw her lack of enthusiasm.

"If we go to the Gates, we'll be that much further from being able to depart these lands," she said quietly.

"Do you feel you must?" Zusamin asked.

"If this new verse of prophecy is truly given, I don't know if I should delay. It spoke frequently of time, and I wonder if that is significant."

"Unless Amrith made it up specifically to make you think that," Witko cut in.

Zusamin's gaze never wavered. "Do you know how you will get there?"

Averlynn shrugged. "I don't. I hoped you might be able to help me."

Zusamin nodded gravely. "I can. And our departure point may not be so far away from the south as you think."

Averlynn cocked her head. "How so?"

"We will use the same point of entry as those who fled the Abandoned Isles in the first place. Near the eastern end of the Snowplains, at the foot of Mount Thinsledon."

39

ALL WILL STAND WITNESS

"He nearly slipped from your grasp, old friend."
"He is not mine to hold."
"Will Melnor return soon? I grow restless."
"Gather strength, Teresh. This war is still only beginning."

20 Halmfurtung 1321 — Autumn

Tavill sat at the head of the valley, feeling sorry for himself.

Lasserain had been a trusted friend. Gone.

Raina had been a steady rock. Gone.

The veil across his memory, once a curse but now, he wondered, had been a blessing. Gone.

Averlynn's army, trusting in his wisdom. Gone.

The sky today was as clear as his vision of both past and future. Winter had peered into the world and then retreated, at least for now. He had a duty again—a hundred loose ends fluttering for his attention. Though they were clear, which of those loose ends to tie first was less so.

He needed to find Averlynn again. He must help the Kalen as best he could. The Prosan, he believed, would still want him dead, so there was no use addressing that issue. The Cariste...

Perhaps it was not *entirely* clear. That they needed to be stopped was plain enough. How to do it—how far to take it—was not. But also plain was that he could do nothing from here.

He had spent four days mourning his losses. Sometimes it took the form of self-pity. He felt he had earned that right. But he pushed that aside. He worried about Raina. Lasserain had said she was fine, or would be, but Lasserain's word was worm dung. He wondered how Averlynn's army fared now, if they continued to push the Cariste back. That thought swelled and grew in his mind, and with a snort he finally stood.

He tested the winds. His sense of smell was as strong as it was before, and his vision had improved dramatically. Not to where it was, but he could see well enough to protect himself. The scent-vision was gone, and he knew this time it was for good. Lasserain, through Tavill's arm, had done his job well.

Tavill bent, paused with his hand outstretched. He sniffed, smelled only cold iron and leather. His bloodlust was gone as well, and for that he did not mourn. In another room he had found weapons fit for the Taur, among them a sword nearly like the one from his recovered memories. It was not his, but strikingly similar with one long keen edge and one jagged saw-edge. It lay on the ground in a massive scabbard, and he grasped it finally, firmly, and belted it around his waist. He felt, with apprehension and some dread, he would need it in the coming days.

That was yet before him. As he strode toward the rising sun he tried to sort through his memories. The problem with having them all rush back at once was that many were in disarray, their contexts buried beneath the sheer weight of them all. He had begun slowly sifting through them, finding clues and placing them in their proper order. The largest difficulty lay in that, before the Rivening, the world's cultures and technologies had progressed sometimes past where they were now. It was not as linear as it would be for the historians, who might identify an epoch by the tools those ancient cultures had used. Those histories always began with the Rivening. Oren, instead, had two global resets, its people reduced nearly to nomads and huts twice by great cataclysms. One, he remembered, had been supernatural. The second, the Rivening...well, he had woken like most of the rest of the world, nearly forgetting who he was. Those memories still lay in the most tangled balls—no, not tangled. More like a stew, scenes and happenings floating aimlessly in a broth.

Those he left alone. More than likely they were supposed to stay that way. Every now and then he would stumble across them, some large and meaty, others the remnants of a crumbled bit of parsley. He dwelt on it only long enough to place it in the stew. Instead he, like the historians, bent most of his focus on the memories after the Rivening.

He let his nose lead him along, staying alert in that sense even while his mind wandered. It was a relaxing exercise, noting a scent and tracking it until he positively identified it, then returning to memories until another scent took his attention.

The large mountains peered at him from across the hills, the ones Averlynn had called the Wall. Even at this distance he felt they were aptly named. She had mentioned them as a possible refuge. He hoped they hadn't needed it. Yet something nagged, something saying that these Cariste shared blood with the Prosan—tenacious, unrelenting. Perhaps the Kalen were not faring as well as he hoped. He turned his steps. With a small army, he knew he could scent them out quickly if they were there. If not, he would turn south.

As the sun rose the next morning, and he continued on his north-east course, he spied against the rising sun a small silhouette flying. And yet, it was not a bird. The distance might be deceiving—he doubted it—but it was much too large. And the wings, for such a large bird, moved too swiftly. Without completely understanding why, he picked up a light jog, following its heading.

As he watched, the silhouette dipped, descended slowly. Just before it reached the ground it extended, almost seemed to split in two. Curious, he ran faster.

Their scent hit him just before he could see them, a strange mix of sun and grass; cold, wet stone; and a musk that he had to search his memories a moment longer to identify.

Dragon.

He is behamien.

She, then?

He slowed his approach, called out in pleasant Cariste in case he was wrong.

His eyesight was perhaps not as good as he thought, as the flying creature streaked toward him like an arrow. He had time for one step backward only before the great wings flared. The behamian wore a pair of swords on his arms, and held them both pointed at Tavill. But in his hesitation Tavill recognized a certain amount of disbelief and respect.

"Why do you call to us so?" he asked in Rinc Nain.

"I didn't know who was ahead," Tavill said calmly. He let his arms hang, near his sword but not threateningly so. The behamian lowered his blades.

The behamian's companion rose from the grasses "Deuel, is it—Oh! The other one!" She said as she jogged forward. She stopped just behind the dragon-son and bowed. Tavill thought her scent suited her well.

His forehead creased suddenly. "'The other one?'" he echoed.

Her hand went to her mouth. "I'm so sorry, I didn't think... I forgot you didn't know. You're..." Her hand lowered as she collected herself. "You're not alone, Tavill. Zusamin is still alive."

At the name, images lost in the stew reeled through Tavill's mind, bright at first but growing grimmer. Lunches and meadows and picnics and parties gave way to clouds and thick darkness, battlescapes, weapons, armor, steel. She had been the other Taur carrying him away from the battlefield—had been there when he first showed symptoms, had first flew into a bloodlust. She had been beside him for long before that.

Pruning... Not plants. Some few of the Taur intervened, cutting out sicknesses, great evils plaguing humans, human societies, civilizations. Assassins? He shuddered at the word—no, they did not strike from shadows. They were an elite few within established armies, able to withstand and mete out justice where humans could not always.

And Zusamin had the gift and calling as well. Together they had aided many in their fights against evil—from rebel uprisings to Marshalls General. They went where needed, not necessarily where asked, and often together. They had grown close, so close, through shared joys and pains.

And then they had been separated when Tavill contracted the plague. She had stayed to continue fighting. She had been...

With Vera. Now he realized why they had seemed familiar. Vera had not looked the same, but Zusamin must have worn her Kalen ring that gave off the true Vera's presence. It would be how she had disguised herself among her own people, and for so long.

Had she thought she was alone, too? How had she concealed it when Tavill showed up? *Why* had she continued to conceal it? Had she, after so many years, rejected him? Forgotten him?

"She is with Averlynn?" he asked, his voice steadier than he thought it would be.

The two glanced at each other. "No," Deuel said. "Averlynn was captured. I was not able to free her along with Catie when I made my escape from the Cariste. I'm sorry."

Tavill gazed southward as though he might see the Cariste army from there. Though the air was clear and he thought perhaps he saw the faint smudge of the trees near the former Kalen outpost, it could also have been a trick of his mind. "Where are they?"

"The Kalen are in the Wall," Deuel said, "but mobilizing south when we left them. We were going to scout the Cariste position. The Kalen want to free Averlynn as well. You could follow along with us, or wait for them to arrive."

Tavill closed his eyes and shook his head. What would wisdom say? It was not as though the three of them would free Averlynn, most likely. They would need the army. He would lose nothing by waiting.

Or did he think so only because of his desire to see Zusamin? In truth, between himself and the behamian—he did not know Catie, she might be capable as well—they might have a better chance of freeing Averlynn as a small force. Even without the bloodlust, he would still have the throat-song. And the behamond, well... They were legendary even among the Taur.

And yet, something called him inexorably northward—as though traveling south was irrelevant. He turned that way, sniffing the breeze but it was against him. "If only I knew..." he muttered. He shook his head. What was more important to witness? What would fulfill his duty? Those were the questions he should be asking—not what suited him best.

"Knew what?" Catie asked.

Tavill turned back. "The Taur are called to witness," he said. "I do not understand why. The Harral do that as well—so why not they?" He shrugged, waving a dismissive hand. She would not know either.

"What are the Harral?" she asked.

Deuel hummed a moment. "Are they what are also called seraphim?" he asked.

Tavill nodded. "The Rinc Nain do not much acknowledge them, though they were once called Elderkendin by them."

"Oh," Catie said. Suddenly her eyes brightened. "Oh! I know why! They don't see it the way you do, Tavill. Time. History. It's all scrunched into a ball for them, they kind of see everything at once, or at least they can. But that's the point: they're too far removed from it. You experience it without knowing how your choices turn out. For the Elderkendin, they don't understand—can't, really—what it means to make the best decision you can with limited foresight. That's why we need the Taur! Illmali is going to stand accusing us of great evil, when—sometimes—in our hearts we desired the best we could do. You and Zusamin will stand in our favor, at least a little, to defend our intentions when maybe our results cannot."

Tavill stared at her. "How do you know this?"

Catie shifted, shrugged defensively. "I was able to see it, briefly," she said. "In Andelen. I had found the Berkarfor, and the fourth one—what is it?"

Tavill knelt before her, bringing his eyes nearer her level. "I know of these. I have underestimated you, and I am sorry. To have found the Berkarfor... You are highly honored, Catie."

"Oh," she said, blushing. She reached out and took Tavill's hand. "Stand up, please. Thank you. I, too, only did what I thought I needed to in the moment."

"What will you do?" Deuel asked.

"I am called northward, to meet with the Kalen who are coming. It will please me greatly to see Zusamin again." He paused, swallowing the lump in his throat. "But not only that, the Kalen army will need me whether we rescue Averlynn or not."

"Very well. Tell them you met with Catie and Deuel, who are still speeding south to locate the Cariste. I will return alone once we have found them, as Catie will be able to communicate with me at some distance while I fly. If we have the opportunity to free Averlynn on our own, do you believe we should?"

Tavill first thought to leave it up to them, to shrug off the question. But, simple as it was, they were displaying their own trust in his wisdom. "Only if the opportunity is abundant, or the danger to Averlynn or the Kalen army is great. As important as she is, I do not know if her life is worth more than yours."

Deuel inclined his head. "Perhaps. Please relay our intentions to Witko and Zusamin as well. They lead the Kalen at the moment."

Catie backed up to Deuel, who wrapped her in his arms. Tavill saw the intimacy there, and it dawned on him that she must be *behamona*. They were a perfect pair, he felt, and he smiled.

When Deuel's wings spread, Catie suddenly held up a hand. "Wait. Do you know who the Ekllar are?"

Tavill cocked his head. "Ekllar is an old Taur word, meaning something obscured—often by deceit. Like a dangerous or harmful secret..." He trailed off, uncomfortable with his sudden association of that word with Lasserain. He cleared his throat. "I believe we used it most often regarding the schemes of Illmali. But it was never a 'who', just a 'what.' Why do you ask?"

Catie's look was grim. "I think it may be a 'who' now. One of the strange things that came to me when I was returning to our time after seeing the vision of the Elderkendin. It was me, I think, but in the future. It seemed I was reminiscing with someone and I said 'remember the Ekllar?'"

Tavill rumbled. "Perhaps. Or there is something coming that will be forever remembered as *The* Ekllar—the dangerous secret that overshadows all others. As The Rivening was."

"Another epoch," Deuel commented.

Tavill nodded gravely. "Time will tell. Oren has had far too many already. I fear what another will bring."

Catie's eyes danced over Tavill, and suddenly she smiled. "I don't know why, but I'm not as afraid. The note I heard, the song the Musician was preparing to play—it was not something terrifying but resoundingly beautiful. Please don't fear, master Taur. Our duty may be hard, but the music it will bring upon Oren will be worth it."

Tavill considered her for a moment, and as he did he couldn't help but smile too. There was a strange peace in her words, and a truth he couldn't quite place. "Then let us perform our duties as best we can," he said with a short bow.

Catie and Deuel both smiled, in their own way—Catie's was broad and shining, his reserved but no less full of meaning—and Deuel's wings propelled them quickly skyward. Tavill watched a few moments until the faint speck of them drifted southward. They would find the Cariste swiftly, he knew. Time for him to find the Kalen.

He turned northward lighter than he had felt for a long time. The sun was higher now, casting shorter shadows, and the land was bright. By noon, he could see occasional movement on the northern horizon—nothing that would stand out unless you were staring at it. And, too, they had the most forward scouts they could have, in the two dragon-children. There would be no one to observe the Kalen army as it filtered southward in pursuit of their leader.

Tavill's heart quickened slightly, now, at the impending meeting. Zusamin's silence when he had been with the Kalen for so long still worried him—worried that her relationship to him had cooled for reasons he may not or would not understand. Instead of rushing ahead he found himself considering stopping for food, to delay what may be a painful reunion.

Our duty may be hard, but worth it. He set his jaw and strode forward, ignoring the closing distance between him and Zusamin. As night fell he smelled them on a rare, stiff breeze from the north. But he did not want to approach at night and so he made a rude camp in a hollow where the air was cold but calm.

He awoke as pale stars still glimmered overhead. It seemed as though his vision still improved by degrees, catching him off-guard at odd moments. As he breathed little clouds of steam rose. The grass was pale again, frosted.

He rose, clambered to the top of the rise. He scented the air, but it was now from the south. As dawn light slowly filled in the roving darkness, he blinked to see the stars glimmering on the horizon as well. But then he realized it was faint bits of weapons or buckles, or faces poorly hidden. He waited until the sky brightened further, that he wouldn't be mistaken for a threat. The he stood to his full height and waited.

He heard Tarafel whinny, and the Kalen stopped suddenly and melted into the ground. Except for Averlynn, who leapt atop her horse and galloped toward him. She reined hard and frozen earth sprayed forward.

"Tavill," she said, her voice quiet but expectant.

"I met Catie and Deuel on the way," he said.

Her eyes cast down. "Yes. I hadn't arrived yet when they left. They shouldn't have..."

"They did not see you from above?"

Averlynn shook her head. "They had no reason to look. If I had escaped immediately after them, I should not have covered so much ground so quickly. They could not imagine I would be so far north so soon. Were they well?"

"They said they will scout the Cariste positions and return. They will know soon enough." He paused as her eyes came back up. "I did advise them not to attempt a rescue unless the danger to you was great."

Averlynn smiled, let out a brief chuckle. "Well, we won't have to worry about that, then."

Just then, movement behind her caught his eye and he stared. Averlynn glanced backward, then returned her gaze with a broader smile. "Our business can wait," she said. "Go meet her, and we can hold council later—perhaps when the behamond return."

Tavill barely heard her, though he was grateful for what words he did hear. Averlynn had only finished speaking when his legs were already moving toward Zusamin. A hundred questions and uncertainties still swirled, but the time had now come to banish or embrace them.

She stepped forward from the Kalen ranks to greet him, and his heart ached to see her. She had changed—the Taur did, though they might not age in the same way men or Kalen did. Centuries stood between them. He could not but help feel the weight of them. And yet, set in the millennia of memories he had reacquired it was strangely still as though they had only parted for a few weeks.

"Tavill," she said in fair mimicry of Averlynn.

Trembling, unsure, Tavill stood. "Zusamin."

She jogged suddenly the few steps between them and embraced him, crying. Tavill wept, uncaring how loud or what the Kalen might wonder or think. Probably they knew. Of all the races, they would understand more than most.

"Tavill, *hat en go taun pende monden,*" Zusamin said.

It took him a moment, through his tears, to translate his own language. None had spoken it fluently since all those who tried to settle here had gone. And it was a familiar form, soft words spoken between closest of companions—or lovers, if their relationship was pronounced so.

He backed away a step, could not take his eyes away. "We must," he said. "I will not function unless I have some few answers, at least. Until Catie and Deuel return with the Cariste position?"

Zusamin placed a hand gently on his cheek. "Of course, yes. But how much—?"

"There was some of my *koridin* left, and it was still infected," he said, his mind frantically thinking back to how much Zusamin had learned while disguised as Vera. "It is gone now. My sight returns, though my scent-vision is gone. But all of my memories have returned. And I was able to read some of our writings from before the Rivening—perhaps more than I realized when I did it."

"So..." She hesitated, glanced around her. All the Kalen stood awkwardly nearby, looking but trying not to. They had not seen two Taur together for an age. Some of them looked young enough they never would have. Zusamin looked toward Averlynn, who smiled.

"Our behamond will return shortly with news of the Cariste," she called to her army. "Let us settle here for now and let the Taur take council. We will move when we have decided firmly our next course of action."

There was a quality to Averlynn's voice that caught Tavill's attention, a distance, almost absence, as though she knew her words and thoughts were opposed. Something to hear later. For now, Zusamin gestured to a small hollow in the ground not far from the main army, visible yet secluded, where some scrubby trees had taken root. They made their way side-by-side, not familiar but close. He waited for her to sit, watching, still in awe that she was there. Finally he sat.

"So you remember me," she said, her eyes struggling to meet his. They did for one brief moment. "Us."

He took a steadying breath. "We both surely believed we were the only Taur left alive, and believed it for long, long years."

She gazed unseeing at the stunted trunks. "Though I arrived here not long after the rest of you, I was in disguise. I never knew the fate that befell our people. I had to stay with the Kalen. As an Isun, I could sometimes go on spiritual pilgrimage. I asked Averlynn and many of the other Rangers about ruins or other peoples. By the time I found anything, it had passed into history. None of them had seen a Taur since landing here. I held out hope for years, Tavill. Maybe two hundred. Hunted as we would have been, I knew we would hide—had taken that exact counsel before leaving the Isles. So I have not lived with the knowledge of our demise, or the despair of being alone, for quite so long as you. But there were many places even I could not go in this land. And I always hoped, just maybe..."

"You hoped to find me."

She closed her eyes, tears wetting the fur at the corners again. "I didn't want to hope for it. Your condition when we parted, I knew in my mind there was no way you, of all, would survive. Not with your *koridin* removed, not only barely recovered from the plague. I don't know why..." She stopped herself, took a deep breath. "Part of me knew why I hoped. Part of me flogged myself mercilessly for such a foolish hope. And yet..." She smiled, turning to look at him.

"There was one part of you that probably knew better," Tavill said. He took her hand but did not caress it. "That our elders knew you might still be alive, and that the two of us might reunite one day."

Her eyes widened a moment as she considered. "Did they tell you this?"

Tavill snorted. "Of course not. I would have torn heaven and earth asunder—" He cut himself off, staring at his hand holding hers. "Why didn't you reveal yourself when I first came to Averlynn?"

She lifted her clasped hands, holding his between hers under her chin. "My first instinct was that it was not time," she said. "That I could not just remove my ring and deal with the repercussions. Great forces move around Averlynn particularly, and I knew that such an action would reverberate. Even when she removed the ring for me, I did not think it was time, but I could not decide that. But also, I did not know what might have happened to you since the Isles. I could tell you were still not whole. It nearly paralyzed me to see it, but it was written all over you."

He snorted, this time with a hint of a smile. "I suppose it was." After a moment, he pulled his hand to himself, gripping hers still in it. He kissed her hand very gently and slid his other hand along her fingers. "What comes next?" he asked.

She blew out a breath. "Well," she said lightly. "When two Taur really love each other..."

He tossed her hand away mockingly. "I said I regained my memories, remember? Even those."

She chuckled, a deep throaty sound from Tavill's distant past. But then she sobered as she glanced toward the rim of their hollow. "We still have our duty," she said, her voice low. "And, I fear, our duty to Averlynn will take us back to the Isles."

Tavill stared a moment, enough to be sure she was serious, then nodded grimly. "There is much to answer for in those Isles."

She glanced sideways at him. "Not so much as you might think," she said.

"Do you know why we made the weapon?" he asked. "The decision, I felt, was made by others. I can't recall it."

She shrugged, shook her head. "I only had suspicions. The plague was as dangerous to us as it was to the Cariste there, so it seems foolish to me that we had done so. Part of why—not all, but part—I go to the Isles with Averlynn is in hopes of finding more."

"And why does she go there?" Tavill asked.

She glanced again to the rim of the hollow, searched it, then lowered her voice. "I have not told her yet. But she is the *Maschen,* Tavill."

Tavill blinked a moment, fumbling through his unsorted memories. Suddenly, it clapped through him like a thunderbolt. His eyes went wide, then shut. *The prophecy she spoke of. I didn't remember at the time.* "Of course she is," he rumbled. He sighed and shook his head. "Lasserain will have much to answer for," he muttered.

"You know of him?"

His eyes snapped to hers. "Do you?"

"Catie and Deuel spoke of him. He is at the seat of some new, great evil. They heard about it in the Clanasoes. Something to thwart the Dricen. It's not clear what they are."

The Dricen, what Lasserain once called the Triumvirate. For being so hidden, it surprised Tavill that behamond would know they existed. He chewed his lip. He did not like all these turns of events, coupled with his own conversation with the behamond.

Suddenly, he noticed Zusamin's turn of phrase. "Did Catie ask you about Ekllar?" he asked.

Zusamin shuddered, shook her head. She froze, and Tavill saw the light dawning in her eyes. "Do you mean..."

Tavill nodded, quickly relating their conversation. "I wonder if it is this. She will remember this struggle, whatever it is. Some battle between Lasserain and the Triumvirs. He seems to be able to move in minds the same way the others can. How could he do that?"

"Perhaps the answer will come in the Isles," Zusamin said.

"But if you haven't told Averlynn she is the *Maschen,* how does she know to go there?"

"She received the fourth verse."

Another struggle as Tavill tried to recall them. When he did, it was his turn to shudder. "Of course. Of *course!* Why must prophecies seem so obvious when they are fulfilled—and impossible to discern when they are not?"

"So no prophecy is at the will of the prophet," Zusamin said with a shrug. "No true prophecy, anyway, could be fulfilled by force or contrivance. And yet, when it is, it is the most natural thing ever."

Tavill took a deep breath and blew it out. "I envy Catie this: with her knowledge, she knows she will survive to remember it."

"So do we," Zusamin said quietly. She took Tavill's hand again, rubbed it with her thumb. "Well, at least one of us will."

Tavill gazed at her, while through his mind flashed the images of all the Taur he had come to this country with. Each and every one had died, sometimes singly, sometimes in batches, until he alone remained and fled. As those images faded and all that was left was Zusamin sitting beside him, he quailed a moment. Could he watch her die? Let her sacrifice herself for him at some critical moment—or, worse, senselessly? "I don't think I can lose you again," he said.

She turned to him, her gaze mildly rebuking. "We will all stand witness, Tavill. Every one. Not only those left alive when the stars fall. I thought you had regained all your memories?"

He grimaced. "Memories, yes. I guess my faith is coming back much slower."

Her hand left his, moved to his back. "We've spent too long worried about the world, Tavill, and not on our purpose in it. We cannot change its destiny, only help guide it to the end. And we were never promised we would all make it to the end—only at least one. Whether it is you, or I, doesn't matter. If you want your faith to return, start by remembering why we were given life in the first place." She shrugged, and smiled. "Everything else falls into place after that."

He returned her smile, but thinly. "I'll work on it." And he would, but maybe after he had enjoyed Zusamin's presence just a little longer.

40

THE WORLD IS CHANGING

"Kanala, the others are arriving."
"Already? Are we prepared?"
"You begin to sound like Teresh. They have much yet to accomplish."
"Still. I will speed these on their way."

21 Halmfurtung 1321 — Autumn

Averlynn sat by the fire across from Witko. He gazed sightlessly into the flames, something Averlynn had been doing since it had been kindled. Her army was settled again. Here and there one tended their bow or sword or clothes. Most sat around similar fires—they had the most excellent of scouts far ahead, and feared no enemy nearby—each with their thoughts.

She sighed and glanced toward the hollow. She could faintly see Tavill's ears poking above the rim, but that was it. Zusamin was just barely shorter, and when they sat together she disappeared.

"Impatient?" Witko asked.

Averlynn whipped around, caught, and Witko chuckled. "I'm sure they wouldn't blame you," he continued, digging a pinky into his ear. He resettled himself. "They'll finish soon enough."

"They have centuries to catch up on," Averlynn said, failing to keep the irritation out of her voice. She closed her eyes. "That was selfish."

Witko chuckled again. "I don't think they'll blame you for that either."

"I do," Averlynn said heavily.

Witko studied her, his grin becoming even more lopsided. When danger retreated, so too did his somber demeanor. He kept turning by degrees into the half-mad Chief she had known before. She wasn't sure she was ready for that to happen, but that was selfish too.

She glanced at him. "If I go to the Abandoned Isles," she began.

"You will," he said, lofting his eyes to the sky. "You must! It's written in rain and cloud, across the very dirt you trod—"

"Witko," she moaned.

"—as you travel on the road..." He shook his head. "You ruined it. What else are you going to do by staying here?"

"Avert the war?"

"Then you should have been named *Avert*-lynn. But you're not. You're a flying torch."

She groaned again. Why had that fool elf written that fool lyric? When she looked helplessly at Witko again she was surprised by the very lucid spark in them as he studied her. "Have you forgotten—or not paid attention?" he asked.

"To what?"

"As a Kalen, for whom names are of utmost importance, you can be such a disappointment sometimes."

"Thank you, I know."

"Fine. A frustration, not a disappointment. Remind us, please, what your name means."

"Little sister to Aver," she said grouchily. Witko frowned. "Daughter of Avako and Erion," she added, mostly to mollify him.

But he continued frowning. "Are you finished?"

Averlynn folded her arms. "Dancer Near Peaceful Water."

"Go on."

"I know, Witko. Yes, I know, and I can't get it out of my head, thank you."

"Not just water, mixed water. Troubled water. Water no one else has tamed, no one else believed could be tamed. In other words, not peaceful yet. And not just Dancer—magic-weaver, guiding star, brightness. But it also means movement, not just near one pool of water or one body of water. You follow the trouble from headwater to mouth, soothing even the slightest riffle."

She curled her lip. "Are *you* finished?"

"Humph." Witko's frown seemed permanent now as he too folded his arms. "And don't think those Taur don't know that about you, too."

"Yes, Witko, I know." They both frowned at the fire. Suddenly Averlynn's lips bent into a smile. "That's why they need to hurry up, so we can share everything we already know about each other."

"Then let us begin," Tavill's voice boomed, making the two Kalen jump.

"I wouldn't think one your size could sneak," Witko said.

"I'm sorry," Averlynn said.

Tavill waved a soothing hand. "I am grateful for the space you gave us. We have caught up on the important things." At that moment Averlynn noticed the joining of their hands. "The rest can wait. There is too much to discuss now. What we do need to discuss is your plans."

Averlynn shot Witko a glance as the Taur sat themselves on the ground next to the fire. "Zusamin told you where I need to go?" she asked. "And you will go back there?"

"Yes."

"I know the way out is in the south. But I wish to know how our people will handle the threats still looming against them, before I leave."

"That may not be your concern anymore," Tavill said, nearly on top of Witko.

"I know I probably cannot win this war before I leave," Averlynn said quickly. "But I want to at least confirm what Amrith said—that they have decided to resist the Cariste."

"How?" Tavill asked.

"Amrith said he had received the next verses of prophecy from Old Raina," she said. "If we find her, confirm at least that part, the rest might fall into place."

Tavill looked troubled. "I would like to find Raina myself," he said. He explained what had happened, from finding Raina to being freed of the bloodlust in Kragnog.

"You saw the Prosan?" Averlynn asked. Witko leaned forward.

Tavill nodded somberly. "They have grown in number, and are ruthless. We should expect so of a people so harshly treated—by the Taur, by the Kalen, by their own people."

Averlynn looked at Witko, who closed his eyes in shame. "We didn't think they would grow so strong," he whispered.

"The Kalen cannot fight both the Cariste and the Prosan, even if they wanted to," Averlynn said.

"They may not have to," Zusamin said. "That mistreatment came later, and they probably view the Kalen as weak. They will strike the Cariste first."

"They did deal the killing blow to a Cariste emissary," Tavill agreed. "Perhaps they hold them in even greater contempt than the Taur or the Kalen."

"So we strike them while their backs are turned?" Averlynn asked incredulously.

If she thought the stare of one Taur was disconcerting, now that she had two it was almost unbearable. But what were they suggesting?

"For them to pursue me so tenaciously," Tavill said gently, "they are a people who do not let insult or injury go. There will be a blood-price, I don't doubt. Aiding them against their greater enemy the Cariste, and granting them land on which to flourish—perhaps make up for years of suppression—may reduce that blood-price to a manageable—"

"We have lost too many of our people already!" Averlynn cried. "We cannot possibly recover as quickly as the Prosan."

Tavill held up a hand. "This conversation is useless," he said. "That is something to be worked out with the Prosan, and by those who injured them—the Chiefs of the Kalen who tried to buy them off." His eyes went plainly to Witko, though they all knew it was not just him.

"Fine," Averlynn said bitterly. "And I'll just run off and never know what happens after?"

"Never is a long time," Zusamin said. She glanced tenderly at Tavill. "And things we think may never happen may yet surprise us."

Early snows drifted lazily from slate clouds, never seeming to touch the ground as a chill wind eddied from the south. Averlynn counted on Catie and Deuel to find the Cariste and come back. Still some hundred strong, the Kalen army would not be hard for the behamond to spot from the air.

The Cariste, in turn, should be headed to The Gates—for now, Averlynn would act as though Amrith was telling the truth. At the very least, the Cariste Commander, Liptieri, should actually be dead or arrived on the scene. It was one, faint point in Amrith's favor, Litpieri being absent.

Of course, even that could be fabricated. She needed Old Raina.

The former site of Amka came and went. Averlynn decided to keep them in the open for now, perhaps until the westward bend of the Waken forced them into the trees. South from there, east of Tekaa Wohan, Tavill had last seen Raina. Well, that was for him to figure out along with Zusamin; they said they could, and she trusted them.

They skirted the Water Plains, making respectable time. The Cariste clearly were as well, surprising Averlynn. Surely Ketzler would still suspect some trap? Or had Amrith as Ravun convinced him so thoroughly?

They were still some days away from sidling into the forest to their left, and Averlynn was beginning to worry in earnest for Catie and Deuel. She trusted them, as far as they were concerned—knew Deuel was especially capable. And yet, encumbered as he had to have been with Catie on his back, had they possibly fallen prey to a Cariste ambush?

The sun sank on the sixth day since they departed with Tavill and Zusamin, and Averlynn's rearguard suddenly called ahead. She wheeled Tarafel, saw the black streak of the behamond coming to land behind them. She spurred Tarafel quickly back to meet them.

"What's happened?" she asked as Catie slid off Deuel's back. They seemed unharmed, but they should have come from the south. "Are we betrayed?"

Catie smiled. "Far from it. The Cariste met the Prosan south of... What was it?"

"Wazé," Deuel replied. "Or so your Scout told us."

"Ravun? Or Amrith?"

"She did not give her name. She fled the battle though. We meant to take her prisoner, bring her to you, but..."

Averlynn's eyes widened. "You didn't kill her?"

Catie's eyes matched Averlynn's. "Oh no, of course not! She's too good for that. She used some magic and eluded us. But she told us Old Raina was camped where Tavill had met her previously," she said with a nod toward the Taur.

Tavill frowned. "Raina does not take part in the fight of her people?"

Catie spread her hands and shrugged.

"She wouldn't," Averlynn replied quietly. "She's...not too old, just weary of it all, I think. And my head spins with calling Amrith a 'she'—he has disguised himself, but he is one of our best Scouts. I'm not sure why he chose the persona he did."

"Ketzler would not imagine a woman capable of such a deceit," Tavill rumbled. "Amrith knows his target well."

"Well, if he is deceiving us, he is keeping it up almost impossibly well," Averlynn said with a sigh. "To fabricate all this just to get rid of me... Well, I can't imagine he thinks so highly of me as to go to such great lengths."

"What do we do, then?" Tavill asked.

The eyes of nearly one hundred four people watched her. "We continue south for now," she said. "When the time comes, Witko will lead the soldiers to The Gates while the rest of us continue to Old Raina—I would still seek her counsel and reassurances before leaving this land and my people."

"What of the behamond?" Zusamin asked, looking to them.

"I came here in part to see my brother," Deuel said.

"We both came to help with this, I think," Catie added.

"'This' what? Our war?"

She shrugged. "Not necessarily. At least, I don't think we're supposed to stay, now. I just knew there was something important to do—when the way south opened?"

Averlynn studied her. "It opened to allow the Cariste access into our lands, some months ago," she said.

"Oh. Well, here we are."

Averlynn let out a chuckle of disbelief. "Well, thank you, I guess."

Deuel continued to stare impassively. "She is often like that," he said, though his voice was tender, as near as Averlynn could tell. "Perhaps what we have done is yet to be realized."

"You have more than helped me," Tavill said quietly, his eyes glittering. "And I think you have shed light onto what has happened here more than you know. The Ekllar are all but exposed, and now we must account for them in our plans."

Catie's eyes brightened. "Oh, so it is a 'who'?"

Tavill nodded, explaining quickly his and Zusamin's suspicions. "They function much like the Triumvirate does—or at least Lasserain did."

Catie and Deuel exchanged glances. "Lasserain?" Catie echoed. When Tavill nodded solemnly she shivered. "We know of him. Zusamin told you? Some others we met had killed him last year, in Burieng. How is he one of the Ekllar?"

Tavill shook his head. "He had visited me more than once since the time you say... He must have been with the Ekllar each time." He gave a short sigh. "To answer you, it is hard to say. The Triumvirs choose the next candidate when the time is ripe. But they are chosen in life; perhaps the Ekllar are chosen in death."

"And chosen from those who will work earnestly and effectively against the plans of the Dricen—the Triumvirs," Zusamin added.

"It sounded like Lasserain certainly did that in life," Catie said.

"And in death," Tavill added. "He used the Cariste to stir up the Prosan, to bring them north to encounter the Kalen and possibly me as well."

"Do you think he used Amrith?" Averlynn asked, alarmed now by all their talk.

"I think Amrith's pride used Amrith," Witko said drily. "That seed was planted long before last year. Ketzler, though..."

Averlynn bowed her head a moment, scratching her jaw. "Are you sure I can leave this land?" she asked quietly. When the silence stretched, she glanced sideways at Zusamin and Tavill.

"I only know you are called to it," Zusamin said. "Whether or not you will is up to you."

She nodded once. "Old Raina first. Do you know where your brother can be found?" she asked Deuel.

"South of the Snowashes," Tavill answered. "He is the only dragon left in these lands." Deuel and Catie shared a worried look that they both quickly erased. Tavill noted it. "I am sorry," he said.

Catie forced a smile. "The world is changing," she said. It sounded like something she had said often to Deuel. "We have only our duty, right?"

Tavill inclined his head. "We may encounter him on our way to Thinseldon," he said, looking to Averlynn. "Certainly they should be able to search him out."

"He will come to me when we are near," Deuel said.

"Very well," Averlynn said. "Outriders in every direction, now, as Ketzler may move quickly south if he can disengage from the Prosan. He may recognize he is overmatched, especially with his army still split and the promise of ambushing the Kalen. I don't want him to run into us from behind. Let's get under cover now—into the Waken—and use up the remaining daylight. Tavill, lead us to Old Raina, please."

Tavill nodded again and turned quickly to lope into the forest, Zusamin and the Kalen and behamond close on his heels.

The wind grew colder, though more due to the approaching Snowashes than winter. It swept down those cooling slopes and through the trees, and Tavill and Zusamin ran with their noses straight into it. Here and there leaves had turned, some fallen and their footsteps crunched as they went. The Gates passed far to their west, but Averlynn felt only a brief twinge of desire to go with Witko and the rest of her army as they turned aside with farewells and well wishes. Harder, perhaps, was parting with Tarafel. He had not been her first mount, but to have gone through such changes, and the rock-steadiness with which he did it... "I will miss you, dearly," she told him. "But I doubt you will enjoy the sea." He nuzzled her and—true to his spirit—turned away as though he knew it was best for her. Witko climbed aboard and Averlynn chuckled: he needed Tarafel more than she, now.

As the days passed the course before her firmed in her mind, aided by advice from the Taur and encouragement from the behamond, especially Catie. The bright and confident behamona held a fascinating perspective, an assurance that Averlynn relished.

Suddenly, Tavill slowed. He scented back and forth, then up. As he continued to stare, the rest of their band stared upward, too.

Then Deuel straightened, his gaze fast to the south. Averlynn looked and saw the broad wings of the dragon above the trees as it banked lazily on currents of air. Catie watched too, a curious smile on her face.

The dragon banked again, aimed directly for them. He came speedily, growing rapidly larger until his wings flared suddenly broadside, then tucked as he dropped through the trees. Averlynn was amazed no branches tangled him, and just before touching down the wings found space to flare again, slowing him and kicking up a shower of dried leaves as he landed. His emerald body glowed, and the neck arched gracefully as he bowed his head.

"Well met, all," said the dragon, its voice a reverse of Aryndurlan's—deep bass with a faint and high-timbre behind it. "A strange party to be traveling so far south, and of such mixed company."

Deuel remained silent, staring into the golden eyes pupiled in indigo. His gaze flickered as though searching, and none of the rest broke the silence. Finally, the dragon's lips curled as though smiling.

"Ah, Deuel," he said. "Forgive me for forgetting—or, not immediately recognizing. I am Berythregal, now." He bowed again, lower this time. "He met the *behamona* Wynthrederan to the north, and of them was I melded."

Deuel now bowed as well, and Catie next to him. "We came to see you," Catie said. "I think we forgot, when we met Aryndurlan, some of our purpose in doing so—" She cut off abruptly as Berythregal's gaze gaze bent on Deuel.

"What is it?" the dragon asked, the high timbre gone entirely now.

"Marethal was in *veythya*, as a wyvern. But he was killed. And now, with Aryndurlan gone..."

Berythregal rumbled, his gaze going distant. "Strange news," he said. He shook his head. "Though I wondered..." Berythregal turned his gaze eastward. "Something stirs. I would call it imbalance, but strangely... It feels more as though imbalance existed, and now that balance has come it throws us off. That, and..." His scales rippled, and his gaze swung back. "The wyverns too are stirring, in Rinc Na."

"But how would that prevent the Call?" Deuel asked.

Berythregal shook his head. "It doesn't, not directly. But the world holds its breath for the completion of some event, I do not know what."

His gaze lifted, scanned the rest of the party until it came to rest on Averlynn. "Ah," he said, and nodded.

Averlynn's eyes went wide. "What does that mean?"

Berythregal cocked his head, his golden eyes flicking to the Taur. "I didn't know if she would be ready..." Zusamin said.

Berythregal cast her a mildly scolding look. "She could not be unless she is who she is—and then there is never a wrong time."

"Who am I?" Averlynn asked oddly, her smile unsteady.

"The Taur would call you Maschen—The One Who Does. Enigmatic, as their wisdom often is, especially of old. To behamond and dragons you are Lendal, Splitter of Light."

Deuel and Catie cast bright eyes on her as Averlynn frowned. "Forgive me, that is no less enigmatic."

"Withdraw Skyalfamold, and draw near."

Tentatively, Averlynn drew the massive sword. Her wrists felt stronger, her time practicing with Amrith not wasted. But it still felt heavy. She stepped forward, unconsciously extending the tip as she approached Berythregal.

"Forgive Aryndurlan that he did nothing about this," Berythregal said. "For the sword only responds to those of its element." The dragon reached out a finger, touched the tip of the sword where the sardonyx bolt terminated. With a warm glow suffusing its length, suddenly the proportions warped, flickered, settled. When Berythregal finally withdrew his finger Averlynn held a sword identical to the original, sized slightly smaller and with a slight curve to the blade. To her hand it felt ten times lighter, and she wielded it with grace and ease.

"To battle the lights, one must be swift," Berythregal said, his voice now a harmonious blend of Wynthrederan and Berygal's. "Though there be four, one must be first—sing the release as the Taur taught you to sing, and plunge it fast into its place, and deep, and do not let go. And after, if you remain true to the rest, perhaps the Call will ring out again."

Averlynn sheathed the sword, surprised to see the scabbard had similarly changed shape to match the blade. She bowed and stepped away. With a glance at Catie and Deuel she motioned to the Taur and turned southward. "We will continue to Raina's," she said. "Meet us there when you can."

They continued, Averlynn keeping one hand on the hilts as they walked. Though not like the senses between Kalen, she still felt some sort of presence of Berythregal through it as they walked. And, occasionally, something like words but expressed through a mix of light and music.

As evening descended, Catie and Deuel loped toward them through the trees, grins still wide on their faces. After Deuel's usually-stony demeanor, his grin looked nearly ridiculous, but also infectious.

So when it disappeared suddenly, and he turned quickly left, Averlynn found herself drawing her sword even before he had his twin blades out. It was another moment before she saw a patch of white to the east that bent as it fluttered.

All weapons were drawn as the flag neared, and she saw Ketzler holding it aloft as he and Karbae descended a small slope toward them. They paused some paces away, then let it droop to the ground.

"What do you want?" Averlynn asked. "Have you lost your army?"

Ketzler placed both hands on the flagpole and leaned forward, but his cocky grin was not gone. "I would rather not shout," he said, his voice quiet enough it barely carried across even the short distance.

Averlynn glanced at Deuel. "Those can cast magics, if I'm not mistaken," she said. He nodded tightly. "Then don't let me get between you and he," she said as she walked forward.

She kept her sword out, made sure his eye noticed it and noticed it was changed. Still his insufferable grin never wavered. Finally she stood only two paces away—close enough to run him through if she had need. "What do you want?"

"You," he said flatly.

Averlynn glanced at Karbae, then up into the hills. She saw then the helmets spread throughout the trees, a weapon here or there rising above some shoulders, could pick out a few longbows.

"I'm leaving these shores," she said. "You don't need to worry about me anymore. What my people do..." She shrugged as indifferently as she could.

"Giving up, then?"

She drew a breath. "My purpose now lies elsewhere."

"Mine is here," he said.

She permitted herself a mocking grin. "I imagine. Not many other places for you to go, is there?"

Finally his grin disappeared as his jaw muscles writhed. He glanced behind him, then behind Averlynn at her companions. "Not much of an army you have," he said. "I don't imagine the rest of your followers left for the Gates already, have they?"

Averlynn was not schooled as well in deception as Amrith was, and she couldn't hold back a nervous swallow. Ketzler's grin returned. "The Prosan mentioned something," he said. "I admit, they fought well at first. But there's usually only so much blood people are willing to shed for a cause."

Averlynn forced herself to breathe evenly. She glanced at Karbae. "And how much are you willing to spill?" she asked.

Karbae glanced sideways at Ketzler, seemed to catch his insufferable smile for herself. "All of it," she said, her eyes flashing.

Averlynn nodded once. "So, what next?"

Ketzler straightened. "You surrender, you and your...ahem...followers, back there. I drop this flag and my army knows not to shoot you all. You refuse and I raise the flag to your demise. Attack either of us, to your peril."

Averlynn glanced back quickly, saw the eyes of her friends intent on her. She thumbed the hilt of her sword. *Magics* Aver had said. She wondered what kind. The words she had memorized sounded promising enough. She felt the hilt warm slightly. "An interesting proposal," she said, twisting her mouth to contemplate while she sent the words like a prayer into the sword.

Goblinsbane, smite them down, with crushing granite rock.

Goblinsbane, split the ground, in earthly confines lock.

The warmth in the handle peaked, the flash—just below her eyesight—lit the woods in the lowering gloom. Ketzler's eye went wide as he dropped the flag and yanked out his sword, ducking to his left—opposite her from Deuel's perspective, she realized as a fireball shot between Ketzler and Karbae.

Defend against the archers!

Peering up the slope, Averlynn swept a line through the dirt at her feet. Halfway up the slope great rock monoliths burst from the ground. Dirt and stone showered off them until they had bodies to resemble the Plains Goblins she knew from Burieng. Arrows ricocheted off their hides, and did nothing to slow their inexorable stride upslope.

With a cry, Karbae had her sword in hand. She ducked another shot from Deuel. Ketzler had his own blade out, then, attacked Averlynn furiously.

But his fury unmade him, as every strike against Skyafamold left a layer of rock on his sword. Within five strokes it looked almost entirely of granite, and he could no longer lift it.

He released the hilt, leapt backward as Averlynn struck again. Karbae jumped between them, but held her sword steady, too wise to attack. Averlynn glared contemptuously, brought her sword to touch Karbae's. Before they could meet, Ketzler yanked her away, out of reach.

Averlynn began to pursue, but paused at a shout from behind her. She looked where Deuel pointed and saw Ketzler's army begin to outflank the stone goblins. Mindless, the golems strode in a straight line. Arrows zipped through the woods, falling short for now.

"We cannot win this battle," Tavill rumbled, striding toward Averlynn. She gritted her teeth, glaring upslope again as his army descended. She pushed her senses through the hilt again, feeling toward Berythregal. She danced backward as another arrow struck close and, as the light began to die from the blade, felt the faintest sense of summer-blue skies and some secret chord. She let her breath out in a burst and turned away: Berythregal would come and give them cover to escape.

As they hurried west and south, she heard a sharp crack like two stone slabs smacking together, followed by an earthen rumble. But as they turned then directly south, she saw Ketzler and Karbae ducking away through the trees, silently away from the assault.

"I'm afraid they are very good as well," Averlynn muttered.

Catie caught her eye and shrugged. "But robbed of most of their power," she said. "I think your people have a chance now—a good chance."

Averlynn shook her head once. "I hope so."

The sounds of battle faded, and the earth and rocks returned to their rest.

They pressed on the next day, and as dusk approached finally spied one of the early Kalenan cabins with smoke curling from its chimney.

"Averlynn, Avako's daughter," Old Raina crooned as they approached her door. "Of all our people, I've missed you the most, I think."

Averlynn bowed her head. "You are too kind," she murmured. "But thank you for saying so, even if you know why I'm here." She lifted her head, piercing Raina with her gaze, awaiting the response.

"Is it because the way to the Abandoned Isles lays to the east?" Raina replied, her eyes twinkling.

Averlynn bowed her head again. Raina motioned for them to enter her cabin; as they crowded in she continued. "I never thought in the remainder of my life to have such distinguished company. Two Taur, two dragon-children, and one specially selected for these times." She shook her head with a smile. "An exceptional gathering."

"How do you know I'm specially selected?" Averlynn asked.

"Skyalfamold, for one," she said, gesturing to the sword Averlynn again wore at her hip. "The prophecy for a second; and your companions, for a third."

"You know of the sword?"

"Amrith told me some, what he had learned from you and from your brother. The rest I learned long ago. There are three others, who I suspect you will meet in the times to come. They call to each other, in their way."

"We'll see them again, then?" Catie said. "Two others—they found it as they were departing Andelen. I had spent some time with them up there."

"Oh yes, you will see them again. All who wield the Shadebreakers will reunite."

"In the Abandoned Isles?" Averlynn asked.

Raina pursed her lips. "That I cannot say. They will meet where they must. Do not search for them, though. You will not need to. But be alert for their arrival—and yours."

"What of this land?" Averlynn asked. She paused to swallow, her throat tightening as she dwelled again on the fact of her departure. "Of our people?"

"I have not heard so much—only plans, laid both cunningly and treacherously."

"Is Amrith turned right? Does he lay an ambush for the Cariste? Will our people survive?"

Raina lifted a hand to slow the barrage of questions. "Those are simple, yet complicated questions Averlynn. Many threads are left to untangle. You know of how the Prosan were treated?" Averlynn nodded, Tavill too out of reflex. "We have had no contact with them outside of depositing our tribute, to know which hate they hold largest."

"They had ambushed the Cariste north of Wazé," Deuel interjected. "Whether by accident or design, that was their first strike. We met the Cariste again just yesterday, but by the power of Skyalfamold repulsed them."

Raina nodded slowly. "The accidents of men are often the designs of the gods," she said. "It will be as it is. But beyond that, there is still this difficulty for you, Averlynn: will you accept your call without knowing what will happen here?"

"Must I?" she asked plaintively.

"Sometimes, yes. You have played a great role already, Water Dancer—without which the present situation would be far, far different. But I perceive that is the end of your role. Sometimes—most times, I find—we can only play the role we've been given with diligence, never knowing the outcome. You have more and even greater roles to advance into, but even those fruits may ripen long after you have gone. That fate is not in our control. All we can do is accept our tasks and work them while we can, to be faithful in them in each moment. But whether you get to plant the seed, water it, or harvest it is only in the hands of the owner of the vineyard."

Averlynn considered those words a moment, and shook her head. "I will not reject the wisdom of the Elders, or the Taur," she said. "Though it pains me to do so. I am happy, at least, that my efforts these past months were not in vain."

"Indeed it was not, precious one," Raina said, smiling. "And if we can send you word, we will."

Averlynn grinned in return. "And when I learn what I must in the Abandoned Isles, I will return as well."

Raina's eyes flicked to Tavill's, and bowed her head. "It will be as it must," she said.

Averlynn's gaze went back and forth, and she groaned. "Keep your secrets, then," she said. "As you say, it will be as it will."

The party stayed that night, warmed by Raina's fire and food, and set out early the next morning under winter-gray skies. They continued along the line of mountains, often in their shadows until nearly evening.

Near week's end they rounded the edge of the mountains, taking the cliff road that Tavill had taken to come north. Here now Averlynn saw the tread of the thousands of feet of the Prosan, and her heart quailed at first. But she remembered the prophecy, took heart in the faith of her companions that this road was the only right and proper one, and bolstered herself with thoughts of her people with wisdom of ages sorting out how to handle the war around them. She had done her part, the part she had been equipped and given; it did not mean she was the only one of ability. For the rest, she would have to trust.

Tavill led them surely, now, through woods in which he had spent so many years by smell alone. Now, with his sight returned, he took in anew forests and glens—though winter-bare—marvelous to his eyes. He had admired it as much as he could on his way north, but with fear prodding him it still had not held the stark beauty it did now.

After several more days the broad Snowplains stretched before them, and they gazed across glittering white to far Thinsledon. Only a faint wisp rose from it now.

Tavill took the lead, guiding them around the deepest drifts. Occasionally they still slogged through deeper parts, but peak winter was still some weeks away when, Tavill said, the snow would fly almost perpetually until spring. They spent the next several gray days with Thinsledon looming ahead of them. Finally at its feet Tavill paused, clambering its slope to a cave high overhead.

"Abandoned," he said upon his return. "I suspect Lasserain was never there, or his accoutrements. Just the bone—though how he got it there I do not know."

"His plans seem to be long laid," Averlynn said. "It had perhaps lain there for years waiting until he could draw you there."

"Waiting for the way south to be open," Catie said. "I was there when Roth Kamdellan spoke the words, and they didn't come from him—from his voice. Somehow, when death was close, he must have overheard their plans or they somehow came through him." She shuddered and was silent a moment. "So the Ekllar knew even then, had a plan for it."

"It worries me that they might still be listening in, somehow," Tavill said as they continued toward the sea. "They could be in any of our minds right now, hearing our thoughts."

There was a moment of silence, until Zusamin said: "So could the Triumvirs."

Catie brightened. "And we've done pretty well so far, despite the possibility. Maybe they're not as all-powerful as they would like us to believe."

"Certainly they could benefit from our doubt and distrust," Deuel agreed.

"Tavill," Averlynn said when they had gone further. "Just because we can get to the ocean doesn't mean we can sail across it."

"Correct," Tavill said. "But I have good reason to believe a way will be made for us." When she continued to stare at him, he smiled. "We have a prophecy to fulfill."

The gray skies eventually met a gray and foamy sea, and great breakers surged over the top of some low cliffs. They went to the edge where the surf pounded the least and looked down. A faint stair was there, a natural series of crags leading down to the water's edge.

"So..." Catie said.

"No, look," Averlynn said, pointing. Near the bottom, the sea rushed in but did not break into surf until a few moments later water spewed as from a large hole.

Catie rubbed her arms. "Easy enough," she muttered.

They made their way down until they came to a kind of landing. The water roared almost continuously, punctuated by great booms from the cave. They pressed on, found wet but level footing into the cave, deep into a recess where light barely made it through. In the back, past a natural breaker, lay a ship bobbing on calmer swells.

They made their way aboard, the Taur's hooves echoing on the boards. Amazed but cautious they inspected the hull, deck, lines, and sails. It was serviceable, just large enough for perhaps fifty passengers, small enough for them to crew alone.

They spent the next few days making ready to sail and stocking up on fish and melting snow for water for their journey.

Finally Tavill declared it ready for sea. With the rest on board and at the ropes, he and Zusamin towed it from the lagoon out into the surf, jumping on board as a wave sucked them swiftly out into the wider sea. The Taur shoved on stout poles while the water was shallow, and the others ran up the sails. They surged through the first few swells, crashed through one final wave as it tossed over the reef, and the wind finally plucked their sheets and ran them away.

Averlynn turned for a moment to watch the land recede, quickly disappearing behind them into a fog. With a deep breath she turned forward again. A few weeks ahead of them lay the Abandoned Isles.

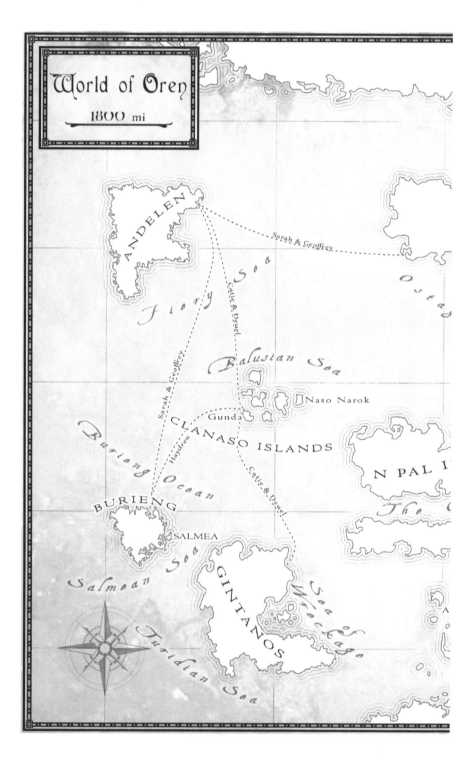

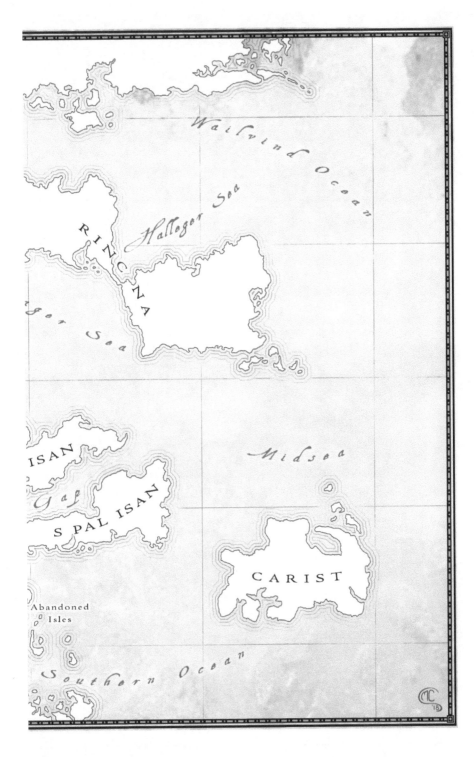

Author's Note on Calendar

I provide here a brief description of the history of Oren, its Ages, and Calendars.

As conquerors, Oren history is told mostly by the countries of Rinc Na and Carist, and the Ages and Times as they understand them are assumed.

The First Age, the Black Age (B.A.), is an unknown age. Some few documents remain in fragments, and there are none who know when it began or how the world looked when it did. Every culture's Creation Myths are guesses at this Age, but little more.

The Second Age, the Magic Age (M.A.), is defined and known as the year when magic was first discovered in Carist, and began to be taught by those who used it best. From start to finish numbers 1,095 years as the knowledge and use of magic grew exponentially. Discoveries were made by many great men and women, daring souls who spoke a language they did not know or understand, and many died in the pursuit. The Age ended with the terrible conclusion of the Wizard War, or War of Magics, that had wrought so much devastation to the lands it touched.

The Third Age, the Age of Discovery (A.D.), began as Cariste and Rinc Nain began to pick up the pieces and embark on a new pursuit: that of sailing to all parts of the existing world. Over the succeeding 2,060 years these two competing countries settled all the known world, either living with or displacing native peoples on the Pal Isans, the Clanaso Islands,

Andelen, and Burieng. Cariste found none living on Gintanos at first, though in the current Age that is soon to change drastically (the first hints of this can be found in *The First to Forgive,* and will come to full fruition in *Sacrificing All Pain).* The Age ended when the settlers on eastern Burieng sent a missive to Carist declaring their autonomy from that home country, and was the first stroke in the most tumultuous age of history.

The Fourth Age, the Age of War (D.W., or During the War) was not a time of constant strife, though strife indeed pervaded every year. In Burieng, Cariste and Rinc Nain fought over the country and were overthrown suddenly by the native Endolin under King Burieng. News of rebellion against the home countries of Rinc Na and Carist spread, and each country in turn declared and fought for their own autonomy from the lands where they had originated. After 896 years all was settled once more, and with only minor exceptions the countries look now as they did then.

Finally, the current Age, after the eight continents solidified, (A.E., or After the Eight). A common calendar was formulated and agreed upon by all Rinc Nain and Cariste, and eventually by the natives as they conducted business with those two peoples. The calendar was conceived and developed by the Rinc Nain, though only those people know it as "the Rinc Nain calendar." It consists of 400 days across 11 months of varying lengths. It begins with **Haschina** (named from legend), on the Winter Solstice in Rinc Na and countries north of the equator; or the first day of Summer in southern latitudes. It continues with **Mantaver** (Month Two), **Thriman** (Third Month), **Halmfurtung** (Half Four Moon, as four Full Moons have come and gone), **Fimman** (Fifth Month), **Monzak** (Month Six), **Savimon** (Seventh Month), **Fulmatung** (Full Eight Moon), **Nuamon** (Ninth Month), **Tetsamon** (Tenth Month), and **Elfumon** (Eleventh Month).

ACKNOWLEDGEMENTS

Time again to remember all who made this thing possible:

My Betas and ARC readers, for their eager anticipation of drafts, and critical early opinions.

The coordinators and designers at GetCovers for their thrilling covers.

Rustymaps, for coming in mid-series and creating such a terrific map.

And, of course, my wife and family for continued support and devotion, and letting me leave the house for a few hours a week to get this done.

About the Author

Daniel Dydek is a multi-genre author, working on his original epic fantasy series *The Triumvirs*, as well as his newest Christian medieval fantasy series, *Spirit Wind*. Besides writing, he also enjoys a personal relationship with Jesus Christ, mountain biking, reading, coffee shops, book stores, and Durango Colorado. He lives in Canton Ohio with his wife and son and two cats.

SUPPORT FOR THE AUTHOR

First, thank you for reading this story on whichever medium you chose—Kindle, KU, or paperback. Your support means dreams come true! If you loved the story, there are a lot of ways to continue supporting the author FOR FREE. Here's a few:

1. Follow on social media

2. Subscribe to the newsletter on danieldydek.com

3. Tell your friends!

4. Leave a review on Goodreads, Amazon, Barnes & Noble, or on your social media. (This is probably the greatest support of all, because we love hearing what people enjoyed about the book! Plus, you know, algorithms...)

5. Request your local library to get a copy

All these things help promote the books, and encourage the author to keep writing stories you'll love!

—The Beorn Publishing Team

The Triumvirs epic fantasy series

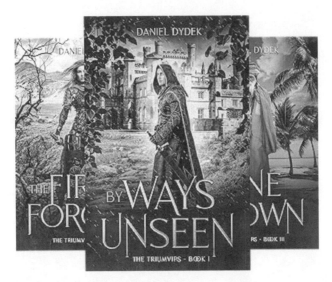

Centuries ago, the world of Oren was ravaged by uncontrolled magic during the Wizards War. In the wake of such devastation and evil, the God of All took three wizards and established for them a Room, of darkness and consciousness, and placed before them a great table whose appearance is of translucent slate, through which they might call up visions of the lands, entering when needed. Few even know these former wizards exist, and their work will always be credited to brave men and women of the world who were faithful in their obedience.

These wizards' task is keeping the peace, of prompting action against the forces of evil. They answer still to the God of All, but retain autonomy. He named them The Triumvirate, and over the centuries twenty-two Triumvirs have guided Oren through wars, famines, pestilences, and the rising and falling of countless empires.

Now, in this current Age of men, will come their most difficult battle.

Amazon search: The Triumvirs Dydek

Spirit Wind Christian suspense series

Cursed with left-handedness, then cursed with fire.

Except the fire seems to comfort, to strengthen, to speak wisdom. Wisdom like:

"The wind bloweth where it listeth, and thou hearest the sound thereof, but canst not tell whence it cometh, and whither it goeth: so is every one that is born of the Spirit."

And so Rae-Anna is borne on itinerant winds, never knowing what danger she'll be asked to face. But she knows this: it will always be demonic. And she will never be alone.

Amazon search: Spirit Wind Dydek

Made in United States
Troutdale, OR
12/04/2024

25852344R00343